Mal Rice

Metallic Dreams

A Horned Helmet Publication

Copyright © 2010 by Mark Rice

The right of Mark Rice to be identified as the author of this work has been asserted by him in accordance with the Copyright, Designs and Patent Act 1988.

No part of this book may be reproduced or transmitted in any form by any means, graphic, electronic or mechanical, including photocopying, recording, taping or by any information storage or retrieval system, without permission in writing from the author.

Published in 2010

Lulu Press Inc.
860 Aviation Parkway
Suite 300
Morrisville
North Carolina
NC 27560

www.lulu.com

ISBN: 978-1-4461-5088-7

Design and layout by Mark Rice © 2010.

Grateful acknowledgement is made for permission to include the following copyrighted material:

Rocking Again by Biff Byford and Steve Dawson, from the Saxon album *Innocence Is No Excuse*, originally on EMI Records. Copyright © 1985.

Planet Girl by Zodiac Mindwarp, from the Zodiac Mindwarp and the Love Reaction album *Tattooed Beat Messiah*, originally on Vertigo Records. Copyright © 1987.

Sausage Party and *Converter* by Hanson Jobb, Udo Von DüYü and Helmut Bang, from the Pink Stëél album *Out at the Devil*, Fistful of Love records. Copyright © 2007.

Front cover pentagram by David Gurrea, © 2004, www.davegh.com. Thank you, David. You rock!

Metal Macabre font © 2009 BoltCutterDesign. StahlSteelRiveted font © 2003 J.F.Y. Daniel Gauthier. Ascent2Stardom font © 2008 Barry Bujol. Thank you to the team at BoltCutterDesign, and to Daniel and Barry.

Epilogue quote by Umberto Eco is his paraphrased version of Carpocrates's Assertion. English translation © 1989 Harcourt Brace Jovanovich, Inc.

Horned Helmet Publications are natural, recyclable and made from wood grown in sustainable forests where tons of gorgeous baby trees are planted annually. The manufacturing process conforms to the environmental regulations of the country of origin.

"For their rock is not as our Rock, even our enemies themselves being judges."

    – Deuteronomy xxxii, 31.

Contents

1.	Stargazer	1
2.	Heavy Metal Thunder	5
3.	Death and the Healing	8
4.	The Ritual	10
5.	Wild Child	14
6.	When Love and Hate Collide	18
7.	Iron Man	23
8.	Spark in the Dark	30
9.	Bonded by Blood	32
10.	A World of Fantasy	36
11.	Big Bottom	39
12.	Room for One More	44
13.	Insanity and Genius	47
14.	High Heel Heaven	49
15.	Violence and Bloodshed	55
16.	Running with the Devil	59
17.	A Cautionary Tale	61
18.	I Come in Peace	64
19.	Parental Guidance	68
20.	Symphony of Destruction	70
21.	All Hell's Breakin' Loose	77
22.	Falling to Pieces	85
23.	Wanderlust	87
24.	Stranger in a Strange Land	93
25.	Coming Home	101
26.	Back in Business Again	104
27.	Take Away My Pain	110
28.	A Warm Place	115
29.	Weaving Sorrow	124
30.	Real World	126
31.	Gypsy Road	130
32.	It's the Little Things	135
33.	In My Dreams with You	149
34.	The Mirror	154
35.	Way Cool Jr.	156
36.	E-Mail from a Shemale	157
37.	Face like an Angel	159
38.	The Morning After	164
39.	The Phone Call	167
40.	Afraid of Sunlight	172
41.	Drop Dead Legs	175
42.	Hiway Nights	176
43.	Electro-Violence	184
44.	Get Workin'	186
45.	Thunderstruck	188

46.	Screaming for Vengeance	190
47.	The Uninvited Guest	192
48.	Little Evils for the Greater Good	194
49.	North	197
50.	Estranged	200
51.	Resurrection	202
52.	Gathering of Freaks	204
53.	Bastard is as Bastard Does	208
54.	Dreams in the Dark	211
55.	Strange Kind of Woman	213
56.	Sink the Pink	215
57.	Some Heads Are Gonna Roll	218
58.	Diary of a Madman	226
59.	Love like Winter	231
60.	Blackened	234
61.	Boys Will Be Boys	247
62.	Man and Machine	250
63.	Armed and Ready	255
64.	Feed My Frankenstein	266
65.	Walk the Stage	280
66.	Big Bad Moon	291
67.	The Writer	292
68.	Makin' a Mess	303
69.	One Helluva Night	309
70.	Hideaway	316
71.	I Am the One You Warned Me Of	319
72.	Losing More than You Have Ever Had	325
73.	Waiting for an Alibi	328
74.	Ballbreaker	338
75.	A Horse with No Name	347
76.	A Dangerous Meeting	352
77.	Prodigal Son	358
78.	Mother	362
79.	Wings of a Dream	365
80.	Warriors of the World United	369
81.	Black Embrace	371
82.	Cold Day in Hell	374
83.	Good News First	378
84.	Great Expectations	382
86.	Róisín Dubh	383
	Epilogue	384

Each chapter in the novel is named after a song. Most are famous, some are infamous, and a few are downright obscure. For any further information, feel free to contact me.

www.myspace.com/metallicdreams

www.facebook.com/SparkMacDubh

www.facebook.com/pages/Mark-Rice-Metallic-Dreams/143919068986750

To Jim,

Kung-Fu Master, fearless beat poet, comrade, fellow coffee drinker, and the soul of Writers Inc.

Enjoy!

Love Mark

for Nana and Papa,
who always believed

Chapter 1 - Stargazer

Dying is the fastest route to fame for an aspiring rock star. The dead man's melodies become profound, acquiring deep mystery and rising into a realm beyond the reach of human criticism. In the stopping of a heartbeat, the rocker is transformed from decadent, depraved hedonist into misunderstood genius. Aye, death and musical stardom go together like Scotland and rain, but I didn't exit Earth as a strategy to boost posthumous album sales. Neither suicide nor overdose, those favourite and most clichéd vehicles of rock 'n' roll demise, transported me out of this world. Perhaps I should feel thankful for that, but I feel only the bite of the black dog named Obscurity.

Snowflakes flutter onto stiffening flesh; the delicate harbingers of death bury my body increment by icy increment. I am the dead of winter. Wind rushes through the bare branches of trees, whispering its pulseless lullaby. If my face were excavated from beneath blankets of snow, its expression would confirm that mine was not a welcomed end. If you afford me the indulgence of turning back the clock half an hour, I'll explain how I ended up in this frozen repose.

Half asleep, I stumble out of my house into a biting wind as snow tumbles from an obsidian sky. Exhaled breaths blossom into ephemeral ghosts, each one haunting for a moment then dissipating into the darkness. Pristine snow has settled atop my fifteen-year-old BMW 316's rust-flecked body, covering all blemishes and restoring the car to its former whiteness. While scraping the windscreen with an empty CD box, I pray that the rusty bastard will start. This is no weather for push-starting a one-ton hunk of metal on a Scottish dirt track, especially dressed as I am, in sky-blue shorts, white running shoes and a navy fleece with *Bodies in Bronze* embroidered on the left breast.

It's just past the middle of the night. My fingertips are numb from the cold. I want to retreat into my house, a thick stone building built in 1608. Its first owner was an ancestor on my mother's side, Mhairi MacFior. Porcelain-skinned, black-haired and beautiful, Mhairi lived happily here, in the countryside seven miles from Bronzehall, with her ten cats. Until she was burned alive for witchcraft, that is. Accused of enchantment, charm, peddling potions and having nocturnal communions with the Queen of Elphame, the fearsome Scottish faery queen, Mhairi was tortured with thumbscrews, flayed with whips, branded with irons, then – after the bones of her arms, legs, hands and feet had been crushed in vices - burned alive. What became of her cats is undocumented. The house remained in my family but lay uninhabited as its architectural black sheep until I moved in six years ago. The building had been untended and ignored for almost 400 years, and it showed. The three-foot-thick walls were intact despite having been swallowed by weeds and ivy. The roof, meanwhile, had disappeared into oblivion. To make the place liveable required more work than any sane person would have been prepared to do. That's when I stepped in, partly out of a sense of family obligation and partly out of a deep affinity for the eeriness of the house with its dark stone, darker past and asymmetrical angles. To my white rabbit Fluff and me, it became *home*.

Snow starts to balance on my hair and clothes. I long to fall back into my warm and welcoming bed. Sleeping seems much saner than braving a blizzard in exchange for piss-poor wages. There are bills to pay, though, and – as Robert Frost once said with eloquence – *I have promises to keep, and miles to go before I sleep*. So, narrowing watering eyes against the wind, I face the pre-dawn elements.

The clouds part, exposing a circle of sky in which two stars blaze like celestial eyes. Gazing upwards, I'm filled with awareness of time. The starlight that penetrates my eyes has been hurtling Earthwards for years, sizzling through the void on its journey. I feel a push against the walls of my mind, as if the Universe is trying to flood my consciousness with cosmic enlightenment. Its efforts are futile, though. My mind is too tired, too worn down, too fuzzy to decipher the messages. As a child, I was filled with understanding and grace. Now, however, my soul is a barren wasteland where the wreckage of broken dreams lies strewn across the sleep-deprived tundra.

As I stretch across the windscreen to scrape its far side, my left thigh presses against the car's door handle and sticks to the frozen steel. When I yank my leg free, a piece of flesh remains stuck to the metal like a pagan warning to the underdressed. The stream of profanity that ensues would make nuns blush and run for cover, kissing their crosses and spouting spontaneous prayers. I scoop up a handful of snow and press the cold powder onto the gash on my thigh. Liquid crimson runs through purest white, spreading outwards like rose petals cast over a winter bride.

At the turn of a key, my trusty, rusty steed splutters into life, coughs twice and does its best impression of a throaty roar. Headlights carve circular trails through the darkness, illuminating the snowflakes that parachute ever downwards in their hypnotic dance. I squelch a foot onto the accelerator. Rustbucket plunges into the snowstorm like a fearless old warhorse.

My soul feels shrivelled, filled with sadness. A degree in Sports Studies seemed like a good idea when I was about to storm into my twenties, yet here I am sixteen years and myriad qualifications later, dressed in shorts and braving a nocturnal blizzard to open a gym where I spend most of my time explaining to customers that the route to a chiselled body is not paved with junk food and alcohol; they nod, but few change their self-destructive habits. Most of them live on the modern Scottish diet of fried food, cigarettes and booze, exercising once a week at most (usually in half-hearted fashion), after which they bemoan their lack of svelteness to me, the captive listener trapped in his gym cage.

My degrees and diplomas are worthless pieces of paper, as is my latest bank statement. When I stared at that aberration yesterday, I realised that my finances were no longer in the red: they had sunk into the brown.

Approaching the outskirts of Bronzehall, I try to psyche myself up for the coming day, but there's not a lot to get excited about; I'll unlock the gym, switch on lights and cardiovascular machines, then sit on a cold plastic chair at a scarred wooden desk, squeezing a mug of coffee for warmth while wondering how the hell my life veered so far off course. It's a futile cycle to be stuck in, but it pays the bills. Almost.

As Rustbucket ploughs onwards through the snow, my mind drifts back in time and remembers how life was supposed to unfold. I was born to be a heavy metal star: the rocker whom hordes of voluptuous groupie whores want to seduce; the guitar hero whom adoring, starry-eyed male fans pretend to be as they play frantic air-guitar in front of bedroom mirrors. In childhood, that was my vision - a vision I shared with my four bandmates, my gang. Our five young minds believed stardom to be our only conceivable destiny.

Things began to go wrong when I was seventeen. My band's twenty-year-old lead guitarist earned seven years in jail for a drug-fuelled spree of violence. The other band members were quick to let go of their musical dreams, but I never did. They did the 'mature' thing: after writing off the band as a teenage fantasy, they got real jobs and made some money. They called it growing up. I called it giving up.

Although I never forgot my dream, it faded to a whisper in the back of my mind. Now, almost twenty years later, electric guitars hang on wall brackets all over my house. Even the kitchen sports a chrome stand on which a spruce-topped acoustic guitar wears the startled expression of an instrument aware of its misplacement; sometimes I think it looks frightened, perhaps worried that when funds are low it may end up in one of my more adventurous stir-fries. Maybe on some level all my guitars are aware that they are reminders of the status my band should have achieved, but never did. Souvenirs of a better time.

(My band's original mission statement was simple: to create music so heavy that it could make eardrums implode. And indeed we did become the architects of riffs the likes of which had never been heard before. No heads caved in, but our melodies brought about a more interesting phenomenon: Bronzehall's teenage girls began to drop their panties for us at a dizzying rate. This led to experiences that made imploding eardrums seem boring by comparison, so we updated the mission statement accordingly, making our new goals twofold: to set out on a heavy metal odyssey and compose music that redefines the genre; to immerse ourselves in as many females as possible along the way.)

I still play guitar every day, but playing all alone floods my mind with images of what could have been and should have been, of my blood brothers, my band, my tribe. Sometimes I cry oceans as my fingers blaze trails of sadness across a guitar fretboard, coaxing out haunted melodies: the sounds of lost dreams.

A stabbing head pain pulls my attention away from musical dreams and back to the road ahead. Like a rat fleeing a sinking ship, my brain seems to be trying to escape through my ears: an unorthodox exit strategy for sure, and a painful one. I skid the car to a halt, fumble for the hazard lights, then climb out in the hope that fresh air will remedy my malfunctions. To my distress, it doesn't. Instead, my legs buckle and I crumble to the ground, arms spread out in a crucifix, eyes fixed on the snowclouds that jostle for prime position like vultures circling their prey. They unleash their cold payload…and wait.

An approaching van slows to a crawl. Its driver hammers out a tuneless symphony on the horn, perhaps to express anger at my 'parking' (which could more accurately be called 'diagonal abandonment') or disapproval of my snowbathing in shorts. On the other hand, he may be attempting to determine if I need help. My hopes of assistance are dashed on snow-spattered tarmac as the van rumbles into the distance.

I hope you crash into the next lamp-post, ya false-hope-giving wankstain. And if you survive the impact, may all your shits be hedgehogs.

My heart, which moments ago hammered my ribs like a pneumatic drill, stops. Blood flow slithers to a halt. I want to gulp gallons of air into my lungs, but they are frozen stiff. Snowflake by snowflake, inch by inch, I feel myself being buried under sheets of icy purity.

So this is my swan song. Half naked, stone-cold sober, miles from my guitars and my blood brothers – hardly an archetypal heavy metal exit. At least I'm in my beloved Bronzehall. Perhaps a dog will piss here and expose my frozen body, scaring the bejesus out of the human who's holding the leash. I hope my blood brothers can be tracked down for the funeral. I'd like one of those long-haired vagabonds to stand up and say, "Spark MacDubh played a mean guitar. We'll miss that blue-eyed daydreamer."

I'm aware of a sound like sand filtering through an hourglass. My consciousness rises out of my body, which, in its snowy sarcophagus, resembles a frozen angel, wavy masses of hair having transformed into white wings. This moment of reflection is fleeting; lifted by an unseen force, my soul ascends through weeping snowclouds and into starsparkled skies, headed for God only knows where.

Chapter 2 – Heavy Metal Thunder

I was ten when I heard the music that ended the first phase of my life and cast me hurtling into a new horizon. Drenched to the skin, I stood on Dunoon's pier peering seawards through diagonal rain, looking for the ferry that would take me home. There, on the everwet west coast of Scotland, I heard it: like sonic scalpels, the sounds of electric guitars sliced through the dreich weather. My body hairs pricked up, each one a willing receiver for the Thunder-God grooves. To my young ears, the sound of these amplified guitars was angelic (although, with hindsight, I don't suppose angels play Gibson guitars at ear-bleeding volume). A voice that suggested vocal chords of polished silver soared alongside razor-sharp overdriven riffs. I knew that I was hearing the future.

After breaking away from the rest of my swimming club, I wandered hypnotised towards the beautiful cacophony, the epicentre of which turned out to be an unremarkable grey stone bus shelter. In Bronzehall, such shelters had a diversity of uses: underage-drinking hideouts; makeshift lovenests; gang hangouts; safe havens from rain; fight locations; toilets; impromptu discos. Some oddballs even used them for waiting on buses. I had never, however, seen them used for *this*.

Fierce guitar riffs, rumbling basslines and artillery drumming boomed from a ghetto blaster in the corner. Three long-haired teens banged their heads in perfect synchronisation with the music, whipping up their manes into whirlwinds that obscured their faces. They wore denim jackets - with the arms ripped off - covered in band-logo patches and conical metal studs. One boy's entire left forearm was wrapped in a leather wristband from which steel spikes jutted, while his adjoining fist was covered by a gauntlet fashioned from burnished bronze. The three hairy beasts were playing invisible instruments: one played air guitar; another plucked the strings of an imaginary bass; the third's arms flailed like a controlled seizure as he pounded an unseen drum kit into oblivion. Aware that I had entered an alternate dimension and was standing on the edge of something scarily visceral, my every particle resonated with the powerful music.

A gangly butterfly swimmer named Barry sprinted over to me, his hazel eyes bulging. "Spark, get your arse back to the pier! Oor ferry's here!"

"I'll be there in a minute. There's somethin' I have to do first."

"If you miss this ferry and get stranded in Dunoon, your Dad will boot your wee balls. If he can find them, that is."

"Fuck off, spunkstain."

Shrugging his shoulders and raising palms to the emptying sky, Barry grunted, "Don't say I never warned you, ya daft bumcrack," then fled into the lashing rain.

The headbangers hadn't noticed my presence. They seemed to

have escaped to another place in their minds: an awe-inspiring place to which I wanted access. Like a zebra among lions, I sneaked into the bus shelter, trying to be calm despite my sphincter flapping like a windsock in a storm. My eyes remained fixed on the swirling masses of denim, leather, hair and studs as, driven by fear and excitement in equal doses, I shouted, "Hello! What the fuck's that music? It's fuckin' amazin'!"

All motion stopped. The three teenage hairballs stared me down like badass hombres from a spaghetti western. I stood as still as stone, my sphincter now vibrating like the exhaust pipe of a dangerously over-revved motorcycle. Wristband Boy swept dark brown hair off his face and held it in his gauntleted grip. Eyes glinting like blue diamonds, he flashed me a smile. "That, wee man, is Saxon! Do you like it?"

"More than like it...I fuckin' love it!" I hoped that my profanity would bestow upon me the coolness that my short, chlorine-bleached hair did not. When the three metalheads grinned and nodded, my fear dissolved into the salty coastal air. Suddenly, I was a welcome gatecrasher at their wild bus-shelter party.

"This album's called *Denim & Leather*," said Air Drummer, his poker-straight blonde hair tickling the arse of his jeans, "and the song you're hearin' is *Princess of the Night*."

"I'm gonnae save up my fuckin' pocket money and buy that fuckin' album as soon as I can," I announced.

Wristband Boy pressed the stop button on the ghetto blaster, removed the cassette tape, slipped it into a clear plastic case and extended a metal, gift-bearing hand in my direction. "Save your money, wee man. I've got the album on vinyl. I can make another tape anytime. You keep this one. There's another Saxon album on side B. *Strong Arm of the Law*. I think you'll like it too."

Overwhelmed by Wristband Boy's generosity, I took the cassette and gushed, "Thank you! That's really fuckin' kind of you. I'll fuckin' treasure this. I'll listen to those fuckin' Saxon albums every fuckin' day. I'm gonna grow my fuckin' hair as long as fuck, just like you three hairy fucks. In fact, I'm never gettin' my fuckin' hair cut again."

The third metalhead, Bass Man, was a sandy-haired paleskin with a spotty face like a join-the-dots puzzle and eyes like melting chocolate. He popped a tape into the ghetto blaster and said, "This, my fuzzy-haired wee friend, is AC/DC. Check oot Motörhead too. Their concerts are so loud that some folk faint. I've heard that some even shit their pants."

"I'll fuckin' do that," I replied. "Check oot Motörhead, I mean, not shit my pants. I love heavy fuckin' metal, even though half an hour ago I didn't know it had been fuckin' invented." Now I was cursing to cultivate coolness. Its effect on my new friends and role models was unexpected but welcome: it *amused* them.

Through floods of laughter, Wristband Boy observed, "You swear a lot for a wee guy."

"Aye," giggled Air Drummer, "your language is fuckin' atrocious."

"What makes you say that, ya cunt?" I asked, beaming.

Wristband Boy collapsed onto the bus shelter's concrete slabs, tears of laughter flowing down his face as fat raindrops bounced off the pavement outside. Once he had regained his composure, he sighed, "You're one of us, wee man. You get it. You *feel* it. Nothin' will ever be the same for you again."

A mind-melting riff burst out of the ghetto blaster. The three metalteers exploded into movement, transforming AC/DC's sonic power into wild kinetic energy. I joined in. Arms flailed, heads banged, hair billowed. My hair was a short, unkempt mop, but I banged my head with abandon until my brain hurt and the muscles on the back of my neck burned.

When the song faded out I explained, "I'm Spark MacDubh from Bronzehall. I swam in the Western Districts championships here this weekend. I'd love to stay here longer wi' you hairy bastards, but if I miss the fuckin' ferry home my Dad will play keepy-uppy wi' my balls."

"You can headbang wi' us anytime you're back in Dunoon," said Wristband Boy. "Go and catch your boat now, wee pal."

"Aye, I will. Have you any heavy metal fashion tips for me?"

"It's fuckin' easy," answered Air Drummer. "Just wear lots of blue denim, black leather, patches and studs. And your idea never to cut your hair again is a good one. Stick to that." His two compadres nodded enthusiastic agreement.

I gave a serious nod, like a spiritual student soaking up the wisdom of sages. "Thanks for all bein' so cool to me. I need to fly."

Wristband Boy punched the air with his gauntleted fist. "We'll see you at the Glasgow Apollo, my wee metal brother. That's where all the best metal bands play when they're on tour." I gave my three gurus high-fives and hugs, then left the cosy comfort of the stone bus shelter and disappeared into wind-driven rain.

Those three hairy creatures were right. Nothing was the same after I discovered the miraculous phenomenon of heavy metal. The world was brighter and louder. *Everything* was better. I was no longer just a kid. I was a heavy metal kid.

And I never did cut my fuckin' hair again.

Chapter 3 – Death and the Healing

Pain skewers my skull and sears into my brain. Eastern mystics believe the mid-forehead area known as the third eye to be the seat of higher consciousness, but mine feels more like the seat of a toilet on which a fat-arsed demon has squatted to shit out last night's napalm vindaloo. Rushing waters crash into the inner walls of my skull and arrange themselves into words. **"Awaken, Spark. Get back on your true path. It isn't too late."** Eyes open. I'm back in my body and high above Bronzehall, dangling from an invisible fishing line and writhing like live bait. A lightning bolt slashes down the sky in slow motion, forks above me, accelerates to a lightningworthy speed and impales my eyes: *I see.* A second bolt of lightning spears my third eye: *I know.* The third flash burns through my chest and into my heart: *I feel.* A fourth strikes my navel then pulses like an umbilical cord to the heavens: *I'm connected.* The fifth lightning bolt hits me right in the balls, jolting my body into an electrified spasm-dance: *oh ya bastard, I'm alive.* Then, as the voltage stops and I'm left hovering high above the sleeping world, understanding floods in: I'm in the grasp of a celestial hand which has – not before time - plucked me up to shake all the fear, doubt and bullshit out of me. Moments ago I was killed by snow and sorrow. Now I'm buzzing with life.

Air whistles past my ears. Falling. Ground leaping up to meet me. Impact. Paving slabs crack as if they were frost-skinned puddles, but I feel no pain. Swarming clouds continue to spill their snowy cargo as I spring to my feet feeling clean, clear and wildly alive. I know my place in the Universe. It's startlingly clear. For long years I lamented what could have been and should have been. Now I understand that focusing on history dragged me out of the present and prevented me from really living. That doesn't matter now. What's important is *what can be.* Vital energy bristles through my body. Like a battery that's been recharged – *overcharged* – I'm bursting with possibilities.

A shooting star trickles down the dark sky and disappears behind a gnarled oak tree, leaving a shimmering starstreak in its wake. Astronomers see shooting stars as specks of spacedust burning up in the Earth's atmosphere. Poets, however, see them as good-luck charms and granters of wishes. I'm with the poets. The star was sent to light my way.

Around the shattered slabs where I landed, snow has melted in a perfect circle. Inhaling fresh winter air, I smell every bird in the trees, every blade of grass, every wild flower, every woodland animal. My eyes drink starlight and digest it into inner fire. Wherever my blood brothers are, I must find them. It's time to revive the band, to do what we came so close to doing all those long and painful years ago.

Resurrected. Recharged. Revitalised. Reborn.

I climb into the car, do a U-turn and head for the countryside. I won't be working in a gym today or any other day. My destiny is calling. And when destiny calls, only a world-ranked idiot hangs up the phone.

It is not too late.

Chapter 4 – The Ritual

Even before puberty arrived with its truckload of testosterone, I had observed girls gravitating towards Bronzehall's gang members, lured by the bad boys' dangerous mystique. What those girls didn't see, but I did, was that most boys in gangs lacked real toughness: they all wanted to be tough, aye, but were actually scared souls wrapped in shells of bravado. I had no interest in such self-delusion; I wanted to be a warrior like my mythological hero Thor, to hone my body and mind into weapons, and to fight epic battles. In the rough end of town, Vikingwood, where I lived, a gang called The Woodie - the longest-established local white-trash warriors - robbed Bronzehall's honest people, dished out arbitrary beatings and stabbings, and spray-painted their logo wherever they roamed. My gang, Blood Brothers, didn't follow The Woodie's blueprint. We didn't steal from people or property, nor did we vandalise walls or punch anyone just for making eye contact. Blood Brothers did one thing and did it well: fighting. It became our drug. We walked away from every battle with our heads high and the wind on our faces, leaving our defeated rivals lying bleeding, battered and broken in pools of blood. When we weren't knee-deep in gory battlegrounds, we spent our time listening to music, talking about music, talking about girls, and, in an unconscious existential way, trying to figure out the Universe. We were cerebral savages. The idea of calling our gang Blood Brothers derived from a ritual I had participated in years earlier.

In my seventh summer, I travelled abroad for the first time, flying with my parents from Glasgow to Vancouver to spend a month in British Columbia with my Canadian relatives. My uncle Jimmy had drawn up an itinerary in which he had taken the bold step of segregating males and females: the women would stay in the urban sprawl of Vancouver, where they could enjoy such womanly activities as shopping, visiting beauty salons and listening to Barbra Streisand, while the menfolk would inhabit a log cabin deep in Nahatlatch Valley's unspoiled wilderness, where we would do manly things like fishing, chopping wood, arm-wrestling and running away from grizzly bears.

    My Uncle Jimmy met us at the airport and drove us back to his house in the Vancouver suburb of Guildford. Soon afterwards, a rusty blue van pulled up at the kerb. Its driver was my uncle's best friend, a grizzled old geezer named Earl Steer, whose log cabin would be the base of masculine operations. Steer was a fitting surname: Earl looked like a thickly muscled hybrid of grumpy bull and weather-worn cowboy, with only hooded hawk-like eyes suggesting a third species thrown into the mix. His tanned face reminded me of a scarred old leather saddle.

    During the drive to Nahatlatch, my cousin Neil and I chewed mint-flavoured gum under vast blue skies. Beside the road, gigantic evergreens impaled the sky, blotting out a low-hanging sun. Slivers of sunlight flickered between branches, whipping the windscreen with stroboscopic stripes of light. Juggernauts with wheels as big as our van rumbled past hauling logs on enormous backs. The smell of pine filtered into the vehicle as country music blared from the radio's speakers. Earl Steer and Jimmy sang along with hillbilly gusto, while my father - a connoisseur of Scottish Highland music - shook his head in slow, bearded sweeps of disapproval.

As Earl steered us along serpentine roads, I drifted into a deep sleep and dreamed of a Native American girl with almond skin and pleated black hair. She walked towards me holding a grey, heart-shaped stone in outstretched hands. I took the stone from her and noticed on it the crimson words *True Love*. Before I could talk to the beautiful young squaw, Earl thudded my head with a heavy hand. "Wake up, Half Pint. We're at the cabin." Unhappy at being wakened from such a symbolic dream, and less than thrilled at the nickname 'Half Pint', I started thinking of ways to get even with Earl.

The log cabin was the pinnacle of rustic, redneck chic: constructed from roughly cut tree trunks, and smelling of chopped wood, fried onions and coffee, its atmosphere was one of honest-to-goodness simplicity, without the trappings of civilised life. I felt comforted by the immersion in nature. All around, trees scratched the sky, dwarfing our dwelling. A wooden pier led from the cabin to the shore of the ice-cold, fast-flowing Nahatlatch River. My father forbade me from going close to the edge, warning that the river contained dangerous currents.

After a hearty meal of salmon and vegetables, I wandered outside, lay on my back and gazed up into the brightest blue sky I had ever seen. It felt like looking into forever. (Years later I would discover that in Buddhist theology the colour blue represents infinity.) Lying in perfect peace on a forest floor of lush greens and rusty browns, I began to understand my Canadian relatives' affinity for this wilderness.

On returning to the cabin, I found a pint glass – full to the brim with cloudy orange liquid – unattended on the picnic table outside. I sniffed the glass's contents: orangey, with the unmistakeable whiff of alcohol. Through the open door, I heard Jimmy asking Earl if he wanted a beer from the cooler. "No," Earl replied, "there's a large gin an' juice outside with my name on it." Smiling, I lifted Earl's drink and gulped it down. *That'll teach you to slap me around the head and call me names, you saddle-faced sonofabitch.*

I fled the scene of the crime, down to the end of the pier. My surroundings started to spin. On the edge of the jetty, my legs gave way and I fell into the fast-flowing Nahatlatch River. Swept downstream, bobbing like a cork, I managed to grab the twisted roots of a riverside tree. After hauling myself out of the foaming water and onto a muddy embankment, I puked then passed out. I woke to find my cousin Neil's face above mine, his shoulder-length brown hair hanging like a help-rope for a drowning man. Neil attempted to carry me back to the cabin, an idea that idea fell spectacularly on its arse when, after only a few feet, Neil's arms gave way and I slammed onto the ground. For the rest of the journey, Neil led the way while I crawled a slow pursuit on hands and knees.

I arrived back at the cabin sodden, filthy and too inebriated to stand up. It didn't take much deductive thinking from the adults to figure out where the missing gin had gone: the evidence was sprawled in front of them, straight out of primary three and literally stinking drunk. My father decided it wouldn't be right to punish me while I was in that state, but he promised to give my arse the skelping of a lifetime the following day. My ginthievery didn't endear me to Earl either; he stopped calling me *Half Pint* and bestowed upon me the more colourful nickname *Asswipe*.

I lay in bed that night, a first-time drunkard at seven years of age, pondering the punishment I knew would arrive on callused palms. In the forest, as if sensing my plight, wolves howled nocturnal laments. The magnificent lunar lullabies of my lupine brethren wooed me into a deep and cleansing sleep.

The following morning, I experienced the simultaneous delights of having my arse smacked raw just as my first hangover made its appearance. Afterwards, with aching head and red-hot rump, I wandered into the woods with Neil. We found a clearing bathed in sunlight and rich with the smell of ferns. After scanning the area, Neil nodded, flipped open his pen-knife and made a diagonal cut across the palm of his left hand. His hazel eyes took on a possessed look as he passed me the knife and said, in a nasal Canadian accent, "Your turn, little cousin."

This was a test of will power. My logical self ordered me not to cut my palm with the bloody knife; it would hurt like hell and was against all my Mum's standards of hygiene. Somewhere deeper than logic, however, a tribal urge flared. We were in an unspoiled place where some indigenous people still lived. Taking part in this ritual would make Neil and me part of that culture and in some strange way keep it alive. All I had to do was cut open my hand. I took the knife and sliced. Blood sprayed from my palm like water from a sprinkler, painting a nearby plant ferrous red. My hung-over head began to pulse. I felt sick.

Clasping my bloody hand in his, Neil bound our wrists together with a length of rope. As our blood mixed, the overflow dripped onto the forest floor. It felt as if we stood interlocked for aeons, but it was probably less than a minute. When Neil unwound the rope and let go of my hand, my head felt like I was no longer inside it. Like an unholy Indian rope trick, vomit was defying gravity in my throat. The forest's vivid blues and greens faded as, unable to cling to consciousness any longer, I passed out for the second time in as many days.

When I came around, Neil was once again frowning down at me, just as he had been the previous day at the riverside. He asked if I was alive. I nodded. Blood was still pissing out of my left palm, so I uprooted a handful of leaves and pressed them onto the gash. Not only was this remarkably effective at stemming the bleeding, it dulled the pain too. Only a few minutes had passed since the ritual, but already I was feeling like a little Native American shaman herbalist. After the anaesthetic effect wore off, my hand began to throb again. I didn't care. The pain would be temporary, but the blood bond would last forever. It was even worth the additional pain that came later: when Neil and I returned to the cabin – dripping trails of blood behind us – and told our fathers the news, they leathered our arses for doing something so *stupid* and *dangerous*. They didn't understand. Neil and I had tapped into something ancient, spiritual and and mystical. We were blood brothers.

Chapter 5 – Wild Child

Swimming dominated my childhood. My father taught me to swim before I had taken my first steps on land. By age five I was swimming daily. My first training session with Bronzehall's swim team happened on my seventh birthday. At ten, I was training twice a day and competing every weekend.

David Tierney was, despite being only thirteen, the fastest butterfly swimmer in Scotland. When my coach announced David's impending move to Bronzehall from a suburb of Glasgow, excitement rippled through the swim team. A few weeks later, the butterfly phenomenon walked onto Bronzehall poolside for the first time. Several male swimmers approached him with grovelled platitudes in recognition of his achievements, but David Tierney – apparently deep in an inner world - stared into the pool and continued to perform his warm-up stretches. His appearance was more Mediterranean than Scottish: shiny black hair; tanned skin; hazel eyes; sparkling toothpaste-advert teeth; long, lean body. After completing his flexibility routine, David lifted his gaze from the water and aimed it at a group of six swimsuited girls, like a big cat eyeing his prey. I saw shadows moving in his eyes, as if demons resided in those dark orbs. Weeks passed, during which David continued to ignore Bronzehall's male swimmers, but the athletic young bodies of the team's girls never failed to awaken the demons in his eyes. He scared the shit out of me.

A month after David's move to Bronzehall, my father announced on a Friday night, through a mouthful of half-chewed Arbroath smokie, that we would be visiting the house of a new swimming-club family after tea. I hoped that the new swimmer would be an as-yet-unplundered female, preferably a juicy-lipped and beautiful one.

A couple of hours later, my father's car pulled into the tree-lined driveway of a plush bungalow in Bronzehall's most affluent street, Weldstone Crescent. I jumped out, sprinted to the front door, rang the bell and waited with a smile spanning my face. My smile disappeared when David Tierney opened the door, his predatory eyes locking onto me and promising malice. I ran back to my father and wrapped my arms as far as they would reach round his massive frame. "Dad, I'm goin' to get a bus up the road. I'm not needed here."

"You will do nothing of the kind, young man. We've all been invited here. David Tierney is a talented swimmer. You can learn a lot from him. The two of you could end up friends."

Tears welled up in my eyes. "Dad, he's Satan! I don't want to go in there!"

My father glowered at me while my Mum shook her head and raised her eyes to Heaven. "You and that imagination," she sighed. "David's not the Devil. I'm sure he's a lovely boy. Please make an effort, son."

I appealed to my father, for that was the only way of overturning one of my mother's decisions. "Please Dad," I pleaded, "don't make me do this. He's pure evil."

My father's frown intensified, the furrows on his brow like waves on an angry sea, his black beard and hair like dark clouds. From within the storm, his soft blue eyes – like glimmers of sky - looked from me to my Mum then back to me. He seemed to briefly contemplate challenging my mother, but chose not to undermine her maternal authority. "You heard your Mum, wee man. Try to get along with David. Do it for me. Please." While I hid behind the ursine protection of my father, David remained at the front door like a grinning gargoyle at the threshold to Hell.

Then it came to me. I knew how to get out of this. It would mean getting my arse leathered, but that was a price I was willing to pay in order to get far away from David Tierney. All I had to do was say something so shocking that my father's only possible course of action would be to drive me straight home and smack my arse pink. "Dad," I gushed, tugging on his shirt, "David's a demon-filled *cunt*. And if you make me go into this hoose, you're a *cunt* too." There. I'd done it. The very word my father considered worse than any other, and I'd just rattled it out twice like a preacher spouting Hallelujahs. It was a stroke of genius. Now my father couldn't force me into the Tierney house without himself becoming a cunt. I smiled, confident that my Dad would drive me home at high speed to dish out immediate punishment. My Mum, meanwhile, stunned almost to the point of collapse by my profanity, was reeling as if she'd drunk fourteen gins.

My father leaned down and whispered into my ear, "A rather transparent ploy, wee man. Do you think it's that easy to pull my strings? Oh, your arse will be getting leathered, you can be sure of that, but at the end of the night or perhaps tomorrow. In the meantime, while you're anticipating the monumental pain that I'll inflict on you for calling me that name, you could reflect on why certain language isn't appropriate for boys of ten."

"Please come in, Mr and Mrs MacDubh," David invited. "My Mum and Dad are in the living room. I'll show you through." Hardly the words of a demon, but I remained on my guard as the unholy adolescent led the way to a living room that smelled of cigars and ladies' perfume. The demonchild was trying to lull me into a false sense of security, but I was too clever to fall for that. His polite butler act didn't fool me.

Mr Tierney was tall and tanned, with bone-white, slicked-back hair and a neat moustache. He told David and me to leave the adults in peace, dismissing us with a hand gesture as if shooing foul-smelling riff-raff. David walked the long hallway towards his room and motioned for me to follow, which I did, my heart racing. When I saw his room's wall decorations – two Blondie posters and a Madness poster – I started to laugh. "What's so funny, ya wee tit?" he scowled. Giggling, I pointed at a Blondie poster.

"That's Debbie Harry," he explained. "A lot o' people think Blondie's her nickname, but it's actually the name of her band."

The mean streak I had seen in David's eyes must have been projected from the dark depths of my imagination; this boy was a mother's dream. A Blondie fan, for fuck's sake. "I don't care if people call her Arseface and her band Big Broon Keech," I admitted. "She looks like a bulldog's arse. And her band's shit." David devoured the distance between us. A hair's breadth from my face, he stared daggers into me, tomato soup heavy on his breath. Pain exploded through my jaw. I tasted blood in my throat. The attack had been fast and ferocious. I hadn't even seen it coming. A second punch sent an unholy triumvirate of snot, blood and hurt pride streaming from my nose. David tilted his head to one side, no emotion or remorse in his expression, apparently weighing up the damage his attacks had caused. He was thirteen. I was ten. He had seniority and bulk on his side, but I was a heavy metal kid. And there was only one thing for a metal child to do in this situation: I booted David's balls. Hard. He fell to his knees squealing, "Ya wee bastard! I'm gonnae fuckin' murder you."

"Murder this, ya wank!" My fierce upwards-swinging kick thudded into my opponent's chin, snapping his head back and sending his body into a slow-motion descent. As he crashed to the ground like a felled tree, I hollered, "T-I-M-B-E-R!" My wounded adversary inched towards his bed, slithering on his side like a serpent and clutching his freshly booted balls. He reached under the bed and fumbled for something hidden there. Moments later, I found myself looking down the business end of a gun. I realised then that my initial instincts about this fucker had been right. He was a lunatic. He was the Devil.

Like a deer in headlights, I stood frozen as David raised the gun above his head and smashed its butt into my face, splitting my top lip open. I leaned forwards and let my blood drip onto the light-blue carpet. Then – to punctuate my sanguinary vandalism with an exclamation mark – I spat out a mouthful of bloody saliva. "Ya wee shite," David shouted, "look what you've done to my fuckin' carpet! My Mum will tear me a new arsehole!"

"I hope she does. That way, after I boot your balls again, I can rip them off then shove one up your old bumhole and one up the new one."

David hammered my left temple with the butt of the gun. The room started to sway. He threw me to the ground, knelt astride my chest and stared into my eyes. "Sometimes," he rasped, "when you can't win a battle, the smart move is to surrender."

"I wouldnae ever surrender, especially to a fanny like you."

"Even if I was kickin' your stubborn heid right in?"

"You couldnae kick my heid in. It's unkickinable. You needed a weapon to get me into this state."

Eyeballing me at close range, David whispered, "I didn't *need* a weapon. I chose to use one. Why risk breakin' my fists on your thick heid? I'd miss weeks of swimmin' training if I did that."

"Why do you have a gun anyway? Have you flipped your fuckin' omelette?"

David's maniacal grin widened. "It's a spud gun, ya wee tit. It shoots potato pellets."

"I thought you were gonnae blow my fuckin' heid right off. Noo I need to change my underpants. The ones I'm wearin' have more skids than Jackie Stewart's driveway, thanks to you, ya wank."

David's tanned cheeks quivered as his shoulders rose and fell to the rhythm of his laughter. "If it was a real gun and I was goin' to blow your heid off, do you think I'd do it in my own hoose while oor parents were in the livin' room?" He had a point. He'd never get away with that.

David explained that he was obsessed with weapons and warfare. Two years earlier, he said, his worried parents had sent him to a psychotherapist who had concluded that David was not psychotic, but hyperactive, hyperimaginative and wild. The head-specialist had advised the Tierneys to involve their son in a strenuous sport to channel his aggressive energy into something constructive, thereby moulding him into a balanced individual. "That's one possibility," I theorised, "but there was also a chance that competitive sport would just turn you into a bigger, stronger, fitter nutjob. I'd bet on that outcome."

Flashing a disarming smile, David put his arm around my shoulders. "I admire you for standin' up to me. You're a tough wee bastard." Happy with David's conclusion, I smiled, dribbling blood down my chin. "Call me *DT*," he continued. "That's what my friends call me." Moments ago we'd been kicking fuck out of each other. Now, apparently, we were friends.

A week later I introduced DT (as I had come to know him) to heavy metal. He got it. He felt it.

We ripped down his Blondie and Madness posters, then replaced them with giant posters of AC/DC's Angus Young and Motörhead's Lemmy, whose sweaty, larger-than-life countenances gazed down from the walls, soundlessly announcing that the new gods had arrived.

Another month passed. Then, as grey clouds wept outside, DT and I became blood brothers.

Chapter 6 – When Love and Hate Collide

At age eleven I felt as though the world was in the palm of my hand. My chlorine-faded brown hair hadn't been cut for a year and had grown into a wavy mane of follicular fabulousness. Both DT and I had qualified for the Scottish national swimming team. Our coaches were becoming increasingly scientific in their approach to the sport. They taught me the principles of propulsion and resistance, which helped me to develop a *feel* for the water. Studying drag coefficients and edicurrents - and applying that knowledge to my swimming technique - maximised my stroke efficiency and made me more aquadynamic. There was no shortage of swimmers hungry for success. I realised that staying ahead of them would be simple in theory but painful in practice: I would have to swim deeper into the pain than they were willing to. With that in mind, I learned not just to tolerate the lactic acid that burned into my oxygen-starved muscles, but to welcome it as a friend. Swimming's secrets were revealing themselves to me. Girls, on the other hand, remained a mystery.

Gillian Kelsey was the girl that most Bronzehall boys my age (and many older ones, some illegally so) wanted to be with. Her eyes were the same shade of blue as Nahatlatch's expansive summer skies. Her long brunette hair rippled and flowed like a shampoo advert's wet dream. With a single smile, Gillian could turn hard-as-stone fighters into jibbering mush. Gill and I had been friends since we were babies. She had come to all my birthday parties. We exchanged Christmas cards every year. Our birthdays were seven days apart, making both of us Pisces children. One day in the school playground, my reality shifted as Gill walked towards me. I noticed the shortness of her grey skirt, and the length and feminine sensuality of her bare legs. I'd always known that she was uncannily pretty in much the same way I'd always known that lions were dangerous. On this morning, however, awareness of Gill's beauty moved to the forefront of my mind for the first time. It felt like being hit in the face by a floating feather followed by a speeding train.

I *wanted* Gillian; that much I knew. I only wished I had the first clue what to do about it. I was good at being friends with girls but too shy to move beyond that.

Eventually, after thoughts of Gill had been tormenting my every waking moment for weeks, I wrote a note asking her to be my girlfriend, then asked my friend George to deliver it. He returned with the same note, the flipside of which had one word scrawled across it in pink crayon: 'YES!'

In the following days and weeks, joy gave way to frustration as I realised the extent to which my shyness was restrictive. It took all my guts just to hold Gill's hand. Every day after school, we went for long walks and talked about everything. I spent most of my pocket money on presents for her, usually heart-shaped things or vinyl records. I longed to take Gill in my arms and kiss her, like I'd seen done in movies but better. Two things prevented me from doing this: shyness and fear of making an arse of it. I decided to wait until she either gave me a signal or – preferably – took the bull by the horns and kissed me. In the meantime, I made do with walking and talking by her side.

The boys of Bronzehall aimed jealous looks at me whenever I was out with Gill. Rather than being bothered by this, it bolstered my certainty that she was indeed the hottest thing in town. What the green-eyed enviers didn't know was that nothing had happened between Gill and me, not even a kiss. Lord knows, I wanted things to happen, but my shyness refused to disappear. Impatiently I waited, hoping for Gill to make a move. Weeks passed. I discovered masturbation, which may have single-handedly stopped me from exploding like a watermelon dropped from a great height. I whacked off as though it was in danger of going out of fashion (not that I was a fashion guru, darling). Relentless yanking, more than anything else during this testing time, saved my sanity.

One morning, after Gillian and I had been boyfriend and girlfriend for six months, our teacher – Mrs Calderwood – announced that a new boy would be joining our class the following week. His name was Iain Bright and he would be moving from Edinburgh. Mrs Calderwood gave us the usual speech about how we should all be nice to Iain and make him feel welcome. It was a futile speech; good-natured kids would always be kind to new arrivals, while demon-spawn children would see them as fresh meat to torture and bully. A two-minute lecture was never going to change the basic nature of anyone, least of all children.

On the Friday before Iain Bright's arrival in Bronzehall, Gill's friend Kim skipped across the playground to me. "Gill says she's been waitin' for you to kiss her, or do somethin' to her, for six months. She's no' waitin' any longer. She says if this new guy Iain is a better fighter than you, she'll go oot wi' him." It seemed inconsistent with my worldview that Kim with the cute smile, dirty blonde ringlets, holy white socks and Jesus sandals could be delivering such apocalyptic news. This type of communication was brought by angels who descended from the sky on dark wings, flaming trumpets raised to their godly lips. That's what I had been told at Sunday school anyway. Today, though, I watched dumbfounded as the Angel of Apocalyptic Announcements turned and skipped away, her grey pleated skirt billowing in the breeze. Unwilling to let my friends see me crying, I ran out of school. By the time I arrived home, my house looked like a blurry watercolour through tear-filled eyes. Struggling to make sense of things, I puked in the front garden. Ten minutes earlier, I had been sitting on top of the world. Now I was hanging on by my fingertips.

I went upstairs to my room, put on AC/DC's *Back in Black* album and sank into the bed. Hell's Bell rang, then the riffs of Angus and Malcolm Young washed over me, making me clean and whole again.

I didn't return to school that day; I couldn't face Gill and no longer knew what to say to her, how to feel about her or how to act around her.

One idea that popped into my head was to pre-emptively dump her. That would teach the bitch, I figured. There was only one problem with that idea: no sane boy would dump Gillian Kelsey. Her long legs, flowing brunette hair, hypnotic smile and oceanic eyes ensured this. No matter what angle I tackled the equation from, there was no way I could ditch her. Reluctantly, I faced the truth that Gillian was destined to be ever the dumper, never the dumpee.

I trawled my mind for other ideas. The only good one that sprang forth was to play another AC/DC album. *If You Want Blood (You've Got It)* soon had me ready for war, prepared to do whatever it took to show Gill that there was no other boy for her.

I found myself disliking this Iain Bright character even though he hadn't arrived in town yet. His impending arrival had created huge waves in the previously smooth waters of my life. This wasn't Iain's fault; he was about to be ripped away from his home and friends, and placed in the unenviable position of being the new child in a new school in a new town. Gillian had named him as a potential boyfriend and me as a potential jiltee, though, which made him my enemy. I didn't want an adversary but the hands of fate had moulded one for me anyway. After all, this was why people went to war: to fight for what they loved. But if two people experience a mutual and immersive love, how could one stand by and watch the other put himself in danger just to prove that love? This seemed like a strange paradox indeed. My meditations spawned three conclusions: Gill loved only Gill; her ego was out of control; gorgeous on the outside did not equate to compassionate on the inside. There was no time to study Sun Tzu's philosophy of war or any other such wisdom. Iain Bright would be arriving in three days, so I had until then to get my game plan in order.

On Monday morning I walked to school as if marching into battle. This Bright bastard was getting knocked out, whether he ended up as Gill's boyfriend or not. It was a matter of principle. If I punched his lights out he would know to stay well away from me, no matter how things developed with Gillian.

Then I saw Iain Bright for the first time, standing alone in the playground like a little lost soul, emptiness and fear in his eyes, thrown to the lions without even a friend to fight by his side. He stood on unfamiliar grey stone, an exile wrapped in a dreich Bronzehall morning. Approaching the freckle-cheeked boy, I stared into his blue eyes. As he averted his gaze downwards, I said, "You're the new kid, eh?"

Iain lifted his head and smiled. His empty eyes filled until they sparkled. "My name's Iain Bright," he replied. "I'm new here today."

"I know all aboot you, Iain Bright. I'm Spark MacDubh." I proceeded to tell Iain about Gillian, about leaving school early the previous Friday, and about the plan to conquer him in battle to prove myself to her. Then I told him how all those plans had dissolved the moment I saw him standing alone, the proverbial stranger in a strange land.

His eyes widened. "So we're friends then?"

"Aye, friends."

Gillian was perturbed by the fast friendship that blossomed between Iain and me. She would have liked us to go to war over her like knights fighting over a beautiful princess, but that didn't happen.

Four days later, she dumped me to go out with a boy from the neighbouring town of Svartglen. She'd met him at a roller disco and he was, by Chinese-whispered accounts of his scented fingertips, a fast mover. Behind a blue curtain at the roller disco, he had kissed Gillian, felt her ripening tits and even slid a hand down her panties, all while Shakin' Stevens sang about hot piano action behind a *Green Door*. I didn't even try to fight for Gill. My leggy ex-girlfriend was a diamond that could cut through even the hardest stone; my heart had stood no chance. Now it was time to heal.

Ironically, Iain was my rock when Gill broke up with me. Just a week earlier, I had planned to tear him to shreds and then kiss Gill like a conquering hero returning to his homeland. Instead, I found myself cursing her and crying on the shoulder of my newest friend. I wrote Gill a note declaring that the only boys who went to roller discos were wee wanks with tiny tadgers. Then, in a perverse echo of previous events, I sent George to deliver the message.

Rather than feeling shy and uncomfortable around the most gorgeous girl in Bronzehall, I found myself feeling authentic and relaxed with my new friend Iain. The more time I spent with him, the more I liked him. He was funny, intelligent, compassionate, escapist and a lot of fun to hang about with. We had both read Douglas Adams's *The Hitch-Hiker's Guide to the Galaxy*. Iain's big brother Tom had the whole BBC Radio series on tape. We listened to it all in one afternoon and laughed until our sides hurt. When I asked Iain what kind of music he was into, he replied, "I don't really listen to music. My big brother's into E.L.O. and Kate Bush, so I know their stuff."

"Come wi' me," I ordered. "I have somethin' to let you hear." I led the way back to my house. In the back garden, my Mum was sunbathing in a skimpy yellow bikini, her long black hair swept into a ponytail. Iain looked startled by the shameless display of oiled female flesh. When she kissed him full on the lips as a welcome, his little face flushed scarlet. If she had kissed him again, I think he would have fainted.

(Having been a peace-and-love-preaching flower-child, my Mum liked to kiss all my friends on the lips. This habit disturbed me but didn't seem to bother my friends. In fact, some of the perverted wee bastards liked coming round to my house on hot weekends because my Mum often sunbathed topless in the back garden and would always greet them with a kiss.)

My mother made ice-cream floats for us all while I slipped a Judas Priest album out of its sleeve and placed it on my turntable. Iain picked up the album cover and stared at it: a razor blade gripped in an unknown hand; emblazoned on the blade, the Judas Priest logo and the words *British*

Steel. As the opening riffs of *Rapid Fire* blasted from my speakers, Iain's mouth dropped open. By the time *Breaking the Law* began three songs later, a new metalhead had been born.

In the months that followed, Iain and I spent all our pocket money on vinyl but never bought the same records as each other. That way we could tape each other's albums and expand our music collections more rapidly. DT's Mum, who owned an upmarket hair-and-beauty salon, helped to boost our music collections; whenever DT dropped hints to her that he fancied a specific album, it would appear in his room – as if by magic – the next day. The inner sleeves of some vinyl LPs began warning that 'Home Taping is Killing Music'. I didn't know what kind of knuckleheads believed that. In the heavy metal scene of the 1980s, home taping kept music very much alive.

Iain Bright and I became blood brothers during his first summer in Bronzehall. We performed the ritual in my bedroom while listening to Judas Priest's *British Steel*, the logical choice for the occasion, as it was the album that had delivered the goods to Iain. As Rob Halford chanted about standing united and never falling, Iain and I sliced open our palms, pressed the bloody incisions together and were united. Our blood dripped onto the album's white inner sleeve. I didn't clean it off. The bloodstain is there to this day, a reminder of an innocent, optimistic time.

Chapter 7 – Iron Man

On a blue-skied April afternoon, Iain and I wandered through Vikingwood Forest to the old swing park in the heart of the woods. Rotting wooden swings hung from rusty chains. A warm spring wind blew flecks of green paint off a roundabout that had seized up long ago. Weeds reached skywards through cracks in concrete. Once, this had been a place of smiles and laughter. Now it reminded me of an old man with mind anchored in the distant past and body somehow hanging together in the present.

Danny Faulkner, a thirteen-year-old with bloodied knuckles and inward-pointing toes, was sitting on a swing, its chains screeching as he worked up momentum. "What are you wee primary-school poofs doin' in *my* swing park? Get tae fuck oot!"

"I think you'll find you're the only poof in this swing park, ya pigeon-toed knobend," replied Iain. Danny jumped off his swing and charged towards me as fast as his knock-kneed gait would carry him. Iain had brought up Danny's pigeon toes and questioned his sexuality, yet I was the one in his line of attack. Perhaps I constituted a safer target on which to vent his anger, as Iain's big brother Tom had a fearsome reputation as a fighter.

Standing my ground, I asked, "What's the hurry, Faulkner? Are you runnin' to catch the spazzy bus?" Iain cracked up laughing. Buffered by my blood brother's amusement, I pushed my luck further. "You couldnae fight sleep, Danny, so get back on your swing or I'll boot your balls so hard you'll have three eyes and two Adam's apples. Your Mum wanted to name you Fanny, but the minister who christened you had a speech impediment."

Danny wasn't in a talkative mood. His right fist smashed into my jaw, knocking me onto my back. Fluffy clouds chased each other across a bleached blue sky as blood trickled from my mouth. Picking up a heavy branch, Danny flashed a toothy grimace then clubbed me across the head. Orbs of light danced before my eyes. My temple began to throb. As Danny raised the branch for a second strike, Iain slammed into his side like the bastard offspring of a juggernaut and an American-football linebacker, a collision which sent Danny skidding on his bottom across cracked cement. When he stood up, the tattered fabric of his trousers and pants offered a view of an arse that may as well have been attacked by a cheese grater.

Iain grabbed my wrist and hauled me to my feet. We ran. I no longer had faith that I would beat Danny Faulkner in a fight that day, but I knew he wouldn't outrun me. After giving chase for a short distance and falling farther behind by the second, Danny resorted to launching the bloodied branch. It soared over my head like a mini-caber, bounced end over end along the tarmac, then lodged against a dry-stone dyke.

Fleeing into the woods, I looked back and shouted, as loud as my gasping lungs would allow, "Ya bullyin' bastard, Faulkner! You think you're big, pickin' on primary-school kids. The next time I see you on the spazzy bus, I'll lob a brick through your fuckin' window!"

"I'm not a spazzy, ya wee prick! I don't get the spazzy bus! You're away to bum-blast each other, ya wee poofs! I'm gonnae batter your fuckin' heids to pulp…" As I ran, Danny's threats faded out of range.

Iain and I didn't stop running until we reached his flat, where I cleaned the blood off my face with hot water and TCP. Soon, the only evidence that I had been in a fight was a bloody lump - the size and shape of half a grapefruit - on my left temple. We told Iain's brother Tom what had happened at the old swing park, hoping for some Western-movie-style redemption. Instead, Tom said, "You're a pair o' cheeky wee bastards. You probably deserved worse."

Disheartened, I left Iain's flat and boarded a bus. DT was the same age as Danny Faulkner and had the advantage of being a demon-driven aficionado of violence: the perfect avenger. On the back seat of the upper deck, I reflected on the beating I'd just received. Halfway along my journey, DT boarded the bus accompanied by an individual as heavily muscled as a prize bull, spirals of orange hair corkscrewing out from his huge head, which, to avoid banging on the ceiling, he had to duck while walking up the aisle. Clear blue eyes gazed out from the giant's milk-white face. Faded jeans with oil stains and rips covered his tree-trunk legs. Over his AC/DC T-shirt was a denim jacket, on top of which he wore a sleeveless leather biker jacket. This struck me as strange; it was a common heavy metal fashion to rip the arms off a denim jacket and wear it over the top of a leather biker jacket, but until now I had never seen it done the other way round. (DT and I had long ago ripped the arms off our denim jackets, then covered them with patches and studs, for aesthetic effect and added heavy metal credibility.)

"This is Ozzy," DT said, indicating his enormous companion. "He's a crazy bastard. Yesterday he asked oor maths teacher for some help. While the guy was leanin' over Ozzy's desk and writin' formulae in his jotter, Oz took oot a lighter and set the fucker's tie on fire."

Certain that DT must have fabricated this story, I turned to Ozzy and asked, "Is that true?"

Without the slightest trace of bravado, the behemoth replied, "Aye. That bastard's never liked me, and his tie was one o' those ones wi' a piano keyboard on it. Someone had to set it on fire. Know what I mean?"

Dissolving into laughter, I told Ozzy, "I wouldnae like you if you set my clothes on fire, especially while I was in them."

"What happened to your heid, Spark?" asked DT. "It looks like a bag o' bashed-tae-fuck spanners." I recounted the violent events of earlier, after which Ozzy informed me that he and Danny Faulkner lived in the same street and had been friends until two years earlier, when Danny, aged eleven, had tried to finger Ozzy's nine-year-old sister. Ozzy's fists had pummelled the life out of that friendship, and very nearly out of Danny Faulkner too.

I began to feel as if I had known the haystack-haired Ozzy a long time. Unable to contain my curiosity about his fashion sense any longer, I asked, "Why did you cut the sleeves off a leather jacket and put it over the top of a denim one?"

"Because he's a big dense bastard, that's why," answered DT. Ozzy's cheeks flushed as Dave lay across the back seat, hands behind his head as a pillow.

"The first time DT came round to my hoose," Oz explained, "he was wearin' a leather biker jacket wi' a cut-off denim jacket over the top. The waistcoat had Motörhead, Saxon, AC/DC and Rainbow patches on the back and AC/DC's logo in studs across the top. I thought he was the coolest-lookin' son of a bitch I'd ever seen, so I decided to follow suit. I borrowed my Mum's garden shears and cut the arms off my leather jacket." DT's laughter erupted so hard that he rolled off the seat and onto the filthy floor of the bus, where he lay in stitches among the fag-ends, empty beer cans and spit.

"Why did you cut the arms off the leather jacket?" I queried. "Were you tryin' to be original?"

"No," Ozzy replied, "I just got confused."

"That's an example of what happens when you have a gigantic heid inhabited by a pea-brain," observed DT.

Ozzy shrugged and formed a tight-lipped smile: a silent admission that Dave had hit the nail directly on the head. Changing tack, I asked, "Are you called Ozzy after Ozzy Osbourne?"

"It's nothin' to do wi' that lunatic. My real name's Alan Oswaldo, so that's where Ozzy comes from. My Mum's Spanish. Oswaldo's a Spanish surname."

"We get our surnames from our fathers, though," I said, aware that I might be broaching a touchy subject.

"Ozzy's Dad was the milkman," grinned DT. "Alan Oswaldo is better than Alan McMilkman. How many Spaniards have you seen wi' milky-bar skin, frizzy orange hair and blue eyes?"

"I don't know who my Dad was," admitted Ozzy, a faraway look in his eyes. "I've asked my Mum, but she never wants to talk aboot it."

Upon seeing the heartbreak in Ozzy's expression, I overflowed with affection for the giant. "That's too sad. I cannae imagine no' knowin' my Dad. And Dave, you're a disturbed human being."

Unfazed, DT grinned. "What's your point, caller?"

"My point is that anyone wi' a heart would feel compassion, but you're makin' jokes aboot the milkman delivering an extra pint up Ozzy's Mum. That's warped."

"Guilty as charged," DT admitted. "Evil, warped and disturbed, but that's why you like me." I shook my head; the facets of DT I liked so much were his wildness, his freedom and his refusal to give a shit what anyone thought of him. He was a truly free spirit. When he savoured other people's misfortune, however, it didn't endear him to me.

Oz frisked his candyfloss hair. "DT makes cruel comments sometimes, but I don't think he means them. And whenever I talk aboot anythin' sad or serious, he makes jokes. I think he does it to lighten the mood, like that's his way of tryin' to cheer me up. He's always there when I need him, though. He'd always back me up in a fight."

I agreed with Ozzy to a degree. DT did use humour as a defence mechanism, perhaps to avoid dealing with difficult feelings, but he wasn't always a pillar of light; I had seen in him a malice which terrified me. I loved DT, aye. He was my blood brother, for sure, forever, but demons lurked in his dark soul, waiting to be unleashed. That much I knew.

Seven weeks later, DT and I left Bronzehall pool after training and discovered a red-faced Ozzy running up the hill to meet us. Gasping for breath, the giant gushed, "You'll love this! I was just on the same bus as Danny Faulkner. I sat beside him and told him the wee guy he beat up in the swing park was my friend. He panicked and said that you'd called him a spazzy, and that you deserved what he did to you. When I reminded him that he'd started the whole thing by callin' you and Iain poofs and tellin' you to get oot o' the swing park, he started shakin'. He was shittin' himself, but his mooth went into overdrive. He shouted that it was none o' my business and that I should let 'that wee poof fight his own battles'."

"I'm not a wee poof," I protested, "or a poof of any magnitude for that matter."

"I know that," smiled Oz. "Those were Danny's words. Anyway, I didn't like the smug look on his coupon or the way he was moothin' off at me, so I grabbed him by the hair and slammed his heid into a metal seat back."

"Did he stop moothin' off at you after that?"

"Of course. He was unconscious."

"Holy shit! You knocked him oot?"

DT piped in, "When Oz hits you, you know you've been hit. That tit Faulkner will definitely be catchin' the spazzy bus noo…if he's no' deid."

Oz flew into a panic. "Oh fuck, do you think I've killed him?"

DT's dark eyes glittered. "I hope so. I hope you've panned his spazzy heid right in. The prick got what was comin' to him."

"Shit, Dave," I gasped, "that's a bit over the top. I don't want Faulkner deid and it was me he beat the shit oot of. Ozzy will be knee-deep in keech if Danny dies. The cops will find Oz easily. He isn't exactly inconspicuous."

"I know," DT agreed, "can you imagine how good it would be on Crimewatch? Imagine the reconstruction: *Did you see a man matching this description on a Bronzehall bus – six and a half feet tall, orange afro hair, bright blue eyes, milk-white skin, and wearing – inexplicably - a denim jacket with a leather cut-off waistcoat over the top? Studs on the back of the leather waistcoat were arranged to spell 'Moröhead'. Presumably, this is a mis-spelling of the heavy metal band Motörhead or, somewhat ironically, a wrongly spelled Moronhead. Police are looking for a frizzy-orange-haired giant who listens to heavy metal music, possibly rides a motorcycle and definitely has spelling issues."* As DT cackled like a crone, amusement expanded inside me. Not wanting to laugh, I bit my bottom lip so hard that I tasted blood, but pain failed to keep a lid on my mirth. I crumbled onto the grass and let my laughter out. "It's no' funny, ya pair o' dicks!" boomed Ozzy. "I didn't want to cave Faulkner's heid in. I only wanted to teach him a lesson. I'm away home to phone the police. I need to find oot if any teenagers have had their heids panned in on buses today."

Ozzy swept down the hill, his hair rippling in the breeze, while DT and I lay howling on the grass. We were still laughing when Oz disappeared into the yellow horizon.

It turned out that Ozzy had not killed Danny Faulkner, but had given him the gift of concussion with overnight accommodation in hospital thrown in as a bonus. To show my gratitude, I offered to become Ozzy's blood brother. We did the ritual in his loft, to the soundtrack of Ozzy Osbourne's *Blizzard of Ozz*. As Randy Rhoads carved sonic sculptures with his axe, Ozzy's blood mixed with mine.

Two weeks later, DT and I hid from the Saturday afternoon sun in Ozzy's loft. We spent hours listening to UFO's *Lights Out* and Rainbow's *Rising*, playing air guitar, drinking Irn-Bru and talking shit with Oz. Dave and I left at tea time. As we walked up the street, Danny Faulkner sprang out from behind a hedge, golf club in hand, and swung it at my head. I ducked in time to feel the 7-iron skiff the top of my mane. Muscles supercharged by an adrenaline surge, I sprinted back to Ozzy's house.

This was the day on which DT's ever-good luck ran out. His screams of agony shook the sky as I shouted through Ozzy's letterbox, "Faulkner's killin' DT wi' a golf club!"

Oz emerged from his house and lumbered up the street as fast as his large frame would move. We found Dave in a foetal position on the pavement, blood dyeing one leg of his jeans magenta. Golf club held high, Danny screamed, "You picked on the wrong fuckin' guy!"

In an emotionless tone, Oz replied, "I didn't pick on you, Faulkner. I gave you a taste of your own medicine. You reap what you sow."

Gritting his teeth, Danny swung the club at Ozzy, who made no attempt to avoid the impact. It struck his chest with a dull thump which bent the shaft of the club but elicited no reaction from the giant. Not a flinch. Not a grimace. Not an ouch or an ohyabass. Just a freezing glare. Oz grabbed the business end of the 7-iron, plucked it from Danny's grip like a father confiscating a toy from a mischievous child, snapped the club over one knee, discarded the broken pieces, then loosed a punch. The blow struck Danny's chin with enough force to uproot a block of flats, sending him soaring into low-level horizontal flight, arms outstretched like a human plane. Danny's impressive aerobatic display ended with an emergency landing on paving slabs. After a loud crack, Danny lay still. Unconscious. Again.

DT rose from the ground clutching his bleeding leg. "Give me that golf club! I'm gonnae shove it up Faulkner's fuckin' arse!"

Danny's shallow breathing showed that was still alive, but the fast-expanding red pool beneath his head suggested that without help he wouldn't be that way for long. "We need to phone this arsehole an ambulance," I urged. "The blood's pishin' oot of his heid."

"Aye," agreed Ozzy, "he'll die if we don't do somethin'. Let's go back to my hoose and phone 999."

"Fuck that," DT protested. "Why risk gettin' oorselves in trouble? If this wank dies, he dies. I'll no' miss him. In fact, I'm gonnae kick fuck oot o' him right noo." Dave limped across to Danny and thundered a boot into his ribs.

"Dave, for fuck's sake," I pleaded, "you're not gonnae get a reaction from kickin' an unconscious body!"

"That's true," he smiled, "but I could pull doon his pants and shove the broken bits o' golf club up his arsehole. How funny would it be if an ambulance arrived and found two halves of a 7-iron stickin' oot o' Faulkner's jacksie?"

"Aye," I agreed, "that would be funny, but the unfunny bit would be if he died and we got done for it, all because you wasted time shovin' things up his arse. There's a word for men who like to stick things up other men's bottoms, you know. This is how it starts. First a golf club, then it'll be a curious finger, and pretty soon it'll be your tadger."

DT's eyebrows jumped halfway up his forehead. "Ya wee bastard, I'm no poofter!"

"Well quit tryin' to jam things up Faulkner's arse then. You're actin' more bent than a fiddler's elbow."

"I am *not* a fuckin' arsebandit! I'm gonnae boot your balls!"

His patience wearing thin, Oz announced, "No one's bootin' anyone's balls. We need to get back to my hoose to call an ambulance. If you two pricks start fightin' wi' each other I'll knock you both oot and you'll be sharin' an ambulance wi' spazzy boy here. Understand?"

Oz and I ran to his house while the injured DT limped behind us, muttering curses under his breath. After Oz called 999, he and I watched from his loft window as the ambulance arrived. Paramedics lifted Danny onto a stretcher, slid him into the back of the ambulance then drove off in a hail of blaring sirens and flashing blue lights. DT didn't watch. DT didn't give a shit what happened to Danny Faulkner.

An hour later Ozzy phoned the hospital, pretending to be a Faulkner family member. A nurse informed him that Danny had sustained a broken jaw, a fractured skull, a major concussion and had needed eighteen stitches on the back of his head.

Cycling home from DT's house later that night, I reflected on the phenomenon that was Ozzy. Gigantic and powerful, yet gentle by nature. Able to cause serious physical damage with very little effort, but harbouring no desire to harm anyone or anything. The injuries Oz inflicted on others were a side effect of hanging around with DT and me. Oz was the personification of integrity and justice, a perfect counterpoise to the remorseless DT, while I treaded a path somewhere between those two poles, careful never to sway too far to either side. I understood that those who pursue good or evil often become victims of – or slaves to – their values. Look what happened to Jesus. Consider Satan's eternal fall from grace. Fuck that!

A pang of responsibility for Danny's injuries shot through me but lasted only a moment, dissipating as Oz's voice boomed into my mind. "You reap what you sow."

I liked having Ozzy as my reaper.

Chapter 8 – Spark in the Dark

My first heavy metal concert was a life-changing event. When Iron Maiden played the Glasgow Apollo as part of their *Beast on the Road* tour, I had just turned eleven, which my parents deemed too young to attend gigs. Luckily, the fourteen-year-old DT, whom my mother and father believed to be a model of virtue, assured them that he would accompany me to the gig and keep me safe.

DT and I arrived at the Apollo to find a queue of metalheads stretching up the street and round the corner. As we flowed into the sea of denim, leather and hair, two mods buzzed along the road on Lambretta scooters. The nearer rider's oversized green parka had a German flag on one arm and *The Who* emblazoned across the back. A red traffic light forced the mods to stop next to the 2000 hairy headbangers whose eyes were locked onto them. I could feel tension in the air, but I wasn't sure what was happening or why.

As the traffic lights turned green, the parka-wearing mod stuck two fingers up in a V sign aimed at the metal throng, then revved up his engine and attempted to make his escape on a scooter with the horsepower of a hairdryer. Not one of his better ideas. The crowd surged like a mighty ocean, engulfing the scooters. An angry army of metal maniacs dragged both mods up a side street and beat them to bloody pulps, while their scooters were stamped into scrap metal, decimated beyond recognition.

I made a mental note not to stick up a V sign at 2000 mods, should I ever stumble across that many in one place. It may look brave and boost street credibility for a fleeting moment, but it wasn't a recipe for a long, healthy life.

Nothing could have prepared DT and me for the spectacle that was Iron Maiden. We had often played their music at deafening volume in dark rooms, but it had been invisible noise. Now, live in three dimensions, we saw the source of that music for the first time: the band – Iron Maiden - a larger-than-life tribe of hairy bastards clad in skintight spandex, leather and studs. Their hair seemed to come alive onstage as it billowed and swirled, absorbing the variegated colours of overhead lights. Walls of black amplifiers pumped out vast noise. Dry ice formed an eerie mist on the stage, giving the impression that the band was wading through a fantastical, otherwordly landscape.

This was Iron Maiden's first tour with their new singer, Bruce Dickinson, who had been drafted in from Samson (with whom he had sung under the inexplicable moniker Bruce Bruce). On this tour, he looked and sounded better than ever before, plus he had sorted out his nonsensical nomenclature.

It was all coming together for Iron Maiden. They had just released *The Number of the Beast*, a true pinnacle of heavy metal achievement. DT and I had skipped school to buy the album on the day of its release, determined to hold the proverbial baby as it was born. Now we were watching Iron Maiden declare sonic and visual domination over all other bands. They were, in a word, *astonishing*.

Life began to make an increasing amount of sense to DT and me. Conceptual puzzle pieces were falling into place. We had discovered that heavy metal need not only be something you listen to. That first Iron Maiden concert drove home to us the vital truth that heavy metal can *be* your life, if you create it. It can bring fans, riches, creative satisfaction, travel and – perhaps most importantly – girls.

Seeds had been planted in two young and fertile minds.

Chapter 9 – Bonded by Blood

DT started the gang because he lived to fight. Obsessed with warfare, he spent endless hours in his room sketching blueprints for weapons, most of which he went on to actually create. Naming the gang Blood Brothers was my idea. I had four blood brothers at that time: my cousin Neil in Canada; Iain Bright; DT; Ozzy. Each of them had only one blood brother: me. When I suggested to DT that every member of our gang should be an actual blood brother to all the others, he frowned and said, "That's a lot o' palm-slicin'."

I stuck out my bottom lip and affected a baby voice. "Is tough man Dave scared o' the big nasty knife?"

"Shut it, ya wee tit. I'm not scared of a bit o' blood."

"I know how to do this ritual with maximum efficiency."

"Share then, genius."

"I don't need to cut myself, so I'll take care o' the music. You need to mix blood wi' Iain and Ozzy, and they need to mix blood wi' each other. The three of you will stand in a triangle and cut your palms. You'll touch one palm wi' Iain and the other wi' Ozzy, and they'll touch their spare palms together."

"That seems a little gay wi' all of us touchin' like that."

"Well you'll love it, won't you, ya poofy bastard?"

A smile broke through DT's facade. "Did I ever mention that you're a wee tit?"

"You've mentioned it on occasion, aye."

The ritual took place the following week. I was, by virtue of being the only one not leaking blood, the official DJ for the occasion. I decided that the track *If You Want Blood (You've Got It)* by AC/DC was the most appropriate lyrical accompaniment to the ritual. Plus it was AC/DC, for God's sake. One can never go wrong with AC/DC. *(If I ever wake up disorientated and unsure of the world, playing AC/DC is the first thing I do, before even drinking coffee. It works. It doesn't matter which AC/DC album you throw on – they all do the job nicely - but anything with Bon Scott on vocals is preferable. No disrespect to Brian 'Beano' Johnson, Bon's successor, who is a fine singer and frontman. Few could have followed in Bon's footsteps as admirably as Beano has done. There's something about Bon's voice, though, that makes me feel rough and clean and raw and energetic and alive in the truest sense. He was my childhood icon and the most confident frontman ever to walk a stage. I often wonder what would have happened if he hadn't drunk himself into oblivion and choked on his vomit. What unsung tunes did he take to the grave, never to be heard? Wrestling with this question has kept me awake many nights and driven me to the precipice where wonder plummets into madness. Bon Scott, you are missed. I digress, though – back to the ritual.)*

DT's house was chosen as the location for the bloodletting. His parents were away for the day, so we had the bungalow to ourselves. Plus he had a Bang & Olufsen sound system which looked like something out of a black-and-white American sci-fi movie and could play music at ear-splitting volume without a trace of distortion. I went to DT's house at noon in order to prepare, having told Ozzy and Iain to be there by 2 p.m. Dave laid a groundsheet in his room to soak up any blood splashes. (He had caught Hell from his mother after our first fight, when my blood had stained his carpet.) DT had just switched on the percolator when Ozzy arrived and observed, "That coffee smells fuckin' magic."

"That," I explained, "is for afterwards. Coffee and cake will be served once we're all officially blood brothers."

"You're a lucky wee bastard, Spark," whined Oz. "You can just sit back and enjoy the show. No bleedin' for you today."

"I've done this ritual more times than any o' you," I replied. "Today I'll enjoy watchin' you pansies grimace in pain."

A shadow flickered across DT's eyes. "I love pain. It reminds you that you're alive."

"Where did you hear that shit?" asked Oz. "In one o' your Vietnam books?"

"Actually, smartarse, it was. There's a lot o' useful information, such as Vietcong tortures, in those books. Did you know, for example, that the Vietcong used to shove narrow glass phials up captured American soldiers' pee-holes, then lay their cocks on wooden tables and whack them wi' hammers, shatterin' the glass and laceratin' the tadgers from the inside?"

I shook my head. "You, David Tierney, as I've observed before, are one warped human being, if you are human. I have my doubts."

"I'll take that as a compliment," replied DT. He burrowed in his pocket, pulled out a handful of crumpled pound notes, stuffed them into my palm and ordered me to go to the shop for cakes. As Oz and I walked up the street, Dave shouted, "Make sure the cakes are Mr Kipling! If you come back wi' some inferior shite, I'll fuckin' shoot you both!" I giggled, guessing that he was talking about his spud gun. With DT, though, I never knew for sure.

Ozzy and I sauntered the half mile to the shops at Svartnatt Square, talking about music as we strolled. On returning to DT headquarters with a Manor House Cake and twelve Apple & Custard Pies, we found a ghost-faced Iain Bright trembling on the living room sofa, an angry bruise rising on his forehead. "What happened to you, wee man?" asked Oz.

"When I rang the bell, that fuckin' maniac DT opened the door and shot me between the eyes. Point blank."

"He shot you wi' a spud gun," I said. "It was only compressed potato that hit you."

"Aye, I know that noo, but I didn't when the crazy bastard pointed the gun at my heid and pulled the trigger. It made a bang and hurt like fuck. I grabbed my heid and started screamin', then lay doon in the garden to die, which seemed like the right thing to do under the circumstances. I was oot there makin' a prize tit of myself, waitin' for my life to start flashin' before my eyes, and that sick fucker DT was laughin' so hard that tears were runnin' doon his cheeks. Eventually, he confessed to shootin' me wi' compressed tattie, then told me to shut the fuck up and quit greetin' like a wee girl. Go and look in his room. You won't believe what the lunatic's up to. I'm no' doin' this ritual, I'll tell you that. There's no way I'm swappin' blood wi' that demonic nutjob. Whatever's inside him isn't gettin' into me."

Leaving the shellshocked Iain in Ozzy's gentle care, I hurried to DT's room. The windows were blacked out. Laid across the floor was a white sheet decorated with a huge pentagram in fresh blood. Five black candles were burning, one on each point of the pentagram. Dave was naked and twisted into an impossible knot on his bed, like a yoga master in a painful posture, or a gnarled tree in a grotesque imitation of humanity. He stared into space, apparently oblivious to the copious flow of blood from the gash on his right hand. Hoping to snap Dave out of his reverie, I slapped his face and asked, "What's the deal wi' the bare arse and the bloody pentagram? This isn't a Satanic rite. You've scared the shit oot of Iain. He doesn't want to do the ritual noo."

DT's darksparkled eyes bored into me like demonic drills. "It looks as cool as fuck, right? It's not meant to be Satanic. Just metal. A pentagram in blood. That's a good song title, eh Spark? *Pentagram in Blood.*"

Without a word, I left DT to bleed alone. In the living room, Ozzy's giant arm was draped round Iain's quivering shoulders as the giant made a valiant effort to console him. "I'm like Luke Skywalker," Oz philosophised, "innocent and good-hearted, but never scared o' fightin' for my beliefs. DT is like Darth Vader – evil, remorseless and tuned to the dark side. Spark is oor Han Solo. That wee tit hovers between good and evil, swayin' either way dependin' on the situation. Imagine how powerful a gang we'll be if we can harness both light and dark sides o' the Force!"

Won over by Ozzy's inescapable logic, Iain asked, "Can I be oor Chewbacca? Chewie's my favourite Star Wars character."

Ozzy gazed at Iain through eyes like deep, still seas. "That's exactly what I was thinkin'. We need a character like that."

Once Iain had stopped shaking, we all convened in DT's bedroom. After instructing Ozzy, Dave and Iain to stand on the circular perimeter of the bloody pentagram, I flicked open DT's knife and began cutting palms. The atmosphere in the room was worlds apart from that of the ritual I had done in Canada, surrounded by nature in the raw. Dave had deliberately created an ambience of fire, blood and devilry.

I lowered needle onto vinyl. *If You Want Blood (You've Got It)* blasted through Bang & Olufsen speakers, dragging us all back to the familiar territory of our most safe and sacred place: the Sonic Fortress of Heavy Metal. I commanded my blood brothers to clasp palms. They obeyed. With humans in place of electrical components, the scene resembled a circuit that could not be broken until I gave the word. When the song finished I raised my fists into the air and announced with epic grandiosity, "Noo we are all blood brothers!" Waving my arms around in wild gesticulations, I added, "The blood ritual is complete! From this moment on, we four will live and breathe for each other! Blood Brothers the gang – the *tribe* – has been born! Nothin' will ever be the same again!"

Later, as we guzzled coffee and ate cakes, I learned two irrefutably constant truths about this perpetually shifting Universe: energy flowed around the blood-brothers circuit whether we were touching or not; and Mr Kipling really did make exceedingly good cakes.

Chapter 10 – A World of Fantasy

Life was bliss as part of the gang. Our four diverse personalities were held together by one common factor: love…of each other and heavy metal. We represented more than friends or family to each other. We were therapists, defenders, compatriots, confidants, creators, composers, poets, lyricists, innovators, jokers, philosophers, discoverers, warriors and much, much more. I felt most at home when hanging out with the gang, perhaps akin to the 'coming home' that many people experience during meditation. Just being around each other was our meditation.

If I needed to talk about the meaning of life and the deeper significance of the Universe, Iain Bright was my man. When I felt the desire to participate in gung-ho adventures, there was no better sidekick than DT, who half-jokingly signed my birthday and Christmas cards 'Your Partner-in-Crime'. During my dark moods, Ozzy lightened my spirits like no one else could. And when we four fought together as a team, our combined force did to adversaries what tidal waves do to sandcastles.

Music had brought us together. Heavy metal was our united vision and our religion. The mighty deities of heavy metal – the Metal Gods - began sending me psychic messages during waking hours and sleep: Blood Brothers must become more than just a gang, the thunderous voices boomed. It was time, the Metal Gods declared, to balance out the destruction that the gang inflicted, and to do so by forming a band and creating music of a heaviness never before imagined. Only *creating* could temper our rampaging bloodthirstiness and stop it from becoming our dominant impetus. *If you let destruction drive you,* the Metal Gods explained, *it will drive you down a one-way road to a violent demise.* 'But we love to fight,' I argued, psychically. The Metal Gods' reply made absolute sense. *You can **love** to fight but you must **live** to create perfect sonic metal that changes the world for the better. You must have equilibrium.*

Seven days after first unveiling my mystic revelations to the gang, I received a phone call from a hyper-excited DT. "Get over to my hoose right away, ya wee tit! It's important!" He hung up before I could reply, so I threw on denim and leather, then cycled from my house in Vikingwood to DT's bungalow in Svartnatt, at the other end of Bronzehall. Dripping with sweat and anticipation, I arrived and hammered the door. Mrs Tierney, who reminded me of a bustier Marilyn Monroe, greeted me with a wide smile and a hug. "David's in his room with his new toy," she said. "On you go through, Spark."

As I walked up the long hallway, my ears were assaulted by a cacophony from DT's room. There was no recognisable melody or tune: just a wall of heavy crunching noise. When I opened the bedroom door, my mouth fell open in awe. DT stood in the centre of the room looking every inch the rock star: cherry-red Les Paul guitar slung round his neck; glossy black hair flowing down his back; red leather trousers so tight they looked sprayed on; an Iron Maiden tour T-shirt (with its arms torn off) covering his torso. The look on Dave's face made it clear that his mind had escaped. He was lost in sound, eyes closed, expression somewhere between serenity and ecstasy. A black Marshall amplifier made every plucked note sound majestic and huge. DT was born to do this, I realised. The Metal Gods, unlike other deities, never make mistakes. They knew that Dave, after acquiring technical skill on guitar, would be a fretboard force to be reckoned with, a sonic and visual hurricane. DT stopped playing and opened his eyes. "What do you think?"

"I think you've got a cherry-red Les Paul and a Marshall amp, ya lucky bastard."

"I told my Dad aboot the Metal Gods' idea to start a band. He isn't convinced that you receive communication from the Metal Gods, or even that they exist, but he does think a band's an excellent way of keepin' us off the streets and oot o' trouble, so he bought me these."

"Are you gonnae get lessons?"

"Aye, my Dad's gonnae pay for a lesson a week. Noo all we need is a bass player, a singer and a drummer. You can fight wi' Oz and Iain over who plays which instrument."

"We all want to be axemen," I pointed out, "but four guitar players doesn't make a band. We'll have to call a meetin' to decide on oor roles."

"This the start of somethin' huge, Spark. I can *feel* it. We should take the fires that were lit inside us at the Iron Maiden concert and fan them into ragin' infernos." Dave handed me his guitar. The noises I cranked out of it weren't tuneful, but they were *loud*. A feeling of infinite power ran through my body as, for the first time, I felt the connection between mind, muscle and music. It was all one and the same. Another piece of the jigsaw which is the Universe fell neatly into place.

When Iain and Ozzy arrived, the arguments DT and I had anticipated failed to occur. Oz wanted to play drums. It made sense for him to be our drummer, as he was a natural powerhouse who made John Bonham look like a stick insect by comparison.

I liked the idea of fronting our band as its singer. Bon Scott was my idol and role model (except for the choking-on-vomit-and-dying stunt). I had no formal singing experience or training, but we were all starting out raw and inexperienced. No one had any argument with me handling vocals, so my role in the band was set.

Unsure of how Iain would react to being forced into the position of bassist, I turned to him and raised my eyebrows. He smiled and said that he often pretended to play bass. DT pointed out that we weren't starting a pretend band. "Nevertheless," Iain maintained, "I've always liked pretendin' to play bass, so I'll just do that."

"Listen, ya wee fanny," DT spat, "if the rest of us learn oor crafts while you drift deeper into your fantasy world, you'll be the spare prick at the weddin'. Do you know what happens to that particular spare prick? It spends all day longin' to fuck some comely bridesmaid's warm, welcoming pussy but ends up goin' home attached to a sore pair o' balls instead."

    I understood that heavy metal was all about escapism for Iain. It was the musical equivalent of the fantasy and sci-fi novels he devoured. Music removed him from mundane reality and delivered him to a better place. Pretending to be a bassist was just another string to his imaginary bow. Buying an instrument, learning to play, rehearsing with a band, recording and touring: those were harsh realities, real-world stuff. Reality and Iain Bright, however, rarely collided.

    As DT began a vicious verbal assault on Iain, Ozzy moved his large frame between them. "Calm doon," he urged. "If we start the band wi' a real guitar player, real singer, real drummer and pretend bassist, that's still progress. It's a start point." DT, who had only moments earlier looked ready to smash his Les Paul over Iain's daydreaming head, visibly relaxed.

I wheeled my bike along the pavement as Iain and I walked home to the rougher side of town. My excitement was tinged with confusion over the surreal proposition of having a bass mime in our band. We walked parallel paths in silence, my glance occasionally straying across to my blood brother; he was there in body, only a couple of feet to my left, but it was clear that his mind was in another galaxy. Throughout the rest of the journey home, I contemplated strategies for bringing Iain's awareness down to Earth and to the gritty reality of forging molten sonic metal.

There was no rush, I decided. This band, as with most worthwhile things, would take time and effort. The Metal Gods agreed. *Good things take time.*

Chapter 11 – Big Bottom

My family and the Tierneys began to spend increasing amounts of time together, both at the swimming pool and away from it. Our fathers became buddies who spent most of their spare time together, listening to classical and Scottish music, drinking whisky and smoking cigars. Our mothers also became best of friends. DT and I were inseparable adventurers.

One spring night, my Dad asked me what I thought about going on holiday with the Tierneys that summer. The room arrangements would be: Mr and Mrs Tierney in one room; my Mum and Dad in another; Dave and me in a third. I gave the idea my immediate endorsement. Wild things happened when I was with DT, so two weeks with him in foreign lands would lead to decadent adventures. Three months later, we boarded a plane bound for the Balearic island of Menorca.

I was thirteen and DT sixteen. He had deflowered six of the swimming club's girls and seven girls from school, while my virginity was very much intact. This holiday, I hoped, would change that. With Dave as my coach, I figured my chances were good.

When the plane's door opened at Mahon Airport, a wave of dry heat swept into the cabin. I stepped out onto metal stairs and saw tarmac baking under the Mediterranean sun. Flanked by palm trees, the runway stretched into a dusty, heat-haze horizon.

After our evening meal at the hotel, DT and I set out on a quest to find hot girls and cold beer. We soon found a bar called Manolo's among the whiter-than-white, flat-roofed buildings of Biniancolla. The owner stood about five feet tall and six feet wide, with shoulder-length black hair and a thick bandito moustache which - combined with his tanned, muscular torso - gave him the look of a Mexican baddie from a Sergio Leone movie, with a hint of Hell's Angel thrown in for good measure. Manolo introduced himself with an easy handshake and a wide smile that put us instantly at ease.

Dave and I sat on high stools at the bar. Manolo asked about my Saxon T-shirt, so we educated him on the nuances of the New Wave of British Heavy Metal, while he poured us a pitcher of the local beer, San Miguel, on the house. Soon, with alcohol infiltrating my mind, I began to think on a different level. "Manolo, did you buy this bar because of its name?"

The Spaniard swept sweat-soaked hair off his face and fixed me with a perplexed gaze. "What are you talking about, gringo loco?"

"Well the bar's called Manolo's and your name's Manolo. There's no way that's coincidence. That's fuckin' destiny!" I impaled the air with the Eureka finger of epiphany.

Manolo grabbed me in a friendly headlock and explained, through garlic-heavy breath, "First Manolo the man. Then Manolo's the bar.

Crazy Scottish hombre!" With the bar's nomenclature issues resolved in my mind, I began to wonder why Manolo's chef was putting round pizzas into square boxes. DT, meanwhile, told Manolo about my ineptitude at chatting up women. Our host poured us another pitcher of beer, which he promised would lubricate my lips and make talking to girls much easier.

 After disposing of the second pitcher of beer, DT and I ordered a large jug of fresh sangria, which looked like blood, tasted like chilled fruit juice and was so easy to drink that we drained the jug dry in seconds. As Mediterranean booze drowned my shyness, every woman in the vicinity - regardless of age, colour, shape, smell or bodyhair configurations - became a potential lover. "What's goin' on wi' your cheeks, Spark?" asked DT. "You look like a tomato, ya poofy wee lightweight." I tried to protest, claiming to be stone-cold sober, but my slurred speech told a different story.

 DT swaggered across the bar and started talking to three girls from Merseyside: two brown-haired, blue-eyed sisters named Melody and Gail, and their gigantic friend, also called Gail. The bronze-tanned sisters were dressed in short skirts, sandals and bikini tops. A comparison revealed that sister Gail had longer legs, curlier hair and a leaner body, while sister Melody had bigger tits and a filthy look in her eyes. Their dark-eyed friend Gail, who easily weighed more than DT and me combined, had alabaster skin and black hair cut in an asymmetric bob. Her green dress could have made a comfortable four-man tent. Dave christened the larger Gail *Mud-Wrestler Gail* and the other one *Sister Gail*, which seemed like a good system to avoid any Gail-related confusion. I was all for equality, so when DT disappeared out of the bar with the big-titted Melody (whom he had nicknamed *Melons*), I invited both Gails back to my room. Sister Gail accepted the offer with an excited yelp, while the less enthusiastic Mud-Wrestler Gail followed behind us.

 In the room, while I boiled the kettle and made cups of tea for us all, Sister Gail stripped down to her red lace bra and panties. My heart raced as I gazed at her sun-kissed curves: an athletic physique with a hint of puppy fat around the tummy, making it all the more soft and feminine. Grabbing a fistful of my hair, Sister Gail kissed me. Over her shoulder, I saw Mud-Wrestler Gail roll her eyes then pick up her cup of tea and wander onto the balcony. I broke away from Sister Gail's rough embrace and joined Mud-Wrestler Gail outside. "I'm fine," she growled, "this always happens. I'm used to it. Melody and Gail end up taking guys home at the end of the night and I'm left on my own. Go inside and fook her. I'll be fine out here with my tea."

 Sister Gail positioned herself on the bed: face down, ass up, legs apart, dark hair following the curve of her spine. I had seen this seductive doggy-style pose a million times in magazines like Men Only and Penthouse, but never in the flesh.

 Weird consciousness shifts began to happen in my mind. An athletic girl in lacy underwear was kneeling half-naked on my bed, ready to be fucked senseless, practically *begging* to be ransacked, yet my eyes kept straying to the enormous girl on the balcony. I *had* to see what lay under her marquee-sized dress. My fuzzy brain couldn't tell whether the beer and sangria were perverting my sexual proclivities or just unlocking them. I had never before wanted to plunder a girl twice my size; perhaps those urges had been hidden deep in my subconscious and had surfed into my conscious mind on a wave of alcohol. The source of the urges didn't matter, though. All that mattered was slipping Mud-Wrestler Gail out of her dress, immersing myself in her rolls of fat, feeling her soft warmth, licking every inch of her immense body, touching her, tasting her, fucking her.

On the bed, Sister Gail pouted then flipped onto her back and spread her legs wide, beckoning me with a finger gesture. I stripped to my underwear then lay on top of her. She eased my pants down with one hand and scratched patterns on my back with the other. Despite getting my dick stroked by Sister Gail, my attention again drifted to the big girl who stood alone on the balcony, sipping tea and staring at the Spanish sky. "I feel bad for Mud-Wrestler Gail," I confessed. "I'm gonnae invite her in." I staggered out to the balcony, my erection jutting skywards as if pointing out star constellations.

Frowning at my hard-on, Mud-Wrestler Gail asked, "What do you think you're going to do with that, exactly?"

"I don't think. I *know*. It's time to take the bull by the horns or, to use a more appropriate bovine analogy, the cow by its hefty udders." I squeezed Mud-Wrestler Gail's voluminous breasts through her dress, then took her face in my hands, pulled her towards me and kissed her. She responded by grinding her groin into my thigh. Through the thin material of her dress, my tumescent tadger probed the soft folds of her tummy. I liked the immersive feel of that. She didn't protest when I undressed her under Mediterranean starlight and led her into the bedroom. Mud-Wrestler Gail in all her naked glory was a mind-bending sight. Under torpedo tits with saucer-sized brown nipples were multi-layered fat folds which moved like waves. When I stood behind her and beheld her wide-as-a-house rump, the deep, dark bumcrack begged me to plumb its depths. I'm not speaking metaphorically either: the sangria may have played a part in this, but Mud-Wrestler Gail's bottom actually whispered to me, in dulcet tones, "Spark, bury your face in the deep crevice between these bounteous buttocks. At the bottom of the chasm is hidden a tight orifice. Lick it. Spit your saliva onto it. Probe it with your tongue. Then, when you feel it loosening and relaxing, impale it on your Scottish cock." The words from the mighty backside fuelled my erection, which swelled so much that I worried it might explode.

Sister Gail, who was in somewhat of a huff by this point, was hiding under the covers. I pulled the sheets off her and tossed them, along with the last vestiges of my inhibition, onto the floor. Standing naked between the two Gails, my tadger was finally in charge of proceedings; it told me –

like a no-nonsense sergeant barking orders at inexperienced troops - what to say and how to say it. Pointing an index finger at Sister Gail, I commanded, "You in the bed, get your bra and panties off! This is no time for shyness or pissy moods!" I spun to face the big girl. "And you, what the hell are you waitin' on? Get into bed next to your friend and kiss her the way you just kissed me! I want tongues, damnit!" Without defiance, the Gails obeyed. Naked, they kissed, the abundant flesh of the larger girl's bottom spilling over the edge of the mattress. After spanking Mud-Wrestler Gail's arse so hard it stung my palm, I jumped on top of the entangled girls. Like true coital champions, they didn't break their kiss. With a pert pink-nippled tit cupped in one hand and a mammoth brown-nippled breast overflowing from the other, I joined in with the kissing. Warm hands caressed my body. As my dick felt the slickness of Mud-Wrestler Gail's gargantuan gash, I realised that she was the girl I wanted to devirginise me. Her bottom alone was like a planet in its own right: a huge, soft, sweaty planet which I was about to land on and claim as my own. I even had a special flagpole standing erect for the occasion. My right hand was wedged underneath Mud-Wrestler Gail's bottom while my left massaged Sister Gail's tit. The smell of female juices filled my nostrils for the first time. After years of whacking off and dreaming about sex, I was finally going to fuck a girl…and what a girl! Not only that, I was going to fuck her petite friend as an encore. Psyching myself up for first entry, I heard the bedroom door slam shut, followed by my Mum's voice - more curious than angry - asking, "What's going on in here?"

I realised that I had, in my libidinous haste, forgotten to lock the door. Like a flash, I jumped off the voluptuous beast I had been preparing to mount. My body flew but my right hand remained jammed under the big girl's arse, held fast by half a ton of rump and additionally anchored by the sharp metal pincers of my scorpion ring, which had become snagged on the sheet. As I floated through the air, the ring - remaining stubbornly hooked onto the sheets - tore off a chunk of knuckle flesh. I landed on the marble checkerboard floor, my erection swaying from side to side as if conducting an unseen orchestra. Butt-naked with blood gushing out of my finger, I stood face to face with my mother. After a glance at me, she stared at the bed and its two naked occupants, one of whom was so spectacularly large that an orangutan's arms couldn't reach round her body. At the tender age of thirteen, this was - by a country mile - the most embarrassing moment of my young life. Covering my erect tadger with a bloody hand, I pleaded, "Get oot, Mum! Please!"

But my mother didn't leave. Expecting her to fly into a rage, I gritted my teeth and waited for the flak. None came. Instead, she calmly asked the girls, "Is he a fast mover? Is he?" The Gails giggled. I had never felt less like laughing.

Put at ease by my Mum's peaceful demeanour, Sister Gail replied, "He's randy, he is. He's been taking on the two of us. He's a randy bastard!"

"I bet he is," nodded my mother. "Is he a fast mover?"

"He's wild," said Mud-Wrestler Gail. "His hands were everywhere. If you hadn't come in, he'd be fookin' me ragged."

My mother's expression frosted over. "Did he mention that he's only thirteen?" I wanted to disappear into a deep hole, never to return. As I scrambled on the floor for clothing with which to cover my blood-spattered nudity, both Gails pulled on their clothes and fled. The sound of a slamming door punctuated my Mum's wordless exit.

DT arrived back an hour later, having, in his words, nailed Melody to her bed. Twice. When I told him the story of my night, he shook his head and asked, "How could you even entertain the idea of screwin' Mud-Wrestler Gail?"

"I must have some Bon Scott genes in me, I guess. *Whole Lotta Rosie* was inspired by a huge Tasmanian woman who fucked Bon into unconsciousness. Somethin' aboot all those pounds of flesh got to me."

"Pounds? POUNDS? Try tons! Mud-Wrestler Gail would chew you up and spit you oot."

"No chance. I'd rise to that challenge in more ways than one. Seriously, Dave, my dick has never been so hard before. Ten minutes after the girls left, it was still like a batterin' ram. That big beauty stirred up things in me…things that need to be unleashed."

Covering his arse with both hands, DT backed up against the wall. "Don't look at me, ya wee uphill gardener. Just keep that thing in your pants until the next fat mama comes your way. And between you and me, I think you should keep your fat-chick exploits from the rest of the gang. Huge girls are like mopeds – tons of fun to ride, but you don't want your pals to see you on one." He swept the hair off his face and and raised a dark eyebrow.

The next morning at breakfast, DT and I sat at a separate table from our parents, at my request, for I couldn't bring myself to look my Mum in the eyes. I didn't know if she had told my Dad or the Tierneys about the incident with the Gails, but I wasn't taking any chances. Avoiding our parents until things had blown over seemed the sensible course of action.

My mother hadn't made the fuss that most mothers would have, although I suspect her reaction would have been different had I been a daughter. The most difficult aspect of the situation to get my head round was the fact that I had stood naked in front of my mother with my balls swaying in the night breeze and my erection pointing up at her chin. She never mentioned the events of that night again. Thank the Metal Gods for that.

Chapter 12 – Room for One More

Blood Brothers the band rehearsed religiously during its first three years. DT's guitar technique improved in leaps and bounds, as did the length and lustre of his glossy black hair. Ozzy bought a second-hand drum kit, set it up in his loft and played the hell out of it. I sang for at least an hour every day and learned to play DT's Les Paul. Iain Bright neither bought a bass nor learned to play one, although he never missed band practice in Ozzy's loft, throughout which warbled noises from his mouth accompanied his frantic air-bass manoeuvres. Despite lacking a bona fide bassist, the band began to sound heavier than a mob informant's footwear. Oz and I were self-taught wunderkinds. DT was a guitar scholar. Iain was wired to the moon.

The nagging prospect of keyboards loomed. We had many disagreements on the topic, each opinion backed up by a solid argument; some academic, others intuitive and emotional. Layering keyboards onto our sound would require a fifth member in the band, and we were wary of upsetting our delicate equilibrium.

At the time, Blood Brothers was a four-piece band. Most successful heavy metal bands had five members, two of whom played guitar, usually one lead and one rhythm. The twin-guitar assault of Iron Maiden, Judas Priest, AC/DC and Saxon had redefined the genre by layering onto it another dimension and increased melodic possibilities, and had done so without keyboards. Ozzy declared that keyboards were just shit and should be left to the poofy new romantic bands. Iain disagreed, citing Rainbow and Deep Purple - two of the true inventors and innovators of heavy metal - as prime examples of keyboard-laden heavy rock.

Remaining a four-piece would keep the band symmetrical, but I couldn't help feeling that it would limit us. Dave suggested a way of solving the keyboard debate: each of us would go home, choose one track to back up the argument for or against keyboards, then reassemble at his house to put forward our cases. Instead of arguing all day and achieving nothing, we would deal with this in DT's Court of Metal.

We reconvened at Dave's bungalow an hour later, each armed with a vinyl LP. DT brought out the white sheet decorated with his bloody pentagram; the once-red symbol had turned, perhaps prophetically, a deep purple colour. As he spread the sheet out on the floor, a smell like the bowels of Satan after a bad Mexican meal wafted from it.

I slid Rainbow's *Rising* album out of its sleeve and plopped it onto Dave's record deck. As *Tarot Woman* broke the silence, I sat cross-legged on the blood-stained sheet and allowed Tony Carey's otherworldly keyboards to transport my mind to a faraway place. Iain, too, looked as if his mind was in a distant cosmos, which was nothing unusual for him: he spent most of his time there. DT wore an expression of pure concentration as he weighed up what he was hearing. Looking bored, Ozzy slumped forwards and rested his huge head on clenched fists. When Ritchie Blackmore's metallisonic riffery began, however, the giant awoke. Futuristic keyboards and technical, neo-classical guitar were joined by Cozy Powell's thunderous drumming, Jimmy Bain's bass and the astonishingly powerful vocals of Ronnie James Dio. The combined effect was a perfect harmony of metal. "That song is fuckin' breathtaking," DT enthused. "I can't believe Rainbow have Joe Lynn Turner on vocals noo. I mean, the posey bastard can sing, but Ronnie Dio fuckin' *roars*."

"That was a great song," Ozzy agreed, nodding, "but I don't think the keyboards help it. I was bored until the heavy riffage started."

"I love it," contributed Iain. "The keyboards are spacey, dude."

DT asked, "What have you brought for oor listening pleasure, Monsieur Oswaldo?"

"From the live album *No Sleep 'til Hammersmith* by a delicate little power trio called Motörhead, I've chosen *Bomber*." Suddenly, the unholy triumvirate of Lemmy, Fast Eddie Clarke and Philthy Phil Taylor were with us in the room. Fast, thrashy, and relentlessly powerful, the track's heavy metal credibility was unquestionable. Afterwards, there was a long silence inhabited by four beaming smiles. "That," Oz announced, "is no-frills heavy metal. Swirly keyboards would ruin that song."

"You're right aboot that," I agreed. "Keyboards wouldnae enhance Motörhead. They're blood-and-guts metal at its rawest and purest." Heads nodded unanimous support.

"The invisible bass player," said DT, "or, to be more correct, the player of the invisible bass, is up next. What do you have for us, Sir Iain of Bright?"

Approaching the turntable, Iain said, "This is *Nino en Tiempo* by Deep Purple." DT and I exchanged confused glances. After a delicate keyboard intro, Ian Gillan's velvet voice soared high above the keyboard's subtle staccato. The track led our ears along twists and turns, through time and pace changes, and across the spectrum of vocal intensity and range.

Afterwards, DT boomed, "Fuckin' stupendous! And by the way, dickheid, that track is actually called *Child in Time*, not whatever Hispanic nonsense you said." I knew that DT was correct: we both knew Deep Purple's repertoire inside out. Iain protested, prodding the back cover of his album as evidence. An inspection revealed that the twat had mistakenly bought the Spanish import of the album, on which all the song titles were printed in Spanish. *Nino en Tiempo, Child in Time,* whateverthefuck; even Ozzy couldn't argue with the keyboard's contribution to that landmark song.

DT was last to play his chosen track. A synthesised wall of noise invaded our ears at brain-pulverising volume. There was nothing delicate about the sound: it was like spaceships hovering above our heads and blasting our brains with sonic weapons. It was divine. When the song was over, we exchanged astounded glances. "I chose that track," expounded

DT, "to prove that keyboards need not be delicate and poofy. The keyboard can be an instrument of extreme heaviness."

Wide-eyed, Ozzy asked, "Who the hell was that? I love it."

"That was *On the Rocks* by Gillan," replied DT, "from the album *Glory Road*. Keyboards were courtesy of Colin Towns, Bernie Tormé played guitar, John McCoy handled bass, Mick Underwood pounded the drums, and Mr Deep Purple himself, Ian Gillan, took care of vocal duties. What you just heard proves that keyboards can be crushing, just as they can be delicate. We should use keyboards only when they enhance a song. If we think they're waterin' doon a particular track, we kick them tae fuck oot o' there."

Iain walked over to the turntable and switched it on again. As *On the Rocks* soared from speakers, he began playing impassioned air keyboards – eyes closed, head bobbing, sandy hair swirling. Deep in his inner world. Iain's mind might be a fun place to visit, I thought, but only if there was an ejector seat to shoot me the fuck out of there if things got too wacko. "That boy's no' right in the heid," observed DT, pointing at Iain. "If he thinks he's playin' air keyboards *and* air bass in oor band he's way off. We need a real keyboard player, a musical prodigy, a genius who'll drag us up by oor bootstraps and force us to improve."

Using Oz's Star Wars analogy, I pointed out that we already had a Chewie, a Darth Vader, a Luke Skywalker and a Han Solo in our band. What we needed was an Obi Wan Kenobi: someone who had already mastered 'the Force' inherent in music. My teenage loins were also in burgeoning need of a Princess Leah over whom to empty themselves, but I kept that thought to myself.

Chapter 13 – Insanity and Genius

Pete Drummond was a reclusive fourteen-year-old whose wiry blonde hair stuck straight upwards as if conducting electrical current. Quiet confidence glimmered in his turquoise eyes. A multi-coloured jazz hat sat at an unlikely angle on the back of his head like a psychedelic Jewish yarmulke.

    Walking towards the door of his school music room, Pete found the exit blocked by a scruffy metalhead with long, sandy hair and a T-shirt on which the words *Iron Maiden* blazed in large red letters. Underneath the band's jagged logo, a lobotomized monster writhed against the confines of a straightjacket. Pete put on his Sony Walkman's headphones, pressed play and relaxed as David Sanborn's saxophone melodies flowed into him. As he tried to shuffle past the headbanger, a thick arm descended to block his way. Frowning, Pete removed his headphones. "I hear you're some kind o' musical prodigy," said the metalhead, "that you mastered the clarinet before you were oot o' primary school, that you can play any instrument, and that you have perfect pitch. Is that all true?"

    "Ehhhhm, sort of," fumbled Pete, "but I don't play string instruments or drums, man. I play clarinet, alto sax and keyboards. What you said aboot perfect pitch is true. I can name any note on hearing it or play any note from memory."

    The metalhead's eyebrows shot upwards and disappeared beneath his fringe. "That's amazin'. I'm in a band. We're the best metal band on the planet."

    Looking unimpressed, Pete said, "Bein' the best metal band in the world is a bit like bein' the gymnastics champion in a spazzy school." The metallist growled, baring his teeth. In a tactical change of tack, Pete feigned interest. "Tell me more aboot your metal band. What instrument do you play?"

    There was a long pause as the metalhead's wrath went off the boil, his attention seeming to drift inwards. Just as Pete began to think the headbanger must be having an epileptic absence, he replied, "I don't play an actual instrument, but my three bandmates do. Oor band's called Blood Brothers."

    "Why are you in the band if you don't do anythin'?"

    "Who said I don't do anythin'? I said I don't play an instrument, but I'm still an integral part o' the band. I pretend to play bass."

    Pete scratched his head. "The difference between musicians and other cats is that musicians actually play instruments. You might enjoy playin' bass if you try it. Otherwise, you're the proverbial spare prick at the weddin'."

    "I wish folk would stop callin' me that," grunted the metalhead. "I want to play bass, but I'm afraid I might hate it, which would shatter the whole beautiful illusion for me."

Pete's forehead furrowed as perplexity hijacked his brain. He recognised a surreal logic behind the longhair's argument, although the boy was clearly a few eggs short of an omelette. Still, Pete was intrigued. "I'm a jazz cat, so I wouldn't really know much aboot playin' your type o' caveman music. Iron Maiden and those other long-haired noisemakers ain't really my thing, man. I'm more of a Miles-type feline."

"I'd like you to meet the rest o' my band. You're exactly what we're lookin' for."

"But I'm a jazz cat," protested Pete, feeling inexorably drawn towards some destiny over which he had no control. "I play stuff by Miles Davis, David Sanborn, Pat Metheny, cool cats like that."

"What do you play on your synth? I've never heard synth jazz."

"Mainly spacey sounds in the same vein as Tangerine Dream and Jean Michel Jarre. That type o' groove takes my mind to a higher place."

The longhair's pupils dilated, eclipsing the blue in his eyes. "When I heard Jean Michel Jarre's *Oxygène* at the London Planetarium it blew my mind. My band could use sounds like that. Oor next rehearsal is on Thursday at eight o' clock in Vikingwood Studio. Please come, and bring your keyboard wi' you. My name's Iain Bright, by the way." Iain extended a meaty hand.

After staring long and hard at the outstretched hand with telltale cuts on its knuckles, Pete tentatively shook it. "I'm Pete Drummond."

"Aye, I know. The boy prodigy. Come to the rehearsal on Thursday. You won't regret it."

Pete's interest in the bizarre bassless metal project began to blossom. He had learned music in an academic way, but had recently become interested in the decadence and self-destruction that was a major part of the jazz lifestyle. He knew that there were strong parallels between jazz cats and headbangers as far as depraved lifestyles were concerned. Hardly able to believe his words, Pete agreed to accompany Iain Bright to his band's next rehearsal.

As the new friends walked outside, Iain angled his head back and gazed at the sky. A cloud in the shape of a giant bird floated high in the blue like a winged spirit. As the weightless force of nature soared over Iain's head, he felt plugged into the Universe. He had found the band's keyboard player; of that he felt sure. A musical prodigy with perfect pitch, *and* a Jean Michel Jarre fan. There were only two words for that. Fuckin' serendipity.

Chapter 14 – High Heel Heaven

There comes a time in the life of every young headbanger when he discovers heavy metal women. Not the abstract idea of them, but the perfume-drenched, spike-heeled, curvaceous, bodacious, outrageous reality of flesh.

By age fifteen I stood 6'3" and lean, while Iain was a stocky 5'10". We both had waist-length hair: Iain's sandy and straight; mine a tumbling mass of dark waves. Having qualified for the national squads in our respective sports (badminton and swimming), we glowed with good health, our elevated fitness levels making us even hornier than other sex-starved fifteen-year-olds. Sex dominated our imaginations, but my brutally cut-short Menorcan threesome was the closest either of us had been to the real thing. Ozzy and DT were eighteen and getting laid regularly, especially Dave, who had plundered more than half the vaginas in Bronzehall Swimming Club and a rapidly increasing number of unchlorinated holes too. Pete, who had taken up the role of keyboard maestro in the band, expressed no interest in sex. He was all about the music.

In the latter half of the 1980s, Zodiac Mindwarp was the coolest human being on planet Earth and its greatest poet too. At a time when the trend in metal was leaning towards LA-style glam with excessive make-up and bubblegum melodies, Zody represented the last bastion of chest-beating, dirty, raw, feral and unashamedly masculine heavy metal. He was the Tattooed Beat Messiah, the Skull Spark Joker, the High Priest of Love with the Untamed Stare. Zodiac and his supremely sleazy Love Reaction scumbags made Mötley Crüe seem like the Osmonds. While the Crüe tried hard to be bad boys, Zody didn't need to make an effort; he just *was* fantastically foul. Paradoxically, he was depraved yet messianic.

Zodiac Mindwarp and the Love Reaction had booked a gig at Glasgow's Barrowlands Ballroom as part of their *Tattooed Beat Messiah* tour. Iain and I skipped school that afternoon to depart early for the mean streets of Glasgow. He wore black leather trousers, white basketball boots, a Judas Priest *Defenders of the Faith* T-shirt and a black leather biker jacket, while I chose faded blue jeans with rips at the knees, tan cowboy boots, a Zodiac Mindwarp T-shirt and a fringed biker jacket with my old faithful studs-and-patches-covered denim waistcoat over the top.

We took the bus into Glasgow and by mid-afternoon were sipping German beer in a biker pub, The Crooked Garage, in the city's Saltmarket area. Some Hell's Angels and their scantily clad girlfriends were monopolising the pool table. The male bikers' grizzled, wizened faces were barely visible beneath thick beards; they looked forty-something, but were probably ten years younger. The biker bitches had the smooth skin and tight curves of women in their twenties, and dirty ones at that. One of the girls was a leggy, larger-than-life blonde brought to life straight from the pages of a comic: thigh-length, spike-heeled black boots; black leather mini-skirt; cutaway T-shirt exposing plenty of taut midriff. The first time our eyes met, she smiled and licked blood-red lips. Whilst enjoying her attention, I was careful not to flirt back. Eyeing up a Hell's Angel's girl wasn't a good idea, especially when the Hell's Angel in question was a few feet away with a pool cue in his hand. Running a hand through her hair, the blonde temptress strutted over to me and asked, "Does the fresh young heavy metal boy want a game of pool wi' a real woman?"

I looked to the bikers for their approval. One of the Hell's Angels, perhaps sensing my wariness, shouted, "It's OK, have a game!" In her high heels, the blonde seductress stood eye to eye with me. She was dressed like the women in my sexual fantasies: slutty, with just the right amount of tease, her red-glossed lips reminding me of the women from *Buck Rogers in the 25th Century*. Until today, I had thought such women only existed on TV shows, in porn movies, in magazines and in my mind, but I was about to play pool with one.

After introducing herself as Kelly, the girl placed the white ball on the pool table's green baize. As Kelly leaned over the table to break, her mini-skirt rode up, uncovering the half-moon curves of a delectable bottom and the white thong which bisected it like dental floss. Buttock floss, if you will. I looked nervously at the Hell's Angels, but they seemed to neither care nor notice as they guzzled beer, told stories and roared with laughter. They were, I thought, like modern-day Viking warriors, right down to their long hair, beards, helmets and steel horses, going where they wanted when they wanted, drinking ale and plundering tattooed fellatrixes along the way. Today their priority seemed to be drinking, so I relaxed and enjoyed the flesh that Kelly strategically bared with each shot.

After two games of pool, Kelly slid a hand through a rip in the knee of my jeans. "You're cute," she whispered, her hand travelling up my thigh. My body turned rigid. Across the pool table, the watching Iain looked as if he had filled his pants. Kelly's teasing at a distance was one thing, but flesh contact was different: it was the kind of thing that could get me dead in a ditch. She strutted to the bar, mumbled something to the bespectacled barman, returned with a black-marker pen, knelt in front of me and began to draw on the left leg of my jeans. First, she drew a face framed by long hair, announcing that it was a portrait of me. Then she signed her name down the other thigh of my jeans, and underlined it with six kisses. Leaning close, Kelly blew on my neck, coaxing up goosepimples. "Meet me in the women's toilet in one minute," she whispered. "Prepare to have your world rocked." She ran the tip of her tongue up my neck and enveloped my earlobe in her warm mouth. My body started to melt, but a primal survival urge screamed at me to get out.

The largest, hairiest Hell's Angel - a wall of leather and oilstreaked denim - stood up and stormed towards me. He wasn't laughing anymore. After exchanging I've-just-pissed-my-pants glances, Iain and I sprinted out of the pub and didn't slow down until we reached the Barrowlands Ballroom, where the gig was due to start in a couple of hours. We spent the next two hours drinking cheap Scottish beer in a quiet old-man's pub called The Templar's Horse. It lacked the curvaceous eye candy of The Crooked Garage, and its warm beer tasted like watered-down cat piss, but this watering hole was a whole lot safer.

By 8 p.m. the metal fraternity had filled the Barrowlands to the rafters. Every red-blooded male was gawping at two delectable females who, apparently devoid of self-consciousness or shame, had handed their long coats into the cloakroom, unveiling bodies wrapped only in lingerie. The smaller girl was a curvy natural beauty with blue eyes, shoulder-length red hair tied in pigtails, and pale, plentiful flesh accentuated by black stockings, suspender belt, bra, panties and high-heeled shoes. The taller girl had high cheekbones, sculpted features and dark eyes. Long brunette hair cascaded down her bronzed back. She was dressed all in white - seamed stockings, suspender belt, panties, lace basque – except for red spike-heeled boots, which added six inches to her height. Any girls with the confidence (or sluttiness) to walk around at a gig wearing only lingerie were begging to be ransacked. It would be rude not to. And I was damned if I was going to let anyone else be the one to do it. "Iain, let's go and talk to these dirty bitches. They're alone…not a Hell's Angel in sight."

Iain's mouth fell open. "Just walk over and talk to the girls that every guy in this joint is starin' at? Are you fuckin' serious, Spark?"

"As serious as a beatin' from a biker gang. We've just escaped death. Today's oor lucky day. We'd be mad not to take advantage o' that. What do we have to lose? We've never seen these chicks before. There's a fair chance we'll never see them again. Look at all these dudes oglin' and droolin' all over the place. Each one of those shitbags will go home tonight and wank until his helmet's bleedin', wishin' he'd had the balls to talk to these delicious examples of vaginahood. Well, fuck that. Iain Bright, wi' you and the Metal Gods as my witnesses, I will fuck one or both of these heavy metal whores before the night is oot!"

"You're right," Iain agreed. "We *must* walk over there and talk to those beautiful bitches. We'll be the ones to grab the bull by the balls."

"The expression is 'take the bull by the horns'."

"You can take the bull by the horns if you want, Spark, but I'll be grabbin' him by his massive bovine balls and hangin' on for dear life." Somewhat disturbed by Iain's homobestial metaphor, but brimming with confidence, I swaggered up to the lacy-lingeried beauties with Iain bouncing along at my heels like a horny gundog. Appreciative of our direct approach, the girls were happy to chat. They turned out to be eighteen-year-olds from rural Montana who were travelling around Europe for a month and catching a few metal concerts in the process. The American girls didn't ask our ages. We didn't tell.

The dark-haired girl, Erin, asked Iain if she could sit on his shoulders during the gig. A smug expression spreading across his face, he replied, "As long as I've got a face, you'll always have a seat."

Following suit, I asked the petite red-haired Jenna if she'd like to sit on me. She giggled and said she would like that very much. Four songs into the concert, the girls descended from our sweaty shoulders to go to the toilet together. Iain and I exchanged smiles, but neither of us said a word. There was no need. We were living the heavy metal dream.

The dusky-haired, white-stockinged Erin sat atop Iain's shoulders for the duration of the concert, while I became a seat to Jenna. My petite rider removed one of her scrunchy hairbands and used it to tie my hair into a ponytail, which she placed over her left leg, allowing her to rub the exposed flesh of pale thighs - between stocking tops and panties - against the bare sides of my neck. Jenna ground her crotch – which steadily increased in temperature and humidity - into the back of my neck in time to the rhythm of Zodiac's music. Twice during the gig, she gripped my hair, increased the tempo of her bucking and let out a series of ecstatic gasps. By end of the concert, despite my balls being sore from two hours of sporting a relentless erection, I was high on the heady scents of perfume and pussy.

The gig was incendiary. Z and his band were louder, dirtier and more fun than any other on the planet. After waiting while Erin and Jenna retrieved their long coats from the cloakroom, Iain and I walked out of the Barrowlands with our arms draped round the girls' shoulders, attracting envious looks from other headbangers. I invited Erin and Jenna to come back with us to Bronzehall. They said they wouldn't have it any other way. This created an interesting quandary: my mother was in London on business for a week, but my father wasn't. In fact, he was on his way to pick us up from the Barrowlands. With no clue how to orchestrate any time alone with the girls, I decided to leave it in the hands of the Metal Gods. I had heard it said that 'luck be a lady'. That night, I prayed for it to be the case. Two ladies, that is. Dirty ones. In lingerie.

When my father's blue Ford Sierra pulled up outside the Barrowlands, I introduced him to the girls and asked if they could come back to Bronzehall with us. He looked the girls up and down, looked at me, nodded. During the journey home the girls talked tirelessly to my father while I sat in silence, racking my brains to devise a game plan. If I didn't think of something, we'd all end up in my house, drinking tea and eating biscuits with cheese while my Dad quizzed the girls about their home towns, families and aspirations. But the Metal Gods were indeed smiling on me that night. At the outskirts of Vikingwood, my father stopped his car in a lay-by and stuttered, "I've just remembered that I have to, erm…go back to the office. There's work that needs done. Look after these lovely girls and make them feel at home, son. I…ehh…won't be home for a good three hours at least." Iain and the American seductresses piled out of the back seat while, bemused, I remained in the front of the car and stared into my father's eyes. He winked, flashed a rare smile and said, "Enjoy yourselves." At that moment, my Dad overtook Zodiac Mindwarp and became the coolest man on the planet.

Metallic Dreams

I led Jenna straight to my bedroom. Iain took Erin into my parents' room. I put on side A of Zodiac Mindwarp and the Love Reaction's *Tattooed Beat Messiah*. While Z addressed me as his Wolf Child and babbled psychometal verse about of the science of mythology, Jenna's legs opened and I slid into her. Staggered by how much better her warm, wet welcome felt than my usual lover (my trusty right hand), it was all over all too soon – lock, stock and a prematurely shooting barrel. Embarrassed, I confessed that Jenna had been my first fuck and apologised for the limited longevity of my lovemaking. She told me not to worry. Guys, she revealed, always last longer on the second, third and fourth fuck each night, due to progressively decreasing sensitivity. Then, dropping to her knees, Jenna took my soft member into her mouth, looked up into my eyes and sucked like a starving aardvark feasting on a line of ants. Pumping my shaft with one hand, she moved the other between her legs and rubbed her pink slit. She slid a couple of fingers knuckle-deep inside herself, then offered the wet digits to my mouth. The smell and taste of her juices, combined with her flawless fellatio, got me hard again. The dress rehearsal was over. It was time for the main performance.

I did last longer on our second union. Much longer. Afterwards, sweat-soaked, Jenna and I raided the fridge. We rehydrated our parched bodies with fresh orange juice then devoured cheese-and-pickle sandwiches. Iain and Erin appeared, breathless and glowing. The girls retreated to the living room, leaving Iain and me to make hot drinks in the kitchen. When my blood brother and I made our way to the living room with a tray of coffees, we found the American girls entangled on the floor in front of the fire, tongues intertwined, firelight flickering on their skin. They looked like a flawless sculpture, one girl bronze, the other alabaster. A mischievous smile spread across Erin's face. "Do you boys know what the mark of a true friend is?"

My mind went blank. Iain's expression was vacant too; he shrugged his shoulders and stuck out his bottom lip in defeat. Suddenly, a horrific thought entered my brain. "We're no' givin' each other a wank, so you can forget that idea! I do love Iain, but yankin' him off would change the nature of oor friendship. We've been friends for years withoot resortin' to that kind of tadger-touchin' nonsense. Blood brothers, aye. Cum cousins, no way!"

"Aye," agreed Iain, "sperm siblings is oot o' the question!"

Jenna giggled, making her pert jugs jiggle. A true friend," she explained, "is one who is willing to share."

Erin slapped her friend's leg. "You're such a bad girl, baby!"

As the reality of what was about to happen dawned on me, my mouth fell open like a castle drawbridge. Iain and I were going to swap girls. Taking Iain by the hand, Jenna led him upstairs. Erin and I remained in front of the living room's blazing fire.

Iain switched on side B of *Tattooed Beat Messiah* and cranked up the volume. As Z sang of Devil chords, the Tower of Babel and celestial majesty, Erin pushed me onto my back and impaled herself on my personal Tower of Babel, which was, appropriately, pointing straight at Heaven. I looked into Erin's dark eyes, squeezed her bottom, penetrated her depths and gazed at her pert breasts as they bounced to the rhythm of her movements. Each time I felt my orgasm approach, I slowed down and took deep breaths to let it subside. As Erin rode me like a cowgirl at a rodeo, Zodiac told the tale of an intoxicated sex goddess from the Heavens. *'Laser-beam lips give me kiss of life. Sex explosion with Baby Midnight. Psychotic, erotic, full of mad energy. Electrons snap when she touch me. Divine, drunk goddess of love, oh yeah. I said you goddess of love, I love you, Planet Girl.'* Z's song was the perfect soundtrack to the Earth-shattering sex that was happening in a small terraced Bronzehall house. Erin's husky moans became squeals. "Oooh, you sexy Scottish fuck, you're gonna make me squirt!" Arching her back, she began to bounce harder. Hot liquid jetted from her pussy, spraying over my balls and thighs, and rolling in little waves up my body. Pushed over the edge, I roared like a wild animal and spurted inside Erin. Rather than climbing off afterwards, she stayed astride me, and I was more than happy to remain inside the sanctuary of her warm body. She kissed my lips and licked rolling beads of sweat from my neck. Wrapped in each other, we lay in front of the fire and let its flames dry the mixed juices from our bodies, my gaze never leaving Erin's fire-reflecting eyes. Then we made love again. This time there was no soundtrack. Erin's heavy breathing and the crackle of logs in the fire was all the music we needed.

    The girls stayed overnight. By the time my Dad arrived home, Erin and I had squeezed into my single bed, while Iain and Jenna were crammed into a sleeping bag on the floor beside us. The room stank of sweaty, booze-soaked sex. As I drifted into a blissful sleep, I understood for the first time what Z meant by *Driving on Holy Gasoline*: I'd been doing it all night.

    In the morning, my Dad retained his crown as the world's coolest man by giving Erin and Jenna a lift to their hotel in Glasgow.

Iain and I never saw those American girls again. It was better that way. More poetic. They live on - brighter than supernovas – in our memories.

Those uninhibited Montana minxes did more than raise our respective manhoods: they were our initiation ceremony into manhood. To Hell with Bar Mitzvahs and other such supposedly spiritual rites of passage. Iain Bright and I stormed into adulthood the Zodiac Mindwarp way, cumming and screaming and spanking and spunking and roaring. We drove on holy gasoline until our engines were engulfed by flames.

Chapter 15 – Violence and Bloodshed

Before unlocking his car outside the Tierneys' bungalow, my father glared at me over its roof. After a long, uncomfortable silence, he opened the doors and we crunched out of the red-gravel driveway, headed for home. From the back seat, I met the reflection of my father's eyes in the rear-view mirror. "When did this start?" he asked. My reply was a puzzled frown. "Please don't treat me like an idiot, son," he continued. "You know what I mean."

"I have no clue what you're on aboot. I'm no' a mind reader."

My father let out a long, slow sigh, as he always did when he thought I was being dishonest. "I'm referring to you and DT taking drugs. When I spoke to him in the hall tonight, his pupils were dilated and he couldn't concentrate on what I was saying for more than five seconds."

"Maybe you were borin' the tits off him. Did you think o' that?"

"Don't piss me off, son. Not while I'm in this mood."

"Dad, I don't know what DT has been puttin' into his body since he quit swimmin', but I swear I've never put an illegal drug into mine. I've been drunk, aye. Shit, you and I have been drunk together. Other than occasional alcohol and regular caffeine, I wouldnae put a drug into my body. You know as well as I do that my swimmin' performance would go doon the shitter if I was gettin' high."

My father swerved his Sierra into the side of the road, yanked on the hand brake and leaned round to look me in the eyes. "Promise me, son, that you've never taken illegal drugs." Without breaking eye contact, I promised.

My father was perceptive. His career as an analytical chemist had exposed him to the physiological and psychological reactions to a range of drugs, while his unpaid job as a swimming coach had offered him insights into human nature. If he thought he had spotted something odd in DT's behaviour, he was probably right.

Earlier that night, DT had drunk a two-litre bottle of cider while I had stuck to Irn-Bru. I had attributed Dave's slurred speech to the effects of the strong scrumpy he was guzzling, as garbled speech is par for the course once a person starts pouring that unholy water down his neck. DT could, however, have ingested or - surelythefucknot - injected anything before my arrival. I made a mental note to ask Dave if he was dabbling with any weird substances. He had quit swimming a few months earlier, so there could be a connection.

Two days later, DT's Mum and Dad set off on a Caribbean cruise, leaving him in charge of their house. As the events outlined below unfolded, I was enduring new levels of pain in Bronzehall's swimming pool. This pieced-together account of the night's events is based on three sources: the verbal account told by my father; DT's version of the story; a police statement.

On his first night in charge of the house, Dave managed to lock himself out. He had left his bedroom window open a glimmer, though, so he angled a plank of wood up to the ledge, climbed the makeshift ramp, prised the window open wider and squeezed through the gap. While he was half in/half out and kicking his legs to propel himself through the aperture, a police car drove past. The two officers in the vehicle watched as the dark-clad intruder wriggled through the window and then switched on lights in the house.

The cops parked in the driveway of the Tierneys' bungalow. The younger officer ran into the back garden to prevent the intruder from exiting via the rear of the house. Hand on baton, the senior officer rang the front doorbell. To the overweight red-faced cop's surprise, the burglar not only answered the door but did so beaming a carefree smile. DT explained that he lived in the house, making it technically impossible for him to have broken in. Even if he had kicked the front door in, Dave continued, it was his property to break. Thinking Dave's explanation implausible, the officer asked for his name and requested photographic identification. His partner reappeared and radioed DT's responses back to the station. His details checked out. A passport complete with grinning photo of the intrepid guitarist was the icing on the cake.

Disappointed that they couldn't arrest the cocky long-haired vagabond, the officers remained at the front door. The younger cop again radioed the station, this time to ask if David Tierney had a criminal record. DT's demons began to awaken. "You've checked me oot and I do live here," he spat. "Noo get tae fuck off my property before I exercise my legal right tae remove you usin' reasonable force. Real crimes are bein' committed in this toon. Drunken husbands are beatin' their wives. Wee twats are stealin' expensive cars just to joyride them for a night and then smash them up. Burglars are thievin' from honest, hard-workin' folk. Meanwhile, you two daft fucks are wastin' your time here doin' busy work. I know what you're all aboot. You want to look conscientious to your superiors, while avoidin' dangerous police work. A delicate balance that, eh?"

The senior officer grunted, "I'd advise you to shut your foul mooth before I shut it for you." He picked up Dave's green combat jacket from the hall floor and began to rifle through its pockets, uncovering enough cannabis resin to keep Cheech and Chong stoned for a month, and a smaller quantity of MDMA, otherwise known as ecstasy. As a satisfied smile spread across his face, the chubby cop asked, "Can you explain what you are doing with these substances?"

"Shovin' them up your fat arse if you don't fuck off! You just performed an illegal search. You've no warrant to search this property. You confirmed that I live here. I, the resident, gave you no permission to enter the hoose or to search my jacket. Quite the opposite – I asked you to leave. I won't make an official complaint aboot your conduct if you turn roon', get into your jam sandwich and fuck off. Trust me, you don't want me to use reasonable force."

"Fancy yoursel' as a hard man, eh? Listen to me, you drugged-up wee bastard. You're coming to the station wi' us now. It'll be easier for you if you come peacefully, but willingly or otherwise, you're coming. Your drugs will be kept and submitted as evidence."

DT's demons had been shaken from their slumber and force-fed several pots of coffee. Now they were thirsty for blood. "It's a fair cop," he said, his voice steeped in mock submissiveness. "I'll come to the station wi' you. Sorry for shoutin'. I get a little…ehhh…excited sometimes. I'll just grab a warmer jacket from my room. Two seconds." Leaving the cops at the front door basking in their smugness, Dave darted through to his bedroom and picked up a bicycle inner tube containing four heavy batteries: a weapon he had invented after discovering that whacking heads with a hard chib (Bronzehall slang for a striking weapon) hurt his wrists, although not as much as it hurt the person on the receiving end of his wrath. Rather than perceiving this pain as karmic retribution and a reason to stop inflicting damage on others, Dave went back to the drawing board to design a chib that could devastate an opponent while causing minimum impact to the wielder. The simple genius of batteries in an inner tube was the result.

DT wrapped the inner tube twice round his hand, leaving the heavy, battery-filled end hanging. He strolled to the front door, keeping the weapon hidden behind his legs until the enemy was in range. The tube blurred into motion, its whooshing journey ending with a crack when it struck the younger cop's temple. Unconscious, he fell to the ground like a dropped sack of potatoes, blood seeping onto the driveway from a new orifice in his head.

Fixing his bloodthirsty gaze on the remaining adversary, DT wound up his arm for strike two. Moving with astonishing speed for an individual of such substantial girth, the heavy cop knocked Dave to the ground with a baton strike to the jaw, then cuffed his hands behind his back and bundled him into the back of the police car. After calling an ambulance for his leaking partner, the cop used DT's green combat jacket, from which the drugs had been removed, to stem the bleeding.

The injured officer made it to hospital alive but a couple of kilos lighter. Dave, meanwhile, was locked in a cell where police officers – two at a time - took turns in beating him with batons. Since his parents were on holiday and couldn't be contacted, the job of bailing him out fell into the hands of my father, who was anything but pleased when he arrived at the police station to find a blood-drenched, semi-conscious, broken-boned and incoherent DT. Rounding up all the cops in the station, my father boomed, "You're a shower of pathetic wee wankers! You think you're tough, handcuffing a teenage boy and beating him wi' your rubber dildos, but there isn't one of you that could go toe-to-toe with that boy in a fight! You're a pack of fucking cowards! If he dies, I'll be back here to dish oot my own brand of justice, Hebridean-style, with a shotgun! I suggest you all start praying to whatever lucky stars you have that it does not come to that!" Leaving a crowd of quivering cops in his wake, my giant father swept out of the station carrying DT's limp form in his strong arms.

After an exhausting swimming session, I cycled home into an orange sunset while Judas Priest's *Defenders of the Faith* blared out of my Walkman and dreams of taking the musical world by storm flickered through my mind. I was, at that point, blissfully unaware of DT's arrest.

Back home, my parents were sitting in the living room and wearing their most serious faces. When my father announced that something bad had happened, I felt sure that someone in the family must have died, such was the sombre atmosphere. "I have to go to the police station to get DT," he continued, "who was arrested on three charges tonight – possession of illegal drugs, resisting arrest and assaulting a police officer."

"Assaultin' a police officer should be applauded, perhaps even rewarded," I enthused. "Most o' the cops I've come across are stupid wanks."

My Dad sighed. "Son, most police officers are indeed insecure, power-hungry wee wankers. That's the personality type the job attracts. But assaulting anyone, regardless of their wanker status, is serious. DT will have to go to court. He could possibly go to jail. He'll get a criminal record."

"He's already got a criminal record. It's a Rod Stewart album. You know what I mean?" Neither of my parents laughed. Looking at their glum faces, I realised that they simply didn't understand a highly developed sense of humour like mine. Granted, this may not have been the right time for light-hearted jocularity, but I was only trying to freshen up the mood, a plan that had fallen flat on its arse in spectacular fashion. Changing tack, I put on my most solemn expression and promised, "The Blood Brothers will have a serious talk to DT. If he doesn't listen to me, I'll get Ozzy to pummel some sense into his stubborn heid."

Stern words would indeed be coming Dave's way. I didn't care what he put into his body, as long as he didn't overdose and die. My worry was that our guitar guru might end up in jail or dead before we got a chance to redefine heavy metal. And that would simply not be good enough.

Chapter 16 – Running with the Devil

Just after midnight on a misty, rain-soaked Saturday, a lone figure staggered across a blue iron bridge, bouncing off its sides like a drunken pinball. Pete Drummond had taken the bus to a jazz club in Glasgow at lunchtime. Twelve hours of heavy drinking later, his body a booze-soaked sponge, he had reached absolute alcohol saturation point. Experience had taught Pete the point at which to stop drinking in order to avoid alcoholic blackout. It was a fine line and an invisible one at that, but he had crossed it often enough to know the danger signs and slam on the brakes in the nick of time.

Pete peered over the edge of the bridge into the rocky ravine hundreds of feet below. His body hair pricked up. The blue bridge spanned the glacial chasm which separated Bronzehall's two roughest neighbourhoods, Valfader and Vikingwood. Whenever he crossed this bridge, Pete worried about a two-pronged attack from ahead and behind simultaneously, making the only escape route the suicidal one: diving over the edge onto jagged rocks far below. This type of strategic attack was unlikely to happen, Pete knew, but he had always been host to irrational fears. (Despite being a promising diver as a child, Pete had quit Bronzehall Diving Club because of one such fear. Every time he had dived off a high board, he had felt convinced that the surface of the water would somehow be bricked over during his few seconds underwater, rendering it impossible to surface and breathe again.)

Ahead, a streetlight flickered, buzzed, then shattered. Shards of glass tinkled onto the path. A dark cloud blew across the moon, blocking out its light. As gloom fell over Pete like a dark blanket, he felt fear seeping in. The harder he tried to push out the terror, the more it streamed into his body, laying down anchors. He about-turned and began to retrace his steps, thanking God that the streetlight on the other side of the bridge was still working. As Pete neared the nimbus of orange light, he saw the silhouette of a tall figure in the mist. Hypnotised, he kept walking. Twin streams of black smoke belched from the mist, carrying the sulphuric stench of a million spent matches. A guttural growl, lower than the sewers of Hell, filled the night air. Hot piss dribbled down Pete's leg. He stood as still as his trembling body would allow, trying not to move nor even breathe. The black trails continued to alternately appear then evaporate, as if the creature was sucking in air and exhaling darkness. *Creating* darkness. Light worked its way around the thing at a safe distance but avoided touching it, as if even light feared this beast.

Pete stared in horror as the creature strode out of the mist, cloven hooves clopping against cement. It stood over eight feet tall, with skin charred black and sizzling in the rain as if freshly removed from a barbecue. An impossibly muscular torso was mounted atop two hair-covered bestial legs like those of a colossal goat. Rain dripped off curved teeth which glinted like polished scimitars. Fire flickered in hollow ocular cavities. Equine nostrils blasted out black gases that smelled like rotting flesh cooking over burning straw. Two bony horns stretched upwards like the sinister opposite of a plant growing towards the light. Pete knew that this was a creature of the night. Hell, this was *the* nocturnal nightmare: the reason humans sleep during the dark hours.

Driven by a burst of adrenaline and an overwhelming desire to live, Pete wheeled on the spot and ran into the darkness at breakneck speed. The thunder of mighty hooves echoed in the gorge behind him. Like little blonde fuses, the hairs on the back of Pete's neck began to frazzle as boiling breath set them alight. 'Fuck,' he thought, 'I've spent all my money, pissed in my pants and noo I've been set on fire, probably to tenderise my flesh before this Devil-thing sodomises the shit oot of it then eats it. This definitely isnae one o' my better nights oot.'

Running as fast as his intoxicated legs would allow, Pete recited a stream-of-consciousness version of the Lord's prayer. "Oor Father, who art in Heaven, hallowed be Thy name. Thy Kingdom come, thy Will be done on Earth, as it is in Heaven. Gi'e us today oor daily breid, and save us fae demons that want tae turn us into char-grilled chicken. Please save my soul, man. I always knew that fuckin' blue bridge was trouble, since the day the bastard thing was built! For Thine is the Kingdom, the Power and the Glory, raise your glasses high, just like the Saxon song. Be a cool divine cat and help me. I'm wee Pete. Remember me?"

A jet of fire blasted Pete off his feet. He skidded face-down along the pavement, tearing skin off palms, forearms, chin and knees. Flames leaped from his denim jacket, lighting up the night. The quick-thinking jazz cat rolled into a murky puddle, which extinguished the fire with a fizz. Pete's gaze darted around. He saw no sign of the Hellcreature, although the smell of its infernal breath still hung in the air. Driven by renewed optimism, Pete stood up and ran, faster than he'd ever run before, towards Spark's house.

Chapter 17 – A Cautionary Tale

When the frantic banging on my front door began, Iain and I were basking in the warmth from a roaring fire, sipping large mugs of coffee and listening to Metallica's *Ride the Lightning*. I opened the door expecting to see a local booze-hound stagger into the darkness, but found a bleeding and burnt Pete babbling incoherently about the Devil, prayers, the blue bridge, barbecued flesh, cloven hooves, horns and fire. Chunks of skin dangled from his chin, offering a gory view of jawbone. He smelled more offensive than the worst toilet in which I had ever had the misfortune of shitting. The back of his jacket was burnt out, exposing flesh that looked like a jigsaw puzzle with most of the pieces missing. What remained of Pete's once-blue denim jacket was charred black. Watery goo dribbled from burns on his neck and back. "For fuck's sake, Pete," I gushed, "you need to get to hospital!"

From his comfortable seat in front of the fire, the eavesdropping Iain shouted, "Was it the Woodie? Spark, let's round up DT and Ozzy, then waste every one o' those bamsticks! We've knocked oot every one o' those Woodie wanks and broken a lot o' their bones, but this time we'll permanently handicap the bastards!" The Woodie gang was renowned for dishing out arbitrary violence, but unless they had diversified into arson-based assault, Pete had come up against something very different.

"I met the Devil," Pete spat, blood dripping off his teeth.

"Is he in the Woodie?" asked Iain.

"Bright, you're a fuckin' idiot!" snapped Pete. "This was fuck all to do wi' the Woodie! The Devil! Fire! Brimstone! Hell! Horns! Fuckin' big cloppy hooves!"

I wanted to believe Pete, but this was the tallest story I'd ever heard. Something bad had happened to him, but the only Devil I believed in was the one on my album covers. "Where did this happen?" I asked.

Giving me the look a wise physics professor might give a particularly stupid student who asks what all the fuss was about Einstein, Pete replied, "On the blue bridge," then added, as a whispered afterthought, "obviously."

From the living room, Iain proposed, "Here's what happened - you went to a jazz club, hung oot wi' weirdos and absorbed inhuman quantities of alcohol and drugs. Then, on your way home, you had to cross the blue bridge you've always been afraid of. The combination of intoxication, fear and darkness caused you to project your worst fears into your mind's eye. You got scared and ran."

"Get oot here, Bright, ya fuckin' dickheid!" shouted Pete, spraying a fine mist of crimson rain from lacerated lips. "How the fuck could projected fears get me into this state? Did I project flames onto my jacket and scorch my own body? Take your projection theories and jam them up your fat arse! I was chased by the Devil. I felt his infernal breath on my neck. The bastard wanted to feast on me. I said a makeshift prayer, and I think that's what saved me. This sort o' thing never happened to me before I got involved wi' your fuckin' band. As soon as I start messin' wi' heavy metal, I open the gates o' Hell and get chased by fuckin' Lucifer!"

"Did you know," I asked, "that Lucifer means *Bringer of Light?*"

"Bringer of light, my hairy arse," grimaced Pete, a chunk of skin falling from his chin. "That fucker set me alight!" With that proclamation, he passed out and thudded like a felled tree onto the wooden floor of my hall. Iain and I had been so busy trying to get the story out of Pete that we had overlooked his leaking liquid life.

Having been wakened from her slumber, my Mum stormed downstairs calling Iain and me every kind of bastard for making so much noise when she was asleep in bed. On seeing the burnt and unconscious Pete, she keeled over and landed beside him, her left hand coming to rest on a cervical vertebra that was peeking through a hole in Pete's skin.

I sprinted upstairs to rouse my father from his sleep and found him naked on his back with arms and legs outstretched like a huge hairy starfish. "Get up, Dad! You need to drive Pete and Mum to the hospital!"

With a voice full of menace, my father grunted, "One more noise from you and there'll be blood and snotters flying." He was one sleeping dog it really was safest to let lie, but this was a desperate situation that required desperate measures. Grabbing his beard in one hand and his tadger in the other, I pulled hard with both hands. A roar worthy of a frenzied bear filled the room. I fled downstairs. My butt-naked father gave chase. When he saw the carnage in the hall, his anger evaporated as quickly as it had appeared, replaced by concern for his petite wife and the half-cooked jazz cat who lay sprawled beside her on the floor.

After pulling on jeans and a T-shirt, my father threw Pete over one shoulder and my mother over the other, carried them to his car and drove to Valfader Hospital. Tests revealed that my Mum was fine. Pete, however, was suffering from shock, elevated blood pressure, blood loss, burns, lacerations and serious psychological trauma. He decided against telling doctors his version of what had happened, afraid that they may lock him in a psychiatric ward and throw away the key. Nurses cleaned and dressed his wounds, then administered potent painkillers. On the Sunday evening, Pete was granted special permission to go to the hospital chapel, where he offered silent prayers, hoping to receive a divine sign or some kind of celestial explanation for what had happened. Deafening silence was his only reply. That was Pete's first and last appearance in church. His physical wounds healed in three days, leaving a trail of doctors amazed at his recovery but unwilling to even whisper the word 'miracle'.

Pete's experience with the Devil shook up his worldview. He threatened to leave the band unless we made changes to the songs we played. We had to drop Venom's *Black Metal* and *Welcome to Hell* from our repertoire, as well as AC/DC's *Highway to Hell*, *Hell Ain't a Bad Place to Be* and *Hell's Bells,* and Iron Maiden's *The Number of the Beast*. We didn't want to stop playing these songs, but Pete was our musical prodigy and far too valuable to lose. In an act of great compromise, we agreed to stop playing all tracks with even the slightest infernal bent, provided Pete promised never to take another drug.

Pete's reminders of the blue-bridge incident were recurring nightmares and a burn on his back in the shape of a coiled-up baby, as if safe in the womb. His story was too fantastical to accept, yet his healing had been so rapid that otherworldly intervention couldn't be discounted. The experience inspired Pete to write the music for Blood Brothers' first original track, *Blue-Bridge Duel*, which melded the dark broodiness of *Black Sabbath* by Black Sabbath with the melodic spaciness of Van Halen's *1984* and Jean Michel Jarre's *Oxygène 4*. After recounting to me every detail of events on the blue bridge, Pete played *Blue-Bridge Duel* for me. Then, overcome by the same sense of oppressive fear I had felt while watching *The Wicker Man* at age seven, I locked myself in my room and wrote the lyrics to accompany Pete's composition.

Chapter 18 – I Come in Peace

Blood Brothers' rehearsal sessions became increasingly coherent affairs. DT's guitar riffs could blow holes in brick walls (and had done, much to the consternation of his parents). Like a funky-looking Jean Michel Jarre, Pete was a whirlwind of fluid movement and space-age sound. Ozzy's drumming was rhythmic thunder. Not a technical drummer in the mould of Rush's Neil Peart, Oz played in the powerhouse style of Led Zeppelin's John Bonham and the awe-inspiring Cozy Powell, although Ozzy played with as much power as those two legends combined. I had taken the seven-days-a-week dedication learned from swimming and applied it to training my voice. As a result, I could hit the soaring high notes that had earned Rob Halford and Bruce Dickinson their respective nicknames of 'The Metal God' and 'The Air-Raid Siren'. Iain still had no bass, but even bassless we were heavier than Manowar in lead suits of armour. We had more hair than Iron Maiden and got more pussy than Mötley Crüe. All except Pete, that is, who still had short, spiky hair and an untarnished tadger.

Lisa Doune never wore make-up, which was no crime as it would only have dulled the peaches-and-cream glow of her complexion. Long, golden hair tumbled down her back, blindingly bright as if harbouring sunlight. Years of gymnastics and good nutrition had sculpted Lisa into a lithe teenage goddess of exceptional beauty. Iain Bright wanted to do unspeakable things with her. Ozzy said he wanted to take her to the cinema, but we all knew what that meant. I thought of Lisa like a sister, but one of those naughty sisters from porn films: a sister who, on the very day she was due to become a nun, would 'punish' me for peeking at her as she showered. God only knows what DT would have done to her if she'd given him an opening, so to speak. He'd probably have sacrificed her to some pagan idol or other while screwing her in an inappropriate orifice and drinking her blood mixed with magic mushrooms. Lisa, however, only had eyes for Pete, consummate musician and shyest male in the world.

    Pete didn't tell the others in the band that Lisa was coming to his house; he didn't want them datecrashing. He had chosen this particular Friday night because his parents were in Findhorn Bay on holiday, so he had the house to himself.

    The doorbell rang, sending Pete into a panic. Without a clue what to talk about, how to act, or what moves – if any – to make on Lisa, he felt out of his depth. He knew how to dress, though: multi-coloured skullcap; sun-yellow shirt; white brogue shoes; grey baggy trousers fit for Miami Vice. Pete opened the door, and his mouth fell open like a Venus flytrap waiting for an insect. Lisa was standing on his front step in a short, figure-hugging black dress and high heels, a dash of crimson lipstick her only make-up. As Pete's gaze found Lisa's muscular legs, his heart rate trebled.

Metallic Dreams

This girl was the number-one wank fantasy of Bronzehall males. And she had chosen him, for Miles's sake.

(Seven minutes before Lisa rang Pete's doorbell, one boy-racer had, while rubbernecking to ogle her body, ploughed his Ford Fiesta XR2i into a stone bus shelter, an altercation that had turned the car into a metal concertina. On surveying the wrecked vehicle and the bloody driver who staggered from it, Lisa had advised, "You should have kept your eyes on the road and your hands on the wheel, ya silly wee pervert.")

Now, as Lisa stood on Pete's porch looking like the personification of allure, and the definition of a lure, she asked the wide-eyed jazz cat, "Are you goin' to invite me in, ya rude boy? Or am I to stand here all night watchin' you dribble like a mental patient?"

"Ehm…sorry. Come in, Lisa," stammered Pete. "You look, eh…really good, like. A hot female feline."

"Thank you. You look very cool. You dress a lot better than your new pals, the Blood Brothers. Stupid name for a band."

"The band's called that because the other four dudes are actual blood brothers," Pete explained. "Long before those lunatics started the band, back when they were just a gang, they did rituals in which they cut themselves and pressed the gashes together. I'm the odd one oot in the band. I'm the only jazz cat and the only one who's not an actual blood brother, although Spark calls me his 'brother from another mother', whatever that's meant to mean."

Screwing up her face as if sucking on a lemon, Lisa said, "That blood swapping sounds despicable…Satanic maybe. I've seen these idiotic bands like W.A.S.P. on magazine covers, all blood and codpieces. They throw raw meat into the crowd during their concerts. That's just sick."

"Spark found oot aboot Native American blood rituals when he was in Canada as a child. It's an ancient tradition. His band doesn't get involved in any demonic shit. In fact, we don't even play any songs wi' the word 'Hell' in them any more, at my request, after an incident I don't want to talk aboot on a first date."

"All in your own time," cooed Lisa. "I've spoken to Iain and Spark lots o' times. They both lift weights in the sports centre. Sometimes they spectate when I'm at gymnastics trainin' there."

Frowning, Pete grunted, "I bet they do, the dirty bastards."

"I've never met the older guys in the band. What are they like?"

Pete wondered why Lisa was asking him about the twenty-year-olds Ozzy and DT. He knew that most teenage girls in Bronzehall gravitated towards older males with cars, jobs and money: men like Oz and DT. Pete, Iain and Spark, meanwhile, were jobless, carless and broke. They did, however, have bicycles, dreams, cool clothes and a lot of hair. *Is Lisa sizing up DT or Ozzy as potential boyfriend material? Is she here with me just to find out more about them?* With the lines of his perennial frown deepening, and his expression implying that tears could burst forth at any moment, Pete replied, "Oz is the most massive human bein' I've ever seen. His frizzy orange hair makes his heid look like a giant microphone. He's a gentle giant unless you anger him. DT, on the other hand, is far from gentle. That cat scares the shit oot o' me. His Mum and Dad have their own businesses. They live in a big detached bungalow in Svartnatt and drive Jaguars wi' personalised registration plates. DT has his own car, a sporty Renault Fuego wi' a sunroof. He wears tight leather troosers and has waist-length, jet-black hair. He's an intelligent and deceptively cultured guy. I've sat in his kitchen wi' him, sippin' tea, eatin' cake and talkin' aboot life in philosophical terms, but that feline can explode at any time. I've seen him and Spark having brutal fights wi' each other. There's always bloodshed and it only stops when one o' them ends up unconscious. It's bizarre, though – Spark and DT hug like long-lost lovers when they greet each other. They really fuckin' *love* each other, but they just aboot kill each other when they fight."

Lisa's lips formed an O-shaped pout, prompting a stirring in Pete's loins and making him realise that baggy trousers hadn't been a practical choice for this date. "Everyone in Bronzehall knows that the Blood Brothers gang never lost a fight," she said. "It's local legend. Blood Brothers once took on the entire Woodie, all forty-one of them, and triumphed. Not content wi' knockin' their Woodie adversaries unconscious, your four friends tossed the limp bodies into a huge pile then toppled a pine tree onto it, breaking hundreds of bones in one fell swoop. Who does that? And what kind of lunatics walk into battle knowin' that they're outnumbered more than ten to one? Your new friends thrive on blood and violence. You're far too sensitive for that bunch, Petey. Why don't you stick to your jazz band?"

"I still play in the jazz band. In Blood Brothers I can musically express other things, though. Withoot those long-haired lunatics, I'd only ever play keyboards in my room. I'm the creative, sensitive artist in their band. I add delicacy and poignancy to their metallic bluster. We're a perfect complement to each other."

After two hours of drinking beer, listening to music and coaxing conversation out of Pete, Lisa sat on his knee. Having realised that no amount of alcohol would give him the confidence to make the first move, she took his face gently in her hands and kissed him. Pete's world spun as Lisa's soft lips touched his. When her long hair tickled his neck, he felt euphoric and sick at the same time. Hoping that Lisa wouldn't notice the mini-marquee that had sprung up in his baggy trousers, Pete adjusted it like a racing driver changing gear; as he jammed his knob into second, he reflected that this never happened to Don Johnson in Miami Vice.

"Can you feel your heart throbbing?" asked Lisa. Pete felt throbbing in a place rather farther south, but he nodded anyway. Then they continued kissing.

"Spark, open the door, ya hairy heavy metal cat! I had a date wi' Lisa Doune last night! I need to tell you aboot it!" Pete was shouting his news through my letterbox loudly enough to wake my whole block.

I opened the front door and raised an eyebrow. "Lisa Doune. Very impressive, young Jedi. Did you let her feel the Force in your light sabre?"

"I had a light-sabre malfunction. We were gettin' on great, talkin' and that. Lisa sat on my knee and kissed me, which was the best thing I've ever felt. Then she slid her tongue into my mooth, her leg brushed against my stonner and I whooshed in my pants!"

"You did *what?*"

Pete nodded, his turquoise eyes contrasting against his reddening cheeks. "I whooshed. I couldnae help it. It was Lisa Doune, you know what I mean, man? I've never been such a happy, horny cat in my life. And I came right in my fuckin' skids." The furrows on Pete's brow underlined the seriousness of the situation, so I bit my lip and suppressed my amusement while he continued. "I don't think Lisa noticed. I told her I had to go to the shitter, then went upstairs to change my troosers and pants. When I came back doonstairs, she asked why I'd changed clothes. I told her those baggy troosers had gone suddenly oot o' fashion."
Somehow, I managed to keep a cage on my laughter as I pictured the situation in my mind's eye. To massage away Pete's shame, I told him of my first time having sex, and of how I hadn't even lasted to the end of one song. That information perked him up for a moment, but then – ever the pessimist - he observed, "At least you got your tadger oot o' your pants. Before mine could embarrass me for a second time, I told Lisa I was feelin' ill and ended the date." I shook my head in amazement. Most Bronzehall boys would have chewed off an arm for one kiss from Lisa, but Pete had faked illness to get her out of his house.

The little jazz cat pleaded with me not to tell Ozzy or DT about his in-pants explosion. I agreed not to, aware that he was intimidated by the older two, even though musically he left them in his wake.

We walked to Iain's flat to tell him about Lisa and the premature geyser that had erupted in Pete's pants. The three of us laughed so hard that it hurt, our tears of joy washing away all of Pete's embarrassment and shame.

Chapter 19 – Parental Guidance

Our parents played an important part in the development of Blood Brothers the band and, more fundamentally than that, the human beings. I regularly thanked the Universe for a mother and father who never forgot that they had been children not so long ago, and that life is about fun and adventure. Unwilling to piss off the neighbours to either side of my terraced house, my Mum didn't allow the band to rehearse there, although she made it clear to my bandmates that they were always welcome at the house.

Supportive of our band right from the start, DT's Dad had kickstarted our musical journey by buying Dave his first guitar and amplifier, then loaning Ozzy money for a drum kit. Mrs Tierney often arrived at our practice sessions with refreshments and snacks for the band.

I had been friends with Iain since the day he moved to Bronzehall. His family were used to me spending time at their flat, where music was only tolerated at barely audible volume. Theirs was one of those calm, peaceful households where one is scared to fart or swear, in contrast to DT's house, where profanity was practically mandatory. Mr and Mrs Bright always appreciated that I had taken their son under my wing on his arrival in Bronzehall. They realised that had I not done so, their son could easily have become lonely, withdrawn and unhappy. Iain's older brother Tom referred to our band as 'a bunch of long-haired wee poofs who couldn't get a bird in a pet shop.'

Mrs Oswaldo allowed the band to rehearse in Ozzy's bedroom, a spacious converted loft with soundproofing of sorts. On weekdays, when I went straight from swimming training to band practice, arriving wet-haired and chlorine-scented, Ozzy's Mum never failed to bring me a mug of tea and toast with peanut butter, while the others in the band got only tea. To ease my conscience about the toast-related inequality, I took Mrs Oswaldo a box of her favourite Thornton's chocolates every few weeks.

Pete Drummond's parents owned Valfader newsagents. They were nowhere near as wealthy as DT's parents, but drove new cars and owned a sizeable house by Bronzehall standards. Mr Drummond, a cue-ball-headed aficionado of jazz, felt a sense of vicarious achievement through his son's jazz virtuosity. Pete's meanderings into heavy metal, however, displeased his father, who feared that his son would soak up metal culture by osmosis, resulting in his inexorable transmogrification into a thing with long hair, outlandish clothes and an aversion to cleanliness. Heavy metal would, Drummond senior believed, dull Pete's jazz sensibilities. When Pete performed live with his jazz band, his father and I were always in the front row, wearing ear-to-ear smiles. We must have looked like odd gigmates, the hairless Mr Drummond in his suit and tie, and the hair-covered me in studded denim and leather. At these times, I used to wonder how Pete's Dad would feel at the front of a Blood Brothers concert. Sick, probably.

Nonetheless, Mr Drummond didn't push his anti-metal feelings too hard on his son, perhaps aware that doing so might result in Pete rebelling and throwing himself whole-heartedly into heavy metal culture, leaving his jazz melodies fading behind him like an ever-more-distant swansong. Mrs Drummond didn't care what music her son listened to or played. She just hoped he wouldn't end up with long hair, leather and studs like the nice but scruffy kids he had taken to hanging around with. More than that, she wished he would stop drinking so much.

Chapter 20 – Symphony of Destruction

The biggest Bronzehall heavy metal band of the 1980s was Drunken Debauchery (not that they had a lot of competition, you understand). I wasn't sure whether their name was total genius or just shit. I'm still not sure. On one hand, the name encapsulated some of the most dominant aspects of heavy metal culture: alcohol, its abuse, and bad behaviour. Each member of Drunken Debauchery was both a trained musician and a booze-sponge, so their moniker was honest. It did, however, place them firmly in the same realm as joke bands like Lawnmower Deth and Spinal Täp. To be taken seriously, you had to have a serious band name.

Drunken Debauchery had one major advantage over Blood Brothers: they played gigs. In a smart career move that gained them massive street credibility, they played a tribute concert to Metallica's bass player, the legend in loon pants Cliff Burton, the day after he died from injuries sustained in a tour-bus crash in Denmark. Entrance to the gig was free. This show of respect and heavy metal solidarity did wonders for Drunken Debauchery's public image.

My band would have to start playing gigs if we were to have any chance of cementing a local reputation like Drunken Debauchery's. Ironically, our shyest member, the keyboard genius Pete, was the only one to have played concerts. DT, Ozzy and I were confident in our abilities within the confines of a loft or studio, but the idea of playing in front of a crowd scared the shit out of us. Pete told us of two psychological techniques that had helped him during his live shows: if an audience was apathetic or hostile he went to an inner place and became oblivious to those who were watching him; when a crowd was on his side, he fed off its energy and let it raise his game. Then, with four words of Zen wisdom, the little maestro Drummond taught us a simple truth about the importance of rehearsing: *practise hard, perform easy*.

DT suggested playing an impromptu live performance in front of a small, carefully selected group of 'fans'. The list comprised Nicole (a Cornish girl DT had met on holiday), Lisa Doune (Pete's Pied Piper of Cum, and Bronzehall's premiere snake-charmer), a girl known as Hotpants Helen (who was related to the guitarist in Drunken Debauchery and had, apparently, a 'soft spot' for me), Karen Green (Ozzy's girlfriend), Audrey More (a fan of Iain), Justine Slave (also a fan of Iain, and seriously underage), Sarah Keen (ditto) and Tom Bright (Iain's big brother). We persuaded Tom to come by promising him free booze and the opportunity to heckle us, which would thicken our skins and give us experience of dealing with verbal abuse at gigs. Humiliating us with insults would be easy for Tom; he thought we were posey twats and never bit his tongue when faced with the chance to take us down a peg or five. In contrast to Tom, the girls would be our verbal and moral support. I wasn't sure how Iain had ended up with three hot underage girls following him like stalkers;

he neither owned nor played an instrument, so how he attracted these jailbait groupies was a mystery to me.

The band's plan was to play five tracks, all covers, because our original material wasn't yet polished enough to air in front of an audience. We chose one track each. I picked *Touch Too Much* by AC/DC, DT chose Saxon's *Princess of the Night*, Ozzy went for *Heavy Duty* by Judas Priest, Pete selected Rainbow's *Tarot Woman*, and Iain chose Iron Maiden's *Aces High*. Only the Rainbow track featured keyboards, so Pete was expecting an easy night.

DT's latest admirer, Nicole, came up on the train to spend a week with him in Bronzehall. I met her for the first time at Dave's house two days before the gig. She stood about 5'6" with a blonde bob hairstyle, juicy Ribena lips, sparkling emerald eyes, a trim waist and an overinflated bottom which strained cock-teasingly against the spray-on-tight jeans that enslaved it. I concentrated hard, psychically willing Nicole's rump to break out of its denim prison. It never did. Psychokinesis my horned helmet. Where was Uri Geller when I needed him?

Dave had told me graphic stories of Nicole's sexual antics, tales I considered to be far-fetched exaggerations until the moment I saw her in the flesh, at which point I believed every word. On the night before the gig, while DT and I sprawled on corduroy beanbags on his bedroom floor and Marillion's *Fugazi* album filled the air, Nicole announced in a matter-of-fact tone, "I like you, Spark."

"I like you too," I replied, "especially your arse. I'd eat my lunch off it. And my tea. Breakfast could pose a problem, as I usually have bran flakes. Fuck it, I'd give it a shot anyway."

DT's lip curled into a sneer. "Watch your step, ya wee tit. She's my bird!"

Narrowing her eyes, Nicole glowered at DT. "I'm not anyone's *bird!* I'm your girlfriend. And Spark, I like you in a little-brother way."

As a dervish of filth whirled inside my head, I asked, "What's your view on incest, Nicole? I'm all for it."

Dave sprang up from the floor, fist clenched, dark eyes birthing demons. "Stick to your high-school groupies, Spark. It's better for your health."

"Nonsense. I could do wonders for my health usin' Nicole as my training apparatus. Holy shit, the workoots I would do on that body."

Like a long-haired lightning bolt, DT struck. As my hands parried Dave's flailing fists, Nicole grabbed him in a headlock and dragged him off me. "You two are meant to be best of friends," she screamed. "You're fucking nuts, the pair of you! Spark, stop trying to get into my knickers. DT, stop using violence as your answer to everything."

"Take note, Dave," I taunted, "Nicole likes me like a wee brother. Long after she's seen the light and dumped you, she'll still hang oot wi' me. Blood is thicker than water."

From under his girlfriend's armpit, DT countered, "Aye? Well spunk is thicker than blood."

"Please quit winding each other up," pleaded Nicole. "I came up to Scotland for a relaxing holiday, not to referee your fights."

Fixing me with a glassy stare and a dragon-like grin, DT spat, "Aye, ya wee prick, stop windin' me up. If Nicole hadn't pulled me off you, I'd be bootin' your balls."

"Really? Nicole wasn't here the first day I set foot in this bedroom, was she? I booted your balls then and I'll boot them again noo, twice as hard, wi' pleasure."

"I'm not anyone's bird," whined Nicole. "How many times do I have to tell you assholes that?"

DT was making no attempt to free himself from Nicole's headlock; his face was reddening by the second, while his backside, covered by red leather trousers, was sticking up in the air like a female baboon presenting to a potential mate. I pointed to his buttocks. "I appreciate the offer of dungfunnel action, my homoerotic brother, but no thanks. No plundering of arses for me tonight. We have a gig tomorrow and I'm conservin' my energy." Underneath a sweet-scented feminine armpit, DT cracked up laughing. Nicole rolled her eyes and set her boyfriend free.

When the night of the gig arrived we were all shitting ourselves except Pete. Iain was the most nervous of us, which I couldn't understand, as he didn't have to worry about hitting wrong notes or playing out of tune. Iain had fashioned a bass guitar out of Perspex: an actual-size Fender Telecaster model, to which he had fitted strings, a strap, even volume and tone knobs, with immaculate attention to detail. I was no closer to fathoming Iain's fantasy Universe, where it was reasonable to spend hundreds of hours creating an unplayable replica bass, but unthinkable to play a real one.

Before the gig, Ozzy approached Iain and spoke in deep, no-nonsense tones. "This will be the first and last time you fake bass at a Blood Brothers gig. For oor first performance in front of a payin' crowd, we need an actual bassist. Either you do it or we'll get someone who can. We're as good as we can ever be wi' half a rhythm section." After pondering Ozzy's words for a long minute, keeping his gaze fixed on the enormous drummer the whole time, Iain nodded acquiescence.

The band looked the part. Between the five of us, we had nearly eleven feet of hair. We were a pumping mass of denim, leather, studs, hair, sweat, blood, muscle, bone, testosterone and attitude, mostly bad.

Ozzy stripped to the waist, revealing his monstrous torso in all its glory. In just faded blue cutoff jeans and Adidas Kick trainers, he looked like a milk-white Incredible Hulk with orange candyfloss hair.

Nicole and Karen had arrived with DT and Oz. The rest of the girls showed up in dribs and drabs, and helped themselves to drinks (either Carlsberg Special Brew or Barr's Irn-Bru). All the Scottish girls were dressed in short skirts. Nicole had once again squeezed into impossibly tight jeans.

Hotpants Helen and I had apparently met once, at Drunken Debauchery's Cliff Burton tribute concert, but – due to being blackout drunk on that night – I had no memory of it. Reliable witnesses informed me that I'd spent hours talking with Helen, kissing her, even letting her hairspray my mane into a massive Mohawk, but it was all a blank to me. Now, in sobriety, I was too shy to speak to her, so I decided to let the music do the talking.

Tom Bright was last to arrive. He appeared wearing mirrored sunglasses, tartan bondage trousers, black Doc Marten boots and a Skids T-shirt. I respected him for the shirt, at least, since The Skids were one of the most criminally underrated bands ever to grace a stage, plus they were Scottish, which gave them added credibility and relevance. Tom was twenty-four, the oldest person in the studio by four years.

Nicole looked long and often at the spikey-haired punk Tom Bright, which didn't go unnoticed by DT. As my nerves shifted into high gear, the shit that was halfway through my intestines began to kick its way down towards the exit. The Metal Gods offered words of advice. *Breathe. Close your eyes. Relax. You have swum competitions in front of thousands of people. You can sing here in front of a few gorgeous gagging-for-it groupies and one pisshead punk. Do not shit your pants on stage.*

Ozzy's thunderous double-bass drums signalled the start of *Heavy Duty*. As down-tuned riffs from DT's Les Paul resonated inside me, my body hair stood up in salute. Dave arched his body backwards to an impossible angle, his low-slung guitar counterbalancing his body. He had practised this pose in his room for years, and it showed. Eyes shut, he pouted upwards, kissing the sky. The girls shook their hair and swayed to our heavy grooves. Iain jumped off the top of a Marshall amplifier, thumb-slapping his Perspex bass as he soared through the air. The unoccupied Pete threw shapes and banged his head like a lunatic, his jeans inexplicably round his ankles. The Iron Maiden T-shirt he had borrowed from me was far too big for him, completely covering the white boxer shorts from which chalk-white legs protruded like human spaghetti. The little prodigy was lost in our sonic boom.

We finished the first song to wild applause from the girls, who jumped up and down, punching the air and whooping. Just as I began to feel the elation of heavy metal stardom, Tom Bright shouted, "I've done farts that were more melodic than that! You're a bunch o' girly-looking, pansy, poofy wee fannies! That boy on the synth's only dropped his troosers so you can all shag him up the arse! I've walked into some sort o' fuckin' homo Heaven!" Internally, I reminded myself that Tom was here as a favour to us, that he didn't really mean any harm. Deep down, though, I knew he meant every word.

The shit continued to work its way through my system.

Pete kicked off his jeans and threw them into the crowd, sparking a denim tug o' war among the girls. He teased out the spacey keyboard intro to Rainbow's *Tarot Woman*. Exactly on time, DT unleashed a staccato burst of machine-gun guitar, louder and heavier than Ritchie Blackmore had played it over a decade earlier. Iain swung his head in high-speed circles, his hair blurring into a tornado of centrifugal ferocity. Half-naked on his drum stool sat Oz, the giant, whose smile drove home to me that finally, after countless rehearsals, we were a real band. Today, eight fans. Tomorrow, the world.

I did my best Dioesque vocal performance throughout *Tarot Woman*. Afterwards, Nicole shouted, "David Tierney, you are a fucking sex God!" Cool as you like, DT leaned on his Marshall amp, swept back his hair, grinned and invaded Nicole through half-closed eyes. Smiling at Lisa, Pete pointed at the slit in his boxers as if to say, 'You're getting it later, young lady!' The darkly mysterious Helen looked me in the eyes, her face inscrutable. Meanwhile, Iain's three groupies had accepted each other; they congregated, presumably around their hero's invisible bass amplifier, and gazed at him, starry-eyed.

Tom Bright slammed us back down to Earth with a profanity. "Fuckin' bollocks! Ye cannae play for toffee! I'm gonnae rape all your wee sexy groupie bitches!"

With the exception of Nicole, the girls looked disgusted by Tom's pronouncement. Nicole, however, blew him a kiss. As her dirty, dangerous mouth pouted promises of Barbie-doll blowjobs, the demons in DT's dark pools began to surface. He stared Tom down like a puma eyeing its lunch. Tom's reputation was fearsome. He had never lost a fight. As an original punk, he had fought mods, metalheads, skinheads, even other punks, and had always been victorious. DT was a different kettle of shark, though.

I scanned the room, wondering what Dave was sizing up as potential weapons. We were surrounded by guitars, cymbals, drums, drumsticks, cables, amplifiers, bullet belts and glass bottles, any one of which he was capable of using to fatal effect. In my mind's eye I saw Tom strangled with a guitar lead, sliced open by a broken bottle, then decapitated by a cymbal. Suddenly, my fight-related daydreams vanished as my shit shot south. While clenching my butt cheeks together and pondering what David Coverdale might do on the occasion of needing a jobbie during a Whitesnake gig, an epiphany hit me: drum solos and other solo spots were invented to allow other members of a band to answer the call of nature. We weren't doing any solos, though, so I focused on holding in my keech for three more songs.

Throughout Iron Maiden's *Aces High*, I sang with divinely inspired fury, nailing every high note with precision. DT crunched out riffs, keeping his dark, predatory eyes locked on Tom. Beaming from ear to ear, Ozzy pummelled his reinforced drums with breathtaking ferocity. Possessed by Steve Harris, Iain planted a basketball-booted foot atop my amp and tortured his unmusical instrument. He occasionally stopped playing invisible bass in order to punch the air and scream silent orders to imaginary legions of fans. Yes, the boy had serious mental problems, but the reality he inhabited looked like fun. Not only that, he had three times as many groupies as anyone else in the band, so he must be doing something right.

When the song finished, Tom hollered, "That singer should be slid doon a giant razor blade intae a swimmin' pool full o' vinegar! He couldnae hit a coo on the arse wi' a banjo, never mind hit a fuckin' note!"

These weren't random heckles anymore. They were specific and directed at my singing. I wanted to think of a funny comeback that would make me look cool in front of my band and the girls, but I drew a blank. The pressure of Tom's slagging, and my inability to concoct an intelligent comeback, drove my keech downwards until it was touching cloth. As I sprinted out of the studio, a reply popped into my mind. "I'm off tae the shithoose for what we call, in heavy metal vernacular, a Tom Bright."

"What the fuck does that mean?" shouted Tom. "Are you takin' the piss oot o' me, ya wee girl?"

Popping my head back into the studio, I explained, "It's rhymin' slang. Tom Bright equals shite. Know what I mean?" Happy to have cleared up Tom's uncertainties, I continued to scorch a high-velocity trail to the shitter.

When I returned a few minutes later, relieved and feeling lighter than air, Tom was unconscious on the floor, blood jetting from his forehead like water from a burst fire hydrant. Beside him lay DT's Les Paul guitar, its neck snapped in two. Nicole was screaming at Dave, calling him a violent bastard, while Iain and Pete stayed a safe distance back from the fracas. Holding DT in a full nelson, Oz boomed, "I love you, Dave, but I can't let you kill that dickheid. You'd fuck up the band's whole future."

My current understanding of events and the order in which they happened is thus. I sprinted to the toilet, in desperate need of shit evacuation. Tom Bright, unhappy with my use of rhyming slang which equated him with the aforementioned shit, began to give chase. DT, fearing for my safety, smashed his precious Les Paul over Tom's head, knocking him unconscious. Nicole freaked out. DT grabbed a glass Irn-Bru bottle by the neck, smashed it against the wall and advanced on his unconscious adversary, jagged weapon in hand. Ozzy restrained Dave, fearful that he might kill Tom. Everyone else began to wish they weren't there.

I had returned from the crapper feeling relaxed and looking forward to the last couple of songs. After briefly reviewing the devastation that had happened in my absence, I suggested to Ozzy that he take Dave home. They bustled out followed by Nicole and Karen, then, with a roar of exhaust, disappeared in DT's Fuego. A few seconds later, Tom opened his eyes and, in true punk style, launched a spit-projectile which landed on the left thigh of my black leather trousers and spread like an egg in a frying pan. Leaking blood, Tom stood up, stole a bottle of Irn-Bru and wavered out of the studio without a word.

Looking at Iain and Pete (who was by then clad only in boxer shorts), I let out a Halfordesque scream. "Heavy fuckin' metal! We've arrived, baby! Blood Brothers forever!" They joined my celebration, howling and yelping as we exchanged high-fives and hugged. I French-kissed Pete's ear and smacked his arse. Feigning disgust, Lisa turned away, nose in the air. Iain's three groupies jumped up and down, their barely teen titties bouncing like ripe little grapefruits. Finally, I made eye contact with Hotpants Helen, who was sipping Carlsberg on the opposite side of the room. Her almond eyes sent out an unmistakeable message: *you are mine tonight to do with as I please.* Gazing straight back, I nodded.

Iain left with his groupies. To this day, he has never spoken in detail about his post-gig activities that night, always choosing instead to plead the fifth, perhaps because deflowering a thirteen-year-old girl and a couple of fifteen-year-olds tends to be frowned upon by the law. The only information he shared was that Justine Slave's name was appropriate, as she did absolutely *anything* he asked of her.

Pete and Lisa drove into the countryside after the gig. They parked at the side of a single-lane road near Kilmarnock and kissed for an hour. Pete's love pistol went off in his pants. Again. He was doing better, though; on the previous occasion, he had lasted only a minute. At this rate of improvement, he might actually get his tadger out of his pants one day.

Hotpants Helen dominated me that night. I discovered that it is indeed true what they say about the quiet ones. In a very unquiet way, she slapped a smile onto my face. It didn't budge for days.

Chapter 21 – All Hell's Breakin' Loose

DT had been experimenting with drugs for six months. To my knowledge, he had done marijuana, acid, ecstasy, speed, horse tranquilisers, cow steroids and enough magic mushrooms to send a herd of elephants into the stratosphere. I avoided taking the moral high ground and dishing out anti-drug lectures, as he never got fucked up before band rehearsals, plus his guitar playing was better than ever. Dave wasn't the sort of guy to be lectured anyway. One had to be very careful taking that approach with him, or one tended to end up wearing the furniture as a hat.

DT's abuse of narcotics and alcohol had resulted in him blacking out in some undesirable locations, including freshly laid tar. The following morning, road workers had arrived to discover the puke-stained, piss-soaked, long-haired vagabond not just in their domain, but bonded to it. "A case o' lager to the man that gets me tae fuck off this road," DT had bartered, then added, whilst the workmen were weighing up his offer, "Hurry up, for fuck's sake. I've got a shite startin' tae keek oot." Within the hour, the freed Dave - true to his word – had returned bearing a case of Carlsberg as a thank you to his dungareed liberator.

I was meditating to the sound of rain tapping my bedroom window when the frenzied knocking started at the front door. On my doorstep, under weeping skies, I found Nicole, drenched, shivering, barefoot and dressed only in DT's Mötley Crüe *Shout at the Devil* T-shirt. Mascara streams trickled down her cheeks: the perfect postergirl for the Alice Cooper school of make-up. The horror-movie doll gazed at me through emerald eyes which lacked their usual sparkle, as if the light behind them had been switched off.

I invited the bedraggled waif inside and put the kettle on. As I sploshed milk into our coffees and stirred them with a teaspoon, Nicole's catatonic gaze followed the swirls and eddies in her mug. On picking it up, she squeezed its sides for warmth while black tears rolled down her cheeks and dripped into the drink. The combination of DT's absence and Nicole's fragile state didn't bode well. Praying for the best, I asked, "Where's DT?"

"God knows. We lost our heroin virginity tonight. Smoked, not injected. As the drug filtered into my system, I stripped naked, lay on my back, spread my legs and ordered DT to fuck me." Reining in all my reserves of will power, I forced the image of a spreadeagled Nicole out of my mind. Her story so far was just another night chez DT; just as he had never been hugely discerning about what he put into his body, he didn't discriminate when it came to putting his bodyparts - and various other questionable objects - into females. Dave's sex life was an intoxicated *Field of Dreams*-inspired fuck-quest; *if they spread them, he will cum.* "He hit his stride," continued Nicole, "fucking me with long, slow strokes. That was when I suggested adding Tom Bright into the equation."

"Please tell me you're jokin', girl."

"No joke. The heroin was numbing me and I wanted to really *feel*. I thought I could accomplish that by getting DT and Tom inside me."

"One in each end?" I asked, my eagerness for clarification overcoming any glimmer of tact.

"No," she replied, "both at the same end."

I raised an eyebrow. "One in the pink and one in the stink?"

Nicole nodded, eyes cast down. "DT went silent and his eyes darkened. I told him that I wanted fucked by him and Tom at the same time, then added that I wanted it to *hurt*."

"For fuck's sake, girl, DT isn't some peace-lovin' flowerchild! He's a hairy, territorial, alpha-male war-machine who won't share his woman wi' *anyone*, least of all the guy whose inconsiderate heid snapped the neck of his beloved Les Paul guitar."

"I just found that out the hard way. Literally."

"Let me guess. Goodbye, Dr Jekyll. Hello, Mr Hyde's berzerker bastard brother." Nicole's dead eyes widened. She nodded, wiped tears off her cheeks with the back of one hand, sniffed, spat in the sink, then gave me a play-by-play outline of events. What follows is the summarised version.

Hordes of falling rocks splash into the waters of DT's mind as he stares at Nicole with disbelief in his eyes. When she confirms her wish to have the guitar-breaking bastard Bright inside her and adds that she wants it to *hurt*, DT flips her onto her knees, grabs a fistful of blonde hair and rams his cock into her unprepared arsehole without even spitting on it first. "You want it to *hurt*, eh?" he asks, perhaps rhetorically, while sodomizing Nicole with such force that her rectum begins to resemble that of a pink-arsed baboon. She screams in simultaneous pain and pleasure, begs him to *stop*, begs him *never* to stop, tells him he's fucking *killing* her, tells him she'll fucking kill *him* if he ever stops. DT doesn't stop. Not until Nicole has passed out on the floor. She wakes to find the denim-and-leather-clad guitarslinger gathering an array of weapons. She tells him she's in a lot of pain. He replies, "You wanted it to *hurt*. Your wish was my fuckin' *command*." Having desecrated Nicole's butthole, Dave adds insult to anal injury. "Ya two-timin' slutbag Cornish whore witch cow fuckbucket! When I get back here you better be gone. And don't bother goin' to Tom Bright's hoose, 'cause I'm goin' there noo. That tit won't be in a fit state to do anythin' except eat soup through a straw." In the split second before DT turns and sweeps out of the room, Nicole sees something in his eyes that shocks her to the core. Tears. The sound of the slammed front door echoes in the hallway, then there is silence. Nicole and DT are over, with a bang. She sobs on his bedroom floor for an hour, curled up like a beaten child, unfurling as her pain gradually transforms into a burning desire for redemption.

After gulping down her mascara-laced coffee, Nicole asked me if I'd mind having a look at her arsehole to gauge the damage. Despite having daydreamed (and nightdreamed) about Nicole's bottom since first beholding its magnificence, I hesitated. "Please," she whimpered, all puppy eyes, like a child asking for a lollipop. I nodded. She turned round, revealing bloodtrails – raindiluted and somehow beautiful – on the back of her suntanned legs. The dark crimson rivers near her butthole lightened as they meandered down towards delicate ankles. After lifting her T-shirt to reveal near-spherical buttocks, Nicole bent over, pulled her butt cheeks apart and asked, "How does it look?"

Grimacing at the sight, I replied, "To put it tactfully, your arse is in tatters."

"How is that putting it tactfully?"

"That was tactful. If I was tactless I'd have said that your arsehole looks like a doner kebab wi' the meat fallin' oot and far too much red chilli sauce on it."

Nicole began to wail. Head in her hands, she sobbed, "You don't want to fuck it then?"

"Are you deranged? How could you even contemplate puttin' anythin' else up there tonight. Other than ice cubes, that is. They'd reduce the swelling and clean oot dirt, spunk and congealed blood when they melt. And the cold would numb the pain a bit."

"Do you have any ice cubes in the freezer?"

"Aye, my Mum always keeps a tray o' them for cold drinks."

The corners of Nicole's mouth curled into a joyless imitation of a smile. "Do it," she instructed. Again, I nodded. And that is how, aged seventeen, just after the witching hour on a typically rainy Bronzehall night, I came to be wearing my mother's yellow rubber Marigold dishwashing gloves and easing ice cubes into the very rectum I had longed to plunder. Strange, though, how different it looked to the one I had seen in my mind's eye. DT's anal reprimands had turned the puckered little flesh starfish of my fantasies into a burst clam with its guts hanging out. The Metal Gods spoke. *Be careful what you wish for. You just might get it.*

As the echoes of the Metal Gods' words faded, DT's voice resounded in my head. *The Devil made me do it.* My inner voice sent a reply. 'Cowkeech. There is no Devil. *You* chose to hurt Nicole. *You* did it.' *The drugs skewed my behaviour.* 'Shove your drugs up your arse. I hold you, David Tierney, accountable for what you did to that beautiful bottom.' *She wanted it to hurt, so I made it hurt. And this is none o' your business anyway. Stay oot of it or I'll hurt you too.* 'Not even in your wildest dreams will that happen. My fists will rain doon on you like divine fire from a vengeful sky.' *Bring it on, Spark. The demons are on my side.* 'You'll fuckin' need them for this fight.'

After inserting twelve ice cubes into Nicole's desecrated hole, I used my Mum's washing-up basin to catch the pinkish-white goo that trickled out. Then, feeling decidedly heroic, I swept the Cornish beauty up in my arms. Glancing down as I carried Nicole up the stairs, I saw a small patch of golden peach fuzz between bronzed legs. My nostrils inhaled the scent of sex and rain. The Metal Gods repeated themselves. *Be careful what you wish for.*

We lay on my bed, Nicole gazing into me with hollow eyes. Even in her wasted state she looked alluring, the frailty somehow magnifying her femininity. "Hold me, Spark," she whispered. "I need you to hold me." I did as requested. Her soft body moulded itself around my hard physique, and I felt the beat of her heart against my chest. Warm, coffee-moistened lips nuzzled into the side of my neck, sending ripples through me and hoisting an erection into my pants. A hot mouth enveloped the rim of my ear. "My pussy's not sore. Fuck my tight little pussy, Spark." The realisation flashed into me that this was all kinds of wrong. DT was my blood brother. We didn't fuck each other's girls. Nicole may be a sexual superstar, but she was trying to *use* me, and – vain prick that I was - I wouldn't go along with that. Even if I were to throw ethics to the wind and fuck Nicole, I'd lose my best friend and blood brother DT, and a chunk of self-esteem too. Gently, I pushed Nicole away. She grabbed my hair, pulled me close and forced her wet lips onto mine. Feeling the point of no return approaching (the point at which my will power fucks off for a game of golf), I pulled away. "Nicole, you're gorgeous. I've been fantasisin' aboot plunderin' every one o' your holes since the moment I saw you, but those things can only happen in my heid. My tadger will hate me for sayin' this, but I won't fuck you in the real world. Ever."

A cartoon Devil appeared on my left shoulder, jabbed my neck with his pitchfork, shook his head in disappointment, then spoke to me. "You, Spark, are an absolute tit. Men dream about occasions like this and they *never* happen. You've got pussy on a plate and you're turning it down. Not just any pussy either, but the golden pussy of the very girl who's been your wank fantasy since you first saw her. If you don't plunder, pillage, pound and pummel that pussy, I'll disown you!"

A haloed, white-robed figure brandishing a rocket launcher appeared on my right shoulder. He aimed his weapon straight at the fork-wielding Devil and fired, annihilating the little horned baddie in a sea of red mush. "Don't listen to that prick," said the Godly midget. "He never owned you in the first place. You're doing the right thing here by being true to your pal and keeping your raging tool under wraps. Yes, Nicole is off-the-scale delicious. Yes, she would be a fuck to tell your grandkids about. Trust me on this, though – both you and she will regret it if you unload your payload inside her."

"How aboot if I let loose some friendly fire *on* her?" I asked. "Would that be technically OK?"

My angelic advisor shook his haloed head. "Semantics and wordplay! Emptying your tanks over Nicole isn't acceptable either. Don't be dick-led, Spark. You've a good brain in that head, so let it lead the way." The angelic son of a bitch affected his most pious expression. His halo gleamed.

"Aye, you're right," I replied. "I know I'm doin' the right thing, difficult as it may be."

"To whom are you talking?" mumbled Nicole.

"Ehm...just talkin' to myself. I was havin' a wee internal board meetin'."

"Talking to yourself shows detachment from the self."

"You'd know all aboot that, eh Heroin Girl?"

Nicole's eyes began to leak again. I hugged her and whispered, "I'm sorry, gorgeous. I'm not judgin' you. You said the other day that I was *like* a brother to you. DT *is* my blood brother. If I fuck your beautiful wee peach-fuzz pussy it will be a blasphemy against a sacred blood oath which I take more seriously than life itself. Had you never met DT, I would rattle you 'til Saturn was spinnin' in your heid and angels were singin' an orgasmic chorus in your soul. But you only want to fuck me because you're angry at Dave, thereby turnin' sex into a weapon. That, beautiful girl, is a dangerous game."

Nails scored my back as Nicole sobbed into my chest, "You're r-r-right, S-Spark. I don't know what's...what's h-h-h-happened to me. I used to be so...so in control and that fu-fu-fu-fuckin' heroin's wrenched all kinds of...fu...fu...fucked-up emotions out of me."

Gritting my teeth against the pain of the furrows being ploughed into my back, I grunted, "Stay here tonight, in my bed. I'll sleep on the floor. You won't be alone, OK? I won't leave your side until you're clean and poison-free."

Dull green eyes rose. Almost imperceptibly, the death's-head doll nodded. "Thanks." As the sonic serenity of Jean Michel Jarre's *Oxygène* filled the room, I wondered what DT was doing to appease his pissed-off demons. Somewhere, a large quantity of faeces had hit a rapidly spinning cooling device. Of that I was sure.

It turned out that DT had found Tom Bright's house empty. Then, desperate to vent his anger, he had gone to Bronzehall police station and destroyed its interior in an act of gloriously cathartic vandalism. An enthusiastic young officer called McBride had tried to apprehend Dave, only to be flattened by a blow from a hill-walking sock that contained six golf balls. Three more officers had charged at Dave and suffered the same fate as their unconscious colleague. Finally, a German shepherd police dog had taken DT to the ground, after which a crowd of officers had neutralised him with batons ('neutralise' being official police terminology for 'beat the shit out of'). The battered, barely conscious guitarist was locked in a cell and a long list of charges was drawn up: breach of the peace; possession of a deadly weapon; assault of police officers; vandalism; drunk and disorderly; resisting arrest; attempted murder.

The darkest of DT's demons were usually imprisoned beneath a shell of sobriety. I had often witnessed alcohol bending the bars of that cage, allowing its occupants to stick out their unholy heads. A cocktail of heroin and anger had unlocked those demons' cages, after which all Hell had broken loose.

Dave's view of the decadence, depravity and delusion of drug culture was overly romanticised. Abuse of drugs and alcohol had long been engrained in rock culture: Jimi Hendrix, Janis Joplin, Bon Scott, Jim Morrison, Elvis, Keith Richards, Phil Lynott, Keith Moon, Ozzy Osbourne, John Bonham. Aerosmith's Steven Tyler and Joe Perry were famously nicknamed the Toxic Twins due to their inhuman drug intake. Dave had smoked or swallowed all the drugs he could get his hands on, but he had never injected. He was afraid of needles. I thought it odd for him to have such a phobia, as he had no fear of knives, baseball bats, guns or explosives. Alcohol, drugs and sex were addictions that DT seemed happy to host. They were not, however, recommended vices for an individual with a weapons obsession and a love of all things violent. An aficionado of aggression must be clean and sober at all times, or devils become flesh.

At the next band meeting, while Dave was in custody, we discussed the possible reasons for his pent-up fury. I remembered him once telling me he felt frustrated that he wasn't a stereotypical heavy metal star. Rock stars were, after all, meant to start out broke, poorly educated and with a penchant for stuffing pairs of socks down their skintight strides to visually make up for any shortfall in that department. DT was, in contrast, well-off, well-educated and well-hung. His use of drugs was an attempt to follow the heavy metal herd. I wished that David Tierney could see himself through my eyes: the fucker had heavy metal credibility in spades. He was the future of the genre, a heavy metal archetype. *He* just hadn't realised it yet.

Chapter 22 – Falling to Pieces

DT avoided jail after his first assault on a cop. His father hired a hot-shot solicitor to prove that the search of Dave's jacket had been illegal, as the police had entered the Tierney residence and conducted a search without a warrant and against the expressed wishes of the resident. As a result, the drugs found during the unlawful search were inadmissible as evidence in court. Dave's solicitor maintained that his client's violence had been motivated by the threatening behaviour of the police, whose refusal to leave his property had caused DT to fear for his safety, causing him to act in self-defence, using 'reasonable force' against the intruders as is legal under Scottish law. The judge agreed with most of the lawyer's points, but declared Dave's show of force 'excessive rather than reasonable'. On that occasion, DT was found guilty of assault and fined £1000.

No slick solicitor, however, could help Dave after his drug-fuelled frenzy in Bronzehall police station. The whole incident, caught on internal security tape, was played in court as video evidence. It clearly showed DT walking into the station and going berserk without any provocation. Only after the station had been redecorated and four police officers lay broken and bleeding did Dave's winning streak run out.

At the trial, judge and jury sat open-mouthed watching the footage of DT's wild rampage. This was not Los Angeles, where rockers threw TV sets through hotel windows in displays of intoxicated excess. This was Bronzehall, a place centuries older than the school that crumbled to make room for the old school. A flicker of empathy for DT showed on the faces of the jury as they watched a large German shepherd dog bounding towards the long-haired berserker and then saw quite clearly his response: Dave's face showed neither fear nor anger as the police dog was released; reflexly, he raised his weapon, but then voluntarily lowered his arm and let the dog take him to the ground; as the canine sank its teeth bone-deep into Dave's left arm – his fretting arm, no less – the guitarist, while screaming in agony, stroked the beast's head with his free hand. Frowning, the judge summoned the clerk of the court and whispered something into his ear. The clerk rewound the tape, zoomed in, and played it again, in slow motion this time. The second play of the video removed any doubt: the accused had taken out humans faster than blinking, but had made a conscious choice not to hurt the animal. The video tape conveniently 'ran out' after the dog felled DT (whose version of the events that happened afterwards varied considerably from the police's). When Dave's sentence was announced – seven years in jail - Ozzy stood up and shouted, "What aboot the bit where you ask if anyone has any objection, speak noo or forever hold your peace? You missed that bit, ya wig-wearin', transvestite old bastard!"

I tugged on the leg of Ozzy's jeans. "Sit doon, ya dick."

Oz continued to scream from his soapbox high-horse. "I have an objection! I fuckin' object! That man David Tierney is oor lead guitarist! Withoot him, oor band's fucked!"

Again I tugged on the faded denim around Ozzy's mammoth legs, whispering from the side of my mouth without moving my lips, like a nervous ventriloquist. "Oz, you don't get to object. That's weddings, not trials, ya big fuckin' spanner."

Turning a deaf ear to my words, Ozzy's rant stormed valiantly onwards. "Are you listenin' to me? I have a fuckin' objection! I'm not holdin' my peace! This whole trial is a fuckin' joke!"

The bespectacled, grey-skinned judge's expression changed from bewilderment to fury. "What is the name of this idiot who dares to use profanity in my courtroom?"

After looking down at me and beaming his fearless smile, Ozzy raised his head, stood up to his full height, puffed out his chest and boomed, "I'm Alan fuckin' Oswaldo, ya bass! Who the fuck are you?" What felt like hundreds of miles below, in the big boy's shadow, I cringed. To my left, Iain was playing air bass to an imaginary song audible only to him. *Lucky bastard, in his alternate world.* A deep frown underlined Pete's spiky blonde hair. It struck me for the first time that he looked like a teenage Oor Wullie minus dungarees and bucket.

(As a short aside, I would like to express my sincere unhappiness about the fall from grace of the Ozzy-sanctioned term 'ya bass' from Scottish culture. It was one of the most useful and versatile expressions ever to pass the lips of any whisky-soaked poet. When travelling abroad, especially in England, it could be used to scare the shit out of the locals and ensure that you be given a very wide berth. For example, roaring in the roughest Scottish accent you could muster, "What the fuck are you lookin' at, ya bass?" It could be used in a polite fashion, such as when ordering a drink at a bar: "I'll have a pint of Strongbow please, ya bass." An additional use was the friendly form, often used on the phone. Consider: "Ozzy, how the hell are you, ya bass?" These are the three main forms of the term: the aggressive form; the polite form; the friendly form. An advanced usage of the term incorporates one or more adjectives between the 'ya' and the 'bass': "Who the fuck are you callin' a long-haired poof, ya speccy, tashy, suity, baldy bass?" To clarify the terms of the previous sentence, 'speccy'='bespectacled', 'tashy'='moustachioed', 'suity'='suit-wearing' and 'baldy'='bald'. I vote to bring back 'ya bass'. The world will be more colourful and vibrant with it back in regular vernacular. Seriously. Use it wherever you are in the world. It will make you feel warm and fuzzy all over.)

The judge didn't share my sentiments on yabassology; he announced in loud, condescending tones, "Well, Alan bleeping Oswaldo, if your foul mouth utters one more word you will do jail time for contempt of court, you belligerent lout! That's a promise! You will not make a mockery of me or my courtroom!" Ozzy gazed into space as the reality of the judge's words hit home. Then he sat down and turned to me, a sheepish grin on his face.

Seven years without DT's twisted exploits would feel like aeons. I had known him for six years and that felt like forever. In the courtroom, tears welled up in my eyes, but I wouldn't let myself cry. Not there.

DT had screwed our band as surely as he had rearranged the faces of young PC McBride and three of his colleagues. What were we meant to do for seven years without our lead guitarist? Looking for a replacement wasn't an option; the chemistry between the blood brothers was unique. We understood each other. We had grown up together. Shit, we were family.

As the shackled Dave was led out of court, he looked back over a defeated shoulder and gave me an apologetic look, an expression that seemed entirely out of place on his face. Silently, I mouthed the words, "You fucking tit."

The four non-jailbird Blood Brothers met many times over the next few weeks. We discussed the future of our band, a future that DT had sodomised as surely as he had Nicole. He was allowed only one visitor at a time in prison, so we took it in turns to visit. Week by week, his spirits began to sag. He had grown up enjoying life's luxuries and was not adapting well to the crash course in spartan living. And there were harder adjustments for our blood brother, most notably getting used to the uninvited advances of other inmates: men whose idea of a good time was attempting to stick their tadgers up his bottom while he was trying to enjoy a refreshing shower. Consequently, DT learned to shower with his back to the wall and his eyes open. The soap stung his eyes, but that was preferable to the sting of an erection jammed up his unwilling and unprepared sphincter.

Iain, Ozzy, Pete and I continued to speculate on DT's demons. He came from a supportive and loving family, had a job in his family business, drove a fast car, had a beautiful girlfriend, sported a phenomenal head of hair and played guitar like a flash bastard. On the surface, he had everything going for him. Internally, however, bottles were smashing off the inside of his skull, leaving slashed synapses and a headful of broken glass.

I was offered the chance to live, study and swim in the United States for the next year. If I accepted, I would live with an American swimming family, train alongside their sons, and attend high school. There were a lot of pros. Coaching techniques in the US were light years ahead of those in Scotland. American sports facilities, both in and out of the water, were far superior to British ones. If TV, movies and American heavy metal bands (especially KISS, Mötley Crüe, Ratt, Van Halen and Y&T) were to be believed, girls in the US were the hottest and sluttiest on Earth. These were all persuasive selling points in favour of moving there. If DT had been a free man, I would have chosen to reject the offer of moving to America, seductive as it seemed. My belief in the band was absolute, and touring would have taken us to the US and beyond anyway.

I still loved Dave, but he had disappointed me and the others on a monumental scale. One day, our dreams had taken flight. The next, DT had dashed them on the rocks. His raging, narcotic-enhanced temper had snatched away the band's bright future, leaving us at a communal loss as to the way forward. At rehearsals, Pete tried programming guitar riffs into his synth, but that resulted in a mechanistic sound that didn't replicate Dave's fluid fretboard gymnastics. Also, the manic energy DT had brought to the band was missing. Granted, he was warped, but we missed him, his black humour, his constant slaggings, his evil grin and his unique guitar technique.

An exchange family was found for me in Virginia. After much meditation on the subject, I decided to go. If I stayed in Scotland I'd end up moping around and wondering what might have been, had DT not been such a berserker.

Iain, Pete and Ozzy didn't react well to my announcement that I was going to America for a year, but I knew that each of them would have jumped at such a chance. I reminded them that I would be away for one scholastic year only, after which - with six years of DT's sentence remaining - I would return to Scotland, to my blood brothers, to my band. One by one, my bandmates agreed that, if I truly thought America was the best thing for me, they would support my choice.

Chapter 23 – Wanderlust

The US was the logical place for me to be: for swimming; for girls; for music. Heavy metal had originated in the British Isles. The dominant early metal bands were British: Black Sabbath, Led Zeppelin, Judas Priest, Deep Purple, Rainbow, Motörhead, Thin Lizzy and Whitesnake. Then came the New Wave of British Heavy Metal, surfed by Def Leppard, Saxon, Iron Maiden, Tygers of Pan Tang, Diamond Head and Demon, to name a few. By 1988, however, the torrent of British metal talent that had burgeoned in the late '70s and early '80s was drying up. Many of the old guard were still going strong, but metal's breeding grounds had moved. Increasingly, the best new bands were coming from the US. The breathtaking innovation of bands like Metallica, Megadeth, Queensrÿche, Dream Theater, Slayer, Testament, Metal Church, Anthrax and Suicidal Tendencies was taking the world by storm. These Americans had absorbed and digested the music of the British bands, filtered it through their own cultural perspective, then recycled it into something leaner, meaner, faster, darker and hungrier.

Two weeks before leaving for America, I plunged into Vikingwood Forest on my way home from Friday night swimming training. The rain had been perpetual all day, but now the clouds had parted and wet leaves sparkled in sunbeams. Steam rose like resurrected angels from the upper limbs of trees. In no rush to get home on such a perfect night, I took a longer route than usual, revelling in the sights, sounds and scents of the woods. On emerging from the forest, I went into Bronzehall's sports centre to see my friend George, who worked in the café there. He served up a couple of jam scones, poured us two mugs of coffee, pulled down the metal shutter in front of the café, scribbled 'BACK IN 15 MINUTES' on a scrap of paper, then blue-tacked it onto the shutter. We sat at a window table overlooking the floodlit outdoor running track. "This has been a shitty shift," George moaned. "It's been deid all night. I've been stuck in here bakin' scones for non-existent customers."

"Never mind. I'll stay wi' you 'til the end o' your shift. It'd be a shame to let those scones go to waste."

"I can always rely on you to blag my baking, ya fat fuck."

"Fat? I'm a muscle-and-blood swimmin' machine. Check this oot!" I whipped off my shirt and flexed my muscles.

"Stop that, ya pervert. Quick, cover yoursel' up and look over there." The invisible trail from George's pointing index finger led to the far side of the café, where a girl sat facing away from us, her long chestnut hair cascading down the back of an orange vinyl sofa. "She's just moved back to Bronzehall after livin' up in Wick for the last few years," explained George. "Been sittin' there drinkin' cups o' tea for over an hour. She's feelin' sorry for hersel' because it's her birthday today and she's lost touch wi' all her friends here. You should go over and talk to her."

"Who is it?"

"Don't you recognise her?"

"Not from the back of her heid. I've never been much of a back o' the heid recognition specialist."

"It's your old flame Gillian, the very girl you didn't have the balls to ask oot, so you sent me in wi' a note to do your dirty work, ya shy prick."

Gill, my first love: the girl who had ripped my heart into pieces and thrown them to the four winds. Immersed in a magazine, she was oblivious to my presence. Old emotions – love and confusion, fear and lust, joy and pain – came swirling back. When George raised the café shutter and went back to work, I approached Gill with tentative steps. She no longer had any power over me, or so I told myself, but my wavering voice told a different story. "Happy Birthday, Gill."

"Spark?" The word shot out of Gill's mouth like a reluctant bullet. She spun round to face me, moistening lilac-glossed lips with her tongue. When she stood up and smiled, my legs began to shake. The Gillian Kelsey of my memories was a gorgeous, long-legged stick insect. This Gillian Kelsey had curves, and spectacular ones at that – what Lita Ford called *dangerous curves*. The girl had blossomed into a young woman. Looking me up and down with iceberg-blue eyes, Gill asked, "What are you doin' here on a Friday night?"

"I should ask you that. I live here."

"When my parents divorced and my Dad moved up north to work, I went wi' him. His contract in Wick's finished, so we're back in Bronzehall. The worst part of it is that he's on a date tonight…wi' my Mum."

"How's that bad? Don't you want to be a family again?"

"I don't want to be *that* kind of family again. It took me years to get over their split, but I did get over it. They were miserable together, always bickerin' over insignificant things but avoidin' real communication. When I was wee they tucked me into bed every night, then, after givin' me goodnight kisses and puttin' on the whole happy smiley family show, they went doonstairs and tore shreds off each other. They probably thought they were protectin' me from hurt and pullin' the wool over my eyes, but I heard the words they threw at each other like poison daggers. I hated goin' to bed. I used to procrastinate every night, hopin' I could act as a buffer between them if I just stayed up. The quiet nights were the worst ones. I used to lie awake in bed, terrified, waitin' for the fireworks to kick off."

"I always liked your Mum and Dad. I never realised what they put you through."

"They both like you for some inexplicable reason. My Dad thinks the sun shines oot of your arse."

"If you'd care to slide that razor tongue o' yours between my butt cheeks, you'd feel sunshine streamin' oot, thus proving correct your Dad's ideas of sun placement."

"If I looked up your arse, Spark, I'm pretty sure I'd find the same stuff that's spewin' oot o' your mooth. You seem to be full of it."

Metallic Dreams

"Face it, girl, your folks just have far better taste than you. Anyway, how come you're all alone in a sports-centre café on your birthday? Isn't a roller disco somewhere missin' a groupie?"

"I probably deserve that."

"You're fuckin' right you deserve it."

"I was a wee bitch back then, wasn't I?"

"Aye. Bitch wi' a capital W."

"I'll make it up to you tonight, on one condition. You have to kiss George on the lips. If you do that I'll come back to your hoose for birthday drinks. We can celebrate all night if you want."

"For a night wi' you, I'd kiss George's unwashed bumhole."

"Ugh! Disgusting! A kiss on the lips will do."

I ran to the serving hatch and said, "Thanks for the freebies, Georgie baby. Lean closer. There's somethin' I want to tell you, but I don't want Gill to hear." As George leaned over the counter, I grabbed him by the ears and planted a noisy kiss on his lips.

After spitting on the floor and wiping his lips on the back of his hand, the startled George shouted, "Ya poofy bastard, Spark! I cannae believe you just did that! Gill, don't go anywhere wi' that arse bandit! Wait for me to finish my shift then come home wi' me!"

Gill and I waved at George, giggling as we fled the café. Outside, her fingers interweaved with mine. We made the five-minute walk to my house last half an hour, walking hand in hand, filling in the space of missing years. By the time we reached my front door, there was no distance between us. Gill had ditched me years before, but I held no ill feeling about that. Tonight, I had rescued her from boredom and loneliness. She was thankful for that; I could see the gratitude glinting in her eyes.

"Do you have anything alcoholic for a girl to drink on her birthday?"

"You'll need to wait a year for that," I joked. "You're seventeen today, not eighteen. I'm no' servin' alcohol to an under-ager."

"No booze, no screws."

"Back in ten seconds." I ran downstairs and raided my father's drinks cabinet, returning to my room with two full-to-the-brim glasses of Glenlivet whisky. Gill was lying on the floor, her white blouse tied in a knot below her breasts, revealing a tanned abdomen. Either her Dad had been taking her on foreign holidays or she had been toasting her body under a sunbed. I lay beside her, feeling very much like a birthday angel. This angel, however, planned to get Gill drunk and ransack her every orifice. I had been Gill's sole salvation, perhaps her soul salvation, as she sat in solitary misery in Bronzehall sports centre, so I deserved whatever goodies were coming my way.

We drained our whiskies then held each other. When I broke the news that I was leaving for America in two weeks, Gill's body stiffened in my arms. "I just got back and you're takin' off," she whined. "That's not fair."

"I'll be back next summer. I'll write to you while I'm away."

"You'll be popular in America. Tall, fit, athletic and wi' a Scottish accent to boot. You should have loads o' sex over there. Get really good at it, then come back and fuck me properly. I want you to be my first and I want it to be great." Gill's words shocked me for several reasons. Firstly, it told me that she was still a virgin. Secondly, she had just given me her blessing to go on a one-year American fuckfest. Thirdly, and most disappointingly, it highlighted that I wouldn't be popping her cherry before leaving for foreign shores.

Scanning Gill's body, I let out a long sigh. "I appreciate everythin' you've said, Gilly baby, but there's no need to wait another year. I'm more than ready to fuck you right noo."

"Aye, I can feel that you're up for the job, judgin' by that thing that's proddin' my tummy. I'm no' ready for sex yet, though, so do as I say, MacDubh, and devirginise Virginia's virgins 'til they're bandy-legged whores. Become a master at it. I'll be here when you get home."

"But I kissed George…"

"Aye, you did. It's just as well you're jettin' off to another continent, eh? It's hard to be a poof in Bronzehall withoot word gettin' aroon'."

"Still an infuriatin' bitch."

"Still a gullible fool."

We spent the rest of the night on my floor, hugging, kissing and gazing at each other with the wonder of children who had grown up five years in a day. In the early hours of the morning, I walked Gill home to her Dad's house, where we kissed one more time. I wandered home with balls sore from hours of unfulfilled expectation. Then, in my room, I closed my eyes, imagined myself plundering Gill's naked body, and whacked off until cumbullets spattered my bedroom wall.

Gill and I saw each other every day throughout the next two weeks, but she refused to come to the airport when I was leaving: she didn't do goodbyes. Secretly relieved (I didn't want to make a tit of myself by crying in the departure lounge), I told her that I understood.

Iain Bright and my closest family came to the airport to see me off. My mother burst into floods of tears inside the terminal building at Glasgow Airport. I hugged her and promised that I would be OK. My father, stoic as ever, displayed no emotion or tears. He handed me a white envelope and asked me not to open it until I was on the plane. My grandmother beamed her loving smile and wished me the best. She, perhaps more than anyone, had faith in me. I wrapped her in a bear hug, feeling young and full of potential, as I always did in her presence. She knew I could look after myself and plot my own course. Despite having been blood brothers for six years, Iain and I said no words to each other at the airport. There were myriad things I wanted to say, but they collided, cancelled each other out and left my mind blank. I embraced my friend then turned and walked towards the waiting plane. Fourteen steps later, I glanced back over a shoulder. My family were walking away, but Iain stood frozen to the spot, staring right at me, his face crimson. In his eyes was the same helpless look I had seen in the playground on the day we met. Little boy lost. Six years ago, I had made that look disappear. Now it had returned and it was all because of me.

When I boarded the plane, a blonde stewardess whose gold-rimmed name-badge said *Candi* noticed me wiping my tear-slicked face on a sleeve. After ushering me to my seat, the buxom, high-heeled Candi sat beside me and asked what was on my mind. I spilled out the story of my band, DT's incarceration, Gill's return, my coming year with an American family, and the expression on Iain's face moments earlier. Gradually, with Candi as my therapist, my pain passed, clearing the way for wide-open optimism.

The envelope my Dad had given me contained two-hundred dollars and a letter expressing tender, heartfelt feelings from a father to a son. As a poet from a long line of poets, he had always found it easy to encapsulate his emotions in writing, despite being notoriously stoic and stern-faced in person. At the end of the letter were some quotes he had selected as appropriate for a son journeying into the big bad world. One stood out from the others. *In a minority of one, the truth is still the truth.* Those words resonated within me. I stared through the window of the Boeing 747. Wet tarmac stared back. Faces flashed through my mind: my Papa, who had been paralysed as a result of a ballsed-up operation, yet still viewed the world with the awe and wonder of a child; my beautiful Nana, full of grace and fire; my Mum, always in bloom, always wearing her heart on her sleeve; my Dad, who could be one hairy, scary big Highlander, but whose default setting was a gentle giant with a soft heart; Gill, whom I was losing for a second time; DT, the wild jailbird with demon-filled eyes, looking at me almost apologetically over his shoulder as he is led, shackled, from the courtroom; Oz, the Scottish Hulk with orange candyfloss hair and natural smile; Pete, the shy, quick-shooting virtuoso; Iain, whom I imagined standing agape in the airport, rooted forevermore to the spot where we parted.

Tears began to flow down my cheeks. Candi wiped them away with a paper towelette while soothing my soul with her soft southern accent and porcelain smile. As I reclined my seat and closed my eyes, Candi whispered, "Ah'd snap you up mahself if ah was twenty years younger." Happy at the thought of that, I drifted into slumber. After a restful two-hour sleep, during which I dreamed that I was lead vocalist in Y&T, I woke with every cell atingle. Symbolically, the dream had foretold that it was going to be a good year.

As I walked off the plane, Candi the Angel of Compassion kissed my cheek. "Thanks…for bein' so caring," I spluttered.

In a heart-melting southern drawl, she replied, "Baby, that's just who ah aym. You have a good year now, y'hear. And don't break too many American girls' hearts." I flashed a smile, took a deep breath and soaked up one last look at Candi: six feet tall; voluptuous body; golden tan; shimmering blonde hair; traffic-stopping smile that must have cost a fortune in dentist's bills. Then I exhaled and walked into America.

Chapter 24 – Stranger in a Strange Land

I arrived in Virginia thinking, as most seventeen-year-olds do, that I knew everything I needed to know. Certainly, I had figured out some useful interconnected truths: nothing worthwhile comes without sacrifice; sacrifice equals pain; pain, when used to extend one's abilities, is a friend; true friendship involves love; love is always pain. My year in Virginia would teach me that I could survive on a different continent from my biological mother and father, far from the friends I had grown up with. My host mother and father would become Mom and Dad, while my two host brothers, Geraldo and Jorge, would become like real brothers to me. I would discover that entering a fresh situation in a new place can bring out one's true self: when no one has expectations of you, it frees you up to be authentic without the fear of disappointing or offending anyone.

Stafford High School had no dress code. My standard outfit for school was a pair of old-school Scottish football shorts, tube socks, basketball boots and a heavy metal T-shirt. During the third week of term, the Principal, Bill Puget, invited me into his office. "You're an excellent student, Spark," he said, his voice deep and eloquent, "but those Scottish soccer shorts you wear are very short."

"That's why they're called shorts. You know what I mean?"

"Yes, I understand the logic of the nomenclature, but your shorts are especially short. Mrs Lanford the mathematics teacher described them to me at lunch yesterday as 'plum-huggers'. She could have chosen a better moment, incidentally, as I happened to be biting into a plum at the time. Anyway, I've gone off on a tangent. I brought you here to tell you that dressing in such a way might attract the wrong kind of girl."

"There's a wrong kind o' girl?" I gasped. "I never got that memo."

Bill Puget gave me a humourless glare and asked me to wear longer shorts to school in future. He seemed to be fearful that I, his Scottish exchange student, would be hypnotised by an American vagina – not just any vagina, but the *wrong* vagina – which would lead me off the academic rails and into the hot, humid location of Pussyville, USA, where I would spend every waking minute, resulting in my grades dropping from A to F in every subject except, perhaps, female anatomy. He needn't have worried. Much as I loved and revered the female form, there was never any danger of anything cocking up my delicate Zen-like balance of study, swimming, weight training, sleep, music and girls.

In Fredericksburg, my home town for the year, I became good friends with two heavy metal dudes. Brian Ferntree was a carefree individual with a penchant for walking around the house naked. Not just his house: anyone's house. Brian's brown hair fell just below his shoulders and he shaved only on special occasions. He drove a GMC van like the one in *The A-Team*, making him instantly stylish in my estimation. The cool-box in the van was always stocked up with cans of Coke, Dr Pepper and Mountain Dew. Brian had been the best basketball player in Stafford County until an opposing player's deliberate foul had seriously injured his knee, forcing him out of competitive basketball. At six foot one, Brian hadn't been the tallest basketball player in the league, but his inhumanly vast vertical jump had given him a unique dunking ability. He had made a science of learning aerobatic basketball manoeuvres which, in addition to breaking the laws of physics, always ended with a dunk. After his injury, Brian threw himself into physical rehabilitation like a man on a mission. Favourite band: Megadeth.

Manie Lucchese had been conceived in Sicily, but his Sicilian parents had moved to the US before his birth. He looked Italian, sounded half-and-half, and refused to shave above his top lip, where a sparse black outcrop of hair resided. He called it a Sicilian moustache. I called it bumfluff. Manie had the same shiny black hair and olive skin tone as his parents, and hair that flowed almost to his waist. His lean 5'6" physique ran ten miles every day, rain or shine. Favourite band: Metallica.

My swimming reached a new level in the US, culminating in my qualification for the national finals in Orlando, Florida. After an uncharacteristically bad start off the blocks, I regained distance with every stroke, but couldn't pull back enough to place in the top three of my event, the 50m freestyle. Those twenty-two-and-a-bit seconds were simultaneously the best and worst moments of my fifteen-year swimming career.

My quests of the flesh were plentiful during my first few months in Fredericksburg. I revelled in sexual exploits that involved cheerleaders (I liked the outfits), hockey players (ditto) and heavy metal whores (need you ask?). I discovered that, for reasons I couldn't fathom, a Scottish accent was a lubricant to American females. It also didn't do any harm to drop into conversations that I was the frontman in a band called Blood Brothers back in my homeland. Some American nubiles claimed to have heard of my band, but they were either lying, self-deluding or perhaps massaging that most frail of things, the male heavy metal ego. A steady stream of American girls' panties (and morals) were thrown to the winds when their owners discovered that I fronted a metal band, even when the girls in question had never heard, or heard of, that band. During the first half of my year in Virginia, I submerged myself not only in chlorinated water, but also in feminine juices. Without shame or remorse, I used girls to further my sexual abilities, while they used me to gain a story that they had fucked a long-haired foreign dude who was lead singer in a metal band. I enjoyed my southern female hosts and wrote home regularly to rub my bandmates' noses in my sexual adventures.

Gill and I wrote to each other every week. Her letters expressed interest in every aspect of my life except sex, so I wrote nothing about that in my communications to her. Six months into my year away, a letter from Gill requested that I be more discreet with the stories I send to the band; in a Vikingwood pub called The Blacksmith's Anvil, Iain Bright had recounted a tale involving me, a whipped-cream-covered cheerleader and her heavy-metal-whore pal, all in a water bed together. The story had made the rounds, eventually reaching Gill's ears. My written reply told Gill that she had no right to be pissed off at me, as she had asked me to have sex with American girls. At that point, Gill's letters stopped without explanation. When I tried to phone her, I got a dead tone.

I decided to drown my Gill-related sorrows in an ocean of southern pussy. Facing the sky, I screamed to the Metal Gods, "Bring 'em all on! Heavy metal whores, cheerleaders, hockey players, dancers, gymnasts, barmaids, chicks so hellishly beautiful they melt steel just by lookin' at it, but let's not leave oot the girls wi' squinty eyes, lopsided tits and funny walks…I'll fuck them all!" The Metal Gods heard my call and answered it; a fast-moving stream of sluts flowed my way, and I immersed myself fearlessly in them. All the physical pleasure, none of the emotional bullshit. Amazing. Then, one sunny Virginia morning, everything changed.

A rising sun reflected off the surface of Ferry Farm's outdoor pool. At 0800 hours, near the end of my team's training session, we were doing a set of 10 x 100m individual medleys (25m butterfly, 25m backstroke, 25m breaststroke and 25m freestyle, in that order). I was leading my lane. During the backstroke leg of the final IM, my fingertips brushed against something in the lane next to mine. On the following arm cycle, as my hand pulled through the water, it cupped a soft object. A high-pitched yelp preceded the words, "My titty! He grabbed my titty!" I recognised the voice of Kimberley Setzer, our swim team's backstroker extraordinaire, known statewide as Backstroke Queen, and the only African-American on the team.

I flip-turned at the wall, pushed off into my breaststroke length and – while gliding underwater – noticed that Kimberley had stopped swimming and was standing in waist-deep water, hands on hips. When I surfaced to breathe, her stare was there to meet me. Sunlight glinted off the rivulets of water that trickled down her dark skin. I swam past Kimberley and, after finishing my freestyle length, stood up and shrugged my shoulders, unsure of the correct protocol in a subaquatic titty-grabbing situation. Scanning my memory banks for a file entitled *Inadvertent Groping*, I came up blank. The best I could manage was, "I didnae mean it, Kimberley."

"Ye didnae mean it, did ye no'?" she imitated, in the worst mock-Scottish accent I had ever heard.

"No, I really didnae."

Moving closer, Kimberley tilted her head and looked into my eyes. "Well I dinnae believe ye. I think ye squeezed ma titty oan purpose!" Again the horrific Scottish brogue.

I felt my cheeks flush as an audience congregated around us. Fighting the rising communal opinion that I was a raging Scottish pervert who had left his own country just to expand his titty-grabbing horizons, I continued to protest. "Honestly, Kimberley, I'd never grab your tit on purpose. Unless you asked me to, like."

A few of the gathered crowd laughed, lightening the mood a little. Pete Malone, my Jamaican swimming coach, announced, "Spark, I'm proud of you for continuing and finishing the set. That's commitment. Kimberley, you wimped out. You need to finish every set, even when there's a sexual deviant in the lane next to you."

I jumped to my own defence. "I'm no' a deviant."

"Whatever you say, mon. Haaaaa haaaaa haaaa!" Pete's belly laugh echoed around the poolside. Soon, everyone except Kimberley was laughing. After an easy swimdown and some stretching, I took a long outdoor shower in the morning sun.

Kimberley Setzer lived on the street perpendicular to mine in Briarwood Estates. I had never walked her home after training for the same reason no male had ever walked her home: unattainability. She harboured a fierceness that scared the shit out of guys. The few courageous souls who had mustered the courage to ask her for a date had been shot down in flames. No explanations, just flat-out rejection. Kimberley stood 5'10" in her bare feet. She wore her hair in waist-length braids which she tucked inside a cap while swimming. Hers was a perfect female swimmer's body: long and lean with subtle curves. Her dark, almond-shaped eyes appeared to have limitless depth, hinting at a vast intelligence within.

I set off on the walk home dressed only in flip-flops and shorts, enjoying the coolness of my wet hair against warm, swim-tired back muscles. A pair of hands fastened themselves over my eyes. "Guess who, ya titty-squeezin' Scottish sex maniac?"

"Kimberley."

She removed her hands and asked, "May I walk you home, groping boy?"

"Ehm...aye, of course. Didn't your Mom and Dad tell you never to walk home wi' perverts?"

"It's lucky for you I don't listen to them, isn't it?"

"It is, as you say, lucky for me. I hope you don't mind my toplessness. It's too hot to be walkin' home fully dressed."

Kimberley's gaze flicked over me, her expression giving away nothing. "I see your body every day in the pool. Don't cover up on my account."

The walk home seemed to last for years. We talked about music, swimming, my host family, American food, American cars and Kimberley Setzer. On reaching her house, we stood by the wooden mailbox at the end of the driveway and talked some more. I was in the middle of a tirade about Scottish bands' underestimated contributions to the world of music when Kimberley leaned forward, kissed me almost imperceptibly, then dashed into her house, leaving just a faint strawberry scent behind. As my lips oscillated with joy, I slipped Bruce Hornsby and the Range's *Scenes from the Southside* into my Walkman, pressed play and floated home in a Kimberley-kissed daze.

During the months that followed, Kimberley and I spent every free moment together. We walked to and from swimming training hand in hand, rain or shine, morning and night. Her dolphin-like propulsion through the water was visual poetry. I had come to Virginia expecting to experience American girls. Check. I had planned to have a lot of sex. Check. Something else had happened, though, which blindsided me: deeply entranced by the beauty of Kimberley's mind, soul and body, I had fallen in love – hook, line and sinker. Kimberley and I discovered that love and sex, when experienced simultaneously, synergistically increased our understanding of the Universe. This was what ancient alchemists had spent their lives chasing: the Master Work; the purification of the soul; the awakening of secret energies and knowledge through sexual practice. Fearlessly we bared our souls to each other. From a physical perspective, our sex was a lot like swimming training: it gave us the ability to go harder and faster, as well as teaching us to control our breathing, pace ourselves and last longer when necessary.

Near the end of my year away, Manie Lucchese discovered how to make pipe bombs. *(Fill a short, hollow piece of metal pipe with an explosive substance such as gunpowder, then flatten both ends of the pipe and fold them up with pliers. Drill a hole in the middle of the pipe and insert a fuse. When the fuse is lit the resultant explosion tears the metal pipe into pieces, throwing shards of shrapnel outwards in all directions.)* After an argument over grades with Mrs Lanford, his maths teacher, Manie decided to blow up her mailbox with a pipe bomb. He took a rucksack full of bombs to the woods behind his house, where he tested them one by one, using the same process each time: place bomb inside fresh cardboard box; light fuse; run like hell. For each bomb, Manie noted amount of gunpowder used, length of metal pipe, diameter of pipe, thickness of pipe walls, length of fuse, and – after the explosion – blast radius. These prototype bombs helped him to master his recipe.

Under cover of darkness, and with Brian and me as passengers, Manie drove to an old wooden house on the shores of the Rappahannock River. He stopped his red 1973 Mustang next to a metal mailbox with 'LANFORD' in white lettering. Bomb in hand, Brian leaned through the car's passenger-side window, lit the fuse, deposited the bomb into the mailbox and slammed its door shut. As the car screeched away, a blast erupted behind us. Brian and I laughed all the way home, but Manie's face was a brewing thunderstorm; the damage hadn't been substantial enough for his liking. The Lanford mailbox was still standing. A bigger pipe bomb would be necessary.

Manie bought the required supplies the next day. As we set to work creating the instrument of destruction in his garage, Manie's Dad walked in. (There were strong rumours of Manie Senior's Mafia involvement, all of which he denied, sometimes a little too vehemently.)

Under the shadow of his father's frown, Manie explained, "It's a physics experiment to explore the relationship between pressure and force." Technically, that's exactly what pipe-bomb theory represents: increase the pressure inside the airtight pipe to such a level that the differential between internal and external pressure causes the pipe to explode, thus equalising the pressure and ensuring that balance is maintained in the Universe. Manie Senior was no slouch, though; he knew a bomb when he saw one and a bullshit artist when he heard one. He made the snap decision that the 'Scottish pervert' must be responsible for the aberration in his son's behaviour, as Manie Junior had never shown any interest in bomb-making until a strange, long-haired Scottish kid arrived in their quiet town. The Scotsman, therefore, must be the catalyst in his son's bomb-building activities. It was simplistic thinking but I chose not to argue with it, just in case the Mafia rumours were true. Concrete boots were just not my style. Annoyed by the way events had unfolded, I walked home accompanied by the melody of noisy nocturnal insects. Manie Senior grounded his son for two weeks and confiscated all metal pipes, gunpowder and other bomb-making paraphernalia.

With Manie's garage out of commission, we needed another base of bomb-building operations. Brian suggested the local recording studio: soundproof; isolated; far away from parents; plus we could play guitar at maximum volume during breaks from bomb-making. After Manie's grounding had been served, we booked the studio for a weekend. Manie brought a hollow metal pipe of roughly the same diameter as the wide end of a baseball bat, then sawed off a piece - eighteen inches in length - and emptied the contents of 64 shotgun shells into it. Unwilling to be anywhere near this behemoth when it blew, I insisted on connecting an extra-long fuse to it.

When darkness fell on Sunday night Manie's Mustang rumbled to the bottom of the Lanford driveway. After placing the bomb into the mailbox with the care of a midwife laying a newborn baby into its mother's welcoming arms, he drove a few feet then pulled into the side of the road to watch the fireworks. Sphincters awaver, Brian and I screamed at Manie to drive away, but he refused. The explosive gardener wanted to see his flower blooming.

A blinding flash ripped through the humid night air. As my eyesight returned, I saw a flaming stump of wood sticking out of the ground. Not content with merely blowing the sides out of the mailbox, Manie had removed every trace of its existence with the mother of all pipe bombs.

We were guilty of tampering with mail (federal offence), destruction of property (usually a state offence but in the case of mailboxes, federal offence), vandalism (county offence) and possibly terrorism (federal offence). None of that mattered as we drove back to the safety of my host parents' house, basking in the afterglow of our destructive activities. After greeting my Mom and Dad with innocent smiles, we microwaved cornbread and made a fresh pot of coffee. Weird colours and shapes danced on my retinas, which were still in somewhat of a huff after the unprovoked assault on them.

That night I slept the sleep of the just, not suspecting that Manie's appetite for pipe-bombing (dare I say his appetite for destruction?) had not been satisfied. Rather, it had been whetted. He went home that night and made a list of other people who had wronged him. Five people made his shit list. Five Fredericksburg mailboxes didn't sleep that night: they sweated bullets, intuitively aware of their impending doom.

The following day, Manie made five giant decimators. Brian and I agreed to accompany him on his spree of devastation on the condition that we would not hang around to watch the explosions. Light fuse, drive away, repeat. No waiting to smell the gunpowder. Reluctantly, Manie agreed. He placed the pipe bombs in the back of the Mustang, where they lay in silence, steeped in menace and gagging for annihilation. Five chunks of cold Kamikaze metal.

Manie's ex-girlfriend Katrina had dumped him in front of his friends, calling him a 'car fucker' and claiming that he preferred his Mustang to her (which was actually true). Her parting advice to him had been, "Enjoy fuckin' your Mustang's tailpipe 'cause you'll never fuck mine again." The pipe bomb devastated Katrina's mailbox, wood and metal splintering outwards in a violent spray which left not even a stump as a witness. Manie laughed so hard during his moment of redemption that he steered his prize red Mustang into a ditch, crushing its nose like a concertina and leaving the back end sticking up at an odd angle, as if waiting for a knight to joust with. I bailed out of the car and ran like fuck into a cornfield, its seven-foot plants providing perfect cover. In situations like that, it's every man for himself. I wasn't going to end up like DT. One jailbird in any band is enough. I didn't look back and didn't stop running until I was back in my street, drenched with sweat and gasping for air.

Brian and Manie didn't run. Manie went into a catatonic state over the damage to his beloved Mustang, while Brian had the presence of mind to remove the pipe bombs from the car and throw them into the ditch.

In a coincidence of pure bad luck, a state trooper happened to be driving along the road at the same moment Brian chose to ditch the pipe bombs. The cop stopped his car, walked up to the wrecked Mustang and shone his flashlight into the ditch, illuminating the weapons of mailbox destruction. Manie claimed that he must have, by chance, crashed his car right next to a crazy bomber's stash. The cop was unimpressed by the story; he had seen Brian dumping the evidence. The trooper handcuffed Brian and Manie together then carefully ushered them into the back of his sedan. He took the pipe bombs as evidence and drove to the local station. Luckily for me, my friends kept quiet about my involvement in Manie's explosive quest for revenge.

A week later, I boarded a plane bound for Scotland.

Leaving Kimberley was the most difficult thing I had ever done. The thought of being unable to touch her dark body and kiss those full lips scared me shitless. Haunted by the feeling that I may never get another chance with her, I slid down in my cramped plane seat, put on my Walkman's headphones and let the bluesy tones of Great White's *Twice Shy* album act as a dam to my emotions. This worked until the track *She Only*; as Jack Russell's whisky-soaked vocal told the poignant tale of a woman torn by loneliness…a maiden who waits endlessly for her man, always wishing that he would come back and stay. My heart s-h-a-t-t-e-r-e-d. I pulled a blanket over my face and hid there until, six hours later, I arrived in Glasgow with eyes more bloodshot than those of the foulest movie vampire. The irony of returning home but feeling lost wasn't lost on me. I hoped my blood brothers could heal my splintered heart and pull me out of my one-way descent into the hopeless location of Quivering Wreckville.

Chapter 25 – Coming Home

As he wrapped me in a bear-hug at the airport, my father asked if I'd left a maiden behind in Virginia. Perhaps my after-sob voice and bloodshot eyes gave away that this was the case, but, not wanting to cry in front of my father, I shrugged my shoulders and feigned apathy. On the drive home, my Dad stopped at a garage and bought me an ice-cold glass bottle of Irn-Bru. It tasted good, but the only liquid with the power to calm my soul's tumult flowed from Kimberley Setzer. I was back in Scotland, but my heart had burst free to remain in America with her.

My blood brothers had never been far from my thoughts during my year away. Iain was the one I'd missed most, perhaps because of the lost look I had seen in his eyes at the airport. Those eyes had seemed to say, 'You picked me up six years ago only to drop me today.' Back in my house – after greeting my mother with hugs and kisses – I phoned Iain, who suggested meeting at Vikingwood Square rather than talking on the phone. I hung up and set off running. After sprinting past several inebriated Woodie members who were drinking from brown-bagged bottles outside the square's public toilet, I saw Iain Bright, hairier and heavier than a year earlier, careering towards me. We slammed into each other like a car crash, squealing like excited lassies. Shoppers stared and Woodie warriors shouted abuse while Iain and I embraced like long-lost lovers, not giving a shit who saw or what insults they hurled.

We walked to Iain's lockup, liberated his Dad's Austin Montego and drove to a new pub called My Father's Beard. After two pints of cider and an hour of chat, my soul began to feel a little lighter. I was still filled with fear that I might lose Kimberley, but, due to being reunited with my blood brother, I was no longer drowning in my fear; I was afloat in it. Iain told me the news that he hadn't wanted to put in letters. Gillian Kelsey had moved away again and was working in a hotel in the far north. (I didn't care, as I could barely remember Gill; Kimberley's waves of love had blurred my memories of – and washed away my interest in – all other lust interests.) DT had become reclusive and refused to see visitors. Blood Brothers hadn't played a note together. Iain still didn't have a bass guitar.

There was good news too. Ozzy was working in a cake factory and playing drums every day. Pete was saxophonist in one jazz band and clarinetist in another.

I reflected on the logistics of getting the band moving again. Our lead guitarist was an incarcerated recluse with six years of his sentence left to serve. The band's 'bassist' had neither a bass guitar nor the ability to play one. Thinking about it made my head hurt, so I decided just to feel my feelings now and worry about rejuvenating the band later.

Leaving the Montego in Bronzehall town centre, Iain and I walked to Ozzy's house. The door opened and the giant filled its frame, dressed in stripey pyjama trousers, tartan slippers and a Motörhead England T-shirt.

Like an untended hedge, his hair was bigger and bouncier than ever. "Spark, ya wee poof! How the hell are you? Come inside and bring that Bright lunatic wi' you." We climbed the wooden ladder to Oz's loft, where we played a tape I'd brought from the United States: Dokken's *Back for the Attack*. Mrs Oswaldo brought us mugs of tea and digestive biscuits. When I thanked her for the *cookies* and told her she was a perfect *Mom*, Ozzy's mouth gaped. Horrified by my unwittingly adopted Americanisms, Oz reminded me that it wasn't *Mom* and *cookies*; it was *Mum* and *biscuits*. I reminded the giant that my year in America had been influential. Stony-faced, he replied, "You're no' in America noo. You're in Bronzehall, so talk properly, ya wee backside bandit."

As we drank tea, Oz announced that he had seen his doctor that morning about a problem with his tadger, which to his amazement had been bright orange when he woke up. "Aye," he continued, "it's hard to believe, eh? Fluorescent! What a fright I got. So I'm sittin' there in the surgery wi' my skids at my ankles while the doctor peers at my penis and goes through a long list o' questions aboot stress, love life, work, family. Happy wi' all my answers, he admits to being stumped and asks for details o' my last sexual experience, so – honest bastard that I am – I tell him, 'I spent last night watchin' porn and eatin' Wotsits.'"

"Holy shit," I cringed, "you had a year to think up somethin' funny and that's the best you could come up wi'?"

"What are you talkin' aboot? I'm serious! Orange donger is no laughin' matter. It's bad enough bein' born wi' orange hair. I thought things couldnae get any worse than that, but then orange pubes started to sprout when I was ten. I didnae like havin' Irn-Bru pubic hair stickin' oot o' my balls, but I could handle it, so to speak. Orange donger, however, is somethin' up with which I shall not put." Smiling at Ozzy's Winston Churchillism, I suggested that he write a song about his orange-tadger experience. "Already taken care of, Spartacus," he replied. "It's a speed-metal number called *Orange Donger of Doom*." This pushed me over the edge. Tears flowed, sides split and laughter echoed round the wooden attic. Somehow, perhaps due to the natural high of being back with my blood brothers in Bronzehall, I had transcended my Kimberley-related sorrow. She and I would work things out. I didn't know how, but we'd figure out a way. Hovering overhead, the Metal Gods spoke. *Have faith*.

Oz sat on his drum stool, picked up his sticks, pounded out an artillery beat and sang with cookie-monster death-metal vocals:

> "Woke up, looked down, orange cock.
> Fuck me! I'm off to visit the doc.
> Before I go I'll have a quick wank in a sock.
> When my Mum walks in withoot even a knock,
> she stares, shakes her heid then faints from the shock
> of seein' the orange donger of dooooooooooooom!"

We all laughed until we were crying. Eventually, when the laughter had abated, I proposed a visit to DT. Oz refused point-blank. He had wasted too much time and money travelling to and from Dave's new home, only to be rejected and ignored. "DT's sunk so far inside himself that he's completely cut off from everythin' else," Oz explained. "He's no' the same wild card you remember. Prison's changed him. He became more subdued each week, like jail was suckin' the life oot o' him. Then he stopped seein' visitors, even his Mum and Dad. How bad is that?"

Internally, I was screaming to see my wayward brother Dave, but I had to respect his feelings. If he didn't want to see anyone, that was his prerogative. Trying to force my presence on him would be unpoetic and unZen, like a rape of sorts. Possibly, seeing his band on one side of a sheet of bullet-proof glass, while he sat just inches away on the other side, was soulbreaking. Freedom and slavery separated by a thin layer of glass, with him on the wrong side.

After drinking more cider in Oz's loft, we walked the two miles to Pete's house. The goatee-bearded jazz cat was dressed in a sharp suit, à la his jazz heroes, and his ever-present skullcap, which was balanced atop his head at an asymmetrical angle. With Pete (and yet more cider) in tow, we walked to the old swing park in the woods, sat on its rusty roundabout and shot the breeze while guzzling our alcoholic apple juice.

Pete told me that Lisa Doune came to all his jazz gigs and hung on every note he blew. When I asked if Lisa ever did any blowing of her own, Pete closed his eyes and shook his head in wide arcs. "Wait a minute," I added, "you won't know aboot that because you never get as far as drawin' your gun. Are you still shootin' holes in your holster, so to speak?"

"I'm not gonnae dignify that wi' a response," spat Pete. "I'll tell you this, though – my gun is a finely tuned weapon."

"Aye, too finely tuned," piped in Iain. "I believe the term is *hair trigger*."

As the chuckling Ozzy's massive arms wrenched the roundabout – which had seized up decades earlier – into movement, spinning it ever faster, Iain and I lay back, howled with laughter and watched the sky revolve at a dizzying rate. Balanced on the centre, Pete removed his jazz cap, frowned and tugged his wiry hair to a standing position. Looking like a young, moustacheless Einstein, he announced, "You three really are serious fannies. Do you realise this? Can you comprehend the fanny status you've achieved, ya musically pedestrian simpletons?" Our laughter's intensity grew as the truth of Pete's observation hit home: we were fannies of the highest calibre and we knew it.

Chapter 26 – Back in Business Again

Dark clouds recede into the horizon, peeling open a sky of ceaseless blue. I left for work today feeling disillusioned and lost. The adventure, spontaneity and wonder of childhood were long gone. Now I've returned to myself, and not before time. After years as numb slave to a pointless cycle, I'm free again. The country road I navigate is flanked by trees whose steepled branches intertwine like lovers' fingers, casting skeletal shadows onto tarmac that winds its way into dawn's pale yellow sun.

On arriving home, I unplug the phone, bounce upstairs and fall into bed, not to sleep but to revel in the glorious feeling of freedom. Under the bedroom window a blue LED clock display says 0907. I'm more than rested and there's world-changing work to do. As the new day's first mug of coffee kicks into my cells, stimulating an enjoyable adrenaline response, I ponder the whereabouts of my blood brothers.

Every couple of months, Mr Tierney and I meet to drink coffee, share news and play with his latest photographic equipment (on which he spends enough to fund a small country). DT now has a farmhouse in the countryside near Bronzehall. After Dave's release from prison, his father took him under a wing and taught him how to run the family business. Prior to jail, DT had acted like an employee (and a wayward one at that). After prison, however, he channelled his energy into learning and mastering the business, aware that one day it would belong to him. He became a workaholic, replacing destructive obsessions with one he considered constructive. Although Mr Tierney has 'retired', he is still company director, accountant and webmaster, while DT handles the day-to-day running of the business. The rural location of Dave's farmhouse allows him to live a reclusive life when not at work. He grows his own vegetables, chain-smokes cigarettes and shares his farmhouse with a golden retriever called Saxon. I've met DT only twice since his release from jail, both times unplanned, both at his parents' house. On these occasions, we exchanged obligatory hellos but weren't able to maintain eye contact, as if our eyes were similarly charged magnets repelling each other. Maybe he feels responsible for the band's abrupt demise. Hell, so he should. I don't know what music Dave listens to these days, or if he still plays guitar. With his long black hair and unkempt beard, he doesn't look like a captain of industry. It is said that you can't judge a book by its cover, but the cover often gives vital insights into what lies within; DT has not lost his metallic nature. Only a person with heavy metal in his soul would name his dog after the Barnsley Big Teasers. DT is still a metal child at heart. I *know* it.

Iain Bright lives in the small rural village of Lingwood in Norfolk. He works as a project manager for a large insurance firm based in Norwich. Much of his work involves travel, especially to India, for which his company pays him well. His musical taste has broadened (he calls it *eclectic*) and his long hair is long gone in favour of a crew cut. Still the escapist, he spends most of his disposable cash on scuba-diving holidays. Anally reprimanding females is his other favourite leisure pursuit. Quite how he talks so many women into dirt-chute sex is beyond me. Perhaps he lures them into his fantasy world, shows them around, then – as they marvel at the wonder of it all – infiltrates their bottoms. I talk to Iain on the phone once a week. He's the same wide-eyed wanderer he always was. He still has no bass guitar.

At age twenty-five, Ozzy married a tiny redhead called Denise, who looked as though she could have been his younger sister. They took a bus to Devon on their honeymoon. Oz paid a full fare for himself and a half fare for his blushing bride, a feat he often bragged about, thus proving that there are advantages to marrying a jailbait-looking girl (other than the obligatory underage-schoolgirl fantasy). They made an odd pair at the wedding, giant Ozzy and his petite wife, but they looked genuinely happy. Oz and Denise moved to England when he was offered a job with Mr Kipling Cakes. He couldn't say no to an exceedingly good job offer like that, after all. Since then, he has lost touch with us all.

Pete has disappeared off the radar. His Mum and Dad haven't heard from him in years, nor have I. A year ago, Mrs Drummond went to the cinema to see a Scottish indie-flick called *The Clearances* and noticed as the credits rolled that the soundtrack was composed by Pete Drummond. She phoned the film's production company the following day and asked for her son's contact information. All they had was an e-mail address. Mrs Drummond sent repeated e-mails asking – *begging* – Pete to come and see his parents. No replies. His father trawled jazz clubs, census records, voters' rolls and phone books, all to no avail. Now the Drummonds are out of ideas. Their beautiful musical-prodigy son has disappeared into the ether.

My work is cut out for me. Pete and Ozzy are AWOL. DT is a reclusive workaholic from whom I have difficulty squeezing a greeting, so convincing him to rejoin the band won't be easy. Inspiring Iain to buy a bass, learn to play it, quit his job, move back to Scotland and dedicate himself to the band poses a monumental challenge. I suspect I'd have an easier time sweet-talking the knickers off a convent full of nuns than talking my blood brothers – even if I can locate them all – into re-forming the band. That's my quest, though. The nuns will have to wait.

After searching the Internet for traces of Ozzy and Pete, and finding nothing, I put on AC/DC's *Live from Atlantic Studios,* drink more coffee and make a phone call. A high-pitched, aristocratic voice answers, "Sir Archibald Larkin speaking. To whom do I have the misfortune of speaking?"

"You know who it is, dickheid. You have caller ID."

"Spark, you peasant. What's happening in the wild west?"

"Why do you insist on pretendin' to be a knight of the realm? Your name's posh enough withoot precedin' it wi' a knighthood."

"My boy, who declared the Queen the only one with the right to hand out knighthoods? We must question authority at every turn. I have always felt very knightly, therefore I *am* Sir Archibald Larkin."

"You *are* an eccentric maniac, that's what you are. I have business to discuss wi' you. Can you meet me today? Not at my hoose or yours. Somewhere wi' no distractions."

"I could meet you in Bar Chew at noon."

"It's a deal, Archie. It'll be worth your while."

"Never call me Archie. It's common. The young vixens prefer Archibald, as do I."

"We both know that if a filthy young seductress clad in stockings, sussies and heels wandered into your bedroom and begged you to rattle her senseless, you'd scream blue murder and run to the hills."

"I would put the minx over my knee and give her bottom a good spanking, the naughty little filly. And even though your last sentence was a cheap attempt to slate my red-blooded manliness, I like that you squeezed two heavy metal references in there."

"I thought you'd appreciate that. See you at noon."

"Noon it is then, Cowboy." (The Woodie nicknamed me Cowboy two decades ago due to my penchant for marching into battle wearing cowboy boots and leather. On discovering this, Archibald resurrected the nickname.)

Archibald Larkin is a music journalist with substantial influence. Afraid to disagree with Archibald's opinions, other rock journalists often read his reviews and paraphrase them as their own. Thus, his beliefs colour the heavy metal zeitgeist. Rock cognoscenti believe Archibald to be responsible for catapulting several metal bands to stratospheric stardom by writing glowing reviews of their debut albums or live gigs. If those reviews had been dismal, they maintain, other journalists would have followed Larkin's lead, condemning the bands in question to obscurity. There are exceptions to the rule, of course: shoddy bands with so much record company moolah invested in hyping them to the limit that they can't fail to achieve commercial success.

Music journalism is a teeming sea of talented writers, many of whom are frustrated musicians, and some of whom feel simultaneously superior to and jealous of successful bands. This irreconcilable mix of emotions has created dangerous press piranhas who think nothing of tearing bands to shreds. Archibald, however, is a different breed. A professor of music loud and electrified, he is a living encyclopaedia of metal who likes nothing better than to light the blue touch paper under a deserving band, then stand back and watch them soar into orbit. He likes artists who put minds, bodies and souls into creating new styles of metalliboom. Archibald Larkin: laser-sharp metal literatus with a heart.

Archibald and I met in the gym six years ago. He stood out due to his outlandish and non-matching training gear. Not that I'm a fashion victim who pains for hours over which outfit to wear to the gym, darling.

In an old-school, sweat-and-sawdust gym, most people wear scuzzy old training gear. Not Archibald, though. While I was training in a Rainbow tour T-shirt one day, he announced that he reckoned Rainbow's *Rising* album to be one of the few truly perfect albums ever recorded. I agreed. A great friendship started that day. Since our first conversation six years ago, we've attended hundreds of concerts together. I chauffeur us to gigs, then get in free as Archibald's +1 on the guest list. A truly symbiotic relationship.

It's no surprise that Archibald isn't in Bar Chew when I arrive at noon; his timekeeping is legendary for all the wrong reasons. I order a large cappuccino from bar manager Jim Zamoyski (or, as I call him, Jimz). I've been providing Jimz with CDs for the bar for years. Because of this, he never lets me pay for coffee. Symbiosis again.

I sit at a dimly lit table in the corner of the bar as the ambient introduction to Pink Floyd's *The Division Bell* eases through wood-finished Wharfedale speakers. Smiling, Jimz gives me the thumbs-up; he knows this is my favourite Pink Floyd album, an opinion he shares. David Gilmour's gorgeous guitar melodies wash over me as I gulp coffee and scribble impromptu lyrics on a notepad. A sharp-suited Archibald arrives, his slicked-back, shoulder-length brown hair held in place by a yellow plastic hairband. After ordering coffee, he proceeds to protest loudly about being charged for it while "that thieving Gypsy" – indicating me - drinks for free. As Jimz grinds coffee beans, Archibald makes his hands into six-guns, shoots me from across the bar, then blows invisible smoke from index-finger gunbarrels. He makes devil horns with one hand and sticks out his tongue in trademark Gene Simmons pose. I'm used to this sort of extroversion from him and have learned to control my embarrassment. It's not expected behaviour from a man in a suit, as is evidenced by the baffled expressions of bar regulars.

When Archibald joins me at the table I tell him about recent events. He nods in contemplative silence as I tell him about my death and resurrection, and of how I feel the Universe flowing through me. Sooking the foam from the top of his café mocha, Archibald raises his eyebrows. "It all sounds very heroic, Cowboy. It reminds me of Dennis Rodman's autobiography. Growing up, he always felt that something big was going to happen in his life, but he hadn't a clue what it would be; it turned out to be playing basketball in the NBA, where the pressure of other people's expectations started to affect him in a negative way. He sat in his truck one night with a loaded shotgun, planning to kill himself. He was listening to Pearl Jam at the time, which would have tempted any sane person to pull the trigger, but something in their music stimulated the realisation in Rodman that he didn't have to conform to anyone else's ideas. That was his moment of satori. From that point on, he let his true self come out without letting the opinions of others sway him. He became free. Does that sound familiar?"

"There are some parallels, aye, but Rodman didn't die. I did, and somethin' much bigger than Pearl Jam resurrected me. Also, there's another huge difference between Rodman and me."

"He's a cross-dressing, short-haired, sexually ambiguous negro and you're a long-haired vagina addict of Viking extraction?"

"Firstly, it's not 'negro', it's 'African-American'. Secondly, the difference I was talkin' aboot is more enormous than any o' those."

Archibald dips an index finger into his mocha, fellates it in a disturbingly homoerotic way, then smoothes out an eyebrow with the saliva-soaked digit. "Pray tell, Spark."

"Rodman had millions in the bank before his enlightenment and millions in the bank afterwards. I'm flat broke."

Grinning like David Lee Roth on acid, Archibald pulls off his hairband and runs a hand through his hair. "Very true," he says, "but you will find your path to riches. There's an old Zen saying that if you find your joy and pursue it, money will come. Heavy metal is your joy."

"Archibald, the Universe spoke to me. It *breathed* through me and it felt beautiful. I know exactly what to do. I'm gettin' the band back together to redefine heavy metal. I won't even watch porn 'til it's done."

Placing hand on chin, Archibald mimics Rodin's Thinker. "In that case, may I have your porn collection? For safekeeping purposes only, you understand. I'll be your Zen master, making sure you stay focused and on track."

"You wouldn't like my porn. It's heterosexual."

"A puerile comment, sir! Many a young vixen is walking differently after being serviced by Sir Archibald Larkin."

"Name one. In all the years I've known you, you haven't rattled one fair maiden, or a foul one for that matter. I like to think of you as a heavy metal monk who sacrifices pleasures o' the flesh in order to keep his mind clear and pure. I know that's idealistic, though. The truth is probably far more sinister. Perhaps you're an aficionado of the male buttocks. Or maybe you like underage girls. Either o' those possibilities would explain why you keep that part o' your life secret."

Archibald tilts his head to the side and pouts his lips in camp fashion. "A gentleman doesn't kiss and tell, not that you would know anything about that, you savage."

I feel a rush of love for Archibald, whose eccentricities endear him to me all the more. "What do you think my first move should be?"

"It's obvious. Talk to Iain and DT about the band. Do whatever you must to convince them this is what the Universe has willed. Then you must find Ozzy. Leave Pete Drummond until last. He'll be harder to find, since it appears that he doesn't want to be found. If the rest of the band is together by the time you find Pete, a man of his musical pedigree will be unable to turn his back on the possibility of creating epic, timeless music."

Archibald asks me to choose my perfect fantasy metal band, with the proviso that only dead rock stars are eligible. I pick: Bon Scott (ex-

AC/DC), vocals; Phil Lynott (ex-Thin Lizzy), bass; Cozy Powell (ex-MSG, Whitesnake, Black Sabbath, ELP), drums; Randy Rhoads (ex-Ozzy Osbourne), lead guitar; Steve Gaines (ex-Lynyrd Skynyrd), rhythm guitar; Merl Saunders (ex-Grateful Dead), keyboards. "Those choices are completely impractical!" shouts Archibald.

"Formin' a superband consistin' o' deid folk is hardly a fuckin' practical exercise anyway," I point out. As the debate rages and fists thump the table, the bar's other patrons look convinced that my friend and I must be out on day-leave from a psychiatric institution to which we will return any minute, strapped safely back into our straightjackets.

Time flies when you're talking shit. Realising that he's half an hour late for a meeting at a Glasgow press agency, Archibald rushes out, leaving me to contemplate the future.

Chapter 27 – Take Away My Pain

On the drive home from Bar Chew my mind drifts to my grandmother, grandfather and father. Ten years ago, while I was in Hong Kong coaching its swim team, my mother phoned in the middle of the night with the news that her father had died. Not having enough money to fly home for the funeral, I performed my own ceremony for my grandfather on Lamma Island, where I was living. I selected a hill overlooking the sea and climbed its steep slopes carrying a boulder that weighed as much as an ice-cream-fed Rottweiler. Neither an easy nor a safe undertaking, it was a symbolic one. The force of grief drove me to do it as both a catharsis and a tribute. After close calls and near falls, I made it to the summit, laid down the rock, chiselled my grandfather's name into it, then spoke from my heart to his soul.

Seven years later, my grandmother and father died within two months of each other, both stricken by colon cancer. My Nana was ninety-three when she left; my Dad was only sixty-one. Not a good year.

Three days before my grandmother died, she went into Valfader Hospital for an operation to remove a growth from her colon. The hospital's policy was not to operate on people of her age, but she was a headstrong woman who insisted on the operation and, as usual, got her way. After the surgery, a white-coated doctor ushered me into a white room that smelled of lemon bleach. We sat facing each other, four or five feet apart as if there were an invisible table between us. As I looked into the pewter-haired doctor's dull grey eyes, he informed me that the tumour had been successfully removed from my grandmother's colon, but that the operating surgeon had accidentally cut through her bowel wall in the process. Toxins from her bowel were now flooding into her bloodstream, causing whole-body swelling which would result in death. I stared over the doctor's head at the clinically clean wall beyond. *Death*. Holy fuck. I wasn't prepared to hear that. The doctor stood up, straightened the fountain pen in his outside pocket, patted me on the shoulder and said, "Our policy is not to operate on people of your grandmother's age, but she insisted. If we hadn't operated, the cancer would have killed her. I'm sorry." He patted my shoulder again then swished out in a hail of white cotton. Alone in that white room, death's waiting room, I cried my heart out. When the tears finally stopped I made my way to my grandmother's bedside. Despite being almost completely blind at this stage, she could still discern shapes and colours. Pointing in my direction, she asked my mother who was there. "It's Spark," replied my Mum, "your boy." (My Mum and Nana had regular arguments over which of them had played the bigger part in raising me, in other words whose 'boy' I was.) My Nana's unseeing blue eyes lit up as she beamed a heartachingly beautiful smile. Raising her arms into the air, she gushed, "Oh Spark, my boy." I leaned over the bed and embraced the strongest-willed woman I had ever known. Tears cut into my eyes like hot razors. I tried to stem their flow, determined to be strong for my grandmother, but my liquid pain leaked out regardless. A person can bottle up only a finite amount of sadness…and I was bursting at the seams.

When my Mum headed downstairs to the hospital café for a cup of tea, my grandmother whispered, "Spark, I have something to tell you. I want you to hear it from me, not from some robot in a white coat. I'm already dead."

Tears flowed faster, blurring my vision. "You're not deid, Nana. I'm holdin' your hand. It's warm. Do you feel it? You're goin' to get better. You'll be home in a few days." A spoken prayer more than a statement of fact. I had seen the power of will before, though, and was channelling my will towards a miracle.

"I'm dead," she repeated. "This body is just a shell. I need you to believe me. Don't be shocked. The rest of the family have been expecting me to die for years, so it won't shock them, but you're the optimist…the sensitive one. That's why you wrap yourself in studs and leather - spiky armour to protect your gentle soul. You've never known a world without me in it, and I know you're scared of me leaving. I also know you'd face Hell and high water to keep me here, but I have to go."

Keeping hold of her hand, I stood up and sobbed, "You're not deid, Nana. It isn't true."

"I am dead. I've never lied to you, Spark. Trust me. The only reason I'm still here is so that you hear it from me. Once you accept it, I can go."

A rush of wind ruffled my hair, heralding the arrival of the Metal Gods. *Be strong. If this amazing human being can be lucid and eloquent at a time like this, you can be strong.* Calmed by the presence of the deities, I whispered, "Aye, Nana. I believe you. Are you really alright?"

"I really am, my beautiful boy. It's just my time to go."

"Where is it you're goin'? What's it like?"

A strangely comfortable silence passed between us as I stood over my grandmother, holding her hands in mine, marvelling at their softness, waiting for the answer that never came. The only sounds were the beep of her heart-rate monitor and the rhythmic drip of my tears onto the hospital bed's white cotton covers. Eventually, she broke the silence. "Your Papa's been waiting a long time for me."

"Please tell Papa that I miss him and love him."

"Of course I will. We've always had an understanding, Spark, haven't we?"

A smile cracked through my sorrow. "Aye, we have. I love you so much it couldn't be measured. And I've always felt your love for me."

My grandmother's pale eyes welled up with tears. Reaching out, she took my face in her hands and whispered, "My boy." It was the last thing she ever said.

I spent the next two days and nights by my Nana's bedside, sometimes sleeping, sometimes eating, sometimes sobbing, always there. I had a dream in which the scene was almost identical to the real world, but with subtle exceptions: I was sitting beside an empty hospital bed while my grandmother stood outside the window and gazed in. The dream confirmed the truth of her words. My Nana's soul was outside the hospital, while her physical shell, which she no longer needed, had been abandoned like a cocoon. The coma-frozen body with the still-beating heart was experiencing a life hangover.

When the monitors connected to my grandmother's body officially declared her dead, I was prepared. She had made sure of that. Even in death that beautiful, strong woman put my feelings before her own. Nothing was left unsaid.

An amazing life. A remarkable death.

Just as I began to adapt to a grandparentless life, my father died. He had taught me to read before I started nursery school, to swim before I could walk, and to respect all life, even the smallest beings. He was my bearlike protector when I was small and vulnerable. Growing up, I couldn't have wished for a gentler, kinder, wiser, more loving father.

My Dad bought me my first bike when I was five: a green Raleigh Strika. He didn't believe in stabilisers, claiming that they gave a false sense of security and prevented a child from mastering the crucial sense of balancing on two wheels. After a few lessons, a lot of falling off, some skint knees and enough tears to fill a small loch, the crystalline moment when ability falls into line with theory happened on a long, straight stretch of pavement near my house. Elated, I built up speed, feeling invincible and heading straight for a busy road. My Dad's voice screamed at me to brake. There was only one problem with that: the handlebars had no brake levers. (I later discovered that the bike's braking system was the back-pedal variety.) I hurtled towards the road, gritting my teeth in preparation for impact with a car. A glance over my shoulder revealed my father accelerating towards me like a charging bull. He dived forwards, interlocked his fingers through the back wheel's spokes and held on for grim life as the bike's momentum dragged him along the pavement like a cowboy roped behind a horse. By the time the bike came to rest, gaping holes existed where the knees of my Dad's jeans had been. His kneecaps and elbows had been scraped to the bone, leaving a gory trail of skin and blood on concrete slabs. To top off the carnage, his face had bounced off the pavement and was bleeding through his beard. The man who climbed to his feet resembled a horror-movie Robinson Crusoe, while I was unscathed. Guilt exploded inside me. I felt sure that I was in for the mother of all skelpings, but I couldn't have been more wrong. My Dad's only concern was that his wee boy was safe. Despite his pain, he was smiling; he had protected me. As we made our way home I apologised over and over, sobbing, and told my father I would magic his injuries all better if I knew how. Limping like a bloody ghoul beside me, he fixed me with a tender gaze and said, in the softest voice I had ever heard escape his lips, "I know you would, wee man. It wasn't your fault. Dry your eyes. You can't make an omelette withoot breaking a few eggs."

The predominant feeling I associate with childhood is one of safety and security. Around my father, those feelings were at their strongest. Time and again that human bear proved that he would sacrifice himself to keep his wild little son safe.

On our way to a holiday in the Scilly Isles, my cousin Peter and I – each five - started to argue over whose Dad was better. Peter's father was a professional angler who held two world records for distance casting. As the crux of his argument in favour of his father's superiority, Peter boasted, "My Dad's the world champion at angling," then sat back with a how-about-them-apples look on his face.

With no hesitation, I hit back with, "So what? My Dad's the world champion at everythin' else." In the rear-view mirror of my father's car, I saw the reflection of his smile. I was never sure what was going on in the mind behind his black beard and wavy hair, but it usually looked brooding and stormy. Occasionally, however, the storm would clear to reveal pure sunshine.

My father was a perfectionist, sometimes to an infuriating degree. Aged ten, I set my first swimming record, in Buckie, Moray District, Scottish Highlands. Climbing out of the pool and feeling like a legend, I said to my father, "Good, eh?"

Stony faced, he looked me in the eyes and replied, "Plenty of room for improvement." That was the end of that conversation.

His perfectionism taught me not to rest on my laurels, that no matter how proficient I become at an activity, I should strive for improvement. I learned that conceit was a dangerous illusion. To this day, I believe there's something immeasurably cool about achieving great things with total humility.

My parents divorced when I was twenty, after which my father moved to England to run his business. We saw each other only five times in the next twelve years. When he was taken into hospital in Wales a week before his death, I made the five-hour drive to see him. His formerly gigantic frame looked frail and gaunt. He had been a Scottish Highland Games champion, a powerhouse who specialised in the shot-putt and hammer-throw events, but the man in front of me couldn't muster the strength to sit up in bed. Fighting back tears, I hugged my father. For the first time ever, my arms went all the way round his body. Before leaving, I promised to drive down again the following weekend with nutritional supplements and a bag of laetrile-containing foods, which would selectively destroy cancer cells and nourish healthy ones. That was the plan. Robert Burns was right about plans.

Four days later, on a rainy Thursday afternoon, I received a phone call at work to say that my father's health had declined rapidly. A nurse with a soft Welsh accent advised me to drive down immediately if I wanted to see him alive again. I heard her words but wouldn't let myself submit to them.

I left work and rushed home to pack for the trip. The phone was ringing as I stepped into my house. It was the same nurse again. This time her tone was softer still. "There's no need to rush now. Your father died a few minutes ago." A long silence followed, as if she expected me to say something. When I didn't, she continued. "I grew close to your Dad while I was looking after him. He talked of you a lot, always with a light in his eyes. I look forward to meeting the one who brought him such joy. Please take your time driving down. No accidents." An iron fist wrapped in a velvet glove.

I hung up the phone, stared into space and crumbled onto the sofa, bawling like a child. Fluff leaped onto my lap, climbed onto my chest and licked the tears from my cheeks. Her little pink tongue kept pace with my flowing liquid sadness until, after nearly an hour, there were no more tears. She gazed up at me through eyes like melting blue glaciers, as if understanding what I was feeling. After reminding Fluff that she was my best friend in the Universe and kissing the Mohawk-like crest of white fur on top of her head, I did something I hadn't done in years: I went swimming at Bronzehall pool, where my father had transformed me into an aquatic baby. Water was my friend before I could walk or talk, and on my father's dying day it became my friend once again. As I ploughed through chlorinated liquid with ferocity born of loss, every stroke felt sacred. I entered the water mournful and lost, but emerged baptised and serene.

I loved my father, even after he and my mother separated and I spent countless nights nursing her broken heart. He came crashing down from the pedestal I'd had him on, but my love for him never wavered and never will.

My Nana, Papa and Dad: three of the most significant people in my life, all gone. I wonder if their consciousnesses, in whatever forms they exist now, are aware of my reawakening. What do they make of my quest?

Chapter 28 – A Warm Place

Thunderheads loom over the fields and forest north of Bronzehall, casting shadows larger than mountains. The stormclouds converge and darken, like great godlike brains congregating to share malevolent thoughts. A wild wind buffets rain into diagonal sheets. Overhead power lines buzz and crackle, coaxing body hair up into electrically charged air. My car's windscreen wipers swish at full speed, yet the scenery on the other side of the glass is a watercolour blur. I can just discern a stone dyke and rusty metal gate, behind which is the road to my destination and, I hope, my salvation. The car hydroplanes on a layer of surface water and glides towards the wall like a hovercraft run amok, then - as if rerouted by a divine hand - veers into the gate. In the brief battle of Rustbucket versus rusty gate, car prevails. Decayed hinges shatter. The gate soars skywards like a kite, spinning end over end and finally coming to rest in a neighbouring field. Pulse booming in my ears, I continue up the muddy trail at Driving-Miss-Daisy speed.

 At the end of the dirt track, a silver Porsche Carrera is parked outside a two-storey farmhouse constructed from massive blocks of grey sandstone. Rain batters out a percussive symphony on the corrugated metal roof of a barn as the voice of the wind whispers, "*Wwwwwwhat are you doing here in that wwwwwwwheeled box of rust wwwwwwwhich has the cheek to call itself a car? Do a U-turn, drive awwwwwwwwway and never return. No one here is buying your daydreams.*" Demons – they're never far away. Once upon a time, debilitating entities named Fear and Doubt controlled me. Those days are past. Go fuck yourselves, demons.

 If this is the wrong farmhouse, a pissed-off farmer may be moments away from greeting me, double-barrel shotgun in hand, with a bang. Here, deep in the heart of nowhere, that's how justice is meted out. A brass Viking head stares at me from the front door. I grab the warrior's pleated beard, lift it and release. The resultant clash sounds like Thor's hammer striking an anvil, which seems strangely appropriate on this stormy evening. There is no movement or sound inside the house as I wait under descending torrents.

 Long minutes later, my optimism diminished but not doused by the relentless deluge from the skies, I squelch back to the car and asphyxiate its driver's seat with my rain-soaked arse. On the far side of a furrowed field (in which a gate juts from the earth like a misshapen javelin hurled by an angry giant), a man clad in green walks into view. Upon seeing my car, he freezes momentarily then begins to gesticulate like a storm-channelling wizard. From out of nowhere, the largest dog I have ever seen - a golden-haired beast with teeth bared and massive head lowered - thuds onto my car bonnet. The dog doesn't bark or growl; he doesn't need to: his unflinching amber stare communicates destructive intent. Rain streams off the canine's long eyelashes as the man in green sprints across the field, leaping over ploughed lines in the soil and hollering words that are lost to the winds. Suddenly, the dog's expression changes; he tilts his mighty head and frowns at me as if I were a bone he has dug up but can't quite remember burying. Then, as if the distant light of recognition has been switched on in his brain, he lets out a howl and wags his tail, spraying water left and right. From the distance, a voice shouts, "Get fuckin' doon!" The dog ignores the command and instead tries to smash through my windscreen with his head. Fearing for my car's structural integrity, I climb out and back away from the vehicle. The dog pounces. Heavy front paws land on my shoulders. A warm tongue laps rainwater off my cheek. A circular metal nametag dangles from the beast's studded collar. Through the rivulets of rain that trickle down the tag, a single engraved word is visible: *Saxon*. Locking eyes with Saxon, I scratch behind his soggy ears, provoking a toothy grin.

As the man in green rushes up the track towards us, he slips and falls arse over tit into sopping muck. Comprehensively covered in a layer of sludge, he rises, staring daggers and wringing muddy water out of his long, tousled beard. When he takes off his flat cap, acres of black hair tumble down his back. Frowning, Saxon turns to me as if silently begging me to defuse the tension in the air. "Saxon's grown into a beautiful boy, Dave. The last time I saw him, he was just a wee ball o' yellow fur. Have you been feedin' him horse fodder? Dogs aren't meant to be that size. He could pull carts and plough fields."

Shaking water off his cap, the green-waterproofed DT snarls, "He's a stubborn bastard, that's what he is. He leaves a trail o' destruction behind him wherever he goes. That tail o' his has smashed ornaments, clocks, glasses and mugs. I tried trainin' him, but it was futile. He sits when I tell him to lie doon and runs away when I call him to heel. And the fucker looks at me wi' absolute wisdom while he's disobeyin' me. He understands *exactly* what I want him to do, but chooses a different course of action just to piss me off. Last Wednesday night, while I was workin' on the laptop, Saxon wandered into the livin' room wi' a look o' pure mischief on his face. I told him to sit. He did a shit. Right there on my wooden floor. And the bastard fuckin' grinned at me as he squeezed it oot. He understood the play on words, I'd bet my farmhoose on it."

"Were you doing a Sean Connery voice at the time? *Hello Shaxshon, I'd like you to shit on the floorboardsh.*"

"No I wasnae, ya tit. And there's nothin' funny aboot gettin' your floor shat on. You wouldnae believe the size o' the things that come oot o' that dog's arse."

"Maybe it's true that dogs take after their owners. You were never exactly good at followin' orders."

"I was no choirboy, that's for sure."

"No fuckin' choirboy? You were born wild and got progressively more oot o' control."

DT lowers his eyes and stares into the mud. "Aye, sorry aboot that. The band was gettin' good too. At least we made oor mark on heavy metal history, even if it was a localised impact."

"That's why I'm here."

Dave winces. "To talk aboot old times? Don't waste your energy. I don't do reminiscin'. The past is past."

I gaze through DT's dark eyes and into his soul. "I'm no' here to wax melancholy aboot the past, blood brother. I need to talk to you aboot the future. Hard as it may be to believe, I died and got resurrected."

"For fuck's sake, say it ain't so," whines DT. "Please tell me you're no' a born-again Christian. I'm no' lookin' for redemption. I've paid my dues and made my peace."

"My resurrection wasn't metaphoric. I was as deid as a dinosaur, buried under inches o' snow on a Bronzehall pavement. The Universe jolted me back to life wi' lightning from Heaven, then spoke a message. Since then, the way forward's been clearer than if it were written in stars."

"I'm listenin'."

"I'll tell you the rest if you fire up some coffee and get me a towel to dry myself off."

Sunbeams stream through a gap in the clouds, delicate fingers of light which massage the countryside below. Tilting back his head, Saxon gazes into the hole in the sky, an inquisitive expression spreading across his furry face. "Look at that dog," grunts Dave, shaking his head. "Five minutes aroon' you and already he's a fuckin' daydreamer."

After unlocking the front door, DT leads me up an iron spiral staircase, points to the bathroom, then fetches me dry clothing (green woolly hiking socks, white joggies and a Saxon *Crusader* baseball shirt) and a towel, which he drapes over a heated chrome towel rail.

The smell of coffee floats into the shower enclosure as I relax under powerful jets of hot water. Refreshed, I towel myself dry and put on gifted clothes. The Saxon shirt's arms, originally black, have faded to pale grey. The picture on the front is cracked and faded, giving the knights on horseback an authentically aged look. When Dave bought this shirt back in the '80s, on Saxon's *Crusader* tour, it looked as big as a tent on him. Now, wearing my blood brother's decades-old shirt like a second skin, I gaze at my reflection in the mirror and experience a strange existential understanding. When this shirt was new, Dave and I were planning world domination, musically speaking. Our best laid plans, however, did more than ganging agley: they fell flat on their arses and didn't get back up.

Saxon's music changed my life over quarter of a century ago when I heard it booming from a bus shelter. *A quarter of a century. Holy shit! What musical landmarks could Blood Brothers have achieved in that time? What stories would we have to tell of life on the road, live shows, hit albums, despicable behaviour, exotic groupies, less-than-exotic groupies and Spinal Täpesque gaffes?* Rather than stimulating sadness, these thoughts fan the flames of my desire to resurrect the band. In quantum physics terminology, my consciousness is shaping my Universe.

It feels comforting to be warm and dry in Dave's house, about to drink coffee with my old pal and blood brother. I believe that dreamsparks still exist, waiting to be ignited, inside all my blood brothers. And belief, wise men say, is the thermostat that regulates success.

I descend the cold iron staircase and find a leather-trousered DT pouring coffee into two mugs on his kitchen table. "Do you recognise the mugs?" he asks.

"Should I?"

"They're pint mugs from the Xoriguer Gin distillery in Menorca. I'm not sure why a gin distillery would make pint mugs. Do you think Spaniards drink gin in pints?"

"Probably, the crazy bastards. I went to that distillery wi' oor parents one day after you fucked off wi' a bird from Birmingham. Free thimble-sized samples were available at the end o' the tour, so I drank six flavoured liqueurs and aboot twice as many gins, then sat cross-eyed in the back o' the car all the way back to the hotel."

"Taste that coffee," DT enthuses. "The beans are from Malabar. After they're picked, they get laid oot on huge coastal platforms to let the monsoon winds blow over them."

"I don't think so. Monsoon winds are strong and coffee beans are light. The beans would end up bein' whisked away into the sea."

DT opens a kitchen cupboard and pulls out a packet of coffee. "Look," he says, jabbing the evidence with an index finger, "it says on the packet that the beans are laid oot to allow Malabar's monsoon winds to blow over them, giving the beans a smooth, slightly salty flavour. Maybe they put sheets over the coffee beans to keep them in place."

"If sheets were laid over the beans, the monsoon winds couldn't get at them. Maybe they just write some poetic nonsense aboot monsoon winds on the packet, hopin' that no one will think too much aboot the logistics o' the situation. Then they charge extravagant prices for their coffee, safe in the knowledge that gullible, pretentious idiots like you will shell oot silly money for the allegedly uniquely prepared beans."

Beneath a frown, Dave's dark eyes glare at me. "Just drink the fuckin' stuff before it gets cold. It's too expensive to waste."

"That's apparently because the beans are laid oot on sheets to allow the monsoon winds o' Malabar to blow over them, givin' their full flavour a hint o' tropical sea air." After flashing a smile at my blood brother, I blow him a kiss.

The topography of DT's forehead changes from choppy sea to still waters. Half amused and half disgruntled, he sneers, "You're still an argumentative tit then, Spark?" Fairly certain that the question is rhetorical, I pick up my mug and take a couple of gulps of what is without question the most delicious coffee I have ever tasted. Whatever lies or exaggerations are told about these beans and their methods of cultivation, my tastebuds are partying.

"There's a type of coffee called Kopi Luwak," I inform DT, "made from beans that have been eaten and excreted by palm civets, which are wee mammals that live in rainforests. And I hear there's another coffee, the rarest and most expensive in the world, made from coffee beans harvested from elephant shit. I wonder what words are used to market coffee beans that elephants have eaten and then evacuated oot o' their colossal dunghatches."

"Well," says DT, raising a dark eyebrow, "you're Poetry Boy. What words would you put on the packet to make such a thing sound palatable?"

"How aboot this: 'Our coffee beans are grown lovingly at the foot of Mount Kilimanjaro in Tanzania, then recycled by one of Earth's most majestic, beautiful and endangered creatures, giving the beans a hint of the strength and wisdom of the mighty elephant.' That sounds pretty good, or at least better than, 'Oor beans are picked by underage, underfed, unpaid plantation slaves, then laid doon for wandering elephants to eat and shite back oot. Taste the hint o' massive keech in your brew.' What do you think?"

DT cracks up laughing. On recovering, he confesses, "I haven't laughed like this in years. You're still a wee tit, but you're a funny wee tit."

"Wee? I'm six foot three. I'm taller than you."

"You could be ten foot eight for all I care…you'd still be a wee tit to me."

I recognise DT's pseudo-insult as a touchingly sincere compliment and take it as such. It's his equivalent of a mother telling her child that he will always be her wee boy and that she will always love him. "Thanks, Dave. I love you too."

His grin widens and the old mischief flashes in his eyes. "You're barkin' up the wrong tree, but I can't blame you for tryin'. I know I'm one sexy bastard."

"You couldnae handle me sexually."

"Please just drink your coffee, Spark. I refuse to get drawn into a conversation aboot bumchummery." DT wanders through to the living room and puts on Rush's *Signals*. Entranced by the flawlessness of the music, we drink the rest of our coffee without exchanging a word. Before today, I hadn't listened to *Signals* for years. The first time I heard the album was as a child in DT's bedroom. A tune can break the laws of physics by transporting the mind to another time and place faster than the speed of light: it can do so instantaneously. I see a faraway look in DT's eyes, and recognise it. He too is remembering a time when we had few responsibilities and truckloads of fun. Leaping out of his seat and curling an index finger, Dave beckons me to follow him, which I do, to a room at the back of the house. A dull metal door with an LED screen and a numerical keypad blocks our entrance. DT presses six digits in rapid succession. With a hiss like air gushing from a stabbed tyre, the security door slides open. I half expect to find a Delorean surrounded by for-dramatic-effect dry ice on the other side, but the sight that meets my eyes is far, far more exciting.

Six guitars hang on wall-brackets: a black and white Gibson Flying V; a black Les Paul (identical in all but colour to the one Dave smashed over Tom Bright's noggin, ending our only gig with a snap of wood and a spurt of blood); a red Ibanez Destroyer; a salmon-pink Fender Stratocaster; a Silvertone Apocalypse Pro Cracked Mirror, as designed and used by Paul Stanley of KISS; and another guitar whose like I have neither seen nor dreamed of. The instrument looks like a Zeus-hurled lightning bolt, blindingly bright with jagged edges which cast off little rainbows of light. "Where did you get this?" I gush. "Mount Olympus? I've just had a guitargasm!"

My partner-in-crime extends his arms towards the godly guitar, palms up and fingers splayed, as if casting a magic spell on the instrument. "Feel free," he says, "but be careful. It weighs as much as a small cow, hence the reinforced steel guitar strap. It's a one-of-a-kind instrument, built from material from outer space."

"You're fuckin' joking?"

"Spark, would I joke aboot this? Why else would I have spent tens o' thoosands buildin' a security vault for it? I discovered a website that sells guitar picks made from Gibeon meteorite. I was goin' to buy one, but then I realised that if I could get a big enough chunk o' meteorite, I could get a whole guitar crafted oot of it. So off I went to Namibia like Indiana fuckin' Jones, bag full o' guns over one shoulder, rucksack stuffed wi' cash over the other. If I told you how much I paid for my fuck-off chunk o' spacedebris it would make you puke. Once I got my piece o' meteorite, I headed off to the highlands of Tibet, where I paid the world's greatest guitar maker an obscene amount o' money to sculpt the fallen dod o' celestial rock into a guitar straight from Heaven. It took him two months to complete the task. I stayed in Tibet that whole time, livin' in a monastery and meditatin' daily."

Looking into DT's eyes for signs of deception, I see only sparkling authenticity. "If anyone else was tellin' me this tall tale, I'd crown him the King of Keechtalkers, but when you tell it...I'm almost not surprised. In fact, I think I always knew on some level that this would happen."

"Aye," agrees Dave, "it was fuckin' destiny." After a thoughtful pause, during which he twirls his beard into a pleat, he asks, "Well, are you goin' to stand there whackin' off all day or are you goin' to play the fuckin' thing?"

Gazing at the instrument, I ask, "What is your name, beautiful creation? I can't play a guitar until first I know its name."

From over my shoulder, DT whispers, "She is called Heavensent, and she is my celestial harbinger of heaviness." Handling Heavensent as carefully as I would a newborn puppy, I lift her down. Dave switches on his Marshall amp – the same trusty old bastard that blasted out our riffs years ago – and plugs a coiled lead into the guitar. As I crank out the opening riff to Black Sabbath's *Heaven and Hell*, a gigantic wave of otherworldly riffage floods from the amp. Every hair on my body rises in salute. Energy shimmers through the top of my skull, threatening to blow it clean off. DT sings the verse as I continue to deal the riffs. When we join forces on vocals during the chorus, I feel like a walking, talking heavy metal monster, spacesent weapon in hand, Metal Gods breathing through me. After sizzling through the rest of the track and unplugging the guitar, I bracket it with reverence, gazing at it the way Buddhists look at statues of Buddha, or perhaps the way perverts ogle nude dancers in titty bars.

"When did you last feel this good?" I ask.

Without hesitation, DT replies, "The night oor band played its one-and-only gig." In my blood brother's eyes I see a look of lost time. I tell him of my roadside resurrection and the Voice, and he doesn't call me a lunatic. Rather, he listens intently, dark eyes shining, demons conspicuous by their absence. Sitting on top of his black Marshall amplifier, DT looks every inch the metal deity, all long black waterfall hair and wild beard. He tells me that he has played guitar every day since moving into the farmhouse. Despite his stratospheric salary, the only two extravagances he allows himself, he says, are cars and guitars. Stream-of-consciousness lyrics gush out of me:

> "My only two vices are cars and guitars.
> I don't waste my money in skanky titty bars.
> I've lived through some rough times and I still wear the scars.
> Once I lay in the gutter, now I fly among stars."

"Pretty good," admits DT. "You always were a poetic son of a bitch. Have you written any lyrics since the band fell apart?"

"Over a hundred tracks. Have you written any music?"

"A few tunes, aye. They're no' polished, but the melodies are oot o' this world."

"What style?"

"Honey-roasted Saxon wi' a portion o' pan-fried Rush, some curried AC/DC, barbequed ZZ Top, well-fired Megadeth and boiled Judas Priest. And glazed wi' a futuristic drizzle o' Jean Michel Jarre, of course."

"Of course. That goes withoot sayin', for fuck's sake. Let's start jammin' regularly, dude - you on lead guitar, me on rhythm guitar and vocals."

After a pause and substantial beard twirling, DT nods. "I'll do it. Are you still in touch wi' the others?"

"Only Iain."

"That idiot was wired to the fuckin' moon. What's he up to noo? I bet he's a professor of philosophy, or writin' sci-fi novels, the airheid."

"He's a project manager for an insurance company in Norwich."

"Fuck me wi' a cactus! Can he play an instrument yet?"

"No."

"Get on the blower to the crazy wee fuck and tell him to buy a bass, or I'll be drivin' my Porsche doon there and givin' his heid the same treatment I gave his brother's."

"I'll get on the case."

"What aboot oor other brothers?"

"I think Ozzy's still in England somewhere, but I don't know where. Pete's disappeared off the grid. The last time I spoke to his Mum, she told me he'd composed the soundtrack to a Scottish movie called *The Clearances*, and that she hadn't seen or heard from him in years."

"Find those fuckers, Spark. I'm too busy wi' my business to invest time in lookin' for them. I'll jam wi' you a couple o' nights a week. Do you have a guitar?"

"I have guitars comin' oot o' my arse. Not literally, of course. That would involve some discomfort. Especially the Flying V and the BC Rich Warlock. No matter how broke I am, I've never been able to bring myself to sell any o' my guitars. I've flogged almost everythin' else of monetary value, but the guitars are sacred. I'd rather go withoot food and shelter than withoot them."

"Sacrificin' for your art suits you. You always were a spiritual wee fuck."

"How did we lose touch for so long, Dave? We used to be inseparable. What happened to all those years?"

"Don't take any of that personally, wee brother. I was selfish. I had to be in order to shake off the clouds that were fogging my heid. I was offered psychotherapy while I was in jail, but I refused to sit in front of a stranger to talk aboot my most intimate doubts and fears. Seven years is a lot o' time to kill, so I became reflective. I analysed myself, my motivations, my behaviour. Introversion and introspection got me in touch wi' my soul for the first time. A funny thing happened then. I felt the Universe runnin' through me and makin' me strong. That's why I didn't make fun o' you when you talked aboot your reawakening. A higher power has been my sole friend for years."

"Not exactly. I was always your friend, always your blood brother, always your partner-in-crime. You just forgot that." Saxon howls in the living room. "And I think Saxon's trying to remind you that he's your friend too. I suspect every one of oor blood brothers would still move mountains for you." DT's face is expressionless, but his dark eyes glitter. Less of the tortured, raging, bratty rock star; more of the Zen musical adept. He walks me to the front door and raises his right fist to shoulder height. Mirroring my blood brother, I lift my scarred right hand. Our fists collide with a clash of knuckles.

"Saxon, I'm goin' home, big boy!" The golden beast gallops into the hall. His tail whacks the metal bars of the staircase as he runs past, creating a sound like the tolling of Hell's bell. Looking Saxon in the eyes, I whisper, "Sit doon." He sits, cocks his head to the side and gazes back at me. "Paw." Saxon lifts a meaty paw and, with uncharacteristic delicacy, places it into my palm. As I squeeze Saxon's paw, a drooling tongue lolls from one side of his mouth. Overcome by affection for the hairy animal, I drop to my knees and cuddle him.

"It's been good doin' this after so long," admits DT. "You come here uninvited, annihilate my fuckin' gate, use my shower, steal my clothes, drink my expensive coffee after offending it, put your lascivious sweaty hands all over my divine Heavensent, then – to top it all off – demonstrate my inadequacy at obedience trainin' via your Barbara Woodhouse display wi' Saxon. How did you get the headstrong fuck to obey you, anyway?"

"No trick. I don't perceive barriers between myself and other animals, so the energy exchange is pure. I feel their energy and they feel mine."

"I won't invite you to 'sit' in my living room, Animal Boy. Come over on Friday night at eight for a jam."

"I'll be here. Thanks for lettin' me play Heavensent."

"I should fuckin' think so! Keep quiet aboot her. You're the only person other than me to have set foot in that room."

"Someone had to rip you oot o' your cocoon. It's a win-win situation when we're together. It always has been."

"That sounded disturbingly homosexual. Quick, Spark, get off my land before your poofiness rubs off on me."

"Too late for that, I reckon."

"Did I mention that you're a wee tit?"

"A few million times, aye." I turn and walk to the car, my smile widening with each stride. As the old BMW engine roars to life, two hairy figures – one human, one canine – are silhouetted in the doorway of the farmhouse. Waving goodbye, I toot the car horn in time to The Cult's *Lil' Devil*, which booms inside the vehicle.

Air vents suck in the smell of rain-drenched pine as I navigate the narrow track to the main road. Above, the dark arc of the sky is punctuated by glistening stars. Finally, the storm has blown over.

Chapter 29 – Weaving Sorrow

A hooded figure tramples through a dense forest in the black of night. Despite the long hike ahead, he doesn't fret; this pilgrimage is an annual ritual of love. Armed with only a halogen torch and knowledge of the woods, he cuts through the arboreal darkness with speed and purpose. Twigs and frozen leaves snap beneath his massive feet, sending small nocturnal animals scurrying back to the safety of their lairs. The smell of Sitka spruce relaxes the travelling man; he pushes his tongue against the roof of his mouth and inhales long, deep breaths through his nose: archer's breaths.

Three hours later, he arrives breathless and sweat-soaked at a clearing where, on the front wall of an ancient church, two circular windows look like stained-glass eyes, an effect enhanced by the row of gravestones which jut from the mossy ground like decaying teeth, and the mist that filters between tombstones like smoke spewed from an eldritch mouth. The man sits under a yew tree that looks older than God, its leafless branches twisted into tortured humanoid forms which reach skywards as if desperate to escape the churchyard. Sheltered by the branches of the tree which has seen over 4000 years come and go, he leans against its massive trunk and finds a sort of comfort. Sleep takes over.

An eagle owl soars across the sky and lands on a low branch of the yew. The bird hoots, jolting the man awake. Heartbeat booming in his ears, he looks up and locks eyes with the nocturnal predator. "Thanks, owl," he yawns. "Were you sent to wake me?" As if comprehending the question, the majestic bird hoots again, once for yes.

Mournful wails drift from within the mist. Rooted to the spot, the man peers into the cemetery and glimpses a delicate female figure knelt above a grave. Spellbound, he is awake in his worst nightmare. "I love you, baby," he whimpers. "I miss you every day." The fragile form looks at him, fades to a translucent wraith, then blurs into the darkness.

The man's tortured roar shakes the church walls. Tears spill from his haunted blue eyes and roll down copper-bearded cheeks. Fascinated, the owl watches the human's every move: he vaults a wall and enters the graveyard; he wipes tears from his face with a sleeve; he walks towards the grave where the spectre appeared moments ago; he drops to his knees and wraps mammoth arms around the Celtic-cross headstone, which acts as a crutch to his wilting frame; angling his head back, he projects his anger at the sky. At God. "You took away my sun, ya bastard! I can't live! I'm stuck in a fuckin' endless nightmare and *you* made it happen! I *hate* you!" Leaning forward and touching his forehead to the headstone, he lowers his voice to a whisper. "Even though you're gone, I love you more each day. I will never stop loving you. I want to join you in death, but I can't. You know why not." Draped over the cross, he sobs. Lights come on inside the church. Multi-coloured streams spill through stained-glass eyes and converge on the stone cross, illuminating its two inscribed words: Infinitely Beloved.

Feeling that he is under a divine gaze, the man remains in his submissive position, aware that God may not take kindly to the criticism that flew Heavenwards mere moments ago. Stooped over stone he waits, God-forsaken, lovelorn. Minutes pass. He isn't scorched by a bolt from the blue or transformed into a pillar of salt. Deciding that divine retribution must not be getting dished out tonight, he strides back to the forest and prepares his mind for the journey home. He is the definition of a broken man: head hanging low, heart hanging lower, wide shoulders slouched in defeat. An opening in a hedge marks the start of his path through the woods. As the man lumbers into the forest, he is surprised to find whispered words floating from his lips, words taught to him by a friend decades ago, words written generations before that by Robert Frost, words written for a night such as this:

> "The woods are lovely, dark and deep,
>   But I have promises to keep,
>   And miles to go before I sleep,
>   And miles to go before I sleep."

He takes a deep breath and pulls off his hood. Curly orange hair springs out in all directions. Then, slowly and sorrowfully, Alan Oswaldo starts the long walk home.

Chapter 30 – Real World

"You've reached Iain Bright. Leave a message." Beep.

"Buy a bass, ya knob-jockey! If you don't, DT and I will be comin' doon to see you, and it won't be a social call. We'll be crackin' jaws and bootin' baws. It's time for you to stop bein' the thorn in the band's side. Time to step up to the plate."

Less than a minute later, my phone rings. When I pick up the receiver, Iain bellows, "What the fuck was that aboot, ya rude bastard?"

"I've experienced an epiphany, an awakening, enlightenment, satori, transcendence, what drunks call a moment of clarity, a revelation, passing through the gateless gate, soul transmutation."

"Have you been on the booze, Spark?"

"I'm as sober as a brick in a freezer. Somethin' happened that reaffirmed every good feelin' I've ever had aboot life. I died in Bronzehall snow, but a celestial hand reached doon, picked me up, shook all the negative shit oot o' me, then set me doon clean and alive and burstin' wi' belief. It's not too late."

"Not too late for what?"

"For the band, fool. We never got anywhere near oor potential. We only played one gig. One gig! And you still managed to walk away wi' three groupies! Can you imagine what we'll achieve once we cut a CD and start doin' tours? We have the ability to change metal music. Well, four of us do anyway. Then there's you, the musical handicap. Buy a bass and learn to play. Please."

"Spark, I'm a daydreamer, as are you, but daydreams don't pay bills. My monthly mortgage payments are whopping. I also have monthly car payments, utility bills, credit cards and a job wi' serious responsibility. How can you get the band back together anyway? Ozzy and Pete are off the radar and DT's a reclusive maniac. Maybe your 'not too late' epiphany referred to somethin' else. Perhaps it's nothin' to do wi' the band. Did you think o' that?"

"It was *my* fuckin' epiphany and it referred to the band!"

After a long sigh, Iain's voice rises an octave. "Spark, there's no band. There's been no band for over a decade. It's just you in a ramshackle old witch's hoose full o' guitars, where you sit tuned to the past, greetin' aboot ancient history."

"Is that right? It may interest you to know that I jammed wi' DT in his farmhoose tonight."

"You're yankin' my chain, ya prick!"

"I'm as serious as a Boston ballad. DT and I are forging metal again. I'll find Pete and Ozzy too. This band is goin' to happen. If you won't play bass I'll find someone who will."

After a long, uncomfortable silence, Iain speaks in icy tones. "Spark, the band was a childhood dream. You might still be a child, but

I've grown up. Dave and you can play guitar in his farmhoose 'til the cows come home, which will be a long fuckin' time since he doesn't have any livestock, but two twats arsin' aroon' wi' guitars doesn't constitute a band."

"Listen, ya dick, I loved your eccentric bass fantasies all those years ago. You were a total hoot to watch, but noo I need someone who can play bass. Could you handle watchin' the band become a hoosehold name, knowin' you could have been part of it but turned it doon? How would you feel hearin' Blood Brothers on your car radio as you cruise to work in your suit and tie one mornin'? Suddenly, you'll have to deal wi' the reality of me, DT, Oz, Pete and oor new bassist bein' bona fide heavy metal stars. That moment will be your epiphany. In your mind, you'll see a picture of a tombstone that reads, 'HERE LIE THE BONES OF A NOBODY WHO WANTED TO PLAY BASS BUT NEVER FOUND THE GUTS. BORN A PUSSY, DIED AN EVEN BIGGER PUSSY.' My band will make its mark on the Universe. Prepare yoursel' for that." I'm using words as Samurai swords, and striking at raw nerves.

"Your heid's in the sky," Iain grumbles. "Tombstones have fuck all to do wi' this. Sounds like you've been on the special mushrooms up at DT's farmhoose."

"Must I spell everythin' oot for you? Holy shit, why can't you read between the lines? I'll spoon-feed you my point, as it obviously zoomed right over your thick heid. Last week I was at Rachel McTurk's funeral..."

"Shame aboot Rachel," Iain interrupts. "She once sooked my cock so hard it swelled up to double its usual size and stayed that way for a whole week. Best week of my life."

"If you'll stop interruptin'," I continue, "I might be able to finish makin' my point. Rachel sucked half the dicks in Bronzehall, and – if rumours are to be believed – chowed doon on a few carpets as well. She was the town bike, yet 427 people attended her funeral, 403 of them male. Men old and young were cryin' like babies. During the ceremony Darran Chabhair, the butcher's son, turned to me and said, 'I don't know if I can go on withoot her.' I replied that I didnae realise he and Rachel had been close. The fucker, and he was greetin' his eyes oot by this point, fixed me wi' a sorrowful stare and said, 'I didnae really know her. She walked me home from the pub one night, then dropped to her knees and gobbled me ootside my hoose. I knew she'd handled more sausage than my Dad, but no one had ever swallowed my tadger the way Rachel did. It opened my eyes to the possibility of perfection. As long as she was alive, there was a chance I would feel those lips slidin' doon my cock again. But no' noo. Never again.' Then Darran really broke doon, holdin' onto me for support and sobbin' into my good kilt jacket."

"Very touching," Iain observes, his voice dripping with sarcasm, "but what does that have to do wi' me? I would never have travelled all the way to Bronzehall for Rachel's funeral, just to stand graveside like a twat, one o' the myriad notches on her well-used bedpost."

"That business suit you wear must be sappin' your already-suspect brain power."

"Fuck you, Spark! Why are you so anti-suit? Not everyone in a suit and tie is an evil, greed-driven automaton."

"You've missed the point once again. If you were to meet a horrific end like Rachel's…"

"How likely is it," Iain interjects, "that I'd be lyin' in a cornfield and jammin' a dildo into myself while listenin' to my mp3 player at such high volume that I didn't hear the approachin' combine harvester?"

"Aye, you have a point, I suppose. You probably turn your music doon to half volume when you're dildoin' yoursel' in the countryside."

"Spark," spits Iain, "I'm a bawhair away from hangin' up the phone. I've had you up to my monobrow."

"Well quit interruptin' and let me make my point. Rachel had an impact on the people of Bronzehall. Many men will miss her. For selfish reasons perhaps, but they'll miss her nonetheless. Grown men, even Jamie Turpin the blacksmith, were wailin' and droppin' onto the ground at her funeral. If somethin' unforeseen were to happen to you, do you think any o' your customers would collapse screaming, 'He gave beautiful insurance quotes,' or, 'That man really knew his way around a policy!'? There's no fuckin' way they would. Your name and actions would evaporate as if you never existed."

In the long silence that follows, I can almost hear the penny dropping in Iain's head. When he finally speaks, his tone is embroidered out of doubt and wrapped in green-eyed tissue. "Need I ask what mark you think you'll make on the world?"

"Successful heavy metal bands play riff-laden music for a living, travel the world, fuck exotic and not-so-exotic girls from Edinburgh to Ethiopia, get practically everythin' for free, create sonic art in its purest form and love every minute of it. If they move on to another plane, they leave a timeless and immortal legacy behind."

"Well, Spark, I've no plans to move onto another plane. I'm already on a different plane from you."

"Aye, I know. I'm on *Heavy Metal Superstar Airlines*, whereas you're on *Ma Maw's Got Bigger Baws International*."

"Ya fuckin' twat! Don't be talkin' aboot my Mum havin' balls or I'll drive up there and boot yours right noo!"

"Again you miss the point. Your Mum has no testicles, of that I'm almost certain, yet even her non-existent testicles are bigger than your testicles, therefore provin' that you have a negative amount o' testicles."

"Grow up! I don't want to hear any more aboot your daft dreams!"

"I'd have thought that if anyone understood dreams it'd be you, Escapist Boy. If you're declarin' heavy metal dreams daft, you better phone Biff Byford, Rob Halford, Axl Rose, Alice Cooper, Angus Young, Michael Schenker and the thoosands of other metal icons to inform them that their lives are illusory and that they really just need to grow up, get real jobs and start wearin' suits and ties, all because Iain Bright declared it so."

"For fuck's sake," Iain whines, "I've got a comfortable life here. Stop tryin' to upset my applecart."

"If you don't get a bass and learn to play it, I'll turn your applecart upside doon and bounce the spilled apples off your fat fuckin' heid until you change your mind!"

"Kiss my hairy arse!"

"That would make your day, feelin' my lips against your chubby buttocks, eh? Four partin' words for you, ya deviant. BUY A FUCKIN' BASS!"

Chapter 31 – Gypsy Road

A stone archway towers over the ancient village of Wytchcoomb. The top of the arch is the favourite resting place of the village's only black cat (how he gets up there, only he knows). Small children congregate around the monolith as twilight stalls the descent of night's dark curtain, granting the wee ones a little more playtime before bed.

The arch leads from nowhere to nothing. It simply *is*. Exuding silent authority, it has the air of a sentinel watching over the surrounding area. The most arcane artefact in the pre-medieval village built around it, the archway has long permeated the collective consciousness of the locals.

I turn left onto a single-lane road, above which branches intersect like crossed scythe blades. There are no streetlights, cats' eyes or road markings here. Just gloom. Five miles later, having penetrated the dark corridor of overhanging trees and under-maintained road, I emerge in Wytchcoomb. Loud heavy metal might be frowned upon in this pre-medieval place, so I mute the car stereo and slow my car to a crawl. The village stirs up my irrational childhood fears of witches, warlocks and devils. Suddenly, a more pleasant thought enters my mind: this is exactly the kind of village where it's mandatory for the local tavern to employ a busty serving wench with a penchant for wearing low-cut blouses and flashing her legs, or more, at thirsty travellers. That's how it is in the films, at least. I decide to track down a pub in the hope that life will imitate art.

The inn isn't difficult to find. Its wooden sign - The Cemetery Gates - swings in the breeze, screeching on chains. The picture on the sign is a grinning skull with flames in its eye sockets: not exactly welcoming. Tiredness, thirst and curiosity about local nubiles overcome my uncertainty. Just before entering, I notice tiny figures dancing around a stone arch in the distance. From my vantage point, it looks like a pagan ritual performed by midgets.

The bar is tended by a dusky woman whose feral green eyes reflect the light from burning logs. Jet-black hair cascades in waves over her shoulders. Full red lips underline lupine cheekbones. Her skin is smooth and sallow, gypsyish. Large hooped earrings jingle as she moves. A sky-blue summer skirt flares over centurion-sandalled feet with red-painted toenails. The second toe of her left foot sports a silver toering with inscribed symbols. Her white blouse, the top two buttons of which are unfastened, almost covers her buxom breasts. I'd estimate her age to be forty something, but it's hard to tell; she could be ten years older. I feel as a parched flower must when soaking up long-awaited rain. She oozes what I long ago defined as *slutability*: the combination of aesthetic appeal and downright dirtiness.

Conservatively dressed countryfolk fill the inn's interior. I expected a hush to fall when I entered, but the assembled locals couldn't be less interested. I'm almost disappointed.

I straddle a high stool at the horseshoe-shaped wooden bar and order a pint of the local stout, Wytches' Brew. The sultry barmaid promises it will put hairs on my chest. My eyes drift to her cleavage and linger there a little longer than is polite. "You must have misheard me, stranger," she grunts. "I said it would put hairs on *your* chest. I didn't invite you to ogle *my* chest."

"Ehm…ahh…err…sorry, ma'am. It was like a Pavlov's-dog reaction. When you said 'chest', I automatically looked at your chest and salivated." I had never before uttered the word *ma'am*, which must have sifted into my subconscious during my year in Virginia and waited there for the perfect opportunity to be regurgitated.

The barmaid raises an inquisitive eyebrow. "Ma'am is it? Very respectful all of a sudden."

"How could I not be respectful? The ancient Celts worshipped the Earth as a goddess called Danu. If you delve far enough back in time, you discover that most ancient cultures worshipped women. Then came insecure pricks who were threatened by the powerful female deities of the old cultures. These criminals systematically destroyed the arcane beliefs and replaced them with a new, male-dominated religion called Christianity. I'm in tune with the ancient ones. Women, as creators of life, should be worshipped. My respect for the divine feminine is limitless."

The barmaid's lips part into a smile. "Are you some kind of academic buff, here to expound preposterous theories about the archway?"

"No."

"So what are you doing out here in the sticks?"

"Gettin' my band back together to redefine heavy metal and put right the world's wrongs."

"How does that involve our village? Wytchcoomb isn't a hotbed of heavy metal, you know."

"I'm here to find an old friend called Alan Oswaldo. We lost touch years ago, but I found oot that he lives here."

"Alan's cottage is easy to find. It's the only one with a thatched roof. It also happens to be the closest house to the archway."

"It's too late to show up at Oz's hoose tonight. Do you have any vacant rooms here?"

"All my rooms are available. Would you like one for the night?"

"Aye, please. It was a long drive. I'll rest here tonight and catch up wi' Oz in the mornin'."

"I'll show you to your room after I've closed the bar and locked up. Right now thirsty locals are giving me impatient looks. I better attend to them. I'm Rosie, incidentally."

"Like the AC/DC song."

"What?"

"Whole Lotta Rosie, one of AC/DC's best tracks. It's bliss to make your acquaintance. I'm Spark." Rosie extends her left hand. A quick scan reveals it to be ringless, so I lift the hovering hand and kiss it. Two burly men in heavy woollen jerseys shake their heads, their scowls warning me to tread gingerly. I grew up on the bloody battlefields of Bronzehall, though, sculpted by warfare, water and the heaviest metal. I don't do gingerly.

Thick wooden beams jut from stone walls inside the inn, imbuing the interior with a rustic ambience. On one wall hangs a faded portrait of a serious-faced, black-clad woman who looks fit to haunt castles. In front of a crackling log fire, an armchair of worn brown leather welcomes my tired body. After a few mouthfuls of refreshing stout, I sink into the chair and fall asleep.

High above a cornfield on a summer's day, I'm flying naked, arms outstretched as the sun beats down on my back. I soar towards a stone archway which is sandwiched between the infinite blue of the sky and the field's shimmering sheafs of gold. Something grips my arm, halting my flight's progress. A feminine voice with a Cornish burr whispers, "Spark, it's late." I open my eyes and see chairs balanced on top of tables. In the fireplace, embers glow where a blaze raged earlier. It feels as though the fire has burned up most of the oxygen in the inn, leaving a warm sleepiness in its place. "You dozed off," Rosie purrs, "and I didn't want to leave you here all night. The remains of your Wytches' Brew will be warm by now. I'll ditch it and give you a glass of our local mead. On the house."

Yawning, I rub my tired eyes. "I'd like that. I've never tasted mead."

As Rosie leans over the table to pick up my glass, buxom breasts strain against the confines of her blouse. She retreats behind the bar and pours golden liquid into a fresh pint glass. "Try that. It's honey mead. Best in the land." I take a sip. The sweet drink glides easily down my throat, leaving no nasty aftertaste. I nod my endorsement. "I make it myself," explains my host, "from our local honey. The recipe's the same one my family's used for over a thousand years. Don't rush your drink. You can take it up to your room." Rosie leads me up a narrow wooden staircase. On reaching a white door of about 5'0" in height, she opens it and ushers me into a room rich with the welcoming scents of oak and vanilla.

"What's the deal there?" I ask, ducking into the room and pointing at the miniature doorframe. "Is your ancestry dwarvish?" Rosie smiles but doesn't answer.

The room is small, claustrophobic and cluttered, with a cosy, homely feeling. Its white ceiling is reinforced by a latticework of oak beams. The top of the bed's wooden headboard has been intricately fashioned into the likeness of a goat's head, around which five symbols are carved. A row of old, leather-bound books on witchcraft and demonology sits atop a chest of drawers. The paraphernalia of modern hotels is conspicuously absent. There is no kettle, no Bible, no television, no wardrobe, no scented air freshener, no shoe-shine machine, no bubble bath, no shower cap...no shower, for that matter. Somehow, I feel comforted by this. Rosie notices me sniffing and says, "The smells of some things in their natural states are far superior to any fabricated aromas."

"I agree. How old is this inn?"

"As old as the mead recipe. As old as the village. A little over a thousand years old. The archway is older still. No one knows how it came to be there or how long it has existed."

"I like the atmosphere in your village. It feels like I've driven back into a simpler time. Thank you for your hospitality, fair maiden."

"You're welcome, Scotsman. Rest now. I'll bring you breakfast in the morning."

Rosie turns and walks towards the door. "Ehm...ma'am," I stammer, "I hope I didn't make you feel awkward earlier when I looked at your breasts. If I did, I'm sorry."

Without turning, Rosie asks, "Did you like what you saw?"

"You were exactly what my tired eyes needed after that long drive."

Whirling to face me, Rosie flashes a smile that manages to be both coquettish and carnivorous. "Would you like me to stay with you tonight?"

"That's not the worst idea I've ever heard."

"There'll be no sex. I don't do one-night stands or fly-by-night sexual encounters. I'd just like to sleep beside you and feel your skin against mine."

"I'd be honoured to lie beside such a divine example of femininity, sex or no sex." In an impeccable display of mind control, I force out all depraved ideas of what I'd like to do to Rosie. If I can keep my thoughts pure, or as pure as possible given the circumstances, I may get to sleep in time to prevent the arrival of the blue balls.

(Blue balls happen when a male gets into a sexually exciting situation for a prolonged duration, but does not ejaculate. The longer the sexual stimulation continues without orgasm, the more severe the case of blue balls that ensues. The testicles get excited as soon as there's the possibility of jettisoning a few million of their wiggly tailed passengers. Sperm production goes into overdrive as the balls gear up for unloading their contents in, or all over, a lucky recipient. When that fails to happen, the excited sperm are shoved out in every direction as new sperm are born into increasingly overcrowded testicles. Pain begins in the balls then moves upwards into the abdomen. Soon, walking becomes difficult. Before long, the lightest brush of anything against the balls feels as if they have been slammed with a sledgehammer. There is only one known cure: ejaculation. Care must be taken when whacking off in a blue-balls situation; on ejaculation, cum fires out like bullets from a gun, painting anything in its line of fire. The principle is much like thunder: if areas of scrotal high pressure exist close to low-pressure external areas, the high-pressure area has to displace its energy in order to maintain equilibrium. Whenever a

girl complains about having to put up with periods, I tell her to think herself lucky she's never had to endure a blue-balls episode.)

After lighting a candle on the bedside table, Rosie sheds her clothes on the floor. Her body is heroically feminine, a synergy of strong muscle and soft curves. A chain of fine gold sparkles around her midriff, a fashion I've found a particular turn-on since first seeing it (on a naked six-foot Amazon blonde in a Playboy magazine I found in Vikingwood Forest when I was ten). Candlelight flickers over Rosie's sallow skin. Shadows on the walls take on lives of their own, becoming hungry incubi animated by malevolent sexual intent. The candle's flame stretches longer, thinner. A change comes over Rosie in the half-light; she appears as a frost-haired cailleach, wide of hip and pendulous of breast, the chain around her waist transforming from gold into thorny twigs that pierce her crinkled skin. The flame grows and begins to gyrate, its swirling lightshow illuminating a lithe young maiden with bosoms that are just beginning to bloom, and the slightest hint of fuzz between her legs. A string of interconnected daisies circles her taut midsection. The youngster fixes her gaze on the flame, which, as if under her command, returns to a uniform shape, as does its mistress. As I wonder if the combination of tiredness, dim light and the effects of mead are affecting my senses, the Metal Gods set me straight. *Believe your eyes, they see what's true. The triple goddess is here with you.*

As naked as the watching candleflame, Rosie approaches me in her original form. Warm breath skims my neck. Fingertips trickle down my arms, conjuring up goosepimples of pleasure which are not the only things on the rise; casting her eyes downwards, Rosie purrs, "Your tumescence precedes you."

"It's mathematical. My tumescence is proportional to the proximity of your presence, goddess. And that poetry was intentional, in case you were wondering."

Rosie's giggle sounds like glass wind chimes. She frees me of my clothes then climbs into bed. Under the covers, our bodies tangle in a union which, despite being non-sexual, feels unfathomably sensual. "Hold me," she whispers, "and sleep."

"May I kiss you, goddess?"

"I grant you one kiss, Scotsman." Rosie's crimson mouth fastens over my top lip. She tastes of honey and wheat. Rolling over and presenting me with the smooth S-curve of her spine, she slides backwards until our bodies meld into one. I blow out the candle, close my eyes and inhale: no perfume; no deodorant; no synthetic smells of any kind; just the heady aroma of womanhood. Rosie was right. Some things in their natural states smell unbeatable. Whole lotta Rosie, indeed.

Chapter 32 – It's the Little Things

Ozzy. The giant. The drumming powerhouse. The iron man. The reaper. *Here.* It feels like aeons since I saw him.

The cottage is framed by an early-morning sky decorated only by a single slash of cirrus cloud. Rough thatch hangs over the edge of the roof like the fringe on a hairy dog. Curtains are neatly tied open in every room. A red-brick chimney contrasts with its blue-sky backdrop. The smell of burning wood hangs in the air. In no particular rush to reach its front-door destination, a cobbled path winds its way across a well-tended lawn surrounded by a white picket fence.

I close my eyes and think of Ozzy's loft in his Mum's house. Unmade bed. Gigantic drum kit. Clothes in two piles on the floor: one clean; one dirty. Hundreds of *Kerrang!* and *Metal Hammer* magazines scattered on the ground, with the odd *Penthouse* and *Men Only* present for good measure. Next to the bed, a sock with the texture of cardboard: evidence of Onanistic activities. The room looked like a bombsite but felt like a cosy den, up there shut away from the world.

Eyes open. A fairytale cottage. Stillness evokes the feeling that I've been captured in a photograph. Even the cirrus cloud pauses as if frozen in time. A wisp of smoke curls from the chimney, breaking the illusion as it disperses into the blue.

Eyes shut: nuclear wasteland of heavy metal paraphernalia and teenage wank fantasies. Eyes open: picturesque country cottage, thatched roof, short lawn bounded by whitewashed fence. "Shurely shome mishtake, Mish Moneypenny. Thish cannot be the shame Alan Oshwaldo. He wash a big animal with no table mannersh, and a lack of attenshion to pershonal hygiene and cleanlinesh that would dishgusht a Vietnameshe potbellied pig. Thish gorgeoush houshe cannot be hish reshidenshe." (When thinking out loud, I do it in a Sean Connery accent (acshent?). I'm not sure why I do this, but it works for me so I'll stick with it. Head doctorsh would have a field day with me, of that I'm absholutely shure, Mish Funnyfanny.)

"Why are you talking to yourself?" enquires a little voice from behind. I spin round to find a tiny girl gazing up at me through eyes like cobalt-blue pools, her pale brow furrowed into a frown. Hair like spirals of fire spills down her back. Dressed in denim dungarees, a green jersey, black boots and suede mittens, she is barely as tall as the fence: waist level on me.

"I was just thinkin' oot loud, wee girl."

"You talk funny," she observes. "You're not from Wytchcoomb."

"You're right. I'm from a cold, wet, wild, faraway land called Scotland, where all the people talk in weird accents."

"That's where my Daddy comes from too!"

Leaning closer, I look into the child's eyes. My gaze doesn't stop at the surface, but passes through her exterior and splashes into her soul. Her emotions wash into me: a wave of serenity laced with sorrow. My heart starts to race. The world swirls. In this child, I sense a depth of feeling unlike anything I've ever encountered. I'm glimpsing the soul of a little Buddha, a guru, a sage. Even before asking the question, I know its answer. "Who is your Daddy, little one?"

"His name is Alan, but I call him Daddy. No one else gets to call him that, just me. We live here." She points a tiny finger at the cottage.

"I know your Daddy. We're friends from a long time ago."

"People say I have his eyes, but that's silly. How would he see if I had his eyes?"

Entranced by her innocence and indisputable logic, I reply, "You're right. It is silly. Grown-ups tend to be very silly because they're full o' nonsense." She tilts her head and nods, as if assimilating the information that adults are actually composed of nonsense. "I'm Spark. What's your name, little one?"

"Sunshower Dee Oswaldo."

"That's a beautiful name."

"My Mummy chose it."

"Let's go and talk to your Mummy so I can congratulate her on such perfect taste."

Sunshower's eyes overflow. Her bottom lip starts to tremble. She arches backwards until her fiery hair, incandescent in the morning sunlight, is trailing on the ground. Gazing up, she points a delicate finger skywards. "My Mummy's up there. In Heaven."

My heart booms supernova.

Sunshower maintains her position as if expecting something to drop to Earth. When that something fails to materialise, tears accelerate from the corners of her eyes. I pluck the little girl up and cuddle her. She weighs almost nothing. "I wish I could bring your Mummy back for you," I whisper. "I would if I could." With precious cargo in my arms, I walk up the cobblestoned path and chap the front door. On the other side, heavy footsteps pound a wooden floor. The door opens and I'm faced by a man even larger than the Oz of old, his wall of muscle now covered by a substantial layer of fat. His afro is still formidable, like dayglo orange candyfloss, and his rough beard looks like copper wool. Ozzy's eyes, once as clear as desert skies and as sparkling as polished glass, host a haunted look. Ghost clouds drift across his eyes. Reflections of the sky, I tell myself, but an upwards glance reveals solid cloudless blue. Perplexed, I stare at my blood brother, his eyes now a washed-out azure, and tell him, "I found this gorgeous creation outside. Yours, I believe."

"How did you find this place?" asks Oz. "I'm ex-directory. I'm ex-everything."

"I used phone books and Internet search engines to look for you, but they led me up blind alleys wi' deid ends. Your old next-door neighbour in Bronzehall told me that your Mum had moved back to Spain. He didn't have her new address or phone number. Eventually, I found you in a database DT's Dad has which contains details of every hoosehold in the UK, even those that think they're off the grid."

Oz looks down at his feet. "After the message in the wheat, I knew you were comin'."

"What message?"

"You know what I'm talkin' aboot, Spark. The crop circle you made last week in the wheatfield five miles from here. That farm's owner is one o' my suppliers."

"I've been at the centre o' some truly weird phenomena recently, but I've never made a crop circle. What made you think I did it?"

"Technically, it wasn't a crop circle. It was a crop pattern in the shape of a gigantic Flying V guitar. In the corner o' the field, like a signature, was a smaller pattern…a coiled-up baby like the burn on Pete's back."

The hairs on my neck prick up. "Maybe it *was* a signature. Do you remember how Pete got that burn?"

"I remember how he *says* he got it, but we're no' talkin' aboot that. I don't want my wee girl gettin' scared." Sunshower observes the interplay between her father and me like a spectator at a tennis match, her gaze flitting between us.

"Oz, I had an experience that makes crop circles, even colossal guitar-shaped ones, mundane by comparison. That's why I'm here."

"I've work to do, Spark. Do you expect me to drop everythin' when you show up oot o' the blue after more than ten years?"

"No, but you could at least invite your blood brother in for coffee and cake after he travelled all this way just to see you."

A low rumble emanates from deep in Ozzy's chest, giving the overwhelming impression that he is not human, but a bear reluctantly wakening from hibernation. "I'll put the kettle on," he grunts, frisking his hair with one hand. "Come in." The house is spotless, as if a team of French maids left through the back door as I arrived at the front. Seeing my surprised expression, Oz explains, "Denise always kept the hoose pristine. I'm just carryin' that on."

"Sunshower told me aboot Denise. I wish I could bring her back, big brother."

Ozzy's eyes recede. "I still haven't got used to it. Every day, I wake hopin' it was a bad dream, then that hope flushes away and I face the day knowin' that the nightmare is real. My life is in your hands."

At first I'm not sure what he means, but a glance at Sunshower - who is perched on my arm and gazing at me through oceanic eyes – makes it clear. "Aye," I nod, "she is beautiful."

"Do you really think I'm beautiful, Spark?" she asks.

"I don't just think you're beautiful. I *know* you're beautiful, wee girl." Sunshower smiles and combs her fingers through my hair.

"You still have a way with the ladies," Oz observes.

"Not wi' all of them," I reply. "Only those wi' impeccable taste."

Unsmiling, the giant glares at me. "Take Sunshower into the livin' room. Strong coffee wi' milk and no sugar?"

"Aye, please."

With my wild-haired passenger dangling from my neck like a lemur from a branch, I walk into an expansive living room where everything is hewn from natural wood: horizontal wall panels; flooring; ceiling; sideboard; coffee table; chairs; sofa. I find the textures, smells and hues of my surroundings more comforting than papered and painted walls ever could be. A framed wedding picture of Ozzy and Denise hangs on one wall. Beside it is a picture of Sunshower, her sky-blue eyes looking out through a tempest of hair. There are no pictures of the family together.

Oz soon appears with coffee and assorted baking on a circular metal tray. As I wolf into the food and grunt my approval, he explains, "Mr Kipling does make exceedingly good cakes, but they're no' perfect. When I finished workin' wi' Kipling, I moved here, altered the Kipling recipes until they were absolutely perfect, then continued doin' the only job I knew. Wytchcoomb's locals can't get enough o' my stuff. I don't earn millions, but we get by."

"This tastes phenomenal," I mumble, spraying fragments of apple pie onto the floor, "and in case you'd forgotten, bakin' isn't the only job you ever knew. You were a drummer once. You were *the* drummer."

"That wasn't a job. It never made me any money."

"It was fun, though, eh?"

"Aye, a wild adventure."

"An adventure cut shorter than your front lawn. Do you still have your drum kit?"

"I sold it before movin' here. When my job wi' Mr Kipling ended I got a redundancy payment, but I didn't know how long that money would last, so I sold everything – drum kit, albums, motorbike. I don't miss them. They're relics from a past life."

Am I living in the past, chasing a dream? To let this dream fizzle out and die would be to slap the Metal Gods in the face. They wouldn't let such a crime go unpunished; black dogs would be sent to hound our unfulfilled psyches, so that each Blood Brother would always wonder, 'What might have been? What could we have achieved if only we had had the guts to follow our heavy metal dream?' I can't bear to suffer such melancholy musings. It is not too late.

"My Daddy's the best baker in the world," says a little voice. Not bragging. Simply stating what she believes to be incontrovertible fact.

"Your Dad is also the most powerful drummer in the world. When he plays drums it sounds like thunder on the tundra." My Thor reference goes over the heads of Oz and Sunshower, but I feel quietly pleased with myself anyway.

"My Daddy can play drums?"

"Your Daddy can play drums harder and louder than anyone else."

Sunshower looks at Ozzy with new wonder in her eyes, perhaps for the first time seeing him as more than just father and provider. She turns to me and asks, "What do you do, Spark?"

"I sing, play guitar, write poetry, compose songs, exercise every day, live with a white rabbit and look at the night sky through a telescope."

"I *love* looking at the stars," she gushes. "My Mummy's up there, you know."

"Aye, I know. Her soul is part of the eloquent celestial symphony of the Universe." Sunshower springs onto my lap and jams her nose against mine, her eyes blurring into out-of-focus oases.

Oz suggests a walk through Wytchcoomb Forest. Sunshower leads the way, running ahead and yelling at the 'big funny-talking Scottish people' to hurry up. Daylight struggles to penetrate the forest canopy while far below, where we wander, all is shadow. Giant Sitka spruce trees spear the sky, their bark and visible roots covered by green moss. After taking us to her favourite arboreal haunts, Sunshower brings us out of the woods near the archway. As I point my camera at the ancient monolith and press the shutter button, Sunshower cartwheels into the frame. "Take another picture," she instructs, so I do. Soon, I have twenty photos of the archway, or – more correctly – twenty photos of Sunshower against the backdrop of the archway; she does handstands, forward-rolls, jumps, cartwheels, aerobatic spins, animal impressions and pirouettes, all caught on pixels. Oz refuses to be in any photos, but he takes one of Sunshower sitting on my shoulders under the archway. I feel at home here, just as I do at Callanish standing stones in Lewis. Give me solitude over bustling cities any day. Ancient places with mysterious stones of indeterminate origin gain my instant reverence.

After suggesting a drink in The Cemetery Gates, Oz starts to tell me the inn's history. "Hold on," I interrupt, "I'm gettin' a communication from the Universe. It says that…this inn…has the oldest mead recipe in Britain…made from local honey…that the owner and mead maker is a gypsy-lookin' woman called Rosie…the kind of delicious serving wench who, in exchange for just one kiss, could make a mortal man sell his mother's soul to Satan. Transmission over."

My blood brother's mouth drops open. "How did you do that?"

"I stayed in the inn last night and sampled their honey mead." Leaning closer to Oz, I whisper, "That's not all I sampled."

"You *didn't*."

"I slept with Rosie," I confess.

"*No one* sleeps with Rosie," Oz panics, his eyes darting around as if fearful that anyone else might hear. "She's a Wiccan priestess, which stimulates both healthy respect and unhealthy fear from the locals."

Burying my face in Oz's frizzy orange mop, I whisper, "I didn't fuck Rosie. I slept with her. Asleep. In a bed. All night. No funny business. No slap and tickle. No hide the sausage. Not even any squirting. Just one kiss."

"Don't you know it's rude to whisper?" asks a wee voice from below. Sunshower folds her arms in defiance.

"You're absolutely right, little one," I giggle. "I was just tellin' your Dad that I slept in this inn last night and that I met Rosie." Satisfied with my explanation, Sunshower unfolds her arms, wraps tiny fingers around my belt and pulls me towards the inn door. I look over my shoulder at Ozzy and shrug. "I guess we're goin' inside. We could use drinks anyway. I'll buy."

Rosie is behind the bar in a figure-hugging cream dress that, while accentuating her curvaceous body, reveals none of it. I expect her to be sheepish, but she greets me with a smile and an untamed hug, then pours four orange juices. "How have things been going?"

"There's been a lot to catch up on," I reply, "some of it painful, some of it life-affirming." Sunshower sucks her juice through a straw with loud slurping sounds.

Nodding, Ozzy adds, "So much has changed. So much has happened. I can barely believe that my life back in Scotland was real. It seems so long ago…so far away… like another world."

I try to project myself into the giant's mind. What is it like to find a perfect lovemate only to watch her die? How does it feel to have a little girl like Sunshower look into your eyes and call you Daddy as she cries for her mother? These are big questions to which I don't have answers.

When we stand up to leave after our drinks, Rosie emerges from behind the bar and kisses me with a ferocity that sucks the breath from my lungs. Shaking his head in slow sweeps, Oz takes Sunshower's hand and leads her outside.

Back at the cottage, Ozzy serves up nut roast, parsnips, potatoes, garlic broccoli and gravy. Sunshower shovels food into her mouth as if she's never eaten before. After the meal, as Oz makes cocoa for his daughter, he tells me that the wee lassie often has dreams in which she receives cosmic communications from her mother. She enjoys this, he says, but becomes melancholic upon waking. He is regularly wakened by a sorrowful little bundle clambering into his bed, howling for the mother she never knew.

After being bathed, towelled dry, plopped into pyjamas and tucked into bed by her father, Sunshower shouts, "Please sing me a lullaby, Spark!" Oz nods his approval, the edges of his mouth curling up a fraction. On Sunshower's pastel-pink bedroom's bedside table are two wood-framed photos: one of Oz; one of Denise. A doll's house at the foot of the bed contains three miniature red-haired people. Above our heads, a skylight window offers a glorious view of the star-speckled night sky.

An idea springs into my mind. "The original version of this song is called *She Is So Beautiful*. I'm goin' to personalise it to make it the perfect lullaby for you, little stargazer. This version is called *You Are So Beautiful*."

Pounding her bed with impatient fists, Sunshower yells, "Sing it, Sparky!"

My softest voice floats forth:

"You are so beautiful.
It's impossible for me to conceal
the undiluted joy you make me feel.
I'm a freebird soaring high with heart pure and true,
yet I would sacrifice my wings in a heartbeat
for you, Sunshower, only for you.
You are so beautiful,
fierce yet loving and wise,
stars reflected in the oceans of your eyes.
An infinite road stretches before me
and hardship will be unfurled,
but your smile will make it all disappear;
you're the most Zen soul
to ever set foot on this world.
For you are like a sea,
you are like a pulsing star,
lighting my way from afar,
your voice a heavenly riff from space,
a cosmic wind, messenger of joy.
And here I stand, a smiling boy.
You are so beautiful,
I'll miss you every day when I leave.
In you, Sunshower, I believe."

Sunshower claps excited hands, a smile spanning her face. "I loved it, Sparky! Thank you!"

I take a humble bow, buoyed by her praise. "Anytime, beautiful girl. When I'm in Scotland and you're here, I'll sing to you down the phone anytime at all." Sunshower jumps out of bed and wraps me in a baby bear hug that nearly snaps my ribs; she's Ozzy's girl all right. I kiss the pale softness of her cheek, whisper goodnight, tuck her back into bed, switch off the light and tiptoe out of the room, leaving the door open a crack to let a sliver of light in.

In the living room, Oz is sprawled on the sofa. "That sounded exceedingly melodic. Are you mellowing?"

"That was my adapted version of a flawless ballad by my compatriot Mike Scott of Waterboys fame. Cannibal Corpse wouldn't be a good bedtime lullaby for your sensitive wee girl."

"Thanks, Spark. I sometimes worry that Sunshower's life in this village is too insular with just me and a few wee pals as companionship. She seems to have taken to you, though."

"It's mutual. I feel things with your little girl that I've never felt in my life. She's amazing."

"Aye, she is. I don't know where I'd be withoot her. Actually, that's no' true. I know exactly where I'd be. Deid." A deep breath puffs out Oz's massive chest, then he exhales and continues. "Denise chose oor baby's name one night while she was pregnant. Sunshower for a girl, Angus for a boy. We fell into a contented sleep, but she went into premature labour in the middle o' the night and began to bleed. When I switched on the light oor bed looked like the scene of a massacre. We're miles from anywhere here, so by the time we reached the nearest hospital she had lost litres o' blood. The doctors managed to save the baby, but Denise slipped away."

Grasping for the perfect words to console my blood brother, I come up empty. I'd even settle for a comfortable silence. The heavy-bastard silence that hangs in the room, however, is far from comfortable. Oz stares at me through helpless eyes, as if silently begging me to do or say something – anything – to make his pain stop. "I love you, big brother. I always have, since we dyed battlefields red together. And after meetin' your spectacular wee girl, I absolutely love her too. I'd smash through mountains with my bare fists for you both."

The giant slumps off his armchair as if the bones have been extracted from his body. He crawls across the floor towards me, the beaming smile I love never further from his face. Wrapping me in tree-trunk arms, he collapses on top of me and sobs, "I miss her every moment of every day." Pinned to the sofa by Ozzy's gargantuan bulk, I rub his huge head like a mother comforting her child. If I need to sit here all night as a literal shoulder to cry on it's a small price to pay for lightening my blood brother's soul. Eventually, when Oz has cried himself dry and the rhythm of his lamentations has slowed, he climbs to his feet looking ashamed. "Sorry, Spark. I didn't plan that."

"There's no need to apologise for tears. I've spilled my share. My Nana, Papa and Dad are all gone."

"Fuck, wee brother, you've had it rough too."

"Aye. Perhaps everyone does. Maybe we're taught as kids that life is all fairytales and happy endings, only to have that illusion smashed by the iron-fisted realisation that life is a rough fuckin' ride on a crazed cosmic bull. One snowy mornin' not long ago, I died on a Bronzehall pavement. Deid and buried under falling snow one moment, yanked hundreds of feet into the air and resurrected the next, wi' the Universe's words echoin' in my heid."

Oz's brow creases. "I thought you'd have outgrown your heavy metal Joan of Arc phase of hearin' voices and headin' oot on insane quests. The voices aren't real, Spark. They never were. We used to indulge you because we wanted to believe in the Metal Gods and in you as their chosen one."

"This was nothin' to do wi' the Metal Gods. When they speak it sounds like thunder in a chrome cavern. This Voice was different, like mighty oceans rushing through my heid. It said in a few words only what was necessary to re-ignite my inner spark, no pun intended."

Fixing me with an exhausted stare, Oz grunts, "Spark, it's all in your heid. You can get medication that'll make the voices stop."

"This was *real*... real enough to bring me back to life when I was stone deid. The Universe told me to awaken and get back on my true path, that it wasn't too late."

Oz ruffles his mass of orange hair and narrows bloodshot eyes. "I believe that *you* believe it, but why would the Universe single you oot just to say that?"

"It communicates usin' brevity, which I dig. Brevity is a virtue."

"What the fuck is brevity? Isn't that the toasted sandwich maker DT's Mum and Dad used to have?"

"That's a Breville, ya dick. Brevity is the ability to be concise but profound. The Universe reminded me that it *cares*. It *loves*."

"How did it do that?" queries Oz, more than a hint of sarcasm in his tone.

"It struck me with five consecutive lightning bolts. The last one hit me right in the balls."

Shaking his massive head, Oz says, "Only you could get hit in the balls by lightning and equate that wi' the Universe showin' you love. What kind of skewed logic makes that connection? The Universe was probably tryin' to neuter you, and I don't blame it."

"You're wrong. I got jolted back to life for a reason."

"What reason?"

"For the *band*, big boy. For Blood Brothers."

"That's dangerous talk. It's *insanity*. I'm too fried to listen to any more o' your shit. I'm off to bed. You can sleep on the sofa. See you in the morning." The giant sweeps out of the room and slams the door.

Ozzy has feelings to process before he'll be ready to listen. As children, DT was volatile to the point of flammability, while Oz was a Zen machine. Now Dave has faced down his demons and found his peace, but Ozzy has become haunted. Perhaps that's the way of it when a man's eternal lover – the mother of his child – dies. Maybe his love continues to burn just as brightly, but - in the absence of a tangible target - flares outwards uncontrollably, draining his vital energy. At least Oz can focus his love on Sunshower. Without her, I suspect his feelings of loss and anger would have destroyed him from the inside out.

As I ponder the complexities of love and death, Ozzy returns to the living room carrying a yellow woolly blanket, which he throws over me and tucks into the sofa with shovel hands. He leans down and kisses my forehead with absolute gentleness. "Thanks for bein' a shoulder and an ear. It means a lot."

"You're welcome, dude."

"After Denise, I didn't want to return to my old life and old places. I wanted to stay in this little village - far from everywhere – wi' my wee girl and the memory of my wife. Who would have thought that the mighty Ozzy, who used to grab the world by the balls and shake it, would hide away from life, like a coward?"

"There's nothin' cowardly aboot you, so don't ever think that. Just existin' and carryin' on after what you've been through is courageous. Maybe we do what's necessary to survive. It's easy to start believin' that certain epochs are all good or all bad, but as Walt Whitman said,

There was never any more inception than there is now,
Nor any more youth or age than there is now;
And will never be any more perfection than there is now,
Nor any more Heaven or Hell than there is now."

"Still with the poetry, eh Spartacus?" Oz attempts to smile, but the result is a grimace.

"The Universe is poetry, Oz."

"Aye, mostly bad poetry. I really am off to bed this time. Please don't sleep in the scud, Poetry Boy. I don't want Sunshower walkin' in here in the mornin' to be greeted by your battle-scarred tadger."

"I'm sure Sunshower has no interest in tadgers. It'll be a few years before you need to worry aboot that."

Ozzy glowers at me, his orange eyebrows heavy above sleepy eyelids. "Thanks for remindin' me I've got that to look forward to, ya tool. Just keep your pants on tonight, eh? Goodnight." He lumbers out of the room, leaving me in darkness feeling sorry for the first unfortunate to have designs on Sunshower Dee Oswaldo.

I fly over western Scotland's mountainous landscape, stopping to hover above the Isle of Skye's Inaccessible Pinnacle, Sgurr Dearg, which looks like the back of a godsized stone stegosaurus. After enjoying an unbroken view of the Cuillins' peaks - jagged rocky spears that impale the sky - I soar north over the village of Portree and beyond, to the petrified stone forest of the Storr, the most otherworldly of all Hebridean scenery. As I gaze down at the enormous shaft of vertical rock that is the Old Man of Storr, an invisible weapon strikes my cheek. I fall through the air like an angel dewinged, arms flailing, the Old Man's pointed top moving ever closer. Two things flash through my mind in the instant before impact: *Angel Impaled* is an excellent song title; annihilation by a gigantic chunk of Torridonian rock is a crushingly appropriate demise for a rocker. In the next moment, rather than exploding like a sixteen-stone bag of guts, I open my eyes and discover Sunshower sitting on my chest, her palm raised and ready to slap. "Finally, you're awake," she says, lowering her arm. "I was bored and I want to play, so I…"

"So you slapped my face redder than a naughty stepchild's bottom." Sunshower nods, giggling. In the morning's streams of sunlight, her hair looks like snakes on fire. "I was dreamin' that I was flying," I explain. "I

Metallic Dreams

had a dream like that in Rosie's inn too. I was flyin' towards an archway but woke up before I could go through it."

"So you don't know what happens when you do?"

"No. What happens?"

"I can't tell you, Sparky. You have to fly through it in a dream."

"What happens then?"

"You have to find out for yourself."

"Really?"

"Yes. Or as you and my Daddy would say, aye!"

I want to unlock the meanings hidden within the last few days: two flying dreams in two nights, after having none for over ten years; the form changes of the beautiful Wiccan priestess Rosie; the enormous Flying V crop pattern in the wheat; the ancient archway. I'll meditate on the significance of these things when I'm safely home, as hindsight is always 20/20. For now, I want to savour every moment of my time in Wytchcoomb.

"My Daddy says you've to make me breakfast. He's gone out with his bow for a walk and a shoot and a think." I lift Sunshower off me, swing my legs out from under the blanket, lay her back down on the sofa as if placing the roof on a house of cards, then head to the kitchen to rustle up something edible for the little one and me. After locating half a loaf and a lump of yellowish cheese (which smells like my socks after a ten-mile run), I fire up the grill and go to work.

Sunshower is overjoyed with her makeshift breakfast of toasted cheese, orange juice and tea. It is, in her words, so simple. I wolf down my breakfast while Sunshower devours hers with daintier bites. She sips baby tea as I guzzle cafetière coffee with the consistency of mud.

Sunshower lies in front of the TV and gazes at cartoons through eyes of liquid-blue innocence. She is the only one capable of manipulating Ozzy. I can *use* her. A pang of guilt smacks my head for even considering such a course of action. Rather than pushing the feeling aside, I challenge it. Sunshower is in a unique position to influence Oz, who has always plotted his own course and been unswayed by others. I would be using her for the right reasons: for putting joy, faith and satisfaction back in all our lives. If my plan works, she will have a happier, more contented father and – by extension – a happier, more contented life. We all use people, but most of us are too deluded or self-righteous to admit it. We use people for sex, for love, for allaying our fears, for massaging our egos, for skills they have which we don't, and for countless other reasons. Slain by infallible logic, the guilt pang ceases to exist.

"Sunshower, would you like to hear your Dad play drums?"

"I'd love it."

"You can make it happen. I need to get the band back together, but your Dad won't listen to me. He listens to you, though."

"I don't want him to give up baking. He makes delicious food and we need the money it makes." A disturbing feeling washes through me:

the tiny girl beside me has higher levels of pragmatism than I. There's enough money in my bank to last perhaps another week. My credit card has soared straight past red hot and is currently melting in my wallet. Where my next cash will come from is a mystery.

"Your Dad can always bake," I explain, "but those big hands of his were born to do more than that. They were sculpted by the Metal Gods, honed into the perfect drumstick-wielding weapons. The drumbeats he pounded oot were the bombastic foundation on which the rest of the band built epic heavy metal structures. Drumming chiselled your Dad's body into a force of nature and his soul into the definition of rhythm. The band was *celestial*. Gods and demons alike danced to oor music. By gettin' the band back together I'm carryin' oot the Universe's perfect truth and channellin' its energy instead of blockin' it oot."

"You do talk nonsense, Spark, but I like you."

"Thanks, wee girl. I like you too. You're a timeless sentient soul who knows all there is to know. How did one so wee get to be so wise?"

Sunshower shrugs her shoulders and replies, "If I concentrate hard on something, that thing comes to me in a dream and reveals its inner workings. Last night after you sang me the lullaby, I dreamed about you."

"And what did that dream reveal?"

"It showed me that high above your head, too high to see from the ground, a thing like a dark cloud with horns is watching you. When you play guitar or sing, the colour of the horned thing lightens."

"That sounds gorgeously symbolic. Play, not just the playing of musical instruments but any kind of play, has the ability to make dark clouds sparkling white and heavy souls lighter than air. Most adults are so uptight that they've forgotten how to have fun and play. People don't stop playin' because they get old. They get old if they stop playin'."

Sunshower stares at a point on the wall, considering my musings. "Was my Daddy happy playing drums in the band?"

"Aye, he had the biggest smile I've ever seen. Even his eyes used to smile – big, blue, sparkly ones."

"He misses my Mummy."

"Aye, he does. When your Mum moved on, his heart splintered. It's still not whole, but your love rebuilds it day by day. You heal."

Sunshower gazes at me and flutters her eyelashes in a way that will get her out of numerous speeding tickets in the future. "If he has me *and* drums, he'll have two things that make him happy."

For a brief moment, I feel like the Devil incarnate for planting the seed in her mind. In my defence, Ozzy was happiest when seated behind his drum kit, thrashing like a wild animal while I screamed the roof off his loft. When the band played, each of us was in his own personal Heaven despite being geographically anchored in rainy Bronzehall.

The bang of the front door heralds the return of the giant from his wanderings. "Did you come doon a beanstalk?" I ask.

"You're an idiot," Oz replies, blood-red bow in his left hand, quiver of arrows over the opposite shoulder. "Did you sort Sunshower oot wi' some breakfast?"

"Aye. Toasted cheese, fresh orange juice and baby tea. Did you make the bread? It was delicious."

"It's my own recipe. Marble rye wi' seeds and ground nuts."

"May we talk aboot the band?"

Ozzy's face morphs into a pained expression I've seen once before, in battle, when Woodie leader Jux – resplendent in new steel-toecapped Doc Martens - booted him in the balls. "You can talk," Oz grumbles, "but I won't listen." Homer Simpson shouts, 'Doh!' while Sunshower lies hypnotised in front of the TV screen, her chin resting on the heels of tiny hands, legs bent to acute angles at the knees.

"I died and got resurrected. The wonder I felt as a child is back. I'm connected to the Universe again. The Metal Gods need me to do their bidding. They need you too. *They* made the crop pattern for *you*, as a sign to tell you to rejoin the band. I'd bet my guitars on it."

A long pause is accompanied by the wail of Lisa Simpson's saxophone. "Playin' in the band was amazin'," Oz admits, "but everything's different noo. You and DT are playin' together again, but I've sold my drum kit and live in a different country, plus I have a business to run and a child to look after. Not only does Iain live in a different country from you, he has never played a bass other than the one that exists in his deranged heid. To top it all off, Pete hasn't been seen for years. His jazz lifestyle probably killed him. Even deid, he'll have more musical talent than you and Dave combined."

"That's below the belt, Ozzy. The Universe wants the band back together. Even with your physical enormity, you can't obstruct the flow of the Infinite. Not for long, anyway. If we don't get the band back together we're slappin' the Universe in the face and tellin' it to shove its infinite intelligence up its arse. Anyone with the audacity to do that will face severe karmic and cosmic retribution."

"We had a band and we had fun," Oz concedes, "but that was a long time ago. Things change. I have a life here wi' my bakery business and Sunshower. That's all I need. My drummin' days are over. Think aboot it. The thing you call a band currently consists of a rehabilitated ex-convict guitar player and a singer who hears voices in his heid and thinks he's a mystic visionary. The ex-drummer is too fat to fit on a drum stool, not that there's one strong enough to support me anyway. The wannabe-bassist is a lunatic who has never played a note. He spends half of his time in this world and the other half escapin' to God only knows where, but he should spend all of his time in a straightjacket. To top it all off, Pete - the musical genius of the band - has done a disappearin' act and is quite possibly deid. Does that sound like a recipe for musical success?"

"When you put it like that, it doesn't sound ideal, but…" Exasperated, I start to bite my lip, scrambling for words to say.

"I'd like to hear you play drums, Daddy," interrupts Sunshower with impeccable timing.

Ozzy glares at me the way one might look at one's shoe after stepping in particularly foul dogshit and treading it into one's white shag-pile carpet. "That's low, usin' my wee girl like that."

Sunshower throws her arms round her father's neck. "Daddy, even when you smile, I see in your eyes that you're crying on the inside. I want you to be *really* happy, to smile for real." The little guru's perception has, like a mental scalpel, cut straight through her father's facade and deep into his inner being.

In an effort to keep the pro-band momentum going, I add, "Ozzy, I'm on this planet to create powerful, beautiful, riff-laden, epic music. For years, I almost forgot that. My soul was asleep and bad-dreaming. Noo it's wide awake and ready to sculpt sonic masterpieces."

"There you go again with the poetic piss," spits Oz.

"Good poetry is symbolic, articulate and vivid. Compare that to the everyday small talk most people make in order to avoid real, meaningful conversation. There's nothin' wrong wi' being poetic or aspirin' to live a poetic life. It should be applauded, not criticised."

Oz says nothing else. He writes his phone number on a piece of paper and stuffs it into my biker jacket's inside pocket. Before leaving the cottage, I hug Sunshower and kiss her cheek. She follows me into the garden, does a handstand on the lawn, drops into a forward roll, bounces to her feet and waves a tiny hand. Her father, whose frame fills the doorway, doesn't wave, nor does he look in my direction. As the opening riff of AC/DC's *Highway to Hell* soars from my car speakers, Ozzy's gaze is fixed on the archway.

Chapter 33 – In My Dreams with You

After a twelve-hour drive from Wytchcoomb to Bronzehall, I arrive home feeling as if I've been out of Scotland for months rather than the eventful three days it has actually been.

I'm now in contact with DT, Iain and Ozzy. Superficially, Iain and Oz have no interest in becoming involved with the band again, but I would bet my record collection that the sparks of old dreams which have lain inside them at a low fizzle are now re-igniting. I know what it is to become distracted from my true path, to feel like a passive part of a pointless world rather than a small yet integral part of the seamless, intelligent Universe. Now I know why life sprang forth in the Universe. Life is the means by which the Universe perceives itself. As we gaze into the Infinite, we provide eyes through which the Universe can look upon its wonder. We are all mirrors.

On arriving home, I'm greeted by Fluff pressing her nose between the bars of her enormous plastic-bottomed house. I lie down and touch her nose with mine. Letting out her happy noise, a low-pitched nasal vibration, she licks my nose from bottom to top with delicate flicks of her tongue: a ritualistic rabbit anointment. (Our story begins six years ago in a pet shop in Bronzehall, where a tiny ball of white fur with translucent blue eyes stood up on back legs and shoved a pink twitching nose between the bars of her far-too-small cage; not only did she attract my attention, she melted my heart. As I slid a middle finger through the bars and stroked the fur on top of her head, leporine eyes eased closed and she drifted into a reverie. The rabbit's fur began to draw static sparks from my fingertips, but the little shocks seemed to relax her. I became transfixed by the energy exchange between myself and the baby animal. As much as I chose Fluff that day, she chose me. I bought her the biggest rabbit-house I could find, one in which she had room to run and jump, to roll in lemon-scented sawdust, to make burrows out of meadow hay: somewhere she would feel like a wild rabbit rather than a prisoner. I rabbit-proofed the ground floor of my house by raising all electrical wires out of the reach of ever-chewing teeth. When I'm at home, Fluff has the run of the ground floor. She is my best friend, companion and teacher.)

I open the door of Fluff's house. Like a furry bullet, she sprints into the living room and runs laps around it. After three days holed up in her house, she has energy to burn.

As I collapse onto the sofa with a mug of coffee, Fluff launches herself onto my lap from halfway across the room. She nose-nudges my free hand, wedging her head under it then making micro-adjustments to her orientation until, happy with her position, she shuts her eyes; I'm forgiven for leaving her these last few days.

An hour later, I plant a gentle kiss between Fluff's ears, lay some fresh uncut hay in her house and plop her into it. She buries herself under the hay, pushing it upwards and backwards with her head until she has created a burrow. "I love you, Little Fluff. You're my best friend." She lets out her happy sound; she understands. I switch off the light and leave her to sleep.

Archibald's mobile goes straight to answerphone. *'You have reached Sir Archibald Larkin. I'm not able to answer the phone right now. Please leave your name, message and phone number after the tone.'* Beep.

"Archie, it's Spark. I'm home again. Thanks for feedin' and waterin' Fluff. The greatest band never to tread the boards is one step closer to bein' a reality."

Less than a minute later, my phone rings. When I pick up the receiver, Archibald's shouts are swamped by down-tuned riffage and tribal drumbeats. Realising that he's at a gig, I tell him to phone me later. When he calls back, he asks, "How was the trip? Did things go well with Oz?"

"He wasn't exactly receptive to the idea of the band. His life has changed a lot. His wife died in childbirth. He's bringin' up their daughter on his own. She's a wise soul, and indescribably beautiful. Her name is Sunshower."

"That's a ridiculous name."

"Pot kettle black."

"Sir Archibald Larkin is a noble name, you peasant. And another thing - your rabbit is wild. Every time I put food into her house, she tried to bite my hand off."

"That's just her showin' affection, Archie. She probably just wanted to play, or to have a wee nibble at your fingers."

"A wee nibble at my fingers? She was trying to take my fucking fingers clean off with those razor rabbit teeth of hers. And how many times do I need to tell you not to call me Archie? My name is Archibald."

"Thanks for lookin' after Fluff, Archibald. I owe you one."

"You're welcome, reprobate. Do you want me to drop in for coffee on my way home?"

"Not tonight, dude. It's been a long day's drivin' and I need solid sack time."

"Very well, Spartacus. I can only speculate as to what you mean by sack time, but I will leave you to it, whatever it may be. Coffee at noon tomorrow in Bar Chew? You can fill me in then."

"Perfect. Thanks again for lookin' after my wee pal."

"Goodnight, peasant."

"Night, dude."

I fall into bed, close my eyes and focus all my energy into imagining the Wytchcoomb archway in my mind's eye. As I recede into the mysterious land between wakefulness and sleep, an idea materialises. I jump out of bed, boot up my PC, plug a microphone into it and make a digital recording of my voice whispering the words 'fly' and 'archway'. I create a fifteen-minute loop of my vocal whispers, overlay it onto Jean Michel Jarre's *Waiting for Cousteau* instrumental, then burn the resulting track onto a CD. After placing the still-warm disc into my CD player, I set it to repeat mode, then press play and fall back into bed. With ambient soundscapes flowing into me, I lapse into contented unconsciousness.

High in a sky of unbroken azure, I soar above a desert. Shapes are inscribed into the desert floor: a hummingbird; a spider; a monkey; a snowflake. I glide over the animals and stop above the snowflake. Its intricate geometry, usually associated with extreme cold, stares up at me from burning sands far below. This is a paradox, a Zen koan with no rational answer, and I have been brought here to learn its significance. The horizon wobbles and sways, molten sands melting into blue sky as if stirred by a celestial spoon. "This place wasn't always desert. It was once a frozen wasteland." The desert blows her hot-whispered reply. *'I was a frozen wasteland once, traveller. Me and the rest of the planet. Try again.'*

Feeling like I have been transported into Carlos Castaneda's peyote-inspired alternative reality, I look around for clues but find nothing. The landscape appears barren and dead, a scorched Earth. Then I have another idea. "Desert and snowflake are both matter, creations of mind, illusions of perception."

'True, traveller,' the desert whispers, *'but I am not looking for vague metaphysical meanderings. I need to hear absolute truth, or you are in for a long hover.'*

Shit. What is the absolute truth? Snowflake. Snow. Desert. Sand. Cold. Heat. Liquid. Solid. Something shifts in my mind. Synaptic walls crumble and dissolve. If a snowflake could fall towards the relative solidity of the desert, it would never reach the ground; its semi-solid, semi-liquid body would be vaporised, leaving behind only its essence. Into boiling winds I shout, "Heat and cold are the same, as are solid, liquid and gas. Your clue was the heat-haze horizon where sand blended with sky in a seamless blend of colour. There are no opposites - only levels. Heat and cold are just levels of temperature, yet we humans tend to think of them as polar opposites, which is flawed thinking. Solid, liquid and gas are levels of matter - not different things, but levels of the same thing. Life and death aren't opposites. They're levels of existence, aspects of being, different expressions of soul consciousness."

After a long pause, the desert blows her reply. *'Traveller, you understand. Now that you have transcended barrier thinking, your spirit can transcend. Keep in mind your new understanding as you journey. Good luck.'*

Before I can offer thanks, I'm sucked into the horizon at breakneck speed. Burning air dissolves my eyes. Skin bubbles and bursts. Long hair, which moments ago flapped noisily in the breeze, catches fire and burns like multiple fuses, with my head - presumably – as the dynamite. Into the horizon's melting pot of gold and blue I merge.

Suddenly, the air around me is cool. I can see again. My hair has regrown. I'm flying over a forested landscape with Wytchcoomb's archway dead ahead. Keeping my focus fixed on the arch, I take a long, deep breath, then exhale and let my soul act as both compass and rudder on the journey. Sunshower's smiling face flashes into my mind's eye. "Your turn now, Spark!" With air whistling through my hair, I pass through the arch. And into another world.

The sky is dark green with a low-hanging canopy of crimson clouds, beneath which rocky ground appears devoid of life. Sulphurous air burns my lungs. Flashes of lightning strike clouds, bursting them open and spilling blood-red rain onto grey rock below. Thunder roars. This place would make the perfect heavy metal album cover.

I walk, not in any particular direction, just enjoying the sense of movement. Focusing on my breathing, I break into a run. Blood pumps faster. Lungs expand. Endorphins flood my system. I feel lung-gom light as my lengthening strides devour the ragged landscape. As the storm dies out, leaving deafening silence in its wake, I reach the edge of a chasm that looks about fifteen feet wide but appears to have no bottom. I drop a rock into the abyss. Silence. It falls forever.

On the other side of the rift is an expanse of neatly shorn grass and a solitary eildon tree. The sky lightens to an olive-green shade. Life flourishes on the other side of the chasm, but my side is barren.

Three horses gallop into view on the opposite side of the ravine. I recognise their riders as my grandmother, grandfather and father. The horses slow to a trot and stop under the branches of the eildon tree. My grandfather dismounts and walks to the edge of the chasm, where he stands facing me. He is dressed in a suit of blinding white and his silver hair is slicked backwards. There are a million things I want to say, but the situation is so surreal that it strikes me dumb.

"You look good," my Papa says. "A bit bloody, though."

"I went for a run in the crimson rain."

"Lovely night for it."

"There wasn't much else to do here. I just felt like running."

"Some things never change, Spark. I loved watching you run like a gazelle every day of your childhood. Anyway, to business. We were alerted to your presence here, which is why we ventured oot into the storm."

"But you're bone dry. I'm drenched."

My grandfather smiles, baring teeth that sparkle like his clothing. "Things on this side are different," he explains. "Back up and take a running jump. You can make it across the divide. It's beautiful here."

I stare down into the bottomless abyss. With a good runnie I could make it across, yet something keeps me rooted to the spot. My Papa paces back and forth, exuding effortless athleticism as he did in his youth. His limp, the result of being shot in the kneecap by a German sniper during World War 2, is gone.

My grandmother and father are both clad in pale-blue robes that resemble those of Shaolin monks. The detail of their faces isn't clear, but the light from their eyes shines across space and time.

Without a word, I turn and run away from the divide. I don't stop running until the chasm is miles behind. Love for my dead family members fills me to overflowing, but I'm not ready to cross that abyss.

Judas Priest's *Desert Plains* booms across the landscape, its riffs shaking the Earth. Ahead, a stone archway filled with shimmering metallic-blue liquid erupts from the ground, symbols of white fire hovering in the air around it. As I sprint archwards, the heavy metal soundscape is replaced by Sunshower's voice. "You have to fly through it in a dream." If this world isn't a dream, I'm hopelessly lost. Launching myself into a fists-first dive, I fly through the archway.

Chapter 34 – The Mirror

David Tierney jolts awake from a nightmare, climbs out of bed and stumbles in darkness across a wooden floor that feels like ice against the soles of his feet. He stubs a big toe on the bathroom door, provoking a tirade of swearing that wakes Saxon. The air turns blue with the profanity of two species, canine howls mixing with human curses. As Dave fumbles unseeingly for the bathroom light switch, Saxon pounces on his back, toppling him from his precarious, one-legged position to a more stable one, face down on the bathroom floor. Rather than taking the direct route of descent, he stops mid-fall for a brief meeting between his chin and the rim of his porcelain toilet. Predictably, the shitter wins the debate, splitting open Dave's chin and knocking him unconscious. Blood filters through his thick beard and forms a dark pool on white tiles.

Saxon sits back on hind legs, unsure of the correct canine protocol in this situation. He takes the safe option and does nothing, thinking it highly possible that his walkerfeedergroomer is just having a lie down.

Two minutes later, a disorientated Dave clambers to his feet, switches on the bathroom light and turns on a hot tap. Cupping water in his hands, he submerges his chin for a couple of seconds then parts his palms and watches crimson liquid splash into the sink. Feeling disturbingly Jesus-like, having turned water red, he opens the bathroom cabinet, takes out a roll of bandage, holds one end under his chin, unrolls the gauze over the top of his head and back under his chin, repeating the wrapping process until blood is no longer showing through the material.

Dave stares at his reflection in the mirror. He looks like a semi-mummified tramp, black beard and gauze covering his face. In his eyes is a look that resides only in those who have been a heartbeat away from Hell and managed to pull back from its brink. He has overcome adversity, transmuted dire into divine, turned profanity into profundity, and has faced and exorcised his demons. Now he is free, but he doesn't see freedom in his eyes: he sees unfulfilled dreams. Unable to hide from himself any longer, David Tierney decides that as soon as his injured chin has healed, he will shave off his beard and bare the face that has been buried - along with his heavy metal dreams - for far too long. For eternities his musical aspirations have bubbled beneath the surface, resigned to a dark and lifeless corner of his being. Time to set them free.

Saxon grabs a bathroom towel with his mouth, tosses it into the bloodpool, barks once and pads down iron stairs to his waiting bed.

Dressed only in boxer shorts, a pale figure hovers over a Yamaha keyboard in the smoke-filled living room of the dingy flat that has become his prison, agoraphobia and neuroses its bars. Here he stays, the musical wizard confined to his protective castle. A shock of wiry blonde hair sprouts from his frown-lined head. Skinny limbs protrude from a pasty body like toothpicks jutting out of a skinned potato. Living on a diet of Pringles, sweet coffee, cigarettes and rivers of booze has not done his health or mental state any favours. If they could, his lungs would sell the rest of his body in exchange for one breath of the outside world's fresh air.

He glances at his watch: 4.07 a.m. Normally by this time of night he has achieved something. Tired eyes look to the keyboard, soundlessly threatening it with violence if this musical dry spell isn't quenched soon. He knows the instrument is not to blame, though; it is merely a tool. Winds howl outside the flat. They are the winds of change and they are calling his name. He can *feel* it.

Tuning his ears to the gale outside, he programs the keyboard to mimic the windsong. The gap between wind and mind diminishes until there is no differential between the electronic sounds inside the flat and those of wild elements raging outside. Human energy melds with primal forces. A long-overdue feeling of freedom fills the man as invisible tendrils snake outwards from his body and tap into quantum energy fields. Bolt-upright blonde hair crackles in the two-way flow of electricity.

For the first time in years, Pete Drummond feels plugged into something bigger than himself. Without leaving the confines of his prison, he has escaped.

Chapter 35 – Way Cool Jr.

Ted Watkin strolls into New York's JFK International Airport and looks around in surprise at the sparsely populated concourse. New York is such a perpetually bustling city that to find its main airport empty feels more than a little odd. No amplified voices boom through loudspeakers. Perhaps, Ted thinks, there has been a bomb scare. No, that isn't it; after a suspected terrorist attack, the airport would be cordoned off while armed police swear on their lives – to anyone daft enough to enquire – that there is nothing to see and that nothing out of the ordinary has occurred. One check-in desk is open, attended by an immaculately dressed woman in thick make-up and bright red lipstick. The scent of Chanel No 5 wafts across the concourse.

Ted's trolley adheres to Airport Luggage Trolley Association regulations, which state that all airport trolleys must have three efficiently functioning wheels and a retarded one, presumably as an equal-opportunity policy for wheels. The trolley pursues its spastic journey, screechily meandering across the floor towards the check-in desk where the doll-like lady is seated. Ted flashes her a smile, removes his passport and flight tickets from the inside pocket of his fringed suede jacket, and slaps them down on the desk. The auburn-haired Teri – for that is what her name badge says – smiles back. Ted recognises her smile as forced rather than authentic. Teri likes well-groomed men who wear expensive suits and smell of designer eau de toilette: the sort of men who use moisturiser and toner on their skin prior to spending half an hour trimming their neat sideburns into a state of perfect symmetry. Ted Watkin is not such a man. His long, straggly, honey-blonde hair would beat even the most stubborn hairbrush into submission or, at the very least, a Mexican standoff. Eyes like polished milk chocolate sparkle through strands of the unruly mane that hangs over his face and torso like venetian blinds, partially obscuring the Megadeth T-shirt which warns that the planet is on a countdown to extinction. So plentiful are the rips in Ted's jeans that they now consist more of fresh air than of denim. Below the faded jeans, which appear to be debating whether to hang together or disintegrate, are snakeskin cowboy boots with shiny metal toecaps. After tagging his bass-guitar flight case and brown leather suitcase, and placing them onto the check-in's moving conveyor belt, Ted walks away from the desk with a glance over his shoulder at Teri. *Gorgeous, but pristine and altogether too uptight. I bet she hates sucking dick. I'd get two blowjobs a year from her at most – birthday and Christmas perhaps.*

As the flight case sails through translucent plastic slats to be loaded onto the next flight to Hamburg, Teri notices Ted's backwards look in her direction. *I bet he'd be a great fuck. He looks like he's been dragged through a hedge backwards, but he's a sexy son of a bitch.*

Before heading into the departure lounge, Ted sneaks a last glimpse at Teri and smiles inwardly. *Bitch wants me so badly she's sliding off her seat.*

Chapter 36 – E-Mail from a Shemale

Manie's e-mail isn't one of his usual updates detailing his 'romantic' conquests and stories of his band – Fatal Visionary - and its organic growth. The subject box of today's e-mail contains the words 'gender transformation surgery'. The body of the message claims that Manie has been taking female hormones for a year and has saved almost enough money for a gender-reassigning operation. I reply to it with the tact it deserves:

'Manie,

Does this mean you will be shaving off the 'tache which has resided on your top lip since high school? There is a demand for hirsute women, albeit a niche market. If you choose to keep the 'tache, along with your titties (which are surely growing nicely after a year of female hormones) and newfound vagina, I'm certain that there will still be a special someone out there just for you. Look on the Internet. It's full of perverts.

Have any of your bandmates groped your melons yet? I'm sure Brian the bufu beast must have given them a good few squeezes. God knows, I would have groped the hell out of them if I was there. Your Dad calls me 'that Scottish pervert', so I'd live up to that reputation. It would be rude not to.

Are you familiar with an underrated AOR band called Unruly Child? Their singer – Mark Free – became Marcie Free after a sex-change operation. He/she still sang beautifully afterwards, if at a noticeably higher pitch. I'm sure Marcie could give you make-up tips and practical advice on making the transformation from masculine heavy metal icon to, pardon the pun, Rock Goddess. (Probably the second most famous all-female heavy metal band from Britain, after Girlschool, is Rock Goddess. Any self-respecting UK metalhead would already know this, but a gender-bending, titty-growing, spaghetti-scoffing, tadger-sacrificing, moonshine-drinking, bomb-making, backwoods-living sonofabitch from Rednecksburg, Virginia may not be aware of such subtleties.)

You have limited time in which to buy a T-shirt proclaiming 'I'M A LESBIAN TRAPPED IN A MAN'S BODY!' Or have you have given up rug-munching in favour of sausage-related activities?

I'm off for a ride on the mountain bike.

Give your paps a squeeze for me.

Later Dayz.

Your Gay Lover,
    Spartacus

P.S. *If your band doesn't make it big you can be Blood Brothers' resident groupie, but only if you shave off the 'tache.'*

I click the *Send* button. The message takes electronic wings and flies.

I return from a cycle in the countryside a few hours later, covered in sprayed-up mud and cowshit, and soaked in sweat. After clicking *Send/Receive* to see if I have any new e-mails, I strip off and hit the shower. As the water turns from cold to hot, the opening riff of AC/DC's *Gimme a Bullet* blasts out of my computer's speakers, heralding the arrival of new e-mail.

Wrapped in a towel and relaxed after a long shower, I look at the fresh e-mail lying in the comfort of its Inbox bed. The subject line: 'YOU'RE AN INSENSITIVE ASSHOLE!' I have long suspected this to be the case, and have been told so verbally on many occasions. Now, for the first time, written verification has arrived to confirm my suspicions. In the body of the e-mail, Manie expounds his disgust at my clumsy treatment of the serious topic of gender transformation. Sure that he's trying to drag out the joke a little longer, I type a stream-of-consciousness reply:

'*Manie, or rather Emmanuelle,*

Thanks for your reply. Please accept my heartfelt apologies for hurting your feelings. Losing a tadger and gaining a gash must be stressful. Please photograph your big new titties and e-mail me the pic. It's not that I doubt what you're telling me; I just need something new to whack off over…oh, wait…it's bad grammar to finish a sentence with a preposition…I just need something new over which off to whack. That's better.

Spark'

Manie's claims *must* be a wind-up attempt. We created pipe bombs together and annihilated mailboxes with our homemade explosives. We spent endless hours listening to heavy metal and going, in the words of Anthrax, metal thrashing mad. We watched porn flicks together. Wait, could that have been a turning point? Is it possible that Manie thought the nasty sluts in those films looked so good that he decided to become one? I understand the desire to dive head first into a curvaceous fellatrix, but *becoming* a woman…perish the thought. Monthly periods, out-of-control hormones, pregnancy, leg-shaving, underarm-waxing, eyebrow-plucking, make-up and, last but not least, relationships with men. Fuck that! I've heard people talking on television about being born a man, yet feeling like a woman trapped in a male body. *Is it possible? Manie?* My thoughts slam back to Earth with a bang as I remember that this is Sicilian-American, metal-loving, red-blooded, bomb-blasting Manie I'm questioning. He's as testosterone-fuelled as anyone. This is an elaborate test of my gullibility, a test I'm not going to fail.

Chapter 37 – Face like an Angel

Safe from the wind's bite, DT and I are cruising to Glasgow in his Porsche. We're travelling at 130 mph, although the ride is so quiet and smooth that it feels more like 30 mph. Silence in a car is an unfamiliar experience for me: Rustbucket's mechanically unsound rumblings are so loud that only the heaviest of metal can drown them out.

Tonight's trip is to see Scottish icons the Sensational Alex Harvey Band playing live. Alex himself is long dead, but his band has continued through various incarnations, all of them entertaining yet lacking the on-the-edge danger that Mr Harvey provided.

SAHB play a blinder. After the gig, I flip a 50p coin. As the silvery heptagon spins end over end, DT calls tails. Tails it is. He selects my first mark of the night: a tall, skinny girl whose lank black hair hangs over a white-corpsepainted face punctuated by black lipstick and eyeliner. After DT has told me my script, I swagger up to the black-clad girl. I'd bet that I know her type of man: shoulder-length hair (dyed black, of course); corpsepainted face; black eyeliner; black lipstick; black PVC jeans; long black leather coat à la Matrix; boots with soles about a mile thick. I'm familiar with such men. I see them at gigs all the time, lumbering about all skinny and morose, expending superhuman effort just to lift their feet and take a step, due to the gargantuan mass of their boots. If any undernourished goth soul is unfortunate enough to fall off a pier while dressed this way, he's a goner; the Mafia couldn't do it better with concrete boots.

Unfazed by my approach, the girl looks me up and down, her perpetual dejectedness unwavering. "Aren't you in the wrong place?" I ask. "Shouldn't you be oot hauntin' hooses?"

Her facial expression changes from apathy to disgust. The shadow of a frown appears beneath her mask of white corpsepaint. Black lips part and the spectre spits, "You're an idiot. Fuck off." She turns and looks away with affected superiority, body language she has practised to perfection.

"It's OK, girl. I understand your pain, even though Mummy and Daddy don't. Your fashion is a statement of rebellion and a badge of individuality. Isn't it weird that millions o' goths worldwide choose a style that's meant to showcase their individuality, yet they all look the same? How can somethin' be unique if it's replicated millions o' times over? Goths are like Big Macs…wherever you go in the world, they're identical."

Her gaze revisits me. For a moment I see thoughts flickering behind her eyes, as if my philosophical utterances have switched on a light in her head, or at least led her to the light switch. Then, her previous expression of borderline hatred returns. "I'm not a goth. I'm a neo-goth.

Shows how much you know, you judgemental caveman prick. Now fuck off. Please."

Her politeness comes as a life-affirming surprise. I've been told to fuck off more times than I've had hot dinners. Never before, however, has anyone added 'please'. I feel obligated to return the courtesy. "Thank you, fair maiden. I hope the rest of your evening is pleasant and relaxing." As I make the walk of shame back to DT, his beaming smile lights my way. "That went well," I tell him. "She's a lovely girl – very polite."

Dave and I look over at Miss Neo-goth, who is staring into space, her face communicating neither superiority nor disgust, nor even apathy. On her face is the unmistakeable look of baffled confusion.

I lay down DT's challenge. His mark is an androgynous short-haired girl of about six feet tall in skintight red PVC trousers, dangerously spiked white heels and a black AFI shirt on which rabbits chase each other in a circle. Other than pillar-box red lipstick, no make-up is evident on her asexual face. It's difficult to gauge her age, but I'd estimate thirty. Too cool to care that smoking in public places is now banned across Scotland, she takes long drags on a cigarette.

DT bounces up to her with gallus strides. I follow him, stopping just inside earshot. "I saw you lookin' at me from across the bar," he drawls, in his best John Wayne style, "and I honestly can't blame you. I'll let you style my hair if you come home wi' me."

Looking puzzled, she asks, "Are you talkin' to me?"

John Wayne morphs into Robert de Niro. "I don't see anyone else here, so I must be talkin' to you."

"There are hundreds o' people here. What's the matter wi' you? Are you handicapped? Do you have special needs?"

Rubbing his crotch, DT replies, "I have special needs you couldn't even *imagine*. You could get arrested for even thinkin' aboot them."

The woman purses her lips and blows smoke into DT's eyes. "Here's an idea," she says. "Go and buy me a drink, slip tranquilisers into it, then heave my unconscious body back to your place. That's your only hope of gettin' into my panties."

"There are subliminal messages hidden in your words. You want me, but you won't admit it to yourself. You mentioned me slippin' *my* tranquilisers into *your* drink. Don't you see what that means? If Freud was here he'd declare that what you really want is *me* slippin' my magnificent appendage into *you*."

"Leave me alone or I'll get a bouncer to slip *his* fist into *your* foul mouth, ya sex pest."

DT shrugs his shoulders then rejoins me. "She sussed you oot quickly," I observe. "She hit the depraved nail right on its perverted heid." We both fall about laughing, looking thirty-something and feeling twelve.

DT chooses my next target. She is everything I go for in a rock bitch: sluttily dressed and oozing heavy metal chic; metallic-blue leather mini-skirt; black high-heeled boots; skinny-fit vest; perhaps 5'6" tall in her extreme heels, which account for at least six inches of altitude, making her barefoot height closer to a petite five feet; a tantalising strip of white waistline visible between skirt and vest; piercing blue eyes; long auburn hair; blue lip gloss and matching eye shadow, liberally applied. Slutability quotient: off the scale.

Motörhead's *Iron Fist* booms through the club's speakers as Dave makes a loudhailer out of his hands and yells the next script into my ear. The slutty goddess smiles as I approach and ask, "Do you want to ditch this place? Let's go and find a hotdog van."

"Why would I want to leave a perfectly good metal club to go to some scuzzy hotdog van? Buy a bag o' crisps from the bar if you're hungry."

"You look like a girl who appreciates a big sausage, that's all."

As her smile disappears, I feel like a bona fide tit. The sting of alcohol in my eyes is immediately followed by a sharper pain in my shin. After licking my lips (which taste of whisky and coke), I limp back to the cracking-up DT. "You're a real charmer," he chuckles. "I hope you feel suitably humiliated. And you've the cheek to call me a sex pest."

The Metal Gods divert my attention away from my throbbing shin and nipping eyes. *Remember that tonight is about Zen training. Killing the ego is an important step in a warrior's progress.*

DT's next mark - in black leather trousers, tan cowboy boots and a tight Ratt T-shirt – has waist-length peroxide hair and heavy make-up that lends her facial features a comic-book look, an illusion furthered by fluorescent pink lipstick. I give Dave his lines and stand back to watch the fireworks, again standing just within earshot. "Do you want a game o' soldiers? I'll let you blow the hell oot o' me. Or if you prefer paintball I've got a splattergun in my pants that's just itchin' to cover you in goo."

The mark leans towards DT's ear and whispers something that makes his eyes widen. She takes his hand and leads him into the male toilet. A minute later, an irate Dave emerges and makes straight for me, his face a crimson mask of rage with smears of pink around the lips. "That girl has a cock!" *Touchdown.*

"She must be one of those special chicks," I reply. "What do you call them again? Oh aye, I remember…men….guys…dudes."

"For fuck's sake," Dave laments, face in hands, "that was every kind o' wrong."

"Och, don't worry aboot it, George Michael. You're not famous yet, so it won't make the papers."

"Papers? Fuck the fuckin' papers! I'm goin' to need therapy!"

"What did he whisper in your ear before leadin' you into the bog? Did he say that he wanted to show you his man-pussy?"

"This isnae funny, ya smart-mouthed fuck!"

(I picked a 'girl' whom I knew to be a man. If I hadn't seen him peeing at a urinal during a previous gig here, I would never have believed it. Many men, I understand, enjoy dressing as women. Transvestism is the technical term to describe

such a predilection. Some transvestites are heterosexual. Some are not. Transexuals, on the other hand, are one gender trapped in another gender's body, as Manie claimed to be in his wind-up e-mails earlier today. Thinking about transexuality drives my mind round in Catch-22 circles. If a person is born male and feels like a female in a man's body, yet is sexually attracted to women, does that make the individual a lesbian with gender issues or a heterosexual male with psychological issues?)

Mincing out of the toilet, apparently neither up nor down, DT's mark gazes at him and winks. "Did you see that, Spark? That fucker just winked at me! I'm gonnae punch his fuckin' lights oot!"

I grab Dave's arm and restrain him. "Some keywords for you, dude – assault, prison, successful business, band, future, karma. You did initiate that toilet situation in a rude way. The phrase *what comes aroon' goes aroon'* springs to mind."

DT stares into my eyes, through them. Slowly, the rigidity in his body dissolves and his muscles relax. "Listen, Spark, I don't know if I'll ever see the funny side of this…if there is a funny side. He had his tongue in my mooth and his hand doon my pants."

"Trust me, there's a funny side to it. Hilarious, in fact."

"We'll have to agree to disagree aboot that. Promise me that if oor band makes it big and releases an autobiography, this story stays oot of it."

"I don't know if I can promise that. This could become as legendary as Led Zeppelin's live-eels-up-a-groupie's-gash story."

"I'm fuckin' serious, Spark! This stays between you and me. If we make it big, I don't want to be thought of as some men's-toilet-lurking poofter."

"Deal. On one condition."

"Name it."

"You stop sayin' *if* we make it big and start thinkin' along the lines o' *when* we make it big."

"That's a deal, Spartacus." DT flashes a smile.

"Good. The story won't go in our autobiography then."

"Excellent."

"I'll save it exclusively for magazine interviews."

"You're still a wee tit, you know."

"I know."

"And you're still no' funny."

"Opinions vary."

Mötley Crüe's *Girls, Girls, Girls* roars through the club. I suggest to DT that he should ask the DJ to play Sabrina's disco hit *Boys Boys Boys*, as it is more topical. He shoots me a freezing glance and spits more profanity my way.

The next hour showers us with relaxing, old-school metal tunes: Ted Nugent's *Cat Scratch Fever*; Iron Maiden's *Two Minutes to Midnight*; Megadeth's *Peace Sells…But Who's Buying*; Testament's *Low*; Metallica's *For Whom the Bell Tolls*; Suicidal Tendencies' *You Can't Bring Me Down*; Ratt's

Round and Round; Van Halen's *Ain't Talkin' 'Bout Love*; David Lee Roth's *Perfect Timing*; Thin Lizzy's *Whiskey in the Jar;* Mordred's *Falling Away*.

Behind me, a hoarse female voice asks, "Is that sausage offer still open?"

I whirl round to find my gorgeous second mark, now seriously inebriated and propped against a pillar. Taking a step back, I ask, "You're not goin' to attack me again, are you?"

She looks deeply into my eyes, her lips forming a lusty, liquored-up pout. "I'll do a lot more than attack you," she purrs. "I'm Angel, by the way."

"Angels are devoid of genitalia."

"Not this Angel." She pulls a small hardback diary from her bag, rips out a blank page, scribbles down a number with an eyebrow pencil, stuffs the piece of paper into the front pocket of my jeans and whispers, "Call me." Angel kisses my cheek then vanishes into clouds of dry ice.

I turn to face DT. "Did you see that?"

Stony-faced, he grunts, "You should have checked to see if she has a cock. You never know in this fuckin' place."

We listen to Saxon's *Denim and Leather* on the journey home. I ask Dave if he thinks it odd that Ozzy is the only blood brother ever to sustain a healthy long-term relationship with a woman. He replies that the rest of us are a talented bunch of social misfits who are unwilling to compromise enough to nurture a stable love life. Ozzy's marriage, Dave proposes, left him in a state of emotional purgatory anyway, so to Hell with committed relationships. I wonder if it is truly better to have loved and lost than never to have loved at all, or if such sentiments are just fodder for power ballads by glam-metal bands.

I arrive home to find one new e-mail, from Brian Ferntree, who has just comforted an upset Manie and assured him that I must have thought his sex-change e-mails were a joke. Brian's message also mentions that Fatal Visionary's bassist, Ted Watkin, is vacationing in Europe with his bass - as always - by his side.

I send two e-mails to Virginia. The first is to Manie: a sincere apology, explaining that I had deemed his e-mails tests of my gullibility. I assure him that no matter what his sexuality and gender, I'm always on his side and never more than a phone call or e-mail away. My next message is to Brian, thanking him for his peacemaking and requesting Ted's mobile phone number.

As I fall into bed a plan starts to hatch.

Chapter 38 – The Morning After

It is one of those uniquely Scottish days in which the weather, apparently in conflict with itself, can't decide whether to be happy, sunny and blue-skied or miserable, dreich and rainy. Clouds roll in, empty themselves, roll away. Sun bakes wet ground dry. Repeat.

Paul Roberts wakes from a drunken slumber and looks at the sleeping redhead to his left. Hazy memories of the previous night sieve through his mind's alcohol-drenched filter. The pain in his head screams, "Swallow a double dose of paracetamols with a pint of water then go back to sleep. Otherwise you're in for the hangover from Hades."

Last night in Paul's apartment was not an average few-drinks-in-front-of-the-TV-with-the-significant-other occasion. Paul's girlfriend, Janine, lambasted his preference for computer games over her, then verbally shredded his standards of hygiene, his irregular shaving, his family, friends, job, even his Weimaraner dog, Yoshimax. Her words hurt Paul, but – a placid soul by nature - he didn't argue back. Not at first. As Janine's tirade stormed relentlessly onwards, however, her ingratitude began to stir up his wrath. He had spent his life savings on buying and refurbishing their flat. A hate-fuelled diatribe wasn't what he expected by way of thanks. Little had Paul realised that Janine's anger and resentment had been brewing for years, awaiting the perfect opportunity to be unleashed. Last night had been that time. What follows is a chronological summary of events.

Paul spent the morning, afternoon and early evening painting the apartment magnolia, then put his two-year-old boy Montrose to bed and read him a story from a Ladybird book that had been Paul's as a child. After kissing the chubby blue-eyed bundle goodnight, Paul liberated a can of beer from the fridge and sat in front of the TV for some well-earned relaxation in the form of the first-person-shooter video game *Zombie Stomp*. When Janine returned home from work to find her boyfriend supping beer and splattering zombies with a rocket launcher, she blew her top. No mention was made of the professional paint job in the hall, the expertly laid wooden flooring in the kitchen or the contented sleeping baby. Paul switched weapon and started to decapitate zombies with laser-precise blasts from his sniper-scoped plasma rifle. Janine would stop whining, he figured, if he ignored her and kept his attention on the game. Furious, Janine yanked the TV plug out of the wall and continued her rant right in her boyfriend's face.

Paul had been a games junkie since coin-operated Space Invaders machines appeared, when he was barely out of nappies. He knew he was as much part of the digital Universe as the physical one, but he resented being told that he spent too much time playing games. He wasn't harming Janine or anyone else.

Janine poured herself a large gin and lemonade, necked it, then poured another. As the booze flowed, so did her verbal venom. Rather than arguing back, Paul decided to get drunk too. Inebriation might, he reckoned, dull the shrill sound of Janine's voice. This strategy worked well until she retrieved his megaphone from the bedroom and began to scream uncensored insults through it at deafening volume. Pushed to breaking point, Paul retaliated. "If I'm really that fuckin' clueless and unable to make a good choice in life, why are you wi' me? What does that say aboot you, ya daft cow?"

"Why do you think I drink so much?" yelled Janine. "I'm numbing the pain of livin' wi' you, ya useless prick!"

"Useless? I helped you to create a perfect baby. I put all my savings into this flat, then spent weeks paintin' and decoratin' it. And I hold the world's all-time high score on Xevious."

"What the fuck is that? Probably one o' your stupid fuckin' video games! Grow up, ya big child!"

"Och, away and shove that gin bottle up your massive gash."

"Ya fuckin' bastard! I bore our child!"

"Aye, and you bore me too, ya fat bitch!"

"Fuck you, ya fuckin' fuckheid! It isn't easy losin' weight after pregnancy!"

"Especially when you drink five gallons o' gin a night."

"I was teetotal for nine months while I was pregnant! Have you forgotten that I gave birth to our baby?"

"That's one way o' puttin' it. Another way is to say that a team of doctors and nurses drove up your massive muff in a bus, picked up oor beautiful boy, then drove back oot again."

"You world-ranked asshole! Maybe my vaginal dimensions are regular and your tadger's the issue. Did you think of that?"

"You're off your trolley! My tadger is legendary. Every minx lucky enough to have received it has soaked her sheets."

"The only way their sheets could've got wet was if you pissed the bed, which wouldn't surprise me, ya fuckin' overgrown baby. To Hell wi' you and your wee wanger!"

"Massive muff!"

"Tiny tadger!"

"Voluminous vagina!"

"Diminutive dick!"

"Fat fanny! Gaping gash! Volvo-sized vulva! Colossal cunt! Oversized orifice! Bulky bush! Parachute pussy! Chasm crack! I can do this all night. I would too, but I'm goin' oot to find a woman who appreciates my cock."

"I'm gonnae fuckin' kill you!"

"How will you do that? Throw me to the bottom of your gash, the gaping chasm of which the Grand Canyon is envious?"

Janine charged at Paul, her nails poised to scratch out his eyes. He sidestepped her clumsy attack and retreated. She launched a Gordon's Gin bottle at his head. He leaned to the side just in time to avoid being hit full in the face by the angry green projectile, which whistled past his ear and smashed on the wall, spraying gin and fragments of glass over the back of his neck. Raising megaphone to mouth, Janine screamed, "You fuckin' prick!" Then, lowering both megaphone and voice, she whispered in a sinister tone, "I fucking hate you." Guzzling brandy from the bottle, Janine slumped onto the sofa. Paul, meanwhile, remained on the other side of the room, never taking his eyes off Janine. He was still staring daggers at her when she passed out in an alcoholic stupor.

Paul staggered from the living room to the spare bedroom (which he had spent the previous week painting and flooring). He picked up a tub of Polyfilla and a tube of superglue, stumbled back to the living room, slid his hands under Janine's skirt and eased down her G-string, mumbling, "I'll fuckin' fix your fat hole, ya bitch." Janine was easy to manoeuvre, like a large rag doll. After spreading her legs, Paul pried open vaginal lips and squeezed Polyfilla into the aperture. When it began to overflow, he reached, reflexly, for his filling knife, then laughed at himself; this job did not require a perfect finish. With drunken dexterity, Paul squeezed superglue round the perimeter of the Polyfilla, where it met soft, pink flesh. As the mixture hardened, he lit a cigarette, plugged in the TV and flipped channels to Discovery Animal Planet, where an intrepid diver was swimming with manatees. Paul liked manatees. He liked all animals. Generally, he liked people too. He had especially liked Janine until she transmogrified into a loud-mouthed harpy who criticised every aspect of his being. After watching the manatee programme, Paul completed *Zombie Stomp,* drained his last six cans of beer, then carried Janine to bed, laying her down with extreme care, as if she were a box of delicate wine glasses.

Back in the present, it's morning. Paul looks to his left, last night's haze clearing in his throbbing head. Suddenly, he remembers the Polyfilla incident. *Please let that have been a dream.* A glance under the covers reveals that it was no dream. Unsure of the best course of action, he hurriedly pulls on joggies, trainers and a Motörhead T-shirt, then leaves the house before the shit, or in this case the multi-purpose surface filler, hits the fan.

Chapter 39 – The Phone Call

A pot of coffee gurgles into being. Sunbeams squeeze through gaps between pregnant rainclouds. Ted's mobile phone number stares at me, tempting me like the apple in the Garden of Eden. It's time to make that call.

Ted answers his phone sounding gruff and hungover. When I explain who I am, a softer demeanour takes over. His voice is husky and deep, like a male Demi Moore. "Oh yeah, Spark. You're that Scottish dude. Brian tells me you sing worse than a tone-deaf Ozzy Osbourne." Laughter roars down the phone then gives way to a bout of coughing.

"Aye, I'm the Scottish dude. How did you work it oot, genius? Was the accent a clue?"

"Listen, asshole. I'm tryin' to recover from a night I can't even remember. If you're callin' to give me a hard time, then you can fuck off. Failin' that, if you have a point, please get to it. I have a bed I need to collapse into."

"Do you realise that you just ended two sentences wi' prepositions? Most Americans have no basic understandin' of the language they purportedly speak. Instead of endin' your sentence wi' *you can fuck off*, you could have said *off you can fuck*. A better ending than *I need to collapse into* would have been *into which I need to collapse*."

"Oh Holy Jesus, I don't believe this shit! Here I am with the worst hangover of my life and there's a pedantic Scottish fuck on the phone givin' me grammar lessons…and that's after insultin' my intelligence. Please, dude, I'm tryin' to be patient. What the fuck do you want?"

"I have a favour to ask."

"Fuck," Ted growls, "you may know a thing or five about sentence construction, but you have a whole lot to learn about tact. In America, if we're gonna ask a man for a favour, we kiss his ass beforehand, you know? Butter him up, massage his ego. Apparently you think it better to offend him instead. That's a novel tactic." Ted's eruption of laughter is cut short by another bout of coughing.

"OK, Ted. Even though I didn't get to know you as a person while I was in Virginia, I always thought you had lovely hair. Could my band borrow your bass-playin' skills for a couple o' days, since you're in the neighbourhood?"

"In the neighbourhood? I'm in fucking Holland, man. I'm nowhere near your insignificant little island."

"You're tourin' Europe, though. What's the closest you'll be to Scotland?"

"London."

"How aboot I meet you in London and drive you up to Scotland? You can sleep at my hoose. I'll cover food costs. Your days wi' me won't cost you a penny. Also, you'll get to play bass wi' Blood Brothers."

"I'll do it on one condition."

"I'm not suckin' your dick."

"You wish that was my condition, you Scottish pervert. My condition is that you take me to see Loch Ness. I've read a lot about it. It would be cool to see."

"You have yourself a deal, redneck. When do you arrive in London?"

"One week today."

"I'll phone you nearer the time and we can make arrangements."

"Whatever, dude." Cough, cough, click. Jerry Springer has a lot to answer for.

My phone rings again. Expecting it to be Ted, I answer it with, "Do they teach you manners in America?"

"I don't know. I haven't been to America," says Sunshower, her voice pure refreshment to my soul.

"Hi, little one. It's good to hear you. How are you and your Dad?"

"We're OK. My Daddy wants to speak to you, but I wanted to say hello first. Hello."

"Hello, beautiful."

"Bye, Spark."

"Bye, wee girl."

Sunshower's small, delicate voice is replaced by Ozzy's booming tones. "I'm goin' to kick your arse, Spark. Sunshower won't stop pesterin' me to get a drum kit. I'm leanin' towards the idea just to shut her up."

"You just made my day, you orange-heided wonder!"

"Don't get too excited. I'm no' rejoinin' the band. Think aboot it – what would happen to Sunshower when we tour? Journey pointed oot on *Faithfully* that the road is no place to start a family. Equally, it's no place to raise a wee girl."

"Oz, the band hasn't even cut a demo yet. One thing at a time, eh big boy?"

"Another thing I've been thinkin' aboot is DT. If the band takes off, and that's a gigantic *if*, Dave'll be aroon' drugs. Puttin' him in that situation's askin' for trouble."

"Dave has more money than the rest o' the band combined. If he wanted drugs he'd be buyin' them in copious amounts, but he's not. I've spent a lot of time wi' him recently. He's as clean as a whistle."

"Maybe so, but his current work environment is far removed from livin' high on the hog wi' a tourin' heavy metal band. I think immersin' Dave in metal again is throwin' a wolf among the chickens."

"I disagree, Oz. Dave is no wolf. Drugs were the wolves and he was a chicken. He paid his dues - seven years locked in the chicken coop. Noo he's a free-range chicken wi' no desire to go back to the coop."

"Spark, can we stop wi' the chicken metaphors?"

"You started it, orange heid! My metaphors were incisive."

Metallic Dreams

In a move which both surprises and invigorates me, Oz bursts into song. "Back to the coop! You will lay when I say you must lay! Back to the coop! Fear the pie when I say you must die! Back to the coop! You chicken! You squawker! You focker!" Recognising an improvised *Disposable Heroes*, one of Metallica's most bombastic songs, I join my blood brother for a rousing end to the chorus. "Back to the cooooooooooooop!" We fall apart laughing, hundreds of miles apart but together.

"Oz, I understand your concerns over DT, but there's nothin' to worry aboot on that front. How come you're such a worrier noo? What happened to the light-hearted giant wi' the heart full o' dreams?" No sooner have I said the words than I wish I could take them back. Cringing, I wait for a reply. It is a long wait.

"You know what happened, Spark." Ozzy's voice is softer, sadder. "My dreams used to be like big, soft, beautiful clouds. Those clouds turned into dangerous, unpredictable bastard-tornadoes that ripped me to shreds, and still do, daily."

"Sunshower's your proof of the beauty o' dreams. You can either give life your best shot or live in fear and regret it later."

"I know you're right, but it's not easy. Do you have *Bloody Kisses* by Type O Negative?"

"Aye. Excellent album. Dark, melodic genius."

"Do you remember what it says on the inside cover?"

"If memory serves, it says *No Hope = No Fear*."

"Do you know how much sense that idea makes to me?"

"You sound nihilistic, Oz. I want to see your optimistic smile again. You're not made of darkness and doom. That's not your inner nature. You know that, I know that, and Sunshower knows it too. She sees into your depths and loves the beautiful soul that's locked in a cage."

"Spark, I'm *tryin'*," Oz sobs. "I really am."

"I know, big boy. I apologise for my lack of tact earlier."

"You're no' renowned for your tact."

"True. And we're no' renowned for oor music, but it's time to change that. Ted, the bassist in my American pals' band, is in Europe. I've convinced him to come up to Scotland for a couple o' days, to play bass wi' us. You and Sunshower could come too. Even if you don't want to play drums, you could just hang oot and soak up the band vibe again."

"I don't think so."

"I have faith that you'll do the right thing."

"You sound like a preacher."

"I am a preacher. I'M THE PREACHER AT THE CHURCH OF HEAVY METAL AND A VESSEL FOR MESSIANIC METALLIC ENTITIES. YOU ARE, ALAN OSWALDO - EVEN IF YOU'RE AFRAID TO ADMIT IT - ONE O' MY CONGREGATION!" Like a baddie in a James Bond movie, I force a maniacal laugh.

"You do realise," Oz observes, "that you're no' right in the heid?"

"I do, aye. I'll call you in a couple o' days. Please tell Sunshower that I love her."

"She already knows."

"Just tell her anyway, pumpkin-heid."

"I'll tell her. Bye the noo."

"Bye."

After hanging up the phone, I make a mental note to learn at least a primitive understanding of tact, something of which I appear to have none.

Desk Sergeant McBride answers the phone at Bronzehall police office. The woman on the other end of the line is babbling in unintelligible fashion. Using calming techniques he learned at police training college, McBride manages to slow the woman's speech to a level where he can decipher most of her words. When the woman says that her boyfriend has filled her in, McBride thinks he must have misheard. "Please miss," he interrupts, "you're not making a lot of sense. Your boyfriend can't have filled you in. If he had, you wouldn't be phoning me to tell me about it, primarily due to being dead. Murdered people tend to shy away from making calls to report the offence."

The woman continues to rant, her voice becoming more high-pitched. Slowly and gently, McBride asks her to summarise the problem. "My boyfriend has filled my vagina wi' Polyfilla and the fuckin' stuff has hardened!"

Desk Sergeant McBride likes to talk. He has never, ever been lost for words. Until now. He flirts with the idea of hanging up and pretending that the call never happened. The crazy woman would, he decides, just call back again. McBride decides that the best thing to do is stay on the phone and say nothing. He was taught nothing about this in training college. Murders, assaults, rapes, breaches of the peace, drug offences, speeding cars, reckless drivers, crowd control, police dogs and horses – all these things he can handle. Polyfilla-filled vaginas, however, are definitely not his domain.

"Hello! Is anyone there? Did you fuckin' well hear what I said?"

McBride realises that her profanity could be construed as a breach of the peace. He toys with the idea of booking her on that charge, tracing the call and sending a couple of officers to her home address to arrest her. That could be, he thinks, a simple end to an awkward situation. Such a course of action would not solve the woman's Polyfilla situation, though. Also, Police calls are recorded, and ignoring the alleged assault would not be viewed kindly by his employers. "Ehhh…miss…ehm, I understand that you must be in distress over the…ehm…odd use of DIY paraphernalia. I'm not sure, however, what law your boyfriend has broken, if any. Police policy is not to get involved in domestic disputes, especially those involving DIY accessories. In all my years on the force, there has been only one exception to that policy, when a Vikingwood man panned his wife's head in with a hammer, making it murder and hence, very definitely, a police matter."

"It's fuckin' rape! My fanny's sealed shut! I'm burstin' for a piss and it cannae get oot!"

"Please stay calm, miss. I understand your distress. Technically, for it to be rape, your boyfriend would have had to insert his…err…penis into you without your consent. I suppose if he penetrated you with a finger or toe, or one of those women's pleasure-giving devices it may perhaps be construed as rape. No part of the rape law mentions home-improvement materials, though. Maybe you should go to A&E at Valfader Hospital."

"I want that fuckin' lunatic Paul Roberts locked up!"

"Miss, if you give me all the relevant information I will speak to my superiors about your allegations. In the meantime, I suggest that you take some photographs of the…ehm…scene of the crime. That will be handy evidence if the case goes to court."

"That's your advice? Take photos of my fanny?"

"Yes, miss. That is my advice. Take photos then go directly to hospital and let medical professionals deal with your…ehm…situation."

After giving Desk Sergeant McBride her details, Janine orders a taxi for Valfader Hospital.

A junior reporter from *The Bronzehall Gazette* wanders into the police station and finds a huddle of senior officers in loud dispute over what sounds like a very delicate situation. Desk Sergeant McBride greets the well-dressed young journalist with practised professionalism. The reporter asks if there are any breaking stories.

There may be, Desk Sergeant McBride confirms, a doozy of a story.

Chapter 40 – Afraid of Sunlight

DT's farmhouse is basking in moonbeams as I ascend its driveway with Skyclad's *Moongleam & Meadowsweet* playing on the car stereo. Saxon appears at the living room window and watches as I lift my BC Rich Warlock guitar out of the boot. It could be my imagination, but the instrument seems to be quietly seething tonight: meditating before unleashing untold riff-laden mayhem. When DT opens the door, we exchange easy smiles but say nothing. I open the living-room door and find Saxon charging at it like a golden bull. His angled-down head slams into my abdomen with the force of a battering ram, knocking me off my feet. The dog pounces, pins me to the floor with powerful paws and licks my face. "Thanks for the wet welcome, golden boy," I splutter. "I'm happy to see you too."

Dave fires up a pot of Monsooned Malabar coffee while Saxon and I wrestle in the spacious living room. On a mahogany coffee table lies *The Bronzehall Gazette*, its front-page headline posing the question, 'BIZARRE DIY ACCIDENT OR DELIBERATE SEXUAL ASSAULT?' It strikes me as the kind of nonsense more suited to the *National Enquirer*. I reach out to pick up the paper, then change my mind and continue playing with my canine friend instead.

Ted Watkin's train approaches Paris just before sunset. Prior to today, he imagined Paris to be full of pretentious pricks and arrogant arseholes. Now, gliding into the city and viewing it through a train window, he is filled with a sense of humble awe, like an artist arriving at the spiritual home of art. As he exits the train and walks onto bustling city streets, strange lyrics and melodies arrange themselves in his mind. He pulls out an A4 pad, sits on a paving slab, and scribbles down words and music as they stream into his head. This, he thinks, is what it means to be inspired.

Ted has been studying music since he was six. His contributions to Fatal Visionary's repertoire have been calculated pieces of precision instrumentation. Until now, music has been a largely academic and mathematical exercise for him. Today, emotional and symbolic understanding of sound floods his mind. On a Parisienne pavement he sits, honey-coloured hair tumbling over his smiling face while he transcribes words and symbols with passion. He doesn't hear the sounds of passing high-heeled shoes clicking on stone; his mind is elsewhere. He is the minstrel possessed, sprawled on the ground, all shining grin, wild hair and fast-flashing pen.

Feeling that it has been too long since he voyaged into the outside world, Pete Drummond stares through his living-room window. For the last few years the Internet has been his main connection to the world, allowing him to download music and movies, to order books and CDs, and to keep tabs on world news. He understands the plight of people so overweight that they are confined to one room of their house. Food is their demon. Pete, too, has his personal demon: the King of Demons. For years after the demise of Blood Brothers, Pete felt sure that the Devil had lost interest in his soul. That certainty crumbled one night when Pete awoke from a nightmare to discover blazing eyes above him and taloned hands fumbling inside his chest. He hurled himself sideways out of bed, but those otherworldly hands ripped something out of Pete: his confidence. The experience shook him up so much that he moved out of his parents' house and into this flat, which he turned into his hallowed ground, surrounded on all sides by occult protection. Here he has remained, writing soundtracks for theatre and film, always inside these walls. His most recent works are sonic pastiches of struggle against oppressive supernatural elements: reflections of his life, externalisations of his dark inner emotions.

Dressed only in faded jeans, Pete lights a Marlboro. The door-knocker raps out the opening rhythm of *Flaming Eyes,* one of Pete's movie scores. He walks along the narrow black-painted hallway and peeks through a peephole on the front door. Satisfied with what he sees, Pete opens the door. "Come in, baby."

A tall, svelte woman enters carrying two bags of supplies. As she swishes to the kitchen, Pete gives her shapely legs a long stare. Lisa Doune has been his godsend throughout recent years. Lisa ditches the shopping bags on a worktop and switches on the kettle. "Petey, are you OK? You look fragile. More fragile than usual, I mean."

"I've had enough o' this agoraphobia bullshit. It's more than agoraphobia. It's also demonophobia or Satanophobia. What would you call that combination of neuroses? Agorademonophobia? Satanagoraphobia? Maybe just plain off ma heid, eh?"

Lisa blinks back tears. "Don't say that, darlin'. You're a tortured soul, as all geniuses are, but I'm by your side through it all."

"I know, Lise, and I love you. Recently, these walls have been pressin' in on me. I've been feelin' claustrophobic but also achin' to go oot into the world. A claustrophobic agoraphobe. What does that make me? Agorademonoclaustrophobic? A fucked-in-the-heid screwup."

"We'll get through this, baby," Lisa promises. "If the Devil exists I don't know what he would want wi' a sensitive soul like you. I'm sure he must have other fish to fry."

"I think the Devil preys on sensitive souls. Rough, tough bastards are too much hard work for him. They're difficult to break. The blue-bridge incident was real. You've seen the burn that bastard left me wi'. And what aboot the night he reached inside me to rip oot my soul while I was sleepin'? That wasn't a dream."

"I know what you think happened that night, baby boy, but it was a vivid nightmare, your imagination."

"I didnae fuckin' imagine it! I hadn't been drinkin' absinthe or some other hallucinogenic crap! I was *there*. It was *real*."

"I want to believe you, Petey, but it's hard."

"I know, Lise. I love you for tryin'. I love you, period."

"By the way, I just saw Spark at the shops. I wasn't willin' to answer questions aboot you, so I avoided him. Lying isn't my forté. He would have been able to tell a mile away that I was hidin' something."

"I miss the Blood Brothers, even though I was never truly one o' them. I was the fifth wheel, the only one in the band who didn't do the blood ritual. Every day, I stare oot o' this flat and wonder where those wild dudes are and what they're up to. I couldn't face them, though. You're the only one I can face. You're pure."

Lisa pins Pete against the wall and kisses him with passion, smearing red lipstick over his mouth. She giggles at the effect then wipes his face clean with tender fingertips. "I'm glad you got over your fear of sex," she whispers.

"I had a good teacher."

"Your agorademonoclaustrophobia I can deal with, but if you were sexophobic I'd have to shoot myself. You're the sexiest man in the Universe, and the most talented." Pete doesn't feel deserving of either title, but he knows that Lisa speaks from her heart. Taking her by the hand, he smiles and leads the way to the bedroom.

Chapter 41 – Drop Dead Legs

I'm in Bronzehall pet shop buying hay for Fluff when the long-legged brunette struts past dressed in a black woollen jacket, above-the-knee skirt, black seamed stockings and high heels. Noticing my wandering eyes and lascivious expression, the female shop assistant glowers at me over the rims of her oval glasses. I delve into my pocket, fish out my last two crumpled notes, pay for the hay and bustle out of the shop.

Grey clouds descend, giving the impression that the sky is falling. The woman moves towards the taxi rank with graceful strides I'm sure I've seen before, a long time ago. As she leaves in a black cab, I jump into my car and follow, the screech of Rustbucket's tyres echoing off stone car-park walls. Several cars are between us, but I manage to keep the cab in view. Ten minutes later, while I'm stuck behind a Ford Mondeo a red traffic light, the taxi pulls up outside a three-storey block of flats in Valfader. Helpless, I watch as the woman enters the building. The traffic lights turn green. I roar into the street and skid to a halt outside the flats. Looking up, I get a clear view of the woman's face through the second-floor stairwell window. *Lisa.* Older but no less beautiful.

I sprint into the building and leap up stairs four at a time. A discordant pattern of knocks is followed by the sound of a door opening and a familiar voice saying, "Come in, baby." *Pete!* I reach the second floor as Pete's door slams shut. I stare at its black surface for long minutes. It will be best to speak to Pete when he's alone. No distractions. No Lisa. In no hurry, I walk back down the stairs and head out into the rain. Good things take time, and I have no time for rejections or reunions right now. London is calling.

DT has transferred £200 from his bank account into mine to cover the costs of my Ted-collecting trip to London. He views this not as money lost, but as an investment in our band's future. It will, we hope, pay for itself many times over.

I drive to the local garage, withdraw £50 from the hole in the wall and fill up the petrol tank of my (t)rusty steed. After paying for my fuel, I do an impromptu tribal dance on the forecourt, praying to the Metal Gods (and to any others who may be listening) that car and driver make it to London intact. Then, in a crossfire of quizzical stares from onlookers, and with Megadeth blasting from car speakers, I head out on my pilgrimage.

Chapter 42 – Hiway Nights

Megadeth's precise speed metal fills the car as it hurtles south at a velocity not just in excess of the speed limit, but likely to make the vehicle fall to bits. Once a mighty metal steed, my BMW is now held together by rust and prayers. Megadeth is the perfect soundtrack to this road trip: I'm no stranger to falling asleep at the wheel during long drives, but it's almost impossible to fall asleep to Megadeth. *Mechanix* announces its arrival with staccato, lightspeed riffs. Dave Mustaine wrote the track during his time in Metallica, before Megadeth's inception. Metallica and Megadeth both have versions of the song on their debut albums. Metallica's song, *The Four Horsemen*, plods like a mid-paced metal behemoth, while Megadeth's rendition, *Mechanix*, surfs into your ears on waves of sheer speed then proceeds to kick the shit out of your brain before bursting out through the eyeballs, leaving you grinning in disbelieving ecstasy. Metallica's version is an easy guitar warm-up, but Megadeth's is serious fretboard speed training.

I wonder if Ted can play with Megadethesque speed and dexterity. Fatal Visionary is a speed metal band, so it's likely that he is a scorching bass player with scary technical abilities. It will be an endorphin rush to play alongside him, and a novelty too, since Blood Brothers has never had a bass player who actually *plays*.

On the cruise through England's lush Lake District and beyond, all my favourite Megadeth tracks get aired. *In My Darkest Hour, Tornado of Souls, Mechanix, Peace Sells…But Who's Buying?, Symphony of Destruction, Crush 'em, Boots, Rust in Peace…Polaris, Into the Lungs of Hell*: riff-laden slices of lacerating, laser-sharp sonic mastery.

London is a shithole of a place in which to drive, and today reminds me why. When I was in my teens, the main obstacle to enjoyable London driving was traffic; the city was a gigantic, perpetual traffic jam. Now, not content with achieving an unparalleled level of congestion, London has added mass confusion into the mix: lanes exclusively for buses; lanes for taxis; lanes for cars carrying more than one person; other lanes with symbols I've never seen. I scrutinise hieroglyphic instructions on the road then give up and decide to make my own rules. A bus lane appears to be the fastest route to my destination, so I swerve into it and put the foot down.

Amid horn-hooting and hand gestures from irate bus drivers, *Mary Jane* animates Rustbucket's inner world, motivating me to show my red-faced antagonists my repertoire of cathartic hand signals: dickhead; fellater; wank; fuck you; victory; and, of course, Devil horns. Fuck 'em. I'm not doing any harm by driving in a bus lane. Folk down here have become so hypnotised by man-made patterns on the road that they've forgotten how to think for themselves. Painted symbols don't dictate my path. An old Chinese monk in Kongxiang Zen Temple once told me that going through life without control over the emotions is like driving a fast car without a steering wheel. This idea seems lost on most London drivers.

I have no clear memories of Ted from my time in the United States. He belonged to the anonymous throngs who walked the high-school halls with downturned eyes, happy to blend in with lockers and carpet, unseen and unnoticed. I'm expecting his hair to be longer than in the yearbook photo, but I'm not prepared for the windswept figure who strides towards my car. Long hair billows as he walks, as if a wind machine is aimed at his tanned face. Mirrored sunglasses cover his eyes, presumably to cover the bloodshot evidence of last night's excesses. Black leather trousers cling tightly to long legs. An old Holy Terror T-shirt hangs loose on his torso. Pointed snakeskin boots clack against broken paving slabs as he struts with the confidence of a musician who has spent decades mastering his craft.

Ted's transformation since high school is radical. He has gone from meek music nerd to rock 'n' roll star with consummate style. Opening the car's passenger door, he leans in and asks, "What's happening, Spark? It's good to hear that you have taste in music, even though your social skills are lacking to the point of non-existence." He flashes a grin. I sense nothing hidden behind it: no malice; no hidden agenda; no uncertainty. This man knows why he's on the planet.

"Thanks for the back-handed semi-compliment, redneck. Your grammatical abilities appear to have improved. You just used two well-constructed sentences in a row. Congratulations."

We stare at each other in silence for a moment, after which Ted says, "Touché, asshole." He throws his suitcase into the boot, lays his bass guitar's flight case across the back seat, then climbs into the passenger seat. Noticing my interest in his flight case, he says, "My bass, a Rickenbacker."

"Like Lemmy's?"

"The very same. You know your metal trivia."

"Inside oot and upside doon. Heavy metal is my religion and I'm the most pious son of a bitch you ever met."

"It's weird that you mention music as religion. I had what I'd describe as a religious experience in Paris. Music flowed through me like water through a fountain. I transcribed it all in musical notation. I'll play it for you once we reach your peasant country."

"I look forward to it."

As we carve north, Ted and I share easy, unforced talk laced with a healthy dose of good-natured taunting. The energy exchange between us is good, with just the right amount of conflict to make conversation funny but not aggressive. A premature sense of loss shoots through me as I contemplate only having the bass redneck at my disposal for a couple of days. I sense that my band could achieve great things with him, given the time. Nevertheless, if all goes according to plan, he will prove to be a useful tool.

Ted slides a Fatal Visionary CD into the car stereo. Their technical metal is staggering: blast-beat drums, rumbling bass, lightspeed twin guitars and bowel-dissolving vocals. Their music is a spring clean to the mind.

Yngwie J. Malmsteen would shit his pants and hang up his Stratocaster if he heard them.

I flash a glance across at my passenger. He doesn't look proud of his band's music. He appears to be weighing it up academically. From the expression on his face, I guess that he would grade it B+, a humility which endears him to me. I doubt that anyone plays faster than Fatal Visionary, but there's a cold, clinical feel to their music. There is no airspace, no light and shade, just heaviness. Perhaps Ted's numinous experience in Paris was emotion smashing through layers of thrash metal academia and into the deeper recesses of his soul.

"I have a feelin' you'll get on well with DT," I tell Ted.

"Isn't he the guy who smashed his guitar over a heckler's head?"

"Aye. The heckler was oor bass player's brother."

"I thought you never had a bassist?"

"We had a guy who pretended to play bass."

Ted looks bewildered. "Do I have to explain to you how Spinal Täp that sounds?"

"No, dude, you don't. Iain's heid was firmly in the clouds. We always hoped he would buy a bass and learn to play, but he never did. That, my American speed-merchant brother, is where you come in." Ted stares into the orange sunset and nods. As we pass a small English lake, he asks if it is Loch Ness. He repeats the question every time we pass a body of water. I begin to feel the way parents of small children must feel when, during long car trips, their children continually ask, 'Are we *there* yet?' After explaining that Loch Ness is in the Highlands of Scotland, several hundred miles north of our current location in the heart of England, I suggest that Ted should wait until we're in the right country before asking again. He slides mirrored sunglasses down his nose, peers at me over their top, then flips up his middle finger. Fatal Visionary's music continues to shake the car's shell.

I ask Ted about Kimberley Setzer. Does he know where she lives? Does she talk of me? Is she involved with anyone? Does she have children? What is she doing with her life? He doesn't have any answers. Word is, he says, that when I returned to Scotland it broke her heart. *And my heart too.*

Night falls as we approach the border. Dark motorway stretches ahead, lit only by green cats' eyes dotted to infinity. To make up for shooting down the heavy metal redneck's Nessie-related exuberance, I pull into a service station in a scenic wooded area to buy us coffee and cake.

As Ted heads to the bathroom, I find a payphone, pull a tattered scrap of paper from my wallet, press a pound into the phone's coin slot, dial the number that's scrawled on the paper, then hold my breath and hope for the best. After seven rings, a soft female voice says, "Hi, you've reached Angel. You know the drill. Leave your details after the beep, bla, bla, yada, yada. If you're extremely lucky and your planets are perfectly aligned, I'll phone you back." Beep.

"Angel, it's Spark. I met you after the gig the other night. If you still want to try fittin' my sausage into your undoubtedly delicious pie, phone me." Not the most romantic message ever left on an answerphone, but short and to the point. Norman MacCaig would be proud of my brevity. Moments later, on realising that I forgot to leave my phone number, I call Angel again and leave a second message.

When Ted and I wander into the café, staff faces visibly drop, their expressions conveying that ordering pots of coffee and Danish pastries at this hour of the night has exposed Ted and me as a pair of lawless rascals. We sit at a window overlooking a pond where ducks float across murky water, metallic-green-headed adults in front, brown fluffy babies behind. Ted takes a bite of his Danish and gazes at the serene scene. "Before you ask," I explain, "those are ducks. Not plesiosaurs, sea serpents or Loch Ness monsters. Wee ducks."

Clutching his stomach, Ted fakes a silent belly laugh then disposes of the rest of his Danish pastry in one bite, his cheeks puffing out like those of an over-ambitious hamster. When he leans back and rests booted feet on the seat opposite, a fat, bespectacled man emerges from behind a till. Pointing at Ted's boots, he barks, "Feet off the seat, son!"

Without looking up, Ted takes a loud slurp of his coffee, gulps it down, then says in a deep Virginia drawl, "Buddy, I'm a payin' customer who is tryin' to relax here after days of travelling. My friend and I are patrons of your café, yet you and your staff have made us as welcome as paedophiles in a kindergarten. Your corporate motto should be 'Service with a scowl'. If you don't get out of my personal space, I'll be shovin' this pointed snakeskin boot directly up your candyass." Too cool to acknowledge his antagonist visually, Ted keeps his mirrored gaze fixed dead ahead.

"Fucking hippies," the man mumbles, backing away from the table. "I don't get paid enough to deal with this shit." He picks up a phone at the till and dials a three-digit number.

I tell Ted to drink up, that it's time to leave. We have music to play, plans to set in motion and arrests to avoid. Seconds later, Rustbucket is speeding north. As a 'Welcome to Scotland' sign emerges out of the horizon, blue flashing lights appear in the rearview mirror. The police car gains rapidly, flashing high-beam lights and sounding its siren. Even when the pursuers are dangerously close to my back bumper, I don't stop. Only after crossing the border into Scotland do I pull over onto the hard shoulder. Hands on batons, two police officers approach my car. The older cop is a jowly, overweight man of about fifty, who looks uncannily like the cartoon character Droopy. He gestures with his baton for me to lower my window. I buzz it open a crack. Droopy says, "I understand that you two individuals caused a commotion back at the motorway services."

"That's untrue, officer. We ate Danish pastries and drank coffee. If anyone was oot o' line, it was the people who run that café. Eleven quid for two coffees and two wee cakes? That's where the expression 'Highway Robbery' comes from."

Droopy looks unconvinced. "The service station's manager called us and said that two hairy gentlemen, who match the description of you and your passenger, had committed a breach of the peace." Droopy's younger, thinner sidekick looks conscientiously at his feet, happy to stay out of proceedings.

"What constitutes a breach o' the peace?" I ask.

"Technically, any type of anti-social behaviour that makes another human being feel uneasy."

"In that case, I contend that the manager and his staff are the criminals. They charged exorbitant prices for their meagre sustenance, then acted as if they were doin' us a favour by robbin' us. From the moment we entered their establishment, they were anti-social and made us feel unwelcome. The manager was so rude that my friend decided to give him a taste of his own medicine, but he did so withoot violence or vandalism. In fact, my friend didn't even make eye contact."

"I find that story hard to believe," says Droopy. "You two look like exactly the kind of rockstar pricks who throw televisions out of hotel windows and smash up roadside cafés."

"Officer," I spit, "I want the badge numbers of your chubby self and your underfed sidekick. The nonsense you just spouted is unacceptable and prejudiced. The rockers you're talkin' aboot get driven in luxury tour buses and limos. They don't drive themselves aboot in vehicles so rusty they could disintegrate into a heap of component parts at the next bump in the road."

Officer Sidekick raises his head for the first time. He frowns at Droopy, who continues to stare me out. What these cops don't know is that I've never lost a stareout. (Once, while reading Michael Moore's *Downsize This*, I went without blinking for eleven minutes just to disprove Moore's contention that anyone who blinks less frequently than once every two minutes must be an alien.) "I would strongly urge you to stop giving me the eye," warns Droopy. "It tends to precede a lengthy stay in hospital."

Still staring at my antagonist, I snarl, "You just crossed the border into Scotland, you fat cartoon fuck. Even if your claims contained a grain of truth - and they do not - you have no jurisdiction here. Scotland is a warrior nation and I come from a long line of badass Scottish bastards. My father was a Highland Games professional in his youth, as was his father before him. Either o' them would have picked you up and tossed you across this motorway like a chubby caber. Luckily for you, I've got more control over my temper. Make no mistake, though, if you say one more fuckin' word I'll get oot o' this car and you'll be cannon fodder. And please put your dildo back in its holster. You'll need a lot more than that to knock me oot."

Metallic Dreams

In my peripheral vision I see Ted's jaw drop. Officer Sidekick's face morphs into that of a blow-up doll: mouth open in characteristic 'O' shape, as if an electrical probe has been shoved up his arse and switched on. Droopy's left cheek starts to twitch. He opens his mouth as if to speak, but no words come out. As the stareout continues, anger boils in Droopy's eyes. I gaze back, Zenlike, daring him to call my bluff. He blinks. I stamp on the accelerator pedal. Rustbucket lunges forwards, spraying dust over the stunned cops who shrink in the rearview mirror until they are specks in the distance…and then nothing.

"That was fuckin' great," Ted enthuses, "like Braveheart, man! What was that bit about, *'I am a warrior from a warrior nation'*? That was phenomenal. You have cojones as big as basketballs, man – serious balls." In a mock-Scottish accent, he spouts, "Ah'm fae a warrior nation, so dinnae darken me wi' your fat shadow again or ah'll shove that police baton up your chubby arse! We are the Gods of the Infernal Haggis and we cannae lose a fight!" Rustbucket hurtles ever north, filled with the sound of laughter.

Whether we jam tonight or not, I want Ted and DT to meet. Once some personal chemistry has been created, musical chemistry will follow. As Rustbucket draws up outside Dave's farmhouse, a golden beast runs in front of the headlights then recedes into the darkness. "That," I tell Ted, "is the Loch Ness monster. Only joking. That's Saxon, Dave's puppy."

"*Puppy?* That thing's a fuckin' polar bear! It's enormous!"

"*He* is enormous. If you call Saxon *it*, he'll get upset. And upsettin' him is not a good idea." As I step out of the car, Saxon plants his front paws on my shoulders and gives my cheek a vertical slurp. I embrace my hairy friend, scratch behind his ears, then carefully lay his paws down on wet stone. Ted remains in the car, shaking his head in a movement I interpret as, 'I'm *not* getting out of the car to be attacked by *that*.' Noticing that the farmhouse door is ajar, I lead Saxon into the kitchen, then motion to Ted that it's safe to come in. On entering, the redneck gushes, "Now *this* is what I imagined a house in Scotland to look like. Thick stone walls, iron-and-wood interior, fields and forest all around."

From above, a voice announces, in grandiose style worthy of Count Dracula, "Welcome to my humble abode! You will stay a while, yes?" A clean-shaven DT, reeking of Fahrenheit aftershave, descends the spiral staircase in tight red leather trousers, black motorcycle boots and a white sleeveless T-shirt with a flaming heart on the front. Fifteen years have dropped off him in as many days. It's amazing what losing a gigantic beard (which could have been habitat to several species of woodland animal) and refinding lost faith can do for a dude. "Cool pair o'strides," says Ted, without sarcasm.

Flashing his far-too-white smile, DT replies, "Nice snakeskin boots."

"May I please interrupt this mutual fashion-admiration extravaganza," I interject, "before it veers into all-oot arsebanditry? There's coffee to be drunk and riffs to be born."

"Ya cheeky wee shite," DT cackles. "You go and make the coffee, since you're far too unfashionable to be included in this conversation anyway. Ted and I will adjourn to the living room and get to know each other."

Stamping one foot, I raise my right arm in a Nazi salute and adopt my best Third Reich voice. "Heil Tierney! I vill get right onto my coffee-making duties und leave you two girls to svap fashion ideas. You vill probably be giving each ozher hair-care und fellatio tips by ze time I arrive vith ze beverages."

In the kitchen, while waiting for the Monsooned Malabar coffee to filter, I wrestle with Saxon and end up covered in dog-drool. When I deliver the tray loaded with coffee and plain-chocolate digestives to the living room, Ted and DT announce that tonight will be dedicated to hanging out, relaxing and talking. If we were to start jamming now, DT explains, it would end up lasting all night, and he has an important meeting in the morning. It feels like the right time to inform DT that I have tracked down Pete. Unsurprised by the news but eloquent as always, he barks, "Get the wee fucker for tomorrow's session in the studio."

When the subject of band management arises, Ted informs us that Fatal Visionary recently hired a new manager: an old school friend from Virginia called Todd McTagger (whom I once called Hold McTadger during an argument over places in the lunch queue). Todd worked for a music PR company, moved from there into A&R, and for the last five years has been in artist management. His hard-nosed attitude helped him to break several metal bands into the big leagues. Within six months of being hired by Fatal Visionary, Todd had secured them a contract with an independent record label and had lined up gigs in thirty-seven of the fifty states. Most of these were support slots with established metal acts, but on their tri-state Delaware/Maryland/Virginia home turf, Fatal Visionary had a solid enough reputation to sell out headline shows. They were able to quit their jobs and concentrate on their first love: writing and playing music.

DT and I look at each other and share a telepathic moment. Our band is only 40% complete, but that's a technical detail, and one we will remedy even if it means facing Hell and high water. Above and beyond our self-belief is something else. I feel invisible runes scattering. The Universe is coming into alignment for us, clearing space for our imminent arrival. Our time is coming. I *feel* it.

Suddenly, I realise who our band manager has to be. Paul Roberts grew up two doors down from me in the same block of Vikingwood terraced houses. We were inseparable friends until his family moved to Bahrain when I was ten. During the formative years of Blood Brothers, Paul was browning under a Middle Eastern sun. Aged twenty, he moved back to Bronzehall and came straight to my house with an ice-cold glass bottle of Irn-Bru under each arm. Orange liquid flowed, Alice in Chains's debut album spun on my father's Linn record deck and excited words were exchanged. We dissolved ten years in as many minutes.

I propose Paul as band manager. Scowling, DT storms out of the room. He returns holding a newspaper. "Is *that* the dude you're suggesting should steer oor band?" he asks, tossing the paper at me. "Say it ain't so."

I recognise the headline, having seen it here before and chosen not to read the story. As my eyes flick over the front page, I realise that the star of the story is indeed my lifelong friend Paul Roberts, not a namesake. The age, address and location all fit, as does the photo. Paul's girlfriend alleges that he sealed her vagina shut with a Polyfilla/Superglue mixture. In response to the accusations, he is quoted as saying, "The girl went nuts. She drank herself into oblivion, attempted to take my head off with a gin bottle, then filled her fat fanny with multi-purpose surface filler, intent on blaming it on me. Based on the diameter of that particular cavity, it probably required three tubes of the stuff. I was framed. I wouldn't touch her minge with a bargepole, never mind wasting my DIY materials on her. I have a good mind to start a countersuit or, at the very least, to fill her big mouth with Polyfilla so I won't have to listen to her squawking any more." Beneath the story is a photo of Paul looking as though he has just fallen out of bed: black hair shooting out of his head at unplanned angles; an expression of sleepy confusion on his face; mouth hanging open as if wanting to speak but waiting on vital instructions from a bewildered brain.

At first I'm stunned, but when the initial shock wears off I start to laugh, tickled by the story's preposterousness. Paul's no-holds-barred (no holes barred?) response beats the hell out of the nonsense that usually fills the Bronzehall rag.

I throw Ted the paper to let him read the story. Soon, he too is in floods of laughter. Shaking his head, DT says, "How's that funny, ya cruel pricks? Havin' an orifice plugged is no laughin' matter!"

Times have changed. As a child, DT was El Sicko. He revelled in other people's misfortunes. Perhaps in prison he had orifices stuffed, unconsensually and unceremoniously. His sense of humour is as intact as ever, but the sickness has been sucked out of it, leaving it purer and more innocent. I conclude that - unlikely as it seems - DT and compassion have become acquainted.

Chapter 43 – Electro-Violence

A winter sun blazes in the cyan sky above Pete's flat. Staring at it for as long as my retinas can handle, I see solar flares curling into space, torching anything unfortunate enough to lie in their paths. The part of planet Earth on which I stand, however, feels no evidence of the nuclear furnace in the sky. Here, all is frozen. Older Scottish natives who have lived through world wars describe days like this as *crisp* or *fresh*. I describe days like this as *fuckin' freezing*.

    A grizzled old man in a long houndstooth coat and flat woollen cap shuffles along the pavement towards me. His slow, deliberate steps make delicious crunching noises on frost-covered stone. Eyes like moons look out from his deeply lined face. Smiling, he observes, "It's crisp today, eh?" I recognise it as a rhetorical question; he doesn't want to chat about the weather. Bowing to his experience, I nod my head.

    I bound upstairs to Pete's flat, hoping that the brisk movement will warm my body. It doesn't. A glass peephole fisheyes out from the door, offering a distorted view of a hallway in which hundreds of weird symbols are carved on black walls. Eye to the glass, I bang my fist twice against the door. A spindly figure in boxer shorts flashes into view at the far end of the hall, then disappears. I bang the door again. A minute passes. The figure reappears, this time in blue jogging trousers and a T-shirt. He darts along the narrow hallway with jerky diagonal movements, as if dodging gunfire. A turquoise eye jams itself to the other side of the peephole. Eyes separated by only a thin layer of glass, we wait.

    The door doesn't open.

    Crouching down, I open the letterbox and shout, "It's Spark! I need to talk!" A buzzing sound starts inside the flat. I grab the door handle to try it. Pain erupts up my arm. Involuntary muscle contractions force my grip closed tighter than a vice. I feel my bodily juices starting to boil. Alien sounds spew from my mouth. Then, as suddenly as the torture started, the pain ceases and my grip relaxes.

    After staggering back to the car, I take a pad and red felt pen out of the glove compartment. My violated right hand refuses to function, so I write the note with my left. Soon, I'm the proud owner of a blood-red message that looks as though it was written by a deranged five-year-old with killing on his mind.

'PETE - BLOOD BROTHERS ARE PLAYING IN THE STUDIO TONIGHT AND TOMORROW NIGHT FROM 8P.M. UNTIL MIDNIGHT. PLEASE COME.'

    I want to add something about the electro-torture, but writing left-handed is difficult so I stick to the bare essentials. Plus, I *need* Pete. The band needs him. Criticism of his extreme home security measures won't motivate him to get re-involved with the band.

Outside Pete's door, I tentatively touch the letterbox to check for voltage. To my relief, it's not live. I lift the flap and drop my note through with a tingling hand.

Chapter 44 – Get Workin'

Ted and I arrive at Bronzehall recording studio half an hour early. When Colin, the studio's owner, greets me with a strong handshake, I realise that full sensation has returned to my right hand: no excuses for bad guitar playing, then. In addition to producing albums by myriad musical artists, Colin has played as a session drummer with several big-name acts and has toured extensively with his own band. His appearance is worlds away from that of the metal monsters who have hired his studio: neatly pressed beige trousers; blue button-up shirt; silver hair trimmed short and brushed into a neat side-shed. Colin's face has a weathered look, like treated wood. Small, round glasses give him a bookish air. When I introduce Ted and explain that he is filling in on bass duties for a couple of days, Colin shakes his hand and asks, "Are you a bass mime like Iain Bright? That boy was a lunatic. Excellent at throwing shapes, though. I have to give him that. Every band should have a gimmick, but a fruitcake bass mime's more of a handicap. It's a bit like the Happy Mondays guy Bez, who dances aboot like a tit but doesn't play an instrument or sing. Soaked in style yet lacking substance."

Ted shakes his head. "My bass playing will blow your tiny Scottish peasant mind."

Fearing that Ted may be on his way to a boot in the balls, I interrupt. "What Ted's tryin' to say, Colin, is that he's honoured to be in your studio and that he wants to impress you with his musicianship tonight."

"He won't have to do much to impress me more than your previous 'bass player'. I saw the look in that boy's eyes when he was jumping off amplifiers. He was a loon, a nutjob, a basket case, not the full shilling, et cetera, et cetera. He's the Village Idiot."

Ted nods, his expression indicating that he believes Colin's description of Iain to be truer than mine. "I was classically trained," Ted explains, "so my bass abilities are technical *and* flash."

Colin shakes his head. "Music is all aboot feel, aboot expressing emotion, aboot soul. Some o' your heavy metal compadres play fast, technical music just to prove that they can play fast, technical music. If you play an instrument withoot the burning desire to communicate emotion to the world, you're just wanking. It becomes a self-indulgent activity in which the musician only cares aboot gratifying himself. When I play in front of an audience, I make love to them. There's a world of difference."

As he sets up his gear in the studio, Ted's slickness with amps, cables, effects pedals, and all things powerful and electric becomes obvious. He straps on his bass and begins to play, spinning his head in rapid circles. His long hair swirls like rotor blades. If his head spins any faster, he will surely achieve flight. Ted's left hand blurs across the bass's fretboard, while the fingers of his right pluck out low, gut-dissolving notes.

Colin appears with a tray of coffees. After sipping our steaming potions, we kick off with Metallica's *Fade to Black*. Initially, due to the lack of drums, DT and I have trouble staying in synch. By the end of the track, though, we have stopped listening for drumbeats and begun using Ted's rumbling, bottom-end bass rhythms as our sonic map. I'm happy to see Colin nodding approval. He isn't a metal fan, but he appreciates good musicianship in any form.

During the next three hours, we spend as much time talking as playing. One challenge is finding tracks we all know, other than the back catalogues of Metallica and Megadeth. Ted was weaned on classical music followed by speed, thrash and power metal. After discovering the NWOBHM (New Wave of British Heavy Metal), DT and I soaked up older metal like Rainbow, UFO, Deep Purple and Led Zeppelin. Since those early days, I've opened my mind to music of myriad genres; I hate labelling, as music - like people - can't be boxed. Dave, rather than keeping up with modern developments in metal, has gone back in time to delve into rock ancestry such as Velvet Underground, Iggy Pop, Cream, Blue Cheer, Black Oak Arkansas, Jimi Hendrix and Grand Funk Railroad.

The common ground the three of us discover includes tracks by Megadeth, Alice Cooper, KISS, AC/DC, Judas Priest, Mordred, Queensrÿche, Metallica, Testament, UFO and the Sensational Alex Harvey Band. DT and I are surprised that Ted has heard of Alex Harvey and even more shocked to discover that Fatal Visionary has covered three SAHB tunes during live shows. As Ted plucks the opening bass riffs to SAHB's *Faith Healer*, Colin jumps out of his swivel chair and waves his arms in a frantic attempt to get our attention. He tells us that he knows every Alex Harvey track and offers to fill in on drums. Not ones to look a gift drummer in the mouth, DT and I nod. With Colin in the hotseat, we kick into *Faith Healer* for a second time, following it with *Boston Tea Party* and *Last of the Teenage Idols*, one of my favourite tracks of all time. Colin's drumming lacks the awesome power of Ozzy's, but his timing is perfect and he adds subtle technical flourishes of his own, which always enhance – never detract from – the track as a whole.

Wide smiles dominate our faces by the time we finish jamming. Even the perennially cool Ted can't suppress his grin. Colin reveals that he was a friend of the late, great Alex Harvey, perhaps the most underrated of all the dead rockers. We pack up our gear while Colin prepares another round of hot beverages. He sits atop a Marshall amp and recounts his tales of life on the road with the legend Alex Harvey. Nursing mugs of coffee, DT, Ted and I sit on the floor and listen to Colin's stories like tribesmen gathered around their shaman. I feel like a child soaking up experience from a wise one. It is good to feel that way: open to the possibilities of innovation and sonic perfection.

Chapter 45 – Thunderstruck

Day two of rehearsals. Colin has set up audio-recording equipment. DT's digital camcorder is mounted on a tripod and waiting. Guitars have been restrung and down-tuned. DT arrives dressed in black leather trousers, motorcycle boots and a white puffy shirt with black crisscross ties at the neck, looking like a mixture of Steve Vai and Jack Sparrow. Ted is also wearing black leather trousers, along with snakeskin cowboy boots (which I have yet to see off his feet, even when he sleeps), mirrored sunglasses and a Blind Guardian tour T-shirt. Opting for comfort rather than flashiness, I've dressed in old faded jeans, desert combat boots and a blue tie-dye Mötley Crüe T-shirt. Excitement hangs palpably in the air, sending little electric shocks through me.

Angel arrives in matching metallic-blue mini-skirt, basque and lip gloss, her auburn hair tied in pigtails. DT flashes me a smile and makes a breast-squeezing gesture with his hands. Ted's jaw drops, ruining his carefully cultivated coolness. His mirrored eyes follow Angel as she sashays across the studio, grabs a fistful of my hair and kisses me. When I come up for air, DT gives me the thumbs up while Ted peers over his sunglasses to gain a better view of events, his mouth still hanging open. Colin appears, gives Angel the once over, then introduces himself.

Leaning into my ear, Ted says, "I've been stayin' with you for the last two days and you didn't ever mention a girlfriend, never mind a girlfriend like *that!*" His mirrored sunglasses are perched atop his head, a reflective hairband for his golden locks.

"Technically, she's no' my girlfriend. This is a first date of sorts."

Ted's eyes bulge. "What the hell kinda date is this, man? It's not exactly romantic."

"It was her idea. She wanted to come and check oot the music I play. Will you help me to impress her tonight, compadre?"

"Yes sirree, I surely will."

"How aboot you, Monsieur Tierney? Will you take it up a notch tonight?"

Dave's dark eyes twinkle under the studio lights. "I'm goin' to make an arse of every solo and every riff. I'll make sure we sound shit. Why should you end up wi' that goddess, when my legacy from the night you met her is the horrific memory of that toilet incident…and the prospect o' future psychotherapy bills?"

"Dude," I plead, "please play well and make us look good."

DT cackles. "Never fear, ya wee tool. I'll play my ass off. When that hot bitch sees the way my fingers scorch across the fretboard, she'll want them scorchin' up her skirt to do some high-speed strummin' and fretless friggin'."

"Angel isn't a groupie," I growl. "She doesn't like me for my guitar skills."

"Fuck off," sneers Dave. "She doesn't like you for your sparkling conversation, that's for fuckin' sure. Anyway, enough talk. Let's do this."

Angel and Colin arrive with steaming mugs of coffee as DT, Ted and I warm up with Anthrax's *Madhouse*, which suits my voice perfectly. Low-end vibrations from Ted's bass almost liquify our insides. DT is on breathtaking form. Angel's eyes follow me the whole time, never faltering. Gazing back at her, I shoot sonic fire from my guitar and lust from my eyes.

Ted requests AC/DC's *Gimme a Bullet* next, to get into a slow groove. His bass line is an easy foundation to follow. By the time we hit the second chorus, DT and I are soaring on the high-end of the audible range, while Ted owns the low range.

A roar like a thousand thunderclaps shakes the ground, toppling DT's tripod and leaving the camcorder's lens pointing up Angel's skirt. Dust crumbles from the ceiling. Striplights shake loose from their fastenings and smash on the ground. I learned in Virginia to stand under a door frame during an earthquake, so I motion for the others to follow me to the exit. Like fleeing heroes in a disaster movie, we run in a chain. The wobbling ground tries to throw us off balance, but we make it to the front door upright.

Night has fallen, bringing cold stillness with it. The noise isn't coming from outside the studio. The earthquake is localised within the building. Its epicentre seems to be studio two, a small one used mainly for music lessons.

Curiosity overcoming fear, I rush back inside and peer through the small square window on the door of studio two. What I see on the other side robs my lungs of breath. As apocalyptic booms shake me off my feet, a smile spreads across my face.

Chapter 46 – Screaming for Vengeance

On a clear spring morning in rural Norfolk, a padded envelope drops through the letterbox of a quaint cottage and thuds onto the floor. The sound wakes Iain Bright, who mumbles incoherently as he stumbles downstairs naked. As a child, Iain was chubby. Daily badminton training during his teens trimmed off the fat, leaving him leaner and fitter than at any time before or since. Since giving up badminton, he has lifted a lot of weights, done countless underwater scuba explorations and eaten mountains of food, all of which are reflected in his physique: he is compact and densely muscled, with a layer of excess fat that somehow suits him.

Iain rubs fists into sleepy eyes, yawns, stretches, farts, sneezes seven times in rapid succession, then bends down and picks up the newly arrived package. He recognises the handwriting on the front. He makes his way to the kitchen, lays the envelope on the dining table, then stares long and hard at it, daring it to piss him off. After two mugs of sweet black coffee and substantial envelope-staring, Iain opens the package. Inside are a DVD, a CD and a piece of parchment on which blood-red words are scrawled: *'Some gifts for your enjoyment, you scuba-diving sodomite. Love Spark'*.

The best-case scenario, Iain thinks, is that Spark has burned him a porn DVD and a CD of mixed metal. He spreads out the discs and note on his kitchen table, like evidence from a crime scene, then frowns hard at them. They give away no clues. Worse than that, they seem to be mocking him.

Iain jogs upstairs and zips through his morning routine: brush teeth, shave, shit, shower, suit, tie, spritz of aftershave, cereal, chocolate croissant, coffee, out of the house like a shot. Today, however, there is one addition: he grabs Spark's CD from the kitchen table on his way out. The whole repertoire takes seventeen minutes. He fine-tuned his morning routine after attending a course in time management. Iain was quietly ecstatic at being able to shave five minutes off his previous record of twenty-two minutes. Increasingly for him, life is about maximising efficiency and cutting loose the superfluous.

Setting off for work in his red Audi TT convertible, Iain lowers the roof to enjoy the glow of morning sun on his face. On the passenger seat rests Spark's CD. The words 'LISTEN AND WEEP' are scribbled on it in large, over-confident letters that taunt Iain as if they were the bastard MacDubh himself. As Iain tries to focus on the treeline sandwiched between blue sky and fields of yellow oil-seed rape, he hears Spark's voice, as clear as the sky above. "Play the CD, Suit Boy. Don't just look at it? Are you scared? Stop starin' at the fuckin' thing or you'll end up crashin' your fine automobile." Iain picks up the disc and slides it into the car stereo. Twin guitars, sharper than razors, paint an aural canvas that takes Iain's mind back two decades. It is *The Hellion*, the instrumental intro to Judas Priest's *Screaming for Vengeance* album, but the riffs that carve their way into Iain's brain today are not cranked out by Judas Priest. These riffs are bigger, sharper...like sonic blades. Iain hadn't thought it possible to make a Priest riff any heavier. On this spring morning, however, he has been proved wrong. This cover version has upped the ferocity several notches. The blueprint has been, in the words of the underrated metal band Sword, metalized. As *The Hellion* blends seamlessly into *Electric Eye*, Iain's ears and brain are fully engaged. He makes mental notes. *Great riffing – laser-sharp and full of emotion. Beautiful twin-guitar assault. Wall-crumbling bass. Powerful, precise drumming. This must be a German power metal band.* A voice soars over the metallic maelstrom: an unmistakeable voice which Iain hasn't heard singing in a long time. *Spark.*

For a moment, Iain feels happy that his friend and blood brother is part of something so majestic. Then the demons start to bite, injecting harsh realisations that hurt more than any venom. It doesn't make sense, doesn't add up. There's bombastic drumming and – worse than that – there's bass. Phenomenal bass, technically accomplished and louder than Hell. A circular thought pattern swirls in Iain's brain like a Zen koan without an answer. *Spark...Blood Brothers...bass...fucking bass...bastards...Spark!* Iain's scream of rage ruptures the early morning stillness. "Spark, you traitorous motherfucker! I'm the fuckin' bass player in the band! Ya dirty backstabbin' bastaaaaaaaaaaaaaaaaard!" He ejects the CD and frisbees it into dewy underbrush at the side of the road. As he stamps on the accelerator pedal and vents his wrath on the road ahead, Iain feels a smidgeon of regret at having discarded the disc. It is much more difficult, after all, to create than to destroy. Somewhere in the angry red mist that fills Iain is a glimmer of wonder: wonder at what other tracks were on the CD; wonder at who was playing drums; most of all, wonder at what fucking imposter was filling his rightful slot on bass.

Chapter 47 – The Uninvited Guest

Pete Drummond stares at the occult symbols carved into the walls of his apartment. Dark thoughts etch deep lines in his forehead as he takes a long draw of his cigarette. Outside, birds sing in celebration of spring's arrival. Feather-shaped cirrus clouds drift across the infinite blue. The smell of honeysuckle blossom sneaks in through an open window, adding a sweet edge to the smoke canopy that hovers at head height in the room.

For years, Pete revelled in his solitude here. It felt liberating to be safe from the Devil and free from the hassles of the outside world. This flat - with its magical symbols, musical instruments, cigarette-smoke cumulus and faint whiff of Lisa's perfume - was his place of alchemical transformation: here he had mastery over his fear, having spent years like a nervous prey animal waiting on that *thing* to reach inside his chest and tear out his soul. Lisa visited daily, her love unfaltering. Whenever she enveloped Pete in her arms, mouth and welcoming body, he lost all sense of where he ended and she began. For a while Lisa and music were all he needed, but his desire to see family and friends grew over time. He loved those disbelieving bastards.

Pete has musical autonomy now, but composing and recording by himself can't measure up to the vast energy exchange of five sonic forces in perfect synchronisation. Blood Brothers' music had always been greater than the sum of its parts, perhaps due to the unique chemistry between the members of the band, or even a form of divine – or infernal – intervention. Whatever the cause, strange cosmic synergism had occurred when the band played together. Rush's *Turn the Page* rushes from speakers, Geddy Lee expounding about the impossibility of existing in isolation. A science lesson from childhood pops into Pete's head: any living organism placed in a vacuum, away from sunlight and stimulation, rapidly withers.

Being confined to an inner world, both psychologically and literally, has influenced Pete's recent musical compositions, which have been dark and brooding pastiches of discordant rhythms and mutated Jarresque keyboards. An exception happened two weeks ago when he temporarily dropped his invisible armour of psychic protection and allowed a raging storm to surge through his fragile body. The untamed forces of nature animated Pete, reminding him how it feels to be spontaneous and unharnessed. Now he feels the urge to break out of his safety zone, to re-enter the world, to channel its beauty into timeless soundscapes. Therein lies the conflict. Having been touched by demonic energy, and bearing the mark to prove it, Pete will never again step outside the protective orbit of his flat.

By studying the principles of Enochian occult protection, Pete learned how to make his property impenetrable to evil entities. He then inscribed walls, floor, ceiling and doors with the magical symbols necessary to create a protective shell around the flat. He ponders the symbols in his black hallway. They make no rational sense, looking very much like the products of a madman's mind. Pete has forced himself to believe in their power, but his faith is second-hand and passed down from others; it is not the comforting first-hand faith he has longed for. Staring at wyrd shapes, he lowers his barrier of psychic protection and opens his mind. Something begins to filter in. *Salvation?*

The front door explodes into a thousand shards of wood that fly inwards like jagged arrows with destructive intent. The high-velocity splinter shower leaves Pete resembling a pincushion. Spikes jut from puncture wounds. Blood trickles down his pale-skinned body. Chunks of masonry drop from the decimated doorframe, crumbling into dust on impact with the ground. A dark figure, gigantic in girth and height, wades into the dust cloud. The behemoth strides into the hall, pulls a black sack over Pete's head, clamps a hand around his throat, plucks him off the ground and tosses his body over a massive shoulder. Then the descent begins. *This is it. Down, down, eternally down. I'm beyond the help of psychic protection, beyond redemption. Lisa, I love you.* The sensation of love clears Pete's frayed mind, granting him a fleeting lucidity. Slung over Satan's shoulder, he casts his eyes down to the sliver of a gap between his chest and the black sack. The sight he glimpses through that narrow aperture throws two questions into his mind. *Why is the Devil wearing Levis? When did he get such a fat arse?* As Pete ponders these peculiarities of demonic existence, his abductor pulls a drawstring at the bottom of the sack. It tightens around Pete's neck and everything turns black.

Chapter 48 – Little Evils for the Greater Good

"Spark, I watched the DVD of your band's rehearsal. I'm speechless. Who would have thought that a lowlife scumbag like your bad self would have abilities like those? I humbly request to be your noble champion."

"If you mean champion the way I think you do, Archibald, then I decline your offer. You'd love to have me as your helpless princess in the tower just so you, the journalistic prince, could woo me with glowing, flowery prose aboot Blood Brothers bein' the most innovative musical outfit in history. As repayment for your beneficence, you'd expect me to bend over and let you thunder up my exit chute."

"My good man, I know you can't help yourself from having homoerotic thoughts about me, but please keep them unspoken. I was merely offering to spread the word of your band to the masses, since I am in the fortunate position of having considerable influence in that sphere."

"Are you offerin' because you genuinely like the band or because we're friends?"

"Spartacus, I follow only one journalistic rule – I write from the heart. Unlike most writers, I refuse to be influenced by fashion or nepotism. I tell it as my ears hear it and my heart feels it."

"The band still has some major problems. Ted flies back to America tomorrow, leaving us bassless. Then there's Pete 'Howard Hughes' Drummond, the reclusive maniac."

"You've come this far on your admirable quest to clean up the post–grunge mire and change the world for the better. I see the same burning self-belief in you that I've seen in icons like Gene Simmons and Angus Young. They lead, but are never led. I have faith in you." I mumble some heartfelt thanks and agree to meet Archibald in Bar Chew in an hour.

DT is working from home today, so I have just enough time to squeeze in some dog-wrestling and coffee at his house before meeting Archibald. Hailstones ricochet off Rustbucket's roof like icy bullets as I park in my usual spot in front of the farmhouse. It must surely be my imagination, but I'd swear that the brass Viking's pleated beard is curling in the wind, and that under my incredulous gaze the Norse warrior's metal lips part into a bloodthirsty grin. Dave opens the door holding an index finger to his lips. "Ssssshhhhh," he whispers, then beckons me inside. We tiptoe to his guitar vault, where a body with myriad puncture wounds and a black sack over its head is tied to a wooden chair. A black-clad Oz has an electronic device pressed into his own neck, distorting his voice into a demonic death-rattle. "Your soul is ours, Pete Drummond. We put a mark on you a long time ago. Now I have come to reclaim your soul. If you sit still, it will all be over in a flash. Either that or a long, infinitely painful eternity. It amounts to the same thing. There is, for you, only one alternative."

Metallic Dreams

Pete is in a hell of a state. A model of pure religious-hostage chic, his head hangs slumped forward, muffled sobs the only hints of life within. Congealed blood is crusted around multiple holes in his skin. I can't help feeling as though I'm watching the scene on CNN days before the unfortunate hostage is beheaded by Jihad-stirring extremists. A semi-liquid mixture of blood, tears and snot slithers down Pete's chest as the sack quivers in time to his sorrowful sobs.

Placing a huge hand on Pete's shoulder, Ozzy booms, "You were once part of a heavy metal band! Only by rejoining this band and contributing to their ascent can you escape the eternal fiery abyss. The choice is yours, Pete Drummond. This is the fork in the road."

DT wears a look of admiration, happily watching Ozzy's Oscar-worthy acting performance. It's exciting to be in the same room as Pete again. Admittedly, the circumstances are less than ideal, but that'll teach the wee bastard to give me electric shocks.

Pete raises his black-sacked head and whimpers, "May I ask you somethin'?"

"Proceed!"

"When did you start wearin' jeans and drivin' a car? Why?"

A panicked look crosses Ozzy's face as he flounders for a response. Affecting a deep voice with, inexplicably, a Yorkshire accent, DT growls, "My fellow demon and I sometimes wear human garb and drive human vehicles because horned demons tearing across the skies on flaming wings are slightly conspicuous. There are rare times when it is advantageous to show our true forms, but humans have an inconsiderate tendency to die of shock when we do so."

The black sack nods. "That makes sense. What's your interest in the band?"

"You humans," DT continues, "like to make bets on the outcome of the future – the stock market, horse racing, reality TV shows and all manner of other bets. In my dimension, we also enjoy making bets on future outcomes, but we wager on different things - wars, famines, plagues and heavy metal bands. Officially, we are not allowed to intervene in a way that influences these outcomes, but rule-bending happens, just as it does in your dimension. Unethical demons have been known to offer immaculate musical ability to a human in exchange for that individual's soul, an illegal exchange which sways the betting odds very much in that demon's favour. Difficult as this may be for you to believe, I watched you and your band improve by the day, then made a bet that you would become the biggest band ever to walk your planet."

I can almost feel Pete's frown through the black sack. "Why did that demon chase me on the blue bridge then? He wasn't offerin' me musical ability. He was tryin' to turn me into a flame-grilled snack."

Maintaining his Yorkshire accent, DT replies, "Demons couldn't tempt you with promises of immaculate musical ability because you already had that. The demon you encountered on the blue bridge was my enemy.

He knew I had wagered on your band, so he came to Earth that night to rip out your soul and feast on it, thus destroying your band's future. Good idea of yours to pray like that. It saved your soul and kept alive my chances of winning my wager. That demon marked you, though, Pete Drummond – a mark that will always remind you that beings beyond your ken, from a dimension outside your scope of understanding, are watching you."

Oz pipes in, "The time has come now for your band to rise. You, Pete Drummond, will be part of this ascent. Either that or we will transport your soul to Hell now, leaving your pathetic broken shell of a body here, tied to a chair and dressed only in skid-scorched underpants and a headsack. My advice to you is to stay alive, Pete Drummond. Put your creative energy back into the band. Take it to the stars."

As Pete nods, a small voice filled with childlike wonder floats from his mouth. "Why did you choose a human form with such a fat arse?"

DT and I fall into silent hysterics. Looking more than a little offended, Oz booms, "Silence! Don't sass a demon, boy!" He unties Pete's arms, flings his body over a shoulder and stomps out of the house.

Aghast, I turn to DT. "You have officially lost your fuckin' marbles, Tierney."

Beaming like an innocent child, he says, "You wanted Pete back in the band? Kazam! He's back in the band. And now, for my next trick…"

Chapter 49 – North

For once, Archibald is on time. I find him perched on a high stool in Bar Chew, taut and upright, eyes scanning left and right like a raven looking for morsels. "Please take this guy to a faraway table, Spark," pleads Jimz. "He'd argue with his fuckin' shadow." Archibald follows me to a table in the far corner.

"What did you say to piss Jimz off this time?"

"I merely pointed out that Pink Floyd has never had a strong singer…and that they would have been better with Ronnie James Dio."

"You know that Jimz is the world's biggest Floyd fan. Why did you wind him up like that?"

"When I arrived he was listening to *The Wall*. After telling Jimz that it's one of the most overrated albums in history, I mentioned Floyd's lack of vocal prowess and said that Dio would have done it immeasurably better."

"Why does everythin' wi' you always have to come back to Dio?"

"Dio was the best singer ever to grace this planet. There will never be another like him."

"That's just your opinion. Other people have equally valid opinions. Jimz happens to have Pink Floyd at the top of his pile. Why do you need to start arguments?"

"Debates, not arguments. Articulate debate stimulates parts of the brain that small talk doesn't."

"So does having a pint glass smashed over your heid. You may want to think aboot that the next time you feel like startin' an argument in a Bronzehall pub."

"Fair point, Spark. Anyway, to business."

"I'm not sure where to start. The rehearsal went phenomenally, as you saw on the DVD."

"How did you get Ozzy back behind the drum kit?"

"Ted, DT and I were playin' oor second session in Colin's studio when a bone-shatterin' noise rocked the whole building. We thought it was an earthquake or the end o' the world. It turned oot that Oz had walked into the empty studio next to oors and switched on a wall of Marshall amps along wi' every microphone in the studio. He set the mics up in a semi-circle aroon' the drum kit, then turned the amps up to eleven and proceeded to beat seven shades of shit oot o' the drums. I'd have been less surprised to find Keith Moon behind that drum kit. The walls and floors were shakin', and striplights got shoogled oot o' their fittings. Colin went off his heid at Oz. After Ozzy apologised and Colin calmed doon, the giant filled in on drums for the rest o' the rehearsal."

"What changed his mind about being in the band again?"

"There were a few factors at work, but in the end it was serendipity."

"How so?"

"Well, Sunshower loves the idea of her Dad playin' drums in the band. I knew that if she pestered him enough, he wouldn't let her doon."

"Was that what swayed him?"

"No, although it helped. Oz trains with an archery club in Wytchcoomb. They use the local school's gym hall three nights a week. One night, as he was walkin' through the corridors of the school, he noticed a sign on a noticeboard. It said, in big black letters, *Dreams Without Action Stay Dreams*. After training, he couldn't get the slogan out of his big orange heid. He realised that his dream of a life wi' Denise was deid, that there was nothin' he could do to revive it. The dream o' the band, however, was one which – with action – could be brought back to life."

"Serendipitous indeed. Do you think the sign was put there by God?"

"I think the sign was put there by the school janitor. Ozzy had probably walked past it a hundred times withoot noticin' it. On this night, though, the time was right. We all receive signs from the Universe, but usually they're symbolic signs, the meaning of which we're left to interpret. In Oz's case, the Universe probably figured it had to use a literal sign wi' big bold letters in order to communicate wi' the big fat fuck. The lips of wisdom are closed, except to the ears of understanding."

"Anyone watching that DVD would think the four of you had been playing together for years. You were tight."

"I know. We had miraculous chemistry. Oz hadn't played drums in years, but he slotted right back into it. After rehearsal he was so fired up that he broke the law in order to secure the band's future."

"I don't think I want to hear this."

"I think you do. When the band makes it big, this story will become legend. A balaclava-clad Oz, dressed in black, smashed his way into Pete's flat like the Incredible Hulk, then hijacked him. He pulled a black sack over Pete's heid and drove him to DT's farmhoose, where they tied him to a chair. I arrived to find Pete lookin' like a hostage in the Middle East. Speakin' through a voice transformer and playin' the role of demon, Oz told Pete that the only way to retain his soul was by rejoinin' the band."

"And he bought that?"

"Pete's experiences with the Devil changed him. After feeling hands of fire fumbling inside his chest, he was so scared that he shut oot the world for years. Fear o' the Devil made Pete a prisoner in his own hoose. Oz and Dave knew that if they pulled off their stunt properly, they could make him do *anything*."

Archibald gawps. "That's despicable."

"Whatever it takes, dude. Finally, things are fallin' into place for the band. Granted, we've taken the arse-over-tit route, but that's always been oor way. The only route to progress is through struggle."

"Very philosophical of you, Zenboy. As it happens, I agree. If you spend your life avoiding difficulty, no growth occurs, which makes for a static, unsatisfying existence. To risk everything in pursuit of your dream is an impressive quest." Archibald and I sip coffee as Pink Floyd's *Run Like Hell* fills the space between us. A look of concern chisels itself into my friend's face. "How many laws do you think you all broke today?"

In my head, I run through the obvious ones: kidnapping; assault; breach of the peace; breaking and entering; destruction of property. Probably others. Man-made 'laws' are irrelevant, though. The only real laws are those of the Universe itself. In pursuit of a higher spiritual quest, sometimes it is necessary to plumb the depths of Hell. Archibald frowns at me, waiting for his answer. *How many 'laws' did we break today?* I look my friend in the eyes and shrug my shoulders. "How many laws did we break? How many fallen angels can dance on the heid of a pin? How long's a bit o' string? Who gives a fuck?"

When I get back home, the sleeping Ted doesn't respond to verbal stimulation or prods in the ribs from my index finger, so I take him a mug of strong coffee and his pack of cigarettes. That does the trick. Within the hour, we are heading north, Fear Factory in our ears, Loch Ness on our minds. A wild Highland wind streams through Rustbucket's open sunroof, buffeting our hair into flight.

Far ahead, the sky is cold and blue.

Chapter 50 – Estranged

One sea-blue wall of Iain Bright's living room wears a generous spattering of red pasta sauce. Jagged fragments of an obliterated china plate sink into the deep-pile carpet. Oblivious to events in Iain's residence, the sun blazes, sending out heat and light to all organisms in its little corner of the incomprehensibly vast Universe. Deep within its primal consciousness, the star ruminates on its thankless task. *Perhaps turning supernova would be fun. Once upon a time, the humans on the third planet from me – which they call Earth - used to worship me. They acknowledged my selfless generosity in their rites, rituals and beliefs. Those were good times. Then humans became obsessed with accumulating material things. Human imagination created new deities that better suited their planet-plundering agendas. Their shallow spirituality veered ever farther from the truth. Now, the humans who promulgate these invented religions take money from others of their species, promising eternal happiness in return. The greedy bleed the gullible. I'll show them true power – let's see if their invented gods save them when I send out solar flares to boil their oceans and char the planet's surface.*

  Deciding that it is falling into the peculiarly human habits of self-pity and anger, the star reminds itself that it is cosmically above such petty emotions, gives itself a kick up the arse, and burns a little brighter. In synch with the solar changes, Iain's dark mood lightens. The DVD he received from Spark is playing at high volume in the corner of the room. Twenty minutes ago, Iain sacrificed his lunch to rage, launching bowl and contents at a living-room wall. In a display of steely discipline, he left the disc running.

  Initially, the sight of Spark riffing like a bastard and singing flawlessly stimulated in Iain feelings of blood-brotherly love and pride. Seeing Ozzy thundering blast beats on a drum kit was, as always, awe-inspiring. DT was almost unrecognisable: beard gone; sparkling smile back; innocence glimmering in his eyes. Pete was nowhere to be seen. When Iain saw the swaggering dude on bass - all suntan, smile, sunglasses and whirling golden mane - he felt as if his guts had been wrenched out without an anaesthetic. He erupted. A living-room wall soaked up the brunt of his wrath, as walls have a habit of doing when a Scottish male loses his temper.

  Iain's feelings of anger, betrayal and jealousy subside to a low simmer as Blood Brothers' cover of the KISS classic *Creatures of the Night* stomps from speakers. As Spark prowls the studio like a guitar-toting predator with instrument set to *kill*, his voice echoes off Iain's sauce-splattered walls. In Spark's eyes is a cold blue light that Iain hasn't seen in his blood brother since childhood. He knows what this means: Spark is once again illuminated by self-belief, and this time it looks undousable.

  The band's performance is tight, as if they have been on the road for years. Watching the motley bunch of hairy animals on his television screen is the most traumatic event Iain has experienced, yet he knows he must suffer through it. As he sips the morning's second mug of coffee, his anger dissipates and his face returns to its natural pale hue. Thirty seconds after the DVD has ended with a roaring rendition of Megadeth's *Tornado of Souls*, Iain is in the driving seat of his Audi, accelerating towards Norwich. On a mission.

Chapter 51 – Resurrection

"Have you found a job yet?" asks my mother, peering at me over the top of her round, brass-rimmed glasses.

"I'm puttin' all my energy into music. I'm too busy wi' that to get a regular job. Never again will I work for anyone else and rely on them to put food in my fridge."

"I admire your determination, son, but you haven't made a penny from the band yet. How are you going to make a living?"

"Mum, I ran *Bodies in Bronze* for a piddly amount o' cash. By the time my bills were paid, I didn't have enough left over for food. Every month, I spent more than I earned."

"I understand that, but now you're making nothing." Ouch. When patronising doesn't work, she goes straight for the jugular.

"I just started doin' one-to-one personal training wi' a glamour model called Vikki Suxxx, who has featured in all the UK's major adult magazines. She's easy on the eyes and pays me well for keepin' her in shape."

"There's a name for what you're doing and it's not personal training. Look at that Vanessa Feltz – she got a personal trainer but never got any thinner. Before you know it, she's given the husband the boot and the personal trainer's her lover. I don't believe there was ever any training being done there, except possibly training her to open those fat legs wider. I don't want my beautiful boy being a gigolo, selling himself to some harlot. You're better than that."

"Vikki isn't a harlot. She happens to have a body that millions of people like to see naked, but that doesn't make her a slut. Actually, she's intelligent and shy, and would never pay for carnal pleasures. The only ridin' she does wi' me is on oor mountain bikes."

"It sounds suspicious. I think she's trying to get her claws into my boy."

"Mum, you think all women are tryin' to get their claws into me."

"Well, most of them are."

"I wish."

"Are you making enough money to pay your bills?"

"Aye, just. I get a cooncil tax rebate due to Bronzehall District Cooncil thinkin' I'm gainfully unemployed. What I make from trainin' Vikki is pocket money."

"Son, this all sounds very cloak and dagger. I didn't raise you to screw the system."

"How did you raise me then, Mum? To have a dream then give up on it? To settle for a miserable hand-to-mooth existence?"

"No, but…"

"What do you think Dad would say? Would he applaud me for listenin' to the Universe and re-ignitin' my musical dreams or would he tell me to get another shit job and knuckle doon to a joyless existence? Would he say that all he taught me aboot havin' an open mind and the courage to chase a dream was like Santa Claus, the Tooth Fairy and the Easter Bunny – myths to steer attention away from the intrinsically dull and pointless lives that most people settle for?"

My mother gives me a long stare. "You're a smartarse, Spark. You must get that from your father because it certainly didn't come from me."

"Come on, ma. I'll take you oot to Bar Chew for lunch."

En route, we discuss the band, future gigs, tours, recording sessions, female love interests and Pete. My Mum has always adored Pete in all his shy sensitivity. The only thing she doesn't love about him is his smoking habit, which I promise her I'll try to rid him of.

Ozzy has wallowed in the depths of despair and loss. DT has faced twisted personal demons and exorcised them through sheer strength of will. Pete's personal journey has taken him to Hell and back, metaphorically and perhaps literally too. I fell into a lifeless rut in which I, like Bill Murray's character in *Groundhog Day,* repeated the same day over and over again, except I didn't get to fuck Andie Macdowell at the end. My blood brothers and I are now moving in the same direction again…all except Iain, who neither faced his demons nor fell into the void. He surprised us all by smashing out of his fantasy cocoon and excelling as an insurance executive. The chemistry of the band can only be perfect when all five are together. A crackpot Iain may be, but we need him.

Back home after an enjoyable hour eating, drinking and chatting with my mother, I brew a pot of coffee and take a mug to the sleeping Ted. Butt-naked except for his snakeskin boots, he wakes with a start, grabs the mug from my hand, slurps down the contents, lights a cigarette and has a short coughing fit. "Stick on some wake-up music, Spark, preferably Helloween. Those German fucks really know how to wake a dude up!" Selecting *The Keeper of the Seven Keys, Part 1*, I crank up the volume.

Unheard by Spark or Ted, who are immersed in loud Teutonic metal upstairs, the phone rings and its answering service records the voice of Iain Bright. "Spark, ya fuckin' wankstain, I've bought a bass! Put that in your self-satisfied pipe and smoke it!"

Chapter 52 – Gathering of Freaks

Paul Roberts, DT, Ozzy and Pete are seated in my living room while I make coffee in the kitchen. Paul and I grew up in the same block of Vikingwood terraced houses and have known each other since we were babies. His clear blue eyes and shock of black hair feature in my earliest memories. My bandmates are meeting our prospective manager for the first time, Oz having travelled up from England for the occasion.

Archibald is late as usual. This will be the others' first experience of him. They're not finding his tardiness endearing. As I carry coffee and a selection of Ozzy's cakes into the living room, Archibald bursts through the front door and breezes into the room, dressed immaculately in a dark-blue suit, white shirt and azure silk tie. Without a word of introduction, he kicks off his shoes, removes his suit jacket, unfastens his belt, drops his trousers, steps out of them, folds them, hangs them over a radiator then starts to mince around the room, pouting like a Parisienne stripper. He unbuttons his shirt, baring the whitest chest on the west coast of Scotland. I'm used to this kind of eccentric behaviour from him. The others, however, stare open-mouthed as the journalist struts around the room like a sun-starved Mick Jagger in black socks and boxer shorts.

As Archibald attempts to squeeze into the narrow gap between DT and Ozzy on the sofa, Dave growls, "What the fuck d'you think you're doin', pal? You must have got the wrong end o' the stick. This is a band meetin', no' some kind o' benders' buffet."

Sweeping hair off his face, Archibald glowers at Dave. "Sir, you have never met a *less* homosexual man. I have a voracious appetite for voluptuous vixens."

Shaking his huge head, Ozzy climbs off the sofa and sprawls on the floor like a sleepy lion. Rather than sliding sideways to fill the vacant space on the sofa, Archibald remains tight to DT's leg. "In case it slipped your notice," Dave spits, "I'm no' a voluptuous vixen, so get your poofy leg tae fuck away from me before I snap it like a twig." Archibald shimmies aside, silent for once.

"Despite his unnerving eccentricities," I announce, "Archibald understands the media's role in heavy metal better than anyone I've met. Listen to what he says and show him respect. He can help us. I'm honoured to have him on oor side. You should be too."

"I discovered today," Archibald declares, "that there is already a band recording under the name Blood Brothers and another band recording under the name The Blood Brothers. Legally, your band can neither gig nor record under either name."

"You're no' makin' a good first impression on me," snarls DT. "First you try to poof me up on the sofa, then you kill oor band name, you effeminate foppish twat. We were usin' that band name first."

Ozzy glares at DT and booms, "If a certain person hadn't ended up in jail we'd have been recordin' under that name years before those other fuckers stole it! Arsehole!" DT and Oz share a long stare, invisible daggers flying between them. This is what I feared might happen: old unresolved issues raising their stinking heads.

Hoping to prevent bloodshed, I intervene. "Oz, we've all made mistakes and paid oor dues. The band could have replaced DT when he went to jail. Oot o' loyalty to him, we chose not to. If he hadn't gone berserk and been incarcerated, the band could have gone doon any number o' paths. Perhaps we'd have sold more albums than Metallica and Led Zeppelin combined. Maybe we'd be drippin' in riches and gettin' so oot of oor heids that we'd be drivin' Lamborghinis and Bugattis into the swimmin' pools of oor Austrian castles. Another possibility, of course, is that the inter-band friendships would have fragmented, leavin' us hatin' each other. Yet here we are, sittin' in a room together after all life has thrown at us, still friends and brothers."

"Eloquently put, Spark," says Archibald, clapping his hands. "Spoken like a leader."

"Why don't you just pick another band name?" asks Paul. "The name of a band doesn't matter anyway."

"You, sir, could not be more wrong," argues Archibald. "The name of a band is paramount to its success. Name creates image. Image sells bands. Many an untalented band with a great name and a strong image has become disgustingly wealthy. You'd have an easier time finding a whore with a heart than succeeding on musical ability alone. MTV put paid to that. Do you think Metallica would have achieved such a monumental level of success if they had called themselves Pink Frock? What if Mötley Crüe had called their band Nÿce Böys? Or, perish the thought, imagine Guns 'n' Roses had called themselves Buns 'n' Toasties."

Paul nods. "I stand corrected."

"Speaking of buns an' toasties," bellows Oz, "get me some more of that cake in here! It's fanfuckintastic! Whoever made it is a goddamned genius." I head to the kitchen to load a tray with the next round of snacks while Archibald puts on a *Monsters of Metal* DVD. The gurgle of filtering coffee is drowned out by Strapping Young Lad's *Relentless* storming out of speakers like a thousand charging rhinos. With an expression like Wurzel Gummidge trying to do sums without his thinking head on, Oz scratches his head and admits, "I can't think of a name for the band."

Half an hour passes. None of us can think of a name. Pete's pale lips part into a smile. "We're the opposite of a think tank…we're a thick tank. A stupid pool. We've been tarred by the idiot brush. We fell oot o' the spazzy tree and hit every branch on the way doon." On the TV, Hammerfall are belting out *Hearts on Fire* as if their very hearts, and their pants, are indeed on fire. Heads in the living room bob rhythmic approval, Ozzy's afro swaying like a hedge in a breeze, while DT's glossy hair flows like a black waterfall.

Suddenly, it hits me: I remember a picture I created on my PC three years ago using Vue d'Esprit 3D modelling software. Back in those dark ages, I often spent entire days on the computer, crafting covers for hypothetical albums by my dead band; usually vast, open landscapes and sweeping skies. One picture stood head and shoulders above the others: a rust-coloured desert stretches to the horizon; the only sign of life is a single tree whose bare branches reach up into a sky of washed-out blue with a fine dusting of cirrus clouds; a stone archway rises from the sand, casting a long shadow that stretches towards the horizon like a finger pointing to the future. After completing the picture, I pained over a title for it. Eventually, the perfect name came not from inside my mind, but from somewhere in the air. Perhaps it's true that half of an idea resides in a person's mind while the other half floats in the ether, the complete idea only able to be born if the individual is in the right place at the right time, culminating in the magical marriage of the two halves.

I didn't remember my picture when I saw the Wytchcoomb archway, or after the otherworldly dream in which I flew through the arch. And I know why: the memory of the picture had descended into my subconscious to wait until the time was right to emerge. I announce that I have our band name and explain the symbolism of the picture to my bandmates. The barren desert represented my life at that time. The tree was me, alone and reaching skywards in vain. The archway was a portal which represented the possibility of travel to a better place. The vast sky was evidence of an infinite Universe filled with limitless intelligence.

Oz hammers the floor with a fist, shaking the room. "Never mind all that flowery shite! What's the name?"

After a long, deep breath, I unveil, "Transcend Everything."

DT's smile almost blinds me. "Phenomenal! A band name *and* a statement of intent. Fuckin' genius."

Running hands through tangled hair, Pete nods. "I'm forced to agree wi' Dave, although it's wrong that you came up wi' the name, Spark. I'm supposed to be the genius in the band."

"Don't cry, Pete," I console. "You *are* the band's musical genius and prodigy. I'm its poet and prophet."

Ozzy's eyes widen and – I must be mistaken – miniature lightning storms rage in them. "Spark, you've just christened oor first album! *Poets and Prophets.*" I pounce on the giant, straddling his substantial torso and hugging him for all I'm worth. "Get off me, ya flamin' homosexual," he bellows, flinging me halfway across the room.

Archibald rises from the sofa. "Well, sirs, you have chosen what I have to admit is the best band name I've ever heard. You have also picked a perfect title for your first album. That's some of the hard stuff out of the way. Your next challenge is to write timeless music of unparalleled melody and power, then to refine it until you have defined a sound that must, true to your name, transcend everything. That, my good men, is one hell of a lofty goal." Smiling like a pervert at a porn shoot, he salutes the band.

Metallic Dreams

Fluff sprints into the living room, hurdles Ozzy's legs and springs onto the window ledge, twitching in mid-flight. She stares through the window, ears raised, body poised, nose sniffing thirteen to the dozen, eyes fixed on something outside as she lets out a high-pitched whine: her scared sound. As her fear becomes louder and more frantic, I peer outside, hoping to learn what is frightening my wee friend. All I see are evergreen trees silhouetted against a darkening sky. Maybe Fluff's sensitive hearing has detected a bird of prey's flapping wings, or perhaps she smells a fox. Picking up my fur-covered friend, I hold her to my chest, cover her eyes and gaze outside again. In the trees, a couple of feet above eye level, two spheres of fire flare into existence. I blink hard, sure that my imagination must be running wild. On opening my eyes, I see nothing but trees and sky.

Chapter 53 – Bastard is as Bastard Does

In Bar Chew, Pete is waiting for me at a window table. In front of him, a coconut-scented candle's flame billows in the draught that heralds my arrival. Pete lights a Marlboro and tuts – actually *tuts* - at me when I tell him that cigarettes will prove harmful to his health in more ways than one if Jimz sees him smoking in the bar. Pete's blonde hair has been trimmed short; he now looks more Oor Wullie than Albert Einstein. Years have fallen off him since the hijack incident. The lines on his face are a little less deep. His turquoise eyes have a newfound clarity. He has started to eat fruit and vegetables daily. His alcohol consumption has declined but hasn't disappeared. The Marlboros, however, are still present in force. Perhaps smoking is the one vice necessary to keep him on enough of an even keel to be a creative and functional part of the band.

It feels good to be sitting opposite my pal and seeing his gentle smile again after too many years apart. I tell him about Angel: mind of a rocket scientist; musical sensibilities of a metalhead; dress sense of a Penthouse Pet. This is the final year of her PhD in Physics. Six months from now, her business cards will read *Dr Angel LaRocque*. Pete reckons her parents must be disappointed in her chosen career, since - based on the name they gave her - they were obviously hoping for a stripper or a porn starlet.

Jimz motions for me to approach the bar. "What's the deal wi' your pal Pete? I told him last week no' to smoke in here. If I ban him from Chew, it's a ban from every pub in toon. That's how Pubwatch works."

"Pete's been in a parallel Universe for a while," I explain. "He didn't leave his hoose for years due to agoraphobia and various other mental fuckups."

"*Fuckups?* I'll give him the fuckin' up of a lifetime if he doesn't put oot that fag. I'll be the one who gets fined if an environmental health inspector walks in here and finds that wee dick puffin' away. Tell him to go ootside wi' his fag or stub it oot, otherwise I'll ban him from the bar and put my boot up his arse."

"Roger, Jimz. I'll deliver that message once you've poured me a free refill o' your fine coffee. And a whisky on the hoose would be appreciated."

"You really are a blaggin' bastard, Spark," sighs Jimz. "I'll bring the drinks over to your table. Make sure that ignorant wee twat isn't smokin' when I get there."

"Thanks, Jimz. You're a good dude. I'll make sure you get free tickets and backstage passes to my band's gigs."

"Is that meant to be a present? Sounds more like a punishment."

Back at our table, I tell Pete that Jimz has promised to thunder a boot up his arse if he doesn't extinguish his cigarette immediately. Raising his eyebrows, Pete asks, "The whole boot?"

"I didn't ask, but I think the whole thing, aye. If I were you, I wouldn't take the chance. Put it this way, he wasn't talkin' aboot subtle sexual stimulation."

Pete stubs out his Marlboro on the wall, leaving a charred circle on the crimson paintwork. Jimz appears with our drinks, flashes Pete a withering stare, then retreats behind the bar. Pete stares at the cigarette-burnt wall for silent minutes. Suddenly, he whirls to face me and says, "I feel like I can walk again after years in a wheelchair." Our eyes merge into a sea of understanding. My joy transmutes into guilt as I remember the hijack incident. "What's wrong?" asks Pete. "You look like someone just pissed in your coffee."

"I was thinkin' aboot the lengths we've gone to in order to kick-start the band again." Not a word of a lie.

"Michael Jordan, man," says Pete. "Whatever it takes, remember?" I wonder if Pete's comment indicates his endorsement of leaning towards the dark side on occasion, to further our mission. The Metal Gods' mighty voices echo in my head. *Little evils for the greater good.* It strikes me as a classic song title, so I pull the whisky-spotted paper napkin from beneath Pete's glass and scribble the title on it. It strikes me as an Anthraxesque song title: the song they never wrote…the song we will write.

After a few more drinks in Bar Chew, Pete and I walk to his flat to lay down melodies and brainstorm lyrics. As I make coffee to stimulate my synapses (and sober up Pete's), spacey synth sounds fill the flat. My mind layers imaginary guitar riffs over Pete's melodies. I write down the musical notation to the combinations that work best.

Within a couple of hours, we have three tracks down in rough form. Pete, DT and I are now rehearsing together three times a week. Having bought and reinforced an enormous drum kit, Oz is practising daily in Wytchcoomb and coming up to Scotland every second weekend to play with the band. Iain Bright is taking bass lessons and dedicating seven hours of each day to learning the craft. He doesn't know that Ted isn't a member of the band; it's in our best interests for Iain to believe that Ted has stolen his bass throne. The Metal Gods agree. *Little evils for the greater good.* Pete and I share ideas on lyrics for the song named after that particular sentiment. We soon have a first draft nailed down.

'Little evils for the greater good
and the growth of our transcendental neighbourhood.
We'll cut the brakes on your car,
fill your bed full of snakes.
Watch us rise from afar,
doing whatever it takes.

Architects of riffs that shred and flay,
we slay those fool enough to stand in our way.
Commandeering Lucifer for musical ends,
we're sonic Vikings with a message to send.

It's all little evils for the greater good
when we hijack your sisters and strip them nude,
spread their legs wide, make them squirt to our beats,
then finish them off with gymnastosexual feats.

The 'free' west pillages on foreign soil,
choosing weak scapegoats to attack.
Storms in, kills their culture, sucks out their oil,
paints its soul blood-red then putrid black.

It's all little evils for the greater good,
immoral, unethical, relentless and crude.
Dismember those who stand in your way.
The fruit of the Devil is here to stay.

We do little evils for the greater good.
We're harder than metal and there's fire in our blood.
Balanced on the knife edge between Heaven and Hell,
we sharpen its blade with the stories we tell
of our little evils for the greater good.
We transcend everything – make way for the flood.'

    Pete walks to his synthesizer, lights a Marlboro and lowers his fingers onto the keys. Music floats through the room: the sound of hurtling at lightspeed through space, past thousands of stars, each playing a different Jean Michel Jarre melody. Eyes closed, Pete sways to the music like a flame aware of its own delicacy. Casting my mind back to our ill-fated gig as Blood Brothers all those years ago, I see in front of me the same Pete, the same musical prodigy, the same innocent soul, the same gentle lamb hanging out with wild, hungry wolves…the same friend.

Chapter 54 – Dreams in the Dark

Enigma's combination of drum machines, synthesizers, chanting monks and coquettish French female vocals penetrates my inner space like a relaxing breeze. Drifting away from the mundane and closer to the celestial, I fall into bed and wait for sleep.

A green sky arcs above red rocky tundra. Surreal shadows sweep across the landscape like a tide. The air smells musty and arboreal, but there are no trees here. No life. My body hair pricks up as fear tries to hold me still. Like prey. No, *as* prey.

I start to run. Boiling air burns my lungs. Peals of thunder shake the ground. A tornado swirls out of the horizon, its undulating tubelike form carving through rock, sucking it up, pulverising it and spitting it out hundreds of feet in the air, to fall as hot red sand that sticks to my watering eyes. Blinking feels like having my eyes massaged by a cheese grater. Driven by a desire to outrun the encroaching fear, I sprint through falling sandclouds. Not for the first time, I wish I was a camel. Burning sand lines my mouth and throat, yet still I run, aiming straight at the centre of the tornado. The source of my fear is here, approaching from behind; I *feel* it. Shove me between a rock and a hard place anytime. It beats running blind between a soul-shredding demon and a force of nature capable of ripping my physical body apart.

Rock is ripped from the ground with a deafening crunch. My heart rate accelerates to an impossible level, which isn't a concern since my heart is about to be wrenched apart along with the rest of me. The soles of my Mizuno running shoes melt, their molten rubber bonding to the soles of my feet. In this moment, I have to choose my obliterator: demon or tornado. Choosing the latter, I launch my body into horizontal flight and surrender. The tornado sucks me in at bone-crushing speed, tearing apart every atom of my physical self. Outside, I can sense the demon spitting psychic venom.

I have no eyes, yet I see. High above the terrain, I'm at one with the tornado. Its force is my force, its power my power. Surveyor of all before me, I *see*. The eye of the storm.

An old story of a Japanese wrestler drifts into my consciousness. No other wrestler could beat him in training, such was his strength and skill. In competitions, however, debilitating nerves prevented him from winning a single bout. When it mattered most, his confidence dropped faster than a teenage Tokyo whore's panties. An old Zen master heard of the wrestler's predicament and decided to pay him a visit. The old man watched the wrestler train and was impressed by his abilities. Later, the Zen master spoke simply and humbly to the wrestler. "If you want to be truly great, sit on the beach all night and look at the sea. Do not avert your gaze from the water until daylight. Return to me when the morning sun is whole in the sky." The wrestler couldn't understand how this would achieve anything, but he bowed to the old man's wisdom and set off for the coast. That night, he sat gazing at the moonlit sea. At first all he saw was dark water and all he heard was discordant noise, but as his eyes adjusted to the darkness and his ears tuned in to the rhythm of the mighty ocean, his breathing began to resonate with the movement of the waves. By the time the sun peeped over the horizon the next morning, the wrestler had become one with the mighty waves. He had visualised himself first as small waves rolling into shore, then as bigger waves smashing in more powerfully, and finally as huge tidal waves that covered all the land. From that day on he was unbeatable. He became the best-known wrestler in Japan and was known as Great Waves.

I jolt upright in bed, sweat pouring from my brow, cheeks burning, sand lining my mouth and nose. Words of yellow fire appear in my mind's eye: *I own your music.* Then, suddenly, it is dark again.

Chapter 55 – Strange Kind of Woman

"Show me your spectacular new titties!"

The former Manie's face scowls inside a webcam window. "Spark, I thought you were gonna be compassionate and understanding about this." He's right; I did say that. It's weird, though. I'm chatting to the guy with whom I used to watch porn movies, but he's no longer a he: he's a she. My request to see his paps wasn't driven by perversion, but by the same indefatigable curiosity that makes it impossible not to look at a horse's tadger while passing its field. One doesn't want to look, but one just can't help it. I don't rubberneck at car crashes, but I can't pass a bull mounting a cow without ogling the scene in strange awe. Animal magnetism, perhaps. Anyway, back to the tits. "Sorry, dude…ehm…I mean, dudette," I stammer. "What do you want me to call you noo?"

"Emmanuelle, as I told you in the e-mails you considered a joke."

"Really?"

"Really. Emmanuelle."

"Sexy. Just like the softcore porn flick starring Sylvia Kristel, the dirty Scandinavian minx."

"Keep your hands where I can see 'em, you Scottish pervert," giggles Emmanuelle. "My Dad was right about you all along."

"*Emmanuelle*. This'll take some gettin' used to. You're the guy wi' whom I used to blow up mailboxes, watch porn, listen to metal, do mechanical work on your '73 Mustang, headbang in your garage."

"I'm still that same soul. As a man, though, I wasn't comfortable in my skin. Now I am."

"When I met you, you were a wee Sicilian-American boy who couldn't even grow a proper 'tache. Noo look at you - a big pair o' paps and a vagina. My little boy's all grown up!"

"Is that your idea of compassion and understanding?"

"Aye. That's my soft, sensitive side. You should see my rough, brash persona. Anyway, what style are you sportin' doon below? Hairy bush, landing strip, artistically shaped design or fully waxed?"

"That's none of your business, deviant."

"I don't see what the fuss is aboot barin' your funbags for me. We used to play basketball topless."

"I'm not showin' you my breasts."

"How aboot if I promise no' to whack off? It'll be an educational experience rather than a sexual one."

"OK, a quick glimpse. And keep your hands above the keyboard where I can see 'em!" Emmanuelle lifts her T-shirt and reveals one of the finest pairs of tits I have ever seen, like twin cantaloupes. Under normal circumstances this would be a huge turn-on, but the owner of these breasts was a dude when we first met. My adaptation to this metamorphosis is just beginning, as is Emmanuelle's. She pulls down her shirt and once again I'm looking at her olive-skinned face and long, black hair.

"That's a stunnin' pair o' titties. Well done."

"It's amazin' what a few thousand dollars' worth of surgery and several gallons of female hormones can do. On a different tack, how did you get on with Ted?"

"Great. The guy's a phenomenon. Super easygoing most of the time, but a monster once his bass is strapped on."

"He loved his time with you. He showed me the DVD of your rehearsal – pretty tight for a bunch of amateurs. Did you find your present?"

"What present?"

"Ted left you a gift in the top drawer of your chest of drawers."

"I haven't looked in there since he left. I'll go and look the noo. Let's close this video conference. I'll e-mail you later."

"Remember our deal, you Celtic criminal. No bashin' the bishop while thinkin' about me."

I lean closer to the screen, until only my lips and some surrounding facial hairs are showing in my webcam window, and whisper, "I promise," then blow Emmanuelle a kiss and shut down the PC.

In my top drawer I find a few sheets of rolled-up paper inside a brass ring. Beside them is an envelope with *Spark* written on the front in sweeping calligraphy. I tear it open and find a card with the following message inside:

'*Spark,*

Thank you for being such a gracious host. I know we didn't get off on the right foot when we first talked on the phone, but you're my kind of dude. Loch Ness was breathtaking. The thing you reckoned to be a floating log was definitely something more seamonsterly, I'm sure of it. You made one of my oldest dreams come true. I hope I can help you to achieve yours. These papers contain the music that flooded into me on the streets of Paris. Do with it what you will.

Your Snakeskin-Booted Buddy,

Ted.'

I unroll the paper scrolls and find myriad musical notes dotted across the pages. It looks like a complex composition, but I'll take the time to figure out how to play it. Pete, the savant wee bastard, will look at the music once and play it perfectly. I sense that sleeping greatness rests on these parchments, waiting to be blasted into life.

Chapter 56 – Sink the Pink

Sunshower is doing handstands on her front lawn when DT and I pull up at the kerb in his Porsche. Oblivious to our arrival, she continues her acrobatics, the flared bottoms of her dungarees flapping in the warm breeze. The sun melts into an orange horizon, painting Wytchcoomb with a hazy glow. A gentle wind carries the smell of freshly cut grass. Only one thing seems atypical for such an idyllic rural setting: the thunder that roars inside a picturesque thatched cottage.

As DT bounces up the garden path, Sunshower freezes and eyes him suspiciously. When she notices me, her face blossoms into a smile. "Spark! My Daddy didn't tell me you were coming!" Before I can reply, she has launched herself into my arms and wrapped herself around me like a monkey on its favourite tree.

"This strange-looking man is DT, my partner-in-crime. He's been friends with your Dad and me for a very long time. A fine guitar player he is, but lacking in politeness and tact. Notice how he hasn't even said hello to your gorgeous self yet."

DT's face takes on the look of a scolded child. His eyes dart from side to side as if looking for an answer. I kick him up the arse, jolting him into speech. "Ehhhh…I didn't mean to be rude. You must be the Sunshower about whom Spark has told me so much. My name is David, but my friends call me DT. I'm at your service, fair maiden." Dave takes a deep and dramatic bow, laying one arm across his waist while the fingertips of the other trace circular patterns in the summer air. His black hair spills over his face, reflecting the day's last rays of sunshine.

"I like your shiny hair and your tight red trousers," says Sunshower. "Spark says you're a man, but your hair looks like a woman's."

Dave's mouth falls open. "What aboot Spark? His hair's longer than mine. Does he look like a woman?"

Turning her attention to me, Sunshower rustles tiny hands through my hair, kisses my forehead, then turns back to DT. "No, Spark's definitely a man. His hair is like a big lion's mane." I place Sunshower down on the path. She runs indoors shouting news of our arrival to her father.

"That's where lookin' after my personal grooming gets me," grumbles DT. "You live like a wild animal and you're all man to her, but I'm just an androgynous thing in shiny troosers."

"It's like that Roy Walker game show that used to be on TV – Catchprase. Sunshower's only sayin' what she sees. Don't fret, though. You're a scorchin' guitar player wi' a farmhoose paid off in full, a loyal and gorgeous dog, a profitable business and a fast car. You have lots goin' for you."

"Aye. You're right. I am pretty sexy, eh?"

"You're a sexy bastard," I nod, "due in no small part to lookin' like a woman."

"Fuck you, caveman."

"You'd love to, Manicure Boy."

Ozzy appears at the front door and finds Dave and me wrestling on the lawn, an endeavour not made any easier by our laughter or the tightness of our trousers. "What the hell are you two spanners up to? I've got neighbours, you know. This isn't Bronzehall. This is a respectable rural community. Get off the grass and come inside, ya pair o' paps."

I grab a handful of grass cuttings, stuff them down the front of DT's trousers and dash into the house. When Dave reaches the living room, scratching his crotch like a man who has just emerged from a poor choice of whorehouse, I'm sitting on the sofa with Sunshower on my lap. He scowls, frowns, scratches his head, scratches his crotch again and sticks out his tongue. Giggling, Sunshower sticks her tongue out in response. "So what's this big news you couldn't tell me over the phone?" asks Oz. "What's so important that you had to drive all the way to deepest Wytchcoomb?"

"We have some gigs."

Oz ruffles the orange haystack he calls hair. "I expected that. It isn't the biggest news in the world. What's the deal wi' Iain, though? We need a bassist for the gigs."

"Iain's bass playin' is almost up to standard. He doesn't know it yet, but he'll be in the band for oor gigs. We have support slots lined up for twelve dates along America's east coast."

Oz and Dave look at each other then glare at me as if I've just suggested plopping their balls into a deep-fat fryer. Sunshower jumps off the sofa, does a handstand and screams, "America! I'm coming too!"

Avoiding the eyes of my increasingly scary bandmates, I wince. Attempting to break the US before making a name for ourselves in our home country isn't a truly original idea. Others have tried. Most have failed. Def Leppard did it, though, so we have a chance.

Ted phoned me from Virginia a week ago with an offer of a tour on America's eastern seaboard in support of a German band with whom he's friendly. Eager to prove himself as band manager, Paul Roberts faxed back a signed tour contract within the hour, behaviour which treaded the invisible line between genius and outright insanity. Paul and I haven't enough cash to get the band and its gear to Aberdeen, never mind America. And if DT and Ozzy think touring in America is the worst of their worries, they've got – in the immortal words of Judas Priest – another thing coming.

The menacing stares of Messieurs Tierney and Oswaldo - who look as serious as twin heart attacks - cause my stomach to start sloshing like a washing machine. Sunshower is dancing furiously and shouting, "America! America! We're all going to America!"

Metallic Dreams

"Spark," grunts Oz, "this is a bad move unless the band we're supportin' is big enough to expose us to a mass audience."

DT brushes imaginary dust from his leather trousers, his mouth turned down into a scowl. "You made me drive all the way doon here to hit me wi' this shit! I guess you expect me to pay for this stateside trip? Fuck sake, Spark, what's in your heid? Who offered us the support slot withoot even hearin' us?"

Gazing into the simmering coals of Dave's eyes, I reply, "Here's a wee clue. One o' the dudes in the band is called Udo…"

Ozzy's surliness is replaced by childlike excitement. "Udo Dirkschneider? Accept? You got us a support slot wi' Accept!" He lumbers over to the sofa and wraps his gigantic arms around Sunshower and me, jamming our heads under his cavernous armpits. It has been a long day's baking; I can smell it. "You beauty, Spark! I never doubted you for a moment!"

"Ehm…I hate to shatter your illusions, but it's not Accept. The band we're supportin' is more…ehh…current. More cuttin' edge. They're an up-and-comin' bunch called Pink Stëël - not huge sellers yet, but they've cornered a niche in the market and have a…cult following. The guy I communicated with is their axeman, Udo Von DüYü, whom Ted knows pretty well. When Ted showed Udo the DVD of oor rehearsal, the dude liked it so much he wanted us as his support act on the tour."

The giant stares out at the sunset, his mind deep in the land of Oz. Through bared teeth, Dave spits, "I've never heard o' Pink Stëël, but that's one o' the worst band names ever. Do they have a website?"

"Aye."

"Show me it! Right noo!"

"Aye," adds Oz, "show us it." Leading us to his PC, he sends Sunshower into her room to draw a picture. She begins to object but, after a heavy frown from her father, goes along with his wishes. I sit at Oz's desk and type Pink Stëël's web address into the browser. As the page loads, my heart races like a dehydrated camel with an oasis in its sights. A picture of two gaudily dressed, heavily made-up and evidently excited metalheads appears on the monitor. Below them, in shocking pink, is the word 'Enter'. I click to gain access. Bold pink letters appear on a black background: 'GAY HEAVY METAL AT ITS HARDEST!'

All is quiet. With my arsehole flapping like a cheap umbrella in a typhoon, I keep my nervous gaze fixed on the screen. I feel a rush of air from my left and turn in time to see Ozzy's tombstone fist hurtling towards my chin…

Chapter 57 – Some Heads Are Gonna Roll

In a Lingwood living room, Iain Bright launches himself off a Marshall amplifier, head twisted away from his body, knees bent at an acute angle, reminiscent of Pete Townshend on steroids. At the apex of Iain's ascent, his head slams into the ceiling, which for a moment contemplates giving way to the cranium, then decides that the ceilingly thing to do is stand its ground, stay hard and let the human do the compromising. Bass vibrations shake the walls as Iain lands face-down on the floor. Unconscious.

Iain comes around with an aching head, a carpet burn on his left cheek and a mouthful of Scandinavian rug. Detaching his tongue from the floor, he spits out the stubborn rug hairs that are loathe to leave the drooly warmth of his mouth. He wavers through to the kitchen on unsteady legs, splashes a handful of water onto his burning face, curses the stinging that follows, swallows a couple of painkillers, then brews a fresh pot of coffee.

As the kitchen walls start to wobble, Iain makes a mental note not to jump off amplifiers without first checking that the ceiling is of sufficient height to allow such a manoeuvre. Being a showman was easy before he had to worry about playing an instrument. Tonight was his first attempt to combine the flash aerobatic stunts of his air-bass days with his newfound musical ability. A smile spreads across Iain's face as he remembers a couple of legendary onstage disasters: Gene Simmons's hair bursting into flame during a KISS fire-breathing extravaganza gone wrong; Blackie Lawless's buzz-saw codpiece exploding during an early W.A.S.P. show, burning all the hair off the unfortunate frontman's nether regions, singeing his sack and coming a hair's breadth from blowing his conkers clean off. Even the best showmen get it wrong on occasion and those are usually the most memorable incidents.

The floor in the living room now appears to have a tide. Blue carpet waves ripple towards Iain, a sensation he finds enjoyable if far from normal. He staggers outside to ask his next-door neighbour for a lift to hospital, but passes out on the front lawn.

A long, serpentine driveway leads to a stone castle with turrets silhouetted against a sky of violet fire. As Iain approaches the castle's front wall, a wooden drawbridge creaks a slow descent. He crosses the drawbridge and walks under a raised portcullis, its sharp iron spikes poised just inches above his head.

In the main hall, chopped logs burn in an open fire, casting everchanging shapes onto walls of stone. After combing the castle for people or food, and finding neither, Iain sits in front of the fire. He tunes his ears to the sound of its crackles as his eyes follow the graceful orange-flame bellydancers on the walls. To his left, a hidden door slides open with the grate of stone on stone. Stairs lead downwards from the newly exposed gap in the wall. Iain plunges down the steps into a cold dungeon with five cells, each containing the stone bust of a dead rock star. In the first cell rests an eerily lifelike bust of Bon Scott, legendary AC/DC singer; mode of death: asphyxiation on vomit after drinking enough alcohol to pickle a brontosaurus. The next cell contains the stone head and shoulders of Phil Lynott, Thin Lizzy founder and frontman; mode of death: heart failure and pneumonia following a heroin overdose. KISS drummer Eric Carr stares lifelessly from the third cell; mode of death: cancer. Next door to him, balanced on top of a ceramic white toilet, is Randy Rhoads, original guitarist with Ozzy Osbourne; mode of death: plane crash. In the farthest cell from the light is a scruffy-bearded Kurt Cobain, Nirvana frontman; mode of death: shotgun blast to the head while out of that head on heroin.

As the floor starts to shudder, Iain grabs rusty metal bars to keep his balance. The outer surfaces of the stone busts crumble and fall away, revealing flesh heads. Bon Scott's head blinks, spits out a mouthful of stone dust and says, "G'day, mate. We've been waiting a long time for you."

"This must be a dream," gasps Iain. "You're Bon Scott. Well, you're his noggin."

"Well observed. My illustrious colleagues and I are here, in Concussion Castle, to give you some nuggets of advice which just may keep you alive and well on your journey. You've probably already realised what my friends and I have in common."

"You're all heids! Disembodied heids. Rock-star heids."

"You missed one vital point. We're heads of *dead* rock stars."

"Aye, I know that. Disembodied heids tend to be that way…deid, I mean."

"Exactly right, mate! And dead rock stars can teach you a whole lot more about the world into which you are about to hurl yourself than living ones can. We didn't learn from our mistakes, but you can. We can teach you the most valuable lessons of all - strategies for staying alive and succeeding in a business where most legends are dead ones."

"I know what you mean, Bon. Like Jimi Hendrix. He was an alright guitar player, a bollocks singer and had only a handful of good tracks, yet look at the legend he became."

"Right again, mate," agrees Bon, nodding as if his neck were a spring. "Look at Cobain down there for an even better example. His band was shit. They couldn't write a good track if the sheet music was a cow's arse and their pen was a banjo. Kurt couldn't carry a tune in a bucket. Now kids who hadn't even been born when he died are wearing T-shirts with his moaning, eye-linered face on them."

From the other end of the dungeon, Cobain shouts, "Hey asshole, I fuckin' heard that! I have three words for you, Bon – *Back in Black*, the second-biggest-selling album of all time. Over forty-million units sold. It was the first album AC/DC recorded *after* you died and the band replaced you with Brian Johnson. Coincidence? Or a better singer?"

Bon flies into a rage. "I'd come down to your cell and kick your bollocks if I had feet...and you had bollocks! You impressed no one with your whinin' about how terrible it was to be a huge rock star. If you didn't like the fame and attention, why did you get involved in the first place, ya fuckin' drongo?"

"Bon, Kurt, please don't fight," Iain pleads. "It's amazin' to see you and I'd like to get my advice noo, just in case I'm due to wake up soon."

All five heads nod. Bon starts the lesson, his accent a seamless mixture of Scottish and Australian. "OK, Iain mate. Every pleasure has an aftermath. With heavy metal success comes many temptations. Choose your poisons – and your quantities – very carefully. Any substance you abuse will abuse you right back. This is especially true of booze, drugs and women. The one thing you can and should throw yourself relentlessly into is the music. It will never let you down or bite you back. The more you put into it, the more you get out of it. Lesson over."

"Thank you, Sensei."

Phil Lynott beams a smile. His black moustache glitters in the light from a flaming torch on the wall. "Hello there, ya wee gobshoite."

"Ehm...hello Phil...I mean Mr Lynott."

"Do you know why oi called you a gobshoite?"

"An affectionate term?"

Phil's laughter echoes so loudly that the other heads wish they had hands with which to cover their ears. "Oi do loike ya, son, make no mistake. But oi called you a gobshoite because your band has never covered a T'in Lizzy song. That's a travesty you'll have to be fixin'."

"I'll speak to Spark and see what we can do."

"Do that. And always be true to yourself. People are smarter than you give them credit for. They can tell if you're fakin' it. Don't try to look or sound American to crack the US. Don't jump on any musical bandwagons. Build your own wagon and make it original. Most bands that try to jump onto a bandwagon land on a hearse."

"Aye, I see what you're gettin' at."

"Well take moi words to heart and you'll be foine, Iain lad."

"Thanks, man."

Eric Carr's smooth American voice floats from the adjoining cell. "Iain, I'll keep this simple. The use of a tank or other large war paraphernalia as part of your stage set can never be a bad thing. War never goes out of fashion. Incorporate epic images of war – of good versus evil – into your lyrical and musical themes. Over and out."

Iain nods silent thanks to KISS's dead sticksman, then moves along to the next cell, from which the shy and retiring Randy Rhoads gazes through hazel eyes. He, more than the other heads, exudes peace and love. Altering his demeanour appropriately, Iain whispers, "Hello, Randy. I love your work wi' Ozzy Osbourne. What can I learn from you today?"

A soft voice replies, "Master your craft. Always seek to improve your ability as a musician. Never rest on your laurels. There's always scope for improvement. Wherever you go on tour, find yourself a teacher and learn, learn, learn. That will keep you humble and inspired. Dying young is not glamorous."

"Thanks, Master."

"You're welcome, young Jedi."

Kurt Cobain's throaty, cigarette-hoarse rasp breaks the silence at the arse-end of the dungeon. "I didn't learn as much as the others from my time in rock 'n' roll because my time was so limited. I did learn this, though – shootin' yourself in the head with a shotgun is not a good idea."

Silence fills the dungeon as Iain and the other heads bounce Kurt's words around in their minds, looking for their profound wisdom…and not finding it. Iain decides that Kurt has not enlightened him with any knowledge that wasn't blindingly obvious. "Ehh, I don't want to sound ungrateful, Kurt, but tell me somethin' I don't already know."

"Read between the lines, you cheeky little fuck. Death does wonders for your popularity and album sales, but if you're not around to enjoy the fruits of your hero status, what's the fuckin' point? I became a musical icon by dying, and how did my missus mourn? Did she sit around dressed in black, listening to Nirvana and sobbing? Did she pepperoni! Instead, Courtney snorted a line of cocaine that stretched from Hollywood to Hell, then sucked a line of dicks that was even longer. I'm a goddamn legend on Earth now, but reality is that I'm just a head, and one with a layer of stone over it most of the time. Stay alive, even when the alternative seems tempting."

"I plan to, Kurt. Thanks."

Cobain nods, the ghost of a smile fluttering over his lips.

"I have a question I'd like you all to answer," says Iain. "What do you miss most? If you had arms and bodies again, what would you most like to do?"

Coughing, Cobain answers, "I'd smoke a pack of cigarettes."

Bon shouts, "I'd fuck a whole women's rugby team. The fatter the better!" Unified laughter echoes around the dungeon.

Randy Rhoads says quietly but assuredly, "I miss my guitars. I'd play them all until my fingers were sore."

Phil Lynott casts his eyes down and admits, almost apologetically, "Oi'd inject heroin roight into moi arm. Oi know it was moi downfall, but oi fuckin' loved it."

A tear runs down Eric Carr's cheek as he says, "I'd put on my KISS make-up, sit at my drum kit on top of the tank and play the gig of my life with Gene, Paul and Ace, my brothers in KISS. They took me in and made me one of them. They gave me a home. And I left them." In the silence that follows, all eyes in the dungeon are tearsparkled and focused on Eric. Iain gets the feeling that if they had bodies, the other stars would be giving Eric Carr a group hug.

After thanking the heads for sharing their wisdom, Iain makes his way towards the stairs. "Hey gobshoite!" shouts Lynott. "You can channel me anytoime you need me."

"What do you mean?"

"Oi mean that oi'm a feckin' great bass player and an even better frontman. If you ever need me, oi'll let you channel me t'rough your body for a whoile."

"Like possession?"

"A bit loike that, except you'd be in charge of when oi come. There is one t'ing, though – you have to be concussed. That makes your brain more receptive to channelling. Before goin' onstage, whack yourself on the head with somethin' hard, and t'ink of me whoile you do it. That should do the trick."

"Are you fuckin' serious, Phil? What if I pan ma heid right in?"

"Then you'll be joinin' us dead rock stars sooner rather than later."

"Ehh…thanks. I might just take you up on those channellin' shenanigans. Can I channel the other four too?"

"No, only me. Oi'm the only real soul here. The other four are just manifestations of your imagination…loike dreams created by your subconscious based on information you already know. The actual souls of the other four are elsewhere."

"OK. Thanks."

"You're feckin' welcome, moi lad. One more t'ing, son. If you're havin' slap and tickle with gorgeous slutty groupies – especially ones with big, juicy arses - feel free to channel me."

"Thanks for the offer, Phil, but female arses are my domain. I'll manage them fine on my own. And by the way, I used your chat-up line from *Live and Dangerous* when I was in Devon on holiday, but changed the nationality part from Irish to Scottish. I walked straight up to this long-legged local beauty and asked if she had any Scottish in her. She said no and scanned me up and doon as I stood there lookin' dashing in my kilt. So then I asked her if she'd like some Scottish in her."

White teeth glint under Phil's black 'tache. "Oi bet that sealed the deal, eh lad? Oi bet you had her legs in the air in no toime after that."

"Actually, no. She slapped my face. Hard."

"Oh, the slap. Well you'll get a lot of them from feminist women. Oi got an awful lot of slaps for usin' that loine…oi also got an awful lot of pussy, though. It evens itself out."

"Well, I may channel you for musical support durin' oor gigs. Women I will handle alone, though."

"It's up to you, gobshoite. The offer stands. If you ever boite off more than you can chew, sexually speaking, oi'm just a bang on the head away."

Iain nods complicity, safe in the knowledge that he'd die before offering up his vaginal sacrifices to anyone, even the mighty rocker Phil Lynott. He waves goodbye to his five new friends. On realising that they can't return the gesture, he cringes. Scraping sounds fill the dungeon as Iain ascends the stairs. A glance over his shoulder reveals five stationary stone busts in torch-lit cells, all traces of life gone from their countenances.

Mike Stone, Iain's next-door neighbour, kicks the heap of flesh with its mouth in the dirt. Iain fails to respond, stirring Mike to bundle his body into a Land Rover and drive to hospital at breakneck speed.

X-rays show Iain's cranium to be intact, a testament to its hardiness, but his concussion is severe. The attending doctor orders that he be kept in overnight for observation.

I open my eyes and find myself surrounded by wooden shards from a broken chair on the floor of Ozzy's office. Oz and DT are leaning over me, worried expressions on their faces. Under the force of Ozzy's furious fist, something had to break. I'm relieved that it was the chair and not my face. My vision blurs. I taste blood in my throat. Everything feels unreal. I know this feeling. A bruised brain is swelling inside my skull. Welcome back concussion my old friend.

"I'm sorry for punchin' you, Spark. I couldn't help it, though. You pissed me right off. Just as you talk me into reinvestin' my faith in the band, you get us a tour wi' a bunch o' German knob jockeys."

"Your faith gave us faith," adds DT. "Your unshakeable belief made us believe in this band again. When you brought Ted to us, things really came to life. Fuck sake, you even got Iain to play bass. You're the captain o' this ship and we all know it, but when you announce that you've signed us up to tour America in support of Teutonic tadger tormentors, the sea under that ship starts to feel worryingly choppy."

"That's why I punched you," says Oz, "oot o' frustration. I've got so much hope in Transcend Everything that it's unbearable at times. One moment you lead me to believe we'll be tourin' America wi' Accept, then you rip that image away and replace it wi' visions of us sharin' showers wi' German arse bandits."

"Aye," agrees DT, "I'm far too sexy to be trapped on a bus wi' uphill gardeners."

"Dudes," I plead, "you're bein' judgemental. You need to *hear* these fuckers. Their music's amazin' and their lyrics are as good as Spinal Täp's. Gayer, it's true, but very funny."

"For fuck's sake, Spark," whines Dave, "please tell me this is a wind-up."

I look into my blood brothers' eyes: first into Ozzy's blue oceans, then into Dave's dark pools. "Have faith in me. I haven't signed oor arses up to be rented all over America. It's a tour. What would you say if I'd got us support slots wi' Judas Priest? You'd be droolin' like over-excited mental patients. Remember, though, that Rob Halford's gay. He's a walkin', breathin' metal deity, aye. He's one of oor heavy metal heroes, for sure. He also happens to be so flaming that the sun's dim by comparison.

So quit bein' so fuckin' homophobic and start seein' this for what it is – a real tour. Pink Stëel's music is excellent, so it shouldn't matter where they choose to park their penises."

A pained look crosses DT's face. "Oh fuck, can you imagine Pink Stëel's groupies? It'll be a pile o' pansy bastards in pink lycra and lipstick!"

Oz smiles. "You'll fit right in, Dave, wi' your silky womanesque hair and your pink leather troosers."

"They're red!" screams DT, climbing onto a chair to give us a better view of his skintight strides.

I shake my head. "Ozzy's right. They're pink."

"They're fuckin' red!"

DT's face turns the same shade as his trousers. He dives on top of me and wrestles me to the floor. Flipping him over, I pin his arms to the floor with my knees, leaving my crotch hovering ominously above his face. "I'm gonnae shove some pink steel in your homophobic mooth right noo!"

The next thing I'm aware of is the sensation of flying backwards through the air. As I bounce off a wall and land in a heap, Oz booms, "I'll have none o' that in this hoose! Even pseudo-poofy behaviour is unacceptable here!"

It's time to let the music speak for itself. I've brought a CD with four Pink Stëel tracks on it: *Sausage Party*, *Converter*, *I'm Comin' Out (All Over You)* and *Johnny Are You Queer?* Helmut Bang's bass drum kicks off *Sausage Party* in a style reminiscent of Spinal Täp's *Big Bottom*. Hanson Jobb's spoken-word introduction follows, sounding like an anally fixated Accept, a sausage-smoking Scorpions, a rectum-loving Rammstein. '*Zees eez not a Tuppervare party. Eet'z not a pool party. Eet eez definitely not a party of five. I have a question for you – who vants to go to a sausage party?*'

DT stares into space, a pensive look on his face. Hanson starts to sing: a high-pitched, high-voltage, throaty scream. '*No girls, just boys. I'm gonna throw a sausage party all ze men vill enjoy.*' I notice Dave's pout edging towards a smile. I've known him long enough to read his nuances; he's digging the music and seeing the humour in the lyrics. Shaking his head, Ozzy announces, "Paul Roberts is gettin' fired as oor manager right after I part his plums wi' my boot."

A little face framed by big hair peeks round the door. "Sparky, will you sing me a bedtime song? I'm sleepy."

"Sure, wee girl. I'm on it."

Happy about my temporary reprieve from my blood brothers, I jump to my feet and take Sunshower's hand. Star-constellation pyjamas cover her delicate frame, the baggy sleepwear dwarfing the little stargazer. After tucking her into bed, I kneel at her side and sing improvised lyrics to the tune of White Lion's *When the Children Cry*.

"Little girl, big blue cryin' eyes,
mind of a Buddha, and wonder in your soul.
You emerged into a family,

where a Dad must be more than a Dad,
without a book of rules.

Where did you come from?
Where has your mother gone?
A world on the brink of despair,
you have the power to repair.

When Sunshower cries,
all the angels sigh.
When Sunshower fights,
angels scream in the night.
When Sunshower prays,
it lights the angels' way.
And when Sunshower sings,
the new world grows wings."

Yawning, Sunshower rubs heavy, half-shut eyes. As she drifts into sleep, I whisper the words that flow into my mind.

"Sunshower, moonflower.
Eyes of blue, hair of dark fire.
Mystic dreamer, spirit dancer, little Zen master,
wild and free, innocent you rescue me."

A little sigh ruffles the duvet. I lean over the bed, kiss Sunshower's cheek, then tiptoe towards the door. A new photo frame on the bedside table catches my attention. In the silver rectangle is a photo of me playing my BC Rich Warlock. I float out of the room feeling lighter than air.

Chapter 58 – Diary of a Madman

"I did more than compose music, eat, sleep, smoke and make love wi' Lisa durin' my hibernation," expounds Pete. "I experimented wi' the *effects* of sound, usin' mysel' as a guinea pig."

"And what ground-breakin' discoveries did you make?"

"Shove your sarcasm, Spark. I'm *serious*. It all started when I was readin' a book aboot the pyramids of Egypt. The author proposed a convincin' alternative theory of the pyramids' construction. The ancient Egyptians employed specific sounds to levitate the giant stones and move them into place. Isn't that theory a lot more feasible than the bullshit most orthodox Egyptologists spout aboot thoosands of gigantic, multi-ton stone blocks bein' carried and put in place by underfed slaves in blistering desert heat? Think aboot it – how could malnourished, sun-scorched dudes have heaved hoose-sized stones across the desert, then *lifted* them hundreds of feet into the air and laid them doon wi' laser precision?"

"I've wondered that myself, I have to admit."

"Exactly! They didn't do it. That's just the dogmatic pish that's still widely accepted despite bein' unproven and scientifically unfeasible. Usin' sounds of a very specific pitch and frequency – the Sounds of Power – the pyramids were built from memory, manifestations on the fourth dimensional level, and they were built *from the top doon* in seven days. I discovered that the pyramids connect the consciousness of oor evolutionary pattern wi' the logarithmic spiral."

"You need to get oot more, Pete."

"Bein' trapped indoors wasn't the worst fate in the world. I had time to ponder the mysteries of existence. So what do you think aboot usin' power sounds to build superstructures, Electric Boy?"

"It sounds theoretically possible. If radio waves can be sent through air, then why not huge stone blocks? Everything's made of energy."

"Exactly! The principle is the same. Only the scale differs. So I set oot to find the exact frequency, pitch and volume of the sounds that can levitate objects. I wanted to use sound to defy gravity. I haven't managed to do that yet, but I made other discoveries along the way. Go and stand at the mid-point between those two big amps." Pete points an index finger and I stand in its line of fire. He sits on a wooden stool and fumbles through the smoke-yellowed, dog-eared pages of a notebook. Slowly and methodically, he smoothes out a specific page. He takes plastic ear plugs out of his pocket and pops them into his ears. Moments later, a low-pitched rumble emanates from the amplifiers. Before I know what has hit me, there's keech in my pants. Pete grins, his hair volting upwards as he pulls the plugs from his ears and asks, "What do you think, man? Cool or what?"

"I think I've done a shit in my pants. That's what I think. Not cool, Drummond. Very far from cool."

"That's why I wore earplugs. I went through a few pairs o' pants when I was testin' oot that sound. I made careful note o' volumes, pitches, frequencies and synth settings. Everything got documented, man. I repeated my trials thoosands o' times to make sure none of it was a fluke."

"Fuck sake, dude, couldn't you just have told me aboot this? Did you have to make me keech my troosers?"

"Would you have believed me?"

"No."

"Well there's your answer, cat."

"It's been a momentous few years for you. You've scored a movie *and* found a noise that makes people shit themselves. Your Mum must be proud."

"Sarcasm is the lowest form of wit, man. The broon note – that's its technical name – wasn't my only discovery. Stand still and I'll show you another one."

"Fuck that! I'm goin' home to get cleaned up."

"Stand still!"

"OK, OK, calm yourself. I dread to think what's goin' to happen this time."

Once again, Pete inserts earplugs and stares down at his notebook. Much twiddling of synthesizer knobs ensues. I can't hear any sound, but I feel my insides vibrating. A sense of well-being overcomes me, followed by a magnificent erection which - before I have a chance to reflect on its unexpected presence – ejaculates, prompting a horrified shriek. Pete lifts his hands into the air, fingers upstretched. "How much of a genius am I?"

"Genius? Fuckin' genius? You raped me, ya wee bastard!"

"It's not rape. Years ago, when Lisa was sittin' on my knee, I came in my pants, but that wasn't rape. And I wasn't rapin' mysel' the thoosands o' times I tested this frequency."

"Well it might no' technically be rape, but it's rude to make a dude cum in his pants withoot his consent. In fact, it's borderline gayness."

"Vamoose, Spark. You're startin' to stink the place up."

"You know what? Your skills as a host leave a lot to be desired. Maybe instead o' readin' books by rogue Egyptologists and messin' wi' frequencies o' sound like a deranged Einstein, you should read some books on etiquette. Try becomin' a wee bit more of a people person."

"I'll pass. I've got this far withoot any real social skills. Noo please fuck off before I have to fumigate the flat."

"Do me a favour, eh? Warn me the next time you're gonnae pull any stunts like that."

"I will. I'll show you my other discoveries another time, man."

"Nothin' that'll make more bodily fluids shoot oot o' me, I hope?"

"I discovered a sound that brings on an extreme headache followed by projectile puking. There's also a sound that convinces me I'm one o' those machines that cleans chewin' gum off paving slabs, but the feelin' wears off after an hour or so."

"You're jokin', right?"

"Serious as an accident in your pants."

"For fuck's sake, Pete. We can't have fans leavin' oor gigs wi' soiled underwear, then spendin' the next few hours cleanin' chewin' gum off pavements wi' their teeth. How'll that help us redefine metal? You're one screwed-up individual, Jazz Boy."

"Takes one to know one, as some cats say. Anyway, time for you to go. My livin' room's startin' to smell like a Sikh's jobbie."

"Could you be more racist?"

"That's not racist – it's a factual observation. I shared a flat wi' a Sikh once and you did not want to go near the toilet for aboot a week after that fucker had been in there. It'd make your eyes water and your nostrils burn. I think it was his diet…all that ghee."

"I'm off before this conversation gets any worse. I won't forget the sonic assaults, ya wee bastard. When we're rich I'll sue you for damages."

"When we're rich I'll let you."

As I walk to the door with straight-legged strides, Pete lowers his eyes to his notebook and reads aloud. *"I've found the 'brown note', a frequency of sound that brings about involuntary relaxation of the anal sphincter and makes people shit uncontrollably. I remember seeing an episode of South Park in which Cartman and Co. set out to find the brown noise. Their plan was to use it during a worldwide recorder concert, thus making the whole world shit itself at the same time. It made funny viewing, but up until now I reckoned the existence of such a sound to be a fanciful myth."*

I arrive back at my house and find Iain sitting on my front step. "You smell like shit," he quips.

"I don't smell *like* shit. I smell *of* shit."

"What shat on you?"

"I filled my pants at Pete's hoose."

Iain shakes his head. "Spark, what age are you?"

"It wasn't my fault. It was…ehh…it's a long story. Anyway, what are you doin' sittin' ootside my hoose like a gay stalker?"

"I had a couple o' holiday days to take and it looked like a nice night for a drive, so here I am."

"How long did it take you?"

"AA Route Planner said it was a ten-hour drive, but I did it in six."

"You reckless son of a bitch. Blackfoot wrote their song *Drivin' Fool* aboot you. Make us a pot o' coffee while I shower."

"Good idea. You smell like a skunk's sack."

After disrobing upstairs, I examine the damage to my underpants and jeans. The denims may be salvageable, but the pants are a write-off. Burning them would be the best option - burnt at the stake for olfactory offences. I open my bathroom window and launch the pants. They land with a satisfying crinkle atop a gorse bush.

I'm not partial to frequent washing, but it feels good to wash the unholy combination of shit and spunk off my body. I head downstairs wrapped in a saltire towel, my wet hair dripping a trail of waterspots on the carpet behind me. After gulping down a mouthful of coffee, Iain asks, "Do you fancy a ride on the mountain bikes?"

"When?"

"Tonight. My bike's in the car and it's a perfect night – dry, still and very dark."

"Deal."

Iain and I scorch along the Covenanter's Trail on our mountain bikes, their halogen front lights carving cylindrical holes through the darkness as we navigate the twists and turns of the boulder-strewn track. The only sounds are our breathing, the whistling wind and the crunch of tyres on dry stone. Pulling up parallel to me, Iain asks, "Would you have sex wi' Rob Halford?"

"He's one o' my heroes, but I wouldn't have sex wi' him. Would you?"

"Of course not. Would you kiss him? Imagine you and I are backstage after a Judas Priest gig, drinkin' Evian and eatin' fun-size Mars Bars. Suddenly, Halford strides in wearin' chainmail underpants and says he'd like to kiss you. How would you respond?"

"I don't think Halford wears chainmail underpants."

"For the purposes of this investigation, he does. Quit stallin' and answer the question!"

"As long as it was just a kiss, I'd do it."

"I knew it, ya toley terroriser!"

"I'd even kiss him wi' tongues and let you video it, then I'd upload it onto the Internet myself. It'd be a laugh, me kissin' the Metal God. Would you no' kiss him?"

"There's no way I'd kiss any man, Metal God or otherwise. That's just flat-oot poofy." Iain pauses for a few seconds, the pregnant pause of a man deep in thought. Then, in a matter-of-fact tone, he admits, "I'd let Halford suck my dick, though."

Shocked, I turn to look at my blood brother. My bike careers off the trail and slams into a boulder, catapulting me over the handlebars and into the night air. After a brief flight, I land in a jaggy bush which finds itself wearing me in the same way Tom Baker used to wear his multi-coloured scarf in Doctor Who. "Ya fuckin' dick, Bright! Why did you have to say that? I'm a pincushion here."

Pulling me out of the bush, Iain says, "I wasnae jokin', Spark. I'd let Halford suck my dick. It's no big deal. I'd let pretty much anyone suck it."

"Let me get this right. Accordin' to your insane logic, I'm gay for hypothetically kissin' Halford, yet you'd put your tadger right into his mooth and not see that as remotely homosexual. Is this nonsense what you're proposin'?"

"Aye. I could close my eyes and pretend he was a woman. I couldn't do that if I was kissin' him and his stubble was scratchin' my face. Therefore, you're gay and I'm not."

"So you don't like the thought of Halford's beard scratchin' your face, but you'd be happy to have it rubbin' against your balls? You're deranged. Seek help."

"At least I can stay on a bike, ya wee girl. I'll race you to the Auchengilloch Monument. Last one there buys the takeaways from Chew." Before I have a chance to accept or decline his challenge, Iain has saddled his bike - like a cowboy mounting a horse - and plunged into the darkness. I rescue my crashed bike from its point of impact and hurtle a pursuit, my gaze locked onto Iain's red tail light.

Chapter 59 – Love like Winter

There's a saying that the rain in Spain stays mainly on the plain. Today, the air in Stair smells mainly of despair. I detected the faint scents of pine and burning logs as I drove into the picture-postcard Ayrshire town. The comfort that these aromas usually arouse is doused by the black cloud that hangs above Angel today. We sit at a wooden picnic table outside a country tavern called The Stair Oot, a centuries-old stone building engulfed by climbing ivy from which the occasional white flower blooms. Dressed in bleached jeans with rips at the knees and buttocks, Angel is atypically devoid of make-up. In her eyes is something far from the warmth and affection usually resident there. I can't quite get a handle on it, but there's a new storm brewing in those summer-blue eyes. "Are you OK, girl? You seem distracted."

"Just sufferin' through some thoughts in my head."

"Physics stuff?"

"Personal stuff."

"Anythin' I can help you wi'?"

"No. Let's just eat? I'll unscramble my head myself."

"If that's how you want it."

"That's how I want it."

Throughout the meal and coffee afterwards, talk is awkward and forced, the atmosphere thickening as conversation thins. By the time we leave the tavern, I'm desperate for solitude. "Will you take me shopping?" asks Angel.

"Shoppin' on a perfect summer's day like this? Seriously?"

"I don't feel like bein' around nature. I need some retail therapy."

"If you must, then I guess so. I want you to know, though, that I'm doin' this under duress. I expect rewards of a coital nature." Angel doesn't reply. Her eyes moisten; the storm I predicted is arriving and appears to be moments from a downpour. Nothing is said for the rest of the drive to Kilmarnock.

As we walk past an Ann Summers shop, I attempt to lift Angel's spirits by suggesting that she go in and try on some outfits. "Is sex *all* you think about?" she growls.

"I think aboot music too."

"Is that supposed to be funny?"

"For fuck's sake, girl, what happened to your sense o' humour? It feels like you've had a personality bypass."

"You know I'm goin' through some personal shit, yet you resort to hurlin' insults and kickin' me while I'm down."

"I offered to talk aboot it wi' you and you refused. It's no' my fault you're feelin' doon."

"Isn't it?"

"Are you sayin' I'm the cause o' the black cloud over your heid?"

"Never mind."

"Fuck that! I *do* mind. You can't go accusin' me o' messin' up your heid. I've never wronged you, Angel."

"It's not *you*. It's just *things*."

"What things?"

"Drop it. Let's just go into the shop." Angel sweeps into the store, auburn hair billowing behind her. I follow at a safe distance, not wanting to be caught under her brooding black stormcloud when it bursts.

In my element among slutty outfits, lacy lingerie, furry handcuffs and all manner of weirdly shaped sex toys, I wander over to Angel with a naughty-Policewoman outfit over my arm and a rampant-rabbit vibrator in my hand. "I have the perfect idea for cheerin' you up tonight."

Angel flicks hair off her face. "Is that what I am to you? A sexual plaything? A personal porn star for the wannabe rock star?" Her outburst draws anxious glances from other shoppers. Speechless, and more than a little offended at being called a wannabe, I shrug my shoulders. Angel screams, "You're not even denyin' it! I've hit the nail on the head! I'm just a warm, wet vagina wrapped in a pretty package, is that it?"

"Your vagina *is* spectacular, I won't deny that. I also can't deny that I find you both aesthetic and functional."

"Aesthetic and functional! You make me sound like a fuckin' coffee table. The first thing you ever said to me was a sausage-related euphemism. Things haven't changed."

"Why do things have to change if they're perfectly good the way they are? You weren't averse to my advances back then. And I've never been less than honest wi' you."

A bulky, black-haired woman in a black leather mini-dress, fishnet stockings and high heels emerges from behind the counter and struts towards us with surprising grace for a woman her size. Her name tag says 'Nikki' and her almond eyes are narrowed like those of an eagle about to dive-bomb a newborn lamb. "Quieten down or leave the premises! I have a business to run here. If you continue to create a scene I'll phone the police."

"Oh no, Nikki, not the dreaded Killie constabulary. Those lazy sons o' bitches would take at least an hour to arrive, if they'd even bother to arrive for such a petty complaint. Anyway, the police don't get involved in domestic disputes unless they escalate into violence."

"Sir," Nikki pleads, lowering her voice and smiling nervously at the other shoppers, "please be reasonable. I don't want any trouble. I'm sure you don't either."

Raising my hands, I admit, "You're right. I wouldn't want you to open a pack o' those pink furry handcuffs, clamp me to the radiator and punish me for bein' a bad boy."

Angel's stormcloud bursts, showering her with sorrow. Her mouth morphs into an upside-down smile. "First you treat me like a sex toy on legs! Then you start flirtin' wi' this heffer! Fuck, Spark, you're a prize asshole!" She blazes out of the store, leaving stunned shoppers in her wake.

I turn to Nikki and grimace. "I'm sorry she called you a heffer. It's no' like her to be nasty like that. You're no heffer. You're a voluptuous, sexy woman."

Cheeks reddening, Nikki says, "Thank you. Maybe you should go after her." I glance out of the shop and see Angel disappearing into throngs of Saturday shoppers.

On a high shelf is a box labelled 'Vibrating Vagina'. Throwing shame to the winds, I reach up, grab the box and slam it onto the counter. "Ring this up in a hurry please, Nikki. Throw in some lube too. I've a feelin' I'll need it." As she stuffs my purchases into an Ann Summers bag, Nikki winks a mascara-laden eye. Smiling, I sprint out of the shop in hot pursuit of my heavy metal hottie.

Chapter 60 – Blackened

High-velocity hailstones exfoliate DT's face as he runs from his car to the farmhouse door. After an unsuccessful stab at the lock, his key slides in and turns with a click. He steps into the hall, kicks off his cowboy boots, grabs a towel from a radiator and rubs his hair to a state of near dryness. Saxon gallops into the hall to greet Dave, who tosses his soggy towel over the charging animal's head. After careering into a wall, the dog paws the towel off his head and gives DT a furry frown which communicates with absolute certainty that payback will be dished out in due course.

A red LED number 3 is flashing on Dave's answering machine. He sits beside the phone and listens to his messages. The first is from Spark: incoherent ramblings about having lost Angel in Ayrshire, followed by some mention of a vibrating vagina. Shaking his head, DT thinks it unsurprising that Spark's bird is trying to escape.

The second message is from Ozzy, expressing his doubts about touring America in close-quarters confinement with homosexuals, and Teutonic ones at that. Sunshower's little voice shouts, "Hello, Mr Woman's Hair!" Again DT shakes his head. "Everyone's a fuckin' critic."

In the final message, a deep voice talks in short, snappy sentences. "Paul Roberts here. I'm glad you're OK with the Pink Stëël tour. I've found the perfect recordin' location for the album. Trust me on this, it's oot o' this world. Talk soon."

DT dials Paul's number. "I got your message. What's this spectacular location you've found for us?"

"Blackness! I was in Edinburgh for a meeting yesterday. Afterwards, I went for a drive on some country roads and stumbled upon Blackness. It's a coastal town as picturesque as anywhere on the planet, plus there couldn't be a more heavy metal place name. None more black."

"All very good, man," says DT, "but where in this wee coastal toon are we goin' to record the album by which all metal albums will be measured? I doubt there's a recordin' studio there."

"Blackness Castle."

"I'm sure the owner won't want a bunch of reprobates fillin' his castle wi' deafenin' noise."

"That's already taken care of. I was walkin' along the beachfront at Blackness and this old country gent was oot wi' his two dobermans. The dogs wouldn't leave me alone, which convinced the man I must be worthy of his attention, as he reckoned his dogs to be excellent judges o' character. We sat on the dunes and had a long chat. He turned oot to be a very likeable old geezer and the owner of the local castle. Based on the way he blethered to me for ages, I reckon he gets lonely livin' alone in the castle wi' only his dogs as company."

"Forgive my bluntness, but how much will this cost? Castles cost a small fortune to rent oot for a one-day wedding, so it'll cost a mint to hire this place for as long as we need to record the album. No doubt you expect me to fund the whole thing. I agreed to pay for oor flights to America, but I'm no' an endless supply of money."

"That's the beautiful part. The old man, Mr MacLeod, offered us use o' the castle for free. He's off to Japan later in the year and fancied me as a hoose-sitter. When I proposed recordin' the album there, he loved the idea of his estate becomin' part o' rock history. I still need to sign a contract to take responsibility for any and all damages to MacLeod's residence while he's away, so none o' your rock 'n' roll wrecking sprees, please, Mr Tierney."

"Ya wee beauty! Well done, Paul Roberts. You've redeemed yoursel' in style."

"By the way, I just faxed Pink Stëël a contract that gives Hanson and Udo legal rights to use your bottom as they desire for the duration o' the tour. They mentioned somethin' aboot you bein' the fillling in their sandwich, whatever *that* may mean. Also, Hanson wants some hair-care tips from you."

"Again wi' the fuckin' hair! Since when was it a crime to look after one's appearance? The rest o' the fuckers in the band could take a leaf oot o' my personal-grooming book."

"You've actually got a book on that?"

"No, arsehole, I don't have a book on it. I was speakin' figuratively."

"Well, I have some demonic pacts to sign in blood. I better go and get busy."

"Do me a favour and never joke aboot infernal pacts aroon' Pete. He reckons the Devil tried to rip oot his soul. Just don't mention sellin' souls to Satan, just in case. Noo get your lazy arse back to work on oor behalf. Begone from this phone line!"

"You're a real charmer, Dave. I'll talk to you soon."

DT hangs up the phone, shuts his eyes and inhales a slow lungful of air through his nose. His body relaxes as he is filled by the feeling that he, Spark and the rest of their band of misfits are on the cusp of greatness. He dials Spark's number and gets his answerphone. "Spark, ya wee tit, I have some good news. Phone me back."

On arriving home sans Angel and finding an answerphone message from an excited-sounding DT, I call him straight back. "What's this monumental news, Dave? Did you find a woman wi' bigger tits than Oz and glossier hair than you?"

"This is serious!"

"What is it? I haven't heard you this worked up since the first time you got your hole."

"This is an even bigger deal than that. Your pal Paul Roberts has found us a place to record the album. It's a countryside location and we're gettin' it free for a month."

"Free? What kind o' place did he find us for free? It's bound to be a ragged, rotting shed wi' weeds sproutin' where floorboards used to be."

"You would think so, but it's rather more grandiose than that. I'll let him tell you aboot it."

"Where is it?"

"Ruin the surprise? I don't think so. Paul came through for us, that's all I'm sayin'."

"Well if you won't tell me, I'm off to phone Polyfilla Boy."

"Wait, Spark," says Dave, his voice low and full of gravitas. "There's a feelin' coursing through me that we're teeterin' on the precipice of heavy metal greatness. All we need is the courage to dive in. Know what I mean?"

"I do, my partner-in-crime. That's the feelin' I've had since my resurrection. That's why I was willin' to do whatever it takes to get the old gang back together. Everythin' we need is either inside us or up there in the generous Universe waitin' to be grasped."

"I feel the way I used to on the way to gang fights," observes DT. "It's the same mix o' nerves and excitement."

"I love you, DT. Soon the world will know oor names, but let's stay humble."

"Aye, definitely. I don't feel big-heided anyway. I feel blessed."

"Me too."

"Right, I've got work to do. My business doesn't run itself. Go and see Paul. You won't be disappointed."

"OK. Rehearsal at your farmhoose tomorrow night?"

"Aye, at 8 p.m. See you then."

"Adios."

The drive to Paul's flat, a fifteen-minute excursion at speed limit, takes me seven minutes. He opens the door, a wide smile splitting his face. As we embrace on the landing like long-lost brothers, a meaty forty-something woman sporting a salmon jumpsuit, white trainers and peroxide hair with black roots waddles down the stairs. On seeing us, she stops, takes the cigarette out of her mouth and stares. "This isn't what it looks like," says Paul.

The woman raises thinly plucked black eyebrows, replaces the cigarette between her lips and continues on her downwards journey, mumbling, "Whatever," as she disappears out of sight.

Paul pulls out his mobile, dials a number and presses the speakerphone button. A deep voice with a lilting east-coast Scottish accent says, "Ronald MacLeod speaking."

"Mr MacLeod, sir, it's Paul Roberts. I met you on the waterfront the other day."

"Hello, Paul. How are you, my boy?"

"Good, thanks. I'm with Spark. I was wonderin' if I could bring him over to Blackness this evening. If you're not too busy, that is."

MacLeod's laugh echoes around the stairwell. "It's been a while since I was too busy. I've read every book in my considerable library at least three times. A couple of young visitors tonight would save me from the fate of immersing myself yet again in well-worn, yellowed pages. Be here for 9 p.m. I'll order some fine food for us all."

"We'll pay for the food, Mr MacLeod."

"Nonsense, my boy. It's rare that I find a person to connect with. The locals prefer their gossip and small talk, something I don't partake of. I'm certain they have their theories about the eccentric old recluse in his castle. You and Spark bring your lively souls here. I'll provide the food."

"If you insist, sir."

"I do. See you boys soon."

Paul and I weave a trail from west coast to east, spearing through diagonal rain in his sky-blue Ford. Our conversation ranges from his Polyfilla exploits to my loss of Angel in a shopping precinct. Despite facing legal action, Paul sees the funny side of the Janine situation.

As we pass a sign welcoming us to the ancient hamlet of Blackness, the rain eases off and I catch my first glimpse of the castle, perched on a rock above the sea like a dark defender. Paul turns to me, smiles and veers off the road, heading straight for a birch tree. With a stamp on the brakes, he grinds the car to a halt inches away from collision. "For fuck's sake, Paul, keep your eyes on the road when you're drivin'! It'd be criminal to wrap us roon' a tree when we're this close to success. Marc Bolan I am not."

Despite his large physical size, Paul looks like a toddler who has just been told off by his mother, right down to the petted lower lip and hung head. "Sorry, Spark. I just wanted to see the look on your face when you saw Blackness Castle for the first time."

Gazing up at the turretted fortress above white-tipped waves on a rough sea, I can't help but be awed. The castle looks menacing and moody, imposing and impervious.

Paul reverses the car back onto the road, then eases forwards towards our destination. Outside the castle's locked security gate is an intercom system. Paul lowers his window, extends an arm and presses the buzzer. On top of the high metal gate and adjoining fence, I notice sharp spikes. MacLeod's voice booms through the intercom speaker. "Intruders, you have twenty seconds to remove yourself from the property! Twin cannons are aimed at your position. After the cannonballs strike, hungry guard dogs will be loosed to feast on your remains!"

My arse starts to waver as Paul reaches for the intercom again. His index finger rattles the button, drilling out panicked Morse code. "Mr MacLeod, it's Paul Roberts!"

"Ten seconds!"

Paul reverses down the hill at breakneck speed then brakes so hard that our heads merge with the headrests. We sit in silence, eyes forward, hearts hammering. Just as I'm about to start chastising Paul, the castle gate opens and a gold Rolls Royce emerges. It cruises down the road and stops in front of us, its gleaming grille a chrome grin. An old man clad in a kilt - MacLeod of Harris ancient tartan - leaps out of the Rolls Royce with a catlike motion which belies his apparent age. His clean-shaven face wears the etched lines of a long life, yet his eyes shine like newborn blue stars. The sparse strands of white hair on his shiny dome flutter in the breeze. "Boys, I am sorry. Please forgive an eccentric old man with a questionable sense of humour."

I jump out of the car, ready to bury my boot between MacLeod's aristocratic balls. The Metal Gods intervene. *Castle in the country, first album, gifts from Heaven. Don't fuck it up, hothead.* Instead of parting MacLeod's plums with my foot, I offer him an outstretched hand. "It's an honour to meet you, Mr MacLeod. Do you have a spare pare o' clean underpants in your humble abode?"

MacLeod takes my hand in a vice-like grip, his colourless lips forming a smile. "You must be Spark, the rock 'n' roll reprobate about whom Paul warned me. The leonine mane and determined look in your eyes gave it away." He releases my hand and bows in dramatic fashion. "Ronald MacLeod at your service. Please follow me back up to the castle. Food and beverages await our return." He swishes into the Rolls Royce and zooms up the hill in high-speed reverse. Paul follows. The two cars ascend nose-to-nose, their front bumpers a hair's breadth apart. MacLeod's eyes crinkle at the corners, his grin beaming down at us.

"Did I mention that Ronald MacLeod is an eccentric maniac?" asks Paul, his eyes fixed forwards, knuckles white on the steering wheel.

"You omitted to mention that snippet of information."

"Oh, OK. Ronald MacLeod is an eccentric maniac."

"Aye, Paul. I figured that oot on my own. An eccentric maniac wi' a castle, though, and an interest in bein' some sort o' kilted Sugar Daddy to oor band."

"Play that metal music, white boy. Don't Sugar Daddies have to get sucked? Isn't that the derivation o' the term? They share their wealth in exchange for regular suckings?"

"Aye, I believe you're right. As band manager, the suckin' of any benevolent Sugar Daddies is your responsibility, so you better get your mooth muscles into shape. You'll be the one shovin' your heid up that kilt o' MacLeod's to sook his tadger like it's a Zoom ice lolly."

MacLeod brakes and sends his Rolls Royce into a 180° spin. Paul skids to a stop a midge's whisker from the vintage car's rear bumper. Flinging himself out of his vehicle like a parachutist exiting a plane, MacLeod shouts, "How about that manoeuvre, boys? That's one I learned in Vietnam! Of course, I wasn't physically *in* Vietnam. It's an expression, like *When in Rome, do as the Romans do*. You don't have to be in Italy to put that idea into effect."

"Aye," I nod, "just as every man has a Jap's eye on the end of his taj, even though the vast majority of tadgers are not Japanese and none o' them feature an actual eye."

MacLeod fixes me with the stoic gaze of an old man who no longer has fear of anything. "I hope that wasn't a racist comment, young Spark. I have many Japanese friends. In fact, it's thanks to them that I'm vacating the castle for a month."

"*Jap's eye* is no more a racist term than *Devil's advocate* is a slight on Auld Nick," I explain. "I once had an intimate liaison wi' a girl whose nether regions could have comfortably housed a fleet of trucks and had room left over for a trucker's café. When I mentioned to her that she had a vagina like a wizard's sleeve, that wasn't derogatory to wizards. I like wizards, as it happens."

MacLeod raises his eyes to the sky and ponders my words. "Yes, yes, young Spark, I'm rather partial to the practitioners of magick myself. Your statement didn't cast aspersions on wizards, although I'm fairly certain it was derogatory to the young lady's orifice."

"You didn't see the minge in question, Mr MacLeod. My observation was purely factual."

Rolling his eyes, Paul pleads, "Spark, can we please change the subject? How is it that you bring every conversation roon' to vaginas and sex? Mr MacLeod is a gentleman. I'm sure he doesn't want to hear your crudity."

I look into MacLeod's eyes. "Country gentlemen wi' castles and Rolls Royces can easily take advantage of shallow women who are impressed by such things, eh Mr MacLeod? I bet these walls, if they could talk, would tell stories of many firelit carnal excursions." I cock a quizzical eyebrow at MacLeod. He smiles, raises and lowers his eyebrows twice in rapid succession, then disappears with improbable speed through the castle's arched doors.

"Spark, please behave," pleads Paul. "We haven't signed the contract yet. Quit talkin' like a depraved sex maniac."

"Get real, Paul. Auld MacLeod has seen more pussy than you, me, Oz, DT, Pete and Iain combined. I'll guarantee that. He's a suave James Bond old motherfucker if ever I saw one. A Martini-sippin', Rolls-drivin', castle-ownin', kilt-wearin', virgin-deflowerin' old son of a bitch. I doubt that rememberin' his conquests of the flesh is a bad experience for him."

"Aye, well tone it doon a bit at least. I don't want him pullin' oot o' this because he's worried aboot you turnin' his castle into some sort of east-coast heavy metal slut groupie bordello. Deal?"

"Deal, although I don't think MacLeod will worry aboot us havin' too much pussy in the castle. He'll probably hide cameras in every room to record the action."

Paul turns and heads for the castle's arched entrance doors. "One-track mind," he mumbles as he breezes inside.

Standing in the high-ceilinged stone cavern of the main hall, I feel small and very young; the castle *reeks* of the arcane. Open fires blaze at both ends of the great hall, the smell of burning peat taking my mind back to my Hebridean family on the Isle of Lewis. A shiny metal suit of armour with broadsword and shield stands guard at the base of a wide stone staircase. At the top of the stairs hangs a larger-than-life painting of Ronald MacLeod in tartan trousers, black shoes, white ruffled shirt and gaudy red jacket, his right hand resting on a wolf-headed wooden walking pole while a long-haired Scottish deerhound sits to his left.

As Paul and I stand at the base of the stairs and stare at the magnificently self-indulgent portrait, MacLeod's voice booms, "The creature you see before you was spectacular, truly a force of nature. And so was the dog." His laughter echoes round the hall, lasts for a handful of heartbeats, then ends as suddenly as it began, replaced by a pained frown. "His name was Grey Man of MacLeod. A denser, more stubborn animal never walked the planet, but he was the most loyal and loving companion I have ever known. I miss my big grey boy."

I'm tempted to walk across the grand hall to hug MacLeod, whose tearsparkling eyes reflect firelight. Instead, I offer empathy. "I understand how attached one can get to animals, Mr MacLeod. My first goldfish died when I was six. I was so inconsolable that I had to take two days off school. I continued to keep fish after that, but losin' them never got any easier. For the last few years, my best friend and closest confidante has been a rabbit."

MacLeod nods. "Magical creatures, rabbits. Five decades ago, they were running riot on the grounds here, so I took out my shotgun to dispose of the little rascals. When I had my first rabbit in the crosshair, it turned and looked straight at me. There was no fear on its face…just a gentle, playful expression, its wee pink nose twitching as it stared up the barrel of my gun, ears pointing to the sky. At that moment I fell helplessly in love with the furry beast. To this day, I've never shot one." MacLeod gazes at the portrait on the wall for an absent minute, blinks a few times in rapid succession, then snaps back to the present. "Come, boys. Let's have some sustenance. Then I'll give you the tour."

We sit at an enormous wooden banqueting table in the dining room. Paul and Ronald munch roast-pork dinners from antique china plates and sip red wine from pewter goblets, while I eat a vegetarian-friendly meal of mixed vegetables and a mountain of roast potatoes. "Do you fancy drivin' home tonight, Spark?" asks Paul. "I'm in the mood for hooverin' substantial quantities o' this excellent wine, and you prefer coffee to alcohol anyway."

"Fine by me, Paulo. It's probably best for me to drive anyway, considerin' your lack o' finesse behind the wheel earlier. I'll keep us on the road."

MacLeod disappears and returns with a large silver platter on which he has balanced an oversize cafetière of coffee, a tankard-sized mug, a jug of milk and a crescent of plain-chocolate mints. I devour coffee and chocolate as the other two pour alcohol down their necks with increasing abandon.

MacLeod licks wine-purpled lips and announces, "I want to lay down a few ground rules. When you're staying here, please clean out the fires thoroughly at the end of each night. Keep the place clean. I don't want to return to a pigsty. You can drink yourselves into oblivion if you so desire, but I don't want any illegal substances on the premises. That's basically it. The contract will cover damages, but I have faith that you'll take good care of the place. How does that sound?"

"More than generous, sir," replies Paul. "It's a gesture the band and I appreciate immensely."

"That's good," nods MacLeod. "It will do wonders for my reputation as an eccentric old aristocrat. Perhaps the locals will begin to see me as an altruistic philanthropist, eh? Do you have any more questions for me before I show you around?"

"I have one," I announce. "Do you mind if we have girls in the castle? It'll be just the band and Paul here most o' the time. We'll be all aboot the music, but we'll need some playtime too, especially after we finish recording. It'd be a waste not to take advantage o' such a seductive location."

Ronald smiles. "Of course you may have women here. In fact, they'll probably clean up most of the mess you make. That's if they're young ladies and not disreputable hangers-on. I don't imagine your band is famous enough to attract that type of female?"

"Groupies? Not yet, Mr MacLeod. Most girls run away when they see us, not towards us."

"More fool them, young Spark!" booms MacLeod, waving his goblet around theatrically, spilling crimson rain on the table. "You seem like a very level-headed, health-conscious young man…one who could give a woman a seeing-to she'd tell her grandkids about!"

Feeling my face flush, I stutter, "Ehh…ehm…aye, I do my best. Paul's pretty adventurous in that department too. He invented some novel uses for DIY paraphernalia."

MacLeod dribbles wine down his chin, wipes his mouth on a napkin and stares goggle-eyed at Paul. "I don't even want to imagine!"

"You don't have anythin' to worry aboot, sir," claims Paul. "And ignore what Spark said aboot me and DIY equipment. He's one o' those creative guys whose imagination is in permanent overdrive."

"Is that right, Polyfilla Boy?"

Paul thumps the table. "Spark, enough!"

Floating to a standing position, MacLeod says, "Time for the tour, boys, before you start tearing lumps off each other. Follow me." Full of enthusiasm, he shows us every nook and cranny of the castle, a task which takes the best part of an hour. It seems like the kind of place where skids on the toilet never occur, slumber is always rejuvenating and meals are mouth-watering feasts. It's far removed from my humble Bronzehall beginnings, yet I feel as if I have returned home. Perhaps MacLeod's hospitality has played a part in those feelings, but I can't help thinking there's more to it than that.

At the castle door, Paul and I thank our kilted host. After shaking MacLeod's hand, I give him my most sincere bow. Darkness has dropped. As I start up Paul's Ford, Ronald MacLeod stands in the arched doorway, a blazing fire visible behind him. He raises his right hand in a gesture which is part salute and part wave. Feeling like an excited child, I wave back and ease the car towards the spiked gate, which opens as we approach. I step on the accelerator and cleave through watery darkness, bound for home.

A little over an hour later, I drop Paul off at his house then climb into Rustbucket and drive home. A dark spectre is slumped on my doorstep, shoulders hunched, sodden hair obscuring facial features. The figure sweeps drenched hair aside, revealing the face of an angel. "I've been waitin' here for hours, asshole."

"Serves you right, Angel. You stormed oot of Ann Summers, leavin' me standin' there like a twat. Then you ignored my phone calls all afternoon. Noo I find you on my doorstep lookin' like the abandoned butt-sex lovechild of Alice Cooper and Mortiis."

"Thanks."

"It wasn't a compliment."

"I know."

Blinking rainwater out of my eyes, I open the door. While I brew coffee, Angel towels her hair dry. Shadows under her eyes hint at lost dreams and found worries. After downing a mug of coffee, she disappears upstairs without a word. Ten minutes later, wondering if she is coming back down, I head upstairs and find her lying on her side in my bed, knees pulled up to her chest. "You didn't say you were headin' to bed, Angel."

"I didn't realise I had to ask for permission."

"You know somethin'? You're no' the same carefree girl I met. Sort oot your attitude or go the fuck home. The world's full o' moany bastards, but this hoose is my hassle-free castle."

"Very caring of you."

Hoping that a good night's sleep will lighten Angel's dark mood, I lie down next to her and close my eyes. The mattress begins to oscillate. Angel buries her face in a pillow, which muffles her sobs. When I cuddle her from behind, she prises my arms off her body then moves away.

I leap out of bed and open the wardrobe. Like a ritual, I pull a box from an Ann Summers bag, remove its cylindrical pink contents, insert batteries into the device, squeeze a Brazil-nut-sized dollop of lubricant onto my fingers, rub it over the opening of the synthetic pink orifice, and flick the switch that brings the machine buzzing to life. A moment later, I'm balls-deep in it, which initially feels a little selfish with Angel lying in tears only a few feet away. In my defence, though, I tried talking, consoling and compassionate cuddling, all to no avail. Now I've grown tired of trying. I just want to fuck. As the mechanical muff pulsates and sucks, I feel fleeting shame for getting so much pleasure from a non-human hole, but that feeling passes as the relentless receptacle sucks me over the edge and into ecstatic outpourings. I fling my spunk-filled saviour back into the wardrobe from whence it came, then fall into bed and shut satisfied eyes.

Stripes of sunlight flood through vertical gaps in my bedroom blinds, bleaching the lime-green walls. I'm alone in bed. With a yawn, I pull on a pair of joggies and head downstairs in the hope of finding Angel there, sipping a mug of coffee and back to her usual light spirits.

On the kitchen table is a note:

'Spark,

I had some great times with you. I wish you and your gang all the luck in the world.

I know you're in lust with me. That has always been obvious. I don't doubt that you like me as a person and that you're entranced by my intellect. You're not in love with me, though. I don't think you're able to fall in love: something is missing. Unfortunately for me, I fell for you. If there's one thing I know in an uncertain Universe, it's that I have no intention of continuing to give you unreciprocated love in the hope of one day receiving yours in return.

I'll look out for Transcend Everything's inevitable rise and will feel blessed to have been there at the start of it.

I cannot see you again.

Angel.'

As I frown at the note in an attempt to uncover its deeper significance, I realise that there is no deeper significance. Angel has called a spade a spade. Not only that, she's right. I'm not in love with her, nor could I ever be. We had good fun and stellar sex. We shared a love of heavy music. We were good friends. *'I don't think you're able to fall in love: something is missing.'* Then it hits me like a falling building. Something is indeed missing, but it's not – as Angel thinks – something internal and intangible. The thing that's missing is Kimberley Setzer. I never fell out of love with her. Can I fuck other women? Aye, 'til the cow jumps over the moon and solves the elusive Unified Field Theory. Can I be friends with other women? Definitely, as long as they're easygoing Zen females. Can I be *in love* with another woman? No way in Hell.

I pour a large coffee and sit on the kitchen floor to ponder my dilemma. I've been in love twice, first as a boy, with Gillian Kelsey: a childlike yet legitimate love which was never consummated. Kimberley, however, was the real deal. I fell head over heels for her. We had sex that doesn't fade over time: sweat-soaked sessions that left our bodies sizzling for hours afterwards. We experienced the sort of physical intensity that writers of erotic fiction struggle to describe in words. Unless you've *had* it, it's impossible to *write* it with any authenticity.

My mind drifts to Kimberley: eyes like dark chocolate; long, braided hair; smooth-skinned athletic body; full lips and astonishingly pink tongue. In my mind's eye, I see her naked body. I feel her strong legs wrapped around me as she welcomes me inside. Now I'm horny. And alone.

I head upstairs to my computer and log into instant messenger. My longtime e-friend Shaquanna, a self-proclaimed BBBW (Big Black Beautiful Woman), is online. Soon, thanks to the wonder of webcams, we are looking at each other and exchanging easy chat. She listens to my woman-woes in an empathetic yet detached way, her huge breasts quaking as she nods an understanding head. "Baby, listen to Mama. L-u-u-u-r-v-e ain't all good. What you need is to git your cracka ass to Cocoa Beach when your band gits to Florida…let Mama take care o' you." Shaquanna raises a chubby index finger tipped by a long, red nail. After flicking her tongue over the fingertip, she fellates it down to the knuckle, keeping onyx eyes locked onto me.

"That's a talent I could put to good use," I admit.

She licks purple lips. "How long have ah bin hearin' that shit from you, muthafucka?"

"Eight years."

"We've been chattin' fo' eight years! You know more of mah intimate secrets than anyone. Ah've watched you playin' with that beautiful white cock while ah frigged my pussy 'til ah was damn near slippin' off mah seat, but ah've nevah seen you in da flesh. Dis pussy's hungry for you and ah ain't waitin' forevah." Her southern drawl washes over me like a warm shower.

"The last date of my band's tour is in Miami. I'll rent a car and drive straight to you in Cocoa Beach as soon as the gig's finished."

"You betta git dahn to Cocoa Beach, cracka! You bin juicin' Mama up all these years. Ah got a game fo' us to play. Ah wanna be your slave biyatch and you, fine cracka that you are, will be a plantation owner who loves to use and abuse his nigga slave girl. Ah wanna git spanked hard, ah want mah hair pulled, ah want choked, ah want belted, ah wanna git fucked rougher and harder than ah evah bin fucked befoah."

"Jesus!"

"Leave him outta this. He'd just be disapprovin'. What's goin' oan wit' your mouth? You look like you're catchin' flies."

"I can't do that racist talk. That's horrific."

"You watch horror films and enjoy them. They're horrific."

"Aye, but that's different. You're a human bein'…and a woman. I can't talk to you that way. I wasn't raised like that."

Metallic Dreams

"And ah wasn't raised to be a slave or a victim or to let anyone call me nigga. Not evah. We're playin' a game, cracka. Ah ain't askin' you to buy a plantation and reintroduce slavery. It's make believe. But ah want you to make it believable."

"I will fuck you seven ways 'til Sunday, Sha. I'll have you squirtin' like a fire extinguisher. I'm happy to punish you, spank you, pull your hair, whip you, belt you, lick you, fuck you, even slap you senseless if you want that, but I don't feel good aboot usin' racist talk. I understand the power o' words. Some words should never be aired."

"Eight years ah bin puttin' up wit' your teasin'. It's time ah got mine. Ah ain't askin' you to join the Klan. If ah thought you *were* a racist sonofabitch, we wouldn't be friends. It's role playin', muthafucka. We're actin' roles. S'all good. Let's practise now." Spurred on by the taboo nature of the game, I'm filled by strange excitement. Shaquanna stands up, offering a clear view of her white panties. The contrast between white cotton and bountiful folds of cocoa-coloured skin is torture to my lust-filled loins. Sha squeals, "Oh masta, what are you doin' in a poor slave girl's room when ah'm standin' here in just mah panties?" She squeezes her enormous breasts together. "What's that, masta? You want me to take off mah panties too? Oh, you bad man! Ah'm just a cotton-pickin' slave girl who ain't old enough for those kinds o' relations. Ah still have mah cherry."

Getting into the spirit of the game, I shout, "Well, kiss your cherry goodbye! Prepare to have your jailbait jungle pussy deflowered! Rip those panties off!" Shaquanna turns away, affording me a perfect view of her bubble butt. She bends forward, slides her panties down over wide hips, then spanks her bottom, making it shake like jelly.

I whip out my tadger and start to stroke its burgeoning hardness. "Turn roon' and show me that pretty underage slave slit." Sha turns, her webcam window filling with hairless brown pussy. She pulls moist labia apart, exposing her deliciously pink interior. "That's what I'm talkin' aboot!" I yowl.

"Ah see from the state o' your manhood that dis slave girl's got you all hot 'n' bothered. What you gonna do with that big white thing? Please, masta, don't take mah flower!"

"Silence, slave! I own your black ass. You work on my plantation, serve my meals and clean my crapper. Noo your savage body's aboot to be impaled by the white spear of enlightenment." I'm frantically yanking now: any harder and my cock would come off at the root. Breathing deeply, I teeter on the edge of orgasm without toppling over.

Sha's middle finger is a blur of motion over her clit. "Oh masta, you feel so good in mah tight little virgin pussy. You gone an' done it now. Ah got the taste for that big white cock o' yours and ah'm gonna fuck it 'n' suck it 'n' have you spurtin' all over mah beautiful body." Two of Shaquanna's fingers disappear, coaxing squelching sounds from her pussy. She's in the zone, pistoning in and out of her soaking hole. "Oh, you bad man, you've fucked my tight little pink pussy and now you wanna shoot your hot cum all over mah big brown titties!" Sha holds her labia open and starts to smack her clit hard. As she screams in orgasm, a jet of ejaculate squirts from her depths. Her legs buckle and she collapses onto the floor. No amount of deep breathing can stop my explosion now. Cum shoots out like liquid lightning, painting my keyboard and monitor. When my tremors stop I'm wearing just a smile. "You bad boy! Ah've got an idea for when you git to Florida."

"Tell me."

"Dis will juice me up mo' than evah! Ah'm soakin' just thinkin' abaht it. Ah'll e-mail you my home address. Aftah your concert in Miami, drive your ass down to Cocoa Beach. Ah'll go to bed early and leave the patio doors unlocked so you can slip into mah house and take me in the night. Make it scary an' excitin'. Ah'll be the slave girl and you'll be my masta who's sneakin' into my sleepin' quarters to do unholy things to me."

"What if you're asleep when I get there?"

"Sometimes you're slow on the uptake, cracka! If ah'm sleepin', then smack my black ass awake, or slap mah face with that big white dick, or pull mah hair, or choke me...make it hurt, make it real. And you were nowhere near racist enough tonight. Ah wanna be humiliated, dominated, abused and *really* scared. Ah don't want it to feel like we're playin' a game. Ah wanna feel like you'll *slaughter* me if ah don't do everythin' you command. E-mail me the date of your Miami concert an' ah'll be sure not to lock mah patio doors that night. When we meet in da flesh ah want psychotic wild sex, not restrained lovemakin'. Unleash the wild animal ah know's inside you. Take it up a notch. Now git gone, cracka." Sha's webcam window turns black. A beep tells me she has logged out.

The Metal Gods give me orders. *Take it up a notch? Do better than that. Take it up 666 notches.*

I step into my shower. As my body gets cleaner by the second, my mind fills with Shaquanna-related filth.

Chapter 61 – Boys Will Be Boys

Ozzy, DT, Iain, Pete, Paul and Archibald move across Glasgow Airport's concourse like a wave. Behind them, Sunshower is on my shoulders, gripping my hair in her tight little fists. Disapproving looks follow us as we cross the International Departures terminal. The poorly hidden thought behind most travellers' faces is, *'Please God, let them be on a different flight from us.'* The ever-inquisitive Sunshower asks, "Sparky, what will we eat when we get to America?"

"Always thinkin' wi' your belly, little one. America is home to the fattest people in the world. It's also full of all-you-can-eat restaurants. We can eat food from China, India, Mexico, Thailand, Europe, anywhere. Also, I'm pretty sure it's illegal no' to eat a few hundred donuts and cherry pies while you're in the country."

"I think I'll like it there."

"Aye, wee beauty. I think so too."

"Will I be able to watch you and my Dad playing your concerts?"

"No. We'll be playin' way past your bedtime, and in some strange places too."

"Dangerous places?"

"Only dangerous if you're a man like DT wi' long, glossy hair and tight troosers. Anyway, danger runs and hides when it sees your Dad. He's hired a nanny from a New York agency to come on the tour wi' us. When the band's onstage she'll give you lessons on the tour bus, then tuck you into your bunk and read you stories."

Sunshower's lower lip slides out like a loose drawer. "A nanny? You mean a babysitter! I'm no baby!"

"We both know that you're a wise, arcane soul in a young body, but the humans have laws against girls of your tender age bein' left alone. Your Dad could be arrested and put in jail if he left you unattended while playin' gigs. Would you want that?"

Her petted lip trembles. "No, I wouldn't. I love my Dad."

"Aye, I know. So do I. So you can see why a nanny's essential. You never know, you just might like her."

Sunshower's mouth says, "It's possible, I suppose," but her frown says, 'It's unlikely.'

I wrap my arms around the fiery-haired child. "Don't worry. We'll make sure you have lots of fun wi' us durin' the daytime. Just wait 'til you meet the guys in Pink Stëel - Udo, Hanson and Helmut. You'll like them."

"I heard my Dad and DT saying they were worried about sharing a bus with a bunch of sausage munchers."

"The guys in Pink Stëel are from Germany, spiritual home of sausage."

"But what are my Dad and Mr Woman's Hair worried about? Are they scared that the Germans will get all the sausage and leave none for them?"

Laughing, I reply, "That's *exactly* what they're worried aboot."

Sunshower and I catch up with the others in the departure lounge. Ozzy turns to me and asks, "What nonsense are you fillin' my daughter's heid wi' noo?"

"Spark doesn't talk nonsense," defends Sunshower. "He's been telling me about all the different food we're going to eat in America."

Sensing that this conversation could go badly wrong, I change the subject to the band's proposed setlist for the tour, while our instruments get tagged and placed on a conveyor belt which whisks them away through hanging plastic slats, headed for the plane to America. Pink Stëel offered us the use of their amplification and drum kit for the tour, and we accepted with gratitude; it'd be cheaper to buy a small Scottish island than to transport Ozzy's gargantuan drum kit and our amps to the United States.

Team Transcend Everything snakes its way to the departure gate. We are carcrash TV: fellow travellers can't help watching from a safe distance, but they're careful not to get too close.

DT has temporarily handed the reins of his company back to his father, who continued to show up at work every day after his 'retirement' and is happy to be back in the business's driving seat. Ozzy's bakery business is on hold until his return, much to the annoyance of Wytchcoomb's locals. Iain's bosses had earmarked him for a trip to India to project-manage the opening of the insurance company's second call centre there. He knew that asking for a month's leave at that point, especially for the purpose of going on tour with a bunch of longhairs, would go down like a lead balloon (dare I say a Led Zeppelin?). Creativity was necessary, so Iain announced that the stress of the India project had sent his blood pressure through the roof; a doctor friend wrote Iain a note to that effect, which he then presented to his bosses. Unhappy but helpless, they were forced to grant him medical leave. Pete invited Lisa to come on the tour, but she was unwilling to, in her words, 'use up the rest of her annual leave sleeping on a stinking bus with a bunch of perverted deviants.' Fair point. Archibald chose to do what Lisa wouldn't: he used his holidays to join us on tour and be present at the live birth of Transcend Everything, a busman's holiday for him. He plans to document the tour with written words, photographs and video. The tour couldn't have come at a better time for Paul, who was happy to leave Janine, the Scottish justice system and the press far behind.

On the plane, I'm sandwiched between Sunshower in her window seat and Pete next to the aisle. The jazz cat takes a Bic pen from his pocket and taps out spastic rhythms on a plastic fold-down table. "What's the matter wi' you, little brother from another mother?" I ask. "Are you drummin' or fidgetin'?"

Pete's eyes ice over. "Somethin' doesn't feel right."

"That's the kind o' talk that sends people into panic on a plane. Everything's fine. There are no bombs on board, no suicide kamikazes, no imminent terrorism of any description. Anyway, we've got Oz." The giant reclines in his seat and closes his eyes, wires from his mp3 player's earphones hanging from his ears like black veins infusing him with sonic life.

The lines on Pete's brow wriggle like worms on a fishing hook. "You're probably right. I'm no' worried aboot anythin' specific, man. I've just got a weird feelin'. I'm an intuitive cat, like."

"I know you're a sensitive son of a bitch, Pete. I also know that when you've nothin' to worry aboot, you worry aboot your lack o' worries, convinced that there must surely be things to worry aboot and that you must have overlooked them."

The ice in Pete's eyes melts. He smiles, exposing nicotine-stained teeth. "What are you tryin' to say, Electric Boy?"

"I'm no' *tryin'* to say anythin'. I'm flat-oot sayin' that you're a serial worrier. Look at wee Sunshower. She's oor mascot, the perfect good-luck charm. Wi' her aroon', nothin' can go wrong." Sunshower is filling in a word puzzle with a pencil, cocooned in her inner world, a trait she inherited from her Dad: they both have the ability to concentrate on one thing with immaculate precision, oblivious to everything around them.

"You're right," Pete nods, "but it's hard to change your basic nature. I'm a worrier. You're a depraved pervert. Those are the hands God dealt us."

"Aye, and Iain's a space cadet. Look at him." Iain has twisted his body sideways in a fishlike contortion to provide him with a better view of the dark-haired stewardess who's swishing down the aisle. He bobs his head, but I'm not sure whether he's nodding in apprecation of the woman's rear or keeping the beat to a song heard only in his mind. When Pete and I start to laugh, Iain whirls round to stare at us, frowning so hard that his forehead wrinkles like an elephant's arse. To the horror of the family in the row behind him, Iain flips up a fuck-you middle finger.

Archibald, meanwhile, has taken off his shoes and trousers, pulled on an eye-mask and fallen asleep, hands down his boxer shorts. DT and Paul are immersed in conversation, their faces masks of seriousness.

Sunshower finishes her word puzzle, leans her head on my arm and falls asleep. Following her lead, I shut my eyes. Images flood my mind: smoky clubs, amplified guitars, thunderous drums, gay German glamsters, filthy metal vixens, tour-bus escapades, open roads, Mom & Pop diners, sweet southern accents, the voluptuous Shaquanna, roadside bars and, most of all, the sound of roaring, rapturous applause.

America, lock up your daughters. And while you're at it, lock up your mothers, sisters, daughters, wives, girlfriends and grandmothers. And just to be safe, lock up your female livestock too. Transcend Everything is coming and we're taking no prisoners.

Chapter 62 – Man and Machine

Udo is in a fine mood for fulfilling his role as Teutonic ambassador to Scottish metallists entering the United States. He arrives at JFK Airport dressed in skintight pink spandex trousers, black cowboy boots, a Judas Priest *Ram it Down* T-shirt, a red sparkly scarf and mirrored Aviator sunglasses. His long sandy-blonde hair is topped by a military-style cap of black leather. Make-up fails to mask the heavy five o'clock shadow around his crimson-lipsticked pout. If Rob Halford had been born twenty years later, and in Düsseldorf instead of Birmingham, he'd look like Udo.

"Spark, du bist ein sexy beetch! Vilkommen to ze United States." Udo kisses me on both cheeks, then plants a kiss square on my lips. My compatriots hang back looking horrified.

"Danke schön, Udo," I reply, smiling nervously. "It's good to finally be here. The petrified stalwarts behind me are my band…and friends…and mascot. The males aren't very in touch with their gay selves."

Nodding, Udo scans the entourage. "Velcome everyone. Helmut und Hanson could not be here. Ve vill meet up vith zem later. Right now, I vish to treat you all to a meal."

Ozzy springs to life like a robot that's just been plugged into a high-voltage power socket. "Food! Noo you're talkin'! Let's do it, ya bass!"

Udo performs an effeminate pirouette, throws one end of his glittery scarf over a shoulder and struts towards the exit. Pushing a mobile wall of rumbling trolleys and flight cases, my gang follows. Beneath a cloudless sky waits a gleaming tour bus with blacked-out windows. A metallic-pink phallus covers its entire side. Under the mammoth member are the words 'Good Times – Fuck Shit Up'.

Clamping a hand over Sunshower's eyes, Oz explains, "There's a naughty word on the side of the bus. No lookin'."

"But what's the picture, Daddy?" She tries in vain to pry her father's huge hand off her face.

"Ehh…it's a huge metal sausage," Ozzy stammers. DT stares open-mouthed as reality hits him full in the face with the force of a twenty-foot titanium tadger.

Udo leans out of a bus window, peering over the top of his sunglasses. "Vas ist der hold-up, you sexy Scottish men? Are you going to just stand zhere all day admiring my appendage, or are ve going to eat?"

As we load our gear onto the bus, I whisper into Archibald's ear, "I bet you can't wait to get your troosers off on this bus, eh?" Shaking his head, Archibald disappears up chrome stairs onto the vehicle.

"Spark, this is all just a laugh, right?" panics DT. "These guys are a comedy band, eh? I mean, they're not really gay German metalheids, are they?"

"I reckon there's a Spinal Täp situation goin' on here. The Täp blurred the line between parody and reality when they released an album and played live gigs. They actually wrote their own songs and played their own instruments. All of a sudden, people were confused. Was Spinal Täp a real band arsin' aboot? Or were they a bunch o' jokers pretendin' to be a real band? Or somethin' else entirely?"

"Aye, but they weren't pretendin' to be *gay*." DT cocks a black eyebrow, like a heavy metal Roger Moore.

"Who says these dudes are *pretendin'* to be gay? Maybe they've pulled the perfect double bluff – real homosexual German metalheids pretendin' to be Americans pretendin' to be a gay German metal band. Clever stunt if they pull that off…"

"Fuck, man, don't say that," DT groans. "My heid's hurtin' just thinkin' aboot it."

"A sore heid's the least o' your worries. A groomed pretty boy like you could easily end up wi' a sore arse on this tour bus."

"If even one o' these shirtlifters tries it on wi' me, it's on your heid, yours and Paul's. If I'm asleep and my sphincter receives any kind o' defamation…"

"I think you mean desecration, Dave."

"I fuckin' know what I mean, Poetry Boy! I mean defamation!"

"Dave, defamation means to injure a reputation. Your butthole can't be defamed unless it has already earned fame. Is your brown ring renowned?"

"OK, smartarse. Maybe defamation wasn't the exact word I was after. Reputation-related injuries aren't the ones I'm worried aboot. Aye, so as I was tryin' to say, if any arse bandits climb into my bunk in the night and try to…"

"I understand. You don't want any defamation of the bumhole. You'd hate Udo and his gang to think your arse is anythin' less than spectacular. I don't think you need to worry. It's a fine arse. They'll love it."

DT runs a hand through his hair. "You will always be a wee tit."

Udo's head pops through the open window and unleashes a barrage of verbal abuse in German. While DT and I have been debating on the kerb, everyone else has boarded the bus. Ozzy's oversized head appears next to Udo's. The giant drummer shouts, "Get on the bus this instant, ya pair o' fannies! That aeroplane food wouldnae fill a sparrow! I'm starvin' and when I get this hungry, I start bootin' balls!" DT and I jump aboard. The door hisses closed behind us as the bus rumbles into motion.

Floor, walls and ceilings are decked out in black velvet. Indicating the décor with a sweeping hand gesture, Archibald asks, "Is this what you call gay chic?"

Udo jabs both thumbs into his own chest. "Zees eez vat you call gay chic."

"Yes, yes," nods Archibald, "your garb is colourful, I'll give you that. You remind me of a big-haired, multi-coloured, sober version of Pete Way."

"Ja, und more handsome I hope?" Udo tilts his head to the side and pouts crimson-glossed lips.

Archibald squirms, his hazel eyes wide, pupils darting from side to side. "Ehh...I'm not really qualified to rank men. I've always been more into the minxes."

"So you say, ya blatant poofter!" shouts DT.

Udo drapes an arm round Archibald's shoulders. "I vas not trying to recruit you to ze homosexual team, Archibald. I vas merely fishing for a compliment."

"Well, you *are* a very attractive man," croaks Archibald, his voice rising an octave. "If I was the sort of man who got turned on by looking at other men's bottoms, your rear would be right up my street."

Ozzy walks past carrying Sunshower on a muscular arm. He glares at Archibald, shakes his head, then continues exploring the tour bus, muttering, "Light in his loafers, that journalist. I knew it since the first time I met him, when he whipped off his troosers and squeezed his half-naked self against my manly physique." Dave rolls off his seat, clutching his sides and howling with laughter. Hovering between a smile and a sneer, Archibald's lip quivers. Udo, meanwhile, is grinning like a pervert at a pool party. The bus hurtles onwards into a red sunset.

A deep Teutonic voice booms through the bus's speakers. "Ich bin Volfgang und ich vould like to velcome Transcend Everyzhing onto our mobile manbus. Ve vill soon be arriving at Big Billy's Diner, vhere Helmut und Hanson vill meet us. Estimated arrival time eez ten minuten from now. Over und out."

When the Stëëlmobile skids to a halt, its big wheels throw up a dust cloud which blots out the half-sun on the horizon. A black Pontiac Trans Am growls in the car park of Big Billy's Diner. A dark-tinted windscreen obscures the driver, but it would be difficult to miss the man on the bonnet of the car. Black hair sprouts from his head like quills from a porcupine, a marvel of hairspray and patience. His leather-trousered legs are spread wide across the car's bonnet, like a homosexual version of a Whitesnake video. Reading my mind, Iain shouts, "Check it oot – Tawny Kitaen wi' a tadger!"

Ozzy is first off the bus, his belly ruling his mind as usual. The rest follow in an orderly line, Udo taking up the rear, so to speak. The man on the hood of the car lifts his round sunglasses, gives our motley arrangement of humanity the once-over and asks, "Zees must be ze Scotsmen, ja?"

Udo nods. The Trans Am's engine cuts out. An electric window buzzes down and from the car's interior a voice says, "Who needs Big Billy vhen ve have all zees Scottish meat?"

Ozzy turns to me and spits, "Spark, I don't know how the hell you talked me into bein' part o' this travellin' tadgerfest."

A cowboy-booted foot kicks open the diner's door from the inside, sending flecks of red paint flaking into the breeze. The owner of the foot is a tall, muscular man with a grey, wolfish moustache and long silver hair which is kept out of his eyes by a blue bandana. His black leather 'cut' waistcoat's patches tell a story: he is a nomad member of the Highway Hellhounds motorcycle club, which means he is not allegiant to the gang of any one specific area. Nomads travel perpetually, visiting various Hellhounds clubs along the way but never staying more than a day or two in one location. For such riders, nomad is a literal description: they are iron-horse-riding stalwarts of the open road. The nomad struts towards us like a modern-day gunslinger, tanned arms hanging loosely by the sides of his faded denims. In his gunmetal eyes is the half-present, half-elsewhere look that tells me he has been to the edge. In a thick New England accent, he shouts, "Run from pain and it will follow you as surely as the sun sets! Dive deep into the pain and you will find joy! Embrace pain! Here comes the pain!"

Ozzy clenches his huge right hand into a fist. DT's dark eyes narrow to slits and lock onto the aggressor. Red speckles appear in Iain's blue eyes, a phenomenon that used to occur during gang fights, when the bloodlust was upon him. The hairs on the back of my neck prick up as my right leg starts to twitch, ready to unleash bone-shattering kicks. A dude with long, poodle-permed brown hair and a powerful physique climbs out of the Trans Am and silently glides behind the nomad. With a practised-to-perfection manoeuvre, he reaches around the biker's waist, unfastens his belt and jeans, and yanks them down, exposing the man's surprised tackle to the last rays of the equally surprised setting sun. Ozzy's meaty hand once again covers Sunshower's eyes. Udo looks at the nomad's appendage in the quality-controlling way I look at grapefruits in the supermarket. Archibald's eyes widen, his mouth a poorly concealed smile. Jeans round his ankles, the nomad wheels on the spot to face his permed nemesis, then hesitates, as if unsure whether priority should go to pulling up his jeans or attacking his disrober. That momentary indecision is his downfall. A metal motorcycle helmet driven by a fist crashes into his head, knocking him senseless. He stumbles backwards into the diner's wall and collapses in a heap of denim and dust.

The curly-haired avenger lifts the bare-arsed stranger and carries him across the car park, dropping him next to a sky-blue chopper with twin exhausts of gleaming chrome. The victor jams the helmet onto the unconscious biker's head with the pronouncement, "He should have been vearing a helmet."

When the nomad's faculties return, he straps the helmet under his chin, pulls up his jeans and rides into the horizon, the roar of his bike's exhaust dimming to a low hum as man and motorcycle melt into the last sliver of sun.

Flexing his biceps, the poodle-permed prizefighter introduces himself. "Ich bin Helmut. Helmut Bang, if you please. Honoured to meet you, Schottischers."

DT leans into my ear and whispers, "Not a bad right hook for a bent shot." As Dave and I giggle like children, Helmut throws his arms round our shoulders and ushers us into the diner. And like that, with a Bang, we meet Helmut.

Chapter 63 – Armed and Ready

The Stëëlmobile tour bus draws up outside the venue of our first concert: an S&M club called Rubber Up in a seedy suburb of New York City. The club's entrance is located in a narrow alleyway between buildings of dirty red brick. Above the main door, a blue tubular neon sign buzzes at sporadic intervals, like an oversized bug zapper. If a fortune teller had told the teenage me that he'd play his first official gig in New York City, he'd have been tempted to believe her. If that same fortune teller had informed the young MacDubh that the gig would be in support of German homo-metallists in a pervert-magnet club called Rubber Up, he'd have whipped off her bandana and tugged on her hoopy silver earrings until she refunded his money. Yet here we are.

The alley is packed with bodies squeezed into tight black rubber and leather. As the crowd parts like the Red Sea to make way for the Stëëlmobile on its arrival, Iain spouts, "Fuck sake, I thought *we* were weirdos. Then I met these manhole merchants." He waves an accusing finger in the direction of Udo, Hanson and Helmut, adding, "No offence to you butt pirates, like. Anyway, just when I think I know weird, I see *this!*" He indicates a pair of pierced and tattooed deviants who are trying in vain to launch themselves through the darkened windows of the tour bus. "You don't get this kind o' lunacy in rural Norfolk."

"Ze people you see out zhere," Udo explains, "vear zheir hearts on zheir sleeves. Zhey have zheir perversions vith zheir piercings und tattoos - on ze outside. You, on ze ozher hand, hide your perversions on ze inside."

Pete laughs so hard that he loses control of his mouth and dribbles fresh orange juice down his shirt. "Udo's sussed oot the Bright cat already. He's an observant feline, that Von DüYü."

"What Udo said aboot my perversions isnae true," protests Iain.

"It is true, dude," I interject. "I've known you since we were wee boys. Udo's right on the money. You're brimming wi' perversions. If I were to split you open doon the middle, perversions would come spillin' oot."

"Aye," pipes in DT, "they'd be wrigglin' aboot on the floor, lookin' for new hosts to infest."

"Fuck ye all," spits Iain. "Wanks the lot o' you…wanks and poofters." His tantrum only serves to intensify the laughter on the bus.

Sunshower stays on the Stëëlmobile with her babysitter, Marisol, a raven-haired Hispanic twenty-one-year-old from Queens. A New Yorker since birth, Marisol sounds no more than a year out of Puerto Rico. Ozzy and I give Sunshower hugs and kisses, then follow the rest of the troop off the bus and towards our awaiting destiny.

We unload our armoury of guitars and head for the club's door like warriors marching into battle. As we march up the alley, hedonistic hands slap our backs and spank our arses. Steam rises from rusted drain gratings as a tattooed hand opens the club's door, a hulking steel thing fit for a vault. Raising an eyebrow, DT asks, "Is this the only dark alleyway you'll be squeezin' into tonight, Udo?"

"Eez zat an offer, David? Eez your rear entrance open late? Ich may pop in." Udo lifts his sunglasses and winks at the speechless DT.

"We've a gig to play, Dave," I remind him. "Save the gay flirtin' for later, eh?"

"Fuck off, ya smart-mouthed prick!"

"Stop bickerin' like women, you two!" orders Ozzy. "Oor only previous gig ended in disaster. Let's no' repeat it. Once we've blown the brains oot o' these sado-masochistic weirdos and made it safely back to the comfort o' the bus, *then* you can quibble like wee bitches. Right noo you should be clearin' your minds and psychin' yourselves up for unleashin' Transcend Everything onto the world."

Hanson nods, causing his porcupine-quilled hair to sway and bend. "Ve vill have plenty of time after ze show to joke around und get to know each ozher better. Have a vonderful time on stage tonight und don't be too gut. Ve have to follow you, remember."

Albert, the club's owner, closes and bolts the door behind us then shakes our hands as if we were visiting dignitaries rather than long-haired Scotsmen with every intention of blowing the roof off his building. An old friend of Udo, Albert is a small, sandy-haired, bespectacled man with beady, darting eyes and a general appearance that imbues him with more than a passing resemblance to the serial killer Ted Bundy. He leads us to a bare-walled office above the club and explains that it will have to do as a dressing room. A brass letter-opening knife is balanced on top of a pile of unopened mail on a wooden desk. Two skylight windows offer a glorious view of the darkening sky.

Wolfgang enters, his shaven head tattooed with an eagle above one ear. His official roles are driver, roadie, guitar technician, drum technician, tour manager and security officer. He grabs my BC Rich's flight case in a gorilla-like arm, its muscles writhing like thick ropes under tanned skin. Noticing my frown, he says, "Do not vorry, Scotsman. Ich vill set up your gear for you." Guitar in hand, the stocky German disappears.

Iain says, "Do me a favour, Spark. Hit my heid…hard. Scone it a beauty!"

"No chance. The way I'm feelin', I'd pan your heid right in."

"Impossible. My heid's famously thick. Think aboot the gang fights we had. I had bottles, baseball bats, chibs, logs and bricks broken over my hard heid, but it never cracked."

"I'm no' doin' it, especially right before we're due to hit the stage."

"Hit my heid, for fuck's sake! Do it and you'll see somethin' oot o' this world. You'll no' believe it."

"In case you hadn't noticed, life has become pretty odd recently. I was deid on a Bronzehall pavement and got resurrected. Transcend Everything's on its first tour - in America, not Britain – in support of a band who may or may not be homosexuals from Bremen, Germany. Oor manager has fled Scotland amid allegations of sealin' his girlfriend's gash shut wi' Polyfilla and Superglue. After years of isolation hidin' from the Devil, durin' which he experimented wi' sonic frequencies that induce altered states, Pete has finally ventured ootside his flat. We've been offered an epic Scottish castle as the location to record oor album. My most recent sexual experience was wi' a vibratin' rubber vulva. After decades o' make believe, you've finally become an actual musician. To top it all off, we're joined on tour by a semi-naturist journalist who just may be the key to exposin' us to the world. So, dude, it'd take a lot to surprise me."

"This'll surprise the Hell oot o' you. Just smack my heid! Full force. Fist or weapon."

"No! I'm no' puttin' the band in jeopardy."

"Fuck this! If you want somethin' done right, you need to do it yourself!" After a long sigh which sounds like air being let out of a tyre, Iain sprints at the wall. His head slams into brick with a sickening crack. He rebounds like a rubber ball, goes into freefall and thuds onto the ground, blood trickling from a horizontal gash on his forehead. I slap his cheek in an effort to bring him around. His eyes loll open, their liquid blue swirling clockwise, gradually morphing into a dark brown.

Ozzy pours a bottle of water over Iain, who jolts to life shouting, in a thick Irish accent, "What the fuck do ye t'ink ye'r doin', ye fat fuckin' gobshoite? Oi was havin'a lovely wee nap there!"

Like a snake spraying venom, DT spits, "I always said that heid-in-the-clouds wee bastard Bright was a brain-damage case. Noo it's official. Listen to me, Bright. If you don't go oot onto that stage and play a blinder, you'll be findin' oot what brain damage really is…care o' my right boot."

"Aye," agrees Ozzy, "you're no' gettin' oot o' the gig noo, no matter how many walls you run into, ya nutjob."

Iain starts to climb to his feet, but falls back to the floor with the scream of a banshee. The room is filled by a sound like dry branches being trampled by heavy horses as Iain's bones snap violently and rearrange into new shapes. Torso and cranium split open, offering a gory view of his insides, yet no blood spills out. His body stretches six inches in as many seconds, as if an unseen force has turned it to putty in order to manipulate its shape. Reminiscent of David Banner's metamorphosis into the Incredible Hulk, Iain has burst through his jeans and shirt. Unlike Banner's transformation, however, Iain has not gained bulk, but has stretched longer and leaner.

Iain opens his eyes and continues his Irish tirade. "The atmosphere here is loike a feckin' coffee mornin'! Loight a foire in yer bellies! Oi'm the rocker and oi need to get out onstage to rock! Hurry up and get your fat Scottish arses ready!" Black bristles emerge from the skin above his top lip, pushing through until a thick, black moustache sits there like a proud paintbrush. Iain's reddish-brown crew cut grows out into a shimmering black afro as his pale skin tans to a milk-chocolate shade. Bone by bone and molecule by molecule, our friend and blood brother transforms into a figure we all know and love…and have missed.

Tears pour from DT's startled eyes as he backs into a wall, arms oustretched in a Jesus Christ pose. Six stunned stares surround the changeling, their owners startled into silence. Pete retreats into a corner, drops into a foetal position and starts to mutter incantations. Archibald fumbles in his bag for a camcorder and starts to record the bizarre proceedings.

Iain's lips part into a smile we've seen on a hundred album covers and magazine fronts. Staring back at us is one of the most recognisable, familiar and beloved faces in the annals of rock. It is a face long gone from the Earth, yet in the spartan office of a New York S&M club it beams at us in all its moustachioed glory. In our humble makeshift dressing room stands the iconic Philip Lynott. "What are ye all starin' at? Oi haven't waited over twenty years to hang around a feckin' changin' room wit' ye all! Oi need to get out there and rock!"

I feel driven to say something profound, but what comes out is, "Eh, Iain…or Phil…or whatever unholy alliance is goin' on in there…I can't wait to hear and see you rockin'. It'll be better if you put on some clothes that fit, though. The geezers who frequent this joint will have a field day wi' you if you walk onstage wi' your tadger hangin' oot o' the hole in your troosers."

Looking down, the shapeshifter notices that his tallywacker is indeed poking through a rip in jeans which are now half-mast on newly elongated legs. He jettisons the jeans and climbs into a pair of soccer shorts. Beside the barefoot Lynott, I start to give the speech I've rehearsed a million times in my head. The words have been different each time, but the intention always the same: a pep-talk for my band on the eve of our live conception. Gazing through skylights, I feel the Universe flow through me. "As we step onstage together for the first time this millennium, let us not forget oor heritage, or oor love of and for each other. Are you wi' me?"

"Oi'm fuckin' wit' ya!" shouts Lynott. Everyone else remains silent, their eyes locked onto the Phil-thing.

Pete mumbles something about Devils then restarts his chants, tracing magical symbols in the air with his fingertips. "For fuck's sake, Pete," I implore, "why would the Devil send us Phil Lynott? Trust me, this is a gift from the Metal Gods! We need to take this bull by its heavenly horns and ride the fucker."

Pete lifts his head and stares at me through leaking eyes. "I don't like your cattle-botherin' metaphor, but I suppose you're right. I've seen the Devil and looked into that cat's fiery, soulless eyes. What happened here is a long fuckin' way from normal, but it lacks the sulphuric stench of Satan."

"Exactly. So let me ask you reprobates once again, are you wi' me?" Silence, almost deafening in its intensity. My bandmates are still gawping at the shapeshifter. At a stratospheric pitch, I scream, "A-r-e y-o-u w-i-t-h m-e? DT! Oz! Pete! Iain! Are you fuckers alive?"

Their attention finally torn away from Sir Phil of Lynott, my compatriots turn to me. Punching the air, Ozzy booms, "I'm wi' you, ya bass!" Above us, right on cue, thunder roars.

I continue my impassioned speech, emboldened by memories of Wallace's horseback speech to his troops during *Braveheart*. "Decades ago we bled on battlefields together and triumphed over all oor enemies. We've dealt wi' the deaths of loved ones. For years we drifted apart geographically and emotionally. Noo, having faced doon all oor demons, we're together again, stronger than death or life or all the demonic entities in the Universe. Let us take the stage as brothers, unify oor energy and blast these motherfuckers' heids off wi' riffs of an intensity never before unleashed." Five sets of knuckles clash, then we head to the stage.

A sea of hair, tattoos, rubber, leather and pierced pale flesh surrounds the stage as a limp-wristed Marilyn Manson cover of the limp-wristed Soft Cell track *Tainted Love* struggles to make itself heard over the raging storm outside. I call a band huddle. "The original plan was to open wi' AC/DC's *Back in Business Again*. Considerin' that Phil Lynott's seen fit to return from the deid to join us, I reckon the least we can do is open wi' Thin Lizzy's *The Boys are Back in Town*."

"Feckin' roight we should," agrees the Iain/Phil thing.

DT scratches his chin and purses his lips, his usual body language when he is about to veto one of my ideas. His doubts remain unspoken, though, perhaps out of reverence for Phil Lynott. Dave's frown melts and he nods his head. The club's lights go down, cloaking us in darkness.

As DT cranks out the opening riff to the Thin Lizzy masterpiece, Lynott props a foot up on an amp and slaps bass strings with a dark thumb, creating rumbles which - combined with Ozzy's drum beats – provide a perfect rhythmic foundation. The crowd is nonplussed. Even the bass-playing, therianthropic Lynott-thing hasn't grabbed their attention. Lookalikes are ten-a-penny in the rock business and our watchers have no idea that they're in the presence of the real Phil Lynott.

Phil and I share a microphone stand, heads tilted upward as his thick Irish accent blends with my pseudo-American singing voice. The BC Rich Warlock around my neck is, for the moment, just a low-slung fashion accessory. DT's head spins in rapid circles, his hair swirling like a black cyclone as scarred fingers scorch across the fretboard of the otherworldly guitar Heavensent. Ozzy's blue eyes are underlined by a wide smile, his massive arms a blur of rhythmic motion as he pounds seven shades of shit out of Helmut's drum kit. Pete stands stage left, leaning on a Marshall stack and smoking like a man without a care in the world.

Silence greets us after the first song, so I call another group huddle. "That was a perfect performance and these shrink-wrapped sodomites haven't even flinched. Time to pull oot the secret weapon!"

DT sweeps silken hair away from his face, flips up a middle finger at the crowd and says, "Fuckin' right. Let's give these deviants what they want."

Pete's left hand grips a bottle of Jim Beam while his right nurses the dying embers of a cigarette. After sucking a final draw from the Marlboro, he flicks it into the crowd. A tall, vampirically white man's hairsprayed black Mohawk catches fire, lighting up like a Roman candle. The screaming human torch's female companion throws her jacket over his head and starts to pound on it in an attempt to douse the flames. Pete takes a relaxed swig of bourbon, leans into a mic and advises, "Stop, drop and roll." Then he starts to play.

DT and I grab cowboy hats from sidestage, don the headgear and announce our presence with crunching metal riffs. Faces in the audience light up with recognition, although I'd bet my BC Rich they've never heard the song played like *this*. The tide turns in our favour as all five members of Transcend Everything chant the opening strains of *Macho Man*. We take the Village People's standard and make it our own: a little less gay, a lot more metal. In the crowd, fists punch the air in time to our rhythms. Some eldritch countenances have broken into smiles. A few rubber people have even started to bounce up and down. The Metal Gods speak. *Good. You've got them by their tattooed tadgers and pierced pussies. Don't let go now.*

By the end of *Macho Man* we're going full-steam ahead and the crowd is moving like an ocean. DT reaches into the maelstrom and yanks a blonde, dreadlocked girl up onto the stage. On her left arm, a tattoo of a horned fire-demon with blank cavities for eyes stretches from shoulder to elbow. She looks as if she hasn't washed for weeks, which is probably one of the reasons Dave chose her: he always did like the dirty ones. He rips off her PVC basque, exposing a lithe body with tan-lined titties. She starts to sway, more flower-child than dominatrix, as Pete's keyboards soar.

Honouring one of my heroes, the chrome larynxed Biff Byford, I close my eyes and sing.

> "I'm standing in the dark, let the music start.
> I can hear you call out my name.
> I see the flashing lights cutting through the night.
> The spotlight is shining on you.
> I've always been around.
> I've never let you down.
> I've seen it through right from the start.
> We'll be rocking together, rocking again.
> Rocking again!"

Rocking Again is an old Saxon standard, but it feels as if it was written for us, penned for this night. DT's riffs blast out of Marshall amplifiers, restyling the hair of the people near the front. Phil climbs onto a stack of amps and adopts a legs-apart stance. Ozzy has become one with the thunder that rages outside. Pete strips down to his underpants in a show of solidarity for our topless dancer, then joins her onstage, pirouetting and gyrating. I launch into my guitar solo. My riffs hang in the air with improbable ease for such heavy bastards, jousting with DT's razor-sharp sonic sculptures. After a minute of fretboard sparring, DT and I synchronise our shredding into unstoppable stampede of sound.

The five band members are connected to a common energy source, hard-wired together like synapses of a larger organism. Hair flows like multi-coloured waves. Muscles twitch, powering fast-moving fingers. Giant drumstick-wielding hands are a blur of motion. Larynxes howl as dry ice belches onto the stage, drowning our lower halves in clouds. Overhead spotlights roll and swirl, following our movements like airborne predators stalking stagebound prey.

By the time we've blasted through adrenaline-fuelled renditions of AC/DC's *Hell's Bells*, Megadeth's *In my Darkest Hour* and our own *Little Evils for the Greater Good* and *Orange Donger of Doom,* the crowd has lost its pseudo-cool; icy exteriors have melted, exposing true natures. Smiles extend from wall to wall. Crowd surfers are passed around by upstretched arms. Heads bang. Hair billows. Black-booted feet stomp sado-military support of our music.

I notice Pete waving his arms around like a drowning man. When I stride over to see what the problem is, he slides a hand into his pocket, plucks out a pair of earplugs and hands them to me. His ears are already plugged. After inserting my earplugs, I return to the front of the stage. Waves of keyboard noise wash over the crowd. Erections spring up in trousers, straining against tight rubber confines as the cock-charmer Drummond arouses flesh snakes with his lilting melody. A glance to my left confirms that DT's aroused member is threatening to burst through the taut confines of his red leather trousers. The Phil-thing is also sporting a stormer and grinning proudly. On his drum stool, a baffled Ozzy looks down in horror as his shorts expand into a mini-tent. Stage left, the trouserless Archibald stands hands on hips, his erection pointing into the heart of the crowd.

With my BC Rich down-tuned to Hell, I crank out the opening riff of Judas Priest's *Desert Plains*. DT grabs our topless dancer who, lost in her inner world, is oblivious to the erection that is pointing at her like a spear hungry for blood. Taking her right hand, DT guides it to his straining lovebone. She drops to her knees and rubs Dave's stiff serpent through a layer of leather. Ignoring my frantic facial gestures to indicate that I'd appreciate his guitar support, DT throws the topless girl over a shoulder in true caveman style, then carries her behind the wall of amps.

As I launch into my most reverential Halford vocal, taking on guitar duties all alone, I can just discern DT through a cloud of dry ice. He drops his trousers, bends his female admirer over, mounts her from behind and starts to fuck her like a bionic jackhammer. It could be an optical illusion caused by wandering dry ice or cigarette smoke, but it looks as though he is pounding her so hard that smoke is belching from her pussy. His technique is like that of a jockey: holding her hair in one hand and spanking hell out of her rump with the other. Judging by the ferocity of DT's assault, he's near the end of the race and still has a few horses to overtake; if this was the Grand National, he'd be fined for whip abuse. Pete wanders behind the amps to watch the coital union, nodding as he takes a relaxed draw of his cigarette.

When Dave re-emerges onto the stage, boner-free and smiling, I growl, "You unprofessional prick, are you finished wi' your sideshow?"

"Aye. For noo."

"This is oor last track o' the night. Good o' you to join us for it. You try being Glenn Tipton *and* K.K. Downing sometime, ya tit!"

"Lighten up, Spark, ya jealous bastard. Let's unleash the new riffs." After flashing a smile, DT grabs me by the hair and kisses my cheek. In that instant, all is forgiven. We prepare to let loose our most recent, most savage song: a beast with razor riffs and teeth like a vampire shark. Dave and I created the guitar parts and lyrics first, after which Pete composed spacey keyboard melodies to perfectly harmonise with our vitriol-laced riffage. The result was an inspired blend of ambience and aggression. The track deserved a title that heralded our arrival. It's more than a song: it's a statement of intent.

I raise my arms and point index fingers at Pete. He recognises my signal and launches into the keyboard intro to *These Are the New Riffs*. DT, Phil and I jump onto the drum riser and hold our right fists in the air. The behemoth Oz stands up - dwarfing the rest of us - and stretches out his right arm. Our fists slam together. The flesh on our arms goosepimples just as it has countless times back in Scotland when bitten by the wolfwind from the north.

DT and I jump off the drum riser, run to the front of the stage and unleash synchronised riffs like long-haired ninjas firing sonic shuriken stars with laser precision. Ozzy's feet kick out double-bass booms that rumble through the building; I soak up the energy and transform it into frenetic fretboard fingering. Phil is right on the money, all Lynott grin and flashing fingers. We have the crowd eating out of our hands.

When the track ends we ditch our instruments and congregate at the front of the stage. Topless and sweaty, we wrap arms around one another, Scorpions-style, and do a group bow. Amid roars from the crowd, my four bandmates disappear backstage. I'm not ready to leave yet, though. Wild emotions are flooding through me. "Thank you, perverts and rubber-clad, depraved deviants of Noo Yawk! We should have been here years ago, but things got rough and we took some hard blows, unlike oor friends in Pink Stëel, who gave some. I'm honoured to have shared this night wi' you. You are all witnesses to the rebirth of a dream. As a result, you are part o' that dream. I love each one o' you. No matter how big Transcend Everything becomes, we will always return to this dark, dingy venue to play just for you. That is a promise. I hope you enjoy my Teutonic, tadger-loving friends Pink Stëel. Goodnight." I press my palms together, as if praying, and bow in a gesture of heartfelt thanks. The wave of noise that erupts from the crowd almost knocks me off my feet. Stretching my arms out into a crucifix, palms facing the crowd, I bask in their energy.

A dark cloud materialises at the back of the hall, gradually morphing into a shape like a minotaur with diagonal horns and fires flickering where its eyes should be. The thing points a dark digit at me. The sweat on my body turns to ice. Shivering, I flee backstage as the crowd continues to roar, apparently oblivious to the otherworldly entity. Udo, Hanson and Helmut are congratulating my bandmates on a job well done. I sprint past them, upstairs to the office, and dial The Cemetery Gates. A child with a barely pubescent voice answers, identifying herself as Rosie. I'm about to challenge her when the Metal Gods intervene. *Her words are true. Believe your ears. The maiden will allay your fears.*

"Rosie, it's Spark! If a demon wi' fires for eyes and horns stickin' oot of its heid is stalkin' me, what should I do?"

"Well, *is* a demon with a horned head and fires for eyes following you?" asks a little voice.

"Aye. There's nothin' hypothetical aboot the shittin' I just gave my pants. This thing's real."

"Have there been any other strange occurrences?"

"Iain turned into Phil Lynott, the deid frontman o' Thin Lizzy."

"Is he pretending to be someone else to boost his onstage confidence?"

"He's way beyond pretendin'. He transformed into Phil Lynott – half a foot taller wi' afro hair, a thick 'tache, an Irish accent, dark skin, the lot. We watched his metamorphosis. Bones snapped and re-formed, skin tone changed, eyes switched colour, he *became* Phil Lynott."

"If this is a prank call, I'll make sure you never see my adult form again."

"I swear on Sunshower's soul, this isnae a prank."

"In that case, it sounds like possession, but I've never heard of the host actually morphing into the possessor. Adopting personality traits, yes. Fully fledged transformation, no. Only in mythology."

"Iain asked me to hit his heid before we went onstage. When I refused, he ran into a brick wall and knocked himself oot. That's when the changes started."

"Supernatural activity like his transformation will show up on the radar of every soulless entity. Demons, you see, do not reside in our dimension, nor can they see us under normal circumstances. They occupy the same time and space as us, but in parallel dimensions. Occult occurrences open a temporary window between dimensions, allowing travel into – or out of - our reality."

"What would a demon want wi' us?"

"That's not the pertinent question. Knowing why a demon has come won't save you, but knowing how to protect yourself against it might. Are you familiar with the pentalpha?"

"No."

"It's a five-pointed star within a circle, each point touching the circumference."

"The same as a pentagram?"

"You may know it as such, yes."

"I've got them on at least seventeen of my album covers. What good is usin' a Satanic sign against a demon? Isn't that a bit like throwin' apple pies at Mr Kipling?"

"The pentalpha is a misunderstood symbol which has been much maligned since the inquisition. Before that, it was recognised as a symbol of truth, protection, infinity, eternity, and the cycles of life and nature. A purer symbol never existed. Believe not the perversions of the Christian church, which claimed it to be an evil sign. The five points of the pentalpha's star represent the five elements in the Universe – fire, water, earth, air and spirit, with the surrounding circle there to unify and harness the elements. It is beyond coincidence that there are five points of the star and five members of your band. In your case, the pentalpha is doubly relevant, as it channels the Universe's forces and also unifies the five disparate energies in your band into a single unified force."

"But will it protect me from demons, Devils, that kind o' shit?"

"Carving a pentalpha into your body is your only immediate protection from demonic forces, so hurry. The entity you experienced may hunt with haste."

"Thanks, Rosie. I better start carvin'."

"Go and do that, Scotsman. Blessed be."

Grabbing the brass letter-opening knife from the desk, I pierce my chest with its point. A rivulet of blood trickles down my body. After carving a circle that stretches from upper chest to mid-abdomen, I slice a five-pointed star inside it. The skylight windows resonate with my screams. They shatter, showering the office in shards of glass. Booted footsteps echo in the stairwell. The office door swings open and Ozzy appears, trailed by the rest of the band. Open-mouthed, they gaze at the gushing design on my torso. Without hanging about to offer an explanation, I run past my blood brothers, leaping down the stairs six at a time. I re-emerge onto the stage looking like a member of an underground Scandinavian death metal band (minus the obligatory spiked wristband, ornate sword and battleaxe). DT's dreadlocked dancer is still onstage. She drops to her knees in front of me and – like a wildcat drinking from a stream – licks flowing blood from my body, painting her tongue gory red.

Lyrics I wrote in a bygone era flow through me, a nearby microphone transmitting the growled words around the arena.

> "Heavy metal whore,
> Kneelin' on the floor,
> Gaggin' for some more,
> Filthy little goer,
> Bend over some more,
> I'll impale your back door.
> Skirt hiked up round your waist
> So everyone can have a taste.
> Legs spread gymnastic-wide,
> Always want it deep inside.
> Pussy waxed baby-soft,
> Tag-teamed in Ozzy's loft.
> Fake tan, dyed-blonde hair,
> Metalheads all stop and stare.
> Slowly stripping for Blood Brothers,
> Out of reach to all the others.
> Groupie bitch slut spunkbucket,
> Show an orifice, we'll fuck it."

A jet-haired seductress in a red rubber catsuit climbs onto the stage and joins the sanguinary feast, which now looks a lot like a Manowar album cover: a sweaty, kilted warrior standing tall after battle, while submissive slut-vixens kneel at his feet, tending his wounds in evident worship. My attention, however, is not focused on the jousting tongues which flicker over my body, but on the empty space where the horned apparition stood just moments ago. Perhaps my pentalpha drove it away, or maybe the demon existed only in my imagination. It's possible that my exhilarated post-gig mind imagined the Devil whose image was placed in my mind's eye years ago by Pete. Something turned the sweat on my body to ice, though. I didn't imagine that. It happened, however, before I had arcane protection carved into me. Now I'm demon-proofed. My fear disappears and my badass self – which had fucked off to whimper in a corner – takes control again, ready to take on anything.

Looking down, I notice that the dark-haired girl has fangs. Prosthetic. Probably. She doesn't bite; there is no need, as my blood is flowing freely, its red lifeforce smeared over the faces and tongues of the women at my feet, giving them the look of fierce lionesses devouring prey. Looks, however, can be deceptive; the energy from these females is healing. Their saliva stings as they lap at my wounds, but the pain brings forth pleasure. I let out a deep roar, like one lucky-bastard tomcat being groomed by two particularly fetching bitches.

Chapter 64 – Feed My Frankenstein

"What the fuck was that display aboot?" demands Oz. "Is it a frontman thing? Do you need more attention than the rest o' the band?" His eyes are wide, forcing creases into his pale brow.

"Aye," adds Pete, "after all your talk aboot the importance of avoidin' lame heavy metal clichés, you go and pull a sub-Mötley-Crüe stunt like that!" He takes a draw of his cigarette, opens his mouth to let smoky clouds drift out, then grunts, "Why don't you go and burn doon some churches wi' your black-metal friends in Norway? That'd be just as fuckin' original. Arsehole."

As blood oozes through the blue towel that's wrapped round my torso, I point an accusing finger at DT and ask, "Why are you all pissed off at me? What aboot that unprofessional knobend? He's the one that walked offstage in the middle o' the gig to get his hole." DT shrugs his shoulders then resumes brushing his hair.

"Dave's behaviour was oot o' line," Ozzy agrees, "but yours was worse. He didn't break any skylight windows. You're lucky Albert thought that was storm damage or we'd be payin' for them. And another thing, DT didn't deface his body wi' occult symbols. You carved yourself up and had women feedin' on your blood. Do you always have to go one better?"

"That's not what it was aboot."

Eyeing me through hovering smoke clouds, Pete asks, "What exactly was it aboot then, Spark?" He sucks the last life from his Marlboro and stubs it out in a glass ashtray. Smoke spirals upwards through skylights and into the night.

Butt-naked, Phil Lynott wanders across the room and drapes an arm around my shoulders. "Moi man here was jest raisin' the feckin' awareness of the band, isn't that roight, Spark? Ye see, playin' great feckin' rock music is one t'ing, but it's usually the other stuff that gets people talkin' about ye – the drugs, the women, the booze, the bad behaviour, the black magic…even if it's all faked. Moi man here's publicity stunt will make sure they talk about us for more than just the music."

"Phil's right," I agree. "All publicity's good publicity, especially in heavy metal. Dirty, depraved, destructive, self-desecratin' behaviour is an accelerator pedal to album sales. I wasn't tryin' to outdo any o' you, especially not that vain prick over there who spends more time brushin' his hair than playin' guitar." DT ties his hair into a ponytail, raises an eyebrow, flashes a smile and flicks up a middle finger at me.

"Feckin' Joisus! Oi feel a fierce warmth in moi belly! Oi t'ink oi'm about to drop the biggest shoite in history. Clear the way to the shoitehouse, boys!" Lynott thunders a path into the toilet, then slams and bolts the door.

Metallic Dreams

"As far as I can see, Ozzy's the only one here who's blameless," I contend. "DT fucked off for a whole song to fulfil his carnal desires. Pete the fuckin' Pied Piper of Penis played the mad scientist. Iain…ehh…I'm still not sure what he did, but it's the single weirdest thing I've seen in my life. I carved a pentalpha into my body. Oz, meanwhile, played drums like a pro, even when his stonner was threatenin' to burst oot of his shorts like a wee orange-haired Incredible Hulk."

"Strawberry blonde," objects Oz. "My pubic hair is strawberry blonde."

DT laughs, spraying Evian water onto the office floor. "Strawberry blonde my arse! You're a blatant ginger."

"Aye," agrees Pete, "you're as orange as can be, big man. Sorry aboot that."

"Ah, you can all fuck off," slams Ozzy.

Pained grunts emerge from the toilet, increasing in volume until we can't hear ourselves talk. It sounds as if a rabid werewolf is chewing through the wooden door. Suddenly, with an ear-splitting bang and a flash of white light, the toilet door shoots across the room, smashes against a brick wall and falls to the floor in a heap of splintered wood and broken hinges. Iain – not the Lynott hybrid, but the stocky, pale-skinned Iain of old - staggers through the open doorway and collapses face down on the floor. "Ah'm fuckin' starvin'," he pleads, "and if I don't get food soon, I'm deid." Then he passes out, bare arsecrack to the sky.

DT thuds a boot into Iain's side. No response. Ozzy pours a bottle of icy water over the unconscious bassist. Nothing.

Udo, Archibald and Paul stroll into the office, cackling about something or other to do with the lack of good grammar in heavy metal. Udo's eyes light up when he sees Iain's backside. "Ooh, and eet eez not even my birzhday! Du bist too kind."

"This isnae a jokin' matter," warns Oz. "Iain's no' lyin' there face-doon, arse-up to tantalise you. He's unconscious…or maybe deid."

"Vhere eez ze sexy chocolate man who played bass for you during ze show? Und who vas zhat man anyway?"

"That man's gone," Oz replies. "Iain had a bout of stagefright and had to…ehh…recruit some help. That's no' important noo anyway. Do you know First Aid?"

"Ich bin ein First Aid expert!" Udo approaches Iain's posterior and spanks its right arse cheek.

Leaning into my ear, DT whispers, "They must do First Aid differently in Germany."

By rolling Iain onto his back and holding an index finger under his nose, Udo determines that he isn't breathing. Pulling open Iain's mouth and pinching shut his nostrils, Udo descends like a striking cobra. Iain's chest expands then falls. Udo rises, gasps for air, and drops back into position to fill Iain's lungs once again.

Iain jolts awake wearing the confused expression of Frankenstein's monster shocked into life. Pointing at Udo, he shouts, "That shirtlifter had his tongue in my mooth! And why am I naked? What are you all starin' at? What the fuck just happened?"

"You had stopped breathing," I explain. "That shirtlifter, as you call him, just saved your life."

"Ja, und ze tongue thing – I vas just clearing your airvay," adds Udo, his eyes aimed down and right, avoiding Iain's stare.

DT whispers, "Like I said, Spark, they must do First Aid differently in Germany." As Dave's shoulders bounce to the rhythm of his laughter, I can't stop myself from laughing with him.

"Oh, fuckin' hilarious!" bellows Iain. "I'm lyin' in the buff on the floor, bein' mooth-raped by a jobbie jabber and you two pricks think it's funny! I hope you both get gang-banged by a bunch o' banjo-strummin' hillbillies when we're doon in the southern states. That'll give me a chance to laugh at your misfortune, ya wanks. I'm surprised you weren't whackin' off while watchin' Udo havin' his way wi' me."

Udo says, "A simple thank you vould have done."

Paul walks to the centre of the room and announces, "Udo, we all appreciate what you did for Iain, as will he once his embarrassment wears off. Thank you. Transcend Everything just played a blinder of a gig. We took an audience that was totally against us and turned them aroon'. That's no mean feat. Somethin' extraordinary happened here tonight. Let's no' get caught up in fightin' again. Focus on what you've achieved and overcome. Transcend Everything is no longer just an idea. It's flesh."

Tossing back his hair, Udo adds, "Ja, ja, your manager eez right. Vell done with ze gig. Iain, you ungrateful schvein, ze next time you stop breazhing, it von't be my tongue zhat I use to unblock your airvay." With eyebrows raised and lipsticked mouth in a camp pout, Udo rubs the crotch of his leather trousers with slow, deliberate strokes, then swishes out of the room like a speed-walker on hairspray and hormones. Frowning, Iain stares at the door, red lipstick smeared across his mouth.

While the rest of us change into fresh clothes, Iain lies still. "Get up," Oz commands. "I want to see my wee girl. I'm no' hangin' aroon' this shithole all night waitin' on you."

"I cannae move," moans Iain. "I've no' even got the energy to sit up. Help me, Oz."

"Nice try, ya wee poof. You'd love to feel my big, strong hands on your naked body. Keep fishin'…I'm no' bitin'."

Tremors ripple through Iain's body. "I'm deid serious," he jitters. "I can't move. This is me tryin' to sit up. I just shake." To the amusement of DT and Ozzy, I dress Iain, dragging clothes onto his leaden limbs while Archibald records the proceedings with his camcorder, muttering inappropriate narrative along the way.

The opening strains of *Converter* curl up the staircase as we head down to the club to watch Pink Stëël doing what they do second best.

Paul and I sandwich Iain between us. With his arms flung round our shoulders, we drag him to the bar, the toes of his boots scuffing along the ground behind him. To celebrate having completed our debut gig as Transcend Everything, we order three pitchers of beer. Onstage, Hanson snarls, "You've got a boring life and some boring wife, but I know that you're a liar…" We kick back and relax, enjoying the over-the-top histrionics and glam/sleaze swagger of our German friends. An hour and a half later, Pink Stëël delivers the one-two knockout punch of *I'm Comin' Out (All Over You)* and *Sausage Party* as we drain our twelfth pitcher of beer.

After the show, the tour bus rumbles off in the direction of Hanson's favourite all-night diner. Pouring beer down Iain's throat was not one of my better ideas; it has failed to revive him from his cabbage-like physical state, but has succeeded in slurring his speech to the point where he sounds like a Glasgow drunk on the late-night bus, both in accent and in frequency of profanity. "Ah'm fuggin' starved, Spark…need fuggin' food, no' cheap pizzy American fuggin' beer. Spark, take me tae food, ya fuggin' bass! Ma body feels like fuggin' cement."

"Just be a wee bit patient," I tell him. "We'll be at the diner soon."

Flashing a grin in Iain's direction, DT says, "And to keep your mind occupied until we arrive there, Monsieur Bright, you could wonder aboot the last place Udo's mooth was before he clamped it over yours." Dave's glassy eyes reflect myriad points of light from halogen bulbs on the ceiling. He looks happy and satisfied. In contrast, Oz is deep in introspection. Wearing only a pair of dungarees, the giant sits in a hunched position, resting his huge arms on oak-tree legs.

"Where's your mind, Oz?" I ask. "You look miles away."

"Ach, Spark, does it ever seem futile to you? Pointless? Doomed?" His watery blue eyes fix on me.

"Does what ever seem futile? The band?"

"Aye."

"Dude, my life has more purpose noo than it's ever had. Remember oor first show as Blood Brothers all those years ago? We had to cut it short, but it still felt like a success. Tonight we had more to be concerned wi' than a pissed-off punk heckler. Oor bassist shapeshifted into a deid rock star, DT walked offstage in the middle o' the set to empty his sack into an admirer, Pete did his version o' the Indian rope trick wi' a synthesiser and a couple o' hundred cocks, and I had a moment o' spontaneous self-mutilation. Yet through it all, we rolled wi' the punches and played a successful show. We transcended oor self-doubts and vaulted the hurdles that fell in oor way. How's that for purpose?"

Ozzy straightens up and parts his lips into a half smile. "Aye, I suppose when you put it like that, we did OK. It always feels as if this band's balanced on the edge of a blade, though. Like we're never more than a bawhair away from self-destruction."

"I feel that too. Maybe it's just creative tension. A lot of iconic musos made incendiary music together, but had difficulty bein' in the same room withoot killin' each other."

"Blackmore and Gillan in Deep Purple…"

"Aye, Ritchie Blackmore and pretty much everyone he's ever worked wi'."

"Mike Patton and Big Sick Ugly Jim Martin in Faith No More. James Hetfield and Dave Mustaine in Metallica. Ozzy Osbourne and Tony Iommi in Black Sabbath."

"All good examples, Oz. You see what I'm talkin' aboot. We're in the privileged position of havin' real love and affection for each other, which should minimise the number o' fights. This band consists o' five very different personalities, each wi' its own strong energy. When those energies combine, crazy shit happens."

"Aye, but there's crazy shit and then there's turnin' into Phil fuckin' Lynott? That goes a wee bit beyond the 'crazy shit' tag!"

"It does, and Iain knew exactly what he was doin'. I'll get to the bottom o' that mystery as soon as he regains enough strength to talk aboot it. It's a hell of a way to conquer stagefright, eh?"

"Aye, maybe so. I'll tell you what, though. I already have one beautiful wee girl to look after. I'm no' goin' to babysit you overgrown five-year-olds too. You all need to keep your shit together."

"I know, Oz. Dinnae worry. I'll act as chief babysitter."

Ozzy covers his eyes with a gigantic hand and shakes his head from side to side in slow arcs. "You'll be chief babysitter? Fuck me sideways wi' a hedge trimmer, Spark. The lunatics have taken over the asylum!"

"Stop worryin', big boy. I'm at the wheel o' this vehicle and you're its rhythmic engine. My drivin' gets a little wild sometimes, but I swear I'll keep us on the road and steer us to oor destiny." Beaming a smile, Oz wraps me in a bear hug.

Brakes squeal as the bus slows to a halt. Hanson's head pops round a black velvet curtain, his eyes narrowing to slits as he observes Ozzy and me in our embrace. "Are you two batting for ze Pink Stëël team now?"

DT looks amused by Hanson's question, so I decide to wipe the smug smile off his face. "Hanson, only one person in oor band uses women's hair products. The same individual also gets his nails manicured at his Mum's beauty salon. If any member of oor band is battin' for your team, he'd be prime suspect. To his friends he's DT, which stands for Dirtchute Tickler."

"I'll tickle your dirtchute wi' my boot!" shouts Dave. "I get my nails manicured to help my guitar playing!"

"Well you need all the help you can get on that front," mumbles Pete.

"Don't you fuckin' start!" yells Dave. "I keep my nails immaculately trimmed so that my fingers always make clean contact wi' the fretboard."

Metallic Dreams

Adjusting his jazz cap, Pete says, "It's just as well you don't play saxophone then, eh? You'd be wearin' glossy pink lipstick and claimin' that it gave your lips a better contact wi' the reed."

DT spits, "Drummond, you're a midge's bawhair away from gettin' your wee musical-prodigy balls booted!" Pete sits cross-legged and smiles like a little turquoise-eyed Buddha while Oz and I sit back to enjoy the fireworks.

Intervention comes not from a divine source but from a gay one. Wolfgang's guttural voice booms, "Ve have arrived at Joe's Famous All-Night Diner! Ze bus vill depart from here in one hour. Enjoy your sustenance."

Ozzy offers to stay on the bus with the sleeping Sunshower so that Marisol can eat in the diner, but the Hispanic beauty declines. I can't blame her; most nice Puerto Rican girls would give our wayward ensemble a wide berth. Oz promises to bring her back some take-out food in a doggy bag. She thanks the sticksman and flashes him a smile.

We flock across a rectangular car park into the spray of red light from an illuminated sign. Iain's limp body is slung over one of Oz's powerful shoulders. When Udo opens the door of the brightly lit diner the smell of fried onions rushes out along with strains of John Cougar's *Jack and Diane*. A short, wiry man of close to fifty attends to the burger, chopped onions and sliced green peppers that sizzle on a square metal grill. His skin tone and dark stubble hint at Greek or perhaps Turkish ancestry. Short salt-and-pepper hair pokes out from under the rim of his white chef's hat. He gives us the once-over and quips, "I didn't know the circus was in town." His accent is pure Brooklyn.

"Eet eez good to see you Joe, you asshole schvein," says Udo.

Joe smiles. "It's been a while. I figured you and your merry band of ass invaders must be handcuffed to a bed in some East Village apartment."

Hanson runs a hand through porcupine-like hair. "No such luck, Joseph. Ve played a gig tonight with our friends from Scotland who vill, ich suspect, decimate your entire menu tonight."

"Good gig?" asks Joe.

"Ja, ja, killer gig," replies Hanson. "To use ze vords of ze gorgeous Jermaine Jackson, ve put ze hurting on ze patrons of Rubber Up."

"Good for you, boys. Pick your tables and sit. I'll come over and take your orders once this burger's cooked."

Hanson leads the way to two tables in the far corner of the diner. We pass a suntanned blonde girl of about twenty in a red and white chequered summer dress. Her blue eyes follow us as we wander past, but she looks unfazed by our hungry, hairsprayed hordes. Balancing a baby on one knee, she holds the bouncing boy with her left hand while stabbing salad with the fork in her right.

Soon, I'm tucking into a half-pound vegeburger, a bowl of blue-cheese salad and a mug of coffee. Oz's rack of ribs takes up half the table.

Pete hand-feeds Iain French fries. Conversation ends, replaced by the sounds of untamed feasting.

The blonde bombshell a few tables away pops open the top two buttons of her dress and pulls down one side, exposing a pert breast with a puffy pink nipple. The girl lifts baby to teat and the lucky wee bastard starts to suck like a child possessed. Unable to drag my gaze away, I miss my mouth with my mug and pour roasting coffee down my front. It soaks through my shirt and into the fresh pentalpha scar. Cursing, I pull the shirt away from the burning incision. Elbowing Ozzy in the ribs, DT points at me and bursts into childlike laughter. The Germans, meanwhile, are unaware of the natural and innocent – yet strangely erotic – breast-feeding scene.

Iain struggles to his feet and stumbles to the girl's table, crumbling onto the seat opposite her. Head slumped on the table, he mumbles a few words. She replies, apparently nonplussed by her uninvited guest. Words pass back and forth for a couple of minutes, but I'm out of earshot and can't even guess what's being said. Iain fishes out some bank notes from his pocket and counts five of them onto the table. The girl takes the money, nods and exposes her other breast. Iain wriggles under the table, pops up next to the girl and begins to suck on her available nipple. She rubs his head with maternal strokes.

Joe sprints to our table and gushes, "I've been dreamin' of doin' that to her since she was fifteen. If only I'd known it was that easy…"

Springing out of his seat, Hanson rubs Joe's shoulders and asks, "Hast du had secret fantasies about me too, Joseph? Ve may be able to come to an arrangement." He plants a kiss on Joe's cheek.

Joe jumps backwards, red lipstick glistening on his face. "There ain't enough money in the world, son!"

When Iain's feeding frenzy has come to a close, the girl pulls a paper napkin from a metal container on the table and wipes dribbled breast-milk off his chin. Holding a mug of black coffee under the teat at which he so recently suckled, Iain squeezes the girl's breast and directs its spray of milk into his drink, which he then stirs with a chunky index finger. Looking unshaken and unbothered, as if breast-feeding strangers is a commonplace occurrence for her, the girl buttons up her dress, picks up her strawberry milkshake and sucks it through a straw.

At Pink Stëël's table, Wolfgang and Helmut are disagreeing over the relative merits of Accept's contribution to the world's metal scene. Wolfgang reckons Accept influenced metal more than their countrymen the Scorpions, albeit in less quantifiable ways. Helmut is visibly angered by this claim, his voice rising a few octaves as he screams the Scorpions' praises. "Ich didn't hear any Accept songs being played vhen ze Berlin vall vas knocked down. I vonder vhy zhat vas? Perhaps eet eez because Accept has alvays been a low-rent Judas Priest rip-off." He aims an O-shaped pout of defiance straight at Wolfgang.

Metallic Dreams

"Zat eez preposterous!" shouts Wolfgang. "Ze Scorpions only wrote zhat *Vind of Change* bullshit, complete vith vhistling, as a calculated, formulaic soundtrack to ze Berlin vall coming down. Eet vas almost guaranteed to become ze soundtrack to freedom und to become a giant hit vorldvide. Zhey sold out!" As the verbal battle continues between the Teutonic tadger ticklers, Archibald decides to start a debate at our table. The topic is the dumbing down of metal.

"Most people are threatened by intelligence," I propose, "but not by stupidity, which is precisely why Joe Satriani and Amorphis sell fewer albums than Guns 'n' Roses and Mötley Crüe."

"That's true, and intelligence comes in many forms," observes DT. "Heavy metal played well is extremely technical, especially the sub-genres of power metal, death metal, speed metal, thrash metal, classic metal and Viking metal. Musical intelligence is as valid as mathematical intelligence, literary intelligence, visuo-spatial intelligence and emotional intelligence."

"I agree with DT," I add, "but I suspect that some o' the metal bands who exhibit a lack of literary intelligence are only doin' so to counterbalance their prodigious musical intelligence. No one likes a smartarse, after all."

Pete blows a cloud of cigarette smoke high into air and says, "Jazz musicians are true artists who exhibit virtuosity, improvisational skills and lyrical talent, withoot ever dumbin' themselves doon for a target audience or lookin' pretty to get on MTV. Heavy metal bands consist of either vain pricks who didn't get enough attention as kids and will do anythin' – even dumbin' themselves doon - to get attention, or nerdy smart kids who were bullied at school and noo want to prove their toughness to the world by wearin' leather and studs while singin' aboot death, motorcycles, dirty women, drugs, booze, Hell, the Devil and the occasional dragon or rainbow. People are threatened by genius."

"Some bands," I contend, "Jackyl and Danger Danger bein' prime examples, feigned stupidity in an attempt to appeal to the lowest common denominator. Tracks like *She Loves My Cock* and *Slipped Her the Big One* have a lyrical pseudo-stupidity that draws attention away from the understated complexity of the songs' sonic arrangements."

Screwing up his face, Oz asks, "What language is Spark speakin'? Does anyone know what the fuck he's on aboot? Does anyone think *he* knows what he's on aboot? Answers on an electronic postcard to www.mentaldeficiency.com."

"OK, big boy," I giggle, "I'll put it in layman's terms. Let's take a metal band of genuine genius – Kings X. Theirs is complex music which goes beyond the 'verse, chorus, verse, chorus, guitar solo, chorus' structure that's the norm. They tell poignant stories with clever lyrics. Their music is original, yet they struggled to put the next meal on the table. Aqua, however, sang some bullshit aboot a Barbie Girl in a fuckin' Barbie World, wi' a tune that sounds like it was written by a deranged three-year-old let loose on a Fisher Price keyboard, yet they still fell arse over tit into money.

Most metal bands that display real genius fail to achieve commercial success, despite – or perhaps because of – wearing their prodigious talents on their sleeves. Rush is a notable exception to that rule."

"What do you have against stupidity?" asks Ozzy. He slurps his coffee and gazes at me over the top of the mug.

"Nothin'. I just can't respect anyone who feigns stupidity in an attempt at coolness. Fake thickos don't impress me. Genuine idiots, on the other hand, can be endearing. Take you as an example - I love you."

Oz slams his mug down on the table, splashing coffee over the rim. "Watch it, smartarse!"

"I'm jokin'. You have rhythmic intelligence and culinary intelligence in spades."

"Aye, very good. Slag me off then kiss my arse when you think I'm aboot to pummel your heid in. That's self-preservation intelligence right there."

"What about the poor grammar you mentioned earlier, Spark?" asks Archibald. "What's the most annoying example you can think of, off the top of your head?"

"Ah fuck," I reply, "why did you have to get me goin' on this? OK, Whitesnake's *Ain't No Love in the Heart of the City* is a perfect example. I'll put the subject matter to one side, since I don't give a shit aboot the lack of compassion prevalent in urban areas. Purely from a grammatical point of view, why the hell does David Coverdale sing *ain't*, for fuck's sake? He's from Saltburn by the Sea. People there don't go aroon' sayin' *ain't*. Cov never wrote the song – it was written by Michael Price and Dan Walsh, and originally recorded by Bobby 'Blue' Bland in 1974 – but that's no excuse. Cov changed the song's arrangement and guitar solo, so he could just as easily have corrected the lyrics. If ol' Cov had sung *Ain't Any Love in the Heart of the City* it would have been grammatically imperfect but would've at least made some kind o' logical sense wi' regards to the sentiment he was tryin' to express. To put the words *ain't* and *no* together, however, is a double negative, so they cancel each other oot and, in effect, imply that there is indeed love in the heart o' the city. The track's title, therefore, is completely at odds wi' its intended message. I happen to know that Cov's a well-educated, eloquent man, so why would he commit such crimes against grammar and logic?"

Pete blows a smoke ring which expands into a grey halo over his head. "Oh, please, wise one, tell us why Coverdale would do such a thing. To give us your sage wisdom so freely and selflessly is truly our blessing."

"I'll tell you why, ya sarcastic wee twat. Cov deliberately committed premeditated acts of feigned idiocy in an attempt to be cool. The blues was originally slave music featurin' lots of *ain't* and *ain't no* song titles and lyrics. The people who invented the blues had received practically no instruction in the correct use o' the English language. Intelligent they may have been. Musical intelligence they had in excess. Most o' them, though, did not get a formal education. American English is a shabby, bastardised dilution of proper English anyway. Even educated Americans tend to have a poor grasp of English, but the slaves who worked their arses off on plantations never even gained a formal education in the bastardised version o' the language. Their English, therefore, was a bastardised version of an already bastardised language. Double bastardisations, unlike double negatives, do not cancel each other oot."

"What does that have to do with Coverdale?" asks Archibald.

"Coverdale loves the *idea* of the blues wi' its mythology and folklore. He hired Micky Moody and Mel Galley, two phenomenal blues guitarists, to play in early Whitesnake, then wrote songs wi' titles like *Walking in the Shadow of the Blues*. He was obsessed wi' the imagery associated wi' the blues. Cov may have grown up in Saltburn by the Sea, but by the time Whitesnake formed, he wanted to sound like a Delta bluesman who had grown up hard and lived on the road, guitar strapped on his back. *Ain't No Love in the Heart of the City* is a blues title, whereas *There's No Authentic Affection in Highly Populated Urban Areas* has no blues credibility. David Coverdale wanted the cachet of a bluesman without actually *bein'* a bluesman. When Cov sings *Ain't No Love in the Heart of the City*, he's not bein' authentic – he's bein' pretentious. The phrase *sho'nuff* is in the lyrics. I mean, for fuck's sake, *sho'nuff*? What in the name o' Lucifer's coalbucket is that aboot? If Robert Johnson had sung those same words they would have been believable. When Cov sings them I cringe."

DT forks a mouthful of apple pie into his mouth and washes it down with coffee. "Alright, Spark, I can't disagree wi' anythin' you've said. The big question is…do you like *Ain't No Love in the Heart of the City*?"

"Aye. That's the worst thing aboot it. I fuckin' love it. The melody is gorgeous, Coverdale's vocals are smoother than velvet, the guitar solo is emotive and emotional, and Neil Murray's bass line is spectacular. That's what makes it all the more annoyin' – I sing along to it and get pissed off at mysel' for collaboratin' wi' Cov in the use o' shambolic grammar."

Pete explodes into laughter, spraying ice cream onto the table. "I've got an idea for a grammatically anal cat like you," he chuckles. "Why don't you correct the bad grammar in heavy metal? You could fix the grammar and syntax in the tracks you love, like a heavy metal editor, then re-record them in their new, grammatically correct format."

"Actually, wee man, that's a good idea. From this point on, wi' you and your stupid jazz hat as my witnesses, I'll correct the mistakes in heavy metal lyrics, whether they're the products of genuine ignorance or deliberately faked stupidity. And Transcend Everything's lyrics will avoid the bravado, machismo and pretentiousness that are all too prevalent in metal. We've always written from the heart and always will."

"What aboot *Little Evils for the Greater Good*?" asks Pete, raising his eyebrows. "What evils have you done in the name o' the band, Vegetarian Boy? What aren't you tellin' us?"

A bloody pentalpha has oozed through the fabric of my shirt, reminding me of the demonic apparition from the club. Ozzy and DT frown a soundless warning to keep my mouth shut about their abduction of Pete. I give a blanket answer. "The lyrics of *Little Evils for the Greater Good* are aboot the lengths to which some folk will go in pursuit o' their dreams."

Pete's voice comes from the middle of the cloud of smoke which obscures his features. "Aye, but what lengths would you cats go to in order to make this band a success? Whatever it takes, like Michael Jordan?"

"I'd go through any amount o' pain, sufferin', heartache and effort for this band. We've all faced doon personal demons already."

Pete nods. "There's somethin' I never told any of you aboot my decision to rejoin the band. There was some…coaxin' involved."

Oz and DT stare warnings at me. I can almost hear their voices in my mind: *'Don't say a word, Spark! Don't fuck it up noo. Pete's here, he's happy, we're finally on our way. Keep your mooth shut.'* "Och, I don't need to know *why* you're here, Pete," I gush. "I'm just happy that you *are* here."

After gulping down the remnants of his coffee, Oz lets out a loud burp then shouts, "The band!" He raises a scarred fist. Knuckles clash above the table. Below our united arms, the landscape is a graveyard of plates, bowls and soiled cutlery, with ceramic mugs standing as headstones.

Iain bounces across the room like a baby gazelle, parks his arse on a bench-seat next to Paul and asks, "What did I miss?"

Paul replies, "Just a band meetin' and a debate over poor grammar and syntax in heavy metal lyrics. Actually, it wasn't as much a debate as one o' Spark's tirades."

Iain blinks clear, refreshed eyes. "I'm glad I missed that."

Feeling anger rise from my core, I spit, "Oh really, ya perverted, titty-suckin' fat fuck."

"There's no need for that," grunts Iain, looking moderately offended. "There was nothin' sexual in what I did."

"You paid a mother - who's probably young enough to be your daughter - to let you suck breast-milk straight oot o' her nipples. How's that no' sexual?"

"When I saw her breast-feedin' the baby, a gut feelin' told me that if I could get some breast-milk, it would restore my strength. I somehow knew that it was the one substance capable of boostin' my energy back to normal. Actually, I've never felt better. It's sobered me up too, so that's a wee bonus!"

"It's the colostrum," explains Paul.

"The what?" asks Oz.

"The colostrum," repeats Paul. "It's a substance wi' miraculous health-givin' properties and it's found in breast-milk. I learned aboot it after Janine gave birth to oor little miracle Montrose."

A mischievous grin spreads across DT's face. "Colostrum, eh? Are you sure it wasn't…ehm…what's that stuff called again? Ehh…oh, aye –

Polyfilla!" Cracking up laughing, he adds, "You totally misunderstood the Polyfilla instructions. When the box says that it's suitable for fillin' cracks, it doesn't mean *those* cracks."

"Aspiring comedian, eh?" queries Paul. "A little free advice, Tierney. Don't give up your day job."

Pete's gaze alternates between Iain and the beautiful mother who is cradling her baby a few tables away. A puzzled expression on his face, he asks Iain, "How did you talk her into it?"

"I just told her the truth and offered her fifty dollars for a feed."

"Just like that, cat?"

"Aye, just like that."

Paul announces, "That fifty bucks you gave her means you're $352.17 dollars doon for the day, as Albert deducted $302.17 from oor fee, to cover the cost of a new toilet door after you destroyed the one in his office. That money's comin' oot o' your share o' the tour takings. We're no' subsidisin' your oddball lifestyle. At this rate, on the tour you'll spend…" Paul pulls a calculator from the inside pocket of his jacket and punches its buttons, "…$3626.04 on shitter doors and…$600 on breast milk. That's a grand total of $4226.04 by the end of the tour if you continue on your present course. Takin' into account that band members are contracted to make $200 per head per gig, then you'll make a net loss and end up owin' the band $1826.04. By the time your food and beverages are added to those losses, you'll be over $2000 in the red. That'd be quite an achievement. I suggest that you grow up, otherwise you'll find yourself on a flight home and replaced by a bass player named Ted from the acclaimed Virginia speed metal band Fatal Visionary."

Iain grinds his teeth. "What kind o' bullshit is that? Have you any clue what I went through tonight for the good o' the band?"

Paul runs hands through his black hair and exhales. "Oh, poor you. Dry your fuckin' eyes! When I listened to Thin Lizzy as a wee boy, I used to draw a moustache on my face wi' black marker then stand in front of my mirror and pretend to be Phil Lynott. You got to actually *be* him for a night. Then your wish to be kissed by a gay German came true. After that, Spark poured a gallon o' free beer doon your throat. And to to finish off a thoroughly awful night, you drank breast-milk straight from the puffy pink nipple of an all-American blonde who's fit for a David Lee Roth video. Tough life you have there!"

"I did it for the good o' the band," replies Iain.

DT strokes his chin. "I sincerely doubt that to be true. You pulled that supernatural stunt for the same reason you wouldn't actually play bass until this year – *fear*."

"I was afraid, that's true," admits Iain, "so I used the tools available to me in order to get through the gig and be a legitimate part of the band."

"You're still no' a legitimate member of the band," argues DT. "That wasn't you onstage in Rubber Up. It was Phil Lynott."

Iain replies, "I don't remember too much aboot it, like one o' those dreams that starts to fade as soon as you wake up, then disappears completely. My memory o' tonight's gig is that it was nearly all me, wi' just a little help from Phil, sort o' like he was my drivin' instructor who used the dual controls a couple o' times just to keep me right."

Ozzy asks, "So if it was mostly you, how is it that you looked exactly like Phil, talked like Phil, walked like him, plucked bass like him?"

"No I didnae," protests Iain, then – after a reflective pause – asks, "Did I?"

Around the table, heads nod. "You should play the rest o' the tour as yourself," I suggest. "You'll be better off financially, you'll have less chance o' seriously injurin' or killin' yoursel', and you'll gain the experience. What's the point o' livin' the life if you cannae remember it?"

Iain replies, "Do you think Ozzy Osbourne or Nikki Sixx remember much aboot their tours?"

A shape like a dark raincloud materialises in the same space as our table, morphing into an ethereal figure in a hooded cloak. Pointing a long talon, the spectre turns clockwise with its arm outstretched, like a sinister version of spin the bottle. When the ghostly digit reaches Pete, it stops. The cloaked head turns to face me, red fires blazing in its empty eye sockets. A piece of ice bounces off my forehead and shatters on the table. "Wake up," grunts Oz. "You were away in your land o' daydreams again." The shadowy presence is gone.

"Did anyone else just see a hooded wraith?" I ask.

Oz wrinkles his brow. "Where?"

"Here at oor table."

Ozzy shakes his head so hard that his hair swirls like a haystack in a hurricane. "Spark, you need to start drinkin' decaf. Your overstimulated heid's seein' things."

Hanson leans over the divider between our tables and asks, "Vhere did ze guy go who vas playing bass with you tonight? He reminded me of someone, but ich cannot remember who."

Iain replies, "He came from a faraway place, that guy. He travelled a long way to be in that club tonight. Lucky for me he did, because that was the worst bout o' nerves I've had since Justine Slave told me her real age after I'd been nailin' her for six months…allegedly."

Hanson tosses back his hair and thrusts his nose high into the air in a Caesar-like gesture. "Ich have no interest in stories about sex vith vomen. Ze reason ich asked about zat man eez zhat ich have eine beschnittenbeule to give him."

"Eine whit?" asks Iain.

"Eine beschnittenbeule." Hanson's eyes indicate his crotch.

"Ehh…I don't think that guy's in the market for one o' those," panics Iain. "He's into ladies, definitely!"

Rolling his eyes, Hanson squeals, "Zhere is no vay he eez zat vay inclined – ze moustache, ze lustrous hair, ze pouting und preening. Zat man likes ze sausage, even if he claims ozhervise. Und ich habe eine German one for him." Udo leans across his table and slaps Hanson's arse. As the two pals crack up, I notice that they even laugh with German accents.

"There you have it, Bright," says DT, "further persuasion, if you needed it, to be yourself in future. You know what I mean? That is, unless you fancy the idea of morphing back into your body only to discover a human brotwürst ram-raidin' your rear."

Iain's eyes mist over as he stares into space, nodding slowly and repeating, as if entranced, "No, I don't fancy that at all. No, I don't fancy that at all. No, I don't fancy that at all. No, I don't fancy that at all. No, I don't fan…" His mantra is broken by the jug of water that's launched over his face by Oz.

After paying the bill and offering Joe heartfelt thanks for his hospitality, we file out of the diner and onto the Stëëlmobile, which shudders to life and rumbles into the night.

Chapter 65 – Walk the Stage

The Stëëlmobile rumbles down America's east coast, leaving a trail of ringing ears, smiling faces and willingly used bodies of both genders in its wake. We've played eleven gigs, all riproaring successes. Bonds between the two bands have become cemented, but thankfully not semen-ted. Shoving thirteen souls into the pressure-cooker environment of a rock 'n' roll tour bus – close proximity, no escape - can have only two possible results: rifts and riots can break out; true community can form. Luckily, the latter has been the case on board Pink Stëël's phallic juggernaut. By day, the Metal Gods have been guiding me, but my dreams have been haunted every night by a dark being with eyes of fire.

Helmut is the only member of the entourage who doesn't travel on the bus, preferring instead to pilot his beloved Trans Am, although he sleeps on a bus bunk. When DT asked Helmut why he chose to travel that way, the German confessed to being a control freak: behind a drum kit; in a vehicle; in the bedroom.

Against all our expressed wishes, Iain has continued to self-concuss. Eleven gigs, eleven Lynott appearances. After making the discovery that colostrum - the substance in breast-milk responsible for his fast recovery - could be bought in freeze-dried powdered form, Iain bought a tour's supply of the stuff, derived from goats. Each night, prior to his channelling activities, he has prepared a colostrum milkshake. The odd concoctions have worked a treat, but I'm concerned that he's using Phil as a crutch to avoid the responsibility of being a fully fledged member of the band.

The dudes in Pink Stëël now know about Iain's shapeshifting. At first, they couldn't figure out how the mysterious, moustachioed figure kept appearing at each gig. Then, five dates into the tour, they witnessed Iain's metamorphosis from stocky Scottish paleskin to lanky Irish chocolate-skinned rocker. The open-minded Germans were less stunned by the live-to-walking-dead transformation than I expected. Maybe in Pink Stëël's daily flow of weird experiences it was just another day.

Excess bodyfat has dropped rapidly off Oz, whose nightly pummelling of Helmut's drum kit has burned untold thousands of calories per gig. This - combined with a high-protein, no-alcohol diet with a vastly reduced cake intake - has resulted in our sticksman's gigantic muscles emerging to the surface day by day as if being chiselled by a celestial sculptor. To the untrained eye, Oz could now be mistaken for an albino bull standing on its back legs and wearing a frizzy orange wig. From a distance, anyway. Up close, his clear blue eyes give the game away.

Prior to leaving the UK, DT printed and laminated an 'Age of Sexual Consent' list detailing the minimum legal age for sex in each of the fifty US states. The document has come in handy on the tour; Dave has fucked his way through an improbable number of east-coast nubiles, but has cross-checked each one's ID against his list prior to getting down and dirty. As the Stëelmobile rolls south across the stateline, DT announces, "Florida's a sexually ambiguous state, Spark. Here, if you're a male under 24 you can rattle any girl of 16 or over, but males of 24 or over can only fuck females of 18 or over. Interestingly, though, Florida's regulations state that 'sexual activity does not include an act done for a bona fide medical purpose'. Theoretically, then, if some starry-eyed sweet-sixteen skank comes backstage tonight and begs me to plunder her cherry, it's not illegal for me to do it, as long as we have a mutual agreement that it's in the interest of improving her health, which it would. Sex is good cardiovascular exercise, as you know, and it lowers cholesterol and blood pressure too."

"Do you only fuck girls that are borderin' on jailbait?"

"Girls are more easily impressed than grown women. I'm pragmatic and horny enough to take advantage of that…and wise enough to check ID before doin' it. I'm *never* goin' back to jail."

"Aye, but askin' for ID before rattlin' a girl isn't exactly romantic."

"Romance is for poetic pricks like you, Spark. I'm all aboot pragmatism, aboot gettin' what's mine. That applies to money, sex, pleasure, acclaim. And who are you to criticise my lack o' romance? You carved yoursel' up and let two heavy metal whores feast on your blood in front of a crowd. Romantic? I don't think so."

"That wasn't supposed to be romantic."

DT raises a black eyebrow and asks, "Care to tell me what it was then, my partner-in-crime?"

"Artwork, usin' my body as a livin' canvas."

"Pull my other tadger, Spark. It's got bells on it. You haven't missed a day's exercise since I've known you. There's no way you'd carve up the body you've put such effort into sculptin' unless you had a powerful motivation to do so."

How do I tell my partner-in-crime that there's a fire-eyed demon haunting me, that perhaps I've lost my mind? Unable to look DT in the eyes, I reply, "It's called sacrificin' for one's art."

Grabbing a fistful of my hair, Dave pulls me close. Saliva sprays from his mouth as he snarls, through gritted teeth, "Tell me, ol' friend, what's really goin' on wi' you? *Tell me!*"

"Somethin' dark and soulless is stalkin' me. I cut the pentalpha into myself as protection against it. Noo that the demon can't harm my flesh, it's appearin' like a malevolent mirage, messin' wi' my heid and hauntin' my dreams."

"Fuck sake, Spark," sighs DT, "there are no demons huntin' you or hauntin' you. There are no demons, period. You've put everythin' into this band. Embarkin' on such an all-or-nothin' crusade is stressful. That stress is causin' you to lose your grip on reality. You don't even have a job to go home to. You burned those bridges."

"Sometimes the best thing to illuminate the way forward is the light from a burnin' bridge."

"Enough o' your Zen philosophy! Listen, stress does weird things to folk. I know. What you see – or *think* you see - is your reality, whether or not it's 'real'. If your mind gets so exhausted that it starts imaginin' demons and dark entities, they'll be as real to you as Angus Young's riffs. My deid grandfather once appeared in my workshop, back when I was workin' seventy-hour weeks and not gettin' enough sleep. I was grounded enough to know that it was my imagination at work, but I entertained the possibility that it may be…just *may* be…my grandpa trying to communicate somethin' to me, so I started lookin' after myself better and gettin' more sleep."

"So what if I'm no' imaginin' this? What if my visions are real? What's the message? Who the fuck's the messenger?"

Dave pulls me close and kisses my cheek. "The mind is a terrible thing to taste, lil' brother…and yours is a deep place. Who knows what lies in its depths?"

"I've wanted to talk to the whole band aboot this," I confess, "but I was worried that it would flip Pete's lid. So I kept it all locked up inside and flipped my own. Demonic irony, eh?"

"Don't say *anythin'* to anyone else," growls DT. "Pete thinks he's in Auld Nick's good books. If you, the fearless metal crusader, start talkin' aboot shittin' yourself because some otherworldly being has you in it sights, you can kiss Pete Drummond goodbye. And that Bright character's mentality is in delicate balance. Fuck knows what goes on in his heid, but at least we've finally got him playin' bass, even though he isn't doin' it under his own steam. He's one loose cannon we shouldn't tamper wi'."

"Dave, when this demon pointed at me after oor gig in New York, the sweat on my body froze. It turned to *ice*."

"Whatever motivated you to carve yoursel' up like a Hallowe'en pumpkin must be terrifyin'. Just remember that real phenomena can happen in response to imaginary stimuli. What matters is what you *think* is real. In jail there were always power struggles goin' on. Periodically I'd be told that my name was on someone's shit list…that I was a deid man. That information provoked intense feelings in me, made all the worse by bein' caged like an animal, unable to run."

I lean closer to DT's ear and whisper, "What if the thing I'm seein' is the same thing that was after Pete years ago? What if it's real? What if it's the fuckin' Devil?"

Leaning backwards, DT looks down his nose at me and narrows his eyes to slits. "Here's what's happenin' – Pete's Devil stories have been percolatin' in your over-fertile heid for years. His self-imposed exile from the ootside world along wi' all the weird occult shit that was inscribed on his apartment walls acted as fuel to the fire that was already ragin' in your poet's imagination. All that otherworldly weirdness sank into your subconscious. Noo it's re-emergin' and manifestin' itself as visions."

"I hope you're right, dude." *I know you're wrong, dude.*

I wander up the bus to see Iain and find him lying in his bunk reading *The Art of War* by Sun Tzu. "May I interrupt you?" I ask.

"You just did, dickheid."

"I want to talk to you about the Phil Lynott thing."

"I've already explained that to you. How many times do you want me to repeat myself?"

"I understand that you've been channellin' Phil. I don't understand the mechanism by which it's been happenin', but none of us can dispute that it has been happenin'. I don't want you to do it tonight. That's a fuckin' *order!*"

"Fuck off, Jealous Boy! You want all the glory in your precious band, eh? You don't want me upstagin' you and stealin' your thunder."

"Listen, arseheid, I'm no' jealous of anyone. Phil Lynott has been a hero to me since I was a wee boy. It's been an honour to share a stage wi' him, even though the crowds have reckoned it's a lookalike soundalike. I'm no' tellin' you to quit shapeshiftin' oot o' petty jealousy. I'm tellin' you oot o' concern for the band's future."

"Tellin' me? Oh, I get it. The mighty Spark, my commanding officer, giver of orders and chosen one of the Metal Gods. That's how you see yourself, eh? Well how aboot this? Take your orders, crumple them into a jaggy ball and shove them directly up your arse!"

Iain turns his attention back to his book. I grab it out of his hands and fling it down the bus. "Listen to me when I'm talkin' to you, ya rude bastard! Every time you channel Phil, you put oor lives in danger!"

Red-faced, Iain springs to his feet and squares up to me. "I've finally figured oot a way o' bein' a fuckin' rock star, ya tit! Why can't you just let me have that?"

"You're no rock star. You've just found another way of *avoidin'* bein' a star. You let a real rocker step into your shoes every night, which is just a different form of the escapism you exhibited as a kid. You haven't even lost your onstage virginity."

"Listen to you! Eleven gigs and you think you're a metal messiah!"

"Aye, well here's the score so far. Spark eleven, Iain nil. You do the maths. Every night after oor shows, I've had buxom nubiles climbin' all over me while you were in your bunk readin' books. You know why? Because not a single one o' those filthy fellatrixes recognised you. Some o' them were juiced up and gaggin' to be rattled by the guy wi' the dark skin and bushy 'tache, the guy they'd seen massacrin' his bass onstage. Most o' those women were prime pussy too. You've missed oot on a wealth of experience, both musical and sexual."

"Fuck off! Pete and Ozzy haven't touched a female either."

"Aye, oot o' choice. They've had no shortage of offers, but Pete only has eyes for Lisa, and Ozzy's still in love wi' Denise."

"How aboot a little appreciation for what I'm doin'? I lied to my boss so that I could be on this tour. Imagine an onstage photo o' me, the real me – not Phil Lynott - were to end up in a music magazine that somehow made its way onto my boss's desk. No amount of explainin' would keep me in a job after that."

"I appreciate what you've done in order to be here, dude. That's why I want *you* - the same Iain who used to headbang in my room wi' me – standin' by my side onstage. If we do this right you won't need to work in an office ever again. You'll have no boss."

"You mean you'll be my boss."

"Not me. The Metal Gods, to whom we must always be allegiant."

"Quit your Manowarish pish, Spark. This band started oot as a democracy, but noo you're actin' like a fuckin' tyrannical dictator."

"When you've shown that you're as committed to the band as I am, then I'll consider relinquishin' some control. You can make a start towards that tonight by goin' onstage as Iain Bright."

"What if I don't?"

Leaning in close, I growl, "Then I'll carve a pentalpha so deep into your fat fuckin' forehead that it'll be forever chiselled on your thick skull."

"Don't threaten me, ya fuckin' maniac!" Iain's face blanches, red speckles appearing in the blue of his eyes. I know these signs well from our gang-fighting years: if I continue on my current tack, words will cease and fists will fly.

Softening my voice, I plead, "Please, Iain, do it oot o' love for oor dreams. Lose your onstage virginity tonight. You don't know what you're missin'."

The pinkness returns to my blood brother's cheeks. His eyes flush back to blue. "I'll mull it over. Noo get me my book and fuck off!" With a grateful nod, I retrieve his book then, as requested, off I fuck.

Pink Stëël and Wolfgang have organised a real-life sausage party to celebrate the end of the tour. It will take place on the bus after tonight's show. The Germans made it clear that we're all welcome to attend and that there will be no compulsion to join in, but warned that they will be, quite literally, letting it all hang out. Archibald has decided to join the party, apparently in order to film video footage. With a dismissive hand gesture, he shushed DT's suggestions that he plans to participate in the sausage soirée.

Helmut has offered me the use of his Trans Am for the night. He plans to abuse all kinds of substances at the party and will be in no state to drive until the following night. No rental car for me. I'll be driving to Cocoa Beach in style.

Paul has booked Transcend Everything into a motel in Cedar Key, a ghost town on the Florida coast. The tour bus will pick us up there the following day and take us to Atlanta Airport in Georgia, from where we will fly home to Scotland.

Tonight's gig is at the Coconut Grove Convention Center in Miami, advertised on their website as 'Quiet. Peaceful. Picturesque.' The Metal Gods disagree. *Not tonight, motherfuckers.* The bus rolls into Coconut Grove at noon. Even through blacked-out windows, the sun is almost blinding. Palm trees sway in the breeze. The scent of sea air mixes with aromas from quiet sidewalk cafés. Somewhat appropriately, David Lee Roth's *Just Like Paradise* flows through the bus's speakers.

The Germans, Archibald, Ozzy, Marisol and Sunshower head to a contemporary art gallery to soak up some culture and eat lunch. The rest of us make our way to Thee Dollhouse, reputed to be the best strip club in the area. Cosmetically enhanced Barbies and heavy metal have always gone hand in hand, so a high-calibre titty bar seemed like a good place to put us in the frame of mind for shredding our audience with sonic firepower. DT asks, "Do you think this is the same Dollhoose mentioned in Mötley Crüe's *Girls, Girls, Girls*?"

"I don't know," I reply. "This is Miami and they were singin' aboot a Dollhoose in Fort Lauderdale."

"Who gives a shit if it's the same one?" says Paul. "What's important is that we have massively mammaried freaks swirlin' roon' poles for us."

"I shouldn't be here," moans Pete. "Lisa wouldn't like it."

DT's brow furrows. "Lisa doesn't have to like it. Lisa's no' here. Not many women would like it. Unless they're women who like livin' la vida lesbo, of course."

Pete shakes his head. "That's not what I meant. Lisa wouldn't like me bein' here."

I loop an arm round Pete's shoulder. "These silicone superheroines aren't replacements for Lisa. This is look-but-don't-touch territory. We'll relax here a while and get focused for the show."

The lines on Pete's forehead move like tortured snakes. "Aye, but Lisa still wouldn't like it," he whines. "I'm here under duress."

"Aye," cackles DT, "we're twistin' your arm and forcin' you to ogle voluptuous, tanned vixens while drinkin' Brazilian coffee and smokin' a box o' your beloved Marlboros. That's a rough fuckin' life you have." Pete begins to giggle. We all laugh, all except Iain, whose distracted expression hints at thoughts far from southern Florida.

During the next three hours, the titty-bar gang smokes Dominican cigars and drinks gallons of strong coffee, cooling our heels while long-legged dancers spiral down poles with astonishing athleticism. Paul, the only one present with any experience of UK strip clubs, observes, "The girls I've seen strippin' back home look like rough scrubbers who'd do anythin' for a few quid. These girls look like athletes, as if they eat right, exercise, get enough sleep and lots of sun. I reckon they approach dancin' as if it were a competitive sport."

"Aye," adds DT, "except that female athletes don't usually have 52-inch silicone bags shoved inside their paps."

"Very poetically put, Mr Tierney," I observe.

"Thank you, Spark," grins DT. "You always did appreciate my subtlety."

Rocket Queen by Guns 'n' Roses fades out to be replaced by Def Leppard's *Pour Some Sugar on Me*. Paul nudges me and says, "Another thing aboot titty bars here – they play great music. I once sat in a Manchester club watchin' scrawny waifs strip lethargically to a soundtrack of Stone Roses, Oasis and the Human League. That rates as the nadir of my life."

DT pulls a mobile phone from the pocket of his tattered jeans. "I'm goin' to call Udo to see what they're up to. Yin and yang."

"What's that Dave cat talkin' aboot?" asks Pete.

"I think he's referrin' to the chasm between the other group's cultural activities and oors," I explain. "Thus, yin and yang." Pete nods, removes his jazz cap, scratches his bird's nest of blonde hair, then places the cap back on his head.

After the phone call, DT announces, "The other group are finishing a nouvelle-cuisine lunch in a beachfront gallery where a five-piece orchestra are playing Paganini. We're every bit as cultured as that – smokin' stoges and watchin' juggernaut jugs jigglin' to Mötley Crüe and Def Leppard." He takes a long draw of his cigar and blows smoke down his nostrils like a black-haired dragon. "We've to meet them back at the bus in an hour," he adds, "then we'll head to the venue to start settin' up oor gear."

By 7 p.m. our equipment is set up and crowds have started to flock into the arena as the sun plunges towards a butterscotch horizon. Our dressing-room window offers a view of a powder-sand shoreline onto which foam-crested waves, which my grandfather would have called 'white horses', crash with a sound like rolling thunder. I've been monitoring Iain like a hawk for the last hour, never straying more than a few feet from him, poised to pounce on his slightest move towards self-concussion. "Spark, is there any chance you could fuck off oot o' my personal space?" he grunts. "You've been hangin' aboot wi' German poofters so much that you want a piece o' me, is that it?"

Making a V with the index and middle fingers of my right hand, I point at my eyes then at Iain's, in the military gesture of 'I'm watching you'. Iain sticks up a different type of V sign. "Do you know where that gesture originated?" asks Oz. "The French, if they captured an English archer in battle, would chop off his fingers to prevent him shootin' again. So English archers started stickin' up the V sign at the French as a gesture of defiance. It was their way of saying, 'Fuck you! Look! I still have my fingers! I can still fire arrows right into you frog-eatin' fucks!' Consider yourselves educated." Nodding, Iain sticks up another V in my face.

Wolfgang appears in black leather trousers and tight white vest. "Fifteen minuten until showtime! Ze crowds are arriving fast. Ze hall eez almost full already." Archibald is filming Pete, who is sitting cross-legged and chanting, in some kind of pre-show meditative trance. Paul is visiting a local rock radio station to give an interview.

"Who the fuck's responsible for this? He's fuckin' deid!" An infuriated DT stomps around the dressing room, his previously red leather trousers now shocking pink. The words '**REAR ENTRY**' have been scrawled in bold black marker across the arse. "These are my fuckin' gig troosers! They cost a fortune. Who the fuck sprayed them pink?"

"Maybe it was your manicurist," I suggest, "or perhaps your hairdresser."

"Spark, don't fuckin' wind me up! This isn't the time!"

"Relax, Dave," advises Oz, "you could just face forward for the whole gig and no one would see the invitation on your arse."

"Invitation? What invitation?" DT stands in front of a full-length mirror and looks over his shoulder at the words on his defaced derrière. "Oh, for fuck's sake! I'm definitely no' goin' oot there noo. This isnae funny at all. One of you fucks is gettin' a kickin' tonight."

Pete, still deep in trance, is oblivious to proceedings. A loud debate rages in the dressing room over the source of DT's wardrobe customisation. Finger-pointing and swearing abound, but no culprit emerges. I'm still keeping watch over Iain, ready to attack at the slightest sign of concussive manoeuvres. Pete snaps out of his meditative state, walks to the open window and lights a cigarette while the topless Ozzy does warm-up exercises to get blood flowing into his huge muscles. DT is mouthing obscene threats involving our naked mothers and a pack of sex-starved wolves when Wolfgang's head pops round the door and says, "Five minuten until showtime."

When I ask DT if he has considered the possibility that a homosexual may be to blame for his lurid legwear, he fixes me with a dark glare and says, "That makes a lot o' sense. Those Teutonic toley terrorisers would love to see me onstage lookin' like a backside bandit."

"Like *more* of a backside bandit," I correct.

"Not funny," spits DT. "I'm goin' to soak those gay fuckers' dildos in superglue then roll them in Miami sand. We'll see how funny they find that." Dave's expression lightens, as if a bulb has been switched on behind his eyes. "Watch this! I'm no' playin' the biggest gig of my life wi' a homosexual invitation on the arse o' my troosers. It's time to one-up these benders. I'm gonnae go Blackie Lawless on their asses!"

Ozzy and I exchange horrified gazes and, in synch, shout, "Oh, no!"

"Oh aye! Tonight, my blood brothers, I'm goin' to be Blackie Lawless of W.A.S.P., circa 1984." Grinning, DT digs into his bag, pulls out a lock-knife and cuts the arse out of his trousers.

Taking advantage of my momentary distraction, Iain sprints at the faraway wall of the dressing room. I springboard off a bench and fly Superman-like through the air, landing bang on top of Iain's thick head. He crumbles to the ground, thrashing beneath me as I press the radius bone of my forearm into his windpipe. My three-point choke is executed perfectly, so the harder my blood brother struggles, the faster the oxygen in his lungs gets depleted. In a goggle-eyed panic, he tears at my forearms, scoring their flesh with his nails. Gritting my teeth against the pain, I hang on until Iain's consciousness slips away and he goes limp in my arms. "Quick, Oz, carry this fruit slice oot to the stage before he wakes up! Tonight he's playin' as himself."

"He's deid!" wails Ozzy. "You just broke his neck!"

"Och, he's no' deid. I just choked him oot. He'll come aroon' in a few seconds, so get the crazy bastard onto the stage before he does. He won't shapeshift in front of a crowd o' thoosands." Oz throws Iain over a mighty shoulder and disappears out of the dressing room.

Having squeezed himself back into his newly customised leather trousers, DT parades around the dressing room, arsecrack bared to the world. "Well, partner-in-crime," he grins, "let's blow the roof off this place."

DT grabs me by the hair and kisses my left cheek. A beaming Pete bounds across the dressing room and plants his lips on my other cheek. "Thanks for gettin' me here, Spark. It was a long few years stuck in my smoky flat. This Florida air agrees wi' me. Let's do this, cats!" Arm in arm, we stride towards the stage, three fearless metal musketeers: Dave in all his bare-arsed magnificence; me, resplendent in kilt of MacDubh ancient tartan, desert combat boots and pentalpha-scarred bare torso; Pete, barefoot in outback shorts, vertical hair pricking skywards.

Onstage, Oz is seated on his reinforced drum stool, his eyes sparkling like blue fire. A disorientated Iain is propped against an amplifier, bass guitar slung over one shoulder. Taking his position behind an array of synths and keyboards, Pete lights a cigarette.

The arena lights go down as the stage curtain parts. A modest roar erupts from the crowd as Ozzy pounds out a tribal beat and a circular spotlight bathes the giant sticksman in light. DT and I crank out the opening riff to Iron Maiden's *Run to the Hills*. I'm happy to hear the rumble of bass; Iain looks half dead, but his fingers are on autopilot, flashing across the fretboard and plucking strings with flawless precision. A scorching redhead in the front row bares her breasts as DT sets his guitar to stun for the solo. I run to the side of the stage and instruct Archibald, who is filming the concert, to capture the titties on film. He swings the camera and zooms in until the girl is filling the frame. I give him two thumbs up then run back to my mic stand in time to soar into the stratospheric scream that heralds the arrival of the final chorus. With the audience booming their approval after the song, I smile at Iain. His response is of the two-fingered variety, after which he approaches me and grunts, "I cannae believe you did that, Spark. You could have killed me, ya fuckin' asshole."

"You were never in any danger from me. You're a danger to yoursel' and the rest of us."

"Fuckin' control freak," he mumbles. "I should walk offstage and leave you in the shit."

"Dude, there's a time and a place for bickerin' and this isn't it. Look oot there into the crowd – thoosands o' faces, here to see us…to see *you*. Phil Lynott is their history, but we're their future. You can be part of that future. For fuck's sake, you've dreamed aboot this all your life." Iain gives me a probing stare followed by the slightest of nods, a gesture which I return.

DT's voice echoes around the auditorium. "Florida, it's good to finally be here. We appreciate you shellin' oot your hard-earned cash to come and see us. We are your humble servants and will do all in oor power to make this a night you will *never* forget!" He gazes at the buxom redhead and strokes Heavensent's neck in an unmistakeably phallic way. Smiling back, she shakes her mass of fiery hair. "We have only five words for you," DT continues. "*These Are the New Riffs!*" Pete glides into the song's keyboard intro. As Dave and I flay our fretboards, twin spotlights descend from the overhead rigging, surrounding us in haloes. Heavensent reflects silver streams of light, illuminating faces in the crowd. Ozzy and Iain are tighter than a midge's arse, rhythmically speaking, pounding out beats that keep the rest of us laser-precise. For the guitar solo, DT and I share centre stage, swapping shredding duties faster than Judas Priest's Tipton and Downing with firecrackers tied to their fingers and lit sparklers jammed up their arses. Thousands of hands impale the air, flashing Devil horns, punching sky, even showing the occasional peace sign. When the song ends, ecstatic screams erupt from the crowd. Breasts are bared and bras spatter the stage at an accelerating rate. DT picks up some of the charity chestwear and hangs it from the neck of his guitar. Leaning into his ear, I whisper, "Dude, I need you play guitar like never before. Those papholders might hinder your playing."

Dave kisses my cheek again. "Spark, my partner-in-crime, quit bein' such a control freak. Have faith."

Mirroring DT's smile, I reciprocate his kiss on the cheek, then tell him, "Ol' friend, my faith in you is infinite. I didn't mean to get on your case. Let's do Ozzy's masterpiece." DT's grin widens. He nonchalantly catches a red lace bra that's flying towards his head and uses it to tie his long black hair into a ponytail. "Thank you, Coconut Grove," he hollers. "We'll stop the onstage cheek-kissin' noo, as you'll have gayness in spades once my buddies in Pink Stëél hit the stage. Beware the *Orange Donger of Doom!*" Oz's blast-beat drums signal his composition's arrival. We scorch through the song at supersonic speed, the whole band chanting vocals on the chorus.

Iain has found his stage legs. When he isn't running the width of the stage or leaping off Ozzy's drum riser, he has one foot planted on a stagefront monitor. Pete, the consummate professional, hits every note with mathematical precision. The humidity has turned Ozzy's hair from a spiral afro into something resembling an untended orange hedge. Sweat flies off the drum monster's bare torso as his blurring arms pound bowel-dissolving sounds out of Helmut's drum kit. DT and I, the partners-in-crime, share a mic stand and trade guitar licks.

We rip through covers of AC/DC's *Guns for Hire*, Judas Priest's *Turbo Lover*, Motörhead's *Iron Fist*, Helloween's *Future World*, Rainbow's

Stargazer and Type O Negative's *Christian Woman*. On Blackfoot's *Send Me an Angel*, DT insists that we change the opening lyrics for humorous effect; as my partner-in-crime gives birth to eviscerating riffs, I sing, "Every night I hit the street…and it's fuckin' sore."

    Facial expressions in the crowd range from ecstasy to awed shellshock. Skystretched hands pass crowd-surfing bodies around the arena. Pete dishes out earplugs to the band before his 'White Noise' synth effect jets from powerful amps straight into the souls and crotches of the audience. Trousers turn into tents. Astonished jaws drop. As confusion ripples through the males in the crowd, I announce, "Florida, it has been a joy to be here. I hope it has been as fulfillin' for you as it has for us. We love each and every one of you. This is oor last song of the night. We do *Little Evils for the Greater Good!*"

    As we launch into the final track, a vast wave of sound – like a mighty sea – lifts DT and me off the ground and washes us towards the front of the stage. Only grabbing a bolted-down mic stand stops us from surging over the edge and into the crowd. Fists pierce the air. Buoyed by our sea of sound, brave crowd surfers float above upstretched hands. Voices reach fever pitch. Breasts pop out across the arena. Dry ice absorbs neon light and transmutes it into clouds of variegated colours. Transcend Everything is a unified organism, each of its members a key component of the whole, each one of us plugged into the energy of the others.

    We ditch our instruments and take our places at the front of the stage. Ozzy stands in the centre, dwarfing the rest of us. When we link arms and take a bow, the roar of the crowd almost knocks us off our feet. My four compadres show fists to the audience then disappear into the bowels of the building. I remain onstage, arms stretched out above the crowd, revelling in the vibrationary shower of their energy. Bounteous breasts are bared in mammary salutes while I stand kilted, bare-chested, pentalpha-scarred and smiling, long hair plastered to my sweat-soaked body.

Chapter 66 – Big Bad Moon

Deep in Wytchcoomb Forest, a raven-haired woman in a hooded robe climbs to the highest floor of a cylindrical seven-tier stone tower built on the intersection of seven major ley lines. She unlocks an iron door and walks into a circular room where a scrying orb is turning from black to cloudy grey on an ancient oak table. Staring into the translucent sphere, she narrows feline eyes and opens herself to the flow of magnetic energy that rushes up the tower like a waterfall in reverse. Above her head, a massive thirteen-sided bronze candelabra is suspended from the ceiling by chains. Thirteen lit candles, one at each point of the tridecagon, cast ever-changing shapes onto stone walls. To block out the full moon, black curtains have been drawn across the room's only window. Medieval harp music floats from a room two floors down.

Rosie touches the scrying sphere's surface with soft fingertips. A moving image forms within the depths of the glass: an hourglass descends from the skies to hover above six pairs of footprints in the sand of a white beach; the hourglass cracks; its contents – the sands of time – spill out into the smallest pair of footprints, filling them until they no longer exist.

The curtains screech open. Moonlight floods the room. The scrying orb turns red, burning Rosie's fingers. With a howl, she retracts her hands and turns her gaze to the sky, where the moon's lunar seas have become sunken shadow-eyes in a skeletal face. Crimson liquid oozes from the dark cavities and trickles down the countenance of the lamenting lump of spacerock. As a swan-shaped cloud drifts in front of the moon, a freezing gust snuffs out the candles' flames, shrouding the room in darkness. The scrying orb explodes.

Bleeding from crystal-splintered skin, Rosie drops to her knees on the cold stone floor and descends into the unchained wails of the mourner.

Chapter 67 – The Writer

As Pink Stëël rocks the crowd at the Coconut Grove Convention Center, DT makes use of their vacant dressing room, into which he takes the curvaceous breast-baring redhead from the crowd and her younger sister (whose ID he cross-checks against his laminated Age of Consent list, just in case). He invites Archibald to film the carnal exploits, an opportunity the journalist doesn't hesitate to seize.

Iain is having his first taste of heavy metal stardom's fringe (aka minge) benefits, in the form of a tanned Florida blonde in tight jeans and a stars 'n' stripes bikini top. The patriotic bimbette is as much a product of cosmetic surgery as of nature, but Iain doesn't care; she oozes slutability and he is determined to enjoy the ride.

Ozzy, Paul, Pete and I are sitting in the Convention Centre's V.I.P. bar. Helmut's Trans Am keys are burning a hole in my pocket, such is my desire to jump into the car and burn rubber to Shaquanna's house. It's too early for that, though, so I sip ice-cold Mountain Dew and try with all my might not to torture myself with thoughts of the dark-skinned body that's sweating in the humid Cocoa Beach night air, waiting on my arrival. Scratching his head, Paul asks, "What is it aboot this Shaquanna that's worth drivin' three hours for?"

"Imagine an ass as big as the side of a hoose and as juicy as a ripe watermelon. Add to that a waxed chocolate-brown pussy wi' just enough of a natural partin' in its labia to allow a glimmer of pink interior to shine oot. Visualise hands wi' long, painted nails capable o' tearin' your back to shreds. Obsidian eyes. Full lips. Torpedo titties. Need I go on?"

Paul cups his balls in one hand and rubs his cock with the other, as if trying to make a genie appear. "Oh aye, go on…*go on!* Don't stop noo! Tell me aboot her big broon discs!" He rolls his eyes skywards and makes orgasmic faces. "Take me wi' you, Spark! Let me be your substitute. She may be too much for you."

"Stop it, ya pair o' perverts," thunders Ozzy. "You're depraved." His cut-off dungarees, pale white skin and seven-day beard give him the look of a large Amish farmer.

"You, Spark, are taking the crotch-controlled route rather than the cerebral one," expounds Pete. "That's a dangerous path, if you ask me."

"Well I wasn't askin' you, so piss aff. We all have to give oor tadgers a treat sometimes. It's been a long tour and this is my reward to mysel' for gettin' the band back together and actually achievin' somethin'."

"Your tadger has been gettin' nightly treats on this tour," observes Pete. "You and DT have fucked girls every night and in every hole. You even filled one bouncy-castle-sized woman's navel wi' olive oil then fucked it like an orifice while DT did the same to her hairy armpit. Your dick doesn't need any more treats. It could use a night off to rest."

"Those girls on the tour bus were tasty snacks. Starters, if you will. Shaquanna, on the other hand, is an all-you-can-eat buffet. There's a world of difference." Shaking their heads, Pete and Ozzy exchange disgusted glances.

Marisol and Sunshower enter the bar. The youngster dashes across the polished wooden floor and launches herself into the waiting arms of her father. "Daddy, you were great tonight!"

Oz frowns. "You saw us?"

"Yes! I got all my sums finished and even did some extra English homework. Because it was the last night of the tour, Marisol thought we should come inside to watch your concert."

"I was just thinkin' today that Marisol could use some excitement," nods Paul.

"What is that supposed to mean?" demands Marisol. "Do you think *you* have what it takes to excite me?" Hair cascades over her eyes as she spits words with Latina fire. "For your information, I have eyes for only one man." Her eyes flicker towards Ozzy's bulging arms, linger there a moment, then look away.

An arena security guard - a short, densely muscled man with regulation Marines buzz-cut and a neatly trimmed moustache - stomps towards our group. He stops a few feet away and clicks his heels together. I almost expect him to salute, but instead he addresses the band. "There is a man outside who claims to be a famous rock journalist. He is not carrying press ID, although I did check his driver's licence. This man would like to interview Transcend Everything, but I have told him that he cannot have access to this area without your permission. How would you like me to proceed?"

"Kill him," barks Paul, "he's an imposter. All press interviews have to be organised through me, the band's manager, at least two weeks in advance."

"I don't have the authority to kill him, sir," replies the guard, without a trace of irony. "If you wish, I can kick him in the groin then remove him from the arena for pestering the band?"

"I like the sound of that," says Paul. "Go and boot his balls. Can you recall the name this guy gave you?"

"Yes sir. His name is Buck Fosterman."

I spring to attention. "Buck! I've read two o' his books. The guy's a phenomenal writer. Send him in immediately."

"As you wish, sir." The guard marches towards the bar's security-coded doors, punches in a numerical code and disappears out of sight.

Moments later, a tousle-haired, bearded, bespectacled and drunk Buck Fosterman weaves across the bar. "Hi, y'all," he slurs. "Please forgive my condition. I was in town visiting a friend. We came to this concert for pleasure rather than business, but I *need* to get an interview with you guys."

"It's an honour to meet you, Buck," I gush, shaking his hand. "I'm Spark. I really enjoyed *Boise Rock City* and *Shooting Yourself to Live*. Before we do anything resemblin' an interview, though, there's somethin' I need to get off my chest. You called Helloween a hair metal band. It'd have been less preposterous to call Slayer a 'peace-and-love ballad band' or Poison an 'extreme Viking metal band'. Much as I hate labels, Helloween are – if anything – German power metal. Just listen to them. Their definitive track, *Hallowe'en*, from *The Keeper of the Seven Keys, Part 1* album, is more epic than anything by Led Zeppelin. Helloween took the traditional metal blueprint laid doon by Judas Priest and mixed it perfectly wi' the darker metal of Mercyful Fate and the lyrical savvy of Iron Maiden. The end result was somethin' original, innovative and light years away from the sleazy L.A. hairspray-and-cosmetics-endorsed bands."

Buck runs a hand through his shock of copper hair, lets out a loud belch and grins. "Consider me deservedly chastised. Would you like to flagellate me now or may we start the interview?"

"Let's start."

Marisol takes Sunshower to a table that's out of earshot, presumably to protect the little girl from words unsuitable for tender ears. Buck staggers to the bar and returns with six cans of Budweiser on a blue plastic tray. "You didn't have to buy us drinks," says Pete, reaching out for one of the beers.

Pulling the tray out of Pete's reach, Buck replies, "I didn't. These are for me. I wouldn't wanna dehydrate durin' the interview." As we lounge on leather sofas around a low table, Buck pulls out his mp3 player and presses its record button. "I have to be honest," he admits, "and maybe it's the beer talkin' here, but I hope it's my journalistic honesty and integrity. Tonight, durin' your show, I…oh God, how do I say it? I…ehh…got sexually aroused durin' a keyboard solo. Very aroused! I'm not even a big fan of keyboards. I've had the hairs on my neck and arms standin' on end at gigs, but your band took that up a notch. And that levitatin' trick you did at the end was amazin'."

Adding a splash of Jim Beam to his glass of Mountain Dew, Pete says, "Weird things happen at oor gigs, but they're not tricks. They couldn't be more real. Durin' oor last track, you witnessed the Sounds of Power, which haven't been heard on Earth since they were used thoosands o' years ago to construct Egypt's pyramids. I've been chasin' those sounds for years, and tonight I caught them. I'm glad the music resonated wi' you."

"Your cover versions were impressive," observes Buck, large square glasses magnifying his blue eyes. "Your own tracks, however, were the most breathtaking music I've ever heard…and I have a *huge* CD collection." More guzzling of beer. More of the endearing Bucky smile.

An excited Ozzy booms, "That's what I'm talkin' aboot, ya bass!" His meaty hand envelops the journalist's daintier digits in a handshake.

"I'm Ozzy, the drummer. I'd never heard o' you before tonight, but it's an honour to meet you anyway."

"How did you get your nickname?" asks Buck. "Ozzy Osbourne, I suppose?"

"No, although most people assume that. My surname is Oswaldo, so people have called me Ozzy from as far back as I can remember."

Cracking open the second can of his six-pack, Buck asks, "What about the others? What are your names?"

"I'm Pete, keyboard king, synth maestro and all-roon' musical genius. I'm the highest form of intelligence in the band."

"I'm Paul Roberts, band manager and Spark's friend since childhood."

A mischievous grin spreads across Pete's face. "Paul's nickname back in Scotland is the Polyfilla Kid. He does what it says on the tin."

"Shut it, ya wee dick!" hollers Paul. "And anyway, that's Ronseal's motto, not Polyfilla's! Shows how much *you* know aboot DIY!"

"I stand corrected," submits Pete. "My humble home-decoratin' abilities cower next to your extensive prowess."

Paul pulls the jazz cap off Pete's head, shoves it down the back of his shorts, wipes his arse with it, then places it back atop the keyboard player's wiry blonde hair. "Take that as a warnin'," rumbles Paul. "I may just Polyfilla your bumcrack next time. Or your wisecrackin' mooth. And another thing, Drummond. Hats are for twats."

"Guys," interjects Buck, "can we keep it to the music, please? Where did the name Spark originate?"

"As a wee boy of four," I explain, "I became conscious of the idea that mysterious energy came from electrical sockets. One day, in my grandparents' hoose, I shoved three saliva-soaked fingers into the holes of a plug socket, hoping to soak up its energy. After a loud bang and a flash of light, my fingers were charred black and stuck together. My grandmother took me to hospital, where A&E nurses freed my digits wi' chemicals. From that day on, my grandmother called me Little Spark, which other people shortened to Spark."

"What's your real name?"

"I changed my real name to Spark by Deed Poll as soon as I was sixteen."

"Wow," enthuses Buck, "that's fucking cool! What did you change your surname to?"

"I kept my original surname, MacDubh, which translates literally as 'son of the dark'."

"Fuck yeah," slurs Buck, "Spark, son of the dark. It doesn't get better than that. You are the light born out of darkness." He empties a can of Budweiser in a oner.

"Somethin' changed in Spark after his electric shock," adds Paul. "The fucker started conductin' electricity big time. More often than I can remember, sparks have buzzed oot o' his fingertips and shocked me."

"That's not always a good thing," I add. "It happens all the time when I'm fillin' my car up wi' petrol - static zaps between my fingers and the metal bodywork. Every time I refuel the car, I'm shittin' it in case a spark hits some petrol and blows half the toon sky-high."

"Now that," cries Buck, "would get people talkin' about your band!"

"Aye, it definitely would," I agree, "but I'd rather no' do it."

"Cut an album first," Buck advises. "If you record an album that's as good as your live performance tonight, *then* blow yourself to smithereens, I guarantee that you will be bigger than Nirvana, bigger than Hendrix, maybe bigger than Jesus Christ."

"I'm no' wantin' to turn into Krist Novoselic," complains Pete. "Transcend Everything is here for the long haul, so please be a good cat, Buck, and don't give Spark ideas aboot rock-icon immortality. He already thinks he's died and been resurrected, chosen by the Metal Gods as their angel on Earth, here to do their bidding. Anyway, even if that tit did blow oor home toon to pieces, he'd be left standin' – Spark, the ants and the cockroaches."

"Ehm...thanks," I stammer. "Pete's last comment, Buck, is what's known in Scotland as a back-handed compliment."

Nodding, Buck says, "In North Dakota, where I grew up, it's known as a bitch-slap! By the way, where are the others from the band?"

"Oor lead guitarist, DT, is plunderin' two sisters in oor dressin' room while my friend Archibald, a journalist from Scotland, films proceedings for the archives. Iain, oor bassist, is showin' an all-American girl aroon' Pink Stëél's tour bus."

Buck downs another Budweiser in one go, burps, scrunches the empty can in an inebriated fist, tosses it over his shoulder then burps again. "Rock hoes, ya can't beat 'em...well, not without the threat of a lawsuit. It's crazy how even the shittiest metal bands attract hot women, yet the best rock journalist couldn't get the same girls to look in his direction, even if he was wavin' his Pulitzer Prize around."

"Perception is reality," I philosophise, "especially in metal. A guy who plays in a long-haired metal band is perceived as a wild, crazy, emotionally unstable S.O.B. Wild, crazy, emotionally unstable women dig that because they see the male version of themselves. Journalists who write aboot long-haired reprobates and their depraved behaviour are perceived as nerdy, bookish, cardigan-wearin' academics whose only understandin' of metal is through observation and analysis rather than subjective experience. The same applies to record producers."

"I don't know," ponders Buck. "Mutt Lange has banged Stevie Lange *and* Shania Twain."

"At the same time?" asks Oz.

"I don't think so," muses Buck, "but it's possible. I agree with Spark's comments about journalists missin' out on the hottest women in metal, all because those women are fixated on guitar-toting pricks or drum-beating assholes. It's just not fair."

Clenching a huge fist, Oz asks, "Did you just call me an asshole?"

Backtracking frantically, Buck holds up his hands and spouts, "No, no, that was a sweeping statement, and like all such proclamations there are exceptions. You, Ozzy, are one of those exceptions. In general, though, my statement holds true. Look around at most metal bands, particularly those from California, and you'll observe some misogynistic, chauvanistic, pampered imbeciles. Many of them make great music, it's true, but they're still assholes."

"The other four guys in this band *are* assholes," adds Pete. "You just haven't known them long enough to realise it, Bucky my man."

"What's your journalist pal like?" asks Buck. "Like me?"

I invite Buck to, "Imagine that, rather than growin' up on a Fargo farm, you grew up in a small toon on the rainy west coast of Scotland, where you were raised as a Catholic by parents whose hoose was a perpetual warzone in which curse words flew like bullets and accusations dropped like H-bombs. Then imagine that instead of workin' on a farm, you spent your free time holed up in your room constructing an alternative identity for yourself as an eccentric Scottish gent. Envisage drawin' comic strips and writin' mini-novels, all featuring your aristocratic alter-ego as the star. Visualise disappearin' into this escapist world so frequently that it becomes your reality. Finally, consider that – unlike your childhood icons of Poison, Mötley Crüe and Guns 'n' Roses – the backing track to your life had been cut by Rainbow, Black Sabbath, Deep Purple, Wishbone Ash and Budgie. If you can imagine these things vividly, you'll have an insight into Archibald. He *is* that eccentric Scottish heavy metal gentleman."

"Fascinating," slurs Buck. "I can't wait to meet him. Mötley Crüe was escapism to me when I was a kid on the farm. Upside-down pentagrams and men in make-up were as far from socially acceptable as possible in Fargo. If the guys from Mötley Crüe had shown up on the main street of our town, the hard-workin' farmers would have beaten them to a pulp then burned them at the stake. I gravitated towards bands whose lifestyles were furthest removed from mine. Archibald and I may have had very different upbringings, but there were common factors of guitar-based music and escapism."

"I like Archibald," adds Ozzy. "He's respectful, smart and always polite to me and Sunshower, not to mention that he's documentin' this tour and will be printin' the results once we get back to British shores. He'll help the band in a big way, I think. He has the odd habit of takin' off his troosers whenever he gets a chance, though. He claims it's so they won't smell of smoke, but he does it whether there's smokin' goin' on or not. Right noo, he's in his boxer shorts shootin' video of DT and his two female companions."

Buck looks nonplussed. "I'll meet the others in due course."

Oz shakes his head. "The only way you'll meet DT tonight is if those sisters have a curfew."

"True," I agree, "although Iain's a different matter. He'll be lucky to last ten seconds. He could be here anytime."

"I doubt it," muses Pete. "The Bright cat won't want us analysin' his sexual performance. He'll whoosh in a few seconds, but he'll hang aroon' on the bus for at least a couple o' hours. That way we won't know how long he lasted or didn't last. He likes to think of himsel' as a coital Carl Lewis."

"Carl Lewis was a sprinter, ya dick," observes Oz. "Surely you mean a sexual Daley Thompson."

Buck slurs something about philosophy under his breath. The only words I manage to decipher are *Machiavellianism* and *Marilyn Manson*. He raises his head and asks, "If you had the power to change one thing about heavy metal, what would it be? Like, if you were in control of its evolution, how would you direct it?"

Pete doesn't need any thinking time. "I'd introduce elements from other types of music, especially jazz. I like heavy metal, but I grew up on cats like David Sanborn. His sax playin' makes it clear that he doesn't have boundaries. Metal felines tend to be much more blinkered."

"Even your bandmates in Transcend Everything?"

"No, they're open-minded cats, which is how I can justify bein' part o' this band. To shape the future o' metal, I'd introduce jazz rhythms, spacey Jarre-like synths and indigenous tribal beats from aroon' the world. I'd throw in classical structures too. That kind o' cross-pollination is healthy, my man."

Buck gazes into space as if willing a beer to appear in it. "You mean you'd dilute metal?"

"I don't see it as dilutin'," Pete replies. "It's more like cross-breedin', which research has shown leads to elevated intelligence in dogs, so why not in metal? Open your mind, Bucky baby!"

"I'd crush all rock star egos," announces Oz. "The more successful a band gets, the more humble its members should become. Commercial success is decided by fans. Musicians should always keep that in mind and never let their heids swell."

"That," postulates Buck, "is an impossible change to implement."

"Well you didnae say these changes had to be realistic," booms the drum giant. "You asked what one thing I'd change in metal. That's what I'd change!"

Buck raises his hands in a submissive gesture. "Are your feelings born of havin' to spend so much time around the other egos in this band?"

Ozzy rubs the orange bristles on his chin. He looks first to me, then to Pete, then up at the ceiling. "No comment."

"Very diplomatic," smiles Buck. "How about you, Spark?"

"I'd allow concert-goers to carry electric cattle prods into gigs."

"In God's name, why?"

"I've been at hundreds o' gigs over the years, but I can't remember one durin' which someone in my immediate vicinity didn't fart. Some inexplicable law of the Universe states that in those situations it's always one o' those evil mist farts that singes your nasal space then continues upwards and tries to melt your brain from the inside. Once, as I was watchin' Joe Satriani playin' *Flying in a Blue Dream* in Glasgow Barrowlands, I drifted into his alien world of sound, findin' myself transported into a beautiful sonic cosmos. Then some bastard in front o' me dropped a pea-souper that was the vilest thing I had ever smelled. Walled in on all sides by bodies, I had to stand there inhalin' that inconsiderate fuck's floatin' shit particles. The song was over by the time the mist cleared. That fart ruined my beautiful, transcendent experience. One moment, the hair on my body was standin' on end and electric shivers were spirallin' up my spine. The next, I wanted to rip off my heid and boot it oot o' the buildin', just to escape the stench."

Buck's glasses slip down to the end of his nose; he peers at me over the top of the spectacles. "I almost don't want to ask, and I'm anticipatin' your answer already, but why would a cattle prod be beneficial?"

"It's obvious! I'd zap a couple o' thoosand Volts into every thoughtless bastard who creates an unholy stench. Like Pavlov wi' his droolin' dogs, the cattle prod would reprogram gig-goers to associate fartin' at a gig wi' a post-flatulatory electric shock. Over time, attitudes would change to the point where, as soon as a dude feels a fart brewin', he'd be aware that violent voltage may rip through his body if he lets it oot. The fear o' that searin' pain would force his arsehole shut tighter than Scrooge McDuck's wallet. All of a sudden, gigs would be more fun and more olfactorily pleasant. People would no longer have that naggin' worry aboot who's goin' to fart and how bad it's goin' to smell, all thanks to the cattle prod. I'd probably get some kind of award for introducin' the idea."

There's amusement on the faces of my tablemates. "That's very funny, dude," chortles Buck. "I've been on the receivin' end of a few of those farts in small, cramped clubs, but most of the concerts I review now are held in huge amphitheatres where there's plenty of airspace. Now tell me what you'd really change. A serious answer, please."

"I couldn't be more fuckin' serious! Anythin' that detracts from my enjoyment of a live metal show must be destroyed with remorseless intensity!"

Buck turns to Oz and says, "Let me guess - Spark's a Manowar fan?"

"Aye," answers Ozzy, apologetically.

"I can spot them a mile away," continues Buck. "OK, Spark. If fartin' was banned in the UK's public places in the same way that smoking was, what would you change about metal then?"

"I'd still keep my cattle prod, just in case. There's always one sneaky bastard who thinks he can flagrantly flaunt those kinds o' rules and get away with it."

Buck sighs. "Well, let's put to one side your gravitation towards injecting voltage into olfactory offenders, extreme as I consider it to be. What else would you change?"

"I've loved heavy metal in all its forms since I was ten. Back then, heavy music was just heavy metal. Music that wasn't quite heavy enough to be metal was called rock. The distinction between rock and metal was blurry, but then came the preposterous preoccupation wi' classifyin' music, almost as if each band was an organism which had to be given a species. Music journalists today – and you're one o' the guilty - talk aboot traditional metal, thrash metal, glam metal, power metal, speed metal, trash metal, sleaze metal, nu metal, goth metal, death metal, doom metal, Viking metal, symphonic metal, avant-garde metal, industrial metal, classical metal, black metal, not to forget your favourite – hair metal. I'm not partial to one subgenre – I love it all. Good music is good music. Tryin' to fit changing organisms into static boxes is a loser's game. I'd scrap all the pigeonholin' that goes on and encourage bands to explore the full range o' their potential. I once read that Steve Harris, Iron Maiden's main man, claimed that his band would never write a love song. I love Steve – and, incidentally, we were born on the same day o' the year - so I'm not knockin' him. Choosin' what material Maiden plays is his prerogative, but what if he wakes up one day and looks at the beautiful woman lyin' next to him, only to feel an overwhelmin' rush of creative energy as the Universe channels the most heartfelt and poignant love song of all time through the vessel of his body? What then? Ignore it? Suppress that celestial inspiration? That would be criminal. True artists, such as Joe Satriani and Rush, are never afraid to experiment and push the sonic envelope. They have my infinite respect for that."

A thoughtful expression washes over Buck's face as he nods. "That makes perfect sense, Spark. Geddy Lee once told me that 90% of Rush fans don't consider the band heavy metal, but 90% of non-fans do consider Rush to be metal. That, he reckoned, highlighted the ambiguity in the perceptions of music. It proves the truth of your assertion that music can't be definitively labelled. The quest to obsessively categorise was started by record companies and music magazines. Each subgenre is a specific target market, you see, and marketing men are power players in the music business."

"Have you ever noticed how your own perception of music can vary?" I ask. "If the first track I listen to upon wakin' is AC/DC's *Highway to Hell*, it sounds heavier than Hell. If I listen to the same AC/DC track immediately after Amon Amarth's *Runes to My Memory*, it sounds like a pop song. My relationship with music, like music itself, is on shiftin' sand."

"Yeah," agrees Buck, "I know that feeling. I like the Black Crowes. They usually sound pretty rocky to me, but one night I put their CD on in the car right after listenin' to Slayer's *Seasons in the Abyss*, and the Crowes sounded like Rod Stewart. Not that there's anythin' wrong with that, as Jerry Seinfeld might say. Maybe when you've got a Slayer hangover, every other band sounds like Rod Stewart."

"My band doesn't sound like Rod Stewart, that's for fuckin' sure," I point out. "I like Slayer, but only in small doses. There's not enough light and shade - it's all pummel and no caress. Transcend Everything, on the other hand, understands the importance of melody. When we go gung-ho, though, oor riffs would blow Kerry King's tattooed heid clean off his shoulders."

Buck turns his attention to Paul. "OK, Mr Manager, what one change would you make to metal?"

Paul looks into my eyes and smiles. Suddenly, Paul and I are four years old and halfway up the snow-covered hill above Bronzehall Brae, high above our childhood houses. The sky is a deep frozen blue. The smell of pine trees hangs in the air as we hurl snowballs at each other. Most of our icy projectiles either miss the target or hit a limb and glance off at an angle, fragmenting into a spray of powder snow. Paul launches one with fearsome velocity and pinpoint accuracy, finding the hole in the front of my woolly balaclava. Snow explodes into my eyes. I fall backwards, clawing cold powder out of snowblind eyes like a rabbit digging a burrow. When my vision clears, Paul is standing above me, blocking out the sun. I give him the thumbs-up to show that I'm OK. Looking into my eyes and smiling, he pulls me to my feet. His body language says, '*I got you a beauty there,*' but his eyes say, '*I'm glad you're OK. You're my best friend and I love you.*' I snap back to the present with the realisation that Paul and I haven't changed. The smile he's blessing me with now is the same one I saw as a child on that snow-covered slope, and on so many other days. His eyes are the same sky-blue worlds in which I've seen every emotion. Without breaking eye contact with me, Paul answers Buck's question. "That's easy. I'd make Transcend Everything the biggest metal band this planet has ever seen."

"*That's* a manager," slurs Buck.

"Aye," says Pete, "a manager who wants his 15% of the biggest band in heavy metal history!"

"Fuck off, Drummond," spits Paul. "You wouldn't be here if it wasn't for me. You'd still be hidin' in your flat, scared o' the ootside world, composin' soundtracks to sadness."

"You were fuck all to do wi' it, Roberts, ya big-heided feline! Demons took me hostage and forced me to be part o' the band again! *That's* why I'm here!"

Silence falls over us like a cold blanket. Buck's mouth drops open. After a lengthy pause, I ask, "Did those demons say that you should carve a pentalpha into your flesh? You should. You all should."

Pete snarls, "Are you takin' the piss, Spark?"

"I'm serious. I'll do the slicin' if you like."

"If you try to deface my body the way you did your own, I'll tear your arms oot o' their sockets," promises Ozzy.

"Ditto," says Paul.

Pete adds, "And I'll disappear faster than DT's tadger up a moist teenage twat."

Buck climbs onto the table, kicks over a large glass of Mountain Dew and rips off his shirt, baring a lean torso. "Cut a pentalpha into me! That's a fuckin' cool thing to do! It totally one-ups Don Costa cheese-gratin' himself onstage with Ozzy Osbourne! Carve me, Spark baby!"

I shake my head. "Sit doon, ya tool. I just met you, you're drunk, and you don't need an inscribed pentalpha."

"I know I don't *need* it. I *want* it! Do it!"

"Trust me, Buck," intervenes Ozzy, "this is one o' those drunken ideas that seems great at the time. Like gettin' a lingerie-clad Miss Piggy wi' enhanced tits tattooed on your arm. After you sober up, you'd wonder who had control o' your brain when it made such an off-its-heid decision."

Buck pulls his shirt on, climbs down from the table, guzzles a mouthful of Mountain Dew and spits it straight back out. "Ugh, fuck! That's not beer! Disgusting!" He grabs his mp3 player from the table and stops the recording. "Thank you for the interview. It has been, ehhhhh, illuminating."

We take it in turns to shake Buck's hand, after which Paul asks him, "Did you notice how we all answered your questions succinctly except Spark, who moralised, philosophised and postulated enough for you to write a book on him?"

Buck handles the flammable question with journalistic tact. "That'll be why he's the singer. They always like to do the lion's share of the talkin', like they've got more profound things to say than everyone else."

Pete says, "Actually, Spark's the singer because he's shite at everythin' else." Buck laughs so hard that he slumps back onto a chair. Before long, we're all laughing like long-haired hyenas.

Adopting a perfect Homer Simpson voice, Oz hollers, "It's funny 'cause it's true!" When the laughter has subsided, Buck thanks us again then staggers a wavy course to the exit, where the moustachioed security guard ushers him outside.

Chapter 68 – Makin' a Mess

The Trans Am's engine roars like the bowels of Hell. In a box on the passenger seat is my special outfit for tonight. Accelerator pedal to the floor, I hurtle at 150 miles per hour along an empty highway which smells of dust and seaweed. Low clouds glide swiftly and silently, like wide-winged birds vying for pole position in their eternal race across the sky. Judas Priest's *Desert Plains* thunders from Helmut's car speakers.

Florida's coastline zooms past too quickly to make much impression on me. Dark shapes above. Blur of trees and undergrowth to my left. Crashing ocean on my right. Poker-straight road ahead.

One thing on my mind.

I arrive at Cocoa Beach just after 1 a.m. The 210-mile journey from Miami took a touch under 90 minutes. The beach, which I expected to be littered with buzzing cafés and bars, shows no evidence of human life. White-tipped waves curl into shore and smash on moonlit sand.

Shaquanna's street is a quiet, tree-lined cul-de-sac, its houses single-level residences from which driveways roll out like grey concrete tongues. At the bottom of each drive is a mailbox. I kill the volume on the car stereo and ease slowly along the road, checking mailbox numbers along the way. The only sound above the restrained roar of the car's engine is the chirp of crickets or some equally noisy tropical insect. Mailbox number 46 has its red metal flag raised, indicating that inside is mail waiting to be collected by the postman. Some voyeuristic part of me fancies opening Shaquanna's outgoing mail, just because I can. The Metal Gods shout me back onto the right track. *Quit stalling! There's a big beautiful ebony woman waiting to be plundered only a few feet away! Who gets distracted by mail at a time like this?*

A quick scan of the street reveals no signs of life. All houses are in darkness. I strip off in Shaquanna's driveway, bundle my clothes onto the floor of the car and open the box on the passenger seat, uncovering a green robe and hood: a Ku Klux Klan Grand Dragon's outfit. I didn't tell any of my entourage about the outfit (which I bought from an auction website called KKKBay), as even the open-minded lothario DT would struggle to approve of my participation in this type of game. The KKKBay site claims to sell outfits for 'fancy dress and novelty purposes only': standard rhetoric to legally cover their own asses.

The robe slips on more easily than a kilt. It feels cool and comfortable. I pull on the pointed green hood and adjust it until I can see through the eyeholes. Walking up the driveway towards the house, I catch my reflection in a window and freeze. Having studied US History at school in Virginia, I know about the Klan and understand the terror it can inspire. Their pointed hoods, robes and burning crosses have long symbolised hate, while Klan members have dedicated themselves to becoming fluent in the unspoken language of fear. Analysed objectively, the Klan's fashion is preposterous. I don't think any descendants of slaves around these-here parts would be very objective, however, if they saw me wandering the streets dressed like this.

The Metal Gods speak words of encouragement. *This is a strange game you've got yourself into, but there's no going back now. If you're this scared of your own reflection, just imagine how frightened Shaquanna will feel when you wake her. For her, fear isn't a mind-killer: it's a gash-slickener. She'll cum bucketloads if you do this right.*

Slipping round to the back garden, I peer through windows to gauge the layout of the house. When I try to slide open the patio doors, the stubborn things refuse to budge. Gazing at my Torquemada-like image in the glass, I realise why Shaquanna has locked me out: she wants it to feel like a real break-in. This method actress can only get immersed in a role if the details are perfect. *The Devil is in the details.*

I've heard that the Scottish burglar's favourite technique for bypassing patio doors is to pop them off their runners. Grabbing both sides of the outer door, I lean backwards and lift. The door comes off with a bump. I stumble backwards, narrowly avoiding a fall into Sha's swimming pool, but regain control of my footing and lay the door on the lawn. Then, without a sound, I slip into the house.

In the kitchen I find a knife fit for Michael Myers in *Hallowe'en*. Knife in hand, I tiptoe to Shaquanna's bedroom and push the door open a crack. To my horror, it creaks. A ruffling of the duvet makes me fear that I've wakened Sha, but her movement soon settles to the gentle rise and fall of nocturnal breathing. As I stand against the wall listening to the sleeping figure's delicate sighs, the excitement is unbearable, my heart's pounding audible.

The room is in darkness. I ease the duvet off Shaquanna's face-down body and run my hands over the shape that towers above the mattress like Ayers Rock above the Australian desert. It is said that TV adds 20 pounds to a person. Webcams must deduct 200 pounds, for this bottom seems twice as big in the flesh. I spank its right buttock so hard that the sound echoes off the walls. Shaquanna wakes with a grunt. Before she can form any words, I grab her hair from behind and press the knife's blade to her throat. "Don't fuckin' move, nigga bitch! Don't say a word or I'll cut you an ear-to-ear smile. You bin struttin' your big 'n' beautiful black ass around town, teasin' good, God-fearin' white-bread men like me. Ah bin watchin' you in your skimpy cotton skirts an' low-cut blouses, flauntin' dat body like the nasty hoochie you are. Well it's time for you to pay the piper. Git oan your knees and lift that ass up fo' me."

Slowly, the gigantic ass backs up against my abdomen. Shaquanna starts to sob. "Shut up! I am Grand Dragon McTavish of the Ku Klux Klan. There's no point cryin' now, nigga. Call me masta." After pulling off my pointed hood and throwing it onto the floor, I bury my face between the cheeks of Shaquanna's bottom, my tongue investigating the new territory like a fearless explorer in a virgin land. The smell of coconut fills my nostrils. Sha's skin is slick, as if she has rubbed herself with oil after a late-night shower. Spreading her enormous ass cheeks isn't easy, especially with the added obstacle of keeping the knife secured in the crook of my right thumb. As I press outwards with my palms, the gargantuan buttocks push back against me, driven by gravity and a hard-wired desire to be back in their natural position. Sha's ass threatens to engulf my head and asphyxiate me. With a superhuman effort, I prise her cheeks wide enough apart to allow access to her soft vagina. My tongue plunges into the crevice like an oil-platform drill determined not to stop until it strikes black gold, T-T-T-Texas T, or in this case C-C-C-Cocoa Beach cum. On into the cavern my tongue descends, revelling in this exotic new land of heat and humidity. I rise, take a brief gasp of air, then plunge once more into the abyss. As Shaquanna's clitoris hardens, I hammer the little bud as if the tip of my tongue were a pneumatic drill. My swirls, licks, probes and Morse-code compositions culminate in a crescendo of vaginal contractions and orgasmic vocal arpeggios. And about a gallon of squirt. At first, my gulps can't keep pace with the generous donations; I'm drowning, but there's no way I'm coming up for air until the job's done. Sexually speaking, just as in sport and heavy metal, it's all about commitment, and I'm nothing if not committed. Either that or I should be committed. Perhaps a bit of both. With Shaquanna's juices overflowing from my mouth and pouring down my chin, I guzzle with a vengeance, somehow managing to suck small amounts of air through nostrils that are squashed between enormous buttocks. As my light-headedness veers towards unconsciousness, Sha's rhythmic liquid jets diminish in volume. Ascending, I gasp air into thankful lungs.

"You muthafuckin' cracka bastard! Ah'll git yo' ass buried fo' this! Yo' a dead man!" Sha's voice sounds deeper than usual, which must be because I'm hearing it in all its bassy glory rather than filtered through a microphone, several thousand miles of fibreoptic cable and a PC speaker.

"Shut up, filthy slut! You gittin' exactly what you been gaggin' fo'! Stay still or I'll cut your fuckin' head off and stick it on top of a burnin' cross in your garden just to show your neighbours what happens to nigga bitches that talk back to their white mastas!" After putting my pointed hood back on, I whip off the robe then feel my way behind the kneeling, sobbing Shaquanna. "Quit cryin', bitch. The water works don't impress me." Grabbing Sha's hair from behind, I thrust into her soaking pussy, gradually increasing my tempo from slow and gentle to hard, fast and deep, always with the knife pressed into her back as a cold reminder of who's in control. With each stroke, my abdomen pounds Sha's gigantic bottom, sending ripples up her body. I knew she wouldn't be easy to toss around, but moving her feels like shoving a truck. Her bottom is too large to allow maximum penetration from this angle, no matter how far apart I spread her cheeks. This starts to frustrate me, so I roll Sha onto her back, lift her quivering legs over my shoulders and plunge into her pussy from an angle of attack which allows deeper infiltration than before.

A few hot sweaty, minutes later, determined to get total penetration, I sit on the bed, spread my legs wide and haul Shaquanna astride me. We're face to face at close range, her warm breath goosepimpling my neck, yet the darkness conceals her features. Pressing the knife to Sha's neck, I slide into her again, this time sinking in all the way. Her defiant outburst is punctuated by ecstatic moans. "You cracka bastard…ohhhhh yeah…oooooo…you ignorant Klan asshole! Oh lordy, oh baby Jesus, you'll git lynched fo' this, I'll make sure o' dat! Ooooohhhh my pussy…ooooooooo…say hello to death row, cracka!"

"Silence, nigga, or it'll be a year of sleepin' in a field for you, tied to a post like a dog by night and pickin' cotton on my plantation by day. Who's your masta?"

"You ain't mah masta! Oooooooo…oooohhhhhh…Jesus, yeah, ooooohh my Lord…yo' nothin' but a cracka biyatch!"

I lower my voice to a sinister whisper. "Listen, nigga. After I've impaled your disembodied heid on the sharpened top of a flamin' cross, I'll come back in here, fuck your heidless body, then wash my hands in the blood that'll be gushin' from your neck stump. After I cum up your black ass I'll wipe my cock clean on your livin'-room curtains…maybe wipe my bloody hands on them too."

"Not my good lace curtains!"

"Quiet!" Sweat pours from Sha's voluminous flesh as the intensity of our exertions increases. The engorged tip of my tadger prods soft innards at the deepest point of each stroke. Our fluids mingle, but the humid air won't let them evaporate. The more we fuck, the wetter we get. As I run my fingertips over nipples that feel like football studs, tremors shake Shaquanna's mountainous body, the reverberations surely showing up on nearby seismometers as a localised earthquake: an eight on the Rectal scale.

I push Sha onto her back and withdraw. It's time to employ a little something I learned from a lipstick lesbian who kindly let me practise on her body until I had refined and mastered the technique. (Or maybe she wasn't being selfless; perhaps she just enjoyed the free fingering. Anyway, I digress.) The middle and ring fingers of my right hand slide knuckle deep into Shaquanna's pussy, leaving index finger and pinkie jabbing like Devil horns into the soft flesh on either side. My probing fingers curl upwards until their tips locate Sha's G-spot. It's easy to find: rougher than the surrounding area and about the size of a pound coin. In a wavelike motion, I press my fingertips into her G-spot then ease off, repeating the movement while gradually increasing the intensity and momentum. My fingertips curve into Sha so hard that her enormous hips lift off the bed as her exquisite interior starts to squelch: giveaway signs that the floodgates are about to open. My fingers spear her G-spot like ferocious horny javelins.

The dam bursts; ejaculate squirts from Sha's pussy, ricochets off my palm and sprays over her body. "Thar she blows!"

"Aaaaaaaaggggggghhhhhhh! You're the muthafuckin' Devil!"

"Who's your masta? Who owns this fat pussy?"

"It's mah pussy! It'll nevah be yours." Shaquanna is squirting like a garden sprinkler, her ejaculate falling like hot rain. I'm soaked in the warm liquid from the neck down. "You muthafucka! Oh Lordy, what's happenin'? Hallelujah, it ain't right what yo' doin' to me! It ain't natural, I tell you. Forgive me Lord fo' dis! Praise Jesus and Hail Mary!"

"Whose nigga bitch slave slut are you?"

"Ah ain't no slave! Ah'm a free woman and yo' a dead man!"

"Sacrilegious talk! And sayin' that you 'ain't no slave' is a double negative, incidentally, which means you are my slave. I'm gonna squirt you until you're just a dehydrated bag o' bones!"

Shaquanna unleashes a piercing scream. Tidal waves gush from her gash, building into a sea of squirt which washes over me and splatters the sheets. The bed feels like a shallow paddling pool filled with warm water.

Neighbours must surely have heard the scream and now be in the process of dialling 911 to report an assault. Time for one last depraved deed before making a stealthy exit. "Get on your fuckin' knees, nigga slut! Do it! Present that ass to me!" Sha does as she's ordered, her body drenched in a concoction of sweat, blood, cum and squirt. I ram my cock into her asshole, delighting in its tightness. Amid sobs and screams, she mutters prayers but continues to grind her hips backwards to meet my pistoning thrusts: an Oscar-worthy portrayal of a woman torn between worshipping the Lord and loving the cock. "You don't fool me," I growl. "You love it. You're my bitch. I fuckin' own your arse." Disturbingly, I realise that my accent has reverted back to its natural Scottish, but I can't for the life of me recall how long ago I slipped out of character.

I feel my orgasm approaching. If it was daylight, I would pull out and spurt all over Shaquanna's back and ass, to enjoy the aesthetic contrast of white cum against acres of dark flesh. Right now, though, it's difficult to discern where I stop and she starts. Opting for the choice that feels best, I unload deep inside her dirt chute. Roaring and twitching, I drop the knife and spank the wobbling wonder that is Sha's bottom. Her backwards-bucking hips threaten to knock me off the bed, so I hang onto her rump and ride the waves for all I'm worth.

It's over. I slide out of Shaquanna's arse and wipe my dick on soaking sheets. As I pick my robe off the floor, a shit – an inconsiderate keech that gave no prior warning of its arrival – starts to exit my arse. *Oh well - in for a penny, in for a pound!* I roll Sha onto her back and order her not to move. Standing over her, legs splayed, I relax my sphincter and let the disgusting mixture - which used to be coffee, grapefruits, nuts, seeds and Mountain Dew - splurge over her body. It's not the worst-smelling dump I've ever taken: no après-vindaloo diabolical mess, but it's far from fragrant. "Eat that, nigga! For years Chuck Berry filmed lil' underage white girls shittin' in the toilets of his Southern Air restaurant! Ah'm takin' one back! Hell yeah, I'm claimin' one back for the masta race! How's that fo' takin' it up a notch?" After wiping my arse on squirt-soaked sheets, I pull the KKK robe over my head and vanish into the night.

Chapter 69 – One Helluva Night

Perspective's an odd thing. By the time I near the ghost town of Cedar Key, I can't help thinking that shitting on Shaquanna may have been stepping over some invisible line. Two hours earlier, in the heat of the moment, it seemed like the only thing to do. Jobbies, however, can't be undone once they're done, so there's no point worrying about it. One small keech for man, one giant plunge into the shitter for mankind.

After leaving Sha's house a couple of hours ago, I drove up a dirt track on the outskirts of Cocoa Beach, parked the Trans Am and changed back into my regular clothes, as the Grand Dragon's outfit would have taken some explaining if I were pulled over by an African-American cop with a family history of slavery, and an itchy trigger finger to boot. Now, as my cross-state journey continues, I pass a sign that tells me I'm twenty miles from Cedar Key. Tired from the band's show, tired from my carnal exertions, tired from long hours of driving…just plain tired, my body begins to relax in contemplation of sleeping in a real bed for the first time in weeks. The motel-room arrangements were made according to logic. DT has a room of his own, a lair to share with several of his starry-eyed young metal bitches. Ozzy, Marisol and Sunshower are sharing one large room, as they have become a family of sorts. I'm booked into a room with Pete. Iain has a room to himself because no one would share with him after the unearthly rumble of his snoring came close to inciting murder on the tour bus. Paul plans to wander the ghost town alone by night to soak up its desolate atmosphere, so he too has a room to himself.

Paul explained to me that Cedar Key was, in the 1800s, one of Florida's largest cities until, in 1896, a devastating hurricane ripped the town apart. Cedar Key never returned to anywhere near its former size after that, but it did retain a skeleton inhabitance along with a framework of its original houses, shops and bars, most of which look ready to collapse around their ears. Some ramshackle houses are propped up on wooden stilts that appear to have grown out of the sea; with the slightest provocation, these buildings will into the water descend. The town attracts tourists with passions for ghost towns or fishing, which perhaps explains how a motel can continue to operate here.

It would feel wrong to speed through a sleepy ghost town in a high-octane sports car, especially at night, so I ease my foot off the accelerator. The four-wheeled beast growls past a wooden sign - straight out of the Wild West – proclaiming 'Welcome to Cedar Key'. Rolling tumbleweeds wouldn't be out of place here, but even tumbleweeds avoid these dead, dusty streets.

The main street is a clanjamfrie of buildings, mostly old wooden constructions. I half expect to see a drunken, stetsoned bandit staggering through a swinging saloon door and struggling onto his horse. One grand three-storey building with vertical stone columns looks like a bordello from the old west. In my imagination, a liquored-up non-paying customer flies through an upstairs window and lands in a haycart below, having been tossed out by an irate, formidable madam in a red lacy dress, tantalisingly low-cut to accentuate her ample bosom and deep cleavage.

Without the ever-present dust clouds that the breeze stirs up, this town would be as still as the grave. Perhaps this town *is* a grave and those aren't dust clouds but ghosts.

Our motel stands a stone's throw from the ocean. The two-storey building, which survived the 1896 hurricane and all the hurricanes since, is coated in gaudy blue paint. At first I see no signs of life, but as the Trans Am rolls closer I notice green mist spewing under the door of a ground-floor room. Like a silent ninja, I slide out of the car and approach the mist-obscured door. A brass number is nailed to it: 22. My room. Heart switching from a beat to a boom, I peer through the murky window. Pete is hovering naked in an inverted crucifix position, his feet secured to the ceiling by writhing blue tendrils which have eaten through skin and bone. Less than a foot from the floor, his head has been engulfed by a sphere of yellow fire from which licks of flame curl outwards. Thorny branches have impaled Pete's palms and anchored him to the walls. The skin on his pale body bubbles and cracks, clear liquid running downwards like melting wax. Then, just as I think the situation can't get any worse, I kick the door off its hinges and see *it*.

The dark thing has been, up until now, an out-of-focus nightmare, a fire-eyed wraith that existed in a quantum duality, sometimes in my mind and at other times in some hellish otherworld. Now its features have taken a clearly defined form. Twin horns stretch skywards from a charred head, scraping chips of wood from the ceiling as the beast shifts its weight from side to side on cloven hooves covered with long, coarse fur. In the centre of a thickly muscled back is a black spine, its jutting vertebrae ending in sharp spikes. The room smells of burnt leaves and not-so-fresh graves. Apparently oblivious to - or unconcerned by - my cowboy entrance, the creature continues to face away from me, its attention focused on the inverted Pete.

As I sink into a sea of diabolical fear, one thought floats: *Ozzy*. My giant guardian angel was an engine of destruction when we fought rival gangs. Back then, of course, we knew who we were fighting. Now I don't even know what we're fighting. Dashing from room to room, I stare through windows until I discover Ozzy and Marisol asleep in a double bed with Sunshower wedged between them. My boot goes to work again. As the door flies across the room, I pounce on Oz and slap his tour-bearded face. Opening one eye, he growls, "Are you *that* eager for a ball-bootin'?"

"It's Pete," I splutter, "something's got Pete."

"This better no' be a joke! I'm enjoyin' the comfort of a real bed after two weeks sleepin' on a bunk built for a homosexual midget."

"I'm no' arsin' aboot, dude. Something's crucified wee Pete. Upside doon. Satanic-style. His body's meltin' and a bonfire's consumin' his heid."

Oz raises thick orange eyebrows. "You mean *someone's* crucified Pete?"

"No, I mean some *thing!*"

The giant explodes out of bed and opens his enormous suitcase, from which he removes a smaller, oval-shaped plastic case. He flips open its metal clips, revealing a compound bow, several arrows, a variety of sights, longrods and other archery accoutrements. Grasping the bow in a powerful left hand, Oz jams six arrows down the front of his pants and sprints out of the room.

When I tell Marisol and Sunshower to stay in bed for their own safety, the little girl starts to sob. "I'm scared, Spark. Really scared."

"I'm scared too, wee girl. Freedom is aboot always feelin' your feelings, so it's OK to feel scared. Right noo I need you to stay here and look after Marisol."

Sunshower's eyes dart to Marisol then back to me. She nods her agreement. I kiss her tear-soaked cheek and whisper, "Thanks, beautiful. You're a brave warrior. I love you."

I find Oz standing under the splintered door frame of room 22. He fits a blue metal arrow to his bow, pulls the bowstring back to his chin, and looses the arrow followed by five more in quick succession. The first three arrows thud into the Devil-creature's infernal buttocks, leaving only fletches sticking out. The next three projectiles crunch through the back of the Hellthing's head. All six protruding sections of arrow burst into crimson flames, burning with a sizzling sound then falling as charred ashes on the floor. The stench of sulphur and dead flesh sticks in my throat. "Oz, I don't think humans can hurt this fucker!"

Glaring at me in disgust, Ozzy booms, "Alan Oswaldo can!" He charges the Hellbeast, screaming the battle-cry, "Die, ya bass!" A long-taloned claw swats the enormous drummer through the window as if he were a tennis ball and the creature a professional player striking an easy backhand shot. The defenestration sends fragments of shattered glass and wood flying as the sticksman skids across the car park on his back.

Ozzy has never been knocked out before, but the Hellbeast did it without batting a diabolical eyelid. I run back to Ozzy's room and rifle through the pockets of his dungarees until I find his mobile phone. After scrolling down to Rosie's number, I hit the green call button. Nothing happens. My heart sinks as I notice that the phone has no signal. To make matters worse, the bedrooms in this ancient motel don't have phones. I sprint to the front office and find it locked. Peering through the window, I notice an antique phone. The office door becomes the third to be kicked off its hinges tonight. To my relief, the old phone works. I call Rosie. The female voice that answers sounds older than Wytchcoomb Forest, as old as time. The Metal Gods explain. *Cailleach.*

"It's Spark! The Devil's crucified Pete upside doon and encased his heid in a sphere o' fire, like some kind o' Satanic album cover. The bastard's standin' there withoot a care in the world, just watchin' my wee friend melt. Ozzy sank six arrows into the unholy fucker, but they had no effect. When Oz charged like a bull, the Hellbeast swatted him like a fly."

"Do you have salt?" A voice like autumn wind rustling through fallen leaves.

"No."

"Can you get salt, lots of salt?"

"No. We're in a ghost toon in the sphincter of nowhere."

"Blood! Ozzy mentioned that you all became blood brothers a long time ago."

"Aye, all except Pete."

"He is indisposed anyway, by the sound of it. Blood is the most powerful substance in all types of magic. If you can extract blood from yourself and your blood brothers, then mix it and find a way of inserting it into the demon, that may dispose of it. Focus your attention on something beautiful and spiritual, something in which you and your blood brothers believe. Belief is a powerful force."

"Aye, it's said to be the thermostat that regulates success."

"I hope so, for all your sakes."

"Thanks, Rosie."

"Go, Scotsman. Blessed be."

An idea starts to hatch, born of desperation and love. I run to Ozzy's room, where two arrows are left in his case: one of metallic blue and one with a gold finish. Screaming like Halford in Hell, I grab the arrows and run to the centre of the car park. An upstairs door opens and DT emerges wrapped in an orange towel, his usually groomed hair a ruffled mess. "What's all the infernal fuckin' noise?" he demands. "Some of us are tryin' to have a fivesome!"

"The Devil just knocked Ozzy oot and Pete's crucified upside doon and meltin'!"

DT's eyes sparkle through the darkness. "A fight! Fuckin' excellent! I'm on my way!" Stinking of sweat, sex and perfume, he flies down the stairs and greets me with a wayward embrace.

Dave leads me to Iain's room, in the most remote corner of the motel. I split the door with a flying sidekick and find Iain unconscious on the floor, an empty whisky bottle still in his grasp, blood trickling from a gash on his head. After stabbing both arrows into my chest and rolling their tips in my blood, I dip them into the red puddle around Iain's head, then turn to Dave. "Your turn now, my partner-in-crime."

"No fuckin' way! You're no' cuttin' up my sexy body!"

"Dave, for fuck's sake, we don't have time for your vanity! Go and look into my room!"

DT disappears, returning ashen-faced a few seconds later. "Do it, Spark! Cut me!" I pull the whisky bottle from Iain's hand, smash it against the wall, slice open DT's chest with the jagged bottleneck, then twirl the blood-tipped arrows in his leaking liquid lifeforce. Securing Ozzy's contribution to our blood bank is easy; when the Devil struck him, he flew through the air and hit the ground like a quarter-ton bag of tomato soup, leaving a red trail from his landing point to the spot where he came to rest. To complete the blood brothers' sanguinary recipe, I dunk the arrows' tips into the growing red puddle beside the drummer's motionless body.

Ozzy's bow is soundlessly screaming my name. I pick up the weapon and load the blue arrow. "Think o' somethin' pure, Dave."

"I'm drawin' a blank!"

"You dickheid, think o' the band! Think aboot the wild times we've had together. Think aboot makin' the most transcendent metal album of all time. Think o' these things like your life depends on it, because it does!" Raising the weapon and pulling back the bowstring to full draw, I take aim at the unholy head that sizzles in front of me. Visions flood my mind: Sunshower doing handstands in her front garden; Fluff licking my nose and gazing at me through oceanic eyes; DT's golden dog Saxon bounding across a furrowed field; my parents; Blackness Castle.

I loose the arrow.

The Devil plucks the flying projectile out of the air. Grinning a long-toothed promise of eternal pain, the Beast fixes me with a blazing gaze, its eyes timeless and remorseless: the bottomless fires of Hell.

"Fuck," wails DT, "I'm a lover, no' a Devil hunter!"

"You've been a warrior all your life, ya fuckin' tit! Don't become a cowerin' pussy noo! Focus! This is oor last arrow and it's a golden one, so that must be symbolic o' somethin'. Focus on oor dreams and oor music. Focus on no' bein' tomorrow's turd in Hell's toilet, which you will be if this fucker consumes you. DT, I have bled wi' you more times than I can even remember. We've never lost a fight. This would be a bad fuckin' time to change that. I love you, my blood brother." I suck air through my mouth, hold my breath and load the arrow. Moonlight glints off its shaft as I whisper, "You're metal with a purpose. Fly true." DT presses his palms against my back, unifying our energy. I draw the bowstring, aim, relax my fingers. The arrow flies, whistling with destructive intent. It pierces the infernal creature's rib cage with a sound like a frozen puddle cracking underfoot. Then there's no sound, no movement. DT's hands turn deathly cold. I turn and run, hauling Dave by the arm. We dive into underbrush at the far side of the car park and lie low like children playing soldiers, harking back to childhood days when we spent endless hours on gang manoeuvres in Vikingwood Forest. A car's length in front of us, Ozzy regains consciousness and sits up, his back a latticework of gravel-grazes. All our eyes lock onto room 22.

Dark fire explodes into the car park and beyond, showering us in wooden splinters and shards of glass. Turning to DT, I ask, "Doesn't this look like a King Diamond album cover? The arcane architecture, the dark night, the full moon, and all with a hint of carnage."

"I wouldn't know," he replies. "I'd rather let the dog use my balls as a chew-toy than listen to King Diamond. Anyway, this isn't really the time to discuss album covers."

"Aye, aye…you're right. I think we took that horned fucker right oot o' the game."

"You go and check the room," suggests DT, his head nodding like a broken jack-in-the-box as a gust of wind blows his hair into horizontal flight.

I run across the car park and peek into the annihilated room. There's no sign of the Hellcreature. Pete's destroyed body is on the floor, blood pouring from crucifixion wounds onto charred floorboards. An indistinct hairless mass, he resembles a spent candle.

Grabbing a shard of glass from a shattered mirror, I carve a deep pentalpha into what used to be Pete's torso. "Rosie said that this ancient symbol is powerful protection against evil. Wi' the will o' the Metal Gods and the Universe itself, may the pentalpha's protection work retrospectively on you. It's not too late." A metamorphosis begins. Crucifixion wounds heal as flesh is moulded into shape by an invisible intelligence. Blonde hair sprouts from Pete's head. Eyebrows and eyelashes grow back, as does the trademark jazz beard on his chin. From a melted-shut mouth bloom pink lips, which part to reveal sparkling teeth. Finally, his rebirth complete, Pete's turquoise eyes flip open and first words are spoken. "What kept you, man?"

Standing well back from the scene of the miracle, DT asks, "What the fuck kind o' voodoo did you just do, Spark? He was Hellbound."

"Voodoo? Noo who's gone all King Diamond? The carved pentalpha protected Pete from evil, just as it protected me after oor gig in New York."

"Oh aye," moans Dave, "protect yourself and to Hell wi' your blood brothers, is that it? Couldn't you have told us?"

"I did tell you, ya dick. You told me it was all in my heid, remember?"

Swishing hair out of his eyes, DT scowls, "This is too fuckin' weird for me. I'm goin' back to my room for a massage."

"Check their ID," I shout, but it falls on deaf ears; Dave is racing back to his team of nubiles. Pete, meanwhile, starts to extinguish the small fires on the floor of our room. It is a night of more than one miracle: somehow, the kettle still works. I make tea and loot two packets of chocolate-chip cookies from the front office.

Popping my head into Iain's room, I find him conscious but drunker than Keith Richards on a whisky-tasting holiday. Splayed on the ground, he blethers incoherent nonsense to himself. I stick my fingers down his throat. Brown liquid with the stench of regurgitated whisky and sour coffee shoots from his mouth and spatters the wall. As I pour sweet tea into his mouth, most of it dribbles down his chin, but he manages to swallow a few mouthfuls. After heaving Iain onto the bed and pulling a cover over his body, I head outside to check on Ozzy. The bleeding giant grunts that he is OK and retreats to his room to patch up his wounds. Time for a walk to clear my mind.

As I head along the bay, a haunting whistled melody - which I recognise as KISS's *Only You* – floats on the wind. The source of the tune, silhouetted against the full moon like a human wolf, asks, "How has your night been? Peaceful and relaxin' like mine? There's nothin' like a walk through an American ghost toon under the light o' the full moon. Quite spectacular."

"Peaceful and relaxin' aren't words I'd use to describe my night. Eventful is a more appropriate word."

"Eventful, eh?"

"Very eventful, Paulo. I had an excellent time on my method-actin' sexpedition wi' Shaquanna, although I may have taken things a bit too far. Anyway, after my mission in Cocoa Beach, I returned here and found the Devil crucifyin' Pete upside doon and meltin' his heid, so I impaled the infernal fucker wi' a golden arrow dipped in the blood of all four blood brothers. There's some damage to the motel…well, my room's been blown up…right up…blown tae fuck, you could say…and I had to kick a few doors in…but no extra charges should get added to oor motel bill. Acts o' God or the Devil aren't oor responsibility."

Moonlight flickers across Paul's eyes. "When I agreed to be your band's manager, you didn't mention Hellbeings and carnage."

"The carnage is finished for the night. And Pete's lookin' healthier than I've ever seen him, no' as much as a nicotine stain on his teeth."

Paul and I walk the dusty trail to the motel in silence, the moon shining on our backs, casting long shadows ahead. On reaching the car park, Paul surveys the post-apocalyptic scene, runs a hand through his hair and asks, "Do you know why I like hangin' aboot wi' you, Spark?"

"Because you like lookin' at my spectacular arse?"

"Suprisingly, no. What I like most is that things are never boring."

Chapter 70 – Hideaway

A warm breeze flows over Pete's face, licking him awake. *Spark must have opened the window when he got back from his perverted excursion last night.* In the moment before opening his eyes, Pete marvels at how refreshed he feels; it normally takes him three coffees and five Marlboros to achieve this level of consciousness. He nearly shits himself in fright when he sees the morning sun through the gaping hole where the room's front wall used to be. Decimated glass, wood and masonry litter the car park, strewn outwards from the room. Blackened floorboards peer through a honeycomb of holes burned in the carpet. On a pile of broken timbers that used to be a bed sleeps Spark, trainline gouges cut into his chest.

Pete walks to the bathroom only to find that it too has been obliterated. He squats above the jagged remains of a ceramic toilet to do his morning shit. The motel's owner appears: a skeletal man of sixty-something, bald except for a few swept-back strands of white hair at the sides of his head, cigarette stuck to his bottom lip. "What in the name of God have you done?" he yelps.

"A shit," replies Pete. "Sorry aboot the smell. Your toilet seems to be broken."

The man spits his cigarette butt on the ground and hollers, "What have you done to my room, you smartass? Is this what you rockstar pricks do for kicks when there's no TV to smash – destroy the whole motel?"

Memories of the previous night flood into Pete's mind as he pulls up his pants. "Sir," he replies, "hard as this may be to believe, we're not responsible for this. The Devil did it."

"Tell it to the police!" The man limps to the front office, unleashing a chain of profanity on discovering that its door has been destroyed. He looses yet more curses when he finds his cookie tin empty.

Rushing from room to room, Pete rouses the others then calls Udo's mobile. A guttural voice answers, "Ja, Herr Sausage here. How may ich be of relief to you?"

"It's Pete. There's trouble at the motel. The cops will be here soon and oor story's ten miles too tall for them to believe. We'll hide oot in the disused ammunition store. Pick us up there as soon as possible, eh?"

"Ja, Ja…but ve are still in ze middle of some sausage festivities. Ve may be some time."

"Well, we can't stay oot in the open or the cops will jail us. We'll stay in the ammo store 'til you get here. Try no' to draw attention to yourselves when you arrive in toon."

"How do you propose zat ve avoid being conspicuous in a ghost town when ve are driving a shiny bus with a thirty-foot penis on ze side?"

"Well just be here as soon as you can, eh? That's a cool homosexual cat."

"OK, Peter. Ve von't forget about you."

"Later, knob jockey."

"Indeed, keyboard jockey."

After hanging up the phone, Pete rounds up the troops and grabs the remaining biscuits from the blast space that used to be a room. Spark and Paul screech down a sunlit trail in the Trans Am. Heaving luggage, the others follow in the sports car's dusty wake. Iain's hangover from Hell pulls him to the back of the pack, while DT and his four teenage admirers skip along at the front like carefree flower children. Sunshower rides on her battle-scarred father's shoulders, gripping his mass of hair.

Pete arrives at the ammunition store to find that Spark has already parked the car out of sight and used his boot to sweet-talk the store's door into opening. The fugitives move into the shade at the back of the shop, where Pete divvies up the stolen biscuits and distributes them, along with cans of Coke he liberated from the motel's vending machine, among the group. Staying clear of the sunlight that streams through grimy windows, the assorted oddballs sit in the shadows and wait, like vampires hungry for nightfall. Time drags. No one has much to say, which seems surprising to Pete, considering the previous night's shenanigans. *How did I survive? Why do I feel brighter and more lucid than ever?*

Marisol has been given a respite from her nanny duties, Spark having volunteered to fill that role now that the tour is over. Pete knows that Spark longed to sing lullabies to Sunshower every night of the tour, but, due to performing onstage, wasn't able to do so. Both Sunshower and Spark are making up for lost time now. While everyone else is sedentary, they are dynamos. She uses him as a climbing frame, arm-wrestling partner and human teddy bear. Marisol, meanwhile, is giving quiet attention to Ozzy, who is lapping it up with bashful smiles. DT's four nubiles stick to him like metal to a magnet; the five of them lie in an intertwined tangle and fall asleep.

Iain is barely awake and, by the look and smell of him, barely alive. His last memory of the previous night, he tells Pete, is drinking whisky straight from the bottle. The injury to his head, he reckons, must have been the result of a drunken fall and a hard impact. A concussive impact, perhaps.

Forced to abandon his plans to explore the ghost town by daylight, Paul has resorted to working on his laptop. For the rest of the day, he will not seek ghosts: he and his metal warriors will *become* ghosts.

Two police cars speed past with blue lights flashing and sirens wailing, their wheels stirring up a wall of dust which hangs in the air as if stuck to invisible flypaper. Hours pass. Pete scrawls musical notation on paper as the others doze in the shade, all except Sunshower and Spark, who talk tirelessly in hushed tones, inexhaustibly amusing each other.

Eventually Pete's mobile rings and Udo announces, in clipped Teutoni-English, "Ve vill arrive in ten minuten. Be ready to make a quick getaway."

"I'll rally the troops." Pete wakes the sleeping masses from their siestas. This incites much cursing of the keyboard player, but ensures that the Transcend Everything tribe is ready to shift when the Stëëlmobile rolls into town. After swallowing its cargo, the gleaming bus U-turns and rumbles out of town followed by Spark and Sunshower in Helmut's Trans Am. Devil survivors and sausage admirers hurtle north, headed for – Pete hopes – a sleepy diner and a hearty meal.

Chapter 71 – I Am the One You Warned Me Of

Wrapped in an airy white summer dress with purple polka dots, Sunshower swings excited legs, her hair glinting in the sun. "Drive faster, Spark! Faster!"

"I won't drive faster, wee girl."

"Why not?"

"I'm followin' the bus, so I have to stay behind it. Plus you're too precious a cargo to put in danger."

She flutters her long eyelashes and gazes at me through huge blue eyes. "But you're an excellent driver. You could race ahead of the bus for a while, then slow down to let it catch up."

"Nice try. The answer's still no. What would your Dad say if he saw us hurtlin' up this highway at a million miles per hour?"

She ponders my question with a frown and a tight-lipped pucker. "He'd be angry at you."

"Exactly right. So we'll drive a safe distance behind the bus, at whatever speed Wolfgang chooses."

"Sing to me, then."

"That I can do. What song?"

"I'm in the mood for something soothing."

A tune pops into my head and I start to sing. Eyes fixed on the sky, Sunshower sways from side to side. When I finish she asks, "Whose song is that? It's lovely."

"The song's called *The Sacrament* and it's by H.I.M."

"Who's he?"

"Who's who?"

"Who's him?"

Hoping to redirect the preposterous Abbott-and-Costello conversation, I explain, "H.I.M. is an acronym. It's the initials *H* and *I* and *M*. It stands for His Infernal Majesty."

"I like it. Well done H.I.M. What's a sacrament?"

"You're a sacrament."

"Am I?"

"Aye, you are. A sacrament is a thing with very special sacred importance. An object with the power to change the Universe for the better."

A contemplative expression appears on Sunshower's face, where it remains throughout my acapella versions of *Holiday* by the Scorpions, *Ride On* by AC/DC, *Every Rose Has Its Thorn* by Poison, and *Sunshower, Moonflower*, my work-in-progress inspired by the wondrous wee soul to my right. When I slide Britny Fox's debut album into the car's CD player, Sunshower snaps out of her reverie. She hollers the chorus of *Girlschool* with me while waving her arms around like an over-excited cheerleader. As the riff of *Long Way to Love* kicks in, the bus's indicator starts to flash. The Stëëlmobile angles off the interstate and onto a twisting country road.

Six miles later, we cruise into the car park of a Mom-and-Pop diner called The Country Kitchen.

Archibald is last to spill out of the bus. As the journalist waddles towards the diner's entrance with a newfound bow-legged gait, DT asks, "You OK there, Archie? You're walkin' like you've been rodeo ridin'. Or were you the ridden?"

"I think I've pulled something," moans Archibald, continuing his awkward shuffle across the car park.

"I know exactly what you pulled," grins DT, "and if your John Wayne walk is anythin' to go by, that isn't all you did, ya toley-terrorisin' bumhole botherer!"

"Spare me your juvenile attempts at humour, Mr Tierney," spits Archibald. "They may amuse your kindergarten groupies, but anyone old enough to use a toilet unaided would not find them a source of mirth."

"Hey, wait a minute," continues DT, "if you're injured shouldn't you be bedridden? Oh, aye, I forgot – you already were...last night!" He cackles like a crone and slaps two of his female companions' arses.

Groaning, Archibald speeds up his wobbly walk.

Rather than sitting around two or three tables, we choose high stools at the diner's long, semi-circular serving counter. Archibald places a cushion on his stool and, with a grimace, lowers his backside onto it.

Against one wall is an unplugged jukebox which looks like a relic from the rock 'n' roll era of Eddie Cochran. I almost expect the Fonz to burst through the doors at any moment, pointing six-gun fingers and shouting, "Heyyyyyyy!" The floor is tiled in a red-and-white checkerboard pattern and buffed to a dazzling sheen. Signed photographs of long-dead movie stars hang on the walls. A wall-mounted television plays a rerun of *The Dukes of Hazzard*. I note with interest that every heterosexual male in the diner rubbernecks towards the TV every time Daisy Duke's voice is heard. *That's* the kind of staying power I want my band to have. Even thirty years after that TV show was made, Daisy still makes men of all ages drool like rabid werewolves.

As we sip our beverages and devour generous platefuls of food, *The Dukes of Hazzard* finishes and a local news show begins. A blonde female newsreader with too much make-up and an expression of perpetual surprise reads the day's lead story. "A Cocoa Beach resident has fallen victim to a horrendous Ku Klux Klan attack of a violent, racist and sexual nature. Maya Devoe, 51, claims that a Grand Dragon of the Klan broke into her home and raped her at knife point, as well as performing other lewd and depraved acts on her person. The attacker allegedly shouted racial abuse at Ms Devoe throughout the ordeal, at one point threatening to decapitate her, place her head on a burning cross in the garden, then perform additional sexual acts on her headless body. The attacker is still at large and should be considered extremely dangerous. Ms Devoe gave the following graphic account, which has been censored for daytime TV."

Metallic Dreams

A huge African-American woman in a tent-sized flowerprint dress appears on screen. "Ah was in bed asleep last night, when dis son of a *beep* woke me up by smackin' my *beep* and holdin' a knife to mah throat. The redneck *beep* called me all kinds o' racist things. He pulled mah hair, spanked mah *beep*, and put his face right in mah *beep*. Aftah *beeping* me like a dog fo' a while, he flipped me over and stuck his fingers in mah *beep*. Lordy, ah don't know what happened to me then. Mah bed ain't a water bed, but it sho' felt like it pretty soon. Oh Lord, ah was powerful afraid. Ah thought ah was dissolvin'. The racist *beep* got me on mah hands and knees, then *beeped* me in the *beep*. When ah thought it was all over, the dirty *beep* took a *beep* all over mah big black beautiful *beeps*. He faked a southern accent at the start, but slipped back into a foreign-soundin' one...Scottish, maybe. The hooded *beep* took off in some kinda fancy sports car with New York licence plates. Ah couldn't see his face because it was dark in the room, but I do know dis - he had long hair, real long hair...the mother*beeper*."

My eyes are glued to the television screen. Despite being aware of my bandmates' stares burning into me, I feel colder than ice. Ozzy whispers into my ear, "Cocoa Beach, big African-American woman, sports car wi' New York plates, Scottish accent, knows the technique for makin' women squirt...it could almost be you, eh Spark? In fact, if it wasn't for the Ku Klux Klan angle, it pretty much describes your mission last night."

"It doesn't pretty much describe my night. It *was* my night. Dude, I've made a terrible mistake."

"No!"

"Aye. That news report described the exact things I did to Shaquanna last night, right doon to the Ku Klux Klan outfit. It was her idea to do the racist stuff. She gets a kick oot of it. I was supposed to break into her hoose, sneak into her bedroom and take advantage of her. The Klan robe was an extra touch I threw in just for fun."

"Fun? Do you think that woman had fun?"

"Well, Shaquanna would've found it fun. The whole master/slave role-playin' was her idea. I did the right things to the wrong woman. I hope Ms Devoe got at least some enjoyment oot of it. She squirted a lot for a woman who wasn't enjoyin' herself. There were tidal waves coming oot o' her gash."

DT asks, "Was the defecation planned or was that another poetic touch you added 'just for fun'?"

"What are you talkin' aboot?" asks Oz, looking confused.

"The defecation," repeats DT. "Spark shat on her. On her big broon titties, to be precise, if I've correctly translated the beeps."

Oz shakes his head, prompting me with his eyes to tell him it isn't so. "The keech was a spur o' the moment thing," I confess.

"Spark, you can't tell anyone aboot this," warns DT. "It was a legitimate mistake. I haven't come this far to lose it all again. We haven't recorded the album yet."

"It was an honest case o' mistaken identity. I had permission to do all those things to Shaquanna. It's not rape or burglary to sneak into a girl's hoose and fuck her if you're followin' her orders, is it? I should go to the police and tell them the whole story. A person can't be guilty of rape unless he knows he's rapin', can he?"

"That defence won't fly in court," spits DT. "Listen, Spark, you cannot admit this to the police! You'll fuck yourself and the band in one huge, violent, racist, redneck Klansman swoop."

"But what aboot Maya Devoe? I'd never deliberately harm her. And I'm not racist. I want her to know that."

DT bares his teeth. "Let's look at your list of offences: breakin' and enterin'; assault wi' a deadly weapon; rape in various orifices; lewd and lascivious behaviour; destruction of property; threats of murder by beheading. Add to that the racist elements, which are sure to make it look like a hate crime. Do the maths, ya tit. If you turn yourself in you'll never see daylight again, no matter how convincin' an explanation you have. Bye bye band. Bye bye dreams. Bye bye beloved freedom. Hello life in a Florida jail, gettin' butt-blasted by angry African-Americans who don't take kindly to rednecks rapin' and desecratin' their soul sisters. Or you might just get put to death. Florida still has the death penalty."

My surroundings start to spin. "Shit, Dave. You're right. I'm fucked. I've fucked us."

"Relax," he consoles, "you technically did nothin' wrong. Not consciously, anyway. In the eyes of the Universe, you're still a good guy."

"A good guy?" grunts Oz. "Don't you mean a deviant, twisted bastard? A good guy wouldn't have set up such a sick meetin'."

Like a knight in black leather armour, DT jumps to my defence. "Each to their own, Oz. Spark meant no harm to anyone. The woman was an accidental victim and he was an accidental perpetrator. He's as much a victim as she is." I guzzle coffee, perhaps not the best thing to put into my already overstimulated body. Desperate to make amends to the woman I saw on TV, I wrack my brain for a way of explaining myself to her while remaining a free man. DT asks, "On a technical note, how did you *find* her orifices? She's a lot o' woman. Even her fat rolls have fat rolls. She has more rolls than Greggs the bakers."

"It's a special ability, a Zen thing."

DT cocks a black eyebrow. "And how did it feel to be immersed in a woman that size?"

"Honestly?"

"Honestly."

"Like a combination of swimmin' in a warm pool and jumpin' on a bouncy castle."

"You two are depraved," snarls Oz. "I can't sit next to you any longer." He slides his plate along the counter and changes seat.

The diner door swings open and two state troopers enter. I saw cops like this during my year in Virginia. Born to be troopers. Black moustaches. Mirrored sunglasses. Flat-top haircuts. Chewing tobacco. No-nonsense swagger. The taller trooper stands guard at the door, shotgun in hand, while his partner, brandishing a snub-nose handgun, moves to the centre of the diner and shouts, "Nobody move! Who is the owner of the black Pontiac Trans Am in the car park, NY licence plate COCK-LVR?"

Helmut waves a hand in the air. The handgun homes in on his head. "Sir, we need to search your vehicle."

After taking a relaxed bite of his flame-grilled hamburger, Helmut shakes his head. "No, you may not search my car."

"Sir, if you refuse to grant us access to your vehicle, you will be arrested and your car will be disassembled into its component parts. Now do you want to co-operate?"

Helmut turns to me and holds out a hand. I toss him the car keys and wait, heart in mouth. Helmut hands the keys to Handgun Trooper, who marches outside and opens the Trans Am's trunk. Moments later, he returns holding the green Grand Dragon's outfit in his free hand. Both guns converge on Helmut. Shotgun Trooper barks, "Sir, you must come with us. We are charging you as a suspect in the following crimes…"

I scribble notes for DT on a paper napkin. '*Go to Blackness Castle and start the album. Don't forget the tunes Ted left us. These cops don't know we're a band, so don't mention that. This isn't the kind of publicity Transcend Everything needs. I'll tell the police the truth about Shaquanna and then use my one phone call to contact her, as only she can get me out of this. One more thing, DT, my partner-in-crime, please, please, please cut a pentalpha into your skin, into Ozzy's and into Iain's, just in case.*' I slide the scrawled message along the counter to Dave. Deep furrows appear on his brow as he reads it. Raising his head, he whispers, "Don't do it."

Shotgun Trooper is still outlining the substantial chain of offences. "…lewd and lascivious behaviour, racially motivated violence…"

When I walk towards the cops, Handgun Trooper spins, points his gun at my head and shouts, "Back off!"

"I'm the one you're lookin' for."

"Excuse me?"

"I was drivin' his Trans Am last night. That's my Klan outfit. It's all a big misunderstandin', though. I had planned a role-playin' sex game wi' a female friend, but somehow I ended up fuckin' the wrong woman. It was a case o' mistaken identity. Muff mixup, if you will. I'm a vegetarian. Know what I mean?"

"Based on the foul stench you left at Ms Devoe's house," booms Shotgun Trooper, "the vegetarian part of your story may be true. Perhaps you do love animals. Hitler loved them too. And just like him, you're a white supremacist extremist steeped in Aryan hatred!"

"No, you've grabbed the wrong end o' the stick. The point o' my vegetarian comment was to highlight that I don't cause sufferin' to any sentient beings. If you had even half a clue, you'd have understood that."

My spirited defence is not popular with Shotgun Trooper, who grabs me by the hair and slams my head into the counter, while his partner handcuffs my wrists behind my back. The lawmen bundle me out of the diner and into the back of their car. Face jammed against a window, I glimpse my friends' stunned expressions as the cop car rolls towards my shackled future.

Chapter 72 – Losing More Than You Have Ever Had

As the Stëëlmobile cruises up the east coast into Georgia, shafts of sunlight spear through its skylight windows, but the mood on the bus is icy and sombre. Wolfgang cranks the TKO track *Doin' Time* through the onboard sound system. Despite his attempt to show sonic solidarity with Spark the first-time jailbird, Wolfgang's choice of song is ironic: Brad Sinsel's vocal tells of a man doing time for loving a woman, but loving is practically the only thing Spark *didn't* do to Maya Devoe; it was the other things that caused his problems.

Opening a large cardboard box, Hanson says, "Ich hope zat ze Spark situation eez rectified soon. Ve have gifts for you all, but ze arrest of Spark has taken ze gloss off zis happy occasion. Anyvay, ve had a customised Pink Stëël baseball shirt made for each of you. Ve hope you enjoy." The shirts are classic baseball style: white body, black ¾ length sleeves, Pink Stëël logo emblazoned across the chest. Ozzy's XXXL shirt has *THUNDER* in large pink letters across the back, Dave's has *HOT LICKS*, Pete's has *SPACE SOUNDS*, Iain's has *RUMBLES*, Spark's has *VOICE*, Archibald's has *WORDS* and Paul's has *DECISIONS*. Sunshower's tiny garment sports the word *GORGEOUS*. This prompts the ghost of a smile from the little girl, who has been in floods of tears since watching her confidant Spark being shackled and dragged away, perhaps forever. Sunshower wraps her arms around Hanson's neck, plants a kiss on his blushered cheek and whispers words of thanks into his ear. Marisol's shirt proclaims *HOT LATINA*, a sentiment that all men present, gay or otherwise, heartily endorse.

Ozzy squeezes into his new shirt, which, despite being the largest size available, looks as if it has been sprayed onto his gargantuan frame. As the giant flexes muscles and admires his new acquisition, Hanson shouts, "Zhese shirts make you all honorary homosexuals!"

DT's eyes widen. "I hope we don't have to consummate that role."

With a playful giggle, Hanson spanks his own leather-covered bottom. "Zhat, big boy, eez completely up to you."

The bus steams onwards late into the afternoon, most of its passengers dozing in bunks, exhausted by the events of the last twenty-four hours. Paul asks Udo, "Will you please keep Spark's suitcase and passport, along wi' some money for him?"

"Ja, Paul. Ve must drive back to Florida soon anyvay to collect Helmut's car. He eez still fuming zat ze Police have impounded eet as evidence. Ve vill keep Spark's stuff safe until he eez released."

"If he's released," laments Paul, "which is unlikely considerin' his repertoire of crimes."

"Ja, und even if he could get bail before trial, he vould not be allowed to leave ze country."

"Oor airline tickets are non-refundable and there's nothin' we can do for him anyway, so we'd be best employed gettin' back to Scotland to start work on the album. Thank you for takin' us oot on the road wi' you. It has been an honour and a pleasure."

"You are velcome, Paul. Eet has been fun rocking ze fans like ze proverbial hurricane every night. Transcend Everyzhing varmed up ze fans beautifully for us."

"We reached a lot o' people. Noo we need to keep workin' while we have that momentum. I just hope Spark's momentum hasn't been permanently halted."

"Have faith. Ich feel in my belly zat ve haven't seen ze last of Spark. Ze truth vill set him free, as ze Bible says."

"I hope so, my rectum-raidin' friend. Spark's a vege-eatin', rabbit-lovin', meditatin' Zenboy, but Maya Devoe doesn't know that. To her, he's the white Devil incarnate. I'm goin' to have nightmares aboot Spark ridin' the lightning, I just know it."

"A good album but not a good pastime, Herr Roberts."

"Exactly. I need to find oot where Spark has been taken, but I can't mention the band or the tour. It could undo all oor hard work if the press gets hold of this."

Udo twirls his blonde hair round an index finger. "Paul, you do know zat zhere is a niche market for ze racist music, don't you? If news of Spark's incident vere to…leak out, he vould become an instant superstar to Aryan vhite supremacists. Zhere are a lot of zhese people around, especially in America…"

Paul freezes Udo with a stare. "There's no way on Earth that's goin' to happen."

"Relax, Paul. Ich vas just thinking aloud about how to make ze best of a bad situation, if ze news about Spark reaches ze press…especially ze music press."

"So you propose that we start writin' songs aboot white power and all that shit, to make a livin' from some idiotic ideology in which we don't believe? Meanwhile, Spark stays in a Florida jail as the adopted hero of the penitentiary's Nazi gang?"

"Vell, eet sure beats ze Hell out of getting reprimanded up ze arsche by ze jail's African-American criminals. Vait a minute! Vhat am I saying? Ze anal punishments vould make it better zhan a stay at ze Hilton!" Udo pouts pink-glossed lips. "Ooh, perhaps I could pay Spark a visit und svitch places with him vithout ze guards noticing."

Paul booms, "Dude, this is fuckin' serious! Spark and I grew up together. We've been friends since we were babies. We always knew that somethin' big was oot there for us…somethin' pure…somethin' timeless. This band is it. I will never let anythin' taint it." Laying a hand on Paul's shoulder, Udo nods.

Paul makes phone calls in the hope of finding out Spark's location. He doesn't mention the band. Fourteen calls later, after being passed around from precinct to precinct, and from department to department, he finally uncovers that Spark is in a holding cell in Orlando, close to the scene of the crimes.

As the Stëëlmobile pulls into Atlanta Airport, heavy clouds darken and a wind starts to stir. Heavy metal souls pile off the bus and cross the expansive car park.

The German hosts insist on treating their guests to one last meal before the flight departs. Much food is ordered, but meagre portions are eaten. Even the ever-hungry Ozzy seems to have lost his appetite. Hugs and kisses are given, hands are shaken, heartfelt words of gratitude and friendship are exchanged. Sunshower jumps on Marisol and wraps her in a fierce embrace. When the flight takes off, however, it is not the little girl who sheds a tear: it is her father.

Chapter 73 – Waiting for an Alibi

Sunday, 2.19 a.m., Holding Cell, Orlando

"May I get a guitar to play while I'm in here?"
"No."
"A pad and pen?"
"No."
"A book to read?"
"No."
"A tod mag?"
"I don't even know what that is, but no anyway."
"For fuck's sake, please get me somethin'. There's only so much pacin' up and doon I can do withoot goin' crazy."
"You should've thought of that before you brought your racist misogynistic agenda to America."
"I'm not racist. And I can prove it wi' the one phone call I'm supposed to get."
"You might get your phone call after Sergeant McAllen has spoken to you. He wants to have a…chat with you first."
"Nobody read me my Miranda rights, which makes this an illegal imprisonment."
"You have no rights, asshole."
"I have the same rights as you."
"Really? Maybe you should call your embassy to complain. Oh, wait a minute…you can't, because you're not gettin' a phone call. Now shut the fuck up!"
"How aboot a café mocha and a wee bit o' shortbread?"
"Did you see a sign outside sayin' this was the Ritz?"
"A mug of instant coffee then?"
"I swear to God, you long-haired dickhead, one more word from you and it'll be the tazer followed by my nightstick! You'll have a hard time orderin' coffee after I knock your racist teeth out!" That's the end of that conversation.

The holding cell stinks of stale piss, alcohol, sweat, puke and shit. It's more medieval dungeon than space-age incarceration. A slab of rectangular stone covered with a colourful assortment of stains is the 'bed'. The foul stench that rises from a small circular hole in the corner of the floor confirms my suspicion that the aforementioned aperture is the 'toilet'. A bright striplight on the ceiling flickers incessantly, making sleep a dream rather than a reality. I'm too wired to be tired anyway. Pacing up and down the cell helps to let off steam, but the endeavour is hindered by the eight-feet-squared floor dimensions, which prevent me from getting into my stride. Earlier, in claustrophobic humidity, I paced five hundred laps of this cubic cage, after which I felt better but smelled substantially worse.

Metallic Dreams

Fairly certain that requesting a shower would result in me being stripped, dragged out back and blasted with a high-pressure hose, I decide to stew in my own juices instead.

Sunday, 4.40 a.m.

The loud rat-tat-tat-tat of a nightstick being dragged along steel bars echoes off the walls of my cell. A deep, bassy voice shouts, "Wake up, convict!"

"I'm neither asleep nor a convict. I haven't been convicted of anythin'. In fact, no one has read me my Miranda rights. And please do somethin' aboot that perpetually flickerin' striplight."

"Son, do you think you're in a position to be dishin' out requests? Get this clear - *you* don't tell *me* anything! In here, I'm God."

"Should I pray for a mug o' coffee and a phone call then?"

"Smart-mouthed motherfucker!" A southern drawl, absent until now, sneaks into the voice, its owner shrouded in shadow outside a neighbouring cell.

"May I at least tell you my story?" I ask.

"If you're referrin' to your tall tale of mistaken identity, my officers have already recounted it to me. Of all the stories I've heard from perps, yours is the least credible."

Boot-heels click on stone, the sounds low-pitched and loud, telling me that a weighty person is filling the footwear. A man of about 6'6" with skin the colour of molasses strides to my cell door and stares at me as if I'm a zoo exhibit that has just thrown shit at him. A crew-cut hairstyle and trimmed black moustache lend his face an air of authority. Cratered cheeks hint at severe acne during adolescence. His powerful physique has obviously lifted a lot of weights, but is let down by a belly that has evidently enjoyed too many donuts. Occupational hazard, perhaps. The man's posture is strong: shoulders pulled back; chest up; neck long. Not a dude to get on the wrong side of.

"Are you Sergeant McAllen?"

"Yes, sex beast. My badass reputation precedes me, it seems."

"If you have a lie detector here, wire me up and ask me as many questions as you like."

"I don't have a lie detector. I *am* a lie detector."

"Well ask me aboot what happened. Then, if you're happy wi' my responses, give me a phone call and I'll prove to you that it's all just a misunderstandin'."

The sergeant removes from his belt a large metal hoop which is home to jingling keys of various sizes. He unlocks my cell, slips a gold Desert Eagle out of its holster, points the gun at me and steps into my far-from-luxury accommodation. "Sit," he orders, gesturing with the gun's barrel towards the filthy excuse for a bed. I sit. McAllen crouches in front of me and aims the gun at my head. Holding my wrist in his free hand, he locates my pulse with his index and middle fingers. "Look straight into my eyes as you answer my questions," he instructs, dark eyes boring into me. "Do not look away at any time. Your pulse and pupils are two giveaways. There are twenty-six others. I know them all. For every lie you tell me, I will put a bullet into you." Realising that I have neither leverage nor bargaining tools, I give a humble nod. "Did you have a meeting arranged with an African-American woman in Cocoa Beach two nights ago?"

"Aye." No bullet. So far, so good.

"What was her name?"

"Shaquanna."

"Surname?"

"Prendergast."

"And what were the specifics of this meeting? What was planned?"

"Shaquanna said she'd leave her patio doors unlocked on Friday night when she went to bed. I was supposed to sneak into the hoose, scare the shit oot o' her, then physically and sexually dominate her while spoutin' racist threats. The KKK outfit was my idea, to make things more authentic."

"Had Shaquanna given you permission to have sex with her?"

"Aye, and she wanted it rough. Hair pullin', spankin', slappin', ass-fuckin', chokin', humiliation."

"Why did you break into Maya Devoe's house?"

"Shaquanna told me it was her hoose."

"Why did you perform sexual acts on Maya Devoe after realisin' she wasn't Shaquanna?"

"I didn't realise that until I saw her talkin' aboot the incident on the TV news."

"How could you not realise you had the wrong woman while you were performing the lewd acts on her?"

"Big ebony women are easily confused at night. It was almost pitch black in that room."

McAllen's grip tightens around my wrist. Nails dig into my flesh. His eyes smoulder. "Are you sayin' that all black people look the same?"

"No, that's no' my point. I love dark-skinned women with thick asses. I had arranged to ransack one such fine ass, but somehow I ended up plunderin' a different one."

Relaxing his grip on my arm, McAllen lowers his gun and points it at my crotch. "That's quite a story."

"Please give me one phone call. Shaquanna will confirm everythin' I've said. Also, I'd like to apologise to Maya Devoe. I feel bad aboot what I did to her."

"And so you should. Not content with performin' all kinds of foul acts on her person, your coup de grâce was to shit on her, I believe. Do you think that's an appropriate way to treat a beautiful black woman?"

"Aye, if she likes it."

Through gritted teeth, McAllen spits, "Ms Devoe was very vocally telling you that she did not like it!"

"Aye, but that was the plan! Shaquanna would protest, but I'd be savage and take her by force anyway. I was to have my way wi' her."

"And that's your way, is it? Defecating on a beautiful woman?"

"I'd never done that before. Shaquanna did ask me to take it up a notch, though."

"I can't believe any self-respectin' African-American woman would submit to such humiliation, especially with the spectre of slavery loomin' large."

"It was role-playin' and it was her idea. You must have done some role-playin' in the bedroom yourself?"

"Do *not* try to bring my sex life into this conversation!"

"Please let me apologise to Maya Devoe."

"Is that how easy you think it is? What a world it would be if we could all swagger around swingin' our dicks and stickin' them into any female who catches our eye, with or without her permission. Of course, if she has any objections afterwards, we could always just say sorry." A voice steeped in sarcasm.

"But I thought I was fuckin' Shaquanna. I'm truly sorry for what I put Maya Devoe through."

"Well, loathe as I am to admit it, you're not lying. I don't approve of the filth you've described, but you believe yourself to be tellin' the truth. You might, of course, be crazy and delusional…this 'Shaquanna' may not exist outside your depraved head. If that's the case, look forward to life in a straightjacket and a padded cell instead of life behind bars."

"My phone call?"

"In the morning."

"How aboot a wee cup o' coffee noo?"

"Son, don't push your luck. You're already lucky not to be full of holes right now. The facts stand that you broke into a house and committed various sex acts with a woman against her will while assaulting her and threatening her with death. Your other offence…I don't even want to think about that. It's unlikely that you'll ever see the outside world again, so you'll have plenty of time to ruminate on your actions. Get some sleep now." McAllen stands up, twirls his Desert Eagle round an index finger, slips the gun into its holster, then slams the barred cell door and locks it behind him.

Sunday, 8.19 a.m.

"Time for your phone call, deviant. You may want to say a prayer first because if this doesn't work you're screwed." McAllen handcuffs my wrists and leads me along a corridor to a small office where most of the wallspace is covered by noticeboards onto which black-and-white headshots are pinned. Some of the photos have a large *X* scored through them in black marker, but the majority are untouched. A phone sits on a metal desk in the corner. "Make your call," orders the sergeant.

I dial Shaquanna's number from memory and send out a two-pronged prayer that: I have dialled the correct number; she will be at home. After five rings, as I'm starting to sweat, she answers.

"Shaquanna! It's Spark. I'm in a holdin' cell in Orlando."

"What da fuck did you think you were doin', cracka…fuckin' Ms Devoe like that? You crazy?"

"I thought she was you."

"She's twice the size of me…and ah'm a thick sista! Exactly how big do you think mah ass is?"

"Well, on webcam it looks aboot the same width as a number 78 Bronzehall bus."

"What you doin' breakin' into number 46 anyway?"

"You told me you lived there."

"Ah told you in mah e-mail that ah live at number 64."

"The e-mail said 46!"

"You sure?"

"Of course I'm fuckin' sure!"

"Sorry about that, boo. It must have been a typo. Mah bad."

"A typo? A fuckin' typo?! That typo just might get me sent to the chair!"

"Relax, cracka. They don't use the electric chair in Florida."

"That's a relief…"

"They use lethal injection."

"Oh for fuck's sake, Sha! Help me here. I'm never gettin' oot again unless you tell your side o' the story."

"Ah'll give the cops an explanation over the phone, then drive over to Orlando tomorrow to give a statement."

"Tomorrow? How about noo?"

"How about no? How about ah have work to do, then ah'm going to get mah beauty sleep? Like ah said, ah'll come over tomorrow."

"OK, Sha. Please talk to Sergeant McAllen noo, though." I hand him the phone and slump down the wall, relieved that he's now finding out Shaquanna's not a figment of my imagination. There's still the matter of the defiled and desecrated Ms Devoe, though. In a jury's eyes, I'll look like a white supremacist in a pointy hood who came to America on a mission of sexual, racial and defecatory domination.

Sunday, 10.37 a.m.

"Prisoner, you have a visitor," announces McAllen. "I will monitor this visit. Do not go near the bars of your cell. Stay at the opposite end."

"Shaquanna? I knew she'd come through for me."

"It isn't Shaquanna. It's Ms Devoe, who is in an extremely fragile state. When I explained to her that this is beginning to look like a genuine mixup, she insisted on seein' you face to face. I warn you, prisoner, do nothing to antagonise or frighten her."

"Of course I won't."

Another cop appears and places a blue plastic chair outside my cell. After barked chastisement from McAllen, the officer takes away the flimsy chair and replaces it with a sturdy metal bench.

An enormous woman thunders down the corridor and stops in front of my cell. She looks in at me, looks *into* me, with eyes that look not fearful but tearful. Her skin is flawless and smooth, like dark chocolate. Natural beauty shines from a face decorated only by a touch of lilac lipstick. Straightened hair hangs past her shoulders. Maya's bountiful body strains against the fabric of an above-the-knee denim dress. I find her vast size breathtaking. If Oprah Winfrey ate Queen Latifah, she would look like Maya Devoe. She lowers her weight onto the metal bench. It creaks but doesn't buckle. Maya whispers, "Come closer, child." I'm shocked to hear compassion rather than rage in her voice.

"I want to come closer, but McAllen warned me to stay away from the bars. He thinks I'm some kind o' sexual Hannibal Lecter."

"Shaquanna tells me dat you and she had set up a masta-and-slave sex game. Ah've known dat child all her life. Nevah did think she was freaky like dat, though. Ah believe now dat you ain't a homicidal racist, but ah still think you're a sex maniac, based on the things you did to me. Your goal may have been pleasure, but ah was humiliated and scared for my life."

"I'm truly sorry."

"Yeah, child, ah believe you are. Those were some powerful words you were throwin' around. Words ah thought ah'd heard the back of long ago."

"I'm sorry, ma'am, if those words dredged up bad memories. I never intended any harm to anyone."

"It's ma'am now, is it? You a gentleman all of a sudden? Ma'am makes a welcome change from…what was it? 'Nigga bitch slave slut', ah believe."

My eyes overflow. "I wish I could make it up to you. I'm sorry straight from my heart."

"Ah'm a good church-goin' woman and a forgivin' woman too, but ah need to go to church now to ask the Lord how ah should proceed."

"If your Lord's a forgivin' deity, He'd say, 'Maya, turn the other cheek.' I'm sure of it."

"My Lord can be a forgivin' Lord, but He can smite folks down with bolts of lightnin', or turn them into pillars of salt. Hell, He even floods the world on occasion! Ah need His guidance more than evah."

"Thanks for comin' here, Ms Devoe. I appreciate it."

"Call me Maya. And what should ah call you?"

"Spark."

"Goodbye, Spark. Perhaps you should pray to the Lord too, bein' as it's Sunday an' all."

"Perhaps I'll do that." Maya turns and walks up the corridor, her side profile showing an ass on which one could balance a tray of drinks, and titties like twin Hindenburgs with their noses angled down. As she wobbles out of sight, an erection appears in my stinking pants. I decide to pray later. Now is the time for whacking off.

Sunday, 11.09 a.m.

"What in the name of God do you think you're doin', prisoner? Drop that thing or I'll shoot it clean off!"

Loosening my grip and stuffing my dick back into the olfactorily offensive underwear from whence it was unleashed, I complain, "There's no privacy in here."

"You're goddamn right there's not! This isn't some kinda state-funded sex vacation for foreign perverts!"

"Aye, fair point sergeant. I didn't think a wank would do any harm."

"Your victim didn't come here to get you hot under the collar."

"I know. I apologised to her."

"And got excited rememberin' the other night, is that it?"

"Sergeant, this thing has a mind of its own sometimes."

"You don't say, son! Your sexcapades have made that flagrantly clear. I'll tell you this – if you let the little head make decisions for the big head, you always end up in a world of trouble."

"I'll keep that in mind, sarge."

"You bein' a smartass, Scotty?"

"No way. I'm heedin' your advice. As of noo, the big heid's wearin' the troosers, so to speak."

McAllen removes dark sunglasses and glares at me through darker eyes. Apparently satisfied with my non-smartass status, he marches out of sight, the click of his heels echoing off bare, blood-spattered walls.

Sunday, 9.06 p.m.

I've been awake for thirty-seven hours. Having been deprived of caffeine for the last thirty-three of those hours, my body has reached a state beyond fatigue: grumpiness has superseded tiredness.

The movies' portrayals of prisoners in solitary confinement are lies: I haven't resorted to counting bricks or bouncing a baseball off the walls and catching it in a gloved hand, or even to digging my way out with a teaspoon. McAllen wouldn't give me a baseball or a glove or a teaspoon anyway; he thinks I'd find a creative way of shagging them.

In my cell, I've identified seven distinct stains and a couple that I can't place with any degree of certainty. Smeared shit-skids decorate the walls like clumsy brown brush strokes. Blood-spatters on the stone are configured in such a way that they must be the products of high-velocity beatings. Piss stains are mostly concentrated around the toilet hole, but the dried remnants of the bad aimers and the outright rebels stray farther afield. Some sizeable chunks of snot are stuck to the wall next to the concrete cylinder that passes for a pillow. Pastiches of puke of various textures garnish the cell. One dark stain almost foiled me, but after a careful close-range observation and sniff test, I recognised it as dried bourbon; I can only speculate as to how the bourbon drinker smuggled his bottle into the cell. The unmistakeable markings of dried cum are dotted over the stone bed's surface. Of the two stains that have so far eluded my forensic analytical skills, I suspect that one may be spit, mainly due to its stalactite-like formations on the ceiling, but the blue splodges of the other stain have me puzzled. As I said, the movies tell lies.

Sunday, 10.30 p.m.

A fair-skinned, shaven-headed cop with a blonde beard appears at the bars of my cage. "Prisoner, you have some visitors. Stay well clear of the bars at all times."

"Visitors? Plural?"

"They are either masculine women with disastrous dress sense and deep voices, or something much, much scarier."

For the first time since my incarceration, a smile crosses my lips. "My boys? My Bremen-born bum bandits?"

The cop pulls a piece of paper from his pocket and reads, "They signed in with the names Udo Von DüYü, Hanson Jobb, Helmut Bang and Wolfgang Arschenficken. Friends of yours?"

"Aye, that's exactly what they are."

"You can have ten minutes, but stay away from the bars."

"The gay bars?"

"Pardon."

"Just a wee joke."

"Save your jokes for the trial. We'll see how funny the judge finds them."

"Sorry."

"Remember that I'm watchin' from along the corridor, so no nonsense!"

Moments later, four harbingers of homosexuality sway into view, smelling like a perfume shop and looking like an explosion in a cosmetics factory. "Spark, you smell like an unvashed buffalo," observes Hanson.

"Aye, that's partly me and partly the cell. You all look good. Did my band get away OK?"

"Yes," replies Udo, "und Paul called me today to say zhat zhey have just moved into ze castle. A dude called Colin is zhere vith recording equipment. Pete's girlfriend has moved in too. You look rough, Spartacus. Have you slept?"

"No. Look at this stone-age bed. It's rock-hard and covered in cumstains. And the floor's worse."

"You should not be afraid of ze man-milk, Spark," advises Wolfgang. "Eet eez natural und very good for ze skin. Full of protein too."

"I'm no' afraid of it. I just don't fancy rollin' aroon' in someone else's. Imagine you were imprisoned in a cell that reeked of menstrual blood and vagina juice, wi' posters o' naked women coverin' the walls. Think aboot how you'd feel in that situation. That's pretty much how I'm feelin' in here."

"Ugh," shudders Udo, "zhat sounds awful."

"It's not ideal. Shaquanna's comin' tomorrow to give her statement, though. That could help me."

Hanson asks, "What about ze ozher voman, ze one you vent scheiße on?"

"She was here earlier. We talked. She seems like a gentle soul. Rather than comin' here to vent her anger, she wanted to understand how the mixup happened. She's lookin' to her God noo, askin' Him what the right course of action is."

"Ve have left your suitcase, passport und cash vith ze sergeant," says Udo. "Also, ve brought you a customised Pink Stëël baseball shirt, personalised for you."

"Thanks, boys. Somehow, though, I don't think I'll be needin' any o' that. It's a life of orange jumpsuits, steel shackles and chain gangs for me."

Hanson runs a hand through his black spiky hair then adjusts his mirrored sunglasses. "As Bon Jovi once said, *keep ze faith*. You didn't hurt anyone on purpose und zhat vill come out in ze same vay ve came out of our closets."

"What does that mean?"

"It means zhat it may take some time, but it vill come bursting out vhen ze time eez right."

"I wish I could give you all a hug, but I'll get tazed if I go anywhere near the bars."

"Ve vill take a raincheck for ze hug," says Udo. "Our phone numbers und New York addresses are in ze side compartment of your suitcase. If you ever get out, ve vill be happy to see you."

Tears trickle from my tired eyes. "Thanks for everythin'. The tour was a beautiful rollercoaster ride, but I fear that my seat has come loose and flown off into eternal oblivion."

"Do not cry, hairy Scotsman," pleads Udo. "Ve all love you, as do ze men in your band. Und now you have fans who love you too. As your heroes in Journey vould say if zhey vere here, *don't stop believin'*."

I nod, but the tears continue to flow. "Thank you for visitin'. I love you all. Sorry aboot the tears. I think all your oestrogen is gettin' to me."

The bulldog-like Wolfgang shakes his head. "Ze man who never cries eez like ze frozen loch zhat never thaws. You cannot see or touch his depths." Eyes glistening, the other Germans nod.

"Thanks, dudes. I feel as if I've known you forever."

The blonde-bearded cop stomps up the corridor and announces that the visit is over. My Teutonic friends blow kisses from glossed lips. Once they are safely out of sight, I descend into despair.

Chapter 74 - Ballbreaker

Early on Monday morning, I'm marvelling at the adaptability of the human organism. Neither a morsel of food nor a drop of water has passed my lips since my arrest. Until five hours ago, I hadn't slept a wink in my disgusting cell. After the visit from my German friends, however, sadness choked my spirit. It was then that healing sleep covered me like a heavy blanket, purifying my soul as my body lay in putrefying filth. Now, having been wakened by the stroboscopic flicker of the ceiling light, I feel rested. Last night's sorrow is gone, replaced by something approaching acceptance. Is this how a caged animal feels, initial anger giving way to sorrow which lifts to leave a numb acceptance of its captivity? Fierce freedom-loving souls can't thrive in confinement; I long to be wrapped in shorts, fleece and my old Scarpa hill-walking boots, and to climb high into the mountains of Scotland's Nevis range. In my mind's eye burns a moving picture of the hulking, snow-topped Ben Nevis viewed from the ridge of Carn Mor Dearg as I traverse the narrow arête with careful steps and ascend to the summit of the giant.

If Maya appears in court and says she believes I mistook her for Shaquanna, who *wanted* me to use and abuse her body, the jury may not be so hasty in judging my actions. Even so, I need to get used to metal bars; my future is lined with them or padded walls. My immediate future, that is. Longer term, there could be either freedom or the comfort of a wooden chair into which I'll be strapped while a needle pierces my arm and – like a hellish human-created cobra – injects its killing venom into my body.

Primal survival mechanisms have melted my fear, allowing me to think lucidly once again. Hunger and thirst should be driving me loco, but my body seems to be making do with just deep breaths of humid Florida air, absorbing it and transmuting it into all that I need. Perhaps fasting is responsible for my newfound mental clarity; maybe the energy that usually goes into digestion and absorption of food has been rerouted into honing the mental and spiritual functions vital to sanity and survival.

Heavy boot-clicks echo down the corridor. McAllen marches into view, does a military-style quarter-turn and barks, "Wake up, prisoner! Breaking news!"

"I wasn't sleepin', sarge. I was thinkin'."

"It's a pity you weren't thinkin' on Friday night when you orchestrated your symphony of sick sexual depravity!"

"We've been over this before," I sigh.

"Maya Devoe called a few minutes ago. Apparently, she had some kind of epiphany in church last night."

I grab the cell's bars. "Please tell me this isn't a joke!"

"I'm not known for my sense of humour. I advised Ms Devoe to appear in court, tell her story and let the chips fall where they may, but she insisted that her advice came from a higher source than me. She will – if her conditions are met – drop all charges, makin' you a free man."

"What are her conditions?"

"That's where things take an unpredictable turn. Never in 26 years on the force have I come across a development so unorthodox."

"Just tell me!"

"Ms Devoe has promised to drop all charges if…" McAllen pauses, sighs, rolls his eyes and takes a deep breath, as if he mustering all his strength of will. "Maya is comin' into the station at lunchtime. She can tell you her proposed conditions."

"For fuck's sake, that's torture! Just tell me, McAllen!"

"Sergeant McAllen to you! And no, you can wait and hear it straight from the horse's mouth…not that I'm implyin' Ms Devoe is some kind of equine." He smoulders off into the depths of the station, leaving me deep in wonder. I feel wings bursting through the flesh of my back.

I spend the next few hours breathing deeply through my nose, staring at a single point on the wall and imagining the freedom that lies just a few feet away on the other side. My trance is broken by a large dark shape in my peripheral vision. "Hello, child," says Maya, her voice deep and soft. "The Lord has spoken to me. Ah know what ah must do. Are you familiar with the phrase 'an eye for an eye'?"

"Aye."

"The Lord has said ah should take justice into mah own hands usin' His laws, instead of entrustin' it to the false laws of men."

"I need to make amends for what happened, I agree. I'll give you my heartfelt apologies for as long as you want, Maya."

"You already apologised, child. Dat's not what the Biblical eye for an eye was abaht. It was abaht *redemption*. Only one thing will restore the balance. Ah must do to you exactly what you did to me. Ah need to make you feel how you made me feel."

"That sounds fair, ma'am. I deserve it." Thinking about being engulfed and manhandled by this gigantic mama creates not fear but a stirring in my foul-smelling underwear. If this is punishment, it doesn't feel like it. This must be what's known as landing on one's feet.

"Ah'll be here on Saturday," promises Maya. "Ah'm an early bird, so ah'll be here at sunrise. Once ah'm satisfied dat we're even ah'll sign the papers, freein' you from all legal action. Dat's what the Lord wants. I need to do things His way. Old school."

I mask my libidinous excitement with a serious expression. "If it's what the *Lord* wants, who am I to argue?"

"We have a deal then, child. Ah'll see you on the weekend."

"Aye. And once again, I'm sorry."

The week drags past with nothing to fill its space except cell-pacing, breathing and thinking. *What is the band up to? How is Fluff? What has my Mum been told regarding my non-return? What is Maya Devoe going through?* What I did to Maya must have been immensely traumatic for her, but –

where a lesser woman would have crumbled – she has remained strong and forgiving. Every day my excitement grows over the prospect of release back into the wild. In a world of mixed metaphors, one should not count one's chickens until the fat lady has sung. In the world of heavy metal, I won't taste my freedom until the fat lady has used my body like an amusement park.

Saturday morning arrives. McAllen allows me to use the staff shower room prior to Maya's arrival. An armed chaperone monitors me as I shower, an unnerving experience that feels more than a little like a scene from a gay porn film. The first feeling of hot water on my skin for over a week feels welcome, but I can't relax while mirrored eyes and a steel gunbarrel are aimed at me. Time disappears as I soap myself back to a clean, scented state. My teeth receive the longest scrub they have ever had. After towelling myself dry, I brush the tugs out of my hair. In an unquantifiable way, I'm feeling like a new man. My reflection in a full-length mirror reveals a body leaner than it was two weeks ago, having gone four days without food or water, followed by four days during which meagre portions of steamed rice and vegetables, and the occasional paper cup of water, were my only sustenance. I couldn't even estimate the amount of nervous energy I've burned up by pacing my cell under the spectre of lethal injection. A closer look in the mirror shows that the starvation diet has worked wonders: eyes are clear and blue; hair is lustrous; skin glows; muscles are chiselled; inscribed pentagram has faded to a light pink.

It seems pointless to put clothes on, so I wrap a towel around my waist and wander barefoot into the station accompanied by my chaperone, who lets me use the staff's vending machine. I get two cups of coffee and hand him one in a gesture of solidarity. He is so grateful that he almost cracks a smile.

McAllen struts into the station and enquires, "Are you ready, prisoner?"

"As ready as I'll ever be. Yee-haw!"

"Son, you're not supposed to be lookin' forward to this, whoopin' and hollerin' like some crazed redneck! Ms Devoe isn't havin' her way with you for fun – she's doin' the Lord's bidding."

"Hallelujah, McAllen!"

"Sergeant McAllen, pervert!"

"Sorry…Sergeant McAllen, pervert. I didn't realise that was your full professional title. I knew if we hung oot enough, we'd find some common ground."

McAllen glowers at me over the top of his glasses. "Goddamn Scottish smartass sonofabitch. I'd have thrown the book at you if it was up to me."

"Well, Maya's goin' to throw somethin' at me. Behold the sacrifices I make in the name o' justice and religion."

"I will behold…on our closed-circuit cameras."

"You can't do that," I panic. "It's invasion of privacy, a violation of my human rights."

"For as long as you reside here, you're my property and you have no rights. You're callin' no Scottish Embassy, if such a thing even exists. You already used up the one phone call I so generously gave you. I can't imagine what help a Scottish Embassy would be anyway, other than sendin' you a barrel of whisky and a sheep in case of emergency."

"You just zoomed off Planet Politically Correct wi' that comment. Not all Scottish people are sheepshaggers and alcoholics."

"True," nods McAllen. "Some of them are wife-beaters too."

Shaking my head, I ask, "Where will this Royal Rumble of justice happen?"

"We have an old staff recreation room that's disused. The orders from up high were to install a reinforced bed there specifically for today's encounter."

"God told you I've to fuck Maya in the old recreation room?"

"No, idiot – Chief Levinson told me. I called him to discuss the case because, frankly, I've had no experience of anythin' like this. I've had husbands drop physical assault charges against wives and vice versa, but the complexities of your case, and Ms Devoe's proposals of fire-and-brimstone justice, were beyond me."

"Anywhere's better than my cell. That place should be condemned."

"It's *home* of the condemned, son."

"Sergeant McAllen, I'd like your opinion on somethin'." I flex my muscles in a front-double-biceps pose, then swing my clenched fists down and pull a most-muscular pose. "How do I look?"

"Son, I do not bend that way!"

"Aye, but if you were Maya would you enjoy gettin' some o' this?"

"If I was Maya, you'd have been beaten, shot in the kneecaps, dragged out into the Everglades, tied to a tree, and left for the mosquitoes and the 'gators. I wouldn't be humpin' on you, that's for damn sure."

"Remind me not to piss you off."

"Son, you piss me off every day. Part o' me's glad you might be gettin' outta here. I've had about all the jive-ass Scottish nonsense talk I can take. I will say one thing in your favour, though."

"What?"

"That's a mighty fine head o' hair you have. I've never seen anythin' quite like it."

Fluttering my eyelashes, I ruffle my hair. "Thank you, sergeant, but I respectfully reject your advances. I'm spoken for today and my date will not be happy if you defile me first. She wants me all to herself."

"Levity isn't smart when I'm the one with the Desert Eagle and you're the one standin' half naked in a towel."

A voice through a loudspeaker summons Sergeant McAllen to the front desk. He handcuffs me to a towel rail and leaves the room, locking the door behind him. The blonde-bearded cop arrives, frees my wrist from its constraints, gestures for me to follow him and leads me to a room with floorspace of about twelve feet squared. Wooden cupboards and a corroding metal sink line one wall. A gigantic bed has been wedged into the available space. I fall back onto it and wait.

The woman who appears at the door is not the God-fearing, churchgoing Maya Devoe who visited my cell on two previous occasions. Bounteous brown fleshs spills over the tops of black thigh-high leather boots with spiked heels. A black PVC basque, struggling to contain her enormous girth, squashes colossal breasts together, cultivating a cleavage in which I could park my mountain bike. Her long hair has been tied into a long pleat. Blue eyeshadow, liberally applied, looks like fierce warpaint on a face normally soft and gentle. Red lipstick covers thick lips which are set into an inscrutable pout. I sense fury seething just beneath Maya's stoic surface. Silhouetted against the corridor's lights, she looks like a monolithic angel of vengeance come to do God's dirty work.

After warning me to do exactly what Ms Devoe orders, the bearded cop leaves the room and locks the door. Maya ditches her bag in a corner of the room and stomps towards me, her metal-tipped heels clicking on the stone floor. "Ehm...hi," I stutter, "you look beautiful."

Dropping to her knees between my legs, Maya lifts my towel and wraps a strong hand round the base of my stiffening penis, which, like a valiant Viking aching for battle, stands erect, ready, bloodthirsty. Maya runs the tip of her tongue along my cock from base to tip, blessing its head with soft kisses. She toys with me, teases, traces circles around my glans with her tongue. The thought flashes into my mind that Maya, in basque and boots, looks like a fleshy African-American Wonder Woman: the modern female superhero for a multicultural melting pot. As she fellates me deep into her throat in a single unflinching movement, her eyes roll skywards, revealing white orbs which look more demonic than celestial. The muscles in Maya's mouth and throat alternately contract and relax in a dick-milking motion, prompting an observation from the Metal Gods. *That's a skill she didn't learn in church.* After a breath-holding/sword-swallowing combo, Maya comes up for air. Gasping, she dribbles a trail of bile and saliva on my vertical member, rubs the liquid into the tumescent tadger then once again swallows it whole. When the point of no return arrives I grab Maya's hair and unload down her throat. She swallows – practically inhales – every drop like an alcoholic sucking down free booze. "The Lord is proud of you! Do His dirty work! I'm a bad man! Punish me!"

Maya stands up, balancing unsteadily on thin-spiked heels. She struts to her bag, removes a cat o' nine tails and asks, "What would you know abaht the Lord, you godless redneck honky?" A ferocious lash from the nine-tailed whip rips into my chest. I look down and see red welts rising, a line of blood at the top of each.

Another lash of the whip. "Argh! Fuck! God wouldnae approve o' this at all!"

"Shut yo' mouth, you heathen honky cracka!" Maya raises her weapon-wielding hand high and cracks the whip across my back, forcing a howl from my mouth. Breathing hurts, so I suck in staccato, shallow breaths. "Lose the towel, you muthafuckin' cracka redneck cunt!" Obedient to my mistress, I toss the towel. The whip's leather strips tear into my testicles. Searing pain works upwards into my abdomen. Tears form at the corners of my eyes: an involuntary response to the beating my balls have just taken. "Pussy! Can't take a lil' pain, white bread?" The massive mama lashes my balls a second time. "Wanna try pullin' mah hair now, honky biyatch? Think you gonna cut off mah head and stick it oan a spike now? Ah own your ass, whitey! Understand?"

In too much pain to speak, I nod. Another lash thrashes my scrotum, spraying blood across the wall and giving birth to a silent scream. Maya slams me back onto the bed and straddles me in reverse, her enormous bottom bearing down on my face. Without lubrication or warning, she jams a long-nailed finger up my arse. Her free hand coaxes my cock back to life from its sleeping state, while the uninvited finger remains painfully wedged up my jacksie. When it presses on my prostate I start to cum in explosive jets. Maya continues to wiggle the digit which has gone, like the Starship Enterprise, where no one has gone before. I toss my head back and roar in ecstatic pain. My body starts to twitch in the involuntary way bodies do when stimulated further than nature intended. Still, the finger continues to press on my prostate, keeping my cock hard and – along with the rapid pistoning action of her other hand – making me cum indefinitely. I've heard stories about men going into sperm banks and pretending to be unable to ejaculate, in the hope that stockinged nurses will jerk them off, only to be horrified when their dungholes are infiltrated by nurses' lubricated fingers which locate their prostates, press hard and have them cumming in an instant. I always thought those stories were urban legend, but now I realise that they may be true. My insides feel as if they're being jettisoned out of my cock as Maya continues to pump and press, piston and squeeze, whack and massage, pound and probe. I'm flailing like a trapped animal, but her immense bulk has me pinned to the bed. It would take a crane to lift her off, so in my semi-starved state I haven't a snowball's chance in Hell. My view of proceedings is blocked by Maya's supersized ass. For all I know, she could have pumped me dry and I could now be shooting fresh-air bullets. My orgasmic contractions show no sign of letting up as helpless lamentations burst forth. Just as consciousness starts to slip from me, Maya stops, pops her finger out of my arse and drops my dick, which flops like a dead flower.

Maya swivels to face me. She leans forward and licks blood from the gouges on my chest, staining her tongue crimson. Her saliva stings like vinegar in my wounds. Dark eyes sparkle as she opens the stud fastenings of her basque and lifts it over her head, freeing gallons of Nubian flesh from their tight confines. She reverses her wide-load ass and lowers her hips onto me, engulfing my sleeping dick between sopping pussy lips then bucking her hips like a cowgirl balancing on a bull. In this case, though, the bull is dwarfed by the cowgirl. In a reversal of traditional rodeo roles, it is the bull rather than the rider who faces a life-threatening challenge. As Maya becomes warmer and wetter, my cock twitches back to life and slides inside. "Ooh, fuck Mama like a good honky! You betta make Mama happy. Don't cum until ah say so, or ah'll be takin' the cat o' nine tails to dat cracka cock. Ah'll lash it 'til it looks like szechuan shredded beef!" Maya's breasts jiggle as she moves, sending ripples through the fat rolls below. "Fuck me deep! Impale Mama on dat white cock! Do it, you backwoods hick muthafucka!" I angle my body up off the bed, grabbing Maya's bottom for traction. As she arches backwards the head of my cock achieves touchdown on soft cervical flesh, sending tremors through her body. Sweat runs down her neck, over enormous breasts, and drips onto my chest's whip wounds.

"Grab Mama's big brown titties! Pull mah nipples, cracka bastahd!" Obeying, I grab Maya's nipples and tweak the spark-plug-sized protrusions as if trying to tune into an elusive radio station. I flick my tongue over one nipple, then suck it. "Ooh, yeah! That's mah cracka biyatch! Keep suckin' oan mah beautiful ebony titties! And keep hittin' that spot wit' your cock too, fucka! Ooh! Ooh! Ooh yeah, Mama cummin'…Mama cummin'…Mama ugh!" Gripping my hair with both hands, Maya slams her full weight onto me. The bed's legs snap. The mattress goes into freefall, landing with an impact that knocks the wind out of me. Maya doesn't miss a beat. She continues to grind herself onto me, her vaginal walls contracting like a soft vice. Even after I cum, she keeps bouncing until her pussy's frothing like a well-shaken can of fizzy soda.

Sliding forward, Maya slaps her cavernous cum-dripping cunt over my face. Pitta-bread-sized labia swallow my mouth while rolls of sweaty flab cover the rest of my face. Unable to breathe, I flap my arms and spank Maya's ass with all my might. Ignoring my pleas, she keeps me pinned. "Drown, cracka! Drown in mah sweet black pussy!" Survival here is about sending her into orgasm in record time, so I focus on her clitoris. I alternate between sucking the hard bud and flicking my tongue over it, sending quakes rippling through Maya's body. As her orgasmic shriek echoes off the walls, the lights in my head go out.

I regain consciousness to find Maya lying on top of me in an exhausted, sweaty heap, my face sandwiched between her mammoth breasts. The smells of coconut and leather flood my nostrils. Her heartbeat pounds agonisingly against my bloody chest. When Maya's breathing has slowed to a resting rate, she dismounts me and stomps across the room. From her bag she removes black leather straps which she fastens round sweat-soaked waist and thighs, all the while facing away from me. The tight hoops press indents into plentiful mounds of flesh. It looks like some kind of heavy-duty suspender belt. Focusing my will on lacy stockings being the next item plucked from the bag of tricks, I lie smiling like an over-medicated lunatic, scarcely able to believe my luck. When Maya turns round, my smile vanishes. Between her legs hangs a baseball-bat-sized thing, fixed onto a harness at four points on her waist and legs. "Eye for an eye, cracka! Bend over, boy! You mah biyatch now!"

"Oh God, no!"

"The Lord moves in mysterious ways! You abaht to git an ass-fuckin' you'll nevah forget, you redneck hick racist cracka honky Klan-wannabe muthafuckah! Eye for an eye, ass for an ass!"

"Maya, please dinnae! No' my delicate wee arse!"

"Shut up, biyatch! I'm abaht to skewer you like a kebab! When you mess wit' Maya, you mess wit' the Lord!" She grabs my hair, hauls me to the floor and spreads my legs wide. Skint-kneed and spreadeagled, I'm terrified at the thought of the thing behind me with its sights set on my sphincter.

Maya hammers the phallic vehicle of vengeance home. She may as well have shoved a flamethrower up my arse and pulled the trigger. Panicking, I struggle to escape, but she has my hair in a tight grip and won't let go. Just as I think the pain can't get any worse, she thrusts in to the hilt, forcing my internal organs up into my throat. Holding my hair like reins, Maya rides me like an accomplished equestrian. Desperate for anything to anaesthetise the pain, I yowl, "Any chance of a reach-aroon'?"

"Shut yo' nasty cracka mouth, white Devil biyatch! Ah deal in *pain*! Feel my wrath, honky!" With knees bleeding from being ground into the stone floor, I collapse forwards and lie still. Maya thrusts the strap-on behemoth into me one more time. When it slides out with a slopping sound, I feel liquid trickling from my desecrated arse.

Maya rolls me onto my back and stands with one leg either side of my chest. "Now for mah finalé, cracka. Mama ate a family-size bucket o' fried chilli chicken last night, just fo' you! Ah'm goin' to git you good, sucka!" She pulls gargantuan butt cheeks apart and squats down half way.

It is one of those indecisive jobbies, the type that has difficulty making up its mind as to whether it's solid or liquid. During its short flight from the enormous arse above me, it hangs in the air in a quantum keech state (Schrödinger's jobbie?). I close my eyes just in time to avoid the torrent of squidgy shit that splatters on impact, covering my face, neck and chest. The stench is so vile that I start to gag.

Then, out of the blue, I hear Maya's authentic voice: her soft and gentle voice. "You are forgiven, child. Vengeance is mine. The Lord truly does work in mysterious ways." The door opens then bangs closed, after which a lock turns in the key and spiked heels click ever more distantly. When I've wiped the mess out of my eyes and summoned the energy to rise from the floor, I spy Maya's bottle of anal lubricant. Its label reads *Pablo the Lunatic's Chilli Sauce – Caution: XXX Hot. Avoid contact with eyes*. It should also say *Avoid contact with arse*.

I wrap the towel around myself and waddle to the front desk, blood oozing from my torn arsehole. Twelve cops are sitting in an arc around a monitor, two large Dunkin Donuts boxes open on their desk. As the lawmen drink coffee and munch sugary snacks, contented smiles on their faces, Sergeant McAllen booms, "Well done, son! That was quite a show you put on for the men and me! Maya Devoe signed the papers and dropped all charges. You're officially a free man. I hope you enjoyed your trip to Florida, the Sunshine State. Come back soon." The officers crack up laughing and, for the first time, I see McAllen's smile: a clumsy expression which looks fairly certain it's appeared on the wrong face.

Now that the freakshow is over, most of the officers disperse into the bowels of the station, while two stay and talk in hushed tones about an incident in the ghost town of Cedar Key, where a hole was blown in the side of an old motel by some long-haired rock 'n' rollers who were booked into it for a night. Blood was found in the car park, in several of the rooms, in the main office and in trails up the stairs. Laughing, the taller cop says, "It was probably one o' those Satanic metal bands tryin' to get attention, as their parents didn't love them." His partner nods and speculates that perhaps the rockers were trying to summon the Devil himself. They both have a hearty laugh at that. Taking large bites of frosted donut, the cops glance at my long hair and pentalpha-scarred body as I ease past them in my towel, but their minds fail to make the connection. Either that or they don't give a shit.

After showering again (unsupervised this time), I jam a pair of underpants up my gaping butthole as a makeshift arse-tampon. Dressing in my own clothes again feels good, like returning to my tribe. I retrieve the bottle of chilli sauce from the room of anal ruin, take it to the staff bathroom, rub the fiery liquid into the roll of toilet paper in the cubicle nearest the door, then head to the front desk, where McAllen is sitting like king of his castle. He slides a large mug of coffee across the desk and nods towards a box of assorted donuts. I devour two Boston cremes and a blueberry donut. While washing them down with coffee, I notice the blonde-bearded cop heading into the bathroom. My cue to leave. I grab my suitcase, bid McAllen goodbye and scuttle towards the exit as fast as my shaky legs will allow. A piercing shriek flies from the toilet. Glancing over my shoulder at the frowning McAllen, I shrug and tell him, "The Lord truly does work in mysterious ways. Hallelujah!"

Outside the station's front doors, I inhale sweet Florida air and the sweeter scent of freedom. The Metal Gods intervene. *Don't waste your time gazing at the Florida sun. Get your bloody arse back to Blackness. There's work to be done.*

Chapter 75 – A Horse with No Name

The flight from Orlando to Glasgow is a long one when you're harbouring a hedgehog up your arse. Of course, there is no actual animal wedged in my orifice; that would go against all my vegetarian ethics, not to mention breaking several airline rules. No one has, to the best of my knowledge, pulled a spiky mammal out of his posterior and subsequently hijacked a plane using the cute, jaggy creature as an unwitting weapon of Jihad, but it's surely just a matter of time. Anyway, as I mentioned, there are no mammals – spiky or otherwise – up my jacksie. If you could feel what I'm feeling, though, you would never believe that.

    I sit diagonally in my chair to avoid putting pressure on my raw rectum. I've dressed all in black so that any fresh blood from my backside won't be visible on my clothes. Bloodstains would attract undue attention at the airport, perhaps even generating enough suspicion to warrant a cavity search. That – an unpalatable prospect at the best of times - is unimaginable today. It feels as if the bleeding has stopped and been replaced by a congealing stickiness. In an attempt to transcend my physical discomfort, I close my eyes and meditate.

    As I soar through clear skies above foam-lined waters, a shoreline comes into view, its golden beach backed by a wooden boardwalk and an assortment of shops. Gulls circle above a seafood restaurant, cawing their hopes of an easy catch. It looks like a seasonal town, one of the many in America that thrive during summer months then diminish to a skeleton population for winter, to hibernate until the tourists return the following spring. This would be a good place to rest a while. Healing would happen quickly here. Ignoring that thought, my consciousness catapults me forward, inland from the coast at rocket speed, then faster still. The landscape blurs. Night falls.

    As if placed down softly by a divine hand, I land barefoot on a dirt track, wearing only torn jeans. My faithful BC Rich Warlock is strapped onto my back, horned headstock pointing downwards. Under the starsparkled sky is a wooden shack, outside which an old man with black skin and salt-and-pepper hair plays harmonica. As he moves, his short beard glitters silver in the starlight. In slippers and denim dungarees he prowls the porch, blowing soulful blues melodies into the night. A half-empty bottle of bourbon rests by the door.

    "Howdy, fellow traveller," says the old man, slipping his harmonica into a chest pocket.

    "Ehhhhh…howdy, sir. Where am I?"

    "The question ain't where you are. The question is where you're goin', ain't that so?"

    "Could be. Beautiful night tonight, eh? I haven't seen a night this clear and starry in ages."

"I ain't seen anythin' in gone thirty years. You think I wear these glasses at night to look cool?" A closer inspection confirms that the old man's eyewear is the blacker-than-black shades of the blind man.

"You play a mean harmonica," I observe.

"Thank you kindly, son. You play a mean guitar."

"How do you know that? How *could* you know that?"

"My sight may have gone to Hell, but some things I see more clearly than ever. Play wit' me now."

"I'm not whackin' you off, if that's what you mean. I've had all I can take of you American perverts."

A childlike chortle makes the old man double over. "Play music wit' me – *music*. Git your guitar off yo' back and play. Whackin' off, indeed! Crazy son of a bagpipe! Heh heh!"

I unstrap my BC Rich from my back and wonder what musical common ground the old man and I could possibly have. He looks and sounds like an original bluesman, while I'm a dyed-in-the-wool metalhead. Much rock, however, is rooted in the blues, to the extent that some of it is merely repackaged and regurgitated blues with louder amplification.

The old man asks, "Are you familiar wit' the music of Robert Johnson?"

"I'm familiar wi' hearin' it, but no' playin' it."

"How about B.B. King?"

"The same applies."

"Damn, son, what blues *do* you know?"

"I can play a scorchin' *Mannish Boy* that blows the balls off the original."

"Muddy Waters – excellent! Don't git more bluesy than a bit o' Muddy. An' I'll decide if it blows the cojones off Muddy's version."

I have no leads or amplification, yet when I strum my Warlock's strings I'm nearly flattened by a wave of sound from the side wall of the rustic shack. "What kind o' magic is this?" I ask.

The old man cackles, "Blues magic, son! *Blues* magic!"

As we start to play together, I'm amazed by his ability to sing, dance, play harmonica and drink bourbon from the bottle, seemingly all at once. The bluesman tosses me a metal guitar slide, which I catch and place over my left ring finger: married to the blues. The slide bluesifies the Warlock's lacerating guitar tone, above which the sound of the harmonica is always audible; blues magic, indeed. We alternate on vocal duties, telepathically knowing whose turn it is, then join forces for the final chorus, the old man's deep drawl blending perfectly with my glass-shattering resonance.

As waves of sound flow from mystical amplification, I spin in circles, stamping on the ground to stir dust clouds up into the cool night air. Wooden boards creak and bend under the old man's jig while he blows lunatic melodies out of his harmonica. He may be an old, blind bluesman, but he prowls the night with the agility of a young wildcat. "Git up here an' give me some skin!" he hollers. "That was beautiful! Muddy himself would have pissed in his big ol' pants if he'd heard that!" I jump onto the porch and wrap the bluesman in an untamed embrace. "What you're lookin' for," he continues, "can only be found if you ride the drunken horse to the crossroads. Bluesmen bin' ridin' that horse to those crossroads forever, lookin' for...*Him*. But *He* never appeared. Tonight's the night, though. You gonna find what you bin' lookin' for."

"What am I lookin' for?"

"Don't mess wit' me, boy. We both know who you're lookin' for. When you git to the crossroads, *He* will find *you*."

"How will I know the drunken horse when I see it?"

"Son, if you don't know an inebriated equine when you see one, you got mo' problems than makin' it in music."

"Where will I find it?"

Looking up the starlit trail with unseeing black-visored eyes, the old bluesman points a finger. "Continue up there a ways an' he'll be around. If you're not sure that you've got the right horse, you could always smell his breath, or give him one of those newfangled breathalyser tests. Heh heh!"

"It was fun playin' blues wi' you...educational too."

"Yeah, you make a Helluva noise. Heh heh. Now git goin', kid. I'll see you in the funny papers."

Sniffing the fresh night air, I ramble up a trail flanked by overgrown fields. There are no signs of human habitation other than the old shack which, step by dusty step, recedes into darkness behind me.

A mile or so along the road, a saloon comes into view. It looks like something from the Wild West: two-way shutter doors, a hanging wooden sign, and a large brass spittoon on the ground outside. A huge black horse bursts through the swing doors and collapses on the road, spraying dust in all directions. A bearded man with tattooed forearms steps out wielding a length of wood. "And don't come back until you can pay your tab! I ain't subsidisin' no horse habit!" My instinct is to correct the barkeep's grammar, as his double negative implies that he is happy to subsidise the horse's drinking pursuits. Before I can speak, the man turns and storms back into the saloon.

I kneel beside the fallen equine. The horse's dark eyes are glassy and unfocusing. I stroke his snout, which is velvet-soft against my palms. Warm breath hisses from flaring nostrils, smelling like a mixture of freshly cut grass and cheap whisky. "Hey, beautiful boy," I whisper, "I've been told you're the only one who can take me where I want to go. Any chance of you gettin' up on your feet and takin' me to the crossroads?"

Nothing. A vacant stare. The non-response of the horse who just doesn't give a fuck.

"I need you. I don't know where I am or how I got here. What I do know is that you're my only way oot. Please, big boy, help me get to the crossroads." Foul breath blasts into my face. Glassy eyes see nothing. Not sleeping. Not dreaming. Comatose drunk.

The horse's mouth is filled by an improbable number of large, flat-edged teeth arranged in an inebriated grin. After yanking open his jaws, I uproot a handful of long grass and slide it down his throat. He snaps his mouth shut, narrowly missing my fast-retreating fingers. "If you bite me I will boot your horse balls!" Realising that such an attitude is a trifle inappropriate for someone seeking a favour, I soften my voice. "Let me rephrase that, you big, beautiful equine. I need my fingers for playin' guitar, so please don't bite them. I'm tryin' to do you a favour. It'd be criminal for such a fine horse to choke on his vomit just like Bon Scott, so let's get your stomach emptied and get you back to consciousness." Again I open his jaws and insert the long grass. This time a loud, ganting burp is followed by gagging and a stream of projectile puke. Neighing and snorting ensues, heralding the arrival of a second - more violent - spray of vomit.

The black horse clambers to unsteady feet, looking more co-ordinated but also more pissed off. Glaring at me, he stamps a front hoof on the ground and tosses his head around. With the appropriate amount of panic that imminent attack by a one-ton, pissed-off, pissed-drunk animal generates, I back up, but a fence impedes my progress. The old bluesman's voice echoes inside my head. *Ask and it shall be yours.* Closing my eyes, I scour my mind for what would calm an angry horse. Hoofclops approach. Again, the bluesman's voice. *Think, asshole – think!* A carrot appears in my mind's eye. At the same moment, my back pocket bulges. I pull the carrot from my pocket and extend it like a sword towards the charging black beast. He skids to a halt, his hot, post-puke breath foul enough to wither flowers. After regarding the carrot, sniffing it with some suspicion, and giving the vegetable a tentative lick, the horse rips it from my grip. A cacophony of crunching follows as the dark equine devours his snack. Afterwards, raising himself to his full towering height, he gazes down his nose at me. "Any chance o' you takin' me to the crossroads noo, my beautiful big friend? Please." He contemplates my request then nods his head once.

The horse is far too large to mount the way cowboys do in movies, so I climb onto a fencepost and from there jump onto the mighty equine's back, almost transgendering myself on landing. Whinnying wildly, my new friend plunges into the night, vaulting high fences, accelerating across fields and leaping wide streams as easily as I step over cracks in the pavement. Cold night air filters through my flapping hair. After miles of jumps and swerves, the dark beast slows to a trot at a desolate, nondescript crossroads with flat grassland on all sides.

After dismounting the wonderbeast, I whisper heartfelt thanks into his ear and stroke his muscular back. He responds by nuzzling his warm boozy snout into my neck. Then, rearing up onto hind legs, he traces mystical symbols in the air with his front hooves while his long mane paints irridescent patterns that hang in the surrounding darkness. At first I'm not sure what he's trying to communicate, but it soon becomes clear that the glowing mane-made shapes are sheet music in the air, and my friend's hoof movements are equine approximations of a man playing guitar. When I nod to indicate my understanding, the black horse plants his hooves back on the ground and gallops into the night like a greased bullet.

Chapter 76 – A Dangerous Meeting

BC Rich Warlock around my neck, I sit in the dirt at the crossroads and start to play. There is neither moonlight nor streetlight, but winking stars offer just enough illumination for me to crank out cosmic riffs without putting a finger wrong. As was the case at the old bluesman's shack, there is no need for cables or amplification here. The louder I will my guitar to sound, the louder it becomes. Looking up into infinity, I convert starlight into mystic fretboard patterns. My eerie melodies dance an ascent into the sky.

With a sound like rolling thunder, a dark stagecoach hauled by six white horses emerges out of the horizon. Upon reaching the crossroads, the carriage's wooden-spoked wheels skid to a halt. Feathered plumes on the horses' heads flutter in a gust of warm wind as the Devil unfolds from the stagecoach's interior and plops hair-covered hooves onto the ground. This Devil is no stranger to me: it has been waiting in the wings, stalking me, haunting my dreams, testing my sanity. When we tangoed in Cedar Key I came out victorious. I'm not feeling confident about the rematch, though.

Fire crackles in infernal eye sockets as the Beast reaches a taloned claw towards my guitar. I hide the instrument behind my back. "You're no' puttin' your foul mitts on my guitar. I know the old blues folklore – I play guitar at the crossroads, you appear, I hand you my instrument, you arse aboot wi' it and retune it in some fantastical way then hand it back to me, whereupon I receive the ability to play anythin'. I then achieve monumental musical success, but when the ride is over, you get my soul, isn't that right? Well, I don't believe that bullshit and I don't like your interest in my band."

The Devil sways to and fro, subtle movements like a tree bending in the breeze. Smoke curls from its sizzling torso as if the flesh were cooking before my eyes. Gazing down at me through bonfire eyes, the Hellcreature shrugs cannonball shoulders, but the gesture of innocence doesn't fool me. Baring teeth like rows of sharpened knives, the dark being extends a hair-backed claw in a gesture of friendship. "No hand-shakin' either," I spit. "I don't want your malevolent blessings."

"*Why did you summon me here, mortal?*" My skull vibrates from the inside as if the Beast's words were stars exploding in my head. Its hellish gaze burns into my eyes.

"My band was deid for too long. Deid, that is, everywhere except in my mind. I always kept that dream burnin' at a low simmer, but I couldn't revive the band withoot the other four members. Noo, after years in the wilderness, we're together again. Nothin' is goin' to fuck that up."

The Devil gnashes teeth like clashing swords. Its ribcage expands to full capacity as it sucks in night air. Between the ribs are gill-like fissures through which dancing red flames are visible, inhabiting - and perhaps animating – the otherworldly being. A creature of fire and flesh. *"Without me, little mortal, your band would be nothing more than a distant memory."*

"Your only part in my band's evolution was helpin' Pete to become a jibberin' recluse for years. You only hindered us, never helped."

"On the contrary, I am your only door to success."

"I returned to the motel in Cedar Key to find Pete upside doon in some sort o' Satanic crucifixion. Was that your idea of helpin' us?"

"Mortal, you have much to learn. The music you know as 'heavy metal' cannot succeed without my intervention."

"Eh?"

"There are many dimensions. Energy in each dimension stays mainly in that dimension, but there is some crossover. Success in heavy metal music requires very specific dark energy…energy which is born only in my dimension…in me. The exchange is always fair - my dark energy flows into chosen musicians, putting its infernal imprint on every track they create, but I receive their soul energy at the point of death. Haven't you heard it said that the Devil has all the best tunes?"

"Haven't you heard it said that when angels arrive, the Devil leaves?"

"What know you of angels?"

"More than you might imagine. I am one. For what are angels if not beings whose sole purpose is to carry oot the orders of their gods? And I prostrate myself before the Metal Gods, who channel their wishes through me, their earthly representative."

"Those false gods exist only in your head, testament to your lunacy. I own heavy metal. Your only route to success is through me. I am the Dark and the Way."

"Not for my band. The Metal Gods are primal forces of awe-inspiring power. You, on the other hand, are just some sort of infernal shylock, an otherworldly lender whom I trust as much as I trust earthly bankers, which is not at all, incidentally. You'll loan me a temporary flow of your dark energy, but you get the eternal payoff later, is that your proposal?"

"Exactly."

"Why have you been torturin' Pete for years? Why not the rest o' the band?"

"Some souls are tastier than others."

"You *eat* the fuckin' things?"

"I consume them and make their energy mine. Their brightness brings me closer to the light from which I was cast out so long ago. Pete Drummond's is a key soul. Quite literally. It is the key which can unlock my graceless dimension, forever freeing me."

"Are you sayin' that the biblical story of you bein' cast oot o' Heaven, a fallen angel eternally denied God's grace, is true?"

"That is a parable dreamt up by feeble-minded humans in an attempt to grasp what really happened. The creative forces in the Universe cast me into an empty dimension and took from me my ability to create. I was banished there aeons

ago, long before your planet and its sun began their cosmic rotations, my existence a frozen Hell separate from all light and love. Then, when I had forgotten all but the eternal agony of damnation, I heard a sound…a dark and malevolent noise which drew me to it like a flame to a moth."

"You mean a moth to a flame?"

"No, mortal – I am the flame, the eternal fire, while the music is fleeting like the moth. I heard the sound of the first amplified electric guitar. The thing you know as heavy metal would never have been born without my intervention. I channelled a flow of my dark energy through selected humans, who then filtered it through their souls and let it manifest itself as heavy metal music. Each individual who accepts my energy receives riches beyond his dreams, but I receive his eternal light. Have you never wondered why so many heavy metal album covers feature diabolic scenes? Often, the brightest souls are those most curious about the darkness."

"Pete would never give you his soul."

"When you interrupted me in Cedar Key, I was persuading him to do just that."

"Persuadin' my arse! You were torturin' him, ya horned prickheid!"

"Torture is an ugly word. I do not have the power to tear out a soul and make it my own. Souls have to be given willingly. I can, however, inflict such pain on mortals' bodies and minds that they pray for anything, even the lifeless void of Hell, just to make their pain cease."

"So you thought you'd inflict inconceivable pain on wee sensitive Pete until he condemned himself to oblivion?"

"Well, I am the Devil. What do you expect?"

"A wee bit of integrity would be good. And maybe…" My sentence is cut short by the Devil's interruption. *"Awaken, Spark. Get back on your true path. It isn't too late."* It's the same voice I heard while lying on a Bronzehall pavement with death's icy fingers around my throat. I stare into the bottomless fires of the Devil's eyes. "You? That was *you?* I thought it was a Higher Power…the Universe itself." Crushed, I drop to my knees in the dirt.

The Devil's eyes burn brighter, fuelled by my despair. *"That was me, yes. I sensed your death, just as I do when any heavy metal soul prepares to move on. As your essence ascended from your body, an opening to your dimension opened, which is what openings do best. These portals remain open only a short time. If I had let your soul continue on its journey, Pete Drummond would have remained out of my reach forever, so I used the intelligent strategy. I slammed your soul back into your body, offered some words of inspiration, and jump-started you with five blasts of my infernal energy. Not for nothing did Jesus say that he saw Satan fall like lightning from Heaven."*

"So you resurrected me as bait to draw Pete oot o' hidin'?"

"Guilty."

"How can you manipulate people's lives like that? How can you toy wi' oor dreams?"

"I brought you back to life and out of your slump, did I not? Prior to your death, your soul had been shrivelling for years. Now it blossoms like a wild flower. You should thank me."

"It blossoms because I rediscovered my belief in myself...in my band...in the possibility of transmutin' dreams into reality. I thought my message was numinous, from the Universe."

"Oh, how disappointing it must be to find out that your inspiration came from an infernal source."

My mind is adapting to this information like a computer rebooting after the installation of new software. "You did motivate me to re-form the band, but you did it for your benefit, not for oors, so by my calculations I owe you fuck all. My self-belief was always inside me somewhere. Your words helped me to rediscover my faith, but you didn't create that faith."

"You belittle my role in proceedings, mortal. I saved your soul. Have you no gratitude?"

"I do appreciate your infernal intervention, but I *hate* your reasons for doin' it. Please clarify somethin' for me. You said earlier that all successful metal musicians have made deals wi' you."

"Yes, with one exception."

"Who?"

"The mortal known as Philip Lynott. His was a gentle, poetic soul which I desired so strongly that I tortured him to near insanity. I inflicted constant pain on him in an effort to feast on his soul's succulence. He wouldn't crack, though. Instead, he found ways to numb the pain, ways that led to his ultimate demise."

"But Thin Lizzy sold millions of albums. They had success. Explain."

"As The Who sang, I can't explain, other than to say Lynott is the solitary exception to the rule. I smelled his soul's presence several times recently, always near your band. That is how I located Pete Drummond in Cedar Key. The appearance of Lynott's soul alerted me. Your pentalpha protection was out of range, so I chose to have my 'meeting' with Pete."

"Of course! Iain's drunken fall and bump on the heid. Lynott must have popped into his body again."

"I am impressed that you were able to dispel me before Pete's soul could be mine."

"So why heavy metal? What aboot pop, blues, techno, classical and other musical styles?"

"The energy exchange only happens with heavy metal. Other music has its own intrinsic energy, so it is not my domain."

"Who decides what's metal and what's not?"

"I suspect you already know the answer to that. You of all people know heavy metal when you hear it."

"Aye, fair enough, but what aboot punk?"

"Punk's three-chord excuses for musical compositions contain no darkness. Punk is a pseudo-aggressive realm for childish pretenders. Heavy metal is true. I did not make the rule, mortal. I merely adhere to it. Heavy metal is my loophole out of Hell. Who knows why light has properties of both a particle and a wave, yet is neither? Light itself does not question that paradox. Light simply is. The same is true of heavy metal."

"So why are you doin' this? Are you just a greedy, selfish prick wi' a sweet tooth for tasty souls?'

"There is much more to me than that. I do not have the power to travel to your dimension at will. My dark energy flows there constantly, but events such as the supernatural channelling practised by Iain Bright - and the moving of a heavy metal soul from life to its next plane of existence - have the power to transport my whole being into your dimension for a brief spell. Each soul I acquire increases my power. Once I have Pete Drummond's soul energy, I will burst out of my Hell. Then I will be able to devour souls at will, with or without their owners' consent. I will be able to create worlds, to forge my own reality, to bend the forces of this Universe to my will, to make it mine. You halted my plans. For now, anyway."

"What aboot Mötley Crüe? They sang *Shout at the Devil*, not shout wi' the Devil or make a deal wi' the Devil."

"True, mortal. They did shout at me. Do you want to know what they shouted?"

"Aye, please."

"They shouted, 'Please, Infernal King, give us beautiful women, tons of drugs, lakefuls of alcohol. Help us, Satanic Lord, to sell hundreds of millions of albums even when we can't remember our names. Finally, Dark One, allow us to be consumed by vice-addicted depravity until such time as our souls are consumed by your fire.' That's what those particular humans shouted. And I heard them, loud and clear." Red fires roar in endless eye sockets.

"Led Zeppelin?"

"Mine."

"Guns 'n' Roses?"

"Mine."

"AC/DC?"

"Mine. Bon Scott's soul was most tasty."

"Ya dirty bastard! I love Bon!"

"Perhaps you may meet him soon." The Devil rubs its muscular abdomen with a charred hand. A forked tongue flicks out and runs over the tips of pointed teeth, lacerating itself. Flames ooze from the wounds. After a deep inhalation, the Hellbeast blasts my chest with an inferno from its nostrils.

Expecting to see cooked flesh, I look down. The pentalpha on my torso is glowing white and spinning, the skin around it unaffected by the flames. Buoyed by the knowledge that the Devil can't harm a body that's under pentalpha protection, I growl, "Get back to Hell, hideous demonic spunkstain that you are! I'll see you in the Billboard charts."

"*As one human - whose soul is coming my way - once sang to great commercial success, dream on!*" The sneering Devil climbs back into the stagecoach. An arrow-hole on the infernal torso, *my* arrow-hole, has started to spew a cylinder of fire. The Beast slams its hands together, creating a peal of thunder. White horses snort back to life then drag stagecoach and unholy passenger into the black horizon.

Hands from nowhere shake my shoulders. I try to run, but they have me in their grip. Something covers my mouth and nose, but all I can see is the stagecoach blurring into the dark treeline.

My eyes open. People are huddled around me wearing concerned expressions. There's an oxygen mask fastened over my face. A tall brunette stewardess with a Slavic accent says, "Thank God. You had stopped breathing."

After a few deep lungfuls of oxygen, I remove the mask. "Thanks, miss. I was oot o' my body. Visitin'."

"Visiting?" She looks confused. "Like visiting a friend?"

"No' exactly a friend. An old enemy, to be precise."

Chapter 77 – Prodigal Son

The high fence around Blackness Castle would normally be an easy climb for me, but tonight, thanks to darkness and a delicate physical state, it represents a serious challenge. I could have phoned to inform the band of my freedom and imminent arrival. They like surprises, though, and this should be the mother of all surprises.

Using two small pillows which I liberated from the plane, I cover my hands and pull myself up onto the the fence's sharp spikes. The points dig into my palms, which to my relief remain unimpaled; impalation of one body part per day is quite enough, a sentiment with which my arse would agree. After achieving a state of precarious balance atop the fence, I flip forwards and land with a dull thud on the other side.

Angling my face up to the weeping sky, I enjoy a refreshing shower of baptismal Scottish rain. The window nearest the castle door is open, so I sneak across the gardens and peek in. Ozzy is sitting fireside with Sunshower on his knee. The others are nowhere in sight. I take off my Pink Stëël baseball shirt and hold the *RIFFS* side up to the window. Shaking the shirt around in my best approximation of a headless spectre, I shout, in my best Scooby-Doo-ghost voice, "Woo-woo-ooo-ooo-ooo!"

"Daddy, look over there! It's a headless Spark!"

"Stay here, Sunshower! That heidless Spark's more supernatural weirdness! I'll set the dogs loose!"

The massive front door creaks open and Saxon bounds outside, barking loudly enough to wake the dead. He knocks me onto my aching arse then covers my face in slobber, his golden tail whipping the air. Ronald MacLeod's two dobermans, Dunvegan and Harris, hang back and watch the inter-species loving with pricked-up ears and unconvinced expressions.

Ozzy's face appears at the open window. "Agh! Evil spirit, doppelgänger, begone from here!"

"It's me…Spark!" Squeezing my head between strong front paws, Saxon continues to submerge me in a sea of saliva. Dunvegan and Harris, following Saxon's lead, wash my arms with tentative licks.

"Spark's in America," booms Oz, "in a cell! This is more infernal mumbo-jumbo! Leave my daughter and me alone!"

"Oz, it's really me," I splutter. "The charges were dropped. I wanted to surprise you."

"If you're really Spark, answer this question – when I had the loft bedroom, what did I used to wank into?"

"How many times do I have to ask you no' to end a sentence wi' a preposition? If you're askin' me 'into what did you wank?' then the answer is pretty much everythin' at one point or another, but your favourite receptacle was always the trusty sports sock."

"It is you, Spark, ya grammatically anal prick!" Oz vanishes from view and reappears through the front door. He lifts Saxon off me as easily as I'd lift a chihuahua, then pulls me to my feet and wraps me in a bear hug. The whip wounds on my chest smart under the pressure, but the giant's energy is healing, so I grit my teeth and endure the pain. When I enter the main hall, Sunshower launches herself at me. I catch the little projectile in mid-air and cuddle her. More pain, more healing.

As Saxon runs circles around the main hall, howling like a dog possessed, DT emerges from an upstairs room dressed in moccasin slippers, black satin pyjama trousers and a burgundy smoking jacket, a lit cigar jutting from his mouth. "Shut up, Saxon," he hollers, "we're tryin' to write songs up here!"

"What do you mean *tryin'*, Hugh Hefner?" I ask. "I obviously arrived in the nick o' time. You need help from a professional, as does your wardrobe."

"Spark? *Spark? Spark!*" DT disappears back into the room from which he came and re-emerges moments later followed by Pete, Paul, Iain and Colin. They thunder down the stairs and envelop me in a quarrel of flailing arms and excited bodies. Sunshower bounces up and down on one of Ronald MacLeod's priceless antique sofas while Saxon busies himself chasing his tail in front of a peat fire. In Blackness Castle, wrapped in love, I feel whole again.

"Who's comin' to my Mum's hoose wi' me?" I ask. "I have to pick up Fluff. I can't face one more day away from my wee rabbit."

Bouncing higher, Sunshower shouts, "Me, me, me, me!"

"No," grunts Oz, "it's past your bedtime, little girl."

"Let her come," I plead. "I know it's late, but she's too excited to sleep anyway."

"Aye, thanks to you."

Looking into the deep blue of Ozzy's eyes, I smile at my giant blood brother. "It'll take three hours tops. She can sleep late tomorrow."

"OK," he submits, "you can go, Sunshower. And Spark, I don't need to tell you to drive carefully wi' my wee girl."

"Don't worry. She's more precious to me than the air I breathe. By the way, what did you tell my Mum aboot my extended stay in America? What sort of explainin' will I have to do?" Gazes dart around the room in spastic motions, looking everywhere but at me. "DT, look me in the eyes and tell me what you told my Mum!"

Dave sweeps long hair off his face, holding it in a makeshift ponytail as he turns to me. "Your Mum believes that you were held in America indefinitely under the Prevention of Terrorism Act."

"What? You told my Mum I was a terrorist?"

"Not true at all, man. We told her you were a *suspected* terrorist!"

"Oh, that subtle distinction will make all the difference! How can I face her noo?"

"Would you rather we'd told her the truth? *'Hello, Mrs MacDubh, it's aboot Spark. He's been arrested in Florida for dressin' in a KKK robe, breakin' into a hoose, violently assaultin' the voluminous African-American resident, rapin' her in both the gash and the dirt chute, then - as a finishin' touch – shittin' on her. He's in a holdin' cell in Orlando and may be executed by lethal injection. On the bright side, the band had a great tour.'* Does that sound better?" He cocks an eyebrow.

"Well, I admit that the terrorist story is preferable to that. Couldn't you just have said that I got nicked for speedin'? Or punchin' fuck oot of a security guard who was beatin' up one of oor fans at a gig?"

"Spark," says DT, "we had a band vote, includin' Paul and Archibald. We voted terrorism as the thing you'd most likely be busted for."

"You mean 'for which I'd most likely be busted'. Prepositions, remember."

"You know what I didn't miss when you were locked up? Or rather, when up you were locked? Your perpetual pedantic grammatical criticisms. So as I was sayin', we reckoned you'd most likely be detained for terrorist activities."

"How did you arrive at that conclusion?"

"Och, look at you. Vegetarian diet. Zen meditation. Exercise daily. Wash infrequently. You're exactly the bean-eatin', rabbit-lovin' personality type to get sucked into an animal-worshippin' bomb cult who'd blow up some vivisection lab after liberatin' all the cute furry animals. So there it is - you were a terror suspect."

"Thanks anyway, I suppose. I'll tell my Mum the American police made a horrible mistake."

"So, Spark," frowns Pete, "you were an imprisoned cat and now you're a free feline. How did that happen? We all thought you were locked up for life."

"I eventually got my one phone call, so I phoned Shaquanna, who gave a statement explainin' things. Once Maya Devoe found oot I'd made an innocent mistake, she dropped the charges."

Rubbing his chin and squinting, DT asks, "Just like that? It sounds too good to be true."

I hesitate for a moment, thinking of the pummelling my arse took earlier. "Ehm…well, Maya received a message at church. Apparently, God told her that I was to be forgiven."

"It's great to have you back," grins Oz. "We were startin' to wonder if we were wastin' oor time wi' the album."

"Aye," agrees Dave, "workin' on it every day was startin' to feel like an enjoyable but ultimately unsatisfyin' exercise…like fuckin' a delicious wee minx who's just on the right side of jailbait, but not gettin' to cum."

I smile at my partner-in-crime. "Well, dude, I'm back and I'm celibate. Sex equals trouble. I've been thinkin' aboot all the energy I've wasted daydreamin' aboot pussy, whackin' off into all manner of weird receptacles, and desecratin' women's bodies. If I'd put all that energy into writin' and recordin' music, we'd have aboot twenty albums under oor belts, plus Maya Devoe wouldn't have been rudely awakened by a cracka with a hard-on and a Klan hood. As of noo, I'm all aboot the music, all aboot you, my metal brothers."

With a self-congratulatory beam, Paul announces, "I've been celibate since the Polyfilla incident."

"Aye," I nod, "but I'm celibate by choice. Your celibacy, on the other hand, is the choice o' the female gender. Women don't know what you'll try to shove up them."

Sunshower tugs on the leg of my black jeans. "Spark, let's go and see Fluff the rabbit!" She clamps little arms round my neck as I whisk her off the ground.

"Get your lazy arses back to work," I command. "I want all your musical contributions ready by the time this little beauty and I get back. I have Earth-shatterin' riffs and vocals to layer over your transcendent sonic landscapes." With that, Sunshower and I breeze through the castle's arched doorway and into the cold, wet night.

Chapter 78 – Mother

My mother is standing at her front door, hands on hips, ready for battle. "Is this how I raised you? To be a terrorist?"

"Mum, I wouldn't have been let oot of America if I was guilty of anythin'."

"That Sunday school you went to as a wee boy – that was a good Sunday school, wasn't it?"

"Aye, they were nice people."

"Well, did anyone there ever mention blowing things up? Were they grooming you as a religious bomber, son?"

"No, Mum. Like I said, they were nice people."

"Well, something smells fishy. I spoke to Mrs Roberts yesterday. She'd been over at Paul's hoose doing his washing…how bad is that? The boy's in his thirties and supposed to be your band's manager, yet he still has his mother washing his clothes…so anyway, where was I? Oh aye, Paul's answerphone was flashing when she arrived, so she checked his messages. There was one from the owner of a motel in Florida. He said that someone in Paul's party had blown up his motel and that the incident had been reported to the police and the media. Apparently, the explosion happened in the room allocated to you and Pete Drummond."

"It's a long, weird story, ma. All you need to know is that I didn't blow the hole in the motel."

"Was it your room?"

"Aye, but it was nothin' to do wi' me."

"Look me in the eyes and tell me that, son."

I look through my mother's glasses and into her cerulean eyes. "It was nothin' to do…ehm…well it was technically *somethin'* to do wi' me, but the explosion wasn't caused by me. I was there, that's all."

"So you *were* something to do with it, after all! I remember seeing in your *Kerrang!* and *Metal Hammer* magazines years ago that heavy metal bands in Norway and Sweden were burning doon churches. I hope your band isn't trying to carve a niche for itself by blowing up historic hotels. Believe me, son, that's not a good Unique Selling Point. You'd be better concentrating on the music."

"Mum, you're missin' the point in a big way. Firstly, those church burnings were done as a rebellion against Christianity, which had violently driven oot the indigenous beliefs and faith inherent to Scandinavia. Those countries used to have rich Viking beliefs and their own array of gods…"

"Aye, and I remember you and Iain sitting on the sofa reading aboot the church burnings, saying that you understood those black-metal arsonists' reasons for doing it…that you even *empathised* with them!"

"The Christians stomped in there to eradicate every trace o' the ancient, cherished beliefs while promisin' eternal fiery torment in Hell to anyone who didn't accept their new ways. Christianity crushed the old religion by destroyin' its buildings of worship and then erectin' churches on the same sites, thus establishin' physical and symbolic domination over the old faith. The church burnings in Scandinavia were merely retribution by modern followers of old Viking deities. Bearing the psychic scars of the old wounds, they decided to honour their arcane gods by razin' the Christians' so-called holy buildings to the ground. This sent the Christian peace-and-love-preachin' hypocrites a clear message that their deity has no place in Scandinavia. Trust me, Mum - I know this subject inside oot."

"I know, son. I've seen your album covers."

"We're driftin' way off the point. What I'm aboot to tell you is between you, me and Sunshower, OK?"

Seemingly for the first time tonight, my mother notices the little girl who is gripping my hand and smiling. "Hello, wee girl," she gushes. "Your hair is beautiful! How are you enjoying your time at the castle?"

"It's great, especially since Spark got back! He's my best friend! He sings to me whenever I want, you know."

"Aye, he's a good boy."

Shaking my head in bafflement, I ask, "May I finish my story? I arrived at the motel in Cedar Key to find Pete bein' tortured by somethin' infernal."

"Terrorists?"

"There were no terrorists! Will you get terrorists oot o' your heid! Something not o' this world had Pete suspended in an inverted mockery of Jesus's crucifixion. Pete's heid was in flames as he burned like an upside-doon candle. I phoned a Wiccan priestess friend whose knowledge helped me to save Pete. I sent the Devil back to Hell, but the Beast didn't go quietly. It went oot wi' a boom. A big boom."

A long silence follows, during which my Mum looks deep into my eyes, into my soul, for the slightest hint of a lie. Eventually she nods, then turns and heads into the kitchen, asking, "Tea and biscuits, everyone?" Before Sunshower or I can answer, my mother adds, "It's nearly midnight, Spark. Don't you think it's a bit late to have a wee girl like that oot galavanting?"

"One thing this wee girl definitely doesn't need is beauty sleep," I reply. "Just look at her. Any more beauty sleep and she'll blind us with her gorgeousness!" I throw Sunshower into the air and catch her as she falls back to Earth. She pinches my cheeks and shoogles them, forcing comical noises from my mouth. We both crack up laughing.

"Aye, well you're both aboot the same mental age," observes my mother. "I suppose the occasional late night won't do a child any harm."

Sunshower helps my Mum to prepare our snacks while I give Fluff long-overdue affection. After tucking into savoury biscuits with cheese, a dozen Tunnock's teacakes, homemade rhubarb crumble and a pot of tea, Sunshower and I thank my mother, then give her hugs and kisses. Outside, low-slung clouds are emptying themselves like giant sponges squeezed by a celestial hand. I pick up Fluff's pet carrier and race Sunshower to Dave's

Porsche, which I 'borrowed' for tonight's trip. In the car, in contrast to the dreich Bronzehall weather, David Lee Roth's voice is sonic sunshine. Driving eastwards into a dark deluge, I sing along with Diamond Dave, smiling as I change his words:

"Well east coast girls are hot,
I really dig the flesh they bare.
And big southern girls with holy punishment
do God's dirty work when I'm down there.

The mid-west metal groupies
really make me feel alright.
And fat northern girls with two-ton tummies,
warm Transcend Everything at night.

I wish they all could be Sunshower,
I wish they all could be Sunshower,
I wish they all could be Sunshower girls!

The west coast's sunshine blazes
and half-naked girls get tanned.
I snap off French bikinis on Hawai'i island,
exposin' bare boobs on the sand.

I've riffed all round this great big world
and I've spanked all kinds of girls.
Yeah, but I couldn't wait to get back to Blackness,
back to the cutest girl in the world.

I wish they all could be Sunshower,
I wish they all could be Sunshower,
I wish they all could be Sunshower girls!"

My little passenger is in floods of laughter, curls of copper hair hiding her face as she slaps tiny denim-clad thighs. Into the darkness we plunge, insulated in our silver bubble of warmth and love.

Chapter 79 – Wings of a Dream

The weeks in Blackness Castle sail past. Ronald MacLeod calls to ask if we would mind castle-sitting for an additional month, as he plans to visit Peru and Ecuador after leaving Japan. We grab the opportunity without a second thought. Iain takes the radical step of telling his boss that he has checked into a secluded and exclusive Scottish mental-health resort, a yarn that isn't far off the mark. To the chagrin of Wytchcoomb's population, Ozzy's bakery business is on indefinite hold. Ever supportive of our band, DT's father continues to run the family business. Archibald pops in every few days for first-hand updates on the album. His stories of our tour have found their way, along with pictures and videos fit for general publication, onto Internet music blogs and into UK metal magazines. Each article advises Metaltown to make way for a new sheriff by the name of Transcend Everything.

  The band, Paul, Sunshower, Colin, Lisa, Saxon, Fluff and the two dobermans, Dunvegan and Harris, have become like a single organism inside the secure stronghold of our ancient fortress. Each of us has a key role and several minor roles. I'm vocalist, guitarist, lyricist, composer, coffee maker, dog walker, babysitter for Sunshower (although I often think she's the most grown-up soul in the castle) and companion to Fluff. Ozzy is thunderous drummer, father figure (to the band, not just to Sunshower), cook, baker and Thor's hammer when an argument shows signs of starting. DT is lead guitarist, backing vocalist, composer, hairstylist, dishwasher, heavy metal fashion adviser and business brain. Pete is keyboard player, lyricist, composer, Marlboro smoker, unintentional comedian and all-round sensitive soul. Iain is rumbling bass monster, master of the peat fires, pasta chef and tantrum-throwing hothead. Colin is producer, drum technician, mixer, musical adviser and wise old guru with endless entertaining stories of a life in music. Paul has stepped into the role stated on the back of his Pink Stëel baseball shirt: the decision maker. He views Transcend Everything as a celestial ship which he will never own but must steer towards the brightest stars. (His girlfriend Janine disappeared with dog Yoshimax and child Montrose, but not before torching the flat Paul had bought and decorated.) Lisa is breakfast maker, laundry expert, lover to Pete, and unwitting tease to the rest of the male fraternity (she tries to make love quietly, but we have all heard her ecstatic moans pouring out of Pete's room at night). Saxon's boundless energy appears to be infesting everyone around him. Fluff's affection keeps me on an even keel. Dunvegan and Harris, once protectors of the fortress, have accepted the gigantic Saxon as alpha male. The dobermans, enjoying their newfound loss of responsibility, are becoming more playful by the day. And Sunshower…well, there's only one word to describe her: *bliss*.

The tracks we record are:

1. *These Are the New Riffs* (the opening track on the album, and favourite for the first single);
2. *Blue-Bridge Duel* (a revamped version of the old Blood Brothers track about Pete's fateful night);
3. *Little Evils for the Greater Good*;
4. *Aff-the-Stot Tin* (old Scots for 'out-of-tune song');
5. *Orange Donger of Doom* (Ozzy's mighty song, and live favourite);
6. *Ignited Souls*;
7. *Synaesthesia* (a Pete Drummond keyboard instrumental);
8. *Our Lady of Sporadic Chastity*;
9. *Witch* (which I wrote as a tribute to Rosie);
10. *The Black Isle of Mourning*;
11. *Poets & Prophets*;
12. *Sharks in Seals' Clothing*;
13. *Tripping the Dark Fantastic* ;
14. *Sunshower, Moonflower*;
15. *Skygazing* (the sweeping melodies penned on Parisienne streets by Ted, and given to us as a gift);
16. *The Weight of a Thought*;
17. *The Hauntie* (a poem DT and I wrote decades ago, recently set to music by Pete).

Seventeen tracks and not a filler in sight.

In two cases – *The Hauntie* and *Sunshower, Moonflower* – lyrics were written first and music wrapped around them afterwards, like adding muscle and flesh to skeletons hungry for movement. On the latter track, Sunshower sings evocative backing vocals with a heavenly voice.

The band works in a shift pattern: the rhythm section records by day; when others sleep at night, the nocturnal animals – DT and I - come out to play; Pete prefers to work alone, as he claims that solitude brings out his genius. When Pete finds an old set of Uillean pipes in a cupboard of MacLeod's music room, Colin surprises us all by playing heart-wrenching music on them. As a result, Colin's haunting pipe melodies grace seven of the album's tracks. A perennial source of wisdom, Colin hones our rougher tracks into polished beasts, then adds layer upon layer of harmonic complexity to the songs.

We haven't signed a record deal yet, but thanks to our live performances - along with Paul's tireless radio appearances and PR work during our US tour - three major labels and a host of smaller independent labels have expressed an interest in signing Transcend Everything. Paul, meanwhile, is pitting record labels against each other in an attempt to haggle the largest possible advance fee for the album.

As Colin and I complete the album's final recording session, Iain and Pete enjoy an afternoon's relaxation away from the castle. On his return, a beaming Iain asks, "Guess who Pete and I met in an Edinburgh tearoom today?"

"Jimi Hendrix."

"You're an arsehole, Spark," he informs me, not for the first time. "We met Gillian."

"Gillian Kelsey?"

"Aye and no."

"It's one or the other. Aye or no?"

"Well she *was* Gillian Kelsey, but she *is* Gillian McSweeney. She's married to your old pal George, who was wi' her today. A year ago, she moved back to Bronzehall and bumped into him. He asked us to thank you for breakin' the ice between him and Gill."

"Breakin' the ice? I sent him to ask Gillian oot for me!"

"Accordin' to him, he spent so much time deliverin' written and spoken messages to her on your behalf that he fell in love wi' her. He decided to cut oot the middle man this time and go oot wi' her himself."

"How's that cuttin' oot the middle man? He *was* the middle man. That robbin' bastard stole her from me."

"Firstly," says Iain, "he can't steal somethin' from you unless you possess it. Secondly, you're professin' celibacy noo, so what does it matter who's rattlin' the spectacular Gillian?"

"True on both counts, I suppose. Did they look happy?"

"Blissfully. She's six months pregnant, which confirms that George has done what you couldn't – the lucky fucker has had sex wi' her."

"What do you mean I *couldn't* have sex wi' her? You make it sound like I had a tadger malfunction. She wasn't ready for sex wi' me. That's why it didn't happen."

"Oh aye, it's like that is it? Such is the mighty Spark tadger that women need years to psyche themselves up for receivin' it?"

Ignoring Iain, I turn to Pete. "Well, I'm sworn off sex anyway, so good for George. Good for both o' them."

Pete scratches his chin and raises a blonde eyebrow. "So if Gill had been alone and horny, and had begged us to bring her back here to be ransacked and plundered by the Spark cat in one of his Viking rampages, you'd have declined due to your celibacy?"

"Aye. My mind has to stay pure."

Digging Iain in the ribs with an elbow, Pete rolls his eyes. The unbelievers crack up laughing.

Colin calls a band meeting in MacLeod's music room, which - due to its flawless acoustics - was the natural choice for use as our studio. He walks to the centre of the room and announces, "I saw something today that shook me to the bone."

"Fuck, man," says DT, "quit the melodrama. Just tell us."

"Very well," continues Colin, "although I don't think you're mentally prepared for this." He delves into a worn leather briefcase, pulls out a magazine and tosses the colourful publication onto the centre of the coffee table, where it sits, surrounded by ceramic mugs and crimson candles, like an object of worship at an ancient ritual. It's a magazine I don't habitually buy, but one which is perhaps the most influential music publication of all time. The cover of *Rolling Stone* magazine features a photo of DT and me onstage at Coconut Grove Convention Center: we're sharing a microphone stand, our guitar necks bisecting each other like crossed swords; Dave's long black hair looks shiny enough to be gracing the front cover of *She* or *Cosmopolitan*; the carved crimson pentalpha on my bare torso hovers above the greens and blues of my MacDubh tartan kilt. The bold-lettered headline boasts, **'Transcend Everything – So Good You'll Cum in Your Pants!'** Underneath, smaller text reads, 'Buck Fosterman Speaks to Heavy Metal's Rising Stars'.

Comprehension takes a while to set in. At first, I think that it must be a prank, perhaps one of the novelty front covers that can be bought at photo stores. Colin, however, is not a practical joker: he's all business. The only sound in the room is the delicate flutter of candleflames. Breath is held, as if breathing may shatter the beautiful illusion. The silence is finally broken by the dungaree-clad Ozzy jumping to his feet and booming, "That's what I'm talkin' aboot, ya bass!" After dishing out high-fives that almost rip arms out of sockets, Oz picks up bodies in crushing celebratory bear hugs.

DT unties his mane and shakes his hair loose before punching the air. "It was my keyboard melodies that Buck was writin' aboot," moans Pete, "yet these two limelight-stealin' twats end up gracin' the front cover. Where's the fairness in that? I knew it – I'm destined always to be the unsung hero."

DT pins Pete to the sofa and kisses his cheek. "Aye, you're oor wee hero and we love you! You're just not pretty enough for the cover o' *Rolling Stone*." Running fingers through his hair, DT pouts like Udo. In the worst mock-German accent ever attempted, he preens, "Ich bin ein sexy beetch. Look at mein sexy mänliness. Girls just vant to touch mein höt bödy." He plants a second kiss on Pete, this time square on the lips. Pete's frown dissolves as he lets out a howl then laughs out of control.

I head downstairs to make more coffee for us all. When I return with a silver tray of beverages, the room has quietened. The excitement is palpable. Taking his place in the centre of the room and pointing a finger skywards, Colin announces, "This is just the beginning, and what a beginning! You're all standing at the fork in the road. You have it all to gain…or all to lose. It's up to you. Record companies will fight over you. In fact, those greed-driven fuckers will go to *war* over you. *Poets & Prophets* is, I think, the most impressive album ever recorded. It is an honour to be your producer, mixer and Uillean piper. Taking the sonic diamonds we've created, I will polish them until they're at their full blinding potential. Paul will be at the strategic helm, steering your course through the choppy, shark-infested waters of the music business. We must be a team, a well-oiled machine. It is, my young friends, oot there for the taking!"

Chapter 80 – Warriors of the World United

On the same day that Colin finishes mastering *Poets & Prophets*, Transcend Everything and Nordic church-burners Ramrod Romance play an impromptu gig in Edinburgh. After reading the *Rolling Stone* article and wondering if we'd fancy playing as joint headliners with them at Edinburgh Playhouse, Ramrod Romance contacted the editor of *Rolling Stone*, who contacted Buck, who contacted Paul, who proposed the idea to us. To a man, we jumped at the chance. I often played Ramrod Romance's crushingly heavy *Seeing Through the Eye of Oden* album on the Pink Stëël tour bus, so my band brothers are already converts to the Vikings' cause.

The gig goes like a dream. After a visceral show by Ramrod Romance, a fired-up Transcend Everything blows the roof off the place. Literally. When Ramrod Romance's long-bearded vocalist Johan Tresverd joins us onstage for our last track, a wall-shaking cover of Type O Negative's *Christian Woman*, chunks of cement fall from the ceiling, smashing holes in the wooden stage but miraculously missing our heads. Amid the masonry shower, Johan and I share a mic stand and roar the mantra, "Jesus Christ looks like me. Jesus Chri-i-i-i-st." The irony of the situation hits me: Johan and I - with our pale skins and blue eyes – don't look much like the historical Christ with his bronzed skin and dark eyes. It's likely, though, that Jesus did have long hair and a beard, so between Johan's mass of facial hair and my wavy locks, which hang to mid-thigh, we have at least something in common with the crucified Nazarene. Standing face to face with Johan, I notice that his eyes resemble Earth from space. Cosmic oneness fills me. I feel a connected unity with my Norwegian friend, with our planet, with the whole Universe.

After the performance, bands and entourages head back to Blackness Castle for the night. The Vikings love the place. Johan points out that it is exactly like descriptions of Valhalla's Great Hall, to which valiant warriors slain in battle are carried by winged Valkyries. Gallons of ale are supped. While decimating a tray of Ozzy's baking, Johan suggests that Oz is a good enough baker to do it professionally. From across a wide wooden table, Oz flashes me a grin.

An arm-wrestling tournament ensues. The Norwegians claim that their berserker heritage will see them victorious. Ozzy steams through the qualifying rounds, winning easily but being careful to do so without smashing his opponents' arms through MacLeod's antique dining-room table. The qualifiers for the final are a very drunk Johan and a stone-cold-sober Oz. Johan's bandmates paint Viking runes on his face then chant battle cries to psyche up their frontman for battle. Colin counts down, "Three, two, one…wrestle!" In the blink of an eye, Ozzy slams Johan's arm into the ancient table with such force that the stone floor shakes beneath the sticksman's victory.

Tugging his beard, Johan shouts, "It must be the ale! Your Scottish ale has made me weak!"

"Aye, it's probably just the ale," smiles Oz, flexing a giant bicep.

DT brings a box of Honduran cigars into the main hall, where, in front of a peat fire, we take unhurried puffs of the smooth stoges. When Sunshower climbs onto my knee, I start to blow my smoke high into the air, away from the delicate lungs of my wee pal. The flow of conversation is easy and natural. I'm stunned by the Vikings' command of the English language. External appearances can indeed be deceptive: Ramrod Romance - with their abundance of hair and runic tattoos - look like fearsome berserkers, yet they are incisively intelligent souls with a genuine love of their Scandinavian deities. "You have made us feel very much at home in your castle fit for a king…even a Viking!" announces Johan. "Thank you, hairy Scotsmen. We declare you all honorary Vikings."

"Fuckin' excellent," replies DT. "A few weeks ago we were made honorary homosexuals. Noo we're honorary Vikings too. Does that mean we have carte blanche to rape and pillage the male bumholes of the world?" Laughter echoes around the great hall. As the peat fire dies down to glowing embers, cigars burn down to stumps. Fierce handshakes are exchanged, then hairy metal warriors retire to bed for the night.

The following day, Ramrod Romance and crew stagger onto their bus and rumble away from Blackness Castle. In search of the best record deal, Colin and Paul fly out to Los Angeles to meet record-label executives. Colin has in his possession the master copy of *Poets & Prophets*. From opener *These Are the New Riffs* through to the last slicing riff of *The Hauntie*, band and entourage agree that *Poets & Prophets* is a masterpiece.

Chapter 81 – Black Embrace

A wailed lament rouses me from a restful sleep. I run towards the sound and find Oz doubled over in convulsions at the top of the main hall's staircase. "Sunshower's gone!"

My body hair pricks to attention. "Gone oot o' the castle?"

"Deid."

"She can't be deid!"

Ozzy fixes me with a glare that would freeze worlds. "I'm no' an idiot, Spark. She's cold…her wee body's freezin' and she's no' breathin'."

Leaving Oz, I sprint barefoot along the cold stone corridor, past coats of arms and looming paintings of MacLeod's ancestors. My heartbeat booms in my ears. Sunshower is in a four-poster bed, her spiral masses of hair strewn over a white silk pillow. Her skin is the greyish blue of winter dawn. Silver teartrails are frozen on her delicate cheeks. Overcome by defeat and despair and derailment of my soul, I touch her face with trembling fingertips. A wave of unearthly cold rushes up my arm. Energy bails out of my body as I collapse onto the bed beside my tiny friend. My words are barely whispers. "Wee girl, you were my symbol of light, my muse, my innocent world, my mirror of truth. In you I saw the way." A tear drips from my eye and lands on Sunshower's lips. A spark zaps from her mouth to my third eye, flashing a vision into my mind: my little friend's delicate soul is not in blissful reunion with her mother's, but is drowning in currents of eternal torment. My beautiful wee muse has been damned.

I lean forward and kiss Sunshower's frozen cheek. Energy spirals up my spine, ripping through the top of my head. Kundalini the serpent has been awakened, and He is not happy. His power diffuses from my spine into every particle of my being, driving me to my feet, to action, to run. As I reach the wailing Ozzy - who is being consoled by DT, Pete and Lisa - electricity starts to arc from my eyes into the surrounding air. A bolt of blue plasma blasts Lisa off her feet. "Somebody call Rosie and put it on speakerphone! I'm conductin' like a bastard here. If I touch a phone, it'll short oot."

Ozzy dials Rosie's number on his mobile. After four rings, she answers sounding woozy.

"Rosie, it's Spark."

"It's the middle of the night, Scotsman."

"I'm sorry for wakin' you, but it couldn't wait. Sunshower's showin' no signs o' life."

With a voice like winter wind curving round the bare branches of trees, Rosie whispers, "Do you think the Devil is involved?"

"I *know* it. And I know what I want to do aboot it. If that unholy fuck can enter oor dimension for short periods, it must be possible for me to enter Hell for a visit."

"There is no more dangerous undertaking. When your soul travels out of your body, it stays connected by an invisibly fine rope like an astral umbilical cord. If you open a portal to the Dark One's dimension and then send your soul through the gateway, your soul and body will remain connected by that cord. If the portal snaps shut while you are out of your body, however, it will sever the cord, killing your corporeal body and forever trapping your soul in the other realm."

"I need to go to Hell, Rosie. This Devil's been on my ball-bootin' list for a long time. Noo the Beast's got Sunshower's soul. I can't let that slide."

"I wish you well, Scotsman. I doubt I will ever speak to you again, but I will always hold dear memories of you. Once you enter that dark dimension, you are beyond earthly help. Blessed be."

I instruct DT to run downstairs and bring me the biggest, sharpest knife he can find. He bounds down the stone staircase and returns with a serrated-bladed knife. On its bone handle is an intricate carving of the MacLeod clan crest: a bull's head flanked by two flags, and between them the motto *Hold Fast*. "Lay it doon on the deck," I command. DT tosses the knife. It clatters onto the stone floor by my feet. I pick it up and stab its tip into my chest, then recarve the pentalpha, incising fresh lines into old scars. Blood isn't the only thing that leaks from the cuts: when the carving is complete, blue plasma flashes out of my body, burning pentalphas into the walls. Arcane symbols, ancient stone.

"Spark, what lunacy's happenin' in your heid?" sobs Oz. "My wee Sunshower's deid. You can't bring her back...nothin' can!"

"Ozzy, my big pal, have I ever let you doon? *Ever?*"

"No," whispers the big man, "you never have."

"And I never will."

Staring into space, Oz nods. Guided by the sound of Iain's snoring, which could be mistaken for the roars of an angry lion, I sprint to his bedroom and lift a heavy bronze shield off the wall, holding it high above Iain's head as I say an impassioned prayer. "Phil Lynott, you opened Hellportals all over America. Please do it here in Blackness. Iain, ol' friend, if we ever needed your help we need it noo. I apologise in advance if I pan your thick, stubborn heid right in, although I reckon that's unlikely borderin' on impossible. I love you." A loud pang echoes around the castle as I slam the shield into Iain's sleeping head. Then the shapeshifting begins. Ozzy and DT watch from a safe distance, furrows of concern ploughed into their brows.

I send the Metal Gods a psychic request for their last-minute advice, but now – when I need them most – they are silent. Perhaps the Devil was telling the truth. Maybe the Metal Gods really do exist only in my mind. Or maybe, if the Beast does rule over heavy metal, the Metal Gods whose voices I used to hear are merely minions of the Devil, coaxing and seducing chosen souls into Oblivion. With no voices, celestial or infernal, resounding in my head, I realise that it's time to take sole responsibility for my all-or-nothing course.

As Phil Lynott takes shape on Iain's bed, my friends stare not at the changeling, but at me. "Have faith," I tell them. "I'm goin' to Hell. I've always been headed that way. The Devil thinks he can breeze into oor country, oor Scotland, and steal Sunshower's beautiful soul. Well, there's acceptable devilry and then there's takin' the piss. This time the horned cunt's gone too far. I'm off to pick a fight wi' the bastard in his own backyard." Summoning every ounce of my strength, I smash the heavy bronze shield into my head.

Then, blackness in Blackness.

Chapter 82 – Cold Day in Hell

I'm hovering above my body, which is motionless on the stone castle floor. Iain's therianthropic change into Phil Lynott continues. Limbs snap and reset in jerky movements. Black hair bursts through darkening skin. A look of dark clarity washes over DT's face, his features morphing into a mass of hardened, non-Euclidean angles. He whispers something into Ozzy's ear. They flee the room.

When Iain's transformation is complete, an archway of smooth ice rises from the floor, growing until its apex touches the high ceiling. Deep inside the ice are symbols of fire, seven in total, evenly spaced around the arch's curvature. The infernal hieroglyphs aren't static in the way I'd have expected trapped fire to behave: they *blaze* inside the ice, which, by a miracle of demonic physics, refrains from melting. I guess when you're the gateway to Hell, you can bend the regular laws of thermodynamics in the interest of looking astonishing. The archways I've flown through in dreams were portals that welcomed me to heavenly realms and spiritual tests. This one, however, doesn't invite entry. Each of its seven blinding symbols provokes in me a different draining feeling: dread; debilitating apathy; undiluted rage; despair; uncontrollable lust; deicidal drive; nonexistence. The fiery shapes block my passage more surely than steel bars ever could. I will myself to transcend the feelings driven into me by the flaming symbols with their promises of what lies on the other side, but every time I approach the arch they overpower my mind and hamstring my movements. Devil magic. Fuck.

DT reappears with Heavensent round his neck. Dave's facial features blur into darkness, but his eyes glitter from within the black. Ozzy lumbers in carrying Dave's trusty Marshall amplifier in massive arms. He places the amp on the floor - facing the archway - and plugs it into a wall socket. After connecting a coiled golden lead from amp to otherworldly guitar, DT starts to play. The sounds he produces are unlike anything ever heard on Earth. The melodies seem too beautiful to have been plucked by human hands. I'd have thought this music could only be created by a civilisation older than our Universe, a species spiritually advanced to the point of omniscience. The beauty of Heavensent's melodies is not their only surprising characteristic: they are *visible*. As DT's fingers blur across a spacesent fretboard, dark things emerge from his amplifier: oscillating stormclouds that form shapes. Symbols. Seven in all. They glide towards the archway, where they hang in the air, facing their fiery, ice-encased counterparts. One hieroglyph burns its way out of the ice to merge with its dark nemesis. Entangled together, the shapes spin in the air, then, after a brief battle, implode into nonexistence with a sound like an enormous key turning in a lock. Seven times this process occurs, always with the same result. Then I find myself floating in front of an archway that is just a defenceless block of ice. On first meeting DT, I believed him to be the

Devil. It turns out that I was wrong, but not wildly so; he was the child who would grow into the man in whom the keys to the gateway to Hell resided. Now that he has done his part, it's time for me to do mine. I doubt that DT can see my soul, but just in case he can, I propel myself towards the archway by swimming butterfly through the air: an homage to my partner-in-crime.

On the other side are darkness and biting cold a million times more chilling than the Hebridean wolfwind that tears through flesh and bites into the very essence. Compared to this Hell, a fortnight naked in the wolfwind's gust would seem like a Caribbean holiday. As I fall into black infinity, the archway recedes until it is just a twinkle of light through which an ever-narrowing snakelike protrusion is all that keeps me anchored to my body.

'It's rude to interrupt an infernal being at meal times!'

"I don't make a habit of interruptin' folk when they're eatin', but for you I'm makin' an exception, ya fuckin' wank!" I'm momentarily warmed by a sense of achievement at having entered Hell and called the Devil a 'fuckin' wank'. I wish the rest of the band could have witnessed it.

'You cannot save the little one. Hers is the shining soul I need to free me from my bonds. Pete Drummond's soul is a tasty morsel which I have long desired, but he – like you - was never more than a link in the chain that led to the true key. Sunshower Dee Oswaldo was untouchable to me until you added her voice to your music. That put her on my menu. I will drag out her pain, savouring her suffering as I slowly ingest her essence. Transcend Everything my horned head - you have transcended nothing! I have played you, MacDubh, like a tune.'

How could I have been stupid enough to make Sunshower part of heavy metal history, thus opening her soul to infernal influence? And how can I fight to save her when I don't even have a body? I realise that if I don't get out of Hell, everyone's fucked: DT, Oz, Iain, Pete, Paul, my Mum, Lisa, Colin, Saxon, Fluff...oh God, my beautiful, gentle wee rabbit.

Like a climber on a rope, I grab the astral cord and haul my soul-self back towards the archway's pinpoint of light. As my tugs on the soul-rope become more frantic, the Devil's mocking laugh echoes in infinity. As if able to read my thoughts, the Beast taunts, *'Oh, the furry Fluff – her soul will be the first thing I devour when I smash out of my cage.'*

"N-o-o-o-o-o-o-o-o, you hoof-footed fuck!" I yank harder on the cord, a soul possessed, each burst of energy moving my weightless soul faster through the frictionless void. The icy arch draws closer by the second. Soon I'm close enough to see DT at the foot of Iain's bed, Heavensent glinting like a star round his neck. As I prepare to pass through the gateway, it crunches closed. I find myself not in Blackness, as I'd hoped, but in blackness. Space and time cease to have any meaning. Seconds could be millenia. Light years could be microns, but there's no light in this Hell. What is the unit of distance here? Dark years? That seems right. I'm tumbling through an endless void at the speed of dark. More questions arise. Does the pentalpha on my body still protect my soul, now that the soul-cord has been broken? Am I about to be consumed by a being beyond my ken and sentenced to eternal torment? Or has that already happened?

There is no Devil voice, no space, no time, no love, nothing. I've merged with an infinite darkness, out of time. Movement loses its meaning. One's sense of perspective disappears when one is surrounded by infinite nothingness. As I fall hopelessly and aimlessly through the black, I'm tempted to soak it in, to let it *become* me, but a feeling persists that although I am part of the darkness, it is not part of me. Not yet.

Aeons pass.

Part of my consciousness suggests that surrendering to the darkness might end my suffering. Maybe not, though. Perhaps choosing that path would guarantee me eternity in this graceless void. The conversation from the crossroads flashes into my awareness: the Devil hasn't the power to rip out human souls, which have to be offered willingly, but devilish tactics can be used to achieve their acquisition. Are the rules the same here? I swam into Hell looking for a fight, but by coming willingly I may have served up my soul on a platter.

Suddenly, screams shatter the silence. I recognize the voices of Bon Scott, Jimi Hendrix, David Byron, Ray Gillen, Kurt Cobain and other dead stars to whom I've listened in the living dimension. Their voices are not the confident roars of old, but the howls of the damned. I find that I can focus my awareness on a single soul's cry or on the mass lament of the multitude. I cannot, however, silence their voices. Their screams become my scream, their damnation my torment. Then I hear it…smaller and higher and sadder and more lost than the others. *Sunshower!* I home in on the little voice. Deep in what's left of my being, something awakens. *Become the eye of the storm.*

In a dream, I was the hunted who became the hunter by diving into a hurricane to be ripped apart and reborn as an unstoppable force. That dream's symbolic meaning was, at the time, unclear. Now I understand its significance. It was a manual for the future: for now.

A tiny point of light, infinitesimal in intensity, appears in my soul's eye. I realise that it is the source of Sunshower's sorrowful wails. Summoning the energy of every atom of oxygen I've ever absorbed, every ray of sunlight that ever bathed my grateful skin, every soft kiss I've felt, every word of every book I've read, every rabbit-lick that has blessed my face, every hug from Sunshower, every sonic wave of every song I've ever listened to, I transmute these diverse energies into a unified spinning force. Sunshower's song grows louder, her light brightening a little, as if she can sense my presence.

'*My domain! My realm! I rule here! You are now just a sub-mortal scrap of energy, the spiritual equivalent of a schmuck – the scrap of skin thrown away after a circumcision.*'

Metallic Dreams

A whirling force of nature, I rip up darkness and recycle it. Flooded by memories and dreams, pain and love, and all the music I've heard and created, I grow stronger. Dark particle by dark particle, I devour my surroundings, sucking them up and assimilating them into my vehicle of vengeance. Souls of brave and not-so-brave metal warriors are torn apart by my torque and reassembled as they once were: free from pain and infernal anguish.

'You cannot win! I will stop your spinning stupidity and eat your essence! Fear me! Revere my dark majesty! Only then will you be spared when I extend my omnipotence into all realms!'

Whirling at an ever-accelerating pace, I project words from my soul's voice. "Omnipotence won't be yours. Sunshower won't be yours. You know what will be yours? A sore arse, when I snap off those daft horns and shove them directly up your infernal dungchute." Sunshower's light glows brighter.

'I am ruler here! You are a victim of your own folly! Give yourself to me!'

My soul's voice echoes off the walls of infinity:

"I am the Metal King,
the Warrior Poet,
the Zen mindstate practitioner,
the Water Baby,
the Aficionado of Love.
I walk the knife-edge between reality and dreams.
I dare to revel in courageous humility.
I am the one your worst fears warned you about.
For me, this is just a beginning."

'Join with me now and I will grant you a place at my side! We will reign together! Over time, we will grow in power and rule all dimensions!'

"No deal. You took somethin' immeasurably precious. I'm here to reclaim it. And make no mistake, I will fuckin' finish you." I decimate darkness, all the while feeding vivid dream-memories into the engine of redemption I've become. Sunshower's light gleams, emitting a high-pitched hum like a wet finger rubbing the rim of a wine glass. Love fuels my vortex as I move towards the blinding point of light. *The Eye of the Storm.*

I collide with Sunshower's soul, ripping it into myriad points of brilliant intensity and then pulling the bright lights back into my spiral self, starting a chain reaction. Point by point, I give birth to light. As I extinguish the last dark speck, Hell is filled by a sound like a million windows shattering.

Chapter 83 – Good News First

Striplights burn on a white ceiling above me. Wheels squeal on distant floors. A television transmits inane chatter. The smell of burnt toast hangs in the air.

I'm supine on a hard mattress. Standing at the bottom of the bed and facing away from me is a tall, dark-skinned woman in a figure-hugging dress which shimmers like polished metal. She stretches up to change the station on a wall-mounted TV, her body lithe and pantheresque. Braided black hair with interwoven strands of gold licks the curve of her spine. Sunlight streams through a window, reflects off the metallic dress and dazzles my eyes. "Holy haggis, if I'd known the afterlife would look this good, I'd have made a point o' dyin' ages ago! Please tell me you're some sort o' beautiful Valkyrie sent to transport me to a Valhalla full o' feastin', fightin' and lusty liquored-up maidens?"

My eyes home in on muscular mocha thighs as she replies, "I'm no Valkyrie. I am your queen." Something about her voice: I recognise it, as if from a past life.

"My queen? But I'm no king."

"On the contrary, you're the Metal King."

"Oh fuck. Has someone told Manowar? They won't be happy. So convinced were they of their role as metal kings that they made an album called *Kings of Metal*."

"They were merely keeping that throne warm for you, its undisputed occupier."

"My memory must be shafted. I don't remember havin' a queen. In fact, I don't remember anythin' except musical trivia."

"Have you forgotten your Backstroke Queen?" She turns round beaming a smile that's brighter than the overhead lights. Memories blow into me like a divine wind. *Kimberley!* Blue plasma arcs from my eyes and shatters a striplight. Its broken pieces tinkle onto the floor as glass rain. "You'll have to learn to keep that under control if you want to touch me," warns Kimberley. "I haven't been waitin' on you comin' out of your coma just so you can zap me *into* one!"

Coma. Hell. Sunshower. I remember. "Sunshower! I need to find Sunshower!"

"Take a look to your left, my Metal King."

I turn my head and see Ozzy seated on the adjacent bed, a smiling Sunshower standing behind him. She leapfrogs her father, lands like a gymnast on the floor, vaults onto my bed and wraps strong little arms around my neck. I feel vast love radiating out of her tiny body. "You saved me from that cold, dark place, Spark. You're my best friend."

"And you, little girl, are my light."

Lifting his daughter off me, the clean-shaven Oz says, "I think Kimberley wants a shot." After receiving a nod of approval and two thumbs up from Sunshower, Kimberley kisses me with the force of a love that was nearly lost forever. Sparks fly between our bodies.

"Look, Daddy – little sparks!" gushes Sunshower.

"Aye," nods Oz, "I fear those little sparks will lead to little Sparks."

Taking my face in her hands, Kimberley gazes into me. "It has always been you. You descended from the sky like a horny long-haired angel sent to touch down on Virginian soil, to touch my virginal recesses. I've always been your queen." Lines of electricity dance from my fingertips to Kimberley's bottom, jolting her upright. "You did that on purpose," she squeals.

"You've been in a coma here for two weeks," explains Oz. "That night in the castle, you and Sunshower were ice-cold and death-blue, not a vital sign between you. I laid your lifeless body next to hers and cried at your side all night. At the exact moment the sun came up, the colour returned to your faces and your hearts started beatin' again. Neither of you woke up, but you were alive. I brought you both here, where the coma specialists figured that your bodies were rechargin' after an immense trauma. Sunshower came oot o' her coma a week ago, but refused to leave your side. She could have been sleepin' in a four-poster bed in Blackness Castle, but instead she chose a hospital bed next to you."

Amazed, I turn to Sunshower, who smiles and says, "I know…I'm your light."

"After Ronald MacLeod heard aboot you and Sunshower, he invited us all to stay at the castle indefinitely," continues Oz. "He's home again and we're all still livin' in the castle except DT. MacLeod says he likes havin' some life aroon' the place." Ozzy dials a number on his mobile phone then hands it to me. "Talk to Rosie. She has news."

"The Cemetery Gates."

"Triple goddess. It's Spark."

"Scotsman! It's wonderful to hear your voice again! I didn't think I ever would."

I mimic Darth Vader's heavy-breathing bellow. "Your lack of faith is disturbing!"

"You did choose a somewhat lofty goal."

"I didn't choose it. It chose me."

"I've been receiving psychic thank-you cards in droves, hundreds of them every day. It seems that you not only disposed of the Devil, but also obliterated the dark dimension of Hell, releasing all the souls that were trapped there. I had no idea there were so many dead heavy metal icons. These souls have now been transported to their correct destination, back with their dead families and friends. You have become the hero of your dead heroes."

"Excellent. Hero to my heroes, I can deal wi' that. I bet you wish you'd opened your legs for me, eh?" Kimberley slaps my face with enough force to launch a marsupial into orbit. "Ancient history, Kimberley!"

"Not communing with you coitally," Rosie continues, "is something I will have to live with. Anyway, I hear that your lost love has found you."

"Aye. How good is that?"

"I wish you limitless happiness and love. Blessed be." Rosie hangs up, leaving me smiling like a village idiot.

Sunshower fetches two female nurses: a young red-haired one and an older, rounder nurse who addresses me in a soft Highland accent. "I must insist that your visitors leave, now that you're awake. Even you, little Sunshower. Spark will need food and rest to bring back his strength."

"Please let them stay," I appeal. "I get more energy from these people than from all the food and sleep in the world. They're what I need."

The Highland nurse weighs up my words, her expression stern. After a glance at her younger colleague, who is nodding, she says, "It's against all our policies, but to Hell with policies, eh?"

"Thank you. And by the way, there's no such place as Hell. Not anymore."

Frowning, the older nurse takes her workmate by the arm, as if planning to start a line dance, and swishes out of the room in a hail of white cotton.

Ozzy dials Paul's mobile and puts him on speakerphone. "Oz, ya big orange buffoon! How's Spark? Any change?"

"Aye."

"Well don't leave me hangin' like a tool waitin' for a tradesman!"

"Why don't you ask him yourself?"

"Spark! Are you awake?"

"Aye," I reply, "and fightin' fit. Where are you?"

"I'm in America wi' Colin. I hear you've been raisin' Hell."

"Razin' Hell, aye. Razin' with a 'z', that is. It turns oot I'm the Hellrazer."

"Excellent work. I have two pieces of news for you. Would you like the good news or the good news?"

"Start wi' the good news."

"Well, the good news is that the *Poets & Prophets* is bein' released on Monday and has pre-release orders of almost two million. That's what a tour wi' German butt pirates and a *Rolling Stone* front cover can do for you. Once people start listenin' to the album, word-of-mooth marketin' will send sales even higher into the stratosphere. As soon as you're on your feet again I'll organise another tour, a bigger one, a headlinin' one."

"Are you sayin' over a million people have already paid for *Poets & Prophets*, even though it's no' oot yet?"

"That's exactly what I'm tellin' you, Spark. It's advance orders gone wild!"

"Amazin'! What's the other piece o' news?"

"Somethin' that will rocket the band skywards even faster than the *Rolling Stone* cover did."

"What?"

"A week ago, the biggest web doonload was photos o' the bare beavers of post-rehab pals Britney Spears and Paris Hilton, snapped up their skirts by some gutter-lyin' paparazzi as the pantieless minxes climbed oot of a limo. You, Spark, have eclipsed them and become the world's biggest Internet phenomenon. Half a billion doonloads and coontin', and that's only since this mornin'."

"Me?"

"I've viewed it myself and I can honestly say that you are, ahem…a star in more than the musical sense o' the word."

"Eh?"

"The fastest doonload on the Internet is a sensational sex video in which a Godzilla-sized ebony woman does unspeakable things to a man who looks suspiciously like the frontman of Transcend Everything, right doon to the carved pentalpha on his body. I watched every depraved, disgustin' moment o' the video…five times. Research as a manager, you understand. The title o' the movie is *Leaked Orlando Police Security Tape: McAllen Says, 'Have a Nice Day, Spark.'* Is it comin' back to you, superstar?"

"I suppose I'll be famous for this, and we'll have to keep it quiet that I killed the Devil, as no one will believe that anyway?"

"Spark, as Axl Rose once said, you only have to worry when they're *not* talkin' aboot you. Famous is famous, dude!"

"Aye, I suppose so, but I'd like to be seen as the world-savin' hero, not as the sex slave who got plundered by the world's fattest Christian dominatrix."

"I will always see you as both. Welcome back."

"Thanks. It's good talkin' to you."

"You too."

My stunned onlookers are staring at me in silence. Shrugging my shoulders, I explain, "Florida justice. It was either that or lethal injection."

Chapter 84 – Great Expectations

A petite blonde nurse tiptoes into my room, narrowing her eyes to peer through the dimness. "Spark," she whispers, "are you awake?"

"Aye." I beckon her towards me with a hand gesture.

"You've got a phone call from your band's manager. I've told him not to phone this late in future. Do you want to take the call?"

"Definitely. I'll take calls from that deviant at any hour o' the night or day." The nurse switches on the light, leaves the room, then returns wheeling a contraption which resembles R2-D2 from *Star Wars* with a numerical keypad for a face. She watches me through grey eyes as I hold the phone's receiver to my ear and greet Paul.

"I've done it!" he gushes. "I've figured oot how we can ootsell Michael Jackson's *Thriller* wi' oor album!" Paul sounds on the verge of pissing his pants with excitement, if he hasn't already done so.

"Are you drunk? *Thriller* sold over seventy million units worldwide when Michael Jackson was alive. Then the fucker went and died, and it started sellin' like hotcakes again."

"I know that. So what? Listen, we're notchin' up millions o' sales in America and Europe already. Here's the clever bit – think aboot populations. What's the population o' China?"

"A wee bit over a billion?"

"Closer to two billion! How aboot India?"

"Second biggest population after China. I'd guess half a billion."

"Not even close. It's over one billion. Now imagine doin' extensive tours o' China and India, playin' multiple nights in the big cities like Bombay and Beijing. Do the sums in your heid for album sales. Then there's merchandising – T-shirts, panties, bandanas, lighters, jackets, your Orlando sex DVD."

My mind starts to reel. "Paul Roberts, you're a genius! Get us booked on a tour o' China and India."

"It's already done, baby! We leave a week on Wednesday."

"How did you know I'd be oot o' my coma by then?"

"I didn't *know*. I had *faith*."

"Have you told the others in the band?"

"Those crazy bastards? I thought I'd leave that to you. They're all enjoyin' their R&R. DT is incommunicado for the next week due to the arrival of a blonde female fan from Sweden."

"Has he checked her ID? She could be a jailbait runaway."

"That's weird," muses Paul. "I used that exact combination of words. 'DT,' I said, 'don't be gettin' sent back to jail. She could be a jailbait runaway.' When I asked Dave her age, he gave a troublin' response."

"What did he say?"

"He told me not to worry, that she was squirteen."

Chapter 85 – Róisín Dubh

A white-out sky camouflages the snowflakes that fall towards St Fintan's Cemetery in Dublin. Wind whistles through gaps in an iron fence to flirt with gravestones, its tune a howled lament for the human shells not so far underfoot. Snow has painted over the landscape's usual earthy browns and grassy greens with a purifying coat of blue-white sparkles. Five pairs of footprints lead to the farthest reaches of the graveyard: to plot thirteen of the St Polan's section, to be precise, where five men in long black coats are huddled round a grave. The shortest man, a stocky wall of an individual, drops to his knees and scrapes snow off a flat rectangular stone, revealing the words *Go dtuga Dia suaimhneas da anam. Róisín Dubh.* He nods, confirming that this is the place. His companions close their eyes and place right hands on hearts while he offers a prayer. "You were in limbo too long. Finally, you're where you belong, you disreputable angel. It was an honour to have you inside me, so to speak. As a result, your stagecraft and confidence are instilled in me forever. We love you. We miss you. If you can organise a sabbatical from your heavenly realms to contribute to oor second album, you'll be welcome. Until then, I'll watch the skies in the hope of seein' the darkest angel of all swoopin' doon to Earth. Thank you, Philip Parris Lynott."

The four standing men wipe tears from their cheeks, then turn and walk away. Iain Bright, however, remains crouched at the graveside. As he reaches into his jacket and pulls a flower from an inside pocket, a thorn pierces his index finger. Reflexly, he loosens his grip. A black rose tumbles from his hand, followed by a drop of blood which forms a crimson rose shape in the snow. Twin roses, side by side.

Iain Bright looks over his shoulder and sees his bandmates disappearing into the white flurry. Before following their footsteps, he gazes at the grave and whispers, "*Go dtuga Dia suaimhneas da anam. Róisín Dubh.* May God give peace to his soul. Black Rose. *Téigh go dtí an Dia leis an tsíocháin i do anam, mo Aingeal Dorcha.* Go to God with peace in your soul, my Dark Angel."

Epilogue

"…to escape the tyranny of the angels, the masters of the cosmos, every possible ignominy should be perpetrated…you should discharge all debts to the world and to your own body, for only by committing every act can the soul be freed of its passions and return to its original purity."

– Umberto Eco, *Foucault's Pendulum*

Metallic Dreams

Acknowledgements

Thank you to the heavy metal bands who have had the guts to truly go for it. I applaud your spirit, energy and willingness to put yourselves on the line in defence of our faith. Special thanks to Mark Manning (aka Zodiac Mindwarp), Biff Byford, Leonard Loers, Udo Von DüYü (who was happy for me to portray him committing any depraved act, just as long as I didn't have him hanging out with Republicans!), *Rolling Stone* magazine and BC Rich guitars for their generous endorsements of this project. Hail to you all!

Thank you to Sally Rice, my mother, who has always supported my dreams, even metallic ones. For this, I feel boundless gratitude. I love you, Mum.

Thank you to my peers at Writers Inc: the perfect sounding board for my ideas and wordplay. Without exception, your feedback was helpful.

Thank you to Tom Bryan, extraordinary writer and the only person I've ever met who can keep up with me in the coffee-drinking stakes. Your advice was always constructive. I'm honoured to call you a friend.

Thank you to my friends and family, from whom I have been hidden away for the last few years in order to make this book a reality. You all came to accept and perhaps even understand my nocturnalism, grumpiness and compulsion to write. I love you all.

Thank you to the lands of Java, Dominican Republic, Peru, Brazil, Ecuador, Ethiopia, Colombia, Kenya and (of course) Malabar for their fine coffee, without which this book would have taken at least twice as long.

Thank you to my rabbit Fluff, whose love helped me through many a long night's writing. Every cuddle and face lick was bliss. I miss you more than any words could express. I feel you in every breeze, hear you among the trees. Little Fluff, I love you on a scale that dwarfs stars and galaxies.

Thank you to Philip Parris Lynott, who often visits me in dreams. *Go dtuga Dia suaimhneas da anam. Róisín Dubh. Téigh go dtí an Dia leis an tsíocháin i do anam, mo Aingeal Dorcha.*